THE GOOD APPRENTICE

Iris Murdoch was born in Dublin in 1919 of Anglo-Irish parents. She went to Badminton School, Bristol, and read classics at Somerville College, Oxford. During the war she was an Assistant Principal at the Treasury, and then worked with UNRRA in London, Belgium and Austria. She held a studentship in Philosophy at Newnham College, Cambridge, and then in 1948 she returned to Oxford where she became a Fellow of St Anne's College. Until her death in February 1999, she lived with her husband, the teacher and critic John Bayley, in Oxford. Awarded the CBE in 1976, Iris Murdoch was made a DBE in the 1987 New Year's Honours List. In the 1997 PEN Awards she received the Gold Pen for Distinguished Service to Literature.

Since her writing debut in 1954 with *Under the Net*, Iris Murdoch has written twenty-six novels, including the Booker Prize-winning *The Sea, The Sea* (1978) and most recently *The Green Knight* (1993) and *Jackson's Dilemma* (1995). Other literary awards include the James Tait Black Memorial Prize for *The Black Prince* (1973) and the Whitbread Prize for *The Sacred and Profane Love Machine* (1974). Her works of philosophy include *Sartre: Romantic Rationalist*, *Metaphysics as a Guide to Morals* (1992) and *Existentialists and Mystics* (1997). She has written several plays including *The Italian Girl* (with James Saunders) and *The Black Prince*, adapted from her novel of the same name. Her volume of poetry, *A Year of Birds*, which appeared in 1978, has been set to music by Malcolm Williamson.

Iris Murdoch

THE GOOD APPRENTICE

WITH AN INTRODUCTION BY
Professor David Cooper

VINTAGE

Published by Vintage 2000

2 4 6 8 10 9 7 5 3 1

First published in Great Britain in 1985
by Chatto & Windus

Vintage
Random House, 20 Vauxhall Bridge Road,
London SW1V 2SA

Random House Australia (Pty) Limited
20 Alfred Street, Milsons Point, Sydney
New South Wales 2061, Australia

Random House New Zealand Limited
18 Poland Road, Glenfield,
Auckland 10, New Zealand

Random House (Pty) Limited
Endulini, 5A Jubilee Road, Parktown 2193,
South Africa

The Random House Group Limited Reg. No. 954009
www.randomhouse.co.uk

A CIP catalogue record for this book
is available from the British Library

ISBN 0 09 928525 8

Papers used by Random House are natural, recyclable
products made from wood grown in sustainable forests.
The manufacturing processes conform to the environ-
mental regulations of the country of origin

Printed and bound in Great Britain by
Cox & Wyman Limited, Reading, Berkshire

CONTENTS

TO BRIGID BROPHY

INTRODUCTION

In *Iris*, a memoir of his wife, John Bayley recalls the visit to their home of an Irish monk. The inspiration for the setting up and 'way' of the new monastery from which he comes, the monk explains, was two of Iris Murdoch's novels, one of them *The Good Apprentice*. Readers of the novel may be intrigued, or alarmed, by the image of a monastic life modelled on that of 'Seegard', the cold, damp house where the disintegrating magus, painter and erstwhile Don Juan, Jesse Baltram, lives, Lear-like, surrounded by his curious family of women. Still, the monks must have discerned, like A.S. Byatt, that *The Good Apprentice*, published in 1985, belonged among those 'late baggy monsters' whose preoccupation is religion, albeit 'religion without God', as one figure in the novel puts it. Although the backdrop is not, as it had been in, say, *The Bell*, an institutionally religious one, it is engagement with a 'renewal of life', with 'the good life', which shows through in the aspirations of the central characters, even of the sexually focused, love-addicted pair who mouth those two phrases.

As with many Iris Murdoch novels, opinions may differ as to who *the* central character is, and indeed as to whether it is sensible to identify one. The figures in her books are not, after all, the lonely heroes or anti-heroes who stalk the pages of what she called 'existentialist' novels (Hemingway and Kingsley Amis as much as Sartre), people for whom 'others' are little more than elements, 'givens', of their 'situation'. Rather, they are men and women whose lives, indeed identities, are bound up with, dependent on, one another. In *The Sea, The Sea*, a man resolves to 'become a hermit' – to escape, especially, the society of women – only to find that he cannot live without re-possessing an old love.

For some readers, the novel's focus will be the young man who certainly occupies the most pages, Edward Baltram, tortured, remorse-driven natural son of the painter whom he seeks out in order to receive, as if by 'magic', some dispensation or purification. For others, the focus may be Jesse himself, a man who, though now become a 'cruel mad god', was possessed of a 'greatness of being' of which those who did not know him could form no conception. While Jesse appears only briefly, he is, like other of Murdoch's magi – from Fox in *The Flight from the Enchanter* to Vallar in *A Message to the Planet* – a hub whose spokes fix the other characters in a circle around him. It is, however, Stuart Cuno, Edward's older step-brother, who gives the novel its name. Stuart is not an apprentice who happens to be good at it but, as an interlocutor puts it, someone 'apprenticed to goodness'. The allusion is to the view of Plato – 'our best philosopher', Murdoch often remarked – that goodness is, like a demanding craft, something for which a person must assiduously train. As she wrote in her review of Simone Weil's *Notebooks*, it is an apprenticeship during which, at first, the good is bound to 'appear negative and empty'. It is, perhaps, Stuart's uncertain odyssey – from a blank, inchoate aspiration to goodness ('I'm just a beginner') to appreciation of what that aspiration actually entails – which gathers together the themes and episodes of the novel. This is an odyssey which involves him, stumblingly, with his step-brother's expiation of guilt, his father's love-affair, and – another echo of Plato – with the homosexual temptation presented by the son of his father's mistress, who herself will become peculiarly attached to Stuart.

Whichever of these characters is 'central' or most occupies the individual reader's interest, however, the religious *Leitmotiv* is there to hear. Edward does not just 'feel bad' about the tragic episode with which the novel so arrestingly begins: he is victim to what Murdoch, in *Metaphysics as a Guide to Morals*, describes as 'one of the most terrible of human woes ... remorse', something that is 'no less agonising' when, as in Edward's case, arguably, it is a relatively 'innocent action [which] has produced an unforeseeable catastrophe'. In such remorse, one encounters 'the void ... the anguished experience of lack of balance' which only a spiritual 'renewal of one's life' as a whole can restore. Jesse Baltram is (or was) not just 'charismatic', but a man, a 'god', with 'greatness of being' to whom people turn for a dispensation or 'message' that will enable things to fall into place for them, lend sense to all the 'contingent rubble' of life. He is the kind of sage on whom, further east, are centred those 'techniques for the purification and reorientation' of our energies by which Murdoch had become increasingly impressed. The goodness to which Stuart is apprenticed is nothing so particular and hived-off as the performance of one's duties in life: like the Godhead of the mystics, though 'without supernatural dogmas', it can barely be articulated, yet '*shows* ... as the most important thing', the source and object of 'some sort of spiritual ideal and discipline'. Even the buccaneering 'playboy' Harry Cuno, opposed as his conception of the good life is to his son's, is not without *some* sort of spiritual ideal. Sex, he tries to convince his lover, Midge, is something they have proved to be 'true': not a bit of fun on the side, but a vital, integral aspect of a true 'life as a whole' lived in 'courageous' opposition to the 'false abstractions' of good and evil, body and soul.

'Remorse', 'the void', 'greatness of being', 'purification', 'spiritual discipline', good and evil' – recital of these terms must give the impression that *The Good Apprentice* is 'heavy-going'. It isn't. Much of the book, in fact, is genuinely funny: Harry's and Midge's misadventures getting into and out of 'Seegard', for example, could belong in an American 'screw-ball' comedy. For all her serious intent as a novelist, Murdoch regarded herself, not as the author of *contes philosophiques*, but as a 'story-teller' who, as John Bayley reminds us, wanted to 'reach all possible readers', not least through 'the excitement of her story [and] its pace'. To be sure, there are, especially early on in the book, those 'little chunks of reflection' which, Dame Iris once wrily remarked, readers must 'put up with for the sake of the rest of the work'. But these barely stall the pace of a story – or web of interwoven stories – that soon has those readers anxiously wondering what happens next. Will they or won't they? Will anyone discover what *did* occur by the river? Is she going to leave him?

Nor will those who expect to enter 'the unmistakeable world' of a Murdoch novel, to which literary critics so often refer, be disappointed by the present book. Many of the familiar marks are there. Migrations of middle-class London intellectuals to and from an isolated, watery and faintly sinister retreat in the country. Elements of mystery: Edward's two experiences at a medium's house, the strange clearing or *dromos* in the wood, Midge's ecstatic transformation at 'Seegard', and the final fate of Jesse. Sharp, pointed sketches of some modern 'types': 'coolly' modern, sexually casual and selfish Sarah, for example, or her ghastly feminist mother.

Iris Murdoch knew that her readers entered the world of her novels through different gates: some for the entertainment offered there, others to explore a realm from which they could return with fresh perspectives on the actual world. It is, arguably, the aspiration and achievement of the best art, the novel preeminently, to set up a world which, as Martha Nussbaum expresses it, is at an optimal reflective and emotional distance from its audience. The reader who enters it is sufficiently engaged with its inhabitants for their struggles, failures and successes to bear upon his or her own, yet is at a sufficient remove from them for reflection and emotional response to be unclouded by the pressures on rapid decision and snap judgement which actual life relentlessly and messily exerts. In Murdoch's own words, 'great art is liberating [because] it enables us to see and take pleasure in what is not ourselves', but in what is, nevertheless, recognisably adjacent to the arena in which we move.

'What is at stake' in Iris Murdoch's writings, suggests George Steiner in his Foreword to her collection, *Existentialists and Mystics*, 'is the definition of the Good with a view to conducting our lives in its light' – a Good unencumbered, of course, by 'supernatural dogmas'. With which views on the conduct of life might readers return from the world of *The Good Apprentice*? Above all, perhaps, a sense of the *difficulty* of this conduct, of an apprenticeship to good. For Murdoch, 'the most important thing that has happened to us in the last hundred years' is the atrophy of traditional religion, for it is this which, if honestly regarded, must render the good life so problematic in modernity. Unfortunately, too many philosophers and intellectuals have failed to regard this phenomenon and its implications honestly. In particular, the many thinkers she groups under the label 'existentialist' have persuaded people that the moral condition is something very simple – a matter, merely, of 'sincerely' or 'authentically' *choosing* one's moral commitments, as if these were styles of dress selected to suit one's personality. Religious belief, to the degree it has survived, has itself become a matter of 'choice', of filling a spiritual trolley with whatever mix'n match of doctrines and rituals is to one's taste.

In substituting 'for the hard idea of truth ... the facile idea of sincerity', existentialists lead us away from the three things on which, with a view to conducting our lives, we ought to be focusing. First, the difficult task of *seeing*, of truthful assessment of, our 'situation' – the real condition of a marriage, say, or the precise degree of responsibility for a catastrophe. Second, the need to cultivate a 'humility', a 'selfless respect for reality'. This is both one of the most difficult of virtues and a main component, along with 'love', in the process of 'unselfing' which erosion of belief in a God before whom 'I am nothing' has made all the harder. With its 'solipsistic exaltation of the individual', existentialism denies that 'unselfing' is possible, let alone desirable. Finally, existentialists take pride in emptying the moral life of its 'mystery', a sense of which we should be rekindling. Instead of allowing that moral disagreement and the elusiveness of 'foundations' for moral beliefs may be due to the strangeness, the ineffability even, of the good and its 'magnetism', the existentialists' response is Harry's – 'There isn't anything deep here!' (His brusque advice to the anguished Edward, 'Make yourself function again!' is about as sensitive and helpful as was Sartre's to an equally anguished young man who once sought counsel from him – 'Just choose!')

It is at once the need for, difficulty of, and unity among these three tasks – truthful vision, 'unselfing', and 'a sense of mystery' – which show through in the world of *The Good Apprentice*. Edward Baltram is not going to emerge from 'the void' unless he can accurately gauge his responsibility for the tragedy and appreciate his subjection to obsessive self-pity. Yet he must recognise, too, that going through 'the void' is, inexplicably, the fate of someone who, however unintentionally, has had a drastic impact on the lives of others. Stuart Cuno will not come through his moral apprenticeship unless he can add an ability to 'communicate with', indeed love, other people, to his cool, accurate assessments of their 'situations' and to his intimations of a 'religion without God'. The apprenticeship may be hard – people, he reflects, are always throwing bibles or smashing paperweights when he intervenes with advice – but not hopeless. Stuart takes to heart Midge's diatribe, 'You feel nothing ... You pretend to be going to do something great, but you do nothing'. The day eventually comes when, by feeling something and doing something, he learns from his step-brother that a visit he has paid really did 'do some good'.

One thing with which the reader will not return from the world of this novel is simple recipes for the conduct of life. Pursuit of the difficult tasks or 'techniques' described above can at best attune a person for the 'renewal of life' as a whole, not by themselves provide a blueprint for the management of that life. The good is too inexhaustible, the spiritual ideal too occluded, for easy consensus. Towards the end of Murdoch's second 'Platonic Dialogue', *Above the Gods*, in which the protagonists have argued for various conceptions of religion and the good, Socrates proposes a serene resolution of their differences. 'It can't be so simple!', worries a youthful Plato, 'If only I could get it *clear*!' 'You never will,' replies his friend Acastos, 'Anyway, let's be happy. Come, dear Plato' – and off they go arm-in-arm. *The Good Apprentice* closes on a similar note, when Harry and his two sons are discussing the 'good things in the world'. But what *are* they?', worries Edward, 'We might all mean different ones'. 'Never mind,' replies Harry, 'let's drink to them' – and together they raise their glasses.

THE GOOD
APPRENTICE

PART ONE

THE PRODIGAL SON

I WILL ARISE and go to my father, and will say unto him, Father I have sinned against heaven and before thee, and am no more worthy to be called thy son.

These were not perhaps the actual words which Edward Baltram uttered to himself on the occasion of his momentous and mysterious summons, yet their echo was not absent even then, and later he repeated them often.

The story begins however at an earlier point, on the evening in February when Edward played a disgraceful trick upon his friend and fellow student Mark Wilsden. The magisterial drug which transports its initiates to heaven or to hell had been surreptitiously administered. Mark, who had so loftily disapproved and so peevishly refused, now lay a helpless victim, giggling and babbling upon the lamplit divan bed in Edward's small bedsitter upon the second floor of a shabby terrace house in Camden Town. Edward, no trip for him that evening, clad in his magician's robe of sober power, stood looking down. He had concealed the drug in a sandwich, and watched the metamorphosis with wicked triumph. His sole anxiety vanished as soon as it became clear that Mark was destined to have a happy journey. If he had sent his friend even temporarily to hell he would have felt most uncomfortable. As it was, Mark's face, beautiful at any time, was transfigured by a luminous ecstasy. His brown eyes were large, his full, eloquent lips were red and moist, his skin glowing as if illumined from within. The drops of sweat upon his forehead, the hairs of his elegantly clipped moustache and beard, stood out and shone as if his face had become a priestly mask inlaid with precious stones. With his longish head he looked like an Egyptian king. He looked like a wide-browed, huge-eyed god. He was a god, he had become divine, he was experiencing the Good Absolute, the vision of visions, *the annihilation of the ego*. Edward had heard of this. Such insights could last a lifetime. Mark would be grateful to him later. Edward's own experiences, though picturesque and thrilling, had not been mystical. Mark, whom Edward admired and loved, was a mystical type. Edward, contemplating the transfiguration of his friend, felt quite faint with joy.

Mark, who had been laughing continuously in a low undulating rhythmical giggle which sometimes sounded like a sob, now began to concentrate. He thrust his lips out as he often did when he was thinking

'Edward.'

'Yes, Mark.'

'How things are.'

'Yes.'

'How they are. They are in themselves, they are, I say, *in themselves,* that's the – the *secret*.'

'Yes, indeed they are.'

'No. They are not just in themselves – they *are* – themselves. Everything is – itself. It is a – itself. But, you know, there's – there's only one –'

'Only one what?'

'Anything. Everything is – all together – like a big – it's *shaggy* –'

'Shaggy?'

'Edward –'

'Yes.'

'No – it's all scales, millions of scales and – gills – I can see it – breathing – it's a *fish* – I mean – everything is – it's all one . . . big . . . fish . . .'

Edward tried to imagine the big shaggy scaly fish that was everything. But now his own visionary drug images, stirred up by sympathy, began to float by him as if the little room had become a deep lake full of waving reeds and quaking amoebas

2

with big eyes and dark swollen forms bound in white ribbons, the raising of Lazarus, the creation of the world.

'Oh now it's pingling,' said Mark suddenly. He tried to rise a little, but fell back on the divan. 'It's *pingling,* I can see the sky – beyond – oh the light – all made of angels' heads, like pins, pinheads, all shining, all together, all – unfolding, like a long long – scroll – and the light – it's laser beams – the spears, the spears – hurt so – oh I'm so happy – I'm rising up, I'm flying – And God – is coming –'

'Can you see God? What's he like?'

'He's coming – like a – like a *lift.*'

Mark lay for a while in silence, gazing away into the distance of his vision, smiling, his parted lips bubbling a little. Then he raised his hand solemnly as if blessing Edward. Then quite suddenly he fell into a deep calm sleep.

Edward was disappointed. He considered trying to wake him but decided he had better not. Such sleeps could last a long while however, and by the time Mark awoke the fun might be over.

The telephone rang.

'Edward?'

'Yes.'

'It's Sarah.'

'Hello, Sarah.'

'Could you come and see me? I'm low. Come across and have a quick drink.'

'Oh – all right – just five minutes.'

Edward returned to look at Mark. He looked like a sleeping knight in a picture; or the dead Christ, so handsome, unsullied and unhurt. He pulled a rug over his sleeping friend. Then he put a newspaper over the lamp to shade the light and left the room, locking the door behind him.

Edward's visit to Sarah Plowmain (who lived very close by) that evening was not entirely impromptu. He had recently met her in college, in a 'set' which included Mark, and after her casual 'Let's meet, I'll ring' had been expecting her summons for some days. Sarah was cool. She had waited exactly the right length of time before inviting him for (right again) a 'quick drink'. Edward could not resist such elegant discretion, and he was flattered. It was time to establish this girl; after that they could see, it was not an urgent case. For this move however this was the moment, and Edward believed in fated moments. Besides, Sarah had said that her mother had met or known Edward's mother, and any signal, however faint, from the dark lost planet of his parents disturbed and interested Edward very much.

What young Edward (he was twenty) had not expected was that young Sarah (she was nineteen), who was small and dark and agile like a Russian acrobat, would immediately (how had it happened?) undress him (his clothes had seemed to melt away) and introduce him into her bed, in her little cave-like candle-lit room where a stick of incense was burning in a Chinese vase on the mantelpiece.

Now they were clothed again (had he been asleep?) and they were talking and drinking whisky, which was it seemed the only drink Sarah had in stock. Sarah was smoking, she was always smoking.

'You said your mother knew my mother?'

'They were together at the polytechnic. Your mother was doing art and mine was doing sociology. So that was it, was it?'

'What?'

'You just came to talk about your mother!'

'I want to talk about you too.'

'And my father used to teach your brother. We're connected. It's fate.'

'I'm so sorry about your father.'

Sarah's father, the mathematician Dirk Plowmain, had committed suicide not long ago.

'Yes. But we weren't close. He behaved so badly to my mother, they separated quite a long time ago. Your father behaved badly to your mother too, didn't he?'

Edward was hurt by the allusion which, he felt, went too far for this early stage of acquaintance. He had a strict sense of decorum. He said nothing.

'You're the son of Jesse Baltram, aren't you, not of Harry Cuno? Some people are a bit confused about it.'

4

Edward disliked the tone, but replied amiably enough. 'Yes, but I've never known Jesse, I only saw him once or twice when I was a kid. He dropped my mother before I was born, he was married to someone else anyway –'

'Yes, I bet your ma kept you well clear of horrible Jesse! Except that she made sure you had his name!'

'Then my mother married Harry Cuno and then she went and died. I've always regarded Harry as my father.'

'And Stuart is your brother? He's not Chloe's child, is he?'

'No, he's not my mother's child. He's the son of Harry's first wife, she died before Chloe took over, she came from New Zealand.' For some reason Teresa Cuno, when she was referred to, which happened rarely, was always thus labelled.

'So Stuart and you aren't really brothers.'

'Not blood relations – but, well, we *are* brothers.'

'You mean you're *like* brothers. I'd like to meet Stuart. Someone says he's given up sex before he's even tried it!'

'So that was it, was it? You just wanted to get to know Stuart!' Edward was fond of his elder brother, but they did not get on too well.

'No, no, I want to know *you,* I'm studying *you,* can't you see? And then there's your aunt, Chloe's little sister, the fashion lady who married that Scotch psychiatrist. He's miles older than she is, isn't he? I suppose she was a mother to you?'

'Midge McCaskerville, no, not at all.' Certainly not Midge, his charming young aunt, whom Edward remembered kissing so passionately at a dance when he was seventeen. Margaret McCaskerville, *née* Warriston, his mother's younger sister, was always known by her nickname 'Midge', which she had used during her short career as a fashion model.

'Not a maternal type,' said Sarah. 'I'm told she's changed a lot. She's got fat. How do you get on with Harry Cuno?'

'Fine. Maybe you'd like to meet him too, I'll give a party!'

'Oh good! He's a real adventurer, like an explorer, I've seen his picture, like a pirate, a buccaneer, fearfully talented, a hero of our time!'

'Yes, but not exactly a successful one.' Why did I say that, thought Edward. This smart little girl will think I don't like him. She'll repeat it too. And he *is* wonderful.

5

'I tell you who I'd most like to meet.'

'Who?'

'Your real father, Jesse Baltram, now he's a *great* man.'

'You said he was horrible.'

'I was taking your mother's view. Anyway he can be both, can't he? Lots of men are!'

'I'm afraid I can't arrange it,' said Edward.

'A painter, an architect, a sculptor, a socialist, *and* a Don Juan! My mother met him ages ago. She used to know his wife, May Barnes, before she married him. They've shut themselves up in that grotesque house in the marsh. I know that bit of coast, my ma's got a cottage –'

'Isn't your mother famous for something?'

'Women's Lib Journalism. She's a fire-eater.'

Edward was stirred and upset by this display of irreverent curiosity about his family. Almost any reference hurt. He looked more critically now at Sarah's clever sallow face, devoid of make-up, her cropped hair and ragged dark fringe, her shaggy jersey and narrow dirty jeans, her big glass beads and noisy Indian bangles, her bitten finger-nails and little strong hand, smelling of nicotine, which intermittently squeezed his knee. She was less beautiful than the last girl he had made love to (a tall American just returned to Boston) but was more attractive, gipsyish, cleverer, nastier, more unpredictable, dangerous. Was this perhaps the beginning of *it,* the serious business for which his love life had been waiting? The way she had undressed him had been so deft, like knitting, her soft accomplished body so tactful and authoritative. She was certainly experienced. Was that good or bad?

One of the candles guttered out. 'Can't we have a lamp?' said Edward. 'And need we have the incense? I don't like the smell.'

'Why didn't you say?' Sarah sprang up and turned on a lamp and pinched out the incense. 'I like the darkness. Have you ever been to a seance? Would you like to go? It's an experience. Shall we go together?'

Edward suddenly remembered Mark Wilsden. How had he managed *completely to forget* his friend? The sudden love-making, the weirdly concentrated talk about his family, had translated him utterly. And perhaps the use of drugs affects the memory? This was a sober thought. He stood up.

'Do you believe in life after death? I don't, but I believe in psychic phenomena. All right, Edward, you're going, I'll find your coat.'

'I must rush,' he said.

'Haven't you got a scarf? I could lend you a woolly cap. It's getting awfully cold. I wonder if it'll snow?'

Of course Mark was perfectly all right, would be still asleep. Edward looked at his watch, amazed and relieved to find that his eventful visit to Sarah Plowmain had taken little over half an hour. He came out into the clear frosty very cold night, gulping in the cold and seeing with satisfaction his deep breaths turned into steamy clouds. Running the short distance between Sarah's lodgings and his own he levitated several times upon the glittering pavement. He had wanted to be a ballet dancer once.

Edward panted up the narrow flight of stairs. Putting his key in the door he realised that he was drunk. The key skidded over the painted surface seeking the hole. He found it and opened the door, entered and closed the door. The darkened room with its one shaded lamp was curiously cold. Edward saw at once that the newspaper he had put over the lamp was brown and scorched. He quickly removed it, then turned to the divan. The divan was empty. Edward looked quickly about the room, there was nowhere to hide, nowhere to go. There was no one there. Mark was gone. Then he saw the chair drawn up beside the window and the window wide open.

So it was that Edward Baltram's life was profoundly and permanently altered. At the police station, and again at the inquest he described how he had climbed on the chair and leaned out of the window and seen Mark's body lying in the area below the street, illumined by a light from a basement room. Nobody had seen or heard him fall. He described how he ran moaning down the stairs, out onto the pavement, and down the steps to the basement. Mark's body lay there, huge in the small space, stretched out and broken, a blood-stained sack. The blood smeared Edward's shoes. He knocked at the lower flat. The people there telephoned the police. A fruitless ambulance arrived. Someone went to break the news to Mark's mother. 'What happened?' everyone asked Edward. At the inquest he was asked more detailed questions. Yes, he had given Mark the drug. At Mark's request? Yes. Why had he left him alone? He went out for a breath of fresh air. How long was he away? Ten minutes. Drugs, which he had not had the presence of mind to remove, were found in Edward's room. It emerged that he had, on one occasion, casually sold some of the stuff to a fellow student. Mark's mother, a widow, a powerful and frightening woman, terrible in her grief, declared that Mark abominated drugs and would never have taken any of his own accord. She accused Edward of having murdered her son. The authorities were merciful to Edward. His college suspended him until the next academic year. He saw a hospital psychiatrist who bullied him. He was let off on condition that he gave up drugs and agreed to receive regular psychiatric treatment. This his uncle by marriage, Thomas McCaskerville, who also gave evidence at the inquest, agreed to arrange or provide. The newspapers lost interest in him. Thus Edward passed out of the public eye into his private hell.

DEAR EDWARD BALTRAM,

Think what you have done. I want you to think of it at every moment, at every second. I would like to stuff it down your throat like a black ball and choke you. You told vile unforgivable lies at the inquest. I *know* Mark would never have taken that drug. You gave it to him, fed it to him without his knowing, fed him his death, *poisoned* him as surely as with cyanide. You are a murderer. You killed him out of envy, to destroy something beautiful and good which you knew your mean soul could never equal. You killed my beloved son, blackening for ever my life and the life of his sister. You took his whole life away, which I shall have to live in pain as the years go by. You have got off scot free, but I shall not let you forget. God knows how many other young lives you have destroyed, peddling your poison. You ought to die of shame, you ought to be punished, you ought to be in prison, people like you should be put away. May you pay for this with your life's happiness. I hope that you will never be forgiven and that people will turn from you with horror, I hope and pray that you will never be happy again. My only consolation is that you will never recover from the drugs to which you are addicted, their effects are irreversible, you have destroyed your mind and will live the life of an idiot, tormented by fantasies. I wish my hatred could kill you. I curse you, I condemn you to a miserable haunted life. The claws which I drive into you now will never release their hold.

Jennifer Wilsden.

9

This letter from Mark's mother arrived soon after the inquest. Edward thought of writing to her to say that whatever misery she wanted to curse him with was less than what he felt now and would for ever feel. However he did not write. Another similar letter arrived from her in the following week, then another. It was now March. Mark had been dead for nearly a month.

Edward was entirely occupied with his misery, he had no other occupation. He took the tranquillisers and sleeping pills prescribed by the family doctor. He slept as long and as often as possible, he longed for sleep, unconsciousness, blackness, the absolute absence of light. He found it difficult, indeed pointless, to get up in the morning; curled up, hiding his head, he lay in bed till noon. There was nobody he wanted to see, and nothing he wanted to do except sleep and, when this was impossible, read thrillers. He avidly and quickly read dozen after dozen of the coarsest trashiest most violent thrillers he could lay his hands on. It was at least an occupation to go as far as the library or to the secondhand bookshops in Charing Cross Road. He could, in his state, have readily used pornography too if he had known how to get it. He wandered around Soho and looked into the windows of sex shops and at the photos outside strip joints. But he had not the nerve or particularity of will required to enter any of these establishments. He brooded over the cover pictures of terrible little magazines which had been soiled by eager hands, then slouched guiltily on, afraid of being visible. He wandered a good deal in London, vaguely hoping he might be run over. He stood in underground stations and watched the merciful tube trains thunder in. He did not visit pubs or bars. He had no desire for alcohol, and his old drug was now nothing to him; he could not imagine how he had ever wanted it. All that belonged to a childish phase which he could so gladly and easily have given up, which would be an incident in his past, were it not that now nothing of it could be left behind, he was arrested forever in the place of his crime. Something blood-stained and heavy would travel on with him always, through all of his life. How does one live after total wickedness, total failure, total disgrace? The plough had gone over him and he was dismembered. Grief and remorse were pale names for his condition. He recalled the innocence he had once had which he would never have again; and how happy he had been not so very long ago when, not knowing how blessed he was, he had carelessly thrown away all his possibilities of good. Oh why could not the past be undone, since he regretted it so bitterly and so sincerely? One momentary act of folly and treachery had destroyed all his *time*. He had no time now, only the dead task of passing the hours, there was no live time, no future, he hated everyone. He especially hated Sarah Plowmain, who had brought it all about by that homicidal seduction in her suffocating Sibyl's cave. Sexual desire had left him, he could not conceive of feeling it again. The craving for pornography was something else, and even that was dull and lacked intensity. His fantasy life was deadened, he had become an obsessive machine, mechanically afraid of the police and of men in white coats. All cravings were mean now, since he himself was utterly without identity or value. Only occasionally when he woke from sleep did he for seconds recover his lost self, his happy self who did not know that his life was irrevocably smashed and over. Waking perhaps from a happy dream he would exist for seconds as that old self, the lively self that could anticipate a happy busy significant day. Then black memory would come, the blackness that covered everything, blinding his eyes and annihilating space and time. Thus did day bring back his night.

It was not quite true to say that he hated everyone. One person remained to him, the only one he needed, the only one he loved, Mark Wilsden, his friend, his beloved. Talking aloud to himself Edward would repeat again and again, as the rhythmical moan with which the agonised sufferer tries to soothe unbearable pain, 'Oh my dear, oh my darling, my poor lost one, my poor dead one, come to me, forgive me, I'm sorry, oh my love, my love, I'm so sorry, help me, help me, help me.' So he prayed to Mark. A language he would never have used to Mark alive now seemed the only way to speak to Mark dead, to Mark's image or ghost which was now permanently present, a part of every thought, in the chamber of his mind. Sometimes when he was alone he even pictured that ghost as an unhappy strengthless wraith, crying outside his door, begging to be given back his life; and the transformation of Edward's grief into pity seemed so likely to kill him on the spot that he had to run out gasping into the street where the alien hostile faces of strangers forced him to control himself and survive. Vain love for Mark grew in him cancer-like and was spewed forth in a black private eloquence often accompanied by tears. Only Edward could not cry properly, not as he had seen girls cry in gushing pouring streams. His tears came forth painfully as a small and healthless dew.

Sometimes he tried to think simply that he had committed a sin, was feeling guilty, and should repent; but these familiar ideas seemed abstract and flimsy, unable to take any hold upon the devastation of his life. One moment of absolute treachery had proved everything against him, his guilt was a huge pain which blotted out ideas, and he lived in it like a fish at the bottom of a dark lake. If only he could have, somehow, somewhere, a clean pain, a vital pain, not a death pain, a pain of purgatory by which in time he could work it all away, as a stain which could be patiently worked upon and cleansed and made to vanish. But there was no time, he had destroyed time. This was hell, where there was no time. If only he had been accused of some definite outrage and sent to prison. The idea of being for a definite period, however long, in prison occasionally seemed attractive in a world where all natural desire had ended. He even considered committing some ordinary crime in order to *get* to prison. But the will was lacking. He could not invent anything, not even, at present, his own death.

Like Cain I have killed my brother whom I loved. Perhaps I killed him purposely, out of envy, like someone said, how can I know? Oh forgive me, will not someone forgive me? If Mark were alive in a wheelchair would he forgive me? Surely he would. But he is not alive, and I killed him. Edward heard these thoughts, endlessly repeated, ringing in his head, ringing out as if everyone could hear them, and sometimes he found himself, even when he was not alone, starting to recite them aloud as a mechanical litany, and weirdly smiling when the agony was worst. Oh for any other pain except this one, a

12

merciful pain that would wipe away the *deed itself,* perhaps in a million years, but sometime. I left him alone, the final eternally unpardonable moral failure, the ultimate dereliction of duty. If only the telephone hadn't rung, if only I had not gone away, if only I had left the door unlocked, if only I had come back twenty minutes sooner, ten minutes, one minute . . . Perhaps he rattled the door again and again, calling my name – as now I hear him calling in the night, calling out and crying.

Mark Wilsden had been cremated and his ashes scattered. It was as well. If that smeared and broken body had still existed, buried somewhere, Edward would have had to go and lie upon it.

'LISTEN,' SAID HARRY Cuno, patiently and not for the first time to his stepson Edward Baltram, 'you are having a *nervous breakdown* you are *ill,* it is an *illness,* like pneumonia or scarlet fever, you will receive *help,* you will be given *treatment,* you will get *better,* you will *recover.* Please take this *in.* Please be *patient* and do what you are *told.*'

Edward, sitting opposite his stepfather in the drawing room of the tall house in Bloomsbury to which Chloe Warriston had fled, pregnant with Jesse's child, stared at Harry for a moment, then looked way.

My God, thought Harry, both my boys have lost their senses at the same time, and just when they were doing so well, they seem to want to destroy themselves, Edward with this depression and Stuart with religious mania. They're both in love with death.

Harry Cuno, though he loved both of them, was well known to prefer his stepson to his son. Harry, instinctively placed by Edward as 'not exactly successful', had 'suffered' from being the only child of a famous father, Casimir Cuno, a popular highbrow novelist. Harry had detested his father's books, but greatly valued his success. The unusual surname, of which Harry was also proud, was of Provençal origin. Casimir's reputation was now in eclipse, but he had bequeathed to Harry, together with a lot of money, a versatile ambitious restless temperament, and a cluster of talents, which Casimir had learnt to use, and Harry had not. Sarah Plowmain had voiced a general view in calling Harry an

14

'adventurer', and a 'hero of our time'. Harry was sorry to miss the war. After a stormy sojourn at his father's old public school in the north of England, and a brilliant career as a university student, and after the death of his father in a yachting accident, Harry had played at journalism, at literature, at business, at politics, at *enfant terrible*. He was a disappointed spoilt child. He had published a novel and some poems, been an unsuccessful Labour candidate, set up a short-lived *avant-garde* publishing house. He never *seemed* to fail, and although many years had passed without any further visible achievements, and his sons were now grown up, much was still expected of him, as if he had the gift of eternal promise. There was always something, endlessly put off but still there. He continued to look handsome and young. His career as a husband and father had been similarly clouded and remained suitably picturesque. He had amazed his friends by marrying a shy quiet girl, with timid gentle hazel eyes, from New Zealand ('the girl from far away'), whom he had met at college. When she died of leukaemia soon after giving birth to a son, Harry got over his grief by playing the libertine. If Harry was a playboy, as some said, it was because all his activities, whether serious or not, appeared to take this form. He next married a more notorious young lady, Chloe Warriston, a painter, but more famous for being Jesse Baltram's favourite model. Unfriendly critics said that Harry, having married someone quiet, ordinary and decent, whom he loved, was kept in the real world by the effort. When he married a professional dream girl he was taken over by his obsessions and his feet finally and permanently left the ground. The girl from far away had been a felicitous accident, Chloe was a fate. He saw her at an Arts Club party, and immediately 'recognised' those tragic eyes, peering from among masses of untidy brown hair. He fancied her reputation, and when he married her she was already pregnant. Some said this alien pregnancy was what attracted Harry most. It was a restless marriage, although Chloe loved her opportune pirate whom, she said, she always pictured swarming on board with a cutlass between his teeth. No hand-to-hand combat had been necessary however, since Jesse had

15

certainly abandoned Chloe, and did not later show any interest in his casual offspring. It was Jesse's long-suffering wife May who had, on two to three occasions, asked Chloe to bring Edward, aged five or six, over to see his father when the Baltrams were staying in London. They had already by this time left Chelsea for the country. On these visits Chloe, who had never forgiven her faithless lover and perhaps was still in love with him, left Edward at the door to confront alone the big dark-haired man who looked at him with amused curiosity, the nervously effusive stepmother, and two staring overtly hostile little girls. Harry stayed away from these encounters of which he disapproved, and which after Chloe's early death (Edward was seven) were not repeated. May Baltram later sent two or three Christmas cards to Edward which Harry intercepted and destroyed. That was the end of a matter about which Edward retained remarkably little memory in the motherless years during which he so took for granted Harry as father and Stuart as brother. He could not recall his mother at all clearly, he remembered mainly her large sad eyes as the wasting illness took her away, and his own feeling of a terrible sadness, and a kind of guilt which he had imbibed from the sense of a tension between her and Harry, as if perhaps her reproaches, addressed to those who would survive her, were falling upon him too. Later, as he became more aware of the oddity of his parentage, he protectively clouded her image. A little extra 'family' was provided for Edward by Chloe's younger sister 'Midge', a fashion model, once the smartest woman in London, who amazed everyone by marrying an 'older man', Thomas McCaskerville.

The panelled drawing room of Harry Cuno's house, which had been his parents' and his grandparents' house, was a long room on the first floor with windows at each end. It was painted, had been painted long ago and had pleasantly aged and faded, a darkish green, now made sombre again by an afternoon mist outside. One lamp was on. A fire was burning in the grate. Harry was a large broad-faced fresh-complexioned man, his thick lively hair, skilfully cut, which had only lately faded a little from being 'golden', standing up in a crown above his unlined brow. He had cordial blue eyes which looked with inquisitive friendliness about him. Sitting by the fire, he was leaning forward now with his elbows on his knees. Edward, tall and thin and dark, with a hawk nose and limp dark straight hair which flopped across his face, a little taller than his stepfather, cringed back into his shabby box-like armchair. Harry's words did not, could not, reach him, had no connection with his sufferings, did not concern him in the least. He was having an imaginary conversation with Mark. 'Look, Mark, it was her talking about my family that delayed me . . .'

Harry thought, I've got to do something. We've let him rest, stay in bed, wander about, be by himself, he seemed to prefer that, but he's fading away, he's like a dying animal. If only there was something he *wanted.* 'Why don't you go on holiday? Go with anybody you like, go with a girl. I'll fix it all. Go to Venice. You were talking about going to Venice.'

Edward, his gaze fixed on the corner of the room, slowly shook his head. The double-glazed windows admitted faint traffic noise, at the other end gave glimpses of close misty trees.

'Has Thomas said anything, arranged for you to see him again?'

'No.'

'Curse him, why doesn't *he* do something? He's got some idea in his head. He's so devious. This leaving you alone is no good. You will come to dinner tonight?' The McCaskervilles had invited Harry and Edward and Stuart to dinner.

'Yes.'

'It's for you, you know, to get you out of yourself.'

'Yes.'

'Willy and Ursula will be there.' Willy Brightwalton was Edward's tutor. (Edward was studying French.) His wife Ursula was the family doctor. 'Are you taking those pills Ursula gave you?'

'Yes.'

'Edward, do listen to me, concentrate, take a pull on yourself, get yourself together a bit. Try to put all this behind you. Nobody blames you, you're not guilty of anything, it was

17

an *accident*. Don't be so self-important, everybody isn't thinking about you, if that's what's worrying you. People have other troubles, you've been forgotten. You're free now, you've been through it all and got off. British justice has forgiven you and send you home to get on with your life, so can't you forgive yourself and do just that? You've got every advantage, you're young, you're attractive, you're clever, you're healthy, don't chuck it all away. Happiness, that's what life's about, it's your job to be happy, not to spread gloom and despair all round. Don't be so selfish. Get your courage back, get your narcissism back, get your myth back, straighten you spine and believe in yourself again.'

Edward looked at Harry, or glanced at him, with an expression of faint wincing distaste, huddled himself further into his chair, and resumed gazing into the corner of the room.

Harry, who had only lately see his sons' faces change from the soft vague sweetness of boyhood to the hard anxious definition of manhood, looked with despair and anguish at Edward's weak puckered discontented almost feminine air.

'You want to be a writer, don't you? Well, here's an experience, why not write about it!'

'I couldn't. It's not – an experience –'

'Write a diary about it, about how you feel, you could use it for material later on.'

Edwards shook his head. His whole face was insipid, entirely changed, ugly with weakness. Looking at that change Harry thought, he's very ill.

'You're making too much of it, see it in proportion, see it in perspective, you're sick with self-pity, you want to wallow in guilt, in a way you're enjoying it. It doesn't matter so much. It doesn't matter all that much what you do, personal responsibility is a sort of pretentious notion anyway, it's a fiction, who do you think you are? There isn't anything deep here, God isn't watching you, your job is to make yourself function again, just get going, get back to college, get back to work anyway, and for Christ's sake don't let Thomas talk you into some sort of interesting psychological condition, that could go on forever. Edward, are you listening?'

18

'Yes.'

'This is a small incident in your life, it's almost nothing to do with you at all, you'll see later, all life is accidental, of course we blunder against each other, and there are wicked men, but you're not one. Back up, stop thinking about yourself, *that's* what's wrong, don't let this business lodge in your soul, it isn't anything, it isn't deep, it isn't a great spiritual drama, just shrug it off, toss it away, as if it were a bit of mud or a bit of ash or –' Harry, made increasingly irritable and upset by Edward's silence, leaned forward and picked up a cinder from the grate. He dropped it hastily. It was extremely hot and had burnt his fingers. 'Damn!' He flapped his hand and blew upon it.

Edward watched him with a faint gleam of interest.

'CANST THOU NOT minister to a mind diseased, pluck from the memory a rooted sorrow?'

'No.'

The first speaker was Harry Cuno, the second Thomas McCaskerville.

The scene was the McCaskervilles' dinner party at their house in Fulham, the little gathering which was 'for' the unfortunate Edward. Midge McCaskerville was in the kitchen, Thomas, Harry and Edward in the drawing room. Edward, glanced at occasionally by the other two, had taken a book from a shelf and was sitting in a corner pretending to read it. He had refused a drink. The room, Midge's taste, for Thomas was unconscious of his surroundings, was brilliant with flowers, upon the curtains, upon the wallpaper, upon the oriental carpet, even in plaster wreaths upon the ceiling, as well as serenely and more ephemerally present in jugs and vases. Yet each flower knew its place, and the tall stiff brigades of yellow-eyed narcissi, whose perfume filled the room, did not put the discreet little wallpaper roses in any way out of countenance. Upon the walls here and there, stemming the floral tide, were airy views of Berkshire by Midge's (and Chloe's) deceased father, Cleve Warriston, a minor painter and follower of Paul Nash. Many lamps lit the still expectant scene. Willy Brightwalton, who loved Midge, was helping her in the kitchen. Ursula and Stuart, the remaining guests, had not yet arrived.

Harry and Thomas stood by the fireplace upon an *art deco*

rug embroidered with tulips. Primroses from Midge and Thomas's country cottage crowded upon the mantelpiece. Outside, the east wind prowled, rattling the windows. The curtains were securely drawn. Harry and Thomas, standing close to each other, were conscious of a familiar beam of ambiguous emotion occasioned by proximity. They had known each other for a long time. Harry took a step back. He was dandyish in his bow tie, his broad calm fine-complexioned face ('milk and roses' as Chloe used to say), newly shaved, glowing with health. Thomas, whose ancestors were Jacobites and Rabbis, was thin, with a narrow dog-like jaw and cool blue eyes and a square-cut fringe of wiry light grey hair, and thick robust rectangular glasses which he was rarely seen without.

'Why not?' said Harry.

'The patient must minister to himself.'

'Yes, yes, of course, call yourself a mediator, an enabler of the gods, what you like, but can't you *do* something?' Harry was by now so used to feeling that Edward did not hear what he said that he spoke as if the boy were absent.

The door bell rang.

'Midge will go,' said Thomas in his high fastidious Edinburgh voice. A woman's tones were heard. 'That's Ursula. Stuart will come?'

'He said he would, so he will.'

'What's the latest?'

'He wants to be a probation officer!'

Stuart Cuno, four years older than Edward, had lately startled his family and friends by refusing to continue his education. Established as a graduate student with distinguished honours in mathematics, offered a coveted teaching post at a London college, he had announced that he was leaving the academic world in order to do 'social work'.

'Well, why not?' said Thomas. 'But what *is* it?'

'Well, you should know, no mother, a neurotic stepmother, a father who preferred his brother –'

'I don't mean that –'

'However well Stuart did, Edward was always the star, he was the charmer, he was the one they noticed –'

21

'I mean, what's his idea?'

'Some religious sect must have brainwashed him or something –'

'Why shouldn't he break out and help his fellow-men?'

'It's not just that, it's his attitude, he'll be barefoot in a brown robe next. If it were political I wouldn't mind so much –'

'It's not political?'

'Only vaguely, like helping the under-privileged.'

'Some mathematicians just lose their drive at that age.'

'He was clearing out of maths anyway. He was doing some logic and philosophy stuff for his doctorate, something on Boole and Frege. I thought he was loving it.'

Harry felt something cold touching his hand. He looked down and saw that it was a bowl of olives held by Meredith McCaskerville. Meredith was Thomas and Midge's son aged thirteen. Meredith had straight fairish brownish hair like his mother, which he combed down in neat lines to his collar, and with a fringe like his father. Tonight he was jacketed and wearing a tie. He was a straight-backed dignified laconic boy. He did not look up at Harry but simply thrust the edge of the bowl against his hand. Harry was used to Meredith and fond of him, he appreciated his reticent style, he even imagined they had something of a secret understanding. 'No thanks, Meredith. Is it fun being a teenager?'

'Not much. There are salted almonds if you'd rather.'

'No thanks. Are you looking forward to boarding school?'

'No.'

'Have some more of the mixture,' said Thomas. They were drinking a blend of white port with Carpano and Noilly Prat with liberally added apple juice. Such gluey aperitifs, concocted by himself, were drunk, sometimes under protest, by Thomas's guests.

Meredith, who was *never* called 'Merry', was distinguished by a red wine-coloured birthmark upon his cheek, referred to by his father as 'the sign of Dionysus'. Everyone continually told him how attractive it was. What Meredith thought was not known.

Ursula Brightwalton came in. She was wearing a long stiff black satin evening skirt which made a noise like a small saw, and an old and visibly shabby Chinese jacket embroidered with dragons. As she often announced, she always dressed hastily in something easy. Her dark greying hair was cut in a sensible bob, and her clever thoughtful eyes peered merrily at the world. Her smirking facetious garrulous manner deceived only some. She was a handsome woman who usually looked like what she was, an able and popular general practitioner. Thomas had known her for a considerable time in a medical context (where they did not always agree) and more recently Willy had attracted Edward into his college. Ursula and Willy had a brilliant son Giles, a little older than Stuart, who was away winning extra laurels at an American university, where Willy was about to visit him.

'Hello, Thomas, hello, Harry. What a frightful smell of flowers in here. Shouldn't you open a window? People think flowers are good for them like they think sunlight is, a great mistake. Good evening, Meredith, you've grown. Hasn't he got a grown-up look? What a fine suit you're wearing, all you need is a waistcoat and a watch chain. With a strawberry birthmark and a name like Meredith McCaskerville you can conquer the world. You'll be Prime Minister. Don't you think?'

Meredith ignored this sally.

'Such a soldierly child,' said Ursula to Thomas, 'so upright and self-contained. What does he want to do now when he grows up?'

'He thinks now,' said Thomas, 'that he'd like to be an aeronautical engineer. He wants to reintroduce airships.'

'He'll make a fortune. And how are you, Harry dear?'

'How do you think, with all this. In general I'm resting, like an actor.'

'You *are* an actor, you always were. What a pity you didn't get into politics, you could have used up all that restless ambition. Midge and Willy are in control in the kitchen, they don't need me, can't I have a drink, I've had a terrible day, whisky please, Thomas, not your sugary mixture. Isn't Midge looking lovely in that new dress? No wonder she was voted London's best-dressed woman.'

Going to the drinks Thomas said, 'She never made it to best-dressed woman, she was only a runner-up.'

'He always put her down,' Ursula murmured to Harry.

Meanwhile Meredith, picking up the salted almonds, was offering both bowls with outstretched hands to Edward. Edward, still in his corner, had shrunk as if in the process of some biological change, into a small animal. His lean head had become narrower and descended into a hole between his skinny shoulders, and he had drawn his long legs in against the chair. He clasped the book hard against his chest. His grieving mouth enacted a jerky smile like a little paroxysm and he shook his head. Meredith put the bowls down on the carpet and lightly caressed the sleeve of Edward's jacket; then he picked them up again and placed them on the table and left the room.

Ursula now noticed Edward. She flushed and put her hand up to the neck of her jacket. As she went over to him he shrank into an even small compass. 'Edward, how are you? Are you taking those pills I gave you? Are you *eating*? Harry, is he eating?'

'Sort of,' said Harry.

'Edward, you must eat. I'll come over and talk to you tomorrow. May I?'

'Yes, thank you,' said Edward in a dead voice.

'Is he still staying in bed all day?'

'Not so much.'

'He must eat, he must. We must surround him with – we must surround him – oh *dear* –'

Midge McCaskervile came in followed by Willy Brightwalton. Midge was wearing a long straight blue and pink and white striped silk dress, with a poised undulating collar with smaller closer stripes of the same colours, and a suggestion of a train which slid sibilantly upon the formal tapestry of the carpet. With a flourish she whirled up the train revealing her fine legs in pink stockings, and laughed. Thomas stared at her as if he had never seen her before. Her copious fairish brown hair, which contained many tinges, including red here and there, disposed itself in a decorous graceful mop about her head, tossed mane-like from time to time. She wore little but very careful make-up, whose boldest feature was the deep glossy red of the little fingernails upon her small hands.

24

She rarely wore jewellery. Her eyes, a cordial gentle brown, seemed always to petition and persuade: like me, like me! Her face expressed an almost insistent sympathy. She was friends with everyone, and her little air of self-satisfied animation made people, even as they admired her beauty, smile a little. She had a perfect nose and was often photographed in profile in the 'smartest woman' days. Since then she had admittedly put on weight.

Her self-appointed *chevalier* Willy was comfortably stout and bald. He continually, even in the middle of dinner, combed a long lock of gingery hair over his bald patch, but as often the lock fell away, depending awkwardly over his ear, giving him a slightly mad look. Willy was famous for having, as a child, witnessed his father's death, killed by a camel on a long-planned long-looked-forward-to visit to Egypt. The camel, perhaps mistaking Brightwalton senior for a driver who had ill-treated him, knocked him down and knelt on him. Willy also witnessed the shooting of the camel which happened soon after. When Ursula said 'he thinks about it all the time' she scarcely exaggerated. 'He feels that camel kneeling on his heart.' This tragic business had, in the callous hurly-burly of social life, become a joke, and people warned each other how important it was never to mention camels in Willy's presence, and how mysteriously difficult it was to keep off the subject. Willy, clever, lazy, always anxious, always guilty before his pupils, was a Proust expert, but never managed to finish his great book. He disliked intellectual conversations which he would dreamily break off by murmuring his favourite saying, 'Ah well – *tout passe, toute casse, tout lasse.*' He had lately developed the notion, entertained in fact by no one else, that he was expected to take Edward with him to America so as to 'distract him from his troubles'. Willy especially regarded Harry as having framed such a plan. With a glance now at Edward, whom he had greeted earlier and did not have to attend to now, Willy at once began explaining, 'Pardon, gentles all, I'm afraid, I've told Midge, I can't stay to dinner. I've got to go home and pack, I'm leaving for California tomorrow morning.'

'So soon?' said Thomas.

'I have to go earlier, it's because of Giles, he quite insists, it's my first sabbatical for I don't know how long, I've been looking forward to it so much –'

'It's true,' said Ursula, 'he's like a child waiting for his hols, Willy loves America, he feels liberated there like so many Englishmen, he's longing to see Giles, how I wish I could go! And he *must* go and pack, he's done *nothing*!' Ursula looked indulgently upon Willy's chaste passion for Midge, it seemed even to cause her some satisfaction.

'You're lucky,' said Harry, 'no problems with Giles, he just goes on from one triumph to another. I wonder if you could ask him to write to Stuart and tell him not to be such a fool?'

'Don't go yet, have another drink,' said Thomas.

'I'm afraid Willy got onto the whisky in the kitchen,' said Midge.

Willy cast a glance of dread towards the terrible figure of suffering Edward. He hated it when his pupils had troubles. He always drank the detestable 'mixture' out of politeness. Thomas, perhaps out of some rabbinical ancestral puritanism, had made a positive rite of it. Midge caught Harry's eye and smiled, turned away to look at Edward. She went to him and with a flurry and a soft hiss of the striped dress knelt on one knee, and, with a gesture which resembled her son's, touched his jacket and then laid her red-tipped fingers lightly upon the back of his hand. Edward shuddered and withdrew his hand, then forced a smile. Midge sighed and rose. 'Edward, dear, do come and join us, have a drink.' But the words were uttered tonelessly, without hope of effect, as she turned away.

'Stuart is late,' said Thomas.

'He's probably at a prayer meeting,' said Harry.

'But Stuart doesn't believe in God,' said Midge.

'That doesn't stop him. And to do him justice, I don't really think it's a sect, he's doing it all on his own, he thinks he's got a mission to mankind, he's waiting for it all to start, he's expecting the first miracle.'

'I'll have some jugs of water ready for him in the kitchen.'

'I suppose he reads lots of oriental books like they all do,' said Willy.

'No, he doesn't, he reads nothing, he doesn't like any form

26

of art, he hasn't any friends, he just sits wresting with himself, wondering what the purehearted young idealist does now!'

'It's an out-of-date question,' said Midge.

'He's an out-of-date boy.'

'You said once he wanted to be a solider.'

'That was ages ago, just symbolic, the idea of duty and obedience, and a life of monkish deprivation. He wants to be like Job, always in the wrong before God, only he's got to do it without God.'

'Does he want martyrdom then?' said Ursula.

'I expect so. He'll probably die young, in the sea or underneath a train or –'

'Not suicide?'

'No, no, stupidly trying to save somebody's life. He's a retarted schoolboy.'

'Stuart *thinks* before he laughs at a joke,' said Midge, 'and then if he does laugh, he laughs loudly like a child.'

'No *risqué* jokes when he's around!'

'Is it true he's taken an oath of celibacy?' said Willy. 'How's it done?'

'At his age it's impossible,' said Midge, 'he just lacks confidence. I'll find him a girl. He wants to draw attention to himself. It's a cry for help.'

'No, he takes it all seriously,' said Harry.

'All what?' said Thomas.

'About being good, being perfect!'

'Well, I suppose it was meant to be –'

'Can he do anything for Edward?' said Willy.

'No, he's too self-obsessed, he scarcely knows that Edward exists, and they never really got on –'

'I think Stuart was wrongly advised at the start,' said Ursula, 'don't you agree, Willy? He ought to have done biological sciences. But really he's all right, he's just having a schoolboy religious crisis a bit late in the day, he always was a slow sort of chap.'

'I suppose it's nuclear war,' said Midge, 'the young say it hangs over us all.'

'I confess I don't notice it all that much,' said Ursula, 'but then I'm so busy.'

27

'Stuart is more worried about computers,' said Harry.

'Computers?' said Ursula. 'But they're man's best friends. They're invaluable in medicine.'

'Harry, you've hurt your hand,' said Midge. 'It looks like a burn.'

'It is a burn. What do you prescribe, Ursula?'

'Nothing.'

'Trying to bring home a point to Edward, I picked up a red hot coal.'

'Was he impressed?' said Midge.

'Stuart has moved in on me, he arrived yesterday with all his stuff. He's terminated his grant, and his digs, he didn't have to, typical youthful selfishness at someone else's expense. And of course Edward's been at home since that business. I'm cooking for those two loutish boys now, *and* one's a vegetarian!'

'You love cooking,' said Midge. 'Oh dear, the cheese soufflé will be spoiling. Stuart will have to miss his drink.'

'Drink? He doesn't *drink*,' said Harry. 'He's like a camel as far as serious liquid refreshment is concerned.'

'I must go,' said Willy.

The door bell rang. Midge went.

Willy turned to Thomas. He was red in the face, as if near to tears. Ursula came to him and took his arm. Willy said to Thomas. 'How absolutely lovely Midge looks tonight.'

'Yes,' said Thomas, 'she is so warm, a life-giver.' Thomas sounded insincere, almost ironical, but one never knew with Thomas.

Ursula led Willy to the door and out of the room. She returned. 'I don't know whether it was Midge or whisky or camel!'

Stuart Cuno walked in.

Stuart was as tall as Edward but more robustly made. He had a large pale face and pretty lips and blond hair, golden like his father's used to be, but cut shorter. His eyes were a light amber brown, almost yellow, like the eyes of an animal. Someone had once likened Stuart to a plump white grub with a big head emerging from an apple, but the image was unjust. Stuart was physically abrupt, ungainly, not at home in space,

28

but not unimpressive. Meredith followed him in.

Stuart, ignoring his hosts, was saying to Meredith, 'Yes, we'll fix a day, now I'm settled in we can go running again.' Stuart and Meredith had been fellow joggers for more than a year. Meredith nodded his head slowly and emphatically several times.

Midge called them in to dinner.

'So you think only religion will save us from the wrath to come?' said Ursula to Stuart.

Dinner was far advanced. Meredith had retired to bed. They were eating cheese. Edward, to whom everyone kept turning with kind bright attention, was mainly silent, but had been forced to make a few simple remarks.

'It isn't religion he's got,' said Harry. 'You can't have religion without God.'

'But he said that nothing was more important than the future of religion on this plant.'

'I think he should have a uniform,' said Midge.

'I suggest a sheet,' said Harry.

Stuart smiled.

'You can tuck into the cheese,' said Midge to Stuart. 'I'm terribly sorry I forgot to make you a proper vegetarian dish.'

'I've eaten plenty,' said Stuart. It was true. He was always hungry. 'The cabbage was marvellous,' he added.

'Edward, do have some cheese,' said Midge, 'it's the kind you like.'

'But what exactly is it you're so afraid of?' said Ursula. 'Of course there's nuclear warfare and atomic waste and all that, but you seem to be simply afraid of science.'

'Doesn't science prove free will nowadays?' said Midge.

'I think you hate science,' said Ursula, 'and that upsets me.'

'But of course I've had no education,' said Midge, 'and I can't understand these things.'

'Don't show off!' said Harry.

'You hate mathematics because that's the future,' said Ursula. 'Actually the human race will be finished off by molecular biology, but we keep that dark.'

'I'm tired of this century,' said Harry. 'I want to start living in the next one.'

'Isn't it true that science proves free will?' said Midge to Thomas. 'They used to think that everything was like a machine, and now they think it's all random.'

'I don't think either of those ideas has anything to do with free will,' said Thomas.

'Personally I find the idea of the nuclear bomb attractive,' said Harry. 'Get rid of all that messy accumulated past, all those old ideas and things, shake up the collective psyche. Don't you think, Thomas?'

'I want to know what Stuart's *after*,' said Ursula. 'You're *scared*, there's something you *hate*, and which is making you act in this funny way.'

'Stuart thinks the world is the work of Satan,' said Harry.

'Help him, Thomas,' said Midge. 'Don't just sit mum, you're as bad as Edward.'

Thomas said, 'The devil made everything except one thing which he continually looks for but cannot find.'

'Helpful old Jewish saying,' said Ursula. 'Well, the Greeks said God was always doing geometry, modern physicists say he's playing roulette, everything depends on the observer, the universe is a totality of observations, it's a work of art created by us –'

'Quantum physics is the language of nature,' said Midge.

'Who says so?' said Thomas.

'I do. I heard it on TV. And the subatomic world needs us to rescue it from chaos. It all sounds perfectly mad. No wonder there are terrorists. No wonder we need religion.'

'If Newton hadn't believed in God he would have discovered relativity,' said Ursula.

'There you are!' said Harry.

'A machine can be cleverer than a man now,' said Midge.

'And wiser and better,' said Harry. 'It stands to reason. The computer age is just beginning. Even now a machine can see infinitely more than we can, see it faster, discern more details, make more connections, correct itself, teach itself, learn new skills which we can't even conceive of. A machine is *objective*. It's a matter of flesh and blood, it's a matter of nerve cells, we are puny, we are imperfect, these things are gods. A computer could run a state better than a human being –'

'Aren't we already run by computers?' said Midge. 'Isn't there one at Downing Street which does the budget?'

'They could help us to redesign ourselves, and we certainly need redesigning! They offer us a vision of the human mind, glorified, clarified and fortified, we can learn about ourselves by watching them, improve ourselves by imitating them –'

'Come on, Stuart,' said Thomas.

'A machine doesn't think –' said Stuart. 'A machine can't even simulate the human mind.'

'Why not?' said Harry.

'You mean it's syntactical not semantical?' said Ursula. 'Isn't that what they say now? Or that it has mind but not consciousness?'

'Because we are always involved in distinguishing between good and evil.'

'Surely not always,' said Ursula, 'not even often.'

'Who is to judge the wisdom of a machine, another machine? Human minds are possessed by individual persons, they are soaked in values, even perception is evaluation.'

'But isn't serious thinking supposed to be neutral?' said Ursula. 'We get away from all that personal stuff.'

'Serious thinking depends on the justice and truthfulness of the thinker, it depends on the continuous pressure of his mind upon –'

'That's a different point,' said Ursula, 'the chap's got to be OK, and of course discoveries can be used rightly or wrongly, but the thinking itself can be pure, without values, like genuine science, like maths, like – at any rate that's the ideal and –'

'You can't just switch it on,' said Stuart, 'as you say it's an ideal, science is an ideal, and partly an illusion. Our trust in science as reason is something frail. Wittgenstein thought that the idea of a man on the moon was not only unreasonable, but forbidden by our whole system of physics!'

'Stuart just despises empiricism,' said Harry, 'he's opting for the life of the emotions.'

'You mean there are wicked scientists?' said Midge. 'Or computers could go mad?'

31

'Not just that,' said Stuart. 'It's not just on the outside, about using discoveries, or as if a man just had to be serious and could then switch to being neutral. Being objective is being truthful, making right judgments is a moral activity, all thinking is a function of morality, it's done by humans, it's touched by values right into its centre, empirical science is no exception –'

'All right then,' said Ursula, 'but there *is* an exception and it's mathematics, and *that's* why you're giving it up! It's the only thing which whoever made *your* world didn't make and is always looking for to destroy it, and I'm against him! *You'*d like to destroy it –'

'So it's all relative?' said Midge. 'I'm getting muddled.'

'No, he is,' said Harry.

'Well, maths is an oddity,' said Stuart, 'though it's just our thinking too, and more confused than outsiders imagine. It's impressive, it looks as if it's all there and can't be wrong, we call it a language – But it can't be a model for the mind, it's not a super-mind, computer logic can't be a model for the mind, there's no ideal model and there can't be because minds are persons, they're moral and spiritual all the way through, the idea of a machine isn't in place, artificial intelligence is a misnomer –'

'Now he slips in "spiritual"!' said Harry. 'You want to make everything moral, that's your version of religion, you want to push what's really objective and factual into a corner. But the lesson of our age is the opposite, modern science has abolished the difference between good and evil, there isn't anything deep, that's the message of the modern world, science is what's deep, Ursula's right, mathematics is the pure case, and that's the point, because mathematics is everywhere, it's swept the board, biology is maths now, isn't that so, Ursula, the language of the planet is mathematics –'

'You're drunk,' said Ursula.

'What *are* you afraid of?' said Thomas to Stuart. 'Can you give it a name?'

'Oh – all that, what we've been talking about.'

'But we've been talking nonsense,' said Ursula, 'dinner-time conversation.'

32

'I'm afraid that we could lose our language, and so lose our souls, our sense of truth, and ordinary reality, our sense of direction, our knowledge of right and wrong . . .'

'It's certainly the end of an era,' said Harry, 'the energy which we got from the Greeks and the Renaissance is all used up. New technology is the life force now.'

'How do you mean, lose our language?' said Thomas.

'Lose our value language, lose our central human language which is spoken by individuals and refers to the real world.'

'But there's always *this* world,' said Midge, tapping her wedding ring on the table. 'Isn't there, Edward?'

'We could lose our ordinary sense of an order of the world as ultimate, our self-being, our responsible con-sciousness –'

'We've never had these things,' said Harry. 'It was an illusion, we're waking from a dream, our precious individual being is something superficial, it's just a matter of style, *le style c'est l'homme même*. Good and evil are relative concepts. After the simplest generalities people start talking nonsense about morals.'

'But surely there's such a thing as human nature,' said Ursula, 'and it stays the same. We women know that, don't we, Midge?'

'Women are always a touchstone,' said Harry, 'like litmus paper or dogs before an earthquake, look at them now running round in manic excitement, *they*'re destroying the old order you're so fond of, men are terrified, no wonder Islam is the most popular religion in the world!'

'Spirit without absolute,' said Thomas to Stuart, 'that's what you're afraid of.'

'Yes. Lost bad spirit.'

'No doubt,' said Thomas, 'the real live language will be reserved for the creative few who have all the power, they will be the only individuals left, and the ordinary mob will simply be codified manifestations of a generalised technological consciousness.'

'My dear Thomas, that's how it is now!' said Harry.

'You cynical élitist!' said Midge.

'He's trying to annoy *us*,' said Ursula.

33

'There you are,' said Harry, 'women have to make everything personal.'

'So religion is the answer,' said Ursula to Stuart, 'that's where we started.'

'Yes, something that keeps love of goodness in people's lives, that *shows* goodness as the most important thing, some sort of spiritual ideal and discipline, like – it's so hard to see it – it's got to be religion without God, without supernatural dogmas, and we may not have time to change what we have into something we can believe in – that's what I think anyway – but I'm just a beginner –'

They laughed.

'Spiritual discipline!' said Ursula. 'I think evangelical Christianity is your fate, I can see it all, you'll be a general in the Salvation Army – or else a Jesuit –'

'I can't think why you're so gloomy,' said Midge, 'you seem so prejudiced, all sorts of wonderful things are happening and will happen, we can fly in space, we've cured TB, we shall cure cancer and feed the hungry, and isn't television a good thing –'

'No, it isn't,' said Stuart.

'Well, what about the animal programmes –'

'Even the poor animals are spoilt by that horrible medium, it destroys our perception, our sense of the visual world, and it's full of pornographic muck –'

'Talking of that,' said Midge, who was getting tired of abstract conversation, 'we came back the other night earlier that we said and discovered Meredith watching some absolutely *awful* pornographic video cassettes which he'd borrowed from his little chums! Children watch absolute *filth* these days.'

Stuart put down his knife with a clatter. He flushed red. 'You don't mean real pornography, that Meredith's been watching real pornography –?'

'Well, real, yes, what they call "hard porn" – it was horrid what I saw, absolutely nightmarish, there were these two men and a girl, and a boy with a knife –'

'Don't tell me,' said Stuart, 'what did you do?'

'What do you expect, we told him to stop and to take the

stuff back where it came from, which he did the next day.'

'You mean that child was looking at – but you explained – you told him how wrong it was – you made him see –'

'We expressed our displeasure. Ought we to have beaten him? He said all the children watch these things. And it's not easy to explain to a child, how does one explain these days? Our ancestors would have been shocked at children knowing anything about sex, now we're told to tell them all about it as soon as they can talk! You can't have it every way. Sex is everywhere. As you said, Stuart, ordinary television is full of what you call muck. Anyway, children aren't innocent, psychoanalysis proves that, you can't protect them –'

'They *are* innocent,' said Stuart, 'and you *can* protect them. There's such a thing as being pure in heart –'

'You can't protect them, and I don't really see why you should,' said Midge. 'Of course we told Meredith not to look at that stuff, but I expect he will, and maybe it's a good thing, how much does a child understand anyway. Better to see it now and get bored than come across it later and get hooked. And he's bound to come across it later. Don't you agree, Thomas? It's like being vaccinated. Have the shock early on and then get it over permanently.'

'I couldn't disagree more,' said Stuart. 'I don't see why he's bound to come across it later. Pornography isn't compulsory, people can recognise what's bad and keep away from it. Why should it be assumed that young people are unavoidably obsessed with every aspect of sex? And why do you take it for granted that Meredith will deceive you? What children get used to and regard as permissible at an early age can weaken all their moral defences, it's an early training in cynicism, and as deep and as lasting as any other training. It's not a bit like vaccination, it's more like acquiring an incurable virus, something that degrades and corrupts, and the corruption of children is an *abomination*.'

'You just don't understand children,' said Midge, 'if you did you wouldn't get so cross and red in the face!'

'I agree with Midge,' said Harry, 'one must be more tolerant these days, absolute judgments are a thing of the past, you've got to come to terms with yourself somehow, and the earlier the better. We aren't saints and can't be. We must learn to accept so-called evil as something natural. Scientists have always been gnostics, and if they say there's a basic indeterminacy in human consciousness, then I say that's exactly how I feel! As for corrupting the young, that's what Socrates was accused of! We all have smutty thoughts. Pornography is part of the modern scene, it's something we all really like, and it's perfectly harmless.'

'I don't think Stuart likes it,' said Ursula. 'I wonder if Edward does? What do you think, Edward, you're the youngest person present?'

Edward rose abruptly, overturning his chair onto the floor. He picked the chair up and said to Midge, 'I'm terribly sorry, I'm not feeling very well, I think I'd better go home. Please don't anybody come. I'll just go back –'

'Oh, I'll come,' said Harry rather crossly. 'Come on, Stuart. Our lot for home. We'll have an early night. Don't see us out, we'll quietly steal away.'

'I must go too,' said Ursula, 'I must help Willy pack, he'll have done nothing. Midge will help me find my coat, I think it's upstairs.'

They left the room, leaving Thomas alone with the wine.

After the door had shut upon the Cuno contingent Ursula, closeted upstairs with Midge, said, 'I wanted to see you alone. I'm so worried about Edward, Thomas doesn't seem to be doing anything for him.'

They were sitting on the great ornate ancestral double bed in which, as Thomas liked to announce, many a McCaskerville had been born and died. Midge had shaken off her shoes and pulled up her skirt to reveal the pink stockings. She had undone the invisible buttons which supported the collar of her dress.

'I think Thomas has some plan,' said Midge, 'he usually has.'

'Well, he'd better hurry up with it. Anything could happen to that boy. He needs stronger drugs that the ones I'm giving him. He ought to be inside with some experts.'

'Do you really think so? He wouldn't go. Thomas wants to take him off drugs altogether.'

'Thomas is crazy. Edward could be in for a long depression. I've seen such cases.'

'Stuart seems pretty daft too. I feel sorry for Harry. Just when they were both getting on so well.'

'Oh Stuart and Harry, *they*'re all right. Harry is the perfect hedonist, calmly determined not to be disturbed by the grief of one son and the dottiness of the other.'

'Harry doesn't really believe in neurosis,' said Midge, 'he thinks people should just pull up their socks.'

'I'm not worried about Stuart,' said Ursula, 'he'll be back a little battered in a year or two, sadder and wiser, knocking at the door of the university. Anyway why shouldn't he want to help poor unhappy people, no one seems to give him any credit.'

'Harry wants him to be some sort of top academic.'

'Harry is a snob. Stuart has got a temporary fit of religious mania like boys have at fourteen. He thinks he was immaculately conceived because he can't imagine his mother in bed with Harry. Chloe never like Stuart. Classical bad stepmother, idealised absent mother, that's his trouble. And Harry's wild love life after Chloe died. Actually Stuart is a tough egg. He and Harry are as like as two pins, they're both *Boys' Own Paper* types, romantics who want to be tested, obsessed with courage, have they got it or not, they'd like to be war heroes, it's as simple as that. They should have lived in the nineteenth century. Harry would have been an explorer building the Empire, Stuart would have been a fearless missionary or a controversial bishop.'

'I rather see Harry in Berlin in the jazz age. I must say, I find Stuart exhausting. What did you think of his lecture on pornography?'

'I liked it. What's young Meredith doing now?'

'Reading in bed.'

'What's he reading?'

'*Hydrogren-Propelled Airliners*.'

'He'll be all right.'

'He won't play any of those expensive computer games Thomas got for him.'

'Good child. Never mind them. I'm worried about Edward. At best he'll be in for the dreary business of falling in love with Thomas and then having to fall out again.'

'Harry's afraid he'll become homosexual through being so obsessed with Mark Wilsden.'

'Yes. He's in love with Mark now. Poor boy, oh poor poor boy.'

'Harry was very nervy and nasty tonight, wasn't he. I don't think Thomas was pleased.'

'Harry just uses his intellect to shred himself to pieces, the golden charmer who destroys himself. I can't stand these prophets of doom, gloating over the collapse of civilisation, they're always anti-women. I think Harry despises women, well I suppose most men do. Poor old planet all the same. No wonder Dirk Plowmain shot himself.'

'I didn't realise he shot himself,' said Midge.

'Yes, very stylish. He was a clinical depressive. They're a funny pair, Harry and Thomas, they're chalk and cheese, Thomas an oriental Celt and Harry some kind of archetypal Englishman, two men with absolutely different kinds of minds who fascinate each other.'

'You think they really like each other? I'm never sure,'

'I said "fascinate", but yes, I expect they adore each other! What a pair of egoists! Willy's another of course, in a different style. I must get back. Is Thomas really writing a book about that crazy patient of his, Mr Blinnet?'

'I don't think so.'

'I think that Blinnet man is a fraud. It never seems to occur to humourless psychiatrists that their patients are having them on.'

'Thomas isn't humourless.'

'He's humourless by other means. He's devious, he's *too* deep. Funny finicky Thomas. You know how fond I am of him, and I do admire him. *Quand même*. Tell him to keep an eye on Edward. I'll try to too of course. But it's easier for Thomas. He only has four patients a day, I have dozens.'

'Less than four now. He wants us to live more in the country now Meredith's going to go to boarding school. It's interesting. Harry prefers Edward. I think Thomas prefers Stuart.'

'Yes,' said Ursula, 'Thomas is far more *interested* in Stuart's crisis than he is in Edward's. I don't mean he's irresponsible. But quick crude science is what's wanted here, not snail's pace subtleties. Drugs are the solution, everything else is frivolous. Thomas is moving away from science, he's a traitor, that stuff about all analysis being lay analysis, it's a bad line of talk, and people *listen* to him. He was never much of a doctor anyway, he didn't practice for long. I once heard him say he wanted to forget he'd even been a doctor. He sees his function as priestly, it's all those rabbinical ancestors. It's a substitute for the religion his trendy parents deprived him of. Midge, I'm afraid for Edward.'

'You mean you think he might commit suicide?'

'Of course I think that. One mustn't play with these depressions. I think – don't tell Thomas I said this – I talked with him once about it – that Thomas wouldn't mind a patient of his committing suicide if he were sure this was the deepest desire of his psyche! I stick to the old medical view that it's our job to save life. Do look after Edward.'

'Oh God,' said Midge.

'It'll give you something to do. You do nothing. It's bad for you.'

'I shop, I cook, all right, I have a char, but she only comes some mornings. I don't do nothing!'

'You know what I mean. I wish you'd get yourself some education. You always complain about being ignorant. Why don't you take a college course, there are all sorts. At least it would get you out of the house.'

'No college that would admit me would be worth going to!'

'Then go and help Stuart look after people. I'm serious!'

'Go home, dear Ursula, go home!'

They rose. Ursula's stiff skirt, now liberally covered with particles of Midge's perfume, made its dry sawing noise. They looked at each other. Their clothes were crumpled and their faces, in the bright light which Midge had now switched on, weary, no longer young.

'You look even more beautiful when you're tired,' said Ursula, 'how do you do it? I wish you'd tell Thomas that malt whisky is better for us than those sugary alcohols. Say goodnight to him from me.'

'You can't face him.'

'He's withdrawn. God knows what he's thinking about now. Goodnight, angel.'

When Ursula had gone Midge went into the dining room where, as she expected, Thomas was sitting in exactly the same attitude in front of the decanter of claret. He liked his wine but was a moderate drinker. He had taken off his glasses and had a milder and more vulnerable face. Without looking at her he stretched out his hand.

The dining room was on the ground floor, and now that the noisy conversation no longer filled it, the sound of traffic rising and falling like gusts of wind was audible, and at moments the faint shaking of the windows. Midge, standing beside her husband, took hold of his hand which was becoming wrinkled and spotted, older than its owner. As she still held it, his hand quested beyond the touch and stoked her silk dress. She released him and went round the table, leaning across to look at him with her own amazement, like to that with which he sometimes regarded her. Thomas often startled her as if his appearance were subtly changing, and she were married to several men who happened never to arrive together. He looked sad. She gazed at his fox terrier head and blinking narrowed light blue eyes.

'How tidy your hair is,' said Midge.

'How untidy yours is.'

'Did you just comb it?'

'No.'

'It looks like a wig.'

'Sit down, darling, for a minute.'

'You're tired.'

'Yes. Sit down.'

Midge sat down opposite to him. 'Ursula is very worried about Edward.'

'Yes.'

'But you'll do something.'

Thomas was silent for a moment, rubbing his eyes. He said, 'It's like a chemical process, Edward has got to change and we have to be, for a time, spectators of that change.'

'Tonight wasn't much good,' said Midge.

'It was an exercise, artificial as exercises often are, a formal gesture, perhaps not without value.'

'Oh –!' Midge poured herself out some claret into Harry's glass. 'I think you could make Edward hate you if you seem to ignore him now.'

'He's not ready for me yet. If I tried to corner him now he'd reject me and make it all more difficult later. Anything I said to him now would be an order. People in this sort of shock enact a mythical drama, and circumstances may conspire with them in an almost uncanny fashion. It's a search for solitude and purification. The thing is that he will run away – but he won't do so without seeing me first. That is a structure which must be allowed to develop.'

'Run away?'

'Yes. I must tell Harry.'

'Where to?'

'I don't know. But soon, when he's collected enough energy, he'll *run*, he'll disappear. And I want to know where he's going. That's what he'll tell me when he comes to see me.'

Harry in a black silk dressing gown was seated. Stuart was standing before him. They had just returned from the McCaskerville dinner party.

'I was a fool when I was your age,' Harry was saying, 'I was some sort of crazy absolutist, fortunately I didn't do anything irrevocable about it. I was a romantic, I am a romantic, I was working out my nature, I wasn't in a state of total illusion. You seem to be trapped inside a purely theoretical notion of yourself as good or holy or something, I can't think where you got it from, you weren't religious at school, to which you're sacrificing the precious time in which you could be learning something useful. Why can't you go on studying something worthwhile, you could study and help the poor? You're running away from something difficult to something easy, that's what it comes to. You're a defeatist, you're *bogus*. You're giving up the world because you realise you can't rule it, you can't succeed, you'd like to be a grand professor, a powerful physicist, a great philosopher, you're funking it all, you're throwing it all away, you'd like to know how to blow up the world, but you never will, so the only way you can destroy it is to pretend to give it up. Isn't that it?'

'I don't think so,' said Stuart.

'You aren't unselfish and humble, you're power-mad, a sort of moral Hitler. If you were some kind of artist I could understand it, I went on with my studies, I did well, but in the end I was only interested in what I could invent entirely by myself. That's what makes an artist, wanting to be God. You want to be God, perhaps we aren't so unlike after all, but you're not an artist, you lack imagination, and that's a recipe for disaster. Perhaps you want to be persecuted – but you don't want to end up as a pitiful neurotic, do you?'

'Certainly not,' said Stuart.

'And as for giving up sex, you can't, all you can do is put it off and get neurotic about it! People will think you're impotent or abnormal or a repressed homosexual. Or perhaps you're waiting for the perfect romance, the pure knight who'll deserve the princess, some sort of virginial Valkyrie! Your religious fantasy is just a sexual fantasy in disguise. You can't take a vow of celibacy all by yourself, there's no such thing, you'll just come to grief, you'll end up leaping on somebody and then feeling guilty and the whole business will be mucked up forever. You *are* like me, Stuart, you're full of sex, it's running out of your ears, you're being insincere, you haven't really examined yourself.'

'I know about sex,' said Stuart, 'I mean about it being in my nature, but for me there's just another pattern of living.'

'You can't do it.'

'I don't see why not. Many people do, like going straight from school into a religious seminary, never entering into – all that – at all.'

'All that! You see it as a black pit of pollution and degradation! You want to stay innocent, not to be like the rest of us. I suppose that's aimed at me, you want to be as unlike me as possible. I suppose you see me as some sort of sex maniac. I couldn't conceal things from you when you were a child. I can remember your little white face, judging me. You've just held onto your childish picture of things you can't understand. This fantasy of yours hurts me so much. Do you realise that?'

'Look, Dad,' said Stuart. 'Look, it's *not* against you. I know what you mean about when I was a child – but it isn't anything to do with you, and I *couldn't* will to hurt you.'

'You could unconsciously.'

'I don't believe in that. I do try to understand myself. But in a way that's not important. It's something else, something ultimate and absolute –'

'But this is simply superstition, as bad as believing in God, which you say you don't! Anyway what's fundamental could be evil, or chaos.'

'That can't be so,' said Stuart.

'I admire your confidence! You ought to have persevered with philosophy. You just want to be admired and revered! Why publish the fact that you've given up sex, or rather never had it, if that's true? You can't claim that you'll live forever without it, that amounts to a lie, it's empty pretentious boasting, why at least couldn't you keep your mouth shut?'

'I didn't publicise it,' said Stuart. 'Other people did. I regret this. But someone asked me a direct question and I answered it.'

'Cannot tell a lie. It's the lie in the soul that counts. Don't you see you can't do all this alone? Human nature needs institutions. You can talk about people entering seminaries. Why don't you do that then, become a priest, join the holy brigade? I'd hate it, but at least it would make some sense. Why not go to the church, to some church, ask for help, ask to be directed?'

'That's just what I can't do,' said Stuart. 'I can't go there. I don't hold their beliefs.'

'Neither do most of them now. They might shake some sense into you, knock your pride about a bit. You can't do it by yourself, without a general theory or an organisation or

43

God or other people. A religious man has to have an object, you haven't got one.'

Stuart was struck by this remark and considered it. He said, 'It depends what you mean by an object –'

'All because you've realised you'll never be a great thinker, I suppose hurt vanity makes people do daft things. Or perhaps it's not so daft. You've chosen the higher hedonism, you'll be the false good man, I've met a few, they're a secret brotherhood. Giving up the world, holy poverty, except that somehow or other all the material goods are provided, living on their rich friends – Damn it, I'm supporting you now, and that's just a start. *And* it works, people regard them as superior, defer to them, run to them, look after them, spoil them, they're *gentlemen* of course – while they trip round with saintly smiles and lofty words and unctuous advice, enjoying everybody's troubles, living at ease, having the hell of a good time, admired and loved, oh so high above us ordinary sinners. I tell you they enjoy life, that's what they've aimed at, *they* have an object all right, cherishing themselves, and they're intelligent too. God, how they smile, those selfless vulnerable touching sympathetic smiles!'

Stuart smiled, then laughed. 'One has to take some risks,' he said.

'That's the only human thing you've said!'

'I'm sorry I'm living on you now, I'll move out soon.'

'Christ, that doesn't matter. Well, it's a nuisance, but *that* doesn't matter. It'll all end tears, you'll waste your precious best years, come running after education when it's too late, God you'll regret it. Surely you don't want to be an ordinary little man with a tiny wage, or a sort of tramp living in a tent when you're forty? You'll be a nobody, you won't get back, don't imagine you can! I wish I could make you put it off a bit. Why not travel? Anything that would give you a few more ideas. See the world, I'd pay. Don't you want to go to Nepal, don't you want to go to Kyoto, visit the monasteries in Thailand?'

'No. Why should I?'

'That's what young people with religious delusions do nowadays, you can't even conform to that pattern. At least it

44

would be exotic, you might learn something. You just seem to want to live a life of brutish simplicity. But you can't. Later on you'll break out. And then you might be capable of any crime.'

'I don't think that means anything,' said Stuart, 'you're just expressing emotion.'

'Your religious plan is simply a sexual plan, it's sex by other means.'

'Well, all right,' said Stuart.

'You're a – What did you say? Why is it all right?'

'I don't mind if people call it sex, the question is can I do it, not what it's called.'

'You'll drive me mad. Damn you, you're *young*. I wish I was your age. It's just because you're young and physically fit, you feel you're pure – it's an *illusion,* Stuart! It's all *abstract*. I can't stand by and watch you throwing it all away, throwing away what I so much want and can't have, youth, youth. Oh *damn*. And you make such a self-righteous fuss about it all.'

'I think you're making the fuss, not me.'

'You might at least make yourself useful by saying something, anything to poor Edward.'

Stuart flushed. 'I will tonight –'

'Thomas said once that those in extreme pain are shunned by all. He should know. He hasn't been near the boy. On second thoughts, don't talk to Edward, you'd only feel it your duty to load him with guilt. Go away, go to bed.'

'Dad, don't be cross with me.'

'I'm not, yes I am, but it doesn't matter, nothing matters, just clear off.'

When Stuart had gone Harry banged around the drawing room finding some whisky and pouring it out, splashing it roughly onto the leather top of the desk. He went to the fireplace where the remains of the fire on which he had burnt himself earlier in the day were murmurously collapsing. Illumined by a lamp, he looked at himself in a mirror framed by gilded cupids which Casimir Cuno had bought for his wife as a wedding present. Harry associated this mirror with his

45

mother, a frail gentle pretty woman, daughter of a Cambridge don, who had sacrificed her talent as a pianist to the heavy task of being her husband's secretary. She made the sacrifice gladly, convinced, as indeed Casimir was himself, that he was genius. Romula was her name. She lived long enough to know 'the girl from far away' (Casimir had died earlier), but not long enough to meet Chloe or to witness the eclipse of her husband's reputation. Her piano, never played now, indeed untouched since Edward had strummed on it as a child, was in the drawing room, which was still the room which Harry's grandfather had created, and Casimir and Romula had added to a little, and Harry and Chloe and the girl from far away had left almost entirely unaltered.

Harry gazed at himself in the mirror. Oh to make a new imagined self in place of the failed soiled present self! When he was young Harry had declared as his motto, 'simply the thing I am shall make me live', a bold declaration which he interpreted in his own way; and he had been sincere in saying to Stuart that he was only interested in what he could invent entirely by himself. Yet he was also, as Ursula had observed, ambitious, a sort of disappointed authoritarian. His present lack of interest in politics was rightly seen as a case of 'sour grapes'. He thought of himself as a man of the future, not a mere power-monger but a prophet: for better or worse, the modern consciousness at its most conscious. Time was passing. Could he still believe that his best work lay ahead? From the face in the glass the bland mask of self-satisfaction and energetic *joie de vivre* had fallen away. He saw his tired wrenched older face, marked by drink and sin. He thought, Casimir is dead, and Romula is dead, and Stuart's mother is dead, and lovely Chloe who was so very much alive is dead too, and I shall die. Harry had a terrible shameful secret. He had, recently and privately, written a novel, a long mature novel containing all his best thoughts; but no one would publish it. Using a pseudonym he had tried several publishers. Nobody liked it, nobody would take it, nobody took it seriously at all. Harry Cuno hated failure, hated even more to be known to fail. Suppose they found out. He had another even more terrible secret too.

He became aware that his burnt hand was hurting, it was blistered and throbbing, it would keep him awake. The physical pain, by an old deep grasping of the mind, conjured an image which travelled with Harry. It was an imagined scene. His father had been drowned when out sailing alone on a mildly breezy day in a lonely region of sea off the coast of Scotland. His empty boat, in perfect order, was found later ghosting along by itself. Casimir must have fallen overboard accidentally. Harry knew that his life-hungry father would never have committed suicide. He was a strong swimmer. Harry pictured the man in the sea swimming and swimming, and watching the boat, always moving a little too fast, gradually draw away. Deep painful associations, framed in the deep secrecy of his mind, drew him back to the present. He pictured Stuart's pale unlined calm face, so lately that of a boy, his pale face, his yellow eyes, his 'don't be cross', so reminiscent of childhood. What's the matter with him, he wondered, and why does it upset me so? Is it mania, or to attract attention, or is it some unusual form of *courage*? In that boy, it's not *nothing*, he's got a will, he's tougher than me. Had he engendered a monster? He was hurt in his secret soul by Stuart's judgment of him.

Stuart, dismissed by Harry, went upstairs and knocked on Edward's door. He could see the light was on. There was no answer. He went in.

Stuart had of course seen Edward and uttered words to him since Mark Wilsden's death, but he had not had 'a talk' with his brother. Stuart had been occupied with closing down his academic life moving out of his digs, ordering his mind. He had had, during this time, no close friend or mentor. He reproached himself for not having earlier forced a meeting with Edward, who had made it clear that he did not want to talk to Stuart.

Edward, in pyjamas, was sitting up in bed reading a book. He looked different, changed, smaller. His face had shrunk, it was gathered and stained. Wrinkles had appeared on his forehead and about his eyes, the flesh of his brow was pulled into a painful knot above his nose, which had become sharp and thin. When he saw Stuart he frowned with irritation, and held onto his book with the air of being determined to see his visitor off promptly.

'What is it?' said Edward.

'Can we talk?'

'What about?'

'Oh – about things –'

'What things?'

Stuart looked round Edward's room. There were bookshelves, French posters, a pink azalea on the chest of drawers. The floor and every other level surface was covered with Edward's clothes interspersed with letters, some unopened. He decanted Edward's shirt and trousers off a chair and sat down beside the bed. 'Are you warm enough, would you like a hot water-bottle?'

'No. I'm all right.'

'What are you reading?'

Edward displayed the paperback thriller. 'Harry got me some more of these.'

'You shouldn't read that stuff,' said Stuart.

Edward, instead of getting annoyed, replied reasonably enough, 'I can't read anything else, nothing else would hold my attention.' He rearranged his pillows. 'What do you suggest I read,' he asked ironically, 'the Bible?'

'Well, why not, just a bit now and then. I just mean – like good novels – like –' Stuart, who was not a reader of fiction, could not immediately think of one.

'Don't suggest Proust – I'd be sick, I'd choke and die. Not that that would signify, I'm dead anyway. Do go away, Stuart, there's a good chap.'

'I won't just yet if you don't mind. What a nice plant you've got. What is it? It's like a little tree.'

'It's an azalea, Midge brought it yesterday. She brought some chocolates too. You don't like chocolates, do you? I'll throw them away.'

'Did you talk to Midge?'

'Of course not, she was shivering with embarrassment, she just wanted to make a virtuous gesture and run. No wonder. I'm a stinking corpse. Particle by particle I'm going bad.'

'Don't talk so,' said Stuart, 'what is it, what is *it*?'

'It's no good talking to me,' said Edward. 'Just let me alone, will you? I'm a machine. I say the same things to myself a thousand times a day, I see the same things, I enact the same things. Nothing can help me, nothing.' As Edward spoke these words a strange grimacing uncanny smile, not at all like his ordinary smile, came onto his face.

Stuart shuddered. 'Don't make misery an end in itself. There must be something you can do, some good move that you can make –'

'I can't move.'

'You must find some refuge –'

'Oh I'm in one, it's hatred, that's something to do, hating everybody, hating Harry, hating you. I loathed that abominable dinner party, all false smiles and lying talk. I hated the clothes those women wore and the smell of their faces. It was true though what they were saying, there's nothing deep, the world's turning into nonsense, everything is coming to an end, it'll all collapse into hell and burn and finish, and I'm *glad*. I'm there already burning in hell. My soul is gone, I have no inward soul, it'll all burnt away.'

'But what is this fire,' said Stuart, 'is it guilt, do you feel guilty?'

Edward threw the book across the room. He shouted, 'Go away and stop amusing yourself by hurting me! You grate on my nerves so that I could *scream* – everything you say is just like scraping a wound with a knife –'

'I'm sorry,' said Stuart, 'I just want to understand, I want a sense of direction. All this repetitive misery is bad, it's not truth. I'm not suggesting you just try to jump out of it all, you can't. It's not like a riddle with a magic solution. You've got to think about what happened, but try to think about it in a bit of clear light. The burning has to go on, but hold onto something else too, find something good, somewhere, anywhere, keep it close to you, draw it into the fire –'

'The one thing the devil didn't make,' said Edward, suddenly quiet again. 'Yes. If the devil can't find it I'm sure I can't. You see, nothing connects any more, nothing makes sense, in extreme pain it can't do, there are no *ways* any more.

Do you know what I've discovered? There's no morality, no centre, since guilt can exist outside it, on its own. You don't know what this pain is like. Words don't help, names don't help, guilt, shame, remorse, death, hell, at the level I'm at distinctions don't exist, concepts don't exist. I wake in the mornings and hear the birds singing, and for a second I forget, then I'm back in liquid blackness, everything's black, everyone's a devil tormenting me, all of you this evening, and his mother sending me letters and –'

'Mark's mother?'

'Yes, she sends me letters accusing me of murder, every two or three days I get one. She'd be glad if she knew how much I suffer.'

'You've answered?'

'Of course not. I hate her. I've stopped reading her vile letters. There's two there I haven't opened, by your feet. I meant to burn them. I wish I could burn her.'

'You ought to read them,' said Stuart.

'To punish myself?'

'No. She might have changed her mind, she might regret those letters and be writing to say so. She's distraught with grief. She might even suddenly need you.'

'You want me to pity her. She curses me. I curse her.'

Stuart picked up one of the letters and handed it to Edward. Edward tore it open, glanced at it, and gave it to Stuart. 'You see. This is what I live with.'

Stuart read the beginning of the letter.

You murdered my child whom I loved, he trusted you and you killed him, you broke his body and you shed his blood, he is dead and all my happiness and my joy is dead and will lie there broken forever, lying in blood and broken bones, and never live again, I shall never lift my head again, you have killed my joy . . .

He put the letter back in the envelope and dropped it. 'Yes. She's mad with misery, like you. I expect writing this is a sort of automatic relief, like crying. I think you should write *something* to her, just a few lines, it could change *her* scene a bit.'

50

'Write what? She'd spit on it.'

'Say you're sorry, say you're wretched, anything – it might do you good too.'

'Oh go away, go to hell, you don't understand. Anyway, I'm not a murderer, I didn't intend it, or do you think I did – You *can't* understand, you don't know what it's *like* to be where I am –'

'Ed, don't go on like this,' said Stuart, '*try* something. Sit still and try to make your mind quiet, breathe quietly, say words, aloud, quietly.'

'What words?'

'Any words, like a prayer, or just "stop" or "help" or "peace" –'

'Words without thoughts never to heaven go.'

'I'm not so sure,' said Stuart, 'you see what happened just now. If you're sorry about what you did, suffer with some point. Don't hate, put away resentment, say "stop" to some thoughts, keep your intent pure, live quietly in your pain, quietness is good, reach out and touch things gently, other things, innocent things – it may seem artificial, like a ritual – like when you wake in the morning and hear the birds singing, hold onto that *after* you've remembered, and just think "the birds are singing", and hold that away from the blackness and keep it there, even for a second.'

'What use is a second, it just makes the blackness more black.'

'Find something good *anywhere* and hang onto it like a terrier. Try to sort of pray, say "deliver me from evil", say you're sorry, ask for help, it will come, it *must* come, find some light, something the blackness can't blacken. There must be things you have, things you can get to, some poetry, something from the Bible, Christ if he still means anything to you. Let the pain go on but let something else touch it like a ray coming through from outside from *that* place outside –'

'It's no good,' said Edward, 'you're talking to yourself, you're intoxicating yourself with pious rhetoric. You live in some sort of blank childish place, you don't know how terrible the world is, what it's like for your whole mind to be taken over by *hopeless* darkness and corruption. It's like cancer, what I shall probably die of soon anyway.'

'Or look at something,' said Stuart, 'anything, any existing thing, that azalea for example –'

'Oh go away, go to *hell*, and take the bloody plant with you, I'm going to smash it up and trample on it! If you want it to survive you'd better remove it, *take it away*, and take yourself away, oh God, if I could only weep. Why do you come here to look at me?'

'I'm your brother and I love you.'

'You are not my brother, and you have never loved me, never, never, never, you're a liar. You were always jealous, always watching and calculating – Go away, I loathe your presence, you suffocate me, and take that vile plant or I'll *kill* it!' Edward's whole face was wrinkled now into a reddened grimace of hate and fury, like a primitive mask in a museum.

Stuart got up. He went over to the bookshelves, and inspected Edward's books. He pulled out a book, the Bible, and put it down on the chair beside Edward's bed. Then he picked up the azalea. 'All right, I'll take this away now, but I'll bring it back later. Don't be angry with me. Forgive me. Goodnight, Edward.'

As he closed the door he heard the flung Bible crash against it and fall to the ground.

After Stuart had gone Edward lay back on his pillows for a few minutes, panting with exhaustion. His heart was beating violently and painfully, his head ached, and when he sat up he felt giddy. He got out of bed. Still breathing heavily and hunched up with weariness and spent fury he opened the window, which gave onto the darkened garden, and hurled Midge's box of expensive chocolates out into the night. He turned round for the azalea, then remembered Stuart had taken it. Damp smells of spring, of wet earth and green things growing, which would have made him happy once, came through the window which he closed with a bang. He saw the Bible on the floor and picked it up. It was a fine India paper edition which a religious cousin of Harry's had given to

Edward when he was fourteen on the occasion of his confirmation. Yes, he had been confirmed into the Church of England and had even felt a glow when the Bishop's hand touched him. The book had opened on its fall and many of the frail pages were creased and crumpled. Edward automatically tried to straighten them out, then angrily bunched the book together. He was about to drop it again into the chaos of strewn clothes when a superstitious idea occurred to him. The only use he had ever put the Bible to was occasionally to make a *sors,* to open it at random and extract a message, an absurd or ridiculously apt one, from the verses his finger lighted upon. He did this now, opening the book and pointing quickly. He held the page under the lamp and looked at what he had been vouchsafed. *Destruction cometh, and they shall seek peace and there shall be none. Mischief shall come upon mischief and rumour shall come upon rumour, then shall they seek a vision of the prophet, but the law shall perish from the priest and counsel from the ancients.* Edward laughed, and his laugh, like his smile, was uncanny, as if a demon within him were exulting with gloating scorn. So, he thought, it's *all* ending, it's *all* coming down, all rules, all law, all the old cant of civilisation. It isn't just me who is to perish – it's only me . . . first . . . He looked at his bottle of sleeping pills, harmless things of course, but there were many other methods. Refuge, take refuge. He took refuge in his endless conversations with Mark, his endless *explanations* of why he had gone away, why he had not come back, how much he suffered, with what pain he paid, how much he loved Mark and longed for him – But these conversations were one-sided, simply lonely fruit-less lacerations of the soul. He tossed the Bible away and began kicking his clothes about, searching for his thriller. Then suddenly, as if magically, he saw that something had *appeared,* a yellow card upon which in capital letters were written simply the words DO THE DEAD WISH TO SPEAK TO YOU? Edward felt as if a dart had struck him, something piercing deeply into him from outside. He picked up the card and returned to sit on his bed. He stared at the apt and fateful message. Then he turned the card over. On the back it read: *Mrs D. M. Quaid, Medium. SEANCES every Tuesday and*

Thursday at 5 p.m. There was an address near Fitzroy Square. Edward held the card, then laid it down carefully beside the lamp. Perhaps things connected after all.

It is a terrible thing to fall into the hands of the living God. These words came into Stuart's head as he entered his bedroom. His room, directly above Edward's, the room of his childhood, was unadorned, only lately indeed stripped of the last trophies of that time. His books, hastily brought from his digs, were piled against the wall. He had put his clothes away. He turned on the lamp, turned off the centre light, and sat down on an upright chair. He sat with his eyes open and breathed slowly and was at once rapt into a state of complete quietness. The ability to achieve, instantly, this separated stillness had come to him naturally and spontaneously at school. It had not been connected with any sort of instruction, certainly not any religious instruction. Perhaps it had struck him first simply as a method of escaping from childish misery, banishing certain unsavoury thoughts, an instant nothingness which could diminish such ailments or make them vanish. Later he had apprehended it as something more positive, a kind of lightness, an escape from gravity, an available levitation to a higher viewpoint, a removal from time, wherein huge and complex awareness could be contained in seconds. A huge space opened, accompanied sometimes by intense joy. Honeydew. Occasionally he worried about it, but not often. *This,* whatever it was, was one of the things which had put *it,* whatever it was, which Harry had enquired about, into his head.

Stuart heard Edward's window below open, then close. He sighed, and began to think about Edward. He already knew intuitively about the terrible untouchable sufferings of others. But upon the horrors he did not dwell. He could picture Mark Wilsden dead, and his tutor Plowmain who had blown his brains out. Stuart had never met Mark, and did not like Plowmain or know why he had killed himself. Interested people wondered whether this violent death had 'influenced' Stuart. It had not, it did not concern him. These bloody casualties were for him sad static things, like tombs, upon the road into the whiteness of his own future, a whiteness which was like a different kind of death. His attitude was that of an unreflective soldier, perhaps not likely to survive for long. Of course he could bleed, he could weep; and if it had been his duty to bury the dead he would have done so. But there were grievous and awful things which must remain externally related to his thought, as if in relation to them, he could always only be concerned as an instrument or servant. Stuart pictured the Good Samaritan as being intently reflective at suitable intervals about the man he had helped, so long as he could continue to help him (for instance by sending the innkeeper some more money), but as otherwise dismissing the matter from his mind. Anything in the nature of drama, of brooding or gloating or re-enacting, was alien to Stuart, as was also joyous or gleeful anticipation. In a way he did not want to reflect too much; and was perhaps in this sense, as Harry had said, lacking in imagination. These peculiarities made of his present task of disposing of his life a curiously cramped and narrow problem. He wanted to find a job, some sort of plain service job, white, blank, like the blankness of time as it continually streamed towards him, getting as it were into his eyes; yet also it must be *his* job, since he retained a sense of vocation, of being called to some work suited to his talents, not his old talents, but his new talents, the talents of his new life, which had to be begun soon: for whatever it was, it was to be won or lost now. That much was clear to him, and that much of a drama, he sometimes felt it was too much, gave structure to his reflection. In another context and another time, traditions and institutions might have upheld and guided him. Now, as he was forced to think about himself, the very emptiness of his thought, which he so much valued, made it difficult for him to plan and make decisions.

Stuart had sometimes put it to himself that what he wanted was a (but *the right*) cage of duties. And now at any rate there was a clear duty, to which he had not needed to have his attention drawn by Harry, to 'do something' about Edward. Did he love Edward? Of course: Stuart did not propose to stumble over that question, any more than over the question of whether some twinge of old jealous resentment might not even now make him the tiniest bit glad that his popular brother was in trouble. His connection with Edward was absolute, and as for base thoughts and feelings, he was used to thrusting them down, as if drowning them, with no misgivings about 'repression'. His talk with Edward had not been a success. He had done it as an act of will, something no longer to be put off. He had never before offered anybody so much advice, or put into words and uttered things which he so profoundly believed in. But these things had not reached Edward. Stuart was aware, and here he did seem to stumble, that only love could have winged his words, *such* words, so as to make them reach that objective. Only in a context of love could talk of sin and guilt effectively take place; and *that* was Edward's trouble, was it not? So he should first have convinced Edward of his love. But how could he have done it? Edward was evidently capable, in this emergency, of regarding Stuart as an enemy. It all remained separated, 'abstract', a word which Harry had used, the absolute existence of his brother, his affection for him, his well-intentioned admonitions. Of course Edward was a special case; on the other hand, if he failed in this case would it not be significant? Was this perhaps a crucial test, a kind of entrance exam, the sign for which he had been waiting? Will it always be like this, Stuart wondered, and if it is, *does it matter,* does it matter for *my* plan? He could not clearly formulate this troubling query, which seemed part of the 'narrow' problem of his task. Supposing he were simply *not gifted* for his chosen mission? Was it like some totally unmusical person deciding to devote his life to music? Suppose it should turn out that he could never really communicate with other human beings at all? He had so far communicated very little. So did he now envisage himself *talking* to people in the future, *advising* them? Could something like this be learnt or did it have to be a natural endowment? Supposing he were *dumb,* would it be different or the same? He thought, with Ed, I'll work on it. Stuart had of course always been aware of his father's preference for Edward, which had left those little scars of jealousy; it had pained him, but not as much as Harry or Thomas imagined.

Stuart's capacity to detach himself dated back a long way. 'A cold aloof little boy,' people had said. This coldness was part of Stuart's problem. *Was* it coldness? Sometimes the very same thing seemed to him like a passion.

I wonder if I ought to have *forgiven* Edward, Stuart said to himself, absolved him. Luther said all men were priests. Of course he knew that the idea was perfectly ridiculous, but it did not occur to him to think it presumptuous. After all, he had long known that life was about salvation, and had known for some time that it was his destiny to live alone as a priest in a world without God. His rejection of God went far back into his childhood. Finding himself already baptised, he had refused the sacrament of confirmation, which young Edward took with vague emotional cheerfulness in his stride. 'God' had always seemed to Stuart something hard and limited and small, identified as an idol, and certainly not the name of what he found within himself. Christ was different, a sort of presence, not quite a mystic person. Christ was a pure essence, something which, as it were, he might have kissed, as one might kiss a holy stone, or the soil of a holy land, or the trunk of a holy tree: something which was everywhere, yet simple, separate and alone. Something alive; and he himself was Christ. The identification was unanalysed and instructive, something obvious, where 'not I but Christ' was interchangeable with 'not Christ but I', experienced sometimes as a transparency and lightness, the closeness, even the easiness, of good. This progressive absorbing of the Holy One, as if after a while Stuart might forget his name, went on of course without reference to 'Christianity', and Stuart never 'went to church', though he sometimes sat alone in churches. It was clear that nothing was worthy of *this* except dedication, something lived and breathed, without intervals. Truth was fundamental, his life-oath. Certainty was there, honeydew was there, but meanwhile the dedication remained as a task, cumbersome, detailed, where every minute contained the likelihood of failure. How could such a paradox be lived? Not, for him at any rate, in the academic world. He needed simplicity and order, a quiet monotonous private life. He wanted to be able to be a place of peace and space to others, he wanted to be invisible, he wanted to heal people, he wanted to heal the world, and to get into a situation where this would be something simple and automatic, something expected and everyday. He knew how awkward and conspicuous he was, how he embarrassed people, exasperated them, unnerved them, frightened them. He lacked charm. He was often aware when he entered a room how much he disturbed the atmosphere and broke the tempo. This made it important to find a *place* where he need have no persona, and awkwardness would become something unimportant, taken for granted. Perhaps it would pass off, he was young and could learn. Besides all men are mocked, Christ was mocked.

Stuart's dislike of modern society was made much of by those who wished to explain or interpret his behaviour, especially his attitude to sex. Stuart certainly detested sexual promiscuity, vulgar public sex, the lack of privacy and reticence, the lack of restraint and respect, the lack of reverence, the lack of inwardness. He was afraid of the future, of a world without religion, of crazed spirit without absolute. He was afraid of technology, and of the decay of human language and the loss of the soul. But these reactions were not the prime movers of his asceticism. He was perhaps nearer, though he laughed at it and gave it no force, to Harry's change of a 'higher hedonism'. How high can it go? He wanted to love the world and not to be caught in traps, to have a calm lucid consciousness and an untroubled conscience. In Stuart's conception of his 'task' celibacy held a central place, not just because of the mucky sex life of people he knew and heard of, but because of some more positive conception of innocence. Why *start*? Stuart said to himself. To love without entanglement, that, for him at any rate, meant celibacy. Many others in the past had seen it so, and in this at least he was not alone. He was sorry now that he had, through answering a direct question put to him by Giles Brightwalton, let his resolve become public, a matter for speculation and jokes. His 'innocence' was to be something private and simple, to be like a lonely animal in its lair at night, or as he had sometimes felt at happy times in his childhood, secure in bed, hearing Harry moving about downstairs. That such a picture might seem dull, or suggest a retarded or childish personality, did not dismay him. Perhaps he just was a little childish, and perhaps this was no great matter, even a good thing. The effect upon him of his mother, 'the girl from far away', was something more complex. She had indeed figured in his child mind, and even still, more dimly, as an angel. He could scarcely remember her, his images of her hovered between memory and dream. Her mystic form had been a refuge from a thoughtless stepmother and a neglectful father and a brother preferred by both. *She* knew about love, about how he lacked it. Her name was Teresa Maxton O'Neill, a Catholic, born in Dunedin of Irish immigrant parents. She had seen the great ocean seals basking on golden seaweed at the end of the world. She had seen the albatross.

A disinterested observer might have wondered why Stuart so ardently rejected God, since he did not simply sit and meditate, he also knelt down, sometimes even prostrated himself. Once again, Stuart, recognising no problem, instinctively resolved apparent contradictions. Meditation was refuge, quietness, purification, replenishing, return to whiteness. Prayer was struggle, reflection, self-examination, it was more particular, involving concern about other people and naming of names. Harry had said that Stuart wanted to be like Job, always guilty before God, an exalted form of sadomasochism. Stuart's rejection of God was, in effect, his rejection of that 'old story', to use Ursula's words, as alien to his being. His mind refused it, spewed it out, not as a dangerous temptation, but as alien tissue. Of course he wanted to be 'good'; and so he wanted to avoid guilt and remorse, but those states did not *interest* him. Towards his sins and failures he felt cold, no warmth was generated there. So little did he feel himself menaced from that quarter that in prayer he would even say (for he used words) *dominus et deus*, without attaching the old meaning to those dread sounds. (Perhaps it was important that the words were Latin, not English.) He knew there was no supernatural being and did not design to try to attach the concept in any way to his absolutes. If something, 'good' or something, was his 'master', it was in no personal or reciprocal relation. His language was thus indeed odd as when he sometimes said 'forgive me', or 'help me', or when he commended others, Edward for instance, to the possibility of being helped. Stuart understood the phrase 'love is only of God'; his love went out into the cosmos as a lonely signal, but also miraculously could return to earth. His belief that his supplication for Edward, his concern for Edward, could help Edward was not a hypothesis about actions which he might, as a result of well-intentioned thoughts, later perform for his brother (though this aspect of the matter was excluded); nor of course was he resorting to some paranormal telepathic form of healing. He simply felt sure that the purer his love the more efficacious it would be in some 'immediate' sense which put in question the ordinary pit-pat of time.

Stuart's 'hedonism' was an instinctive craving for nothing-ness which was also a desire to be able to love and enjoy and 'touch' everything, to *help* everything. To this end, celibacy and solitude appeared as essential means. This reasoning seemed to him obvious. Of course when Harry had said of Stuart (as he said, understood differently, of Edward) that he was in love with death, he had meant something more banal, a commonplace of popular psychology. Stuart certainly wanted happiness, his own particular brand of that which we are told all men pursue. He was however well aware, however much his deepest feelings might deny time, that he was not living in a timeless world. He had certainties so tremendous that he was not even concerned about the sin of pride, which he regarded as a low personal matter. But he was also aware that he was young and inexperienced, clumsy and often stupid, and in need of a job. Like everyone else, he must settle down, and earn money. He had not yet been tested. Can a man live with no evil, no shadow, no ego? Has any man ever lived so? He knew his present failings, and that he would descend further into it all, into the mess and muddle of wrong-doing, like everyone else. He was certainly not, as Harry had conjectured, waiting for the perfect romance with the virgin princess. But he was, in all his more mundane fumblings, waiting for something. He had abjured, he thought, all superstition. Yet still, in some way, he was waiting for a sign.

EDWARD BALTRAM WAS crossing Fitzroy Square. It was raining.

It was the day following Stuart's homily and Edward's discovery of the card about the seance. It was Thursday, half-past four in the afternoon. Edward was going to hear the dead speak.

Edward did not exactly believe that this would happen. He was impressed by the strange way in which the card had suddenly appeared on the floor of his room. He had of course later realised how it had come there. He remembered that on that terrible night Sarah Plowmain had said something about a seance, and that it would be 'fun' to go to one. No doubt she had slipped the card into the pocket of his jacket, and he had pulled it out accidentally without noticing. Nevertheless he felt he could recognise the hand of fate, and fate was just what, at that moment, he needed in his life more than anything, some significant compulsion, even if the significance were dark. To be under orders, to have something he must do. He felt weak and fatalistic. But suppose the dead did speak, and in terrible tones, the message of Mark's mother spoken by Mark, denouncing him as a murderer? Might not that drive him into madness? Even then it would be fate, it would be part of a fated punishment, it would be a *step* upon a *road*, which might lead perhaps in the end to some better state, would at any rate lead *somewhere*. The sense of nowhere-to-go, no space, no time, no movement, was a part of his utter and deep misery. He did not really hate Stuart and Harry. He

61

had even listened to Stuart sufficiently to recall some of his advice. When that morning Edward awoke from drugged nightmares to see that the daylight had returned, and to hear the birds singing in the garden, and after he had passed from the moment of not-knowing into the agony of *'yes, it happened, that* happened', he also remembered what Stuart had said about holding onto the birds and keeping them away from the blackness. He tried to do this. He felt at once the pressure of a huge black irresistible force. His effort lasted for a microsecond; then grief blotted out the sound and he returned to his mechanical conversation with Mark and his wailing regret that he could not change the past: oh if only that vile girl hadn't rung up, if only I had come back sooner, if only . . . So little needed to be changed for it all to be different.

I'm so alone, he thought, no one helps me, no one *can* help me, I don't even want anyone's help. But what is to become of me, would I not be better dead? I am simply cumbering and fouling the earth. I am dead, I am the walking dead, people must see that, why don't they run away? They do run away, everyone shuns me. No voice can reach me. I won't be able to think again, I won't be able to work again, I am permanently damaged. I have no free thinking mind any more, my mind is totally poisoned, clogged up with black poison. I am a little machine, no longer a human soul, my soul is dead, my poor soul is dead. He wished that he could shed tears over his soul, his face screwed up for tears, there was a little moisture in his eyes but not the streams that he desired. Yet while he thought these thoughts, explicitly worded, indeed composed, in his mind, his feet were automatically leading him toward a street which he had looked up on a map to be sure that he knew where it was. Even the name, Mrs Quaid, was in his head as he walked, as he marched, for he was a suffering robot.

He consulted the card again, although he clearly remembered the number, and stopped outside a tall brick terrace house, the kind of house of which there are so many, some grand, some dingy, in that part of London. This house was one of the dingy ones. A card similar to the one he was holding was pinned to the side of the door, with the message

First floor hand-written upon it. There was a bell beside the door but Edward saw no point in ringing it since the door was open. He looked at his watch. It was twenty-five minutes to five. He wondered if he should walk around for a bit, but decided it was psychologically impossible. Besides, he had come without an umbrella and his hair and his mackintosh were already rather wet. He went in, mopping his hair with his handkerchief, and climbed some shabbily carpeted stairs. On the first floor there was one door, standing ajar, with a hand-written notice on it saying *SEANCE 5 p.m. Please walk in.* Edward walked in.

He was in the corridor of a flat, with various closed doors and very little light. There was a rather unpleasant dusty sweetish smell which could have been old cosmetics or some kind of dry rot. He felt his heart-beat, holding his breath, and after listening for a moment, coughed. A door opened and in the dim light he saw a woman covered in jewels. That at least was his first impression. Then he saw a small woman with a fat neck wearing a dark red and blue robe and some sort of turban on her head and a great many necklaces. Some of the necklaces were short, cutting into her flesh, others were longer and hung down in rows as far as her waist. She also wore long earrings which glittered and swung. The necklaces clicked a little and tinkled. The woman spoke, 'You're early, dear. But come on in then.' She spoke with a slight Irish accent. Edward followed her.

He came into a fairly large room with three tall windows. The curtains on the windows were drawn so as to admit very little daylight.

'I'm Mrs Quaid.' She turned on a shaded lamp, and Edward saw a semicircle of chairs, heavy furniture against the walls, a fat sofa and two sloppy armchairs, a fireplace with a grate full of ashes, a sideboard with lace and china ornaments, a television set with a shawl over it. Mrs Quaid pulled the curtains more carefully. She said, 'You're new.'

'Yes.'

'Ever been to a seance before?'

'No.'

'You have to pay, you know.'

63

Edward had expected this. He handed over the fee, which was surprisingly modest. He did not find Mrs Quaid very impressive. Her 'jewels', now more visible in the close lamplight, were of the home-made 'folk' variety. He said to himself, these people are all charlatans.

'I'll explain later when everyone's here,' said Mrs Quaid. 'Won't be many today I think. Sit down, sit *there*.' She left the room and closed the door. Edward put his wet mackintosh under the chair. He was struck by the fact that she had chosen his seat.

The dark room was stuffy and smelt more strongly of the corridor smell, perhaps furniture polish covering some more dirty musty odour. The curtains were made of some thick furry stuff to which Edward instinctively attached a word which he did not know he knew, 'chenille'. They seemed dusty and he resisted an urge to go and finger them. A large old-fashioned globe of whitened glass hung from a wire in the middle of the ceiling. The banality of the room seemed ill-omened, even evil. The vases on the dirty lace on the sideboard were exceptionally ugly, grossly so. Edward returned to the familiar misery, the familiar fear. He listened to his breath, then to the distant noise of traffic, but the room continued to feel heavily silent. The dusty sweetish smell troubled his breathing and reminded him of something. He realised what it was: the incense which Sarah Plowmain had had burning in her darkened room, when he was in bed with her and Mark was dying.

Someone entered, slinking silently through the door, and sat down not far from Edward. It was a man who, after a quick glance, bowed his head as if in prayer. Edward could hear a faint panting sound. Several more people, men and women, came in with the same surreptitious tread and sat with bowed or covered faces. Edward was uncomfortable, unable to submit to the mood of the scene, his hair was still wet, his trousers were wet and seemed to have shrunk, he felt cold, a smell of damp wool arose from the collar of his jacket, he fidgeted. At about five minutes past five Mrs Quaid came in, attired as before except that she had put some jewels into her turban. She turned the single lamp down further, turning a switch which made the light reddish and very dim.

Then she said in a matter of fact voice, sounding more like a nurse or social worker than a handmaid of another world, 'Could you pull your chairs round please, push the empty chairs back, make a smaller circle, come round me, that's right.' Chairs were shifted awkwardly over the sticky resistant carpet, some pushed away, others moved forward. Making a more intimate group the clientele settled down. Mrs Quaid went on, 'There are two here who have not before attended a group where we speak to those on the other side, and to them let me speak a few words. You have all come here with private needs and wishes, troubles and desires, grieving for loved ones or seeking for guidance. The success of our communication with what is beyond depends upon your serious and close co-operation. Of course you must be silent, please do not exclaim or cry out or attempt to speak to the spirits yourselves. All communication will pass through me, it can no other. Above all you must concentrate, concentrate upon those whom you love who have now passed over, and upon the efficacy and clarity of the channels of vision as these are revealed unto you. *We* depend upon *you* for this help. When I say we, I mean that we are not alone, I am not alone. To reach to those who live in the light, beyond this world, who are trying to speak to us who are left behind in this dark realm, a spirit guide is needed. My guide is a woman, her name is Mary Geddy, and she lived upon this earth in the eighteenth century, she was a housekeeper in a great house in the west country. She will put us in touch. You may hear many voices, the voice of Mary Geddy and then perhaps of other dear spirits who are waiting to get through. It may not be possible to hear the voices of your loved ones, that matter is in the hands of the spirits themselves, but you may be vouchsafed a message. Sometimes the spirits are visible, this does not happen often. You may also feel tangible presences. Do not touch these or try to hold them. You are requested not to leave until I declare the seance at an end. Sit quiet, do not be afraid, concentrate your minds. Sit first for a while in silence.'

During this speech, of which at one level of his mind he was fully aware, Edward was also thinking, suppose something terrible and nightmarish happens to me, awful enough to drive me mad, to drive me to destroy myself? Should I not quickly now get up and go? He felt very afraid, panting silently with open mouth, his heart hurting him with its beat, yet at the same time he felt a kind of relief at being trapped, he *could not* go, he could do nothing now. He also thought, I'm vibrating with misery and grief, I'm a great electric storm, a destructive disturbance in the middle of this dark room, I shall make it all impossible, I can't concentrate, I shall scream. He tried to think about Mark, to see Mark, to propitiate his spirit. After some little time the quietness round about began to affect him and he closed his eyes. Then Mrs Quaid began to speak again, but this time it seemed to Edward that she was putting on a thick west country accent. It sounded forced, like a bad actress. The voice, supposed to be that of 'Mary Geddy', said first rather incoherently something which sounded like 'children' or 'my children', and then, after a coughing sound, clarified and said, 'I think that there is one here who is thinking of his wife who has lately passed on. She is wanting to come through. Her name is Clara.' There was a faint groaning sound from a man sitting next to Edward. The voice went on after a moment, 'Clara says I am to tell him that she is well and happy, there are many flowers where she is, flowers such as *marigolds*. She says not to be unhappy for her since she is happy and waiting for the one she loves to be with her. She cannot tell more of where she is. She knows he will understand, and asks him to look at her ring which she gave him. She says he is to look after himself and do all things what she told him. There is a debt to be paid. She bids him love her and have faith in the time to come. She bids him *au revoir*.' The man next to Edward, who had covered his face, groaned again and lowered his head towards his knees.

This manifestation was followed by a silence. Edward had listened vaguely to the insipid message. He felt warmer and a little sleepy. Mary Geddy's ridiculously artificial voice started up again but broke off, to be followed after a moment by another voice. This voice sounded real, as if some new person had entered the room and were speaking from near the door. 'George,' the voice said in urgent tones. It sounded like the voice of a young man. 'George, are you there? George, it's me. You promised, you did. I kept my promise. I'll always be with you, always. George, are you there?' The reddish light seemed to be extinguished, or perhaps something had moved in front of it. Edward was suddenly conscious of something which seemed to be coming across the space between him and where Mrs Quaid was sitting. Only now she was no longer there. Something soft seemed to touch Edward's hand, as if stroking it, and a movement of cold air and substance passed close in front of his face. In the almost complete darkness something which had not been there before seemed to be assembling itself inside the ring of chairs. There was a soft sighing sound as of something deflating and a faint sound like running water. Then there was stifled cry, or whimper. Edward flinched back and closed his eyes for a second. When he opened them the red light was visible and the room was as before except that Mrs Quaid sitting in her chair was holding her hands outstretched in front of her. There was a gleam of light and the sound of a closing door, someone had left the room. It seemed to Edward that it was Mrs Quaid who had cried out.

Mrs Quaid adjusted her turban and composed her hands on her lap. Her numerous necklaces glittered faintly. She sniffed and touched her nose with a handkerchief. She said, after a moment or two, in her own voice, 'There may be no more messages today. But we shall wait a little while to see if the spirits have anything more they want to tell us. Be still and concentrate you minds.' Edward breathed deeply and almost at once, as it seemed to him afterwards, fell asleep. The voice of Mary Geddy came to him, recalling him from some dark place. The voice said, 'There is one among us who has two fathers.' It repeated. 'There is one among us who has two fathers.' Edward was instantly alert, sitting forward, peering into the semi-dark toward Mrs Quaid. Mrs Quaid seemed to be humming very very softly, only now he could not see her because a hovering point of light, like a golden mosquito, was moving in between. Edward had noticed, as he entered the room, the big white globe suspended from the ceiling containing, he assumed, an unlit electric light bulb. This globe seemed to have moved a little, and was now lower down above Mrs Quaid's head. The little point of light entered the globe. The globe seemed to be vibrating, to be part of a vibration which had filled the whole room, and as Edward stared at it it was becoming softly luminous and changing colour. Beginning as a pale gold, it had now become a brown or bronze colour, and something was coming out of the inside of it, or rather holes were appearing in it, like empty glowing eyes and a mouth. A deep voice now issued from what now resembled a more than human size spherical bronze head. The voice spoke with some sort of English slightly drawling accent. It said, 'Come to your father. Come to your father.' There was silence filled with vibration. Edward, clenching his fists, his mouth wide open, stared at the apparition. He then clearly heard the voice say 'Edward'; and then, 'Come to your father. Come home, my son.' Edward gave a little sharp cry, like the cry of a bird. The bronze head dissolved and some-how was no longer there and the light in the room changed and Edward could see Mrs Quaid sitting with folded hands. He could not now recall what had just happened, although he could picture it clearly, as something he had actually seen and heard, it was something of a different kind, as if his own head had become huge and the voice had spoken inside it. He uttered his little cry again, turning it into a sob. He saw Mrs Quaid lean forward and touch the lamp. The red light was quenched and the room was revealed in a brighter but still dim glow. Mrs Quaid said, 'The seance is now at an end.'

The people round about him were no longer entranced, they moved, a woman picked up her handbag, a man coughed, someone got up, the show was over. The door opened and people began to go away. Mrs Quaid stood for a moment stretching her arms and breathing deeply, then walked slowly across to the heavy 'chenille' curtains and pulled them back a little and the terrible cold pale daylight of a grey afternoon came into the room. The last clients, trans-formed into ordinary people with coats and umbrellas and shopping bags and ordinary anxious faces and coughs, were leaving the room, shuffling the chairs and making way for each other as they shambled off. Edward was left alone with

Mrs Quaid, who was standing at the window looking out at the street. He searched for his mackintosh, which had been displaced in the movement of the chairs, and put it on. It was still wet. Mrs Quaid said aloud to herself, 'Double glazing makes all the difference.' Then she turned and noticed Edward and made a gesture towards the door, inviting him to go. In the ungracious light she looked tired and much older.

'Mrs Quaid,' said Edward, 'please may I ask you something. If someone – if some spirit voice – comes through with a message – like just now – does it mean that that person is dead?'

'Does it mean what?'

'That the person – that the voice that speaks has to be that of a dead person, I mean, a dead person not a live person?'

'How do I know?' said Mrs Quaid in a petulant tone. 'I am a *medium,* you understand what that means, I only convey what is sent to me by my guide.' She added, 'It's very tiring you know.' She carefully took off her turban and put it on a chair, and smoothed down her wispy grey hair.

'But when you said "There's someone here who has two fathers –"'

'I didn't say anything. I don't know what the spirits said.'

'Someone said my name. You don't know my name, do you?'

'No, of course not, never seen you before in my life.'

'But do living people ever speak like that –'

'I dare say anything may happen to those who are in tune with nature. Now I've got to have my tea.'

'Perhaps I imagined it,' said Edward.

'Perhaps you did. Sorry, dear.'

Edward went out of the room which seemed so dull and lifeless now, and passed out of the open door of the flat and down the stairs. Outside in the street the rain had stopped and the light had changed, become a bright rainy light with the sun shining momentarily through clouds, there was a fragment of rainbow and everything about him shone radiantly in vivid colours, the glittering pavement, the wet railings, the brick fronts of the houses, the clothes of the passersby, the Post Office Tower. Edward walked a few paces, then stood still. Whatever had happened? He felt a painful excitement, a sick ominous feeling of extreme fear, a desire to vomit. Surely he *had* heard that strange voice utter his name? He had certainly heard 'Come to your father, come home.' It must be for him, that message to the one who had two fathers. But suppose he were being summoned by a *dead* father?

'Do you think we should stop Meredith from seeing Stuart?' Midge McCaskerville asked her husband, as she sat on his desk dressed to go out in her smart black mac and blue and red silk scarf.

'Why?'

'He's become so emotional and peculiar, he might preach his religious mania to Meredith – and – well –'

'You think he might spring upon the boy?'

'No, of course not, but I don't want Meredith involved in an emotional friendship with Stuart.'

Thomas, who had laid down his pen, picked it up again. He said, 'I don't see any problem, we might just create one by interfering.'

'I wish Edward would attend to Meredith more, he's very fond of Edward, not much use at the moment of course. Stuart is so sort of unreal and inhuman. Of course it would be difficult, we don't want to give offence. Are you writing about Mr Blinnet?'

'No.'

'Does he still think he murdered his wife and buried her and she's grown into a laburnum tree? What's his latest, if it's not secret?'

'Oh, he tells everybody. An old schoolmaster of his in Manchester is sending out steel wires which enter into Mr Blinnet's head and convey slogans.'

'Slogans?'

'But not of any interest. Like "Eat more cheese". Blinnet is bored by the slogans. Sometimes the schoolmaster manipulates the wires causing pain to Mr Blinnet as a punishment for his indifference to the slogans. Some of the wires are steel and some are made of gold. The gold ones produce small fires inside Mr Blinnet's head, the effects of which are sometimes visible as flames resting on his hair.'

'Have you seen them?'

'No.'

'Poor man,' said Midge, 'I can't imagine what it would be like to think things like that. Mad people are so inventive. No wonder poets are supposed to be mad.'

'Mad people are quite unlike poets,' said Thomas. 'Their fantasies are detailed and ingenious, but somehow dead. Not surprising in Mr Blinnet's case, since he also believes that he is dead.'

'And that he's the Messiah! Of course he's Jewish.'

'He is a quiet unambitious Messiah.'

'He's creepy. Meredith is afraid of him. I wish you hadn't had him here that time the clinic was closed. He smiles that awful bland smile but his eyes stay sharp and inquisitive. And you say he always wears his hat, even when he's with you.'

'When I give up the clinic Mr Blinnet will be a problem,' said Thomas. 'We could live in the country then. When Meredith goes to boarding school.'

'You're not giving up the clinic,' said Midge. 'I hope you're not being taken over by Mr Blinnet, I don't think you want to cure him at all! You'll be late back tonight?'

'Yes. You're out to lunch with your American school pal?'

'Yes, she's put off going home. Don't forget Meredith's school concert, by the way.'

'What flowers will you buy today?'

'Irises and tiger lilies.'

Shifting his mobile chair Thomas stretched out his hand and Midge descended onto his knee. 'Darling Midge, have a nice day.'

'*You* have a nice day. Are you seeing someone this morning?'

'Yes, Edward.'

'*Edward? Really?* Did you tell him to come?'

'No, he rang up.'

'So you were right.'

'Yes.'

'I'm so fond of Edward, I feel I could help him. Shall I see him too?'

'Not yet. Goodbye, mop-head. You look about seventeen.'

'So you talked to Stuart?' said Thomas.

'He talked to me,' said Edward.

'What did he say?'

'He said I should stop reading thrillers and read the Bible, that I should look at azaleas –'

'Azaleas?'

'Well, an azalea. Midge brought me one.'

'Did she, good.'

'And listen to the birds singing, and sit quietly, and breathe, and find something good and hang onto it like a terrier –'

'And did you?'

'Of course not. I threw the azalea out of the window. No, I meant to, but he took it away.'

'Did he touch you?'

'*Touch* me? Good heavens no!'

'Look, I want you to come off those drugs Ursula gave you. Can you?'

'Yes, I mostly have. They make no difference.'

'And if you don't mind, I'd like to see one of Mrs Wilsden's letters, if you get another one, I think you said you'd destroyed them all.'

'Oh, I'll get another one! She's an artist. She keeps saying the same thing without repeating herself. She must enjoy writing those letters.'

'It's a form of mourning, it will pass, deep grief is like a compulsive song.'

'That's what everyone says to me about my thing, it will pass. But it won't. It's gone on so long. I'd have to be another person. What's wrong with me is me. I'm *done for*. You know how if an aeroplane engine stalls at a certain moment it can't rise, it must crash by its own weight, no power can raise it, it's just a heavy dead thing bound to fall back to earth. My engines have failed, I'm falling, I've *got* to fall, I've no energy left, one way or another I'm done for.'

'You can talk. You are full of interesting images.'

'That's because I'm using *your* energy,' said Edward. 'When I leave you I'll be back in that black machine. I'm in it now, all this talk is automatic, it's hysterical, you are producing it. I'm not mentally ill I'm spiritually ill, I never knew what that meant before. It's the fact, the *fact* I have to live with, what happened, what I did. People say, "you have to live with something", but I can't live with this, I can only die with it, except that I don't die. I wake every day in torment, my whole body glows with pain as if I were being electrocuted, only I can't die.'

'Go on, while your eloquence lasts.'

'I'm frightened of everything, I'm frightened of police and doctors, I'm even frightened of you. You won't let them give me electric shocks, will you?'

'There's no question of that. There isn't any "them". There's only me.'

'They could get at me all the same. You know I never told anyone this, I told lies at the inquest. I said Mark had some of the stuff and took it of his own accord. That wasn't true. I gave it to him, I put it in a sandwich. I deceived him, he didn't know he was taking it, he would never have done it knowingly, he hated drugs, he kept trying to make me stop. Mrs Wilsden guessed that of course. That's one of the things she goes on about. Do you think I should go and tell the coroner?'

'No, I don't,' said Thomas.

'I'm glad I've told you anyway. I know anything I say to you is secret. I'm glad I've said it aloud.'

'One must have things to hang onto. Truth matters.'

'I've lost touch with truth.'

'No, you haven't, you've just demonstrated that. Your idea of losing the truth is simply an illusion. Unhappy people console themselves with lies, then feel that everything is falsified –'

'That's me. I'm deprived of every possibility of acting rightly or doing any good. It's a *system* of grief, every grief I've ever had enters into this grief and augments it. There's no cure for remorse like I feel. I haven't any foothold. It's like trying to add up figures in a dream. You imagine I can think,

I can't. You appeal to my intellect, it isn't there.'

'Of course it's there, don't utter blatant lies. Just try to sort the stuff out a bit, get hold of a few concepts. You were glad you told me about something which troubled your conscience. You have a conscience. You can make distinctions. You spoke of grief just now, and remorse. Can you put those things in any sort of order? What's in the centre of it all? Don't answer at once, just try to *think*.'

Edward, sitting in an armchair opposite to Thomas's desk thought, 'Oh well – what I've said – it doesn't help to say the obvious – just what happened and how to unhappen it – what a terrible thing I did – and Mark, whom I love – being – gone –'

'That's a lot of matter. Go on trying. You used the word "love". You can't unhappen what has happened. Mark is dead and the dead have to be loved in a special way which has to be learnt. And your "terrible thing" is full of things which need to be separated out –'

'God, do you want a list!'

'Yes.'

'I'm marked, I'm branded, people can see it, everyone stares at me in the street. I haven't any real being left, it's all scratched and scraped away, people shudder away from me, I stink of misery and evil. When I was coming here I saw Meredith come out of the house, and he pretended not to see me and crossed the road, he couldn't stand the sight of me, that hurt me so much. It's the shame, the loss of honour, that can never come back. I'm ruined and blackened forever, and I'm so young. And it does connect with unhappening. If only I hadn't locked the door, if only I hadn't left him – oh what's the use – I'm not worthy to live – I'm so weary of grieving and trying to cry – all I want is to be walled up in a stone cell and starve and become a little dried up animal and die.' As he said this Edward opened his eyes wide and smiled, the weird uncanny gloating smile which had so much appalled Stuart.

'Your unconscious mind is having a festival,' said Thomas, who had seen such smiles before. 'You're sure you don't want to see a priest? It's always worth wondering whether the remnants of your religion could help. A priest could hear your confession and absolve you. These are rites which need not depend on dogma.'

'No, no priest. So you want me to specialise in feeling guilty?'

'You could put it so! There's got to be some point in all this mess of miseries where something creative could come about. You keep harping on the "terrible thing", and the "fact" and "what happened", but at the same time you keep spending your energy and your resentment in imagining it hasn't happened. Your feeling of guilt, if you can isolate it, can provide the place, and the "style" if I may put it so, by which you can get it into your mind and your heart that it *has* happened – and start from there. That place, if you can attend to it, can change the atmosphere, give you more air and light. Loving Mark could be something positive, only it's no good loving him still alive. And you might *think* about answering Mrs Wilsden, compose a letter.'

'Thomas,' said Edward, 'you haven't *understood,* I haven't got the *strength,* all this stuff of yours just sounds like *poetry,* it doesn't connect with anything I could do or even imagine. I'm sure you're being ingenious and clever and trying to stir me and appeal to me and so on, and I'm very grateful, but it's no use, I haven't any *imagination* left. I've even lost all my sexual feelings. Stuart says he's given up sex, but he's absolutely bulging with it. I think I've had sex permanently taken from me. All my ordinary fantasy life has gone, or rather it's just gone into *that.* I can't do the complicated little things you're parading before me, distinguishing this from that and holding onto the other, I can't. Of course I want to be forgiven, which seems an awful cheat, but no one can. A priest can't, Mrs Wilsden can't, even if she wanted to which she doesn't, she wants to torture me to death. And I *am* being tortured to death, I torture myself, I suffer so much, I couldn't suffer more, but if I could suffer more I would –'

'I don't think I can forgive you,' said Thomas. 'There's something else I can do, but not that. We need priests, we miss them and will miss them more, we miss their power. There will be different priests in the future, different vocations. We shall have to reinvent God, those without justification will have to invent him.'

'Those without justification will not have the energy,' said Edward, 'they won't have spirit enough. I am *spiritless*. God is the invention of happy innocent people. *We* know there is no God, or whatever God-substitute sentimental asses like Stuart like to slobber over. Oh how you make me *talk*. Perhaps I'll hate you for it afterwards.'

'No you won't, dear Edward.'

'All right, but even you can't see what it's like, this fruitless searing burning hell at every conscious moment, it's misery crystallised as pure fear, because it *will* be worse later, like someone waiting his turn to be tortured. Harry says it's irrational, and Stuart says I'm making it an end in itself, and it's true sometimes I can't even see Mark, he's just a name, as if I've thrown him away, as if I couldn't *remember* why I'm in hell, perhaps that's part of the punishment, to be in hell and not even to know why, but I *am* there, and I shall die of it.'

'You *are* dying of it,' said Thomas, 'I mean you are spiritually dying. You said earlier you would have to change yourself into another person. You are doing that, and it's very painful. You say you suffer and can't remember why. The whole of creation suffers in that way, it groans and travails together. You are consciously partaking in that suffering.'

'The whole of creation is innocent, as far as I'm concerned, I forgive it, everything except me.'

'So you think you're alone in hell?'

'You want to interest me, to make me think of other people, but I don't want to be cured and have it all turned into cheerfulness and commonsense by your magic. Your magic isn't strong enough to overcome what I have, it's weak, it's a failing torch. I am permanently damaged.'

'I'm offering you cheerfulness and commonsense. And of course, don't worry, you are permanently damaged and you won't be cured.'

'I thought you were trying to cure me.'

'Well, I am, but not as you imagine, I'm much more ambitious that that. You will always carry this pain inside you. Many people carry such pains. But it will not always be like *this*.'

'All right, I'm changing, but not in a good way, there is no good way, that's what I've *discovered*. It's not like being – like being a chrysalis – it's the opposite, it's the chrysalis story run backwards. I used to have coloured wings and fly. Now I am black and I lie on the ground and quiver. Soon the earth will begin to cover me and I shall become cold and be buried and rot.'

'Yes, yes, a good image. Now listen to me. You are undergoing by accident and by your own fault a spiritual journey which many would consciously purchase at a great price, but cannot buy. Your picture of yourself, your self-illusion, is in process of being broken. This places you in an unusual position, very close to the truth, and the proximity is part of your pain. You say you have no energy, that you are using mine, it isn't so. Your unconscious mind rejoices in the defeat of your proud ego, its malicious pleasure floods you with demonic energy, which you use up in futile exercises of resentment and anger and hate. What I called your eloquence, your flow of imagery, is a symptom of your condition. You hate your damaged self and feel you cannot live with it, yet you desperately cherish it at the same time. You describe your grief as a system. Indeed it is, a defensive system of mutually supporting falsehoods instinctively produced to defend your old egoistic self-image which you cannot bear to lose, you cannot bear its death which seems so like your own. Your endless talk of dying is a substitute for the real needful death, the death of your illusions. Your "death" is a pretend death, simply the false notion that somehow, without effort, all your troubles could vanish. This is where you are, and here a religious believer would pray, and you must try to find your own equivalent of prayer. The word "will" rarely describes anything perceptible, but an act of will is needed here, an act of well-intentioned *concentration*. You, in your thought, in your deepest heart, must check the misuse of your powers, must redirect that strange energy which, although it is so ambiguous, is god-given, given to you by the dark gods. I'm not telling you not to feel remorse and guilt, only to feel it truthfully. Truthful remorse leads to the fruitful death of the self, not to its survival as a successful liar. *Recognise* lies and reject them at every point. You want to unhappen what has

77

happened, you feel anger and hate at what prevents this, and which you see as the cause of your "loss of honour". These old deep "natural" desires appear to you to be irresistible. Check them, see them to be illusions and lies. Move beyond them into an open and quiet area which you will find to be an *entirely new place*. You have never been in such a place before and the person who is there is a new person. You say you live in pain. Let it be the pain of the death of the old false self, and the life-movement of the new real truthful self. We are all wrapped in silky layers of illusion which we instinctively feel to be necessary to our existence. Often these illusions are harmless, in the sense that we can still go on being reasonably good and reasonably happy. Sometimes, because of a catastrophe, a bereavement or some total loss of self-esteem, our falsehoods become pernicious, and we are forced to choose between some painful recognition of truth and an ever more frenzied and aggressive manufacturing of lies. I am suggesting to you that you become aware of your situation and set yourself to will and to pray. Don't hope for anything except the truth, to see guilt and grief in their own being. Live at peace with despair. Live quietly with your sense of guilt, and with the event and its consequences. Sit beside it, as it were, and regard the frightful wound to your self-esteem as the removal of deep illusions which existed before and which this chance has torn. If you keep checking any lie and resisting the anger which deforms the world you will gradually realise that the poor old wounded self, with its furious whining and its hatred of itself and everything else, is not you at all. That self is dying, but another self is watching it die. And gradually you will feed your life-energy, that which the gods send us for better or for worse, animating your newly made self and no longer that gesticulating puppet you once thought was you. Listen Edward – I'm not suggesting something crazy like instant sanctity! I'm suggesting what is in an immediate sense your salvation. I want you to make a good job of this, and you can. You will never efface the experience of the "terrible thing", you will never entirely "recover". Yet also you will partly forget it, you may think of it every day but not all day. What I call your salvation you will be much more likely to forget about as the natural ego grows again. Yet if you even partly achieve it, that too will travel with you as *evidence* of the power of the spirit in the healing of the soul, when with a good will you turn toward truth and whatever light you know, and simply stop that energetic production of illusions which seems at the moment to be your only life force. You keep repeating that you are in hell. It's not a place for souls to stay in, it's bad for them. You are able to get out. If you make even the faintest serious effort you will sense the life of the new being that you can become.'

Edward, who had listened to Thomas's long speech with attention, said quickly, 'Thanks, I know you're trying to impress me and persuade me, I know you're trying something on. I know it's stupid and bad to be so terribly unhappy and full of what you call illusions, but there's nothing I can do about it. One thing's missing in your awfully poetic picture, and that's the motive. I haven't got the *motive,* that's what's missing from your plan for my salvation. Oh God, I feel so tired.'

'So do I,' said Thomas. 'Let's knock off for a bit.' He stood up and stretched his arms out sideways and wriggled his shoulders.

There was a shock in the room like the twang of a bow string. Edward, to whom his surroundings had become invisible, so great had been his concentration upon the *argument* he had been having with Thomas, and his resistance to the force of Thomas's will, now saw the scene, the books, the sunlight upon the figured carpet, a picture of a mill by Midge's father, Cleve Warriston, Thomas stretching, now ruffling his tidy grey hair, then removing his glasses and cleaning them. Edward sighed and pulled himself up from the armchair. He went to the window and gazed vaguely at a prunus tree coming pinkly into flower and some mauve and white crocuses growing in a semicircle round a stone lion's head set in the brick wall. He touched the thick white paint of the window frame and thrust his fingers through the polished brass ring which served to lift the sash. Thomas watched him.

Edward said, 'I remember now, I dreamt last night that

there was a beautiful enormous butterfly in my room and I was trying to open the window to let it out only I couldn't. Then it lighted on my hand and I could feel it biting my hand with its little teeth. Then I shook my hand gently to make it fly. Only it didn't fly. It just fell down onto the floor with a thud and lay there dead.'

'Psyche is a butterfly,' murmured Thomas. 'She is loved by Eros.'

Edward had just recalled that the sash window in his lodgings had had a brass ring just like this one. He hastily withdrew his hand.

Thomas said, 'That room, that room where it happened. You might go back and look at it.'

'You must be a thought-reader, I was just thinking about that room. I couldn't go back there. Is that supposed to be therapy? I'd run mad and jump out of the window. Anyhow I'm going to go away for a while.'

'Where to?'

Edward, who had been pressing his forehead against the glass, drew away, tucking back his long lock of dark hair. He was taller than Thomas and seemed to have become, in the last weeks, exceedingly thin. His long neck protruded forward skinnily from the open collar of his crumpled blue shirt. He picked his way bird-like to this chair, avoiding piles of books on the floor, sat on the arm of the chair, rose and went behind it, leaning to rest his hands on the back. He did not answer Thomas's question. 'Something very strange happened yesterday.'

'Yesterday?'

'You seem surprised that anything *else* can happen to me. So am I. I never really told you why I left Mark that night and didn't get back sooner.'

'You said someone rang up –'

'Yes, it was a girl. I made love to her, we got straight into bed, that was what delayed me.'

'I see.' Thomas, who had been back at his desk, got up and roamed to the bookshelves, examining the books. 'And the girl, do you love her?'

'No, I hate her, she made me a murderer, she's part of the

conspiracy. All right, that's a wrong way to put it, what you'd call a lie.'

'It's not just called a lie, it is a lie. Anyway, what happened yesterday?'

'I went to a seance.'

'How does the girl come in?'

'She doesn't, except that she was talking about a seance, and she must have put a card in my pocket, *this* card.' Edward produced the card. Thomas put on his glasses and inspected it. 'Well, you see the message. I went there, and the medium said that there was a message for someone with two fathers, that was obviously me.'

'And –?'

'And the message was – from my father. It was weird, like a hallucination, only it somehow wasn't, the room was all dark, and there was this great *head*, like a sphere of bronze, sort of suspended, a terrible talking head, and it said, "Come, my son, come home to your father." And it actually uttered my name, "Edward".'

'Are you sure?'

'Yes.'

'How very interesting,' said Thomas. 'What sort of voice did it have?'

'A deep voice, some sort of accent, sort of slow, spoke quite clearly – I suppose it was a trick, a fake – and yet it couldn't have been. Anyway it was a sign. But it must have come out of my mind. Do you think it's just that bloody drug still working in me, some sort of subjective illusion?'

'I can't say.'

'But you know it *wasn't* an illusion, it was something else. I suppose Jesse Baltram isn't dead, is he?'

'He couldn't be, it would be in all the papers, your father is a famous man.'

'How awfully odd it is to hear you speak of him as my father. I never wanted to see him, I made him non-exist. It's worked till now. He was never part of my life. Harry never wanted me to go near those people. And of course Chloe hated him.'

'You saw him when you were a child –'

81

'Yes, Chloe took me over two or three times, when *they* were in London. He was horrible, he sort of sneered at me, a big tall chap with a lot of dark hair. And *she,* the wife, tried to pet me, but it was false, I saw through it all. And the little girls stood like malicious dolls armed with pins. I felt they were all trying to kill me. Perhaps Chloe took me there on purpose so I could see how awful they were.'

'He probably felt guilty at having mislaid you. He may even have coveted you. The women were jealous.'

'Do you think so? You know, now that it's happened and I've started to think about him I can't imagine why I didn't want to discover him ages ago – my real father.'

'In an important sense Harry is your real father.'

'Yes, yes, I know. You won't tell Harry about this?'

'No, of course not.'

'Because you see – he summoned me – and I must go to him.'

'Go to him? What will you do, write, ring up, say can I come? I suppose he's still living in that house he designed, which everyone was so interested in once. What's its name?'

'Seegard.'

'It was in all the architectural reviews.'

'Yes. Everyone's forgotten now. They've forgotten *him.* He's out of fashion. People don't know he's still alive.'

'I read he was still painting, producing a lot of new stuff. So that's where you're going to run away to. I won't tell anyone. Edward, something new has happened to you.'

'No, it *can't* be new, it *must* be connected, it's to do with my mind, it's compulsion, I've *got* to go – and it's to do with death – there'll be a catastrophe, and I'll make it happen.'

After Edward went away Thomas sat motionless in his chair for some time. When Edward was leaving Thomas had touched him, putting an arm round his shoulder, then quickly sliding his hand down to the boy's wrist, feeling for the bare skin beyond the cuff. It had all happened in a moment. Thomas never touched Mr Blinnet, that would be inconceivable. As for Edward and Stuart, he could have hugged them, only that was inconceivable too.

Thomas was not displeased with the conversation, whose strategy he had planned carefully beforehand. Information had emerged, ideas had been planted. Edward would reflect and remember. He had taken the risk of leaving the boy alone with his horrors. Loving care, even authority, tolerated now, would have been rejected earlier. Thomas had to admit the intrusion of accident. The business of the seance was a surprise. Concerning paranormal phenomena Thomas was an interested agnostic. Of course such phenomena were, in ways yet unclear, products of the mind. Whether they were to concern him, and how and why be distinguished from more 'ordinary' illusions, was something to be decided in particular cases. He felt no strong emotions about the problem. About Edward, he would wait and see. A psychotic episode is sometimes of value in altering a pattern of consciousness. Prompted by the patient himself, it can be a beneficent disturbance, releasing healing agencies. Yet such things could be unpredictable too. The 'dialogue' had been quite a success. Edward had been alert, he had attended, responded, argued, defended his position. He had been able to follow Thomas. How eloquent they can be, he thought, the afflicted ones, the soul-wounded, speaking suddenly with tongues, forced by anguish into being poets. He had never heard Edward speak so well. What awful images of pain the boy had spewed out: captivity, machinery, starvation, electrocution, the dying chrysalis, the plunging aeroplane, the dead butterfly. And my weak magic, thought Thomas, pale and wan against that blackness, like a failing torch. So often, in extremity, and especially when guilt is involved, only strong love can heal. But is it available, is it intelligent, intuitive, can it discover the way? God is a belief that at our deepest level we are known and loved, even to there the rays can penetrate. But the therapist is not God, not even a priest or a sage, and must prompt the sufferer to heal himself through his own deities, and this involves finding them. How many souls there are who, encountering no good powers, are never healed at all. Yes, thought Thomas, they can go down, simply surrendered to gravity, unable to rise against the weight. He had, only once, lost a patient. The boy, after endlessly announcing that he would kill himself, did so. The parents blamed Thomas. Did he blame himself? Yes. But the blame was scarcely distinguishable from the grief. How well he understood the identification in Edward's case. That failure did not bring Thomas any new knowledge. Those who help others to play for high stakes with 'spiritual death' must understand the risks. The desire for revenge on fate can turn against the accursed body. Each person is different, the general idea of 'neurosis' a mere hypothesis. Sometimes at least the afflicted have a right to play out the game themselves without drugs or 'scientific' mythology. The 'myth' that heals is an individual work of art. Edward was partly right when he said that he was borrowing Thomas's energy. In fact Thomas, reaching into the mystery of another unconscious mind, was also using Edward's. If the healer identifies with his patient he may mistake his own powers for those of the other. Not everyone is strong enough to 'play'. Thomas no longer believed in 'dreaming along' with his patients, taking over their fantasies and playing the doctor in an endless therapeutic drama of mutual need: the love affair of healer and patient enacting a play of stirred-up egoism. He had so far changed his early assumptions that he sometimes felt he ought to invent a new name for what he was doing. He once puzzled an idle questioner at a dinner table by saying that his special subject was death. Death in life, life in death, life after death; and yet also simply annihilation. To say that the self-destroyer leaves behind all obligations except to his own soul says nothing, merely states the mystery, the enigma. To reach this position is itself an extreme move. The helper, whom Thomas also pictured as the servant, can do little except present a vision, his image of this particular salvation, and try to communicate the spiritual force needed to choose the death that leads to life; must, with his eyes open in the dark, and with all the magnetism of his intuition, find and release that force in the deep mind of his patient, making him understand the sense in which he is dead already. The motive, yes, as Edward said, the motive must be found. In so many kinds of affliction, in so many forms, the *need* for death, its *necessity,* appears to people who never, in their 'ordinary lives', conceived of it at all. Thomas recalled Edward's weird exalted stare, his uncanny smile. A demon who had nothing to do with the well-being of the ordinary 'real' Edward had for a moment looked out. How ambiguous such conditions were. The entranced face of the tortured Marsyas, as Apollo kneels lovingly to tear his skin off, prefigures the death and resurrection of the soul.

Thomas took a comb out of the drawer of his desk and combed down his sleek light grey hair which swirled out so evenly from the crown and made so neat a fringe across his brow. His hair, which always looked ostentatiously neat, was of a radiant grey, not properly described as silver. He absently cleaned his glasses again upon a snowy handkerchief and resettled them firmly before his eyes. His heart was still beating hard from the encounter with Edward, beating for Edward. We do not have mythical fates, even the individual 'myth' is ultimately consumed, it is 'worked away' in living and only in this sense exists. How was it that Stuart had discovered those things so easily? He did not even know that he knew them. Thomas's face, poised and wrinkled up with thought, had a whimsical almost sentimental gentleness. There are some faces which cannot be 'read' with a key. For one face there may be many keys. There are many ways of assembling that enigmatic *Gestalt,* and some of the most convincing ones can be false. In Thomas's case it certainly helped to know that he was half Jewish. He did not look superficially Jewish, but he looked deeply so. The curl of his mouth, even the wrinkles round his eyes, somehow proclaimed it. His way of seeming civilised, super-civilised, even over-civilised, proclaimed it. The Jewishness was on his mother's side. Thomas was indeed, as Harry had indicated, proud of his ancestry. The McCaskerville side, a brave but ineffectual Catholic family, were in their more recent days (which dated from the eighteenth century) a product of the Old Alliance. Their connections with France predated the misadventures of the Pretenders and they followed the white cockade into exile after the battle of Sherrifmuir. McCaskervilles had fought at Bannockburn, and some younger sons died at Culloden. (Such details would Thomas, very occasionally, impart to a sincerely interested enquirer). Some of the exiles intermarried with impoverished French gentry, described as aristocrats. In the nineteenth century trade brought them back to Edinburgh, and later wealth set them free to become, as they pleased, lawyers and doctors. Thomas's father and grandfather, still strong Catholics, favoured the law, and one of his great-uncles had been Procurator Fiscal.

Thomas's father however broke with what was by now a grand air of tradition by abandoning his faith and marrying a Jewish girl, the daughter of a well-known Scottish Rabbi. Both families were horrified. The Godless young people (for Rachel, Thomas's mother, had also quit her ancestral religion) prospered nevertheless and in time, with the birth of the longed-for boy, and in spite of their socialistic atheism, regained the trust and affection of their respective relatives. Those two groups rarely met however, and the child Thomas was discreetly battled over by two powerful clans, against whom he was also defended by his parents. To the relief of the latter Thomas (an only child) showed no sign of a religious conversion to either party. He showed, indeed, no sign of having the slightest interest in religion; in this respect however he was a deceiver. He loved his parents very much, but constantly, out of a kind of tact, concealed from them many of his deepest feelings. This laconic, secretive discretion, which became in the growing boy a major characteristic, was fostered by the tension, never relaxed on either side, between his Jewish and Christian grandparents. Thomas, an affectionate child, was at home with both sides, but the secret romanticism of his heart favoured the Hebrews. His mother's father, a dignified and witty patriarch, a bearded scholar, a Zionist, an expert on Hasidism, seemed to young Thomas a figure out of a fairy tale. He loved the fancy dress, the embroidered caps and shawls, the long table with the white cloth, the candles and the wine and the exotic food, where so many people so often assembled for feasts and rites from which he was not entirely excluded. And yet he *was* excluded, because of his mother's crime, that terrible marriage, in the guilt of which her son silently partook. His mother, whose Slav ancestors had long been Edinburgh merchants, spoke in her parents' home both Hebrew and Yiddish, tongues to which Thomas listened with silent anguish, well aware that it would not be his lot to learn them. He knew in fact, even as a boy, that he was psychologically disabled from any later adherence to either of the faiths whose strong smell pervaded his childhood. Religion remained for him a *princesse lointaine*; or more like a native land from which he was irrevocably exiled and whose half-remembered songs he could sing only in his heart: a kind of fate which indeed he shared with many of his ancestors on both sides.

Both Thomas's parents passionately loved Scotland, and he pleased them by going to Edinburgh University. As soon as his further education permitted however he went south. His mother died when he was in his twenties. His father lived to see his son's late marriage. (And hurt Thomas deeply by saying that he had simply 'married a pretty face'.) After his father's death Thomas took Midge, at her request, and Meredith aged seven, on a little tour of his past, which upset him very much. They visited some McCaskerville cousins who lived in a mediaeval tower and regarded Thomas as a laughable oddity. Thomas went alone to see his Jewish grandfather, still alive and rather mad in a hospital, who failed to recognise Thomas and talked to him in Yiddish. Since then Thomas had not returned north of the border. Sometimes he felt that he hated Scotland; he made no drama of this but it made him sad. There was an alienation of being which he saw, with mysterious difference, continued in his son. Meredith never referred to Scotland or asked to go there. Looking at the silent watchful straight-backed undemonstrative child, Thomas saw the very image of himself. Meredith, unhampered by parental advice on the subject, underwent the mild Anglicanism of his school without comment. His only effective grandparent was Midge's drunken painter father, more recently dead. With this tramp-like figure the child had had a relation friendly enough to arouse pangs of jealousy in Thomas's secretly yearning heart. Thomas's choice of a profession was no doubt influenced by his peculiar homelessness, and by certain conflicting and deep desires, even passions, occasioned by a proximity of religion as a forbidden fruit. This same condition now prompted the interest which he felt in Stuart Cuno.

Thomas had in fact, though spiritually 'destined' for it, meandered into psychiatry by a route which Ursula Brightwalton would have disapproved of even more had she known the details of it. Thomas had studied literature at Edinburgh, wanted to be an art historian, then took a medical degree to please his McCaskerville grandfather, became a general practitioner and hated it. He returned to medical school to study mental illness. Then, nearer to a 'nervous breakdown' than he ever admitted to anyone, he took a short 'training analysis', ostensibly as part of his medical course. He shunned and feared deep analysis and the 'training', though instructive, increased his scepticism. He was now, in a formal official sense, 'qualified', and soon exerted all his considerable ability to impress people in becoming set up, respected, and soon well known as a psychiatrist. Yet all this time, and in the midst of increasing 'success', he felt he was an amateur. On bad days he felt he was a charlatan. 'There's nothing deep involved, it's just a matter of becoming some sort of *ad hoc* expert on misery and guilt,' he said to someone who was set on admiring him, and who then admired him even more. Of course there were many things which Thomas's medical training had taught him, especially about diagnosis and what not to do. About drugs and electric shocks he knew a good deal more than Ursula imagined. He knew whom he *couldn't* treat. More deeply he was aware that he was an unbeliever, he did not share with his colleagues a certain traditional faith in this form of healing. He did not think that he was a scientist.

Such reflections were constantly at work in Thomas's exercise of power, where at times, in his concentration upon an individual patient, he felt that he was making risky guesses. How he *dared* to do what he did, he did not know. Sometimes he wondered whether his reluctance to generalise were not a result simply of laziness. Yet when he was working well he felt sure of his methods, and not only sure that they were right for him. Only in particular situations there came particular certainties. We practise dying through a continual destruction of our self-images, inspired not by the self-hatred which seems to be within, but by the truth that seems to be without; such suffering is normal, it goes on all the time, it must go on. Here, at the extreme points of Thomas's departure from more conventional ideas of health, he had continually, and with increasing doubts, to put himself in question. Thomas, who was crammed with secrets, guarded this one most carefully. He sometimes wondered whether he were not engaged in the wrong occupation. It did appear to him that he helped people. Yet how could this be, when he required of his patients more that he required of himself? Would it not be better if he could teach something of his methods to some others, and then retire to practise dying? Here most obviously he saw the empty scheme of an impossible religious solution. As for teaching his younger colleagues, how could he do so, since he so jealously concealed what he did, and could only do it on that condition? There seemed to be something wrong somewhere.

Without, until recently, even hinting this to anyone. Thomas had been slowly divesting himself of his powers, trying to 'finish' his patients, meticulously of course, and release them or find them another 'place'. He felt that he required an interval, which might prove to be a long one. He wanted to think, perhaps to write, to leave London, to live in the country, to be more alone, and if these things seemed like luxuries he did not care. He felt he was beginning to need his patients, and this was dangerous. He needed Mr Blinnet, had by now come too close to him; without excluding the theory, for Thomas was more sceptical than Ursula imagined, that this clever and interesting man was at least partly engaged in teasing his psychiatrist. It was time to make a change.

And now there were those two boys in a state of crisis. Perhaps this too was some sort of signal. Thomas loved his wife and son blindly and exceedingly, his 'coldness', his critical 'knocking' attitude to Midge, remarked upon by Ursula, was an instinctive attempt to avert the envy of the gods. He was proud of her and continually felt how lucky he was to possess her. Whereas he 'read' himself in Meredith, she remained opaque, radiant like a work of art, full of strange rays. He loved her, he admired her, and in an odd way he pitied her, and this intense pity was stored in the centre of his love. He never forgot his father's remark, but he translated it into another language. The two boys were a bonus, brought to him by his wife as part of her dowry, two extra sons. Thomas, always an exile and an only child, lacked family. He missed his parents, he thought of them every day. He loved Stuart and Edward, but secretly, and with a more detached emotion which included curiosity, whereas about his wife and son he felt none, they were absolutes. With 'the boys' he had felt a pleasure as at watching animals at play, and now his fear for them felt like a fear felt for loved animals. They were both, in different ways, in pledge to death. Was he to redeem them? For both had become, at once, his patients. Thomas was certainly not going to let Stuart escape without giving up a secret or two. He almost looked forward to seeing him in trouble. In this, over which he almost smiled, Thomas experienced in himself the shadow of the old conflict between holiness and magic, so alike, so utterly different. It was as if Stuart had become for him a talisman, symbol of death, an object of awe and envy, yet also provocative of painful anxiety: Stuart, with his curious blankness, so unattractive to some, to Harry, for instance, maddening. Edward had lost all value, Stuart was gorged with it. It was as if Stuart had become an albino, Thomas saw him as something immensely solid but without colour. Would it develop, would it last? Edward's problems were simpler, but also graver. Edward was about to destroy the world, to banish it by flight, as Thomas had predicted, fleeing out of the mess of here to the purity of elsewhere, taking flight as his image of death. But with what a terrible destination. Edward was running away to the most dangerous place of all, and Thomas was not stopping him. Was he not indeed sending this beloved child straight into the underworld?

'I THINK YOU'RE not worrying enough about Edward,' said Midge.

'What's the use of my worrying?' said Harry. 'I could upset myself by imagining it all, but why should I? It won't help me to help him, quite the reverse. You're all crowding round him and saying "Oh, how terrible". He needs to be made to feel it *isn't* terrible, it's ordinary, like what happens to all of us. He needs casualness, not all this portentous caring. He needs to get over it, to cover it with a healing skin of indifference, to *forget* it. And if I forget it for him, that helps him on. Anyway Thomas has got him now, he'll be in love with Thomas, he probably is already. Thomas will make him feel guilty instead of saying it wasn't his fault. God, how I loathe that idea.'

'Thomas is so sort of romantic about death, he wants people to confront things even if it kills them.'

'Thomas is a *voyeur,* he lives off the miseries of others. But it'll all slide off Edward. He's got what we haven't got which will make him recover.'

'What's that?'

'Youth.'

Midge considered this idea for a moment. It came to her with a hint of the gratuitous barbed bitterness which she now increasingly perceived in her lover. She sighed. 'Haven't we got it? Well, I suppose not.'

'Don't cry about it.'

'I'm not crying. I just want to feel we have endless time.'

'We have endless time, my queen, my Cleopatra. He lives eternally who lives in the present.'

'I wish that was true.'

'We live in a golden time, not in mean ordinary time.'

'Yes, but we are surrounded by ordinary time.' That was true enough. Their great deception, which had lasted now for nearly two years, was like a vast mathematical calculation, a jigsaw puzzle of days and hours and minutes, of patterns which varied and patterns which remained the same. It was as if they were astrologers or physicists. Now, for instance, Meredith was safe at school, Thomas was safe at the clinic, where Midge had telephoned him to make sure, Midge and Harry were safe in the spare bedroom of the house in Fulham, *our* bedroom as Harry called it.

'We live in an impossible way,' said Midge, 'but at least that proves one can!'

'Impossible situations can continue, but that doesn't mean they should!'

'Don't needle me. I wish we didn't have to be here.'

'So do I.'

'It's not that I think Thomas might find out –'

'I suppose you'd know if he found out.'

'Of course.'

They looked at each other. Neither was sure. Thomas was capable of anything. Perhaps Midge was too. Lying was so infectious. Sometimes Harry wondered whether Thomas hadn't known all the time, informed by Midge right at the start, forgiven, licensed, at the start. Perhaps they had discussed it. But Harry did not really think this. He said, 'I'm sorry. My place is hopeless now with those two wretched boys at home. They may be there forever. I'm going to get us that little flat.'

'No –'

'You think it's a "step". Well, it is a step. But consider how many steps we've already taken.'

'It would be so expensive. And the idea of a love nest –'

'Well, this is a love nest! We may as well have a comfortable one! Besides I want to cook for you. This isn't just unsafe. It's appallingly bad form.'

'Oh – bad form –!'

'When we're criminals anyway, in blood so steeped – Have some whisky.'

'No, thanks.'

'Of course, you don't want Thomas to smell it on your Judas kisses!'

'Don't. I wish, oh I wish, I wish –'

'That everything was different. But it isn't. You mustn't wish, you must *will*. I wish you'd waited for me, and not married Thomas. God, why didn't you wait!'

'I wish you'd *noticed* me when Chloe died.'

'All right, all right!'

Harry, dressed but open-shirted, bare-chested, was moving restlessly about the room holding a glass of whisky, now standing near the window looking at the rain falling on roofs and chimney pots. Midge, sitting on the bed watching him, was wearing a huge-sleeved robe of red and purple silks which Harry had had made for her and which she wore for him after love-making and only then, and which he now brought with him to their trysts and took away again afterwards.

'We weren't ready for each other then,' said Midge. 'Still it could have happened. I never got on with Chloe, she never invited me or wanted to see me, I didn't live in London. But we did literally see each other. Of course I looked like nothing at all. I had to make myself. You were made by your father, your childhood, your school, your education, your money – I had to invent myself out of nothing. Perhaps that's why I'm so tired now.'

'It's true,' said Harry, 'you were invisible. The little sister who lived down in Kent. And when Chloe died I was crazy. Poor Chloe, she must have been one of the last people to die of TB – she looked – so beautiful, so frail with big sad eyes –'

'While I'm so healthy and fat.'

'Don't be envious!'

'Jealous. She was your wife.'

'Well, what's stopping you being my wife?'

'When she died I was busy inventing myself.'

'And the height of your ambition was to be a fashion model!'

'Don't sneer. You don't know what a long way I had to go. Chloe and Dad always told me I had no talents. But when I was a model everyone in England had heard of me. No one ever heard of Chloe.'

'Oh stop it, Midge —'

'I was a clerk in an office —'

'And then you donned beauty like a robe. Who was the first person who told you you were beautiful?'

'Jesse Baltram.'

'But you never met him!' said Harry. 'You said Chloe took you to Seegard once, and let you in the car!'

'Well — I did meet him —' said Midge. 'I never told you this. Perhaps I shouldn't. Some memories are like lucky charms, talismans, one shouldn't tell about them or they'll lose their power.'

'Tell, tell!'

'Chloe left me in the car like a dog. I was still at school. She was Jesse's model, she always said she was his pupil, that business was just starting up I suppose. She said she wouldn't be long, but she was ages, and at last I went into the house. It's a very strange house.'

'And you met Jesse?'

'Then Chloe said I could stay for lunch. Nobody *talked* to me at all. I sat at a long table. There were some girls and young men who I thought were art students, and some children, I didn't even identify Mrs Baltram, everyone was rather good-looking and dressed in sort of smocks and robes and things.'

'And Jesse?'

'He sat at the head of the table. He had a great narrow nose and a pointed chin and a lot of straight dark hair like a crest. Everyone was talking loudly and ignoring me and I felt very frightened and miserable. Then suddenly Jesse pointed at me with his knife and called out, "Who is that girl?" And there was a silence.'

'Yes — and then?'

'Well, someone said I was Chloe's sister, and Jesse went on looking at me for a moment. He didn't smile. Then he went on with his lunch and everyone started chattering again. Then after lunch we went away.'

'But didn't you see him again, didn't you talk to him?'

'No. That was all.'

'But you said he said you were beautiful.'

'He didn't say it,' said Midge, 'but I *knew* that he *thought* it. He could really *see* me.'

'This makes me jealous,' said Harry. 'That look of Jesse's was probably your sexual awakening. That's why you think it's a talisman.'

'Perhaps.'

'I'm sure you weren't beautiful then. He might have thought you looked like Chloe. That's why he noticed you.'

'You like to think I didn't exist until *you* noticed me!'

'Of course. God, I've had enough trouble with that man in my thoughts!'

'I'd like to see him again. I'd like to see Seegard again.'

'I see little chance of either of us being invited, I'm glad to say,' said Harry. 'I'm never going near that place, and I forbid you to.'

Midge smiled. She liked it when Harry asserted authority over her.

'He's old now,' said Harry. 'He got married late. He had hundreds of girls before, and probably after.'

'He's not all that old, he's still working, I read in a magazine.'

'He's old. Well, he saw more than I did. He only stared at you because of Chloe.'

'I didn't look much like her then. I do much more now. He saw the future. He was a great dominating powerful man, everyone in that room felt his power. I thought he was rather weird.'

'You mean sexy. I detest dominating powerful men. It's true I never thought you looked like your sister. Now sometimes you do.'

'I know I'm just a shadow of her in your life, a substitute, a second-best,' said Midge. But she didn't believe this.

'Don't provoke me! You're utterly unlike her, you're a completely different person.'

'Yes, but when I was young she was everything and I was nothing.'

'All right, now she's nothing and you're everything. I've cast her out of my life and out of my heart too. I can't love a ghost, I love life not death, flesh not earth. Christ, I think more about Teresa than about Chloe! God rest her soul, she's *gone,* as if she'd never been. Be content with that and let her be.'

'Oh I do, I do,' said Midge, huddling into her silk robe. They were silent, both fearing the wrong word, the wrong move, which would suddenly though only briefly (but they had so little time) set them apart in other perspectives, with other judgments, other possible courses of action. They were there, Midge in her red and purple and Harry heroic in his wild shirt, a long spear of blond hair adorning his open chest, like a king and queen, glowing fateful and majestic in the intense rainy light of the room.

'I want a weekend,' said Harry, 'I must have that.'

'The next step.'

'It's ridiculous, we've loved each other for two years, and we've never spent two whole consecutive days and nights together. When Thomas goes to that conference in Geneva, we'll find a hotel –'

'It's too dangerous.'

'Oh, dangerous! I'm hungry, I'm starving, I want you in my home, I want it to be your home, I want you forever – and now I'm asking you so bloody little. You drive me mad! What does danger matter to us!'

'You know it matters,' said Midge. 'You agreed there should be no letters. You were the one who told me to invent all those old friends I was supposed to be lunching with –'

'Yes, but that was at the start. We've spent two years getting over the big bang, recovering from the first shock, settling in and realising it's forever –'

'We are well as we are, we could lose each other –'

'Midge, darling, we *can't* lose each other, if there were a showdown I'd just take you away, I'd never let you go back to Thomas and leave me, *never*. So you can dismiss that from your mind!'

'Don't be impatient with me,' said Midge, looking at him with her painful face. 'It's harder for me. We can't solve this by planning it or just wild decisions. Fate will solve it, and time, a way will be opened, we shall receive a sign –'

'OK, so long as we can't lose! I'm just getting a bit fed up with fate and time!'

'But we have *good* time, *beautiful* time, the eternal present like you said, and whenever we part we know that we shall meet again, and we can look forward – I'm so happy with looking forward –'

'My dear heart, stop evading the issue, you know you're evading it –'

'Even if for all our lives we had only what we have now, living quietly together and harming no one –'

'Oh *shut up!*'

'I don't mean this will happen, I just mean we needn't hurry.'

'You said that when Meredith went to boarding school we could be more together. Well, he's going to boarding school in the autumn. And he's nearly grown up. Isn't that a sign?'

'He's going to boarding school,' said Midge, 'and Thomas is talking about leaving London and living in the country!'

'And giving up his patients and surrendering all that power? He never would. Why should his plans interest us anyway! We're made for happiness, he isn't, he belongs to a different race. It's that ancestral rabbi speaking in that prissy Edinburgh voice. I used to think you married Thomas for security and status and because he was an older man and to get even with Chloe. Now I see you married him for his power.'

Midge made a dismissive gesture but said nothing. Her face was calmer now and she looked upon him with large gentle loving eyes.

'Midge, oh my sweetheart, my angel, I love you so much, I feel your kisses all the time, all our touchings, all our joys, are about me like a net, I nearly swooned with desire during that dinner party, when I sit alone at home and think about you I could bite my hands off. You said wait and we've waited, we must think now, we must *think* about how to do ourselves justice, do our *love* justice, and be really together and really happy – oh such happiness, Midge, it's *possible,* it's *near,* we have only to stretch out our hands . . .'

Midge turned away her face which for a moment wore a look of evasive hunted irritation which Harry knew and dreaded. She smoothed her cheeks and brow with soothing hands. 'We said once that if Thomas ever found out we'd have to stop.'

'You said that once, on the second day, even then you didn't believe it!'

'You said it was a precious compact, and if we could just have what we have now and belong faithfully to each other we'd be in paradise.'

'I said that to persuade you, and you know that I did!'

'I thought you rather liked the secrecy. You said once that our getting away with it was what was so wonderful.'

'If I said that, which I don't remember, I spoke like a vulgar fool, I *never* thought that. Why do you *argue* so, you keep bringing up these little hurtful stupid lists of objections –'

'Perhaps I want you to clear them all away. I want to hear you say it'll be all right.'

'My darling, it'll be all right. Just trust me and let me *lead*. You keep talking about things being dangerous – yes, Thomas *could* find out, and we must be prepared, and now we *can* be prepared. It's time to nerve ourselves to see the *necessity* of being really and openly together. We'll look back and think we were crazy to live like a couple of frightened animals in a hole! You know how much I hate it. You're thinking about Meredith, but Meredith will be all right, he's such a calm grown-up child, and he loves me, I think he loves me more than he loves Thomas. You said I was his hero. Thomas is a cold fish, he'll survive anything, he may even get satisfaction out of pretending to be a victim! He's fey and elvish and secretive, and he's dignified, there's no fun in him. And he's getting old, you must feel it, you must see it now, the romance of the older man is over. You say he hates social life, and wants to stop at home and read, and doesn't talk to you. *We* talk all the time, we *get on* with each other, we make each other exist, we give each other more being. You never really got on with him, you just pretended to. You admired him, you revered him. He's never regarded you as a real person, he's never *known* you, he's superior, he directs you, he pities you –'

'I couldn't bear a scandal,' said Midge, who had put on a vague faraway look during Harry's speech.

'That's a paltry reply, refusing so great, so perfect a happiness for fear of a scandal! Everyone does such things these days, there's no such thing as scandal. We must live with the truth of our emotions. A love like ours is self-justifying. Believe in it, give yourself to it. A love like ours is rare, it's a marvel upon earth.'

'Yes, I know. My darling.'

'Well then – why prefer what's hollow to what's real? That's hypocrisy, keeping up appearances, bowing to conventions, letting all the real love disappear out of life. Our love is the truth, the concrete, the real, what opposes it is abstract and false. We must follow our hearts, that's true, the truth of our whole being. *Sex* is true, Midge, you've recognised it and we've proved it.'

'Yes. You don't believe we should try and be good like Stuart thinks!'

'You're joking. What Stuart wants is not only false, it's senseless, it's an unintelligible fake, one can't think in that degree of detail about morals. Life is a whole, it must be lived as a whole, abstract good and bad are just fictions. We must live in our own concrete realised truth and that's *got* to include what we deeply desire, what fulfils us and gives us joy. *That*'s the good life, not everyone is capable of it, not everyone has the courage. We are, and we have.'

'I think I'll dress,' said Midge. She looked at her watch, then squatted to find her shoes. She peeled off her silk robe and found her petticoat. Harry groaned. He put his whisky down carefully on the chest of drawers. She went on, 'Yes, I know. But I – you spoke about a net that you lived in – what I live in is lies – wherever I reach out my hand I touch a network of lies.'

'Well, don't tell *me* that! You know what I want, openness and truth and you, absolutely and forever! You say this is wonderful now, just picture it without the lies! I hate lying and creeping about being afraid of being found out! *I* don't want it to be like this, it's contrary to my nature, you make me do things contrary to my nature and I *hate* it, I feel demeaned and demoralised, I want to be myself, with you, right out in the open. You want to have it all ways, to love and enjoy me and yet to torment me with abstract morality!'

'I'm sorry –'

'And you're the one who once said "my motto is anything goes"!'

'I remember that. Perhaps I was trying to please you by saying *your* motto.'

'You do me less than justice.'

'I know, you have your philosophy.'

'Midge, you drive me mad! What's the problem? You said that when you're with me Thomas doesn't exist, so all you've got to do is be with me all the time.'

'I had a bad dream.'

'You said that *this* was the only genuine independent creative thing you'd ever done in your whole life, so why don't you complete it? Why do you hack at it all the time? You know I won't leave you, you are safe in my heart, it doesn't matter what you do. So is it all just to hurt me?'

'I saw a man on a white horse passing and looking so balefully towards me as if he would kill me. He looked into my eyes. Then he went on. I've had that dream before.'

'You'd better ask your husband what it means. It was probably him. He's the cause of all the trouble!'

'You used to like him, you used to admire him.'

'I still do. Do you think that I enjoy deceiving him, and finding myself cursing him? You have a talent for saying things which are both hurtful and ridiculous.'

'I can't think why you love me.'

'Oh *God!* My life rests on your love. I love you deeply and tenderly as if we've long long been happily married.'

'Good.'

'Midge –!'

'I know, my darling. But I can't hear you say it often enough. Forgive my – forgive me. It's time you went home. Look, the rain has stopped. I shall cry when you're gone. Then I shall tidy this room and do my nails and make myself up a new face. Just give me your hand, your poor burnt hand, I'll be gentle with it.'

100

'What about my poor burnt heart? God how it hurts me to leave you. Kiss me and kiss me, there can never be enough kisses in the world, give me my food or I shall die of love.'

'How beautiful you look, my lovely dear animal, my love – Harry in majesty!'

'Cry God for Harry, England, and St George!'

'There now, go. I wish I could help Edward. I'd so like to.'

'Leave him alone. He's got enough troubles without falling in love with you!'

God, why do we have to suffer so, thought Harry, as he walked along holding up his handsome blond head with such an air of calm authority and pride that people turned to look after him. He looked like an ambassador. Why can't we be happy as we ought to be and could be, it's an inch away. I love her perfectly, she loves me perfectly, yet I'm in hell, and she's in hell. Why does it have to be? Why can't I make her strong enough? Yet she is strong, maddeningly so sometimes, when she uses her strength against me. And why do I have to play this part which I so detest, sitting at Thomas's table and trying not to look at his wife? Harry was well aware, in these negative conversations with Midge, of the deliberate far-sighted cunning with which he diminished Thomas, Thomas as old, Thomas as cold, Thomas as joyless and dull, watching as he did so hawklike for the tiniest signs of her impatience with her husband, her spite against him as the cause of her woe and the obstacle to her happiness. He would unravel Midge from Thomas, deftly and patiently undo him from her world, invest for her a past in which Thomas did not exist. For her to be able to make the break contempt, even hatred of her husband would be needed, would at least certainly be helpful: a terrible truth at which Harry tried to look calmly. So I am capable of cruelty, he thought, as well as treachery. And then, he wondered as he often did, whatever would Thomas do if he knew, or rather, as he corrected himself, what will he do when he knows? The man was a bit fey. A fierce primitive Scotsman with a dirk? A masochistic Jew? A fierce unforgiving scheming Jew? With Midge, Harry always pictured Thomas as weak, kindly, likely to accept a *fait accompli* with resignation, even perhaps with relief. Midge was afraid of her husband. This was something they never discussed. Harry carefully concealed the fact that he was afraid of him too: an unpredictable and dangerous man whom, this was the turn of the screw, Harry admired and loved. It was a part of what he sometimes thought of as his punishment that he had to live with this incompatible esteem, and refrain from expressing it to his beloved in any terms of praise. Thus he moved like a dancer between a steadying assurance that their secret life could continue, and the envisaging of its felicitous and inevitable end in a liberation into happiness and truth, between calming her into present enjoyment, and working her, edging her, startling her into a grasp of the future. When would he force it all into the open and carry Midge away in his troika? When would the moment come when, if all else failed, he could make her his wife by threatening to leave her? It was still too early for that. But the pressure must be kept up. The love nest. Step by step, and each step inevitable.

PART TWO

SEEGARD

SEEGARD ONLY, AN almost illegible signpost said, pointing away down a muddy track where the country bus had deposited Edward Baltram.

After his cry of 'I've got to go', Edward had had second thoughts. The idea had briefly seemed, after the intense emotions of the seance and his talk with Thomas, like an inspiration, a glowing indicator. He had thought, I'll go to my father, I'll confess to him and he will judge me. In the next day or two however the energy had faded and the project lost its point. It was not so much that Edward felt afraid of it, though indeed he did; it just seemed useless and worthless, as empty of sense as everything else in his miserable life. Why should he take the *trouble* to go to a place where he had no significance and was not wanted and would simply be rejected? Besides, how could he go? He could hardly arrive uninvited, and was incapable of writing a letter. He wished he had never told Thomas about the seance, telling about it had made it momentarily more real. That whole episode now seemed to belong to a kind of dull madness which belonged in his unhappy being like an alien ball of black rags which had somehow been stuffed in under his skin. Those were mean nasty small hallucinations, a sort of mental filth exuded by the soul. He once more occupied himself by lying on his bed reading thrillers, and walking about London seeing ugly deformed people and obscene pictures. Even the dogs were hostile. They could smell him. He was afraid at first that the seance might haunt him and prompt new horrible

103

experiences. But soon he began to forget it and returned to his endless familiar rehearsals of the old pain.

One morning however Edward was amazed to receive the following letter.

Seegard

My dear Edward,

If I may so call you, my husband and I have been thinking about you, and would so like to see you. I wonder if you would be so kind as to visit us? We would be delighted if you could come, even just for a few days, to renew acquaintance, it would be a great pleasure. Please write and say if you will come, any time soon would suit well.

Yours sincerely,
May Baltram.

PS We read of your sad mishap in the paper.

On the back of the letter there was a map showing how to reach Seegard from the bus route and a note:

I am afraid after the recent rainfall, we cannot get the car up the track, but just let us know roughly when to expect you and we'll be waiting for you at the house.

Edward wrote at once saying he would come. He sent a note to Thomas, announcing his departure and asking him not to tell anyone. Then, without a word to either Stuart or Harry, he packed a small bag and melted away. And now the little bus, which had smelt of human company and things not yet irrevocable, had left him, and the sound of its engine had faded away and the countryside, in the cold cloudy light of the late afternoon, was silent and empty.

It was not, in Edward's eyes, an attractive scene. Having been brought up in a city, he looked instinctively for 'charm' in 'the country', but could see none here. The land was exceedingly flat. The recent rainfall referred to by Mrs Baltram had turned the track into a dark muddy rivulet winding between water-logged fields where some greenish crop was rising a little above the surface. A watery ditch running on one side of the track reflected a little light. Above in the huge sky, a larger sky than Edward had ever seen, some brown clouds were being slowly conveyed along by the steady east wind, their activity and altering colour contrasting with the drab earth which so meagrely depended from the round horizon. The atlas, at which Edward had hastily glanced before leaving London, indicated the proximity of the sea, but nothing of that interesting feature was to be seen. A few isolated trees alone gave definition to the mournful expanse where no human habitation was visible. Mrs Baltram's map had announced a walk of 'about two miles'. Edward's town shoes were engulfed in mud as soon as he left the tarmac. He set off walking into the wind.

In his farewells to Edward after their talk, Thomas had asked him to write. He had also said, 'Look, if it's *awful*, return at once and come straight to me.' Edward had not tried to imagine in any detail what 'it' would be like, he had simply tried to hold onto his idea of it as 'compulsory'. Now it was too late for speculation, his thinking paralysed by the appalled sense of time which attends the approach of a crucial but invisible event: the exam paper, the doctor's verdict, the news from the scene of the crash. He was accompanied by, almost as if he relied upon it, his old familiar grief, his wound, a part of his body, a blackness in the stomach, a weary sense of futility as he lifted his feet heavy with mud. The invigorating sense of fate, which he had briefly felt in Thomas's presence and for a short time after, had left him, 'I will arise and go to my father . . .' Seegard had seemed like a significant destiny, at least a novelty, perhaps a refuge. Mrs Baltram's letter had reinforced the hand of fate, but in making the project more real, made it at the same time more frightening, and thereby in a sense irrelevant. Why should he, in his present condition, submit to being frightened by something *else*? Yet to deny her summons was also unthinkable, and Edward did not try to work out any significant relation between it and his wounded state. His exclamation to Thomas, that they 'must connect', expressed simply his sense of being eaten up by a single obsession.

So now he was to meet his father: that enormous dark

105

figure concealed behind the curtain of the future to which by every step he was coming closer. Mrs Baltram's letter had spoken of 'her husband and herself' as inviting him and wanting to see him. But this might be inexact. Perhaps, after reading about his 'mishap', she had written on her own compassionate impulse without consulting her husband, or just taking his assent for granted? Or perhaps she had written out of some idle morbid curiosity such as attracts spectators to afflicted people, as it attracts them to any catastrophe? This, in the light of his vague memories of his stepmother, seemed more likely. He could attribute such coldness to her which, he noticed, he refrained from attributing to his father. The term 'stepmother', occurring to his mind now for the first time, had an unpleasant ring. Stepmothers were traditionally cruel and unjust. Also, for some reason, he could not imagine his father as *bothering* to be idly curious about him, as if this distinguished man would be above such petty concerns. Was this a good thing or not? Did he want his father to feel strong emotions about him? Would he be terribly disappointed if his father, absorbed in his work, were uninterested in him? Yes, of course. Yet would that not be safer? What, here, would 'safe' be? Suppose his father were *longing* to see him, expecting from him, perhaps, something remarkable? Suppose the mention of his name in an unpleasant, indeed frightful, context in 'the papers' had served as a pretext to recall the child who might earlier have seemed lost forever? Well, he would know soon.

How soon was now appalling him as he walked on, slowly because of the muddy ground, along the track leading to Seegard. To Seegard *only*. The wind was sharper and he felt cold in his thin mackintosh. The watery ditch had by now wandered away into a reedy marshy wilderness which had appeared on the left, wherein, as the clouds were parting, small puddles or pools were being touched by the evening sun. On a very slight eminence on the other side, not considerable enough to be called a hill, there was a mass of fuzzy darkness which Edward took to be a wood. Soon the sky above him had become clear, not blue but a sort of pale lightless green, while the horizon was streaked with burning tongues of gold.

His attention was now caught by some portent rising into the air above the wood, a kind of large dark substance like a fast-moving balloon, which kept changing its shape as it moved towards him. He stopped, then realised that it was an immense flock of birds which was executing a very rapid complex dance as it extended, contracted, folded over itself, changed direction and passed with a faint whirring of wings directly over his head. Watching it vanish he realised how dark the landscape had become, though the sky still had light, and how silent it was. He listened to the silence, then detected in it a faint distant murmur, perhaps of a river. The track, already hard to distinguish from its surroundings, was marked by a line of small tormented thorn trees with pallid whitish flowers, and wild rose bushes still bearing a few blackened hips. There was still no sign of any house, and he wondered whether he had missed a turning, a parting of the ways, and were perhaps now heading away into the marshy wilderness to be lost in the dark. He hurried on, looking about him and trying to walk faster. His surroundings were becoming flickering and insubstantial, his eyes failing in what was now certainly twilight. There was a pale presence of mist over the marsh. Then, as if emerging suddenly from behind a curtain of invisibility, there was ahead of him, already not far off, a house, or rather a substantial building, outlined against the fading sky, a humpy mass with a tower at one end. It looked to him, at that first moment, upon that flat land, huge, like a cathedral, or a great ship. He hurried now, gasping with emotion, conscious of time as that edge over which he was about to fall, that window out of which he was about to walk . . . The image of Mark came to him vividly, almost like a ghost, a reminder of his, in all possible scenes, accursed condition; and he felt suddenly that *he* was the thing which was so frightening, he the figure approaching out of the dark, a bringer to that lonely quiet place of some catastrophe or pestilence.

The house was near now and clearer, the twilight haze becoming clarified as if it were dawn not dusk. Edward had, he now realised, seen pictures of Seegard in some newspaper or journal long ago, but had blotted them out of his memory.

107

It was a weird-looking object, indeed very big, consisting of a long high almost windowless building with a pitched roof, looking like a hall, with what appeared to be an eighteenth-century house attached to one end of it by a high corniced wall. At the other end was the tower, a tall thick hexagon of concrete with an irregular dotting of windows. His feet now informed him that he was no longer walking upon muddy earth, but upon a stone pavement, and he was aware of being enclosed on either side by trees, comprising a wide avenue, not impeding but framing his view of the house. He could now see, in the middle of the high central building, a large door standing open and a light coming from within. And then he saw, near to the door, and flattened against the twilit wall, painted there as a frieze or set up as statues, three women.

Edward stopped, then moved on. The women, motionless a moment longer, stepped forward upon the pavement altogether. Seeing them so suddenly in the light from the open door Edward was at once aware of their beauty, their youth, and their resemblance to each other. They wore long full-skirted dresses of some multi-coloured material, approaching the ankle, pulled in at the waist, there were jewels at their necks and their long hair was piled up in heavy crowns. They smiled upon Edward and as if in shyness were silent, so that Edward, feeling that he should speak first, uttered an inarticulate sound.

'Edward, welcome to Seegard'. A hand was outstretched, then another. Edward shook two hands, then three.

'Come inside,' said a voice, 'it's cold.'

'Welcome to Seegard,' another voice said.

'I hope you didn't mind the walk.'

'No, not at all,' said Edward, 'it was a nice walk but awfully – rather – muddy, and I haven't got any proper shoes.' He recalled those, his first words, later as rather feeble and inane. However they served. He followed one of the women in through the door and was followed by the other two. Someone touched his coat.

The main building into which he was now entering was indeed a hall, or rather a very large barn with a high roof with massive crisscrossings of pale wooden beams. As the door

108

closed behind him Edward's first searching look was for a male figure, waiting, but there was none. There were some high-up windows, a conspicuous tapestry, a group of tall glossy potted plants. The walls were of golden-yellow roughly squared stone blocks. Edward noticed a huge tiled stove, a monster such as he had seen in Germany but never in England. In spite of this presence the large space was distinctly cold. A long solid burly wooden table was laid at one end for a meal. The scene was lit by oil lamps placed upon the table or somehow suspended in distant corners. Edward put down his suitcase and again confronted the women. They still looked very young and all alike.

'I am Mrs Baltram. Those are your sisters, Ilona and Bettina. This is Ilona, this is Bettina.' The two girls curtsied, smiling.

Edward had not of course totally forgotten the 'horrid little girls'. Yet he had not in any way reckoned with them or wondered about them. They had been blotted out of the picture which contained his father, and as a smaller figure his stepmother. He had vaguely thought that 'the girls' would be away, perhaps at school, perhaps at work elsewhere, he had never even troubled to work out their ages in relation to himself, and had not, in his final turmoil, thought about them at all.

'We call her Mother May,' said one of them.

'Please call me that.'

'Yes – thank you – how kind of you to invite me –'

'We're so glad that you could come. You must be tired after that walk. Bettina, would you show Edward his room? Then we'll have supper. I expect you're hungry. Oh, would you mind taking your shoes off? They're a bit muddy. Just put them there, in that box by the wall.'

Hopping awkwardly, Edward removed his wet muddy shoes and put them in one of several boxes near a row of wellingtons. The girl named as Bettina had picked up Edward's case and would not surrender it to him. The others laughed. He followed her across the hall toward a curtained doorway.

'Mind the step. It's all a bit complicated here. You'll soon

109

know your way about. This is a muddly bit called Transition. You're in Selden, that's the old house.'

Edward stumbled on. Bettina had picked up a lamp from an alcove and was now leading the way up some stone stairs which felt very cold to Edward's stockinged feet. She paused, holding the lamp high so that Edward could see his way. He saw ahead of him, beyond the girl, a dark corridor and a lighted doorway, and in a moment they were in a large bedroom where another lighted lamp stood upon a table. There was an odd smell.

Bettina put down her lamp and stared at Edward. It was hard to tell her age, she could have been eighteen or thirty. Her brow was large, her calm eyes of an exceptionally soft light grey, but her narrow aquiline nose and firmly pointed chin gave to her face an air of authority and shrewdness. With her necklaces she looked like a Renaissance portrait of a noble lady, or perhaps of a clever slightly effeminate youth. Her hair, of a rather disconcerting dark reddish colour, was elaborately pinned up, but trailing curly wisps drew attention to the transparent whiteness and smoothness of her neck. Looking at her hand, conspicuous now as she rested it on the side of the table beside the lamp, Edward saw that she had dirty fingernails. He was not sure whether this imperfection reassured him or not. He felt, in her stare, weak, undefended, confused, very tired. He said feebly, 'I like your dress.'

'We weave the cloth ourselves,' said Bettina, conceding a smile and spreading out her mauve and white skirt. 'We always change in the evening, we put on our prettiest dresses.'

'I'm afraid I haven't anything special to change into.'

'Oh, don't worry. There's your bathroom. There's hot running water, it comes up from the kitchen. There's even electricity, we have our own generator, but we save it, we prefer oil lamps anyway.'

'Is the sea near?'

'Fairly, but it's hard to get to. Will you be all right? I don't imagine you'll be long, will you? You don't want to take a bath?'

'No, no, I won't be a moment.'

'Have you got other shoes?'

110

'Yes, some slippers.'

'I'll hang around at the bottom of the stairs to guide you back.'

'Will I meet. . . my father. . . at supper?'

'Oh, sorry, we forgot to say, he isn't here at the moment. Leave your lamp here when you come, don't turn it down.'

Bettina picked up her lamp and left with a swirl of her dress. So, no father yet. Edward felt intense relief. At the same time he felt a little puzzled and disappointed.

The room was bare and rather cold and would have looked austere had it not looked also elegant, even grand. The walls were made of pale cream blocks of rather powdery stone, not unlike the stone of the barn only lighter in colour and worked very smooth. The vaulted ceiling appeared to be made of some sort of stone compound of exactly the same colour. The floor was planks of light polished oak, and the heavy panelled door was also of oak. So was the table, round and extremely solid, with sturdy plain curved legs, and a chest of drawers and a rush-bottomed chair to match. There was a honey-brown woven rug beside the double bed, about the head of which hung a frilled white canopy and curtains of *broderie anglaise*. The faint warmth, which just prevented the room from being very cold, came from a paraffin stove in the corner, the source of the curious smell. There was one picture hanging from a nail driven between the stones, and surmounted by a cobweb, portraying a young girl standing with feet apart in a stream, looking at the spectator with a secretive self-satisfied expression, while on the bank a realistically rendered bicycle was lying flat on the grass, and through the spokes of one wheel a large snake was emerging and gazing at the girl. The initials J.B. appeared in the corner. Edward did not like the picture.

The large window, behind long white curtains, was found by Edward's exploring hand to be covered by rather dusty shutters. Unhooking an iron bar and bending one shutter back, he cupped his face in his palms and looked out at the now dark landscape. He saw, making it out as shapes of darkness against a slightly lighter sky, the irregular avenue of trees along which he had approached. He was then evidently inside the building which he had seen from outside as a 'sort of eighteenth-century house'. He replaced the shutter and drew the curtains and went into the bathroom where he automatically turned the electric switch with no result. The lamplight came through the open door revealing a shrine of similar elegant austerity, with a bare stone wall above an extremely large bath. There was also, beside the wash-basin, a square window out of which Edward looked into a court-yard which was dimly lit by an electric light fixed high on the wall on the farther side. The courtyard surprised Edward, looking suddenly exotic, as if he were looking into somewhere far away, perhaps in the south, perhaps in the past, some château maybe. As he looked the light went out, and he felt sure that it had only been left on for his benefit. Feeling he should delay no longer he tidied himself, combed his lank dark hair into a neat curve and put on the slippers from his suitcase; then, before he opened the door, stood a moment and breathed deeply several times.

Bettina, found waiting uncomfortably close on the landing, led him back through Transition which seemed to consist of a series of dark arches and alcoves, and through the curtained door into the hall. Ilona and Mother May (as he later learned to call her) came forward, and the three of them escorted him silently, like people shepherding an animal, to the long table. There was a pause as if for grace, then they sat down. Edward, obeying a gesture from Mother May, sat at the head of the table, with Mother May on his right, Bettina on his left, and Ilona next to Bettina. Mother May said, 'We aren't believers, but we always stand quietly before eating.'

At this stage Edward was still uncertain whether or not to regard the women as his enemies. Perhaps his father had wished him to come, while they, under pretend politeness, were jealous and hostile. Must he not seem, he reflected, an interloper, someone who had got on very well without them, now in trouble running to them for a support he did not deserve, featuring in the attention of the father as a favoured novelty? If this were so how easy, he felt in the strong vibration of their presence, it would be for them to take their revenge. He had heard the word 'sister'. He thought, I have two sisters, Bettina and Ilona, Ilona and Bettina. What will they do to me? He told himself, I am here on a short visit. But what was happening, what would happen, was larger and graver and longer than that.

Ilona spoke first. 'Are you called Edward?'

'Well – yes –'

'I mean not Ed or Ted or Eddie or Ned?'

'Or Neddie!' said Mother May with a laugh.

'No, I've always been called just Edward.'

'Then that is what we shall call you,' said Bettina.

'Now, we have made a feast for you,' said Mother May. 'Every meal is a sacrament, but this is a celebration.'

'A festival,' said Bettina.

'But first we should explain that we are vegetarians,' said Mother May. 'I hope you don't mind?'

'No, no, I'm almost a vegetarian myself, I often feel I should be, I don't mind what I eat –'

'We hope you'll enjoy *this*,' said Ilona.

'Of course, I didn't mean –'

'Shall we help you?' said Mother May. 'You see we always eat picnic fashion here for simplicity. Everything is on the table, in these bowls. Or would you rather help yourself?'

'Oh help me, please –'

'Later on you can help yourself,' said Bettina, 'we have our funny little ways here, but you'll soon fit in.'

Ilona laughed, or giggled, looking at Edward and covering her mouth with her hand, as he had seen Japanese girls do at his college.

Spooning from various bowls, Mother May put upon Edward's plate a mixture of beans dressed with oil and herbs, lentils in a sweetish sauce, a flat rissole made (as he discovered) of nuts, a concoction of scrambled egg and spinach, and a salad composed of various unidentifiable leaves. All of this (as he also discovered) was delicious. The butter was unsalted and the thick crumbly bread self-evidently home-made.

'Will you have wine?'

'Please.'

From an earthenware jug decorated with blue and green

113

geometrical patterns, Bettina poured a reddish liquid into his glass. 'Elderberry wine, last year's vintage. We make our own wine.'

'We make our own everything,' said Ilona, and giggled. Edward was concluding that Ilona was the younger sister.

'Well, almost,' said Bettina, 'not quite.'

'We don't usually have wine,' said Mother May. 'This is a special day.'

'We have special days quite often,' said Ilona.

'But this is a special special day,' said Mother May, smiling.

The wine was delicious too, with a fragrant sweetish taste and quite strong. Edward felt he was drinking flowers. He began at once to feel a little pleasantly tipsy. He looked about the big room. Yes, it was a large mediaeval barn, up in whose shadowy roof the complex of immense beams made a beautiful architectural play, making Edward feel for some reason that he was in a big ship. The high walls of uneven stone were bare except for the tapestry, which hung opposite to the main door across which a heavy curtain had now been drawn. In the subdued light Edward could not make out the subject of the tapestry. The floor was black, paved with huge slabs of slate. The hall, like his bedroom, was sparsely furnished. There were a few large carved chairs against the wall near the stove, two small tables with lamps on, and the thicket of plants growing out of the huge earthenware pots.

Edward was now, as the conversation lapsed for a moment, quite boldly inspecting his three companions. He was suddenly, not unpleasantly, aware of himself as a man in the company of three women. Three *taboo* women, he thought, with an illumination of relief. *This* is part of it all, of the pattern or the destiny or the doom or whatever it is. Mother May's face was markedly, quite positively, calm, as some women's faces are. The quality of her beauty was radiantly serene. With such faces it may be difficult to tell whether this calmness is unconscious, a gift of nature, or whether it is something achieved, a result of wisdom, or is perhaps a mask of perpetual youth deliberately cultivated. Her reddish-blonde hair, lighter in colour than Bettina's, was more neatly piled, her straight nose less assertive, her chin less sharp. Her

114

broader gentler face was pale almost to whiteness in the lamplight, the light grey eyes humorous and kindly. Edward noticed her smiling finely shaped mouth as beautiful, then perceived *her* as beautiful, and decided that she was more lovely than her handsome daughters. Ilona, whose red hair, even untidier than Bettina's, had partly collapsed down her back, had a rounder more childish pretty face, pinker plumper cheeks and a faintly upturned nose. She returned Edward's gaze inquisitively, with an air of mischievous shy mockery which made him look quickly away. None of the three women wore make-up.

'When will my father be back?' he said to Bettina. He found that he was now eating an apple which he had no memory of having acquired.

Bettina said to Mother May, 'When will Jesse be back?'

'Oh soon – soon –'

Edward found that his eyes were closing. He kept trying to open them and they closed again. The three faces flickered as he concentrated on raising his lids. The hall had become a grey sphere in which he was awkwardly swimming, drowning. He said, 'I'm awfully sorry, I suddenly feel terribly tired.'

Chairs scraped loudly upon the slate floor, echoing painfully inside Edward's head. He rose, holding onto the back of his chair. 'I'm so sorry –'

'You've had a big day, Edward, and the wine is soporific. Ilona, will you see Edward upstairs?'

Still clutching his apple and carefully not falling over, Edward followed Ilona across the long empty floor and through the curtain, where she picked up the lamp which was in the alcove as it had been before. Edward staggered up the stone stairs, pulling himself up by a thick rope banister, and found himself back in his lighted room. Ilona had put her lamp on the table beside his, and was now beside his bed, neatly turning back the sheet and blankets.

'There's a hot water-bottle in the bed, we put it in just before you came, I think it's still warm. Would you like me to put hotter water in it?'

'No, no thanks –'

'The window has shutters, see. There are electric switches,

115

but we make a rule not to use electricity except for essential things like the deep freeze and pumping the water. There's an electric torch in the top drawer of the chest, and an extra blanket in the bottom drawer if you're cold. I'll turn off the paraffin heater now. Do you know how to turn off the oil lamp?'

'I'm afraid I don't.'

'You just turn this little wheel to the right. By the way, don't worry if you hear noises in the night.'

'Noises?'

'Oh just owls – and things – I mean owls and foxes and things – and poltergeists and things –'

Edward giggled feebly at this jest. 'I expect I'll survive. Thanks so much.'

'And mind the rats.'

'There are no rats,' said Bettina, who was standing outside the open door. 'Don't be silly Ilona. Now, are you all right, Edward? We rise fairly early. I'll give you a knock in the morning.'

Edward was soon in bed and fell at once into a deep peaceful sleep and heard nothing in the night.

The next morning Edward was awakened by a curious hollow fluting sound which he thought at first was birdsong but soon realised was not. It was music. Knowing at once where he was he jumped out of bed, anxious in case he had overslept, opened the shutters and looked out blinking at the still faint daylight. The sound came from outside. He opened the window and pulled up the sash. Mother May and Bettina and Ilona, upon a pavement directly below him, were playing recorders. When they saw his head thrust out they burst out laughing and ran off. Edward withdrew his head, closed the window and leaned his brow against the glass and groaned.

Breakfast consisted of herbal tea and fingers of hot buttered toast lightly scattered with dry oats. There was also fruit, which Edward refused. He did not feel well and the old misery

116

was with him again. The women wore brown hand-woven dresses and wooden beads.

As they rose Mother May said, 'We must get to our work now. We are very busy here, you know.'

'This place is a power-house,' said Ilona, 'isn't it, Bettina?'

'What do you do?' said Edward. 'I know you weave your own dresses –'

'Oh all sorts of things,' said Mother May. 'We are never idle. We cultivate the garden to feed ourselves, we keep the house spick and span, we make our clothes, we do carpentry, we do embroidery, we paint a little, don't we, we make jewellery to sell, we make Christmas cards, we are not rich, you know.'

'And we mend the beastly old generator when it breaks down, at least Bettina does!' said Ilona.

'We follow Jesse's example,' said Bettina, 'his rule of order and industry. We have a daily routine.'

'Times of silence,' said Ilona, 'times for rest, times for reading, it's like a monastery.'

'You must let me help you,' said Edward. 'I'm afraid I haven't any skills –'

'You'll learn,' said Bettina.

'After all, you're going to stay with us a long time, aren't you,' said Ilona.

'One of you girls should show Edward round,' said Mother May.

'I will,' said Ilona.

'I always do the washing-up' said Ilona.

'I'll always help you,' said Edward. 'I'll dry.'

'We never dry, we just stack. There's so much to do here, we save every possible trouble. For instance, there's Carrying About.'

'What's that?'

'You know, in every house there's always things to be moved from one place to another, upstairs and downstairs and so on, like washing and plates and books and things. Well, we have carrying places where things which are on the

117

move are always left, and anyone passing by carries them on to the next place. It makes sense, doesn't it. These plates, for example, in this big rack. Some are dry, some are not. Someone passing will pick up the dry ones for lunch and put them on the table in the Atrium.'

'The Atrium?'

'In the hall, that's what Jesse calls it – what we call it – it's the Latin for a sort of main living place. And over there you see dry sheets waiting to go upstairs when someone's going upstairs anyway. You'll soon get the hang and know where things live. I mean, it's pointless to keep running up and down stairs all day.'

'I see. Time and motion study.'

'Bettina always says, carry enough, but never too much, otherwise you drop things, anyway I do.'

They were in Transition, the area lying behind the high plain wall which Edward had seen from the outside as joining the hall to 'Selden'. This had originally been a set of fine stone-built byres lying between the house and the barn, which Jesse had started, retaining a lot of the previous structure, to turn into a cloister, open on the east side. Other plans however, concerning the conversion of the stables, had made him decide to make this the kitchen area, leaving the arches and alcoves of the original project still attractively visible. There was a large handsome kitchen, with a long cast-iron cooking stove, the scullery where Edward had been watching Ilona wash up, the wash room with a washing machine and trapeze-like wooden drying frames, and the 'brushing room' full of dustpans and brooms and boots and shoes, which also housed the enormous deep freeze. There was even an 'electricity room', like the engine room of a submarine, dotted with dials and fuse boxes and dangerous-looking stray wires.

'The place needs to be rewired, one thing is always fusing another, only I don't think any electrician would ever understand that mess. We go easy with the electricity. We've been here a long time and many things have changed. We used to entertain a lot, lots of people used to come and see Jesse, but now they don't since the railway stopped. Come on, I've done here, I'll show you Selden. Here carry some of these sheets.

118

We never iron things, ironing is a waste of time.'

Edward picked up an armful of sheets from a shelf in a little arched 'shrine', and followed Ilona along the corridor and up the stone steps toward his own room. At the top of the steps there was a cupboard into which, as bidden, he unloaded the sheets. Ilona had opened a door next to his room, revealing a small pretty room with a settee, a writing desk, a chinoiserie screen, and a greenish picture representing a child as a drowned mouse.

'This is your sitting room, at least not really yours, it's for grand guests. We don't heat it now. The big bedroom is beyond yours.'

The big bedroom was a corner room, even larger than Edward's with an even handsomer bathroom, and a view two ways, towards the trees of the avenue and, at the side, towards the wood on the rising ground which Edward had seen as he approached.

'Where's the sea?'

'On the other side of the house, but it's a good way off.'

'This is an old house, eighteenth-century –'

'Yes, called Selden House, but it was just a shell when Jesse bought it.'

Edward followed her down and out into the courtyard which he had looked at last night.

'All this part, the other three sides, was built by Jesse. It's a fake really, but it looks nice. These two sides are quite thin, just passageways. The bit opposite you is a real house, smaller really only it doesn't look from here. We live over there, those are our bedrooms, like yours.'

'I bet yours is the smallest one.'

'Yes, we call ours East Selden and yours is West Selden.'

The 'fake' courtyard did indeed look nice, with its four eighteenth-century façades, with walls of creamy stone, tall windows below, square ones above, and shallow stone-tiled roofs. The square was cobbled with sea pebbles, and there was an Italian well-head in the middle. Edward looked down and saw a distant gleam of water and the dark form of his reflected head.

'This must have cost a fantastic amount of money.'

119

'Jesse was rich then. It's all gone now.'

Edward heard the familiar sound of a typewriter. 'Who's typing?'

'Mother May. She's making a catalogue of all Jesse's work, it's a big job. Sometimes she writes about the past, things she remembers.'

'So she's a writer.'

'Good heavens, no, it's just for us! The ground-floor rooms on our side are workrooms. On your side they're just store-rooms. Come back this way through Transition. That corridor on the right leads to our place. Just pick up those plates, would you. We'll go through the Atrium and I'll show you the rest.'

Passing into the hall Edward put the plates on the long table and Ilona added a pile of cutlery. He looked up at the tapestry, now clearly visible. Watched by a large stern cat, a smiling girl with a butterfly net was pursuing through a flowery meadow a flying fish which had emerged from a dark round tree.

'We wove it from Jesse's design,' said Ilona. 'We did four different designs. Some Americans bought the other three.'

'It's beautiful,' said Edward. But he found it, like the painting in his own room, rather distressing.

Crossing the hall, her sandals tapping on the slates, Ilona opened another door. 'This was the eighteenth-century stable block, it juts out at the back at right angles to the barn, it's awfully pretty outside. Jesse made a Gothic window at the end.'

'There's another courtyard!' said Edward, looking out of a window.

'Yes, we're parallel to the piece that joins East and West Selden. The wall is plain on this side as you see, Jesse intended to paint a mural on it. It's a nice old paved yard. Jesse was going to close it in with another pastiche, but it's nicer like this, you can see the fen, except that you can't because it's misty. This used to be our dining room before the kitchens moved to Transition, now it's our sitting room, we call it the Interfectory.'

'That's an odd word. Don't you mean Refectory?'

'Well, that's what Jesse calls it. It's our leisure room.'

120

'What a nice room.' Edward surveyed the large long rather untidy room with bookshelves, and numerous much trodden rugs upon the wooden floor, and low slung armchairs of worn red leather, faded and slippery, with long seats and sloping backs, made for long-legged men to lounge in at their ease. There were two old sagging sofas with ragged covers and an open fireplace with the remains of a wood fire and a dark tall many-shelved wooden chimneypiece. On top of the chimney-piece was balanced a long piece of carved wood on which, between interwoven leaves and fruits, was written, *I am here. Do not forget me.* It was a shabby and unpretentious room with brown varnished woodwork, like an old-fashioned snug or smoking room or the study of an elderly don. It might have represented some idea of a room which Jesse had had when he was a schoolboy. It seemed in some way to belong to the past; perhaps the all-powerful Jesse had decreed it as a place of escape from his fretful and peculiar genius. 'It looks comfortable and real,' Edward added. Then, as this seemed to impugn the reality of the rest of the house, 'It's *all* marvellous – and extraordinary.'

'It's a bit of a mess and it needs dusting, Jesse had so many ideas, but we like it.'

A picture in a dark frame slightly askew hung against the faded leafy wallpaper, representing two adolescent girls with staring pleased eyes and bare small breasts kneeling in a stone recess grown over with damp green plants discovered by a terrified boy. Edward did not need to scrutinise the signature.

'I've never seen any of Jesse's pictures, except one, which I can't remember reproduced in a paper. I think I didn't want to look at it. Are they fairies?'

'What?'

'Are they fairies?'

'I don't know.' Ilona said this in the neutral self-satisfied tone used by scientists when scrupulously refusing to answer a layman's silly question. She straightened the picture, dusting the top of it with her finger.

'What's the photo beside the fire?'

Ilona took the photograph off a nail where it hung low down and handed it to him. 'Jesse, of course.'

'Good heavens!' A tall thin hawkish young man with a loop of dark straight hair curving over his brow was leaning against a tree and staring at Edward with an intense sardonic expression. Edward almost dropped the photo, and hastily handed it back.

'Looks like you,' said Ilona. 'Except he's got larger eyes.' She hung it up again. 'The old kitchen is Bettina's workroom. She's a carpenter, we'll just peep in. All those rooms connect, there's no corridor, if she's not there we can go through, there's rooms beyond.'

Ilona tapped gently on a door on the far side of the room, then opened it cautiously. Edward, behind her, caught a glimpse of Bettina with one knee on a chair leaning forward intently over something on a large wooden table. She did not look up. Ilona closed the door softly. 'She hates to be disturbed. That door over there leads to the tower.'

Edward moved towards the door.

'Oh, not now. We don't go there when Jesse's away. Anyhow I expect he'd like to show you the tower himself. And *that* door leads out into the courtyard. It's an awfully draughty room.'

Edward followed Ilona back into the hall.

'There are your shoes, by the way.' She indicated a box by the door where Edward found his shoes, no longer muddy, beautifully cleaned.

'They're clean!'

'I cleaned them. Cleaning shoes is one of my jobs.'

'You seem to have all the dirty jobs!'

'Not at all, there are plenty of dirty jobs.'

'You're all so industrious and so skilled, I shall feel useless. Would writing poetry count as work?'

'I don't think so! Are those your only outdoor shoes?'

'Yes, silly of me.'

'You can wear some of Jesse's boots. I'll find some, your feet seem about the same size.'

'Please don't bother!' Edward quickly put on his shoes, leaving his slippers. 'Let's go outside, look the sun has come out!'

They went out of the main door onto the pavement outside.

The damp stones were becoming overgrown with creeping thyme.

In the bright light Edward gazed at his sister. She looked even prettier now in her brown dress. Her hair, revealed as a mixture of red and gold, was rather vaguely gathered with many visible pins into a thick flat mass which had slid down the back of her neck almost to her shoulders. Her small up-tilted nose was faintly freckled, her chin was small and round. Her complexion was childishly translucent with rounded reddened cheeks. The eyes, with lighter lashes, were dark grey. Meeting Edward's gaze she looked away and a flush ran down onto the thin hair-encumbered neck. She vaguely and ineffectually patted her hair, dislodging a pin onto the ground. Edward picked it up and handed it back to her, and she laughed breathily, covering her mouth.

He said suddenly, 'Did you ever see my mother?'

Not seeming startled by the question Ilona said, 'No, she was just a legend when I was a child. Mother May was talking about her last night.'

'Oh!' Edward pictured that conversation, the three of them at the table finishing the elderberry wine. He said, to close off the subject, 'What can I do that's useful?'

'Nothing. Mother May said you were to have the morning off.'

'Then I think I'll go for a walk. Will you come?'

'No, I must work.'

'I'll walk down to the sea. It's over there, isn't it?'

'The fen's flooded, there's no way.'

'I could walk up to that wood.'

'It's very messy and marshy. I'm afraid there aren't any good walks at this time of year. You could walk up the track and along the road, that's quite nice. Lunch is at two, don't be late, we work a long morning. Did you sleep well last night?'

'Yes, fine. No owls or foxes, no poltergeists!'

Ilona, who was turning toward the door, paused. 'You know there *are* poltergeists, it's not a joke.'

'Oh – come –'

'They're just a sort of phenomenon, sort of chemical, not ghosts.'

'I've heard stories. Perhaps it's not all imagination or fakes. Aren't they supposed to happen where there are adolescent girls?' Edward was instantly acutely embarrassed by this remark.

Ilona however replied calmly, 'Yes, Bettina says I attract them, they come to adolescent girls and virgins. Anyway, Betinna's a virgin too, so no wonder they come here. They're quite harmless, just a nuisance.'

'Somehow I don't like the idea!'

She opened the door to go in. 'Of course if you get one in your bed you're really in trouble!'

When Ilona had closed the door Edward waited a minute or two, listening to the silence, or rather to a vague soft bird and river sound, and establishing some quite new sense of being alone. It had taken him about a second to grasp that this was a new aloneness, but he could not for some time work out what was new about it. It might just be that he was unused to being in the country, and even more unused to being there by himself. He walked a few steps and looked down the avenue at the way he had come yesterday. He has already decided that he was not going to follow his sister's uninspiring advice about walking back to the road. The pavement, broad in front of the house, narrowed between the trees where it ran on, edged by the big white flinty stones, for two hundred yards or so to meet the track. The trees were disorderly, irregularly spaced out and of various shapes and sizes, some enormous yews, three elegant elongated conifers, unawakened oaks and ash trees bleakly in bud, and numerous ash saplings. Some clean stumps declared where, no doubt, elms had once stood. Between the trees was grass which looked as if it had been cut, but not lately. Further back, on either side, were ragged lines of veronica, interspersed with tamarisk. Everything was wet and there was a moist spicy smell.

Turning away from the avenue, Edward walked along the front of the hall and the plain wall which masked Transition and then along the front of West Selden, passing a door in the middle of the façade. Ahead of him he could see a group of dark ilex trees where a path meandered, and on the right a plot with vegetables, two greenhouses, and a curious over-grown rectangle which was probably an abandoned tennis court. On the left were outhouses, a big open wood store, and a yellow tractor. Further on ahead, beyond the ilexes, was an orchard and a grove of tall leafless poplars. Walking upon wet irregular stones, between which sturdy dandelions were thrusting up their green spears, and meeting now the full force of the east wind, he walked round to the back of Selden, and then on to the stables courtyard. The stables, 'very pretty' as Ilona had said, their stone walls decorated with lines of flints which looked like little faces, made another handsome house, long and broad, with a turret and a golden weathercock in the form of a fox. Edward did not dally here for fear of meeting Mother May or Bettina, feeling shy of the former and in awe of the latter. Moving out of sight of the near windows he stood back and looked up at the tower. Any tower has charm, and this one was indeed impressive, but Edward was not sure that he liked it much. The hexagonal walls were of concrete, and covered by erratic stains, certainly accidental, which might be imagined to look attractive. On one face a shaft of small-leaved ivy had been allowed to climb almost to the top. The windows formed a more striking form of decoration, dotted about apparently aimlessly over the surfaces, some being mere slits, the others mostly squares, some large, some small. Each window was framed by a black metal lattice, whose rusting was no doubt the source of the erratic stains. Edward had been disappointed and a little hurt at not being allowed into the tower. Perhaps Jesse had indeed wanted to 'show it off' himself. Or had just not wanted Edward poking around in his work places.

Hoping he had not been noticed, he turned away from the house. Among a few swift clouds the sun was shining. A path at his feet led away eastward between gorse bushes. The sea must be there and not far off. He began to walk down a slight slope and entered at once into a meadow which was covered with small glittering yellow starry flowers. He looked with amazement at the flowers whose almost metallic brightness gave out a light which hung like a yellow powder above the

125

lush grass. They were certainly not buttercups. He thought they might be celandine, and stooped to pick one. As his fingers snapped the frail stem he felt guilty. He stuffed the flower roughly into his pocket and walked hastily on toward a line of willow trees. It seemed to him that he had seen these flowers, this meadow, somewhere before. Perhaps it was in just such a meadow that the secretive girl with the butterfly · net had been pursuing the flying fish. When he neared the willows he saw that they were rising out of water; while the path, now rather wet, turned a little to the left of them upon higher ground. Beyond, Edward now saw what he took to be the sea, but quickly realised was a dazzling sheet of flood water out of which trees and bushes were raising their heads. Upon the water here and there, their enamelled backs polished by the sun, water birds were sailing, ducks, geese, some birds quite strange to Edward, and a distant pair of swans. He walked on, thinking to skirt the flood, but was now increasingly surrounded by dark pools and clumps of reeds and humpy banks of mud. The path had now given up, or else he had lost it, and he was walking upon a black sinewy surface, springy underfoot and less muddy. Then as he looked, trying to see a way, the light changed, the sun was clouded and the water in front of him became dark, almost black. He stopped and looked back. Seegard, upon which the sun still shone, was already far away, now seen to be upon a slight eminence. As Edward turned about, straining his eyes, he was suddenly removed as if his surroundings had been quickly jerked upward. He did not sink, but fell abruptly, vertically, as the surface beneath his feet gave way and his legs descended into two watery holes. He stood for a moment ridiculously, then sat down, his arms and bottom creating similar holes in the treacherous elastic surface upon which he had been walking and which he now saw to be made of thick blackened mats of old reeds suspended above a base of cold watery mud. He struggled up cursing and was relieved to find that he was able to stand, in water not up to the knee, and laboriously lifting one foot after another out of the black sticky compound, to retrace his steps until he was on firmer ground. He was soaked to the waist, but at least the sun had come out again. Then, where the path ought to have been but was not, he was confronted by an expanse of flooded grass, the green tips just above the surface, and, at a distance, a curious semicircle of stone, which he made out to be a partly submerged bridge. Seegard had changed its position too, lying farther off on his right, and some trees seemed to have sprung up to conceal some of Selden. The wood however, upon its low but presumably dry hillock, was now nearer, appearing indeed as the nearest available solid ground. Edward stepped out into the meadow, with water to his ankles but fairly sound going underfoot, and soon crossed the half-drowned bridge over what was evidently a flooded river. Here he was presented with a small dryish slope and indeed a path. The sun was warming and he hoped drying his wet muddy clothes. He turned, shading his eyes, but could not see anything behind him except muddy watery fen. He thought, suppose Jesse has come home while I'm away, suppose I arrive back covered with mud and late as well? He looked to his watch but remembered he had left it in the bathroom. He decided to follow the path a little bit up the hill, and was soon among trees.

The wood, clearly the work of nature not of man, was a wonderful mixture of every sort of tree. There were oaks and ashes and beeches and larches and firs and wild cherries and some of the largest yews Edward had ever seen. It was an old wood. The old tall trees made a labyrinth of colonnades and archways and vaulted halls and domed chambers, and if Edward had not entrusted himself to the little path he would soon have been lost. Some birds were singing, nearby a blackbird and a loud wren. Distant rooks cawed sadly. Occasionally, some sunlight fell upon the path, which was dry and brown, crisscrossed with ridgy tree roots, almost like steps, and scattered with the mysterious dried-up fruits of various trees fashioned into little brown toys and emblems, which crackled pleasantly underfoot. All round about the antique carpet of fallen leaves stretched far away. The path was steeper now and there was a larger light ahead. Edward began to walk faster and after a minute or two he came to a *place*.

Of course the wood was full of places, celebrations and juxtapositions, mossy alcoves, primroses showing off in the dead bracken, circlets of greenery where the sun managed to shine, long fallen trees as clean as bones. But now Edward, coming out into a large clearing, stopped as one who, exploring the palace, accidentally opens the door of the chapel. The elongated oval sward, though shorter, not two hundred yards in length, curiously reminded Edward of the stadium at Delphi. He shivered. The birds were silent here. The grass was short and fine as if prepared for some game. The spreading branches of two enormous yews at the far end framed a black tunnel. Nearer, round the edges of the space, rows of very tall beech trees soared in smooth shafts. The regularity of the trees and the perfect shape of the level grass suggested some work of human intelligence, something perhaps made very long ago, but certainly tended or renewed in recent years. Following the Greek idea, he saw it as a *dromos* or *temenos*, a sacred area. The most striking feature of the scene however, and the one which in a mysterious way identified it, was a large vertical stone rising from a circular stone base which, standing near to the far end of the glade, was framed in the black archway of the yews. Edward began to walk towards it over the short grass, emerging now into sunshine. He stopped close to the object. The lower broader part, which was about three feet high, made of some dark stone, appeared to be a section of a fluted column. The vertical shaft above, of a lighter greyer stone which glittered with points of light, was more roughly cut, a single battered erection, tapering slightly toward the top. It stood, with its base, a little higher than Edward. He came closer, and touched the pillar, stroked it, it felt warm. Looking down he noticed at the foot, where it fitted into its pedestal, cement had been added, perhaps lately, to keep it firm. The surface round about the fluted column was smooth and polished and looked to Edward like marble. As he now walked round the thing he saw something else, something yellow, lying upon the pedestal, a bunch of celandine, the flowers only a little wilted. He looked round at the silent empty grass and at the shadowy wood and at the black cavern under the yews, and began to

128

walk away. Then, yielding to a superstitious craving, he returned and taking from his pocket the celandine he had picked earlier, threw it down near the other flowers. He walked quickly and then, avoiding the yew trees, ran out of the glade.

The path which had led him to the place was now not to be seen, but trusting to his sense of direction he went on down-hill making a slower pace through the undergrowth of the wood, ash saplings and hazels and little thorn trees. As he went, plunging downward, treading upon brittle bracken and dead leaves, he felt something like a physical change, as if a cloud of gas or pollen or some intense infusion were blowing into his face and enveloping his body. His head seemed to be opening up into a vast area, as if it were literally painlessly splitting and being joined to some enormous pale cloudy sphere up above. Thoughts then came in a rush. Of course as Edward had been looking at the house and walking through the celandine and struggling in the fen and making his way to the wood, he had been thinking not only about what he saw and where he was going, but about Mark Wilsden, and more vaguely about Jesse. Whatever Thomas McCaskerville might think about it in terms of 'a change doing him good', Edward had not imagined that coming to Seegard would alter in any way his awful guilty loving mourning for Mark. That must remain private and untouchable and secret. To imagine that some new scene would automatically banish the dark burden which he carried was to be unworthy of the gravity of what he suffered. He merely found some relief in running away and being somewhere quite else where, in a place unknown to those closest to him, he could hug his misery. The 'connection' he had spoken of to Thomas had seemed just that of a continued doom. The idea of Jesse, certainly striking, seemed in that context accidental. Now with an equal obviousness, streaming into him through the top of his head, came the insight that there was no accident, and that he had come to Seegard as to a place of pilgrimage, carrying his woeful sin to a holy shrine and to a holy man. He had never thought of Jesse in such terms before, had indeed avoided thinking of him at all, nor had he seen this in his first hours at the place or in connection with the women. The women, though amazing, were minor figures, not even acolytes. They were another thing. Mother May's letter with its postscript about their having 'read about his mishap' was another thing. Jesse had not summoned his son out of some vague kindly impulse to cheer him up. It would not be like that between *them*. *They* were being drawn to a fated meeting at a crossways. Jesse might well be unconcerned with Edward's needs, but Jesse was Edward's fate and his *answer*. That it might be a dark answer seemed a little less terrible now that the element of accident was removed.

Walking down the hill, Edward could see through the trees the turret of the stables and the golden weathercock fox turning in the wind, not very far away. His geographical misfortunes were not over however. He came suddenly upon a river, a racing substantial river whose sound no doubt he had heard yesterday and in the night. This must be the river which was responsible for the flooded water meadow and whose channel he had crossed on the half-drowned bridge. Here the river ran deeply and swiftly between high steep banks, churning and foaming along with a humming hissing sound of which Edward realised he had been aware for some time. There was no walking through that torrent, or leaping over it. Vexed and frustrated Edward began to hurry along the bank, anxious now about being late for lunch and finding that Jesse had returned. The power was withdrawn from him, he moaned and cursed audibly as he stumbled along, realising that he might have to run all the way back to the drenched meadows and the submerged bridge. Then, round a curve, where the river narrowed, there appeared suddenly, not exactly a bridge, but a sort of rickety wooden structure, rather like a slatted fence or long hurdle, leaning over at an angle and spanning the waters which bubbled huskily through its many holes. It might have been part of some old vanished lock or sluice, or more likely designed simply as a precarious walkway. Edward saw at once that by placing his feet upon the horizontal beam that held the slats together and holding onto the top of the rather jagged and broken 'fence', he could edge his way across. He slithered down the bank and mounted the thing, which swayed unpleasantly as if about to fall over into the stream, and began to move across by cautious steps, the water running over his feet. Almost at the other bank his bridge came to an end, leaving a small gap where deep waters ran swiftly through agitated reeds. He crossed with a long stride, slipped, grasping at long grasses, then squirmed up the wet slope like a snake, plastering his front with mud. He got to his feet and running now upon a grass path passed through the grove of poplar trees and saw the vegetable garden, the greenhouses and the orchard, and the brown walls of Selden made creamy by the sun. He slowed down and cleaned the more evident lumps of mud off his clothing.

'Oh, you're back,' said Bettina, as he came through the main door into the Atrium. 'Take off your shoes, please. I hope you had a nice walk. I looked in your suitcase, I hope you don't mind, you don't seem to have much in the way of clothes, so I've looked you out some old clobber of Jesse's, I've left it upstairs. Lunch is in twenty minutes. We make our own beds here, by the way.'

'Thanks, sorry – Is my father back?'

'Not yet.'

Passing through Transition, which was always rather dark even by daylight, Edward met Mother May.

'Hello, Edward. Have a nice walk? I forgot to tell you that we rest here from three-thirty to four-fifteen every day, we lie on our beds. You don't have to of course, but I tell you in case you start wondering where everyone is!'

'Thanks. When will my father come?'

'Won't you call me Mother May?'

'Mother May, when will my father come?'

'Oh quite soon. Don't worry. We want you to feel that this is your home. Lunch in about fifteen minutes.'

At the bottom of West Selden stairs he met Ilona who was coming along the corridor from East Selden. 'Oh, hello, how was your walk? Could you take these towels to the cupboard next to your sitting room? Lunch soon, so don't be long.'

Edward went upstairs, put the towels in the cupboard, and

131

returned to his room. His bed had been made, his own few belongings unpacked and neatly put away in drawers. Upon the bed were laid out two jackets, two jerseys, an overcoat, a woollen scarf, an old worn pair of corduroy trousers, a flat cap and a woollen beret. Upon the floor stood two pairs of ancient well-polished leather boots. Edward picked up an armful of the strange clothes. They smelt of father. How was it that he had had this need in his heart all these years and had only now discovered it? Still holding the clothes he sat down on the bed.

EDWARD WAS AWAKENED in the middle of the night by a very loud and very unusual sound. It was as if a large amount of glass, say indeed many tin trays loaded with tumblers, had been hurled down a flight of stone steps. He sat up rigidly in the dark, reached out for his bedside lamp, realised there was not one, and closed his fingers on the electric torch whose proximity he checked each night on retiring. He sat a moment upright, breathing fast, then got out of bed. He shone the torch about the room, then went to the door, cautiously opened it, then listened again. He even went to the top of the stairs and shone the torch down, though by now he was fairly sure he would see nothing. Nothing. Silence. No one stirring. A broken window? An accident in a greenhouse? No. Not that sort of thing. He walked quickly back and instinctively turned the electric light switch in his bedroom, though he knew the current was cut off. How he longed for that comforting revealing blaze of illumination as again he searched the room with the small ray of the torch. He did not attempt to light the oil lamp, he still found it difficult. Edward had now been at Seegard for several days, and tonight's disturbance was not his first experience of the oddity of the place. Two nights ago he had heard a different sound, the unmistakable sound, quite nearby, of children's leather-shod feet running upon linoleum. How he knew that was what the sound was, he was not sure. He could not recall any dream which would explain the impression, and he was sure too that he had heard, and not dreamt, the running feet and now that

133

vast noise of smashing glass. He sat on the bed for a while, holding the torch in one hand and containing his violently beating heart with the other. He had not said anything about the feet. Would he now say nothing about the glass, the vibration of which was still ringing in his ears? It was as if he were ashamed of these experiences. His watch said half-past two. He got up all the same and opened one section of the shutters hoping to see the dawn. The moonless night was silent and very dark. Bettina had taught him to distinguish the *gewick, gewick* of the female owl from the long *ooo-ooo* of the male, and he would have welcomed now a sound that he could recognise. But there were no owls, not even a patter of rain, only a powdery velvety silence. He switched off the torch. He did not want to *be seen* – from outside. He waited a while, and had put his hand upon the sash window, which he kept a little open behind the shutters, intending to close it when he did again hear something, very softly at first, then louder, a sort of pitiful wailing, or as it increased almost howling noise, passing him by as if borne on the wind, and quickly ceasing. Edward abruptly closed the window and the shutter and got into his bed and pulled the bedclothes up around his head.

In the past days, and although Edward expected him at every moment, Jesse had still not returned. *How* would Jesse return, how would Edward first sight him? He would not arrive by car, since the track was still very muddy with the intermittent rain. Perhaps Edward would see him walking toward the house, his tall vigorous figure appearing in the distance, an authoritative figure, a king returning to his kingdom. Or perhaps he would be quietly present one evening, appearing for supper, materialising, a threat kept secret by them all to surprise Edward. Or Edward might be suddenly told, quick Jesse is here, he's in the Atrium and wants to see you, run, don't keep him waiting. Or perhaps during a storm he might come in across the fen, coming up from the sea like a fisherman, like a marine monster. The idea of Jesse's *coming* was frightening, sometimes seemed, in the lengthening interval, unthinkable, impossible. Meanwhile, as he waited, Edward had become used to the routine of steady ceaseless work punctuated by strictly timed periods of rest, as in a religious order, a monastery, where a good innocent quiet life goes steadily and monotonously on. Breakfast was at seven, work continued until lunch at two ('Jesse likes a long morning'), then work till three-thirty, then rest till four-fifteen ('Sleep twice a day, and get two days for the price of one, Jesse says'), then work till six-thirty ('We don't have teatime'), then 'leisure', then supper at eight, then 'leisure' again till ten-thirty, then bedtime tasks (washing up supper, laying breakfast, tidying, locking doors). Then the longed-for loss of consciousness. Edward could not say that he had yet acquired any skills, but he had learnt how to perform a variety of unskilled tasks with some imitation of the quiet swift efficiency of which the women everywhere gave him an example. He endlessly, unconsciously, carried things about, knew all the 'leaving places' where things (plates, linen, clothes, tools) were put when they were on the move. He meticulously obeyed Bettina's precepts: never walk empty-handed, always use two hands (after she saw Edward lifting things from one plate to another while holding one of the plates in one hand), carry plenty, but not too much (after Edward had come to grief through excess of zeal). He washed dishes, he worked the washing machine (powered by the precious generator), he dug and weeded the vegetable garden, he filled the oil lamps, he watered the potted plants, on one occasion he helped Bettina to cement cracks in the wall of the stables, he fetched rain water for drinking and cooking ('The spring water is full of nitrates'), he peeled onions and potatoes, he chopped herbs with very sharp knives, he sawed and carried wood, he fed the stoves, he swept the vast slated floor of the Atrium. He dusted. He was touched and secretly gratified to find how extremely *dirty* Seegard was in spite of the ceaseless activity of its inmates. It was full of blackened wainscots and fluffy floors and spiders' webs and bits of vegetables and corners full of old nails and scraps of wood and miscellaneous balls of dirt. Once when Ilona found him eagerly washing some woodwork in Transition she said, 'Oh

135

don't bother, we haven't time for things like that.' The huge construction (Edward could not quite think of it as 'a house') also exceeded human efforts by remaining, in spite of the slightly warmer weather, extremely, almost mysteriously, cold. The big Germanic tiled stove made little impression on the Atrium, and the open fire in the Interfec was never lighted before six-thirty. Edward, soon used to the temperature, did not attempt to animate the paraffin heater in his bedroom. Bettina had promised to teach him the mysteries of the electric generator and of the pump which brought the spring water up out of the well, not the ornamental well in Selden courtyard, but a secret domestic well under the floorboards of the kitchen, where the great cast-iron stove, as long and bulky as a rhinoceros, was continually burning the wood which Edward brought in; this was the only warm room. Bettina had however not yet had time to teach Edward anything, and he was rather relieved about this. In the Seegard city state he preferred the comparative irresponsibility of an unskilled artisan; besides, Bettina might well prove to be a rather exacting teacher. The 'machinery' was said to be 'always going wrong', and Edward did not fancy having to share the blame. Not that anyone had yet blamed him for anything; but the slightly taut atmosphere suggested to him the possibility of failure, of not, after all, 'coming up to scratch'.

It suited him to be told what to do, to be so much employed that he could exist unthinkingly like a slave, like a working animal. At moments when he was tired, when his strained body resented an exertion to which he was unused, he experienced a welcome sense of degradation, as if he were about to escape from his burden of consciousness. He would become a beast, a four-legged thing that faced the earth and humbly offered its bared back to be ridden upon, he would shrink into a rat, a mouse, a beetle, become a dried-up husk like the little tree fruits he had crunched underfoot on the hill, he would crumble to dust and thus escape the torture of being. Yet would not every grain of dust be cursed with a memory? He would become an atom, an electron, a proton – but these were thoughts which led back again into the quivering pain of the reflecting self. Sitting in the Interfectory during his enforced 'leisure' he ached with misery as he covertly watched the women who, when they caught his guilty look, smiled at him encouragingly but did not speak. Silence was not exactly enjoined but was customary. After the urgent purposeful 'powerhouse' activity of the day, leisure seemed deliberately purposeless. Embroidery frames were in evidence, but not much embroidery was done. Mother May often passed the time mending clothes, but leaving off at intervals to relax, her body becoming limp, her beautiful grey eyes vacant, her lips faintly smiling. Edward, stiff in his chair, wished he could emulate this absence. Ilona drew dreamily with pastels on sketch pads of various sizes. Bettina was studying a volume about African crafts. The bookshelves contained, together with a variety of works upon architecture and design, a number of English nineteenth-century novels, all dusty and undisturbed. What indeed could the women have made of these tales of violence? It would have been like watching savages pretend to read. Edward himself beguiled an appalled boredom by trying to write poetry, but could not concentrate, and concealed his enforced idleness by doodling on the paper or writing nonsense.

After the first morning Edward had not again been serenaded under his window, though he occasionally heard, as he worked in the garden, a brief distant sound of a recorder rather unskilfully played, he imagined by Ilona. There was an old gramophone and some classical records in the Interfec, but Edward had not yet ventured to ask for music. He was also tacitly excluded from another rite, the early 'exercises' which occurred before breakfast on the grass beyond the stables, and which, as he covertly observed them, looked to him more like dancing. 'It's Chinese,' Ilona told him, 'sort of swaying movements, rather slow and rhythmical.' 'It's the natural rhythm of the body,' said Bettina, 'not like the violent jolting most people call exercise.' 'We follow Jesse's rule,' said Mother May, 'he is a mystic. Eastern wisdom teaches the unity of body and spirit, how the outer is the inner, the inner the outer.' This information was not conveyed solemnly but with a kind a friendly levity, and when Edward said he would like to join in he was laughed at. 'It takes ages to get the hang,'

137

said Ilona. Meanwhile there had been no recurrence of the festive wine drinking of his arrival night, but Edward, tired and hungry at meal times, did not miss the alcohol. He had also become used to the very simple monotonous vegetarian fare. The evening meal was nevertheless, even on ordinary days, something of a formality, with the women in their pretty dresses and Edward in a long oatmeal smock-shirt belonging to Jesse which Mother May had offered him as 'evening dress' and in which he felt uneasy, although he now wore Jesse's boots without anxiety. They fitted him well. He had established, or been given, a singular right, that of 'taking a walk' during the afternoon rest time, even prolonging it a little. He treasured this aloneness. He had once tried to return to the *dromos* or, as he thought of it the 'sacred grove'. He wondered if there would be fresh offerings of flowers. Who came there? But the river had swollen a little, the stone bridge was scarcely visible and traverse across the wooden 'bridge' looked too hazardous. He had, out of a sort of shyness or reverential unease, not yet mentioned his discovery of this place. He wondered how it related to Seegard. He had also not mentioned the night noises. Nor had he or the women said anything about Edward's 'mishap' which they had 'read about' and which had evidently prompted their invitation. In spite of their continued almost effusive friendliness and evidences of concern and affection, he still felt a little nervous of the three of them, a nervousness quite distinct from his fear of Jesse, and indeed different in quality in relation to each. With Ilona it was easier, and yet, just because he was closest to the 'young one', he felt anxious, as if some power coming from him might harm or taint her. He was conscious of a diffident withdrawal on both sides. Bettina was sometimes, during work, brusque with him, critical, and yet also there was some vibration of a strong emotion, perhaps simply his sense of her intense self-absorbed inwardness. Mother May, being older, had the clearer role, of a benevolent motherly figure. She expressed her affection for Edward in a more direct way, teasing him, moving round him, making a space where he was *with* her. She had not yet kissed him however, and neither of course had the other two. Kisses, so cheap in

138

Edward's student world, were highly priced at Seegard. Mother May's fine transparent calm face, revealing by daylight some tiny line-thin wrinkles, was amazingly youthful yet expressed a confident reserved authority. Sometimes when all three women plaited their hair in the evening, weaving ribbons into the plaits, and letting the long heavy ropes hang down behind, they looked like three young mediaeval princesses. Three cloistered princesses in a castle waiting for a knight, Edward thought with a shudder. He could feel Mother May watching him, as if *waiting*. Waiting perhaps for some assessment which she would make jointly with Jesse. They would discuss Edward, weigh him, sum him up. The queen was waiting for the king. What would she be like, what would she become, when he came back?

Edward gained a certain satisfaction from thinking how completely he had *run away*, and how *nobody knew*. He inhaled his elsewhereness. He tried to relax and let himself be absorbed into the extraordinary Seegard world of what he thought of as 'Bohemian puritanism'. Yet at the same time the old obsessed blackness remained unchanged. When he went walking alone, on duller walks now since he could not cross the flooded river, going along the track toward the road, along the road or into flat fields nearby, although he consciously tried hard to *look* at the trees, the plants, the flowers, the low white clouds moving in the huge sky, he saw as vividly as ever Mark's face, his huge-eyed royal head, and rehearsed the details of that terrible evening. His feeling attached itself to a small picture by Jesse which he had discovered in the empty bedroom next to his own, representing a number of people sitting awkwardly together in a room, obviously in silence, either waiting for or having just heard of a catastrophe: misery crystallised as pure fear. All *this* he thought, as he looked at the countryside and looked back to see the cathedral-like form of Seegard still upon the horizon, is a phantasm, a dream, a veil, something superficially laid over *the turth*; and only dealing with the truth will save me from death. Or transform death into something else. What else? Life I suppose. But do I want life, any life, do I want to be saved? And is there not only one true death, the ordinary one, being slaughtered and done with, where any promised metamorphosis is a mere fiction? To be dead, like Mark is dead. How weak, compared with this, was the idea, constantly, subtly, urged upon him by the three women, that he had come to a house of healing. All this is just magic, he thought to himself, clouds of pretty colours, a delusion, a *wrong path*. But of course – everything, life and death and truth, must now depend on Jesse.

'Quick, quick, come and see, Bettina is teasing a spider!'

Edward stopped chopping basil and dandelion leaves in the kitchen and hurried into the lower corridor of West Selden whence came Ilona's ecstatic cry. He followed her wave into one of the downstairs rooms, still called the Harness Room from the days when, so Ilona told him, the girls had had ponies, but now mainly full of broken furniture. (He had not yet ventured into East Selden, whither he had not been invited.)

Beside a dusty window ledge, Bettina was confronting a large black spider, a very stout spider with a thick body and hunched up legs and prominent stalky eyes which, the impression was irresistible, were *glaring* at his tormentor. A grey hairy curtain in the corner of the ledge, with a deep hole in the centre of it, was apparently the spider's home, which Bettina was preventing him from returning to by means of a feather. The spider tried various devices, pretending to retreat then rushing forward, shamming dead, suddenly shooting up the window pane. All was of no avail. Bettina, smiling, flicked him back, simply barred his way, or deftly picked him up on the feather and deposited him at the other end of the ledge, whence he returned at an angry run.

'Oh, don't hurt him!' said Ilona.

'Of course I won't hurt him.' At that moment a too vigorous movement of the feather swept the spider off the ledge where he fell with an audible plop out of sight among some upturned chair legs. Bettina turned away.

'Oh, will he be all right?'

'Of course he will, silly!'

'Do you think he'll find his way home?'

'Yes, or else he'll make another home, they work fast, unlike some.'

Ilona suddenly cried out almost in tears, 'Oh the poor beastie!'

'Stop it!' said Bettina sharply.

Edward, coming to Ilona's help, said quickly, 'I've never seen a house so full of spiders.'

'Spiders are sacred in this house,' said Bettina.

'All spiders belong to Jesse,' said Ilona, recovering.

'If Edward objects to cobwebs we'll set him to catch all the spiders in the house,' said Bettina, 'and if he hurts a single one he'll be punished!'

'Oh I love spiders, *and* cobwebs,' said Edward hastily.

'That's just as well,' said Bettina.

Edward followed the girls out of the room and on toward the kitchen. The scene with the spider had disturbed him.

'What a heavenly smell of basil!' said Ilona, as they surveyed the scene of Edward's recent labours.

'The kitchen always smells of basil,' said Bettina, 'we grow it all the year round, in the greenhouses and in the house, there's always a pot or two here.'

'We keep all sorts of herbs,' said Ilona, pointing to rows of dried bouquets hanging from beams. 'Mother May knows all about them, she makes up all sorts of medicines, if you need a medicine just let her know.'

'Edward doesn't need any medicines,' said Bettina.

'Did you sleep well?' Ilona asked.

'Yes,' he said 'but –'

'But what?'

'I heard an extraordinary noise in the night.'

'Like what?'

Edward hesitated. 'I heard a sort of wailing – or howling – I couldn't make out where it came from.' He instinctively chose the noise which might be easiest to explain away.

'Sedge warblers,' said Ilona promptly.

'Sedge warblers?'

'Yes, birds, they sing at night, not a bit like nightingales, they can make quite a harsh sound –'

'I don't think –'

141

'Or owls. Bettina can call owls, can't you, Bet? And she can make high notes only animals can hear.'

'You haven't lived in the country,' said Bettina, 'the countryside at night is full of strange sounds. It could have been mating foxes, but more probably it was the wild donkeys.'

'I've never heard of wild donkeys.'

'Well, you're hearing of them now. There are some in the wood. They make the most amazing sounds, especially in spring.'

'I'd like to see them –'

'You won't, they're as hard to see as badgers, and they can be dangerous, quite fierce.'

'So you have super mosquitoes and super donkeys!'

'I told him about the mosquitoes,' said Ilona, 'they're really dangerous, they're a bigger resistant breed, and they can give you awful malaria.'

'You should keep out of the fen,' said Bettina, 'and out of the wood too, at this time of year. Look, why don't you two knock off? I must do a job on that chair. You take Edward for a walk, Ilona, go down the track and along the footpath, there's time before lunch. Go along, go along, Ilona is an idle girl!'

'Wait, Edward, I must find my coatie!'

They set off in boots and coats with the wind behind them. This was the first time that Ilona and Edward had been for a walk together, and they went rather self-consciously down the avenue between the lines of big gawky black-and-white flints.

Edward said, 'I thought at first that these were the ugliest stones I'd ever seen, but now I think they're beautiful.'

'Yes. Jesse loves them. They inspire his sculptures.'

'I didn't know he was a sculptor.' As Ilona said nothing to this Edward went on, 'Do they come from the sea shore?'

'No, they just turn up in the field like – like treasure, like magic things. Just separate from each other and alone. The flints of the sea shore are different, smaller and smoother and more brown.'

'Is there a beach?'

'Well, very stony. The railway used to run along the coast, but that was long ago. We're quite cut off now, it's nice.'

'I wish I could get to the sea. Could one reach it *that* way?' He waved to the right over a field covered with some immature greenish crop.

'No there's *nothing* that way, and the farmer won't let anyone through. I'm sorry it all looks so drab. There's rape in that field –'

'What?'

'Rape, a crop, it makes oil. It'll be a beautiful brilliant yellow in May, you'll see.'

Will I? Edward wondered. 'So you don't own this land?'

'No, only some fen and woodland and the water meadows. We're not rich, you know, we have to work and sell things. I make jewellery –'

'Will you show me? And you weave –'

'Yes, and Mother May makes rugs, and she paints Christmas cards and boxes and does lovely embroidery –'

'And what does Bettina do?'

'She's not so artistic, well, she was an art student, she's a craft person really, she can make any sort of furniture, and she used to make pots – a friend takes out stuff to London to sell.'

'And you go to London?'

'Oh, well, I have been.'

Not often, thought Edward. Does he imprison them?

'I haven't travelled,' said Ilona. 'Jesse and Mother May have lived in Paris, and Bettina has been there. I haven't been anywhere. I wanted to be a dancer once –'

'How odd, so did I! I'll take you to Paris – one day – You're all so clever. But Jesse's pictures, I mean, don't you sell them?'

'We don't want to sell any at present. You've only seen his early pictures, he's been through lots of phases, there was the black and yellow abstract period, and then his expressionist heroic phase, we call it his royal phase, when he did lots of big figures of kings and animals and people fighting, and then his late-Titian phase when he went back to some of his early ideas only everything looked quite different, darker and sort of

143

twilit but absolutely full of light, and then he had a tantric phase with marvellous colours when he was always painting the beginning or the end of the world, some of his work is very erotic, you'll see –'

'I hope you'll show me. When is he coming back?'

'Very soon, I believe.'

'What's that noise?'

'An electric saw. It's the tree men, they're cutting down trees on the other side, there's a lot of forestry inland. We don't like them very much. They're poisoning all the fretty chervil along the road with weed killer, and they destroyed some orchids. Still, they help us sometimes.'

They walked in silence. The sound of the saw was eerie in the empty scene. Edward said, 'You know, I've heard other noises at night.'

'Oh –'

'Yes. I heard a terrible loud sound like a lot of breaking glass. And a sound like – like children running inside the house. I somehow knew they were children.'

Ilona had put on a coat over her plain day dress and turned up the collar, over which a long tress of her reddish hair trailed down her back as far as her waist. The rest of her hair was bunched into a little blue woollen cap. In the coat she looked childish and small, immature, with her cheeks damp and reddened with cold, she could have been a boy of fourteen. She patted her cap, pulling it down over her ears, then replied.

'The breaking glass noise was the poltergeist, that's one of his tricks. It can be very loud. He hasn't done it lately. I thought he'd gone away.'

'You sound as if you know him personally! Did you hear anything?'

'No.'

'And the other, the children?'

'That,' said Ilona, 'is something from the past.'

'How do you mean?'

'You're sleeping in the old part of Selden. Sometimes things from the past come back, quite isolated things, not ghosts. I don't believe in ghosts or spirits of dead people. It's just, like

144

the poltergeist, something sort of mechanical, something natural, which we don't know much about. Perhaps we pick up waves from other minds, past minds, something else heard or saw –'

'I admire the way you take it all for granted. Are you psychic, do you see and hear things?'

'I've heard the poltergeist. I've never seen anything. But Jesse has. He has a great sense of the past. That chest thing there is our pillar box, Bettina keeps the key and the postman has one. If you want to send a letter out give it to her and she'll leave it for him.'

They reached the road. The sound of the electric saw had stopped. It was beginning to rain.

'I don't want to send any letters,' said Edward. 'Don't you want to know whether you've got one?'

'Oh, I don't get any. There's the footpath. But now it's raining –'

'Let's go back.' They turned about to face the east wind. As Seegard came in sight Edward said, 'It's such a strange-looking house, sometimes it seems quite senseless, I mean I don't know how to look at it, and it's as if that makes it invisible.'

'I know what you mean. Jesse meant it to be hard to look at.'

'Perhaps it's something to do with his sense of the past! Ilona, how old are you?'

'Eighteen. And Bettina's twenty-four.'

'I thought she was older, I thought you were younger. Oh Ilona –'

'What?'

As Edward stared at Seegard he felt as if it were about to vanish and he were making it exist. He could not think what it was that he wanted to say to Ilona. Was he glad or sad that she was his sister and not just a girl? He very much wanted to kiss her. Still staring at the house he fumbled for her cold hand and pressed it.

145

MY HANDS ARE growing old, thought Midge McCaskerville, they are dry, the veins are becoming prominent, they are spotted, they will soon be wrinkled. She was sitting in the drawing room of the house in Fulham. The room was full of tulips, yellow tulips which she had bought that morning, parrot tulips which Ursula had sent her. Ursula often sent her flowers. The yellow tulips stood upright in black Wedgwood jugs, the parrot tulips, striped red and white, drooped gracefully from fanciful mauve *art nouveau* vases. Midge had been looking at them intently. She loved the particular silence which the stilled life of flowers could give to a room. Now, as she returned to her task of altering a dress, she could not avoid looking at her hands. She had boldly cut a foot off an evening dress, which, she noticed, she had not worn for some time. She periodically assessed her instinctive relationship to her garments. She had bought two yards of rather expensive material at Liberty's so as to set in two discreet panels to widen the skirt. She enjoyed altering her clothes. In the order of such consolations, flowers came first, clothes second. Thomas had said, joking of course, 'You ought to have been a botanist or a couturier!', but it displayed how little he understood her. Flowers and clothes were for Midge, although she 'busied herself' with them, contemplative matters, they slowed the pace of the world toward a point of absolute repose. When she sewed or arranged flowers she moved very slowly, often pausing. She liked needles and coloured thread and the act of sewing. She had no sewing machine. Thomas had once said he liked to see her sewing, it made him feel calm. She was now looking at her hands, her right hand holding the needle, now still, poised upon the red and black figured silk. The needle, so clean and bright, so sharp and full of purpose. Her hands so stained with mortality. The panels were of plain red silk and looked so well with the red and black material that she considered but rejected the idea of 'making a feature' by letting them into the front and the back. The silk dress, carefully unpicked, trailed over her knees onto the formal oriental daisyfield of the carpet. It was a sunny afternoon, the climbing convolvulus curtains had been drawn well back and the door opened to the balcony, from which a little white cast-iron stairway led down into the garden, where the prunus was in full flower, the crocuses were over, and the roses yet to come. The stone lion's head in the brick wall was to have dripped water into a basin below, but Thomas had never managed to make this happen. Against the walls, about the small sleek lawn, Midge had chosen for her town garden bushy 'old roses' and pretty-leaved shrubs, veronica, euphorbia, buddleia, rhus cotinus, and Japanese maple.

Today was the day when Stuart Cuno was coming to see Thomas to 'have a talk'. Thomas, she knew, had dropped a hint and had been delighted (though he had tried to conceal this) when Stuart had telephoned to say he would come. Ostensibly the conversation was to be about Edward. But Thomas had unusually cancelled a patient (not Mr Blinnet of course) and come back early from the clinic. Thomas was pleased at the prospect of this 'heart to heart'. She thought, he's gloating because he's going to get his claws into Stuart. She felt uneasy at this thought of Stuart and Thomas coming closer together, perhaps becoming intimate. Midge did not altogether like Stuart. She was one of those who apprehended his 'white grub' persona. She saw him as something unnatural, freakish and cold.

'Have you spoken to Meredith about those earphones?' said Midge to Thomas who had just come into the room. 'Ursula says they'll damage his hearing.' She could hear herself speaking in a complaining uncommunicating tone of voice. Yet did Thomas hear this tone? He seemed not to.

'Yes, I did say,' said Thomas. 'That's all right. What are you doing to that dress?'

'Shortening it, widening it.'

'It's such a pretty dress. Did you have your hair done today?'

'No, can't you see!'

Thomas stood at the window, looking at the garden, smiling, the sun on his face, his clever inward face, his shrewd sardonic quizzical self-satisfied face which had once seemed to her so beautiful.

She thought, he is not thinking about me at all, he deserves to lose me, he thinks all my activities are a form of play. And perhaps they are. Except for one. Except for one, except for one. Oh God – how much I pity myself – and Harry – and Thomas –

'Where is Edward?' said Stuart Cuno to Thomas McCaskerville.

'Fled.'

'But you know where to?'

'Yes.'

'And he's OK?'

'That I don't know. Is Harry worried?'

'Not very,' said Stuart. 'He assumes you're in control. By the way, I looked into Meredith's room on the way and I don't at all care for the posters he's put up. Some of them are pretty vile.'

They were in Thomas's bookish study, where Stuart had refused to sit in the armchair in which Edward had sat not long ago. Stuart roved, examining the picture by Cleve Warriston, peering at Thomas's books, admiring the pinkish foam of the prunus tree. These things of course Stuart had seen before, but he seemed to review them now with a certain intensity. He could not be said to be nervous, just restless and tingling with vitality. His thick fair hair, about as long as that of a long-haired dog, was slightly curly and grew well down at the back of his neck. His yellow-amber eyes, animal-like too, were moist as with recent laughter, or perhaps, as a dog's sometimes seem to be, with pleasurable affection; while his rather sweet lips, pink as a child's, were mobile now, pouting and faintly smiling as at some quick play of thought. He was dressed for the warm day, in baggy light brown cotton trousers and a blue open-neck shirt not very well tucked in. He looked for a moment to Thomas just like a lively healthy young man. That this was so noteworthy, given that he *was* a lively healthy young man, suggested to Thomas in what other and strange lights he had lately been viewing his youthful friend. It had taken Thomas a little time to decide that Stuart, in his 'new phase', was genuine; but genuine *what* remained the question.

'So you haven't decided what you want to do, what job I mean?'

'I wish I hadn't talked about all that,' said Stuart, frowning.

'Well, people, will ask questions, including impertinent ones about your sex life.'

'Yes.'

'You still imagine you have to answer all questions promptly and truthfully. But you don't have to announce your programmes, only to carry them out.'

'I shouldn't have said that about chastity,' said Stuart, 'just have got on with it. You're right – and yet I couldn't lie. And I don't want to practise being evasive.'

'Can a man be absolutely truthful? These are problems most people solve by instinct, usually wrongly, without even noticing. But about the job, if you don't mind my asking.'

'Oh *you* can ask. Of course I may not get *any* job, not everyone can now. I thought of something with prisoners – like a probation officer – or some sort of social work, to do with housing or –'

'It's not all that easy to help people,' said Thomas, 'and they can hate you for it. But shouldn't you do something which involves intellectual studies? You've been learning hard all your life, won't you miss it?'

'I expect I'd have to take some training course. Anyway I propose to go on learning, that's the point! One thing I think I've learnt is how to learn.'

'Apprenticed to goodness – a rather special case. But I meant continuous academic learning, learning with books.'

'I want to get away from abstract stuff.'

'Or shouldn't you perhaps read something about your special subject?'

'My what?'

'About religion, theology, metaphysics, that sort of thing.'

'Thomas, you're joking!'

'No, just fishing around. So you're not tempted to write about it yourself, to try to explain –'

'*Write?! Explain?!*'

'All right, I'm not against books, quite the contrary, children now are brought up on computers, not books, that's part of the trouble. But you seem to regard my education as a pile of stuff, possessions, assets to be used not wasted. I don't want academic studies now, I want to start from scratch.'

'Not an easy place to get to. You're sure it isn't sour grapes, because you can't go on being a star?'

'I'm not a star.'

'You got a brilliant first in maths.'

'Yes, but anybody can. I mean if you can think in a certain kind of way at a certain moment you're bound to get a first, it's not like other subjects. But that doesn't mean you can do anything else or anything further, even Newton was done for at twenty-four. All that's a red herring anyway. The modern world is full of theories which are proliferating at a wrong level of generality, we're so *good* at theorising, and one theory spawns another, there's a whole industry of abstract activity which people mistake for thinking –'

'Yes, I understand, but shouldn't there be theorists who can make radical criticisms of theorising?'

'Maybe, but I'm just not interested in that, and I'm *passionately* interested in this other business –'

'Yes. What is it however? Do you imagine that you can save the world simply by proving that it is possible?'

'Everyone seems to want to make a mystery or drama out of it, but it's desperately simple really, just not to enter the machine.'

'The machine?'

'You know what I mean, the usual things, corruption – corruption, you know, it happens so *fast*.'

'Yes. The second bull-fight is easier than the first, Byron tells us he was hardened after two executions.'

'And chastity –'

'Sex is said to be the image, even the substance, of spirit, and by abstention its instrument – but a dangerous one. All spirituality is dangerous, especially asceticism.'

'You think I might break out!'

'Nothing so simple.'

'All that's what I mean by drama and mystification. In order to be of use I've just got to live simply and be alone. There's nothing mysterious about that. Priests have been doing it forever. I could have gone to a Catholic school, into a seminary, on to ordination –'

'Yes, but you didn't.'

'It's a pity about the priesthood – being a sort of obscure parish priest – that would have been bang on, for the job, for the style of it I mean –'

'But why shouldn't you think now about being ordained? Never mind about dogma, it's all being changed anyway. Theologians are working as fast as they can precisely to reach people like you. The theological rescue party is on the way. Soon you will hear the sound of the bagpipes.'

Stuart laughed. 'Yes, but still that's for insiders. It'll take a long time to stop "God" being the name of someone. I don't want any God at all, even a modified modernised one. I've got to be sure he isn't in it somewhere hidden away. God is an anti-religious idea. There is no God.'

'As eastern religions have always told us. Why not –'

'I'm not concerned with the east. I'm western. It's got to be done differently here.'

'Some say that God has gone away to a vast distance, that for a time the Transcendent is silent.'

'That's an act in a play. There is no play.'

'Let's say that God is a permanent non-degradable love object. *Must* we not imagine something of the sort?'

'There are plenty of such things, we don't have to imagine

151

them as a person existing somewhere else, the world is full of them if we look.'

'You mean symbols, sacraments?'

'You will talk jargon –'

'Trees, animals, works of art –?'

'Look, I'm only doing what any man has to do now, manage alone. Only I don't mean that in any sort of dramatic heroic way. I just mean without the old supernatural scenery.'

'People will say if it's alone it must be personal fantasy, without substance. Without mythology or theology or institutions – and I imagine you're not looking for a master or guru –'

'Of course not. To imagine that somewhere at the end of the world in a cave there's a wise man – that's sentimentality, it's masochism, it's magic –'

'You don't want to be under obedience.'

'I am under obedience, but not like that –'

'You're dedicated.'

'It's got to be everything, my whole being, my whole life, not something part-time, not something optional – Just to try to be good, to be for others and not oneself. To be nothing, to have nothing, to be a servant – and for that to be one's whole occupation. It's all, everywhere, as if everything spoke it and showed it – and it's so deep that it's entirely me, and yet it's entirely not me too –'

'Steady on. All that sounds like God. You say there is no God, then you aspire to be God yourself, you take over his attributes. Perhaps that *is* the task of the present age.'

'I didn't say I was God! I just mean the way – the way to –'

'Kafka said there is no way, there is only the end, what we call the way is messing about.'

'Could you say that again?'

'There is no way, there is only the end, what we call the way is messing about.'

'I'll think about that. I just mean I, I privately, am trying to do, at least I'm starting to try to do, something which I'm *certain* about, which is *obvious*, and I see *everywhere*.'

'Everywhere outside you and inside you too. It's dark inside, Stuart.'

152

'You mean original sin. I'm not concerned with those guilt stories. Oh, of course, you mean the unconscious mind!'

'Don't tell me you don't believe in it.'

'Nothing so positive. I don't fancy the idea. It doesn't interest me.'

'Perhaps you interest it. Don't despise the concept. It's not just an abode of monsters, it's a reservoir of spiritual power.'

'Spirits. Magic. No, I don't like what you've just said. It's a misleading bad idea.'

'You say you're not concerned with guilt. Do you imagine you'll never feel any?'

'I mean the feeling isn't important, it may even be bad. One must try to mend things, do better. Why cripple yourself when there's work to do?'

'So you don't envy Edward his extreme situation?'

'No, why should I?' said Stuart, surprised.

'It's one method of breaking up illusions of self-satisfaction.'

'You think I'm self-satisfied?'

Thomas considered this. 'I'm not sure,' he said. 'Your case confuses the concept. I'm waiting to see.'

Stuart laughed. 'My father says I'm a hedonist, I've chosen the higher selfishness!'

'To sleep with a clear conscience every night is indeed enviable.'

'He meant being ostentatiously poor and looked after by rich friends!'

'You imagine that you want to lead an orderly monotonous altruistic life –'

'Say it, a dull life!'

'You object to the idea of it being dull. Part of your energy is that you think well of yourself. So you will want some recognition, even drama, the pleasure of self-assertion, to conquer and be seen to conquer.'

'You're provoking me!'

'You think you're an exceptional person.'

'There's something exceptional but it isn't me. You think I lack humility.'

'You lack the gift of ordinariness, perhaps essential for your

153

programme. To put it crudely, you have a strong ego. Now isn't that horrible? You don't want to be ordinary. You *think* too much to be ordinary.'

'I want to be invisible. In a way I'm not there –'

'Already?'

'I've never had any sense of identity.'

'That's not the same as being unselfish, dear boy!'

'All right – in a way it is selfish.'

'It's choosing a kind of safety. Being alone is safe. Stoicism is safe. Never to be surprised, never to have anything to lose. A source of pride.'

'I don't think I'm a stoic. Really it's worse than that. For I on honeydew have fed and drunk the milk of paradise.'

'Stuart, could you sit down please. I don't like your leaning against that window, I feel you might fall out, come into the middle of things, *there*.'

Stuart sat down in the armchair opposite to Thomas and gazed at him with an exasperating air of good humour. Thomas, who had known his face for a long time, through boyhood and adolescence, wondered at how unchanged it seemed, how clean and smooth and glowing, as if Stuart had kept all his faces, even his baby face, as satiny masks super-imposed through which this lively intelligence and mad-deningly confident self-being was now looking out. Thomas had to tell himself this was after all a vulnerable inexperienced perhaps entirely deluded young man. He examined the golden points of Stuart's well-shaved beard.

'What's this stuff about honeydew?'

'Oh just that it's so wonderful, it makes me so happy, just to think about it all. It's as if one had manna to eat and didn't want to spoil one's palate.'

Thomas laughed, then roared with laughter, while Stuart continued to smile at him, observing his laughter with benign interest. 'Stuart, you're priceless! You've simply elected yourself out of the human condition of indelible selfishness. To remove a mountain is easy, to change any man's temperament for the better is considerably more difficult. But you seem to assume you've done it already just by thinking!'

'Well, what's wrong with thinking,' said Stuart, 'that's a

sort of action too. And why should I bother about my temperament, a jolly unclear concept anyway. One soon comes to the end of psychology, and there's no point in detailed theories about morals.'

'That's what your father said the other night!'

'He meant it's all nonsense. I mean talk about the "spiritual life" and all that is too abstract. It's not a matter of "explaining". All sorts of important things have no explanations.'

'Yes, yes, of course. And mental activity is action too. But this thinking of yours isn't theorising, it's not systematic reflection –'

'Innocence is a strong idea, purity, holiness – Ideas are signals, or pointers, or refuges, or resting places – it's hard to describe.'

'Of course. You are fertile in metaphors. So you pray? Or sort of. You meditate?

'Yes.'

'You invoke help, you invite grace – sort of?'

'Yes.'

'Do you kneel down?'

'Well – yes – sometimes.'

'Am I being impertinent?'

'Not yet!'

'No one taught you?'

'Of course not! Look, Thomas, these are ordinary natural things, nothing odd!'

'And all this came naturally and painlessly out of your vague Anglican childhood. You weren't religious at school.'

'There's such a thing as growing up.'

'What about Jesus?'

'Well, what about him?'

'You said you didn't want a master, but isn't he one you can't avoid?'

Stuart frowned. 'Not a master. Of course he's *there*. But he's not God.'

'All right. Am I tormenting you? Or are you loving it?'

'You keep getting it wrong. I just want to grip onto the

155

world directly, like – like a painter –'

'Like a spider?'

'Like a *painter*. I don't imagine I'm a sort of sage, I don't believe in sages. And there's no programme of action except that one has to earn one's living and I do want to help people. It's rather a state of being.'

'A prolonged adolescence some would call it. Yes, just that blessed sense of growing up, that happy sense that some adolescents have, a conscious superior innocence. To keep that innocence and that vision of glory and that feeling of possibility and power still with you, to establish that light forever, simply not to let it dim – yes, that might seem easy. But oh you'll be misunderstood!'

'I already am!'

'Yes, but it doesn't hurt yet. And you'll be hated. Perhaps you already are. You'll be called timid and impotent and repressed and retarded and childish – never mind. But do you really think you can live by innocence alone?'

'No – there's more –'

'What?'

Stuart hesitated.

'Come on, tell me.'

'"Sink me the ship, master gunner, sink her and split her in twain, let us fall into the hands of God, not into the hands of Spain."'

'What on earth are you talking about, Stuart?'

Stuart said in a low voice as if confessing a secret, 'Courage, just sheer courage – being willing to die. It sounds awfully silly, but those lines of poetry somehow express it.'

'Every adolescent's favourite poem, or used to be. I'm sure, your father loved it, certainly your grandfather did! Forgive me!'

'I'm talking too much.'

'You're talking beautifully, please don't stop. Since we seem to be listing the necessary things, what about love?'

'What?'

'Love.'

'Oh – love.'

'I don't want to be what you might call abstract or literary

156

or sentimental, but isn't love supposed to be fundamental in the matters that concern you, your state of being, your honeydew?'

'I'm not certain about that,' said Stuart. 'I think it has to look after itself, I mean it has to sort of cancel itself.'

'Cancel?'

'It has to un-be itself, so it can't exactly be aimed at –'

'The subject embarrasses you.'

'No, I just can't think about it. I want to go in at the deep end as it were.'

'Fall in love?'

'No, *not* fall in love. That's the shallow end.'

'But can you get to the deep end without starting at the shallow end?'

'Yes, why not. But I'm probably talking nonsense. I just mean I don't want ordinary attachments, intimate friendships or relationships, what's usually called love. Perhaps just the word bothers me, the name, like "God", it's got so –'

'Degraded?'

'Messy. Messed up.'

'If it can't be aimed at you can't decide where you'll "go in". It's dangerous, Stuart. I liked your image of falling into the hands of God – oh, I know you didn't mean *him* – but it's a deep place, an ocean heaving and giving birth to itself, melting and seething in itself and into itself, interpenetrating itself, light in light and light into light, swelling inwardly, flooding itself, every part interpenetrating the rest until it spills and boils over.'

'What's that, sex, the unconscious?'

'A description of God by a Christian mystic.'

'He must have been a heretic.'

'He was. All the best are. There are principalities and powers, fallen angels, animal gods, spirits cut loose and wandering in the void, they have to be reckoned with, St Paul knew that, he was the first heretic.'

'Thomas, do stop making jokes. I'm against fallen angels like I'm against dramas and mysteries and looking for masters and fathers and –'

'Fathers?'

'I mean, I've got a perfectly good ordinary one and I don't regard it as an important symbol.'

'Since we're on fathers, what about mothers? What about yours?'

Stuart flushed a little, looking almost annoyed. 'You want to explain me through my mother.'

'Nothing so simple. I just want to know what you'll say.'

'I don't see why I should say anything. I'm not your patient. I'm sorry I didn't know my mother.'

'Do you think about her, dream about her?'

'Sometimes. But it's not your sort of thing *at all* and I'd rather you didn't touch it.'

'All right, I won't.'

There was a silence. Thomas thought, he'll go now. Can I stop him, do I want to? He looked down, arranged pens and blotting paper upon his desk, his face assuming a cat-like mask of benign detached self-absorption. Stuart looked at Thomas and smiled in a secretive way, began to rise, then sat back. He said, 'It would be ungrateful of me, after this conversation, during which you've been making me talk so, not to ask if you have anything special to say to me.'

'Advice? I thought I'd been giving some –'

'You've just been provoking me, as you admitted, to see what I'd say! Come on, Thomas, you're *thinking*!'

'Of course I think a lot of things, but I don't see any point in uttering them at this stage. Later on perhaps. I'm still puzzled. You are extraordinarily full of yourself.'

'You mean conceited?'

'No, solid, articulated, full of being. I just wonder – you seem to have two aims, one to be innocent and self-subsistent, the other to help people. I wonder whether these will not seriously conflict.'

'Oh maybe,' said Stuart. He got up and resumed his post by the window. He looked at his watch.

'Also, there is more in you than you know of. You are not lord of yourself. Put it this way, your enemy is stronger and more ingenious than you seem to imagine.'

'You and your mythology, how you love these pictures! You think I ought to go to hell and back, you want me to fall and learn by sin and suffering!'

Thomas laughed. 'You want to be like the Prodigal Son's elder brother, the chap who never went away!'

'Exactly – except that he was cross when his brother was forgiven!'

'Which you wouldn't be.' It's time to stop this, thought Thomas. We're tired, and we've both done well, considering what a mess we might have made of it. And here's another dangerous topic. Better leave it at that for now. We've certainly made a start. He rose to his feet.

'I must be off,' said Stuart. Thomas refrained from asking where he was going, what he was going to do, how he proposed to spend the evening. He had begun to feel an intense curiosity about all Stuart's activities and mode of being. He said, 'Stuart, thank you for coming, I enjoyed talking to you. I hope you'll come again when you feel like it, and we could continue this conversation.'

'Oh, I don't think we'll ever talk like *this* again,' said Stuart, 'it wouldn't do. Things can get spoilt by being talked about. But thank you, you've helped me get clearer about some things. Would you tell Meredith I'll expect him about ten on Saturday at the usual place?'

Thomas opened the door and Stuart moved towards it, then closed it and turned back towards Thomas.

'I know you asked me about Christ – I didn't say properly about him.'

'Isn't he one of your signals or refuges? One of those non-degradable objects you say are everywhere?'

'Yes – but also I – I can't take the idea of the resurrection – it spoils everything that went before –'

'I think I understand,' said Thomas.

'I have to think of him in a certain way, not resurrected, as it were mistaken, disappointed – well, who knows what he thought. He has to mean pure affliction, utter loss, innocent suffering, pointless suffering, the deep and awful and irremediable things that happen to people.'

'Yes.'

'There's another thing I sometimes think of in this connection, a particular thing. This may sound awfully arbitrary or bizarre or –' Stuart suddenly became crimson in the face.

'What? Go on.'

'Something a chap at college told me. He'd been to visit Auschwitz, the concentration camp, you know they've made it into a sort of museum now. And he said the most awful thing he saw there were plaits of girls' hair.'

'Plaits –?'

'They say how the Nazis *used* everything at those camps, at some of them anyway, like a factory –'

'Like lampshades made of human skin.'

'Yes – and they cut off the hair of the people to use – to make wigs I suppose – and there was an exhibition there –' He paused, and for a moment Thomas thought he was going to burst into tears. 'There was a great huge pile of people's hair, and there were long plaits, girls' plaits, beautifully carefully plaited, and I thought – that there was a morning – when a girl woke up from sleep – and plaited her hair – so carefully – and –' Stuart clenched a fist and fell silent, breathing deeply.

'And you connect that with Christ on the cross –'

Stuart said after a moment, 'It's a sort of – particular – absolute – thing.' Then he said, 'You know, sometimes I do look for signs, or a sign.'

'Isn't that a form of magic?'

'Yes. I'm just reporting a weakness!' Stuart smiled and the emotion of a moment ago was suddenly quite gone.

When Stuart had left him Thomas sat motionless at his desk while his mind performed some extremely condensed and intuitive thought-acrobatics. He thought, what an amazing thing such a conversation is, how ever do we do it? What is more extraordinary and inexplicable than human consciousness? Yet we all know what it is, we know what the word refers to, we aren't in any doubt about it. And how surprising and moving his thing about the girls' hair. That means so many things. What an outburst of emotion. And his connecting it with Christ. He really has a talent for – for what?

After a time Thomas relaxed. He pictured Stuart's fair doggy cropped head, rather a large long head, and his amber

160

eyes which were so naïvely trustful and yet so clever. He's cleverer than I imagined, Thomas thought, is that a good thing? What is a good thing here? He pictured Stuart's boyish smile. Then he pictured Mr Blinnet's bland smile and his mocking ironical eyes with their deep crazy inner chambers. Then he saw Edward's grimacing smile, the smile of the unconscious mind as it triumphs over the conscious. Would Stuart founder dreadfully somehow upon the rock of his own resolve? 'Sink me the ship, master gunner –' What a touching motto, a *schoolboy* motto! Did Stuart secretly imagine he was an exceptional person destined to change the world? Would he end up sitting in some hospital garden, imagining he was Jesus? Or would he turn out to be dull, not divinely dull, but just a self-deluded common-place fellow? In fact, just like everyone else.

Oh let *that* not be so! thought Thomas. He was beginning to find Stuart immensely interesting, he wanted to chart his progress in detail. He was saddened by Stuart's 'never again'. He had feared something of the sort. Perhaps in spite of his delicately prescient anxiety not to, he had pressed him too far. More likely Stuart had coolly intended to have just one talk with Thomas; at least he must have felt he needed it. He had certainly come to talk about himself and not about Edward. So would they really never talk again? Thomas had looked forward to many such talks. More than that, he had looked forward to just that 'close' friendship with Stuart which Stuart had declared to be outside his programme!

Of course I am a professional meddler, thought Thomas, but this is a special case. If indeed Stuart were to fade into the dullness with which Thomas menaced him, perhaps that would *be* his success? Or would he be overwhelmed, ruined by the forces which he so calmly imagined he could simply reject? Thomas had to admit that the idea of such a collapse interested him; he was already imagining himself coming to the rescue. The dark powers, as the ancients knew, were essentially ambiguous; and thus, as Stuart instinctively perceived, enemies of morality. Blindly, he recognised them; perhaps they recognised him. He would never game for their favours. But I do, thought Thomas, I have to, I do it daily, trying to make

161

benignant allies out of the most dangerous things in the world. When calm resolve and rational morals seem to fail, can not *they*, vehicles after all of spirit, be invoked and charmed into friendliness, before their exasperation with that very failure leads them to destroy the whole structure? I have to try, thought Thomas, I have to play this dangerous game, because I am that sort of healer, and – oh – heavens – because I *love* it! *Flectere si nequeo superos, Acheronta movebo.*

A LITTLE LOUD wren was singing. The sun was shining. Edward was walking along the edge of the river, the *other side* of the river. He had now been at Seegard for nearly two weeks, and Jesse had still not come home. During this time Edward had said nothing to the women about the *dromos*, which he had continually wished to revisit, but in vain because the river had risen so as to make the hurdle bridge impassable and submerge the stone bridge completely. The weather had turned very cold and he did not fancy swimming across carrying his clothes. On several occasions he secretly made his way past the greenhouses and the vegetable garden, along the overgrown but quite authoritative little path which led to the river. Who trod that path? The sight of the rushing stream, now well above the precarious 'footway' of the wooden structure, shaking it and almost carrying it off, made Edward shudder with a kind of almost sexual excitement. Today however (it was 'rest time') it was with a more purposive thrill that, finding the river a little abated, he set his foot on the leaning structure, tested it, and, with the water splashing his feet, edged his way across. And now he was, the word came to him as he walked along, free; yet not really free, but upon a different ground where, perhaps, other enchantments reigned.

The nervous guilty qualms which he felt at, not for the first time, absenting himself for longer than he was 'supposed to' were proof that he was after all a prisoner, a prisoner with the kindest, most beautiful, most loving captors, captors who set

163

him tasks. He found satisfaction in his tasks, the weariness they caused and his sense therein of being a slave and needing to have no thoughts. He slept promptly and well; yet of course thoughts came. He wondered if, perhaps unconsciously, the women were trying to 'sweat his misery out of him'. They had still not questioned him about Mark. Edward did not raise the subject, and they showed so little awareness of it that he sometimes thought that they had either forgotten it or had never realised how terribly he had been wounded. Nor did they seem aware of how intensely and anxiously Edward was awaiting for his father, how dreadful this meeting would seem from which he also so irrationally hoped for healing. These women, Mother May and his strange sisters, hardly sisters but rather as he now saw them elf maidens, *they* could not set him free, and he no longer even desired to unburden his heart to them.

They, as the days went by, began to appear different to him. They were still, as he had first apprehended them, taboo, holy women, and endowed with arcane skills. They had not healed his wound but they had a little soothed it. He sometimes wondered whether he were being affected by the diet, so monotonous and so pure: apples, cabbage, herbs, rice, bran, nuts, beans, lentils, oats, especially oats. ('It's oats with everything here, you know,' Ilona said.) There had been no reappearance of the home-made wine; but Mother May sometimes produced herbal draughts which smelt and tasted of flowers and were said laughingly to produce 'benign thoughts' and 'happy dreams'. Edward felt healthier, stronger, and wondered whether this were a true and proper and *natural* – a word often used at Seegard – recovery; or whether, by some magic alien to it, his most precious possession, the wound, the guilt, the *thing itself*, were being wrongfully taken from him. Was he being quietly deprived of his sense of reality? He remained convinced that for his true well-being, and so that all this at Seegard so far should not seem a dream interlude or worthless demoralising holiday from his *real* task, he needed Jesse: Jesse's wisdom, Jesse's authority, Jesse's love. Nothing else would do. And yet as he thought this deep thought he realised too the frailty of his hope. Perhaps he should now be quite elsewhere, doing something quite else.

He slept, falling like an animal into its lair at night, waking occasionally for a second to hear the river sound, or what he took to be the distant sound of the sea, then sleeping again to dream of the frou-frou of dresses, the clink and swing of necklaces, long tresses unpinned and softly falling, and of women, mothers perhaps, Chloe, Midge, Mother May, even Bettina, leaning above him and merging together. The wind, which tired him so by day, came at night in regular sighing gusts, sounding like some great thing deeply and steadily breathing. The rain pattering or gently stroking the window panes was more like soft footsteps, soft surreptitious padding, not frightening really but strange, like many things that surrounded him, like Ilona's casual reference to 'things from the past'. He had not heard the breaking glass noise again, or the children's running feet. Sometimes there were faint scratching sounds, rats perhaps, or what Ilona called 'mouse-kins'. Something odd and unnerving had however happened two nights ago as he mounted the dark stairs in West Selden to his bedroom. He now knew his way blindfold about the building and preferred running nimbly in the pitch dark to the bother of carrying a lamp. As he mounted the stairs in velvet blackness of blindfold dark something passed him. It did not touch him, but he heard its faint whirring sound and felt the air of its passage. It was, as he intuited it at the time, something spherical, about the size of a football, passing him very close at waist height. Edward raced up the stairs and into his room and hastily struck some matches, dropping several before he was able to light his lamp. He stood tensely listening, hearing the river and the far off *gewick gewick* and *ooo-ooo* of the owls. In the lamplight he noticed that he was less frightened by the episode than he might have expected. Remembering Ilona's jest, he wondered if what had passed him was a poltergeist which occupied his bed by day and had now fled on hearing his approach! He smiled. All the same, he examined the bed carefully before getting into it.

Another source of unease, felt vaguely, now perceptibly stronger, concerned the women. It had come to Edward at the start that the women were not only *essentially* remote from him in some quite special way, but also perfect: calm, wise, beautiful, devoid of ordinary human failings. This idea persisted, coexisting easily with Ilona's childishness and Bettina's brusqueness. It seemed natural that they had never kissed him. Mother May and Bettina had never touched him. Ilona had occasionally touched his sleeve, but with a puppyish gesture, devoid of emotional significance, to hurry him on or draw his attention to something. That these women actually were (how could they not be?) imperfect unnerved Edward as he became aware of it, even frightened him. For instance, they were afraid of the 'tree men'. Perhaps this was something that came over them when Jesse was away, when they apprehended themselves as lonely and defenceless. But Edward did not like to think of a queen, princesses, elf maidens, as mere nervy women. He had not discovered any reason for this obsessive fear except that the tree men were 'rough', destroyed precious plants, and had once quite deliberately (they said) cut down a beautiful very old tree, a huge sycamore, on Seegard land. Perhaps some old feud with Jesse was involved. The absence of information about Jesse's whereabouts and date of return was also, after this passage of time, disturbing in itself. His advent was constantly and confidently promised 'soon'. Edward had not asked where he was or what he was doing; and now refrained from asking from a fear of being lied to. He sometimes thought, and *hated* to think, that Jesse was perhaps somewhere in the south of France with a young and pretty mistress; even had a quite other ménage. And (this thought had only lately begun to torment Edward) other children. *Another son.* This idea was exceedingly painful; and he was distressed, often made agonisingly nervous, by the unexplained lapse of time, the evasiveness of the women, and also of late by their relations to each other and to him which had at first had such a reassuring formality, had belonged to the 'perfection'. Simply put, he felt jealousy in the air. He was a man among three women. Nothing palpable could suggest the vulgar idea that they were 'vying for his affection'; but there was a certain tension. So far no one of them had attempted to establish a special relationship, to gain

166

his confidence or examine his heart. The only 'sorting out' involved was the no doubt natural assumption that paired him and Ilona as the 'young ones'. 'Off you go, children,' Mother May had said yesterday, despatching them to the apple store. Perhaps he imagined it, but he felt that Bettina might resent some implied relegation of herself to the older generation. She was sometimes stiff with him when they worked together, when he played plumber's mate, or carpenter's boy, fetched the materials or held the tools. Yet perhaps this was just her nature, a usual shyness, an admirable reserve. Mother May, so open and cheerful and busy, the Queen Bee as she sometimes called herself, also seemed to his over-stressed imagination to be watching him with some sort of concealed emotion. And though he was 'easy' with Ilona, they became no closer, nor could he see how this could happen. Perhaps they were all simply worrying about Jesse. As he now continually studied them he saw increasingly how different they were. The three women, always similarly dressed (to please Jesse of course) in their plain brown shifts by day and their flowered-benecklaced dresses in the evening, could still look alike, as if occluded by a powdery golden haze of similarity. Yet with sharpened perceptions Edward perceived their individual faces. Mother May's perfect complexion was sketched here and there with a silverpoint of tiny lines, scarcely visible, not to be called wrinkles, not indeed marring but somehow perfecting her pale calm beauty. Her eyes were of the lightest softest grey. Bettina had a larger face, unlike the perfect oval of her mother's, with darker grey eyes, an aquiline nose and strong protruding chin, and a clever reflective mouth. In repose or when concentrating upon work she could resemble a *quattrocento* picture of a young nobleman. Ilona had a smaller perter face, animated and peering like an animal's, with eyes of a bluer grey, and a witty mobile mouth. They all had similar long reddish-gold hair, sometimes put up in coils or buns, sometimes hanging in long plaits. Ilona, whose hair was longest, sometimes wore hers simply tied with a ribbon at the neck and streaming loose down her back. Edward thought a lot about their hair. He had never touched it, not even

Ilona's. He imagined that he could smell their hair. It had a very delicate feral smell.

Trying to recall his previous journey, Edward had now left the river and was climbing up through the wood, where bluebells were making a hazy blue distance between the budding green of the various saplings which were grasping at his clothes. The sun, piercing down from above through the high roof of oaks and beeches, confused the woody interior with blotches of light. Edward blundered on until he came upon a small twig-strewn path, and followed it upward. Soon he could see the larger light ahead, and stepped between beech pillars over a verge of tall grasses onto a level sward of the *dromos*. He stopped perfectly still, breathless with his climb, and with the surprise of his arrival and the odd authoritative being of the place. He stood breathing deeply, moving his eyes, not yet daring to move his head. It was as if he expected to find some enemy there, or some possessor who should challenge his intrusion. Then he remembered the tree men who were hostile to Seegard. But all was exactly as before, the long narrow area was empty, except for the upright pillar upon its low fluted plinth. The grass had grown longer, but was still short enough to count as a 'lawn' rather than a 'field'. The wood was silent, the trees motionless in the quiet afternoon. Looking now to left and right, Edward began to walk slowly out into the open space of the grove. He looked quickly behind him to see if he were being followed and to check whether his feet were leaving prints in the grass. No alien presence, no prints, only his feeling that something was going to happen. He felt excited, a bit frightened, pleased with himself, that he had found the place again. He approached the pillar which the sunlight, striking in a certain way, was making to sparkle. As he walked round it the brighter light now showed up a carving upon one of its faces, a rectangle with curly decoration, some kind of lettering or perhaps an animal form. As he leaned forward to look, he heard the sound, often mentioned in boys' adventure stories, of someone further down in the wood stepping on a twig. Edward shot away from the pillar into the darkness of the arch between the large yew trees. The earth beneath the yews was firm and hard, and bare except for a deep scattering of brown needle-like yew leaves. The arching trees gave no cover, so Edward skidded into the woodland behind the tall guardian beeches on the other side of the grove and fell down promptly into the long grass near to the edge of the sward, at first anxious simply not to be seen, then wanting very much to find out who the visitor was. It was Ilona.

Edward felt no urge to rise or call out. He felt guilty at the idea of being discovered in the place; and he wanted to see what Ilona would do. She walked into the middle of the sward, then looked around her rather anxiously and furtively as Edward had done. Then she took off her shoes and socks and stroked the top of the springy grass with her bare foot. She thrust her socks inside her shoes and laid them down, took off her brown wooden beads and put them too inside her shoes, then walked on toward the pillar. Here she paused again and looked about, then looked up at the blue sky, closing her eyes against the sun. She was wearing her plain brown day dress which Edward thought much more beautiful than her evening robe. Her hair was loose, hanging down her back, a little tangled as usual. She folded her hands, standing motionless for a moment before the pillar as if in respect. Then she produced from the pocket of her dress something which Edward recognised with surprise as a piece of string. She bound this round her waist and hitched the top part of the dress over it, thus shortening the skirt. She raised both hands above her head, joining her fingers like a ballet dancer. The sleeves of the brown dress fell back revealing the lighter softer more vulnerable flesh of her upper arm. Then she began to dance.

That is, Edward told himself later that that was what had happened. It must have been. What it looked like was that Ilona was lifted from the ground by some superior force, a wind perhaps (only there was no wind) and was conveyed to and fro over the grass, the tips of which her feet were barely touching. He distinctly recalled seeing at one moment both of her feet, moving in slow motion, poised well above the

169

gleaming green surface of the grass as her swaying body was carried away along the glade and then back again toward the pillar. Once or twice it seemed as if, like a leaf, she was about to be blown away altogether and to disappear floating into the wood. There was in her movement no sort of exertion, it was as if, with her hair flying round her, she were simply being carried out, conveyed through the air; and yet a sense of volition was there and the purposeful grace of her body, the patterned weavings of her arms, and of her long slim legs under the hitched-up skirt were those of a dancer. She seemed to leap and to subside, to balance, pivot, swing and turn without touching the ground. For something, with something, she *performed*, not seeming to move at random, but executing a choreographic pattern of ecstatic yet disciplined expression. It was a dance of joy, becoming slower and sadder toward the end, as if she felt the breath failing which had lifted her. She began to move, not exactly wearily, for the precision of the movement remained, but as if, by flowing gestures of her hands and her whole body, she were casting away something, like a garment, in which she had been briefly clothed. Her slowing feet first brushed, then entered the grass, and at last she stood, or landed, holding out an arm to steady herself, then motionless with her hands at her sides, near to the pillar. And so the dance was over; and Edward lay back hastily in the grass, from which in his rapt excitement he had risen a little.

Ilona now looked dejected. She began to undo the piece of string around her waist. She had some difficulty with the knot at which she pulled with graceless exasperation, uttering little cross grunts. At last her skirt fell to its full length, and she stuffed the string into her pocket and stood a while with head drooping, seeming bereft of purpose. Then she turned abruptly and began to walk towards Edward. Edward felt, at that moment, utterly afraid of her, afraid of having been a witness of something he ought not to have seen. He shrank down. However Ilona's objective was not Edward. She went to the edge of the bare shady ground under the big yews, and came back holding a single white flower in her hand. She stood again before the pillar, and looked down intently at the flower for a few moments. Edward, gazing through his grassy

170

screen, now saw with horror that glistening tears were rolling from her eyes and dripping off the curve of her cheek onto the ground. She stared at the flower as if she were pitying it, even regretting that she had picked it. Then she laid it down on the dark stone plinth and turned brusquely away. She moved now with a busy scurrying haste, like a little awkward schoolgirl, finding her shoes and socks, trying to put her socks on standing on one leg, failing, then sitting down abruptly, rather irritably, upon the grass. When she had put her shoes and socks on, and her wooden bead necklace, she got up hurriedly and scampered off into the wood.

Edward waited a while before he rose, for he feared she might return and he wanted too for *whatever it was* to be somewhat dissipated before he presented himself, an impious spectator and outsider. He got up at last and walked out into the open. He looked to see where Ilona had picked her flower, and saw a clump of white wood anemones, the star-like flowers displaying upon a tracery of small fernlike green leaves. He felt an impulse to pick another flower, but rejected it. He went back to the pillar and looked at the white anemone lying on the dark plinth. It seemed already to be fading. It made him think of the body of a dead girl. Edward raised his head and looked nervously about him. The scene was peaceful, empty, the shadows of the trees no longer upon the grass. Nearby a blackbird began to sing, reminding Edward that during his visit to the grove the birds had been silent until now. He looked at his watch and following on Ilona's track ran away quickly into the wood.

'Look!' Ilona held up a tumbler of water in front of Edward. It was before lunch on the following day and they were standing in the sunshine on the pavement outside the Atrium door.

Edward took the tumbler from Ilona and held it up to the light. The water was full of tiny almost invisible organisms, variously shaped, some idling, some purposefully roving, some motionless, some whizzing. The tumbler was absolutely crowded with them.

'What is this, Ilona?'

'Just a glassful of our drinking water from the rainwater reservoir!'

'You mean we drink these? Poor little chaps!'

'Well, we boil the water first, so when we drink them they're already – not alive.' Ilona, avoiding the word 'dead', seemed already sorry to have raised the subject. She took the glass back from Edward and poured the water on the pavement.

Edward said, 'Perhaps we are like that, just tiny things in someone's glass –'

'By the way, if you're rescuing moths from the water butt, don't get them on your finger, use a leaf, then leave them somewhere to dry.'

'Hello, children,' said Mother May, returning from the greenhouses with a basket full of lettuces. Bettina followed her, her hands large with mud held out from her sides. Both of them wore their gardening aprons. 'Let's sit down for a moment.'

Recently they had set out some old teak seats, pallid with age and weather, upon the pavement near to the door.

'You all work too hard,' said Edward.

'Perhaps you are making us work less hard,' said Mother May, smiling, staring at him with her gentle light eyes.

'I'm demoralising you!'

'No, no, you are a messenger.'

'Mother May means you usher in a new era,' said Bettina, smiling too but not looking, fingering the mud off each of her hands. The mud fell on the ground in lumps which she neatly gathered together with her boot.

'Oh the birds sing so, they sing *so*,' said Ilona. 'And the collared doves, they say "Oh my God, oh my God"!'

'The swallows will soon be here,' said Mother May.

'Do the swallows sing?' asked Edward.

'Oh *yes*,' said Ilona, 'such beautiful mad muddled songs, you'll hear.'

Edward thought, will Jesse come before the swallows? Oh the anguish, oh my God –

'And the cowslips will be in flower,' said Mother May. 'This place is covered in cowslips.'

'They are becoming rare,' said Bettina, 'but not here.'

'Bettina once slapped some children she saw picking cowslips,' said Ilona.

Edward imagined that scene.

Bettina frowned. Mother May said, 'I must admit we pick a few, a *very* few.'

'Well, they're your cowslips,' said Edward.

'One doesn't feel quite like that,' said Mother May, 'the countryside belongs to everybody. But one does specially love what one has mixed one's labour with, and that's what we feel about Seegard.'

'And one has a *right* to it, too,' said Bettina.

Later Edward remembered this remark.

'And in the summer you go to the sea,' said Edward.

'We used to,' said Ilona.

'There's a ruined village where fisherfolk used to be,' said Mother May, 'and a little abandoned harbour.'

Edward liked 'fisherfolk'. 'I'd like to see a map of the area.'

'I don't think we have one, have we?' said Bettina.

'I don't think so,' said Mother May, 'I can't think where it would be.'

'You don't often go to London?'

'No,' said Mother May, 'if you live in paradise why go elsewhere? London for us represents all the empty idle noisy busyness of the world – here our lives are full of natural true busyness.'

'We try to carry out Jesse's ideals,' said Bettina.

'Jesse was a fiery socialist when he was young, we all were, true socialists, we worked for the good of society on the basis of simplicity.'

'We still are, we still do,' said Bettina. She lifted up her large head, like the head of a fine sleek keen-faced animal, and looked at Edward as if expecting him to challenge this.

'We never tire of hearing Mother May talk of the old days,' said Ilona.

'We exercise the body and the mind,' said Mother May. 'The health of the planet rests upon the health of the individual.'

'Eastern wisdom teaches that the body is important,' said Ilona.

173

'All right, Ilona!' said Bettina.

'We wanted to have a regular arts festival,' said Ilona, 'to express our ideals, with music and poetry and dance, and there's a big exhibition room for painting in the tower –'

'Why didn't you?' said Edward.

'It was too financially risky,' said Mother May.

'Besides,' said Bettina, 'as soon as you start organising something involving *other people* there are corrupt elements.'

'I'm sure you're right,' said Edward, 'you live such a free life here.'

'The girls are free beings,' said Mother May smiling. 'Jesse and I have seen to that. We stand for creativity and peace, continuity and cherishing. Here I think women have something special to give.'

'Mother May thinks that, compared with us, others are barbarians,' said Bettina, smiling at her mother.

'You are civilising me!' said Edward.

'Oh, we've only just started,' said Mother May. 'We'll teach you to paint, we'll teach you to *see* –'

'I think I can see better already. I can see Seegard better, I mean the building.'

'One has to learn to read it.'

'See it as a ship,' said Bettina.

'See it as a cathedral,' said Mother May.

'See it as a little town,' said Ilona.

They laughed.

'People didn't like it,' said Ilona. 'The *Architectural Review* said it was a mess.'

'It is both too complex and too simple for the vulgar taste,' said Mother May. 'One must see its *lines*. The best critics loved it. One has to learn new art forms.'

'"New styles of architecture, a change of heart", was one of Jesse's sayings,' said Bettina.

'I see it as a palace,' said Edward, 'the kind that vanishes!' He added, out of a sheer idle awkwardness which talking to all three of them made him feel. 'You know, my brother Stuart would like this place, it would suit him down to the ground!' The next moment a spear-like pain went through him. Why had he so stupidly, so ill-omenedly, mentioned

Stuart's name? Stuart was the very last person he ever wanted to see *here*. *Here*, on *Edward*'s territory.

Bettina rose. 'I think everything's ready.'

'Come along, children,' said Mother May. 'After lunch, Ilona, why don't you show Edward your jewellery? Take the afternoon off.'

'I like them very much,' said Edward looking at Ilona's anxious face. But he was not sure that he did.

'My style has changed a lot,' said Ilona. 'This is modern stuff, what they like now. Boys wear it too.'

Edward could not imagine himself, or indeed anyone, wearing the peculiar entities, made of steel, copper, aluminium and wood, which confronted him in Ilona's workshop on the ground floor of East Selden. 'How do you keep that on?' he said, lifting a long piece of grainy wood shaped like an elongated bird.

'Oh you put in on your wrist and tie it on with a scarf. Or hang it round your neck with a leather thong, you can tie it here, round the bird's foot.'

'But then the bird will be upside down.'

'Does that matter?'

'Do you make all the jewellery you all wear here?'

'Yes. I used to buy semi-precious stones, but it became too expensive. Then I made my own stones out of Araldite and dyed them. And I ordered Venetian beads and set them with beads of my own. But that's my old style. I still make wooden beads and carve them, I carve all sorts of wood that I find around here – and that pale bleached wood is driftwood. I make the flat bits into pictures if the wood is stained in an interesting way, or into amulets, like this.' She put into Edward's hand a little wooden square with a sort of Celtic animal incised upon it.

'I like that. Does Jesse wear your jewellery?'

'Oh yes. I used to do flower necklaces, cutting the metal and then hammering it, but it took too long. I used to do enamel too, Jesse taught me. Now I mainly do simpler things.'

'Those chains don't look simple, and those coiled bracelets.'

'The chains are easy. I use aluminium wire and copper wire, it's very pliable, you can twist it and plait it and spiral it in hundreds of ways. And I make these funny ornaments out of steel and nickel.'

'I can't imagine how –'

'With tools, silly. There are such things as hacksaws and hammers and pliers and pincers and tweezers and drills and files –'

'Yes, I can see them. And what's that?'

'A soldering iron.'

'And these things here are finished, they're pieces of jewellery? I suppose they could be hung onto the human form somehow.'

'You'd be surprised. This sort of steel triangle is very popular, and this square collar made of aluminium, and this copper anklet –'

'I wondered what it was – sorry, Ilona!'

'It's primitive really, like in Africa. It gets good prices. Dorothy, Mother May's friend, takes what we make to quite expensive shops. Jesse's name helps to sell it, of course, we call it Jesse Baltram crafts.'

'And did Jesse invent all this primitivism business?'

'He is the source of everything we do,' said Ilona solemnly.

It occurred to Edward for a moment suddenly to think, *perhaps Jesse does not exist at all*? Perhaps he's someone whom they invented, or something they just believe in, like God? Or perhaps the word in their language isn't a proper name but means something quite different? He looked across the thick heavily scored work bench at Ilona who was wearing a leather apron and playing with the soldering iron. She smiled at him. The moment passed. He looked at her small brown hands, at the numerous tools in their neat rows, at the glittering barbaric baubles. He said, 'I think you're marvellous, I can't think how you do it.' He thought, her bedroom must be just above this room. 'Ilona, there's such a strange place upon the hill, in that wood, a sort of long glade with a pillar in it.'

'Oh yes, you found that,' she said in quite a casual way looking at him affectionately. 'It's an old place.'

'How old?'

'I don't know. The Romans were there, and the Druids.'

'That stone, that pillar –?'

'The base part is Roman. The pillar is older.'

'Is it yours, your land, I mean?'

'Yes. The pillar had fallen down and Jesse set it up again, the tree men helped him. Some archaeologists were cross with us. But Jesse knew how it had been.'

'What do you call the place?'

'Well, Jesse called the stone the Lingam Stone, and so we call it the Lingam Place.'

'What does "lingam" mean?' said Edward who knew and wanted to see if she did.

'It's just a name that Jesse invented, he invents names.'

'Like Interfectory!' Edward had by now, after questioning his memory, worked out the meaning of that word. By its Latin derivation it did not mean 'eating place' or 'conversing place', it meant 'killing place'. Another schoolboy joke perhaps perpetrated by Jesse upon his innocent family. What did such a sense of humour signify? He went on, 'That thing in the Interfec over the fireplace, that piece of wood, Jesse carved that didn't he? But what does the motto mean, *I am here. Do not forget me.*'

'I don't know.'

'Who is here? Who is speaking?'

'I suppose it's a general love message, something mediaeval perhaps, Jesse is inspired by all sorts of historical things.'

'Ilona, when will he come –?'

'Oh, very soon.'

'And we'll have a festival with wine?'

'Yes, yes. I must go and rest now –'

'May I come up and see your room?'

'No, it's too untidy.'

Thinking about Ilona and her room Edward wandered back to West Selden, and then through the little door in Transition that led out of the back of the house between 'Selden Square' and 'Stable Square'. He took the gorse-bushy path toward the fen, the way he had walked on his first day, which now seemed so long ago. He passed through the celandine meadow where the withered flowers were already overgrown by lush green grass. He looked back, as he had done before, at the irregular shape of the house; the majestic cathedral-like forms of the barn and the tower made sense, but the two jutting courtyards and the domestic village-like tumble of Transition, its messiness visible from this side, were certainly harder to 'read'. He tried to see it as a sort of town, but it gave little satisfaction. Perhaps a ship in harbour with harbour buildings. He set off toward the line of willows. He had of course walked this way several times in the interim but had been stopped by flood water and had never set eyes on the sea. He very much wanted to see the sea, and to find the little harbour where the 'fisherfolk' once were. Today as he passed through the willow screen he saw that the flood had receded a bit, but a low layer of mist hung over the further view. Against the grey cloudy sky above the mist a dazzling flight of white doves, caught by a momentary gleam of sun, flashed over the fen. The dark sinewy mats, upon which he had precariously walked before, were covered now in an intense green sprouting of reedy spears. Between them something like 'dry land' was emerging at last, and Edward could pick his way fairly easily upon humps of dried mud, stepping over rivulets of black water, and finding here and there dark pools where red-beaked moorhens swam jerkily away, flashing their white tails in signals of alarm. As he strode long-legged he was thinking about what he had witnessed in the sacred grove. He had seen Ilona dance. But had she really been, as he seemed to recall, floating in the air? Could that have been simply an optical illusion? Had he here, at Seegard, come to a place where he imagined things that didn't happen – or where things happened which did not usually happen? When he at last met Jesse would it all *come clear* to him, would his judgment of the women, lately become more clouded, be clarified? It was as if Jesse were a prophet or sacred king whose presence would purify the state, making what seemed good be good, and what was spiritually ambiguous into something altogether holy. Yet was not this way of looking itself a product of the Seegard atmosphere?

178

Oh why *can't* I see the sea, thought Edward, if only this accursed mist could roll away. He was close to the mist now, could see it ahead of him, moved by a slight wind in big separated slowly tumbling masses. The mud was still firm to walk upon, but the pools and rivulets were becoming larger. Coarse salty seagrass was growing here and there and a low plant which Ilona had shown him near the house called bog myrtle. A little sun, released again by the low plump clouds, their sides lightened a little by some reflection, perhaps from the sea, brought so much colour suddenly into the dun scene: red stripes upon the reeds, tall almost fern-like mounds of vivid green moss, succulents with thick pointed blueish leaves, orange lichen upon soaked wood, yellow waterlily pads, pink duckweed. A flurry of activity in one of the pools evidenced a mass of young tadpoles. Distantly inland a lark was signing. From toward the sea came an intermittent booming noise, which Edward thought must be made by some bird. Kneeling down upon drying mud to look at the tadpoles, he saw something floating which turned out to be a starling. He picked it up by one long outstretched wing and laid it, so limp and dead, upon a bed of young green reeds. He thought, so birds too can drown. As he rose, with some difficulty, as the mud had become damp under the pressure of his knees, he felt a little giddy, and blinked for a moment against a sensation of flashing lights. He realised he was feeling cold and decided it was time to go back.

It was then that he saw something very surprising not far off upon his left. He took it at first for a post, or a thin tree, an unusual sight in this part of the fen. The mist had moved, slowly rolling itself over in fuzzy greyish-white balls, and the object was only intermittently to be seen. Edward stared, then walked a few paces, cautiously watching his footing, and stared again. He decided that the motionless thing was a person, a human being. A faceless monochrome figure of which he could not tell whether it were turned towards him or not. Jesse perhaps, he thought at once, Jesse landed from the sea, at an abandoned harbour. Or Jesse, newly come from the house, hurrying out into the fen to look for . . . his son. The figure was quite still and now seemed to be looking

179

towards him. A slight shift and lightening of the mist then revealed a figure in trousers, and a blue mackintosh, feet set apart, who might have been of either sex. Edward leapt across a channel of murky water, steadied on an island, looked again and saw a *girl* fairly near and looking straight at him. His first instinct was that it *must* be either Mother May, Bettina or Ilona. They were *the only* women in this part of the world. Only they never wore trousers. Besides he could see that this was a girl with straight not very long brown hair. He could not see the face clearly, but she was certainly not one of his sisters. A girl who was *not a sister*, standing there with her hands in her pockets, out in the misty watery emptiness of the fen, and looking at him, as he looked at her. At that moment Edward lost his balance and slid down the slippery muddy side of the mound upon which he was standing. One foot descended into water. Stepping upon dark earth which yielded like fudge he gracelessly scrambled up onto something like *terra firma*. He looked about again, and again and again, but the mist rolled on and the girl had vanished.

'BEING YOUR SLAVE, what should I do but tend upon the hours and times of your desire? I have no precious time at all to spend, nor services to do till you require. Nor dare I question with my jealous thought where you may be, or your affairs suppose –'

'That'll do, Harry. Besides,' said Midge, 'you always know where I am –'

'Do I?'

'And you have no cause to be jealous. And you are not a slave. *I* am the slave.'

It was one of their days. Thomas was at a conference in Bristol, Meredith was at school. Midge and Harry were in the spare room, Midge was wearing her red and purple imperial robe. Harry had only just arrived. He had taken off his tie. He had let himself in with his back-door key. He liked Midge to wait upstairs like a captive bride. Who saw him enter the house? No one. He came by a tree-shaded back alley through a gate into the walled garden. He wore various disguises. He liked that. He also possessed a front-door key, but that was just symbolic.

Midge was shaken and frightened because she had had a fall. Shopping that morning she had, in the incomprehensible way in which such things happen, caught her toe on a paving stone and fallen violently upon her knees, then full length, her

181

cheek and elbow were grazed upon the pavement, her handbag went flying and disgorged its contents, one shoe came off. People rushed to help her up, to gather the little personal trinkets out of her bag, she felt a fool with her stockings torn and a bloody knee. 'Are you all right, would you like to sit down, would you like a taxi?' people asked, as if she were an old woman. 'I'm not hurt, thank you,' she said, face burning, tears in her eyes, trying to conceal her knee, her ruined stockings. She hobbled away, watched by sympathetic spectators. The shock was not just the impact, but the awful sensation of falling itself, the utterly helpless movement through the air, the foreknowledge of being spreadeagled on the ground, smashed. Supposing one jumped from a high building: a form of suicide she often considered. Harry had been sympathetic, but not at enough length. This evening, even late this evening when he came back tired from Bristol, Thomas would inspect the wounded knee, bathe it and cover it and pronounce some judgment. He would inspect the grazes upon her cheek and her arm, and her hands all rough and reddened by warding off the ground. He would enquire about all her sensations. Of course that was because he was a doctor, yet it was comforting too. Her hands were still hot and smarting, her knee was painful and stiff. She felt even now near to tears.

'Everyone thinks Edward is at Quitterne,' said Harry. That was the name of the McCaskervilles' country cottage. 'But you say he isn't.'

'He isn't!'

'All right, I believe you!'

'Then why do you say "I say" he isn't?'

'I hate to think you might be keeping Thomas's secrets.'

'You don't seem to care much where he is.'

'Of course I do. But I know he'll be all right because he's like me, full of expanding curiosity, absolutely connected with the world. Not like Stuart, Stuart's a Faust *manqué*. He'd sell his soul to be a great physicist. As that can't be arranged, he can't be everything so he'll be nothing. Really he's power mad. If he wants to be *encanaillé* I can't stop him, it's the virtuous pose that's so sickening. And it won't work. He

182

doesn't realise how much people will hate him. A child who's born without hands can cope somehow, be helped by society and praised too. Stuart was born without – something – and he'll be pecked to death for it. No he won't – he might want that – he's just a mess. He'll be arrested for molesting a child. I don't mean he will molest a child, but people will think he has. They'll see him as sinister.'

'Never mind him, *he's* all right. What about poor Edward –'

'Edward is Thomas's business now.'

'You're jealous of Thomas.'

'Amazing discovery!'

'I mean about Edward. And you're jealous of me about Edward. You always keep him away from me.'

'Only for his good. You're such a honey pot. I don't want him to perish with his wings soaked in honey.'

'Edward kissed me quite passionately once after a dance.'

'So you've told me several times, so shut up. Are you going to say you were out to lunch with anyone? What were you doing all day, when Thomas asks?'

'Thomas knows what I do all day, I dust the drawing room, I do the flowers, I paint my nails and shop.'

'I like to think of you as idle and artificial, an idle woman in a harem, a bored prostitute yawning as she waits for custom.'

'You want to think I have no real occupation except waiting for you.'

'Isn't it true?'

'Yes.'

'I wish we'd established earlier on that we sometimes lunch together.'

'It's not too late.'

'It is, we're getting past expedients of that sort, they're out of date. You say you're a rotten liar –'

'But I wouldn't be lying if I just said I'd seen you –'

'You live a sort of permanent double life where everything is true except that it isn't. When you're with me Thomas doesn't exist, when you're with Thomas I don't exist. If the deception succeeds perfectly you can dream that nothing's happening, that you're innocent.'

'I am innocent.'

'Oh, Midge –!'

'I mean, I have no strategy.'

'Exactly, no real plan, no future for *us* – do you realise how unhappy you make me?'

'You could always go away –'

'You know I can't and won't – Oh don't *cry*, for God's sake!'

'My knee hurts.'

These magnetic unstoppable quarrels were a mode of being together, essential when other contacts were in abeyance, self-perpetuating because neither dared to leave any dangerous remark in the air lest it should seem to have some final awful significance, quarrels like physical contact, like wrestling, dealing wounds known not to be fatal, not like love-making, lacking in purpose and achieved repose, nerve-rending, destructive, yet appearing as necessary and unavoidable expressions of their love for each other.

'It's your double-think about Thomas that paralyses everything. You've told me you don't communicate with him, that he doesn't notice you, that he's obsessed with his patients – must our lives depend on his forever being carefully fed with packs of lies?'

'I've got to know more than Thomas, I couldn't bear his knowing it all, I couldn't manage it –'

'Midge, *think*. Are we to spend the rest of our lives being deceivers and fakers? *We*, with *our* love for each other? He's got to know sometime!'

'There's a cold streak in Thomas, if he found out he might pretend not to mind, but then he'd plan a revenge –'

'And murder us! Your trouble is you want everyone to love and admire you, you want both of us, you want us all to go on loving you whatever you do, you can't bear the idea of losing Thomas's esteem. But try to think how much it's worth. You married Thomas in a dream because you were impressed by his prestige, by his power, by his being grand and older. But Midge, you've grown up now, surely, you can see through him. He sees through himself. That's why he keeps talking about retiring. He plays at being a great healer, but in his heart he knows it's all a charade. You said once he'd wanted to be a writer. People obsessed by power envy what artists know by instinct. Psychoanalysis attracts failed artists.'

'Well, it hasn't attracted you.'

'Midge, don't needle me.'

'I'm sorry. I dreamt about that white horseman again.'

'Besides, Thomas is probably a repressed homosexual. Think how fascinated he is by Mr Blinnet and now by Stuart and Edward. He likes those boys he can dominate. He's got Edward hidden away somewhere. Why has he got so many male patients? If you left him he'd bless you, he'd heave a sigh of relief and start life again as a queer. That's what he's made of. You've both made a mistake.'

'I don't think this about Thomas. You've just made it up, it's your latest idea.'

'Women don't realise how many men are homosexual, it's a closely guarded secret. Even that great sex idol Jesse Baltram had a homosexual phase, he was shacked up with some miserable painter who died of drink.'

'He's had lots of women patients, there's that politician's wife –'

'I've told you, all you have to do is be with me all the time and we shall annihilate Thomas, we shall make him not to be and never to have been! I'll invent a past for you which simply rubs him out. You know that's possible. Christ, why can't you just have some bloody courage? All you've got to do is walk through a short unpleasantness with Thomas and reach *me*. Just keep *looking* at me. You can't be that much afraid of him. It's not like walking through a fire. Oh I know, you lie to me about him like you lie to him about me, you can't help it, it's a law of nature. And we both want to believe you. I can't measure what he means to you, I can't *see* it, that's the trouble. If you still want it to be secret there must be reasons. God, do you want to spare his feelings? If you love me that's a nonsense. Can't we be honest and truthful at last, you know how I hate deception. Once we start telling the truth we shall be *gods*. Love must be obeyed in the end, so why not now? The years are going by which we could spend together, why should we waste them in frustration and unhappiness and stupid endless quarrels? You love me, not Thomas. Thomas is just a habit. Of course you're connected with him but *you love me*.'

'If only we'd met earlier . . .'

'Stop saying that, I forbid you to say it ever again, it's an irrelevance, a mindless insult to our love *now*.'

Midge, with her silky robe clutched round her, was sitting on a bed. Harry was standing near the open door, he avoided the window where the soft spring breeze breathing through a slit was gently stirring the curtains. He had now taken off his shirt and kicked off his shoes. He thought, what is she thinking? She thought, what is he thinking? She was thinking, of course I love Harry, I love him absolutely, but if only I could stop worrying and caring about Thomas. Oh why do I have to suffer so when I just want to be happy! If only I could care just a little less. I can't *see* my feeling for Thomas any more, it's become dark and in the dark it's diminishing, like a little animal left somewhere to die and you come every day and hope that it's dead and it's still twitching and it's still breathing, and oh I *mustn't* think about it like that. I must untie myself from Thomas, undo myself, quietly patiently *thoroughly* untie every little bond, cut every little vein. I must make a great blank where he is, make him into a zombie in my mind, then it won't hurt so. I must decide, I will decide, I have decided. Harry was thinking, a little more and a little more, and surely she is helping me, she is trying to. A little more irritation and mistrust and resentment and fear – she must learn to hate him. She must see him simply as a barrier to her happiness. Then she will come. But it's time for a new move too. I'll *force* her gradually along the road. Of course she *has* decided, and I want her to yield at her own moment. But I must force the pace – and she wants me to. I wonder would it be a good idea to send an anonymous letter to Thomas to stir things up?

'Midge, don't feel guilty, I don't. There are things which are my business and no one else's. There are things which are *our* business. I'm sick with love for you, pity me. We must be more together or I'll die. I've found a little flat in Chelsea in one of those huge blocks where no one wants to know anyone, it's much more secret than here, and it'll be just ours alone, and I can cook for you, I so much want to –'

Midge raised her head, tossing back her mane and releasing the clutched robe; she disordered the bed, plucking at it with a distraught hand, and her face wrinkled in frightened evasive anxiety. 'Harry, you mustn't, I won't have it. I won't come –'

'Why ever not? You *will* come – all right, I haven't even bought in yet! And I want that weekend, I *must* have it, just two nights, Christ how little I ask, and you won't even give me!'

'Darling, not the flat, I can't yet –'

'Then the weekend.'

'One night –'

'Midge, you are being *senselessly* mean. You said Thomas would be in Geneva from Friday to Monday, and Meredith's going to Wales with his school chum –'

'One night – this time – you do understand –'

'I love you, my heart turns over and over for you, so I suppose I've got to understand even if I don't! You belong to me, don't you?'

'Yes. Oh my sweetheart, I don't want to upset you and torment you. You know I just say all the awful things so as to get rid of them, so that you can sweep them away and make them not be.'

'Well, that's one way of arguing I suppose!' He knelt down, capturing her hands while the robe fell apart. 'Oh – my queen –' He kissed the captive hands, turning them to and fro, while Midge gazed at his bent head, his glowing hair, with puckered fascination. She let out a wailing sigh. 'What is it, my Cleopatra?'

'Sometimes I feel we're doomed lovers –'

'Shut up.'

'Sometimes it's like acting in a play – a wonderful play – or as if life had become huge like a myth –'

'That's what's called heightened consciousness. All colours are brighter where we are. We are a king and queen when we're together. How amazing sex is, how absolutely *odd*, this total attraction between two people, we're so *lucky*. My little love, my sweet love, when we're in bed there's a moment when heaven tears us apart like the unrolling of a celestial scroll upon the last day on the angel's trumpet. Well, it's that moment in all of our life now, it's our time, to change our being, to transmute it all into everlasting happiness and pure joy, our metamorphosis, like the substantial change of the bread and the wine. The bell will ring for us, my darling, the heavens will open for us – It's all so close now, it's just an inch away.'

'Harry, you do love me, don't you, you will love me always, it's not just an adventure –?'

'Christ, if I haven't convinced you of that –! I want you to be my wife, I want to be your husband, I want to be Meredith's father, I'll love you and cherish you both forever and ever –'

'Thomas used to say you just wanted to destroy yourself –'

'Don't quote Thomas at me! *He* is the destroyer, find out your life-myth and I'll destroy it for you, that's his motto.'

'Yes. Thomas could be a danger to us.'

'No, no, it's a charade. I remember Thomas saying his favourite literary heroes were Achilles and Mr Knightly! He may imagine he's Achilles, but really he's just a feeble version of Mr Knightly. A gentleman of course. That should stop you worrying! *I'm* Achilles!'

' "Said Tweed to Till –" '

'What?'

'That thing about the two rivers that Thomas used to recite. "Said Tweed to Till, 'What makes you run so still?' Said Till to Tweed, 'Though you run with speed, I run slow, for each man you kill, I kill two.'"'

'I remember, Thomas imagined he was Till, I suppose. But he's not. Now stop arguing. Come on!'

Midge got up reassembling her robe. 'I'm just going to the bathroom.'

Harry was unloosening his belt. The window curtains were blowing gently. He thought, I love her, she loves me, yet we're in hell. It's so unjust. We're in a machine, it's mechanical, it's evil. Yet outside, beyond, there freedom, there's happiness, there's goodness. He felt wearied out with the strain of her argument and with his love-longing which had so much sadness in it. He saw again the empty boat receding, sailing away on its own.

Midge emerged from the room and walked across the landing toward the bathroom. She stopped.

There was something at the top of the stairs, a standing figure. It was Meredith, motionless, erect, stiff as a soldier, his eyes wide, his lips apart.

Harry's voice came clearly from the bedroom through the open door. 'Hurry up, darling, I can't wait!'

Midge, her face blazing, stared at her son. Then she lifted one finger and put it to her lips.

BETTINA HAD MENDED the tractor, and now the car, an old Humber, had come out of its garage and was actually sitting on the pavement outside the house, crushing the cushions of sweet-smelling thyme under its wheels. The early afternoon sun was shining. Jesse had not come home.

Today was a special day, Edward had been told. Not a festival day, but the day in the month when Mother May and Bettina went to town (by bus in winter, by car in summer) to buy the few household necessaries which they could not provide themselves. Usually, he understood, Ilona went too, but today she was to stay to keep him company. To keep an eye on him? What did they imagine he might get up to? The question of taking Edward to the town had not been raised. Did they think he'd run away?

The pair left behind had plenty of occupy them. Edward was to weed the vegetable garden, then saw wood, then if there was time begin painting the outside of the greenhouse. Ilona was to 'clean out' Transition, after which there was a pile of mending waiting for her in the Interfec.

'Don't forget my new toothbrush,' said Ilona, 'I want a blue one.'

'Right-oh. Come on, Mother May, get in.'

'Be good, you two children,' called Mother May, climbing in.

'Look, look,' cried Ilona, as the car began to move, 'a swallow!'

The Humber turned laboriously and set off down the track.

Edward and Ilona waved, then turned back toward the house. Edward had a strange free yet uneasy feeling which he wondered if Ilona shared. They stood awkwardly at the door for a moment. Then Edward said, 'Well, I suppose I must get on with that weeding.' He had not told anyone of his girl-apparition of the previous day.

Ilona went inside without saying anything and Edward found a hoe in one of the sheds behind the ilex trees and went on to the vegetable garden where he started to make weak spiritless pokes at the weeds which were now growing lustily between the wispy rows of carrots and onions. He was conscious of a strong physical feeling of anxiety about the length of his stay at Seegard. Was not being here with these women beginning to have something ridiculous about it, like having too prolonged a holiday? In spite of his acute anxiety about his father he did feel rather 'at home'; yet not as one being healed, taking it more as an interval which put off what it professed to effect. The Seegard magic was sedative, making him forget Mark's death, unhappen it. This place, these sisters, this mother, were all a dreamwork he would have to undo. Time itself was becoming a burden, a kind of continuous moral pain. But of course he was waiting for Jesse, that was the point, and before Jesse came there could be no question of his leaving. But did not this unexplained absence indicate an indifference to Edward on Jesse's part, for surely he must know that Edward had arrived? There were so many possible unpleasant explanations – the mistress in the south of France, the alternative ménage, some addiction, gambling or drink. Or perhaps Jesse was in prison somewhere, there was some disgraceful secret. Edward paused; the sun was warm, and even his idle scrapings had made the perspiration run quietly down his temples and onto his cheeks. He smeared the sweat off with his hand, and surveyed the grove of poplar trees, now lightly covered with trembling young leaves the colour of *vin rosé*. Then he saw, beyond some bushes, the flicker of a brown dress. It was Ilona, who had just disappeared along the path which led to the river. So Ilona was playing truant; and there could be no doubt where she was going. Edward dropped his hoe and ran to a point, near the old tennis court, where he could see along the path. Ilona was hurrying, almost out of sight. He did not call out, nor was he tempted to follow her. He feared to disturb her, and to disturb in himself the vivid memory of her dance in the sacred place.

He now stood still for a while, thinking about the girl he had seen in the fen. Would he see her again? Should he go out to the same place to see if she were there? Who was she? No doubt she was some random tripper, people would be on holidays already. What was odd was that in all the time he had been at Seegard he had seen no one else, not even the tree men. Then he was struck by an even stronger emotion, a realisation which brought the blood to his cheeks in an almost guilty rush: it was that for the first time since his arrival there he was *alone at Seegard*!

Edward turned promptly and began to walk back toward the house. He was not sure what he wanted to do, but he was sure that he very much wanted to profit by this remarkable piece of liberty to do something *illicit*, to *find out* something that was hidden. He thought, I'll go to the Interfectory and try to find a map. They said there was no map of the area but I bet there is. Entering the Atrium Edward paused for a moment and listened. Of course there was nothing to hear, but he felt a shudder which seemed to come from the house itself and enter his body. He took off his wellingtons and put on indoor shoes and padded across the slate floor in the direction of the Interfec. He opened the door cautiously and entered the silent room. *I am here. Do not forget me.* He tiptoed across and opened the door of Bettina's workroom. He had never actually entered this room, though he had been as far as the doorway to receive Bettina's instructions or be given things to carry. He admired the big wooden work-table, much bigger than Ilona's, and the wooden boards upon the walls, looking like modern works of art, which supported sets of tools upon hooks. Another art exhibit was a large old dresser bearing rows of pots of paint of different colours, from which Edward that very morning had been give some white paint for the greenhouse. The windows were, by Seegard standards, remarkably clean and devoid of spiders.

He sped across the room and opened the next door. The next room was darker because of the numerous cobwebs upon the window. It was empty except for a large loom. So here the stuff was woven from which the famous dresses were made! Edward knew nothing about looms. He approached it and tried to move a piece of the machinery, to tilt it up, then slide it along, but it would not budge, it appeared to be jammed. Then he became aware of the soft feel of thick dust, and of long trails left upon the wood by his questing fingers. He stepped quickly back and ineffectually dabbed with his fingertips to hide the marks, then rubbed his hands on his trousers. The loom was rigid and very dusty, it had clearly not been in use for a long time. Yet the women always spoke as if they still used it. And those dresses – he had already noticed how much they were darned and mended – their beautiful woven dresses were *old*. Edward hastily retreated, closing the doors carefully behind him, and fled back to the Interfectory.

Here again was the creepy accusing silence, in which Edward stood still a while, moving only his eyes. Then he began to open the various drawers, looking for something or other, oh yes a map of the region, and here indeed, well buried, there was one, an old one evidently as it showed the railway but not the motorway. He hid it again for future use and began to look about for other treasures. He took down the photo of Jesse which looked so uncannily like himself and studied it for a while. The aquiline nose, the straight lock of dark hair, the shape, even the expression of the thin face – only the eyes were different, Edward's being long and narrow, Jesse's larger and more, even surprisingly, round. Of course he won't look like that *now*, Edward thought. The young Jesse looked at him mockingly – perhaps saying 'Yes, young fellow you were conceived last night. What a night it was! You'll be lucky if *you* ever have such a night!' Edward replaced the picture. Then he looked at the door which led into the tower. He had not, since the first day, worried about the tower. The women were clearly determined, doubtless on Jesse's orders, not to let him in. For all Edward knew, perhaps *they* were not allowed in! Edward felt increasingly sure that Jesse did not want Edward to see the tower until he, its

193

master, came back. But now. Edward listened again, then tried the door. It was locked. Well, locked doors have keys, and where do keys live? In pockets, in handbags, in drawers, on hooks, on shelves, swinging from someone's waist – they had to be somewhere, somewhere perhaps near to the door they opened. Edward tried the drawers again, wriggling his hand in with outstretched fingers, but no key. He stood on a chair and tried the ample ledge above the door, dislodging a stack of dust. He looked about. The big dark oak chimney-piece seemed replete with hiding places. He reached up and thrust his hand in behind the carved message *I am here*. And here indeed there was a key. Shuddering with excitement he went to the door and, with some difficulty since his hand was trembling so, inserted the key in the lock. It entered smoothly. He turned it. The door opened.

Edward felt almost faint with guilt and anxiety. He ran to look into the Atrium to be sure there was nobody there. He ran back. He hesitated on the threshold. Suppose Mother May and Bettina were to come back early? Suppose Ilona found him? But Ilona wouldn't tell. Anyway here he was, over the threshold, *in* the tower, standing in the big hexagonal lowest room. He wondered what to do about the door, whether to take the key with him. He dared not shut it. He decided to leave the key in the keyhole and prop the door open with a rush-bottomed stool which was to hand. The idea of being *trapped inside* was vaguely and alarmingly present. The unpartitoned space of the ground floor was clearly an art gallery, the 'exhibition room' Ilona had mentioned. But what immediately caught his attention was the unusual up-and-down design of the ceiling intended, as he soon realised, to accommodate windows at different levels, rising here and there in shafts and boxes to allow light in from above, and also descending presumably to accommodate windows which lighted the superior floor. Edward recalled the irregular apparently random spacing of the windows seen from outside. The 'cubist' or 'coffered' effect, painted grey blue and red, was startling and pleasant. The walls were white, the wooden floor painted grey. The place echoed, and though he walked cautiously, his footsteps made an uncomfortable noise. The room felt desolate and rather damp and the exhibits, to which he now attended, dusty and un-looked-at. There were some smallish pieces of sculpture in wood and stone, a few in bronze, which seemed to Edward's untutored eye rather old-fashioned. Some of the female nudes might once have been thought daring, there were also entwined pairs, some human, some human and animal, including an interesting Leda and swan in a roundel; but if these were the erotica mentioned by Ilona, they were certainly not likely to astonish anyone now. The pictures were more rewarding. Edward inspected the abstracts, fiercely painted in the yellowest yellow and the blackest black he had ever seen, with occasional startling patches of blue and green. The heroic or 'royal' pictures attracted him more, particularly some large crowned heads, with round eyes and beards, richly and thickly painted, certainly self-portraits, and big grotesque heads of women, mournful, tearful or vindictive. Sometimes the bearded king was represented face to face with a large monstrous animal, ferocious or touchingly sad, which he seemed to be questioning. Sometimes the two were enlaced awkwardly falling or struggling together, fighting or embracing. In other versions a council of seated kings con-fronted a magnificent dragon, perhaps their captive, perhaps their captor. There were also large epic pictures, gorgeously and violently coloured, representing battle scenes, decorated by beautiful flags and heraldic clothing, wherein women and dog-headed men mingled, fighting bloodily with knives, battles elsewhere transmuted into erotic tangles, possibly murders, in luridly lit rooms. The 'late-Titian' style was distinguished by a larger sober light a sort of intensely luminous beige, flecked by squares of radiant cream and blue, depicting twilit halls or woodlands where quasi-classical scenes of violence were being enacted, women watching a man devoured by dogs, a girl watching a man caught by a snake, women pursued by humanoid animals, a youth watching a screaming girl becoming a tree; and here Edward also recognised much altered versions of early motifs, the snake emerging from the wheel, a frightening sphinx dis-covered in a stone recess, a winged head caught in a net, drowned animals, appalling adolescents, callous or terrified witnesses, deformed people sitting quietly together, stunned by hopelessness and fear, sometimes now watched through doors or windows by beautiful children, heartless, probably soulless, carrying emblems, flags or flowers, sometimes turning toward the spectator holding up some ambiguous talisman between finger and thumb. The later 'tantric' pictures were distinguished by extremely luminous dark blues and golds, seas of colour in which oval eggs floated, grew, diminished, or exploded. No Christian themes were visible, nor any recognisable portraits of the inhabitants of Seegard, unless their features could be traced in the mourning heads of women. Edward was extremely impressed. The erotic force of the pictures made him feel weak at the knees.

Fleeing from these images he made his way to a fine very ornate spiral staircase which he climbed to the first floor. Here again the room occupied the whole of the hexagonal space, but was separated into different levels according to the position of the windows and the irregular formation of the ceiling below. Where he stepped off the staircase there was what appeared to be an old nursery, absolutely crammed with dusty toys, dolls, animals, puppets, miniature furniture, rather eccentric dolls' houses, tiny pairs of scissors, little hands. As Edward hurried past these and up some steps into what was clearly an artist's studio he thought how odd it was for Jesse to have children playing just where he was trying to work. Then he realised that of course the toys were *Jesse's* toys, the 'nursery' *his* nursery, ancillary to his imagination and his art. Looking back he now noticed some Australasian and African masks propped against the wall, and little gaudily painted figures of Indian gods. The studio, where there was also a large desk, looked reassuringly ordinary since it looked just like an artist's studio with an easel set up, canvases stacked, jars full of brushes, tubes of paint together with a palette lying on a chair. There was no picture on the easel, but a scattering of pen and pencil drawings on the floor. The 'game' played with the ceiling had been modified at this level, where only two steeply slanting shafts accommodated windows which exceeded the general height of the room. All the windows, six of them, were masked by a variety of shades and blinds to modify the light. Here it at once occurred to Edward that out of one of these windows he ought to be able to see the sea. He crossed the room, uncertain of his orientation. There was a fine view inland, along the track to the tarmac road and showing a church on the far side of the road which Edward had not discovered and upon which the sun was now shining. But when he went to the opposite window the mist again obscured the view and he could see only as far as he had already walked, scarcely beyond the line of willows.

He turned to look at the drawings lying about on the floor. These, looking rather old and faded, were mainly of nudes, and he picked up one, representing a nude woman with longish tangled hair and large sad eyes. Edward wondered who the woman was, Mother May perhaps. He realised he had never thought of Mother May as Jesse's model, the idea seemed quite improper. But it did not at all resemble her. It then flashed upon his mind that this might be, then he felt must be, a picture of his mother. He promptly dropped it. Looking more closely at the scatter of drawings, they all seemed to be of the same woman. He picked up another one, and looking at the sad face felt suddenly a unique and special feeling of guilt and sorrow. He had never known his mother, he had never worried about her, she never appeared in his dreams. Chloe had been Harry's wife. He had never thought of her as Jesse's mistress. With an instinctive desire not to be hurt and saddened he had early banished Chloe's ghost. Harry had never wanted Edward to mope or feel deprived, but to be happy, as he, Harry, always contrived to be. How good Harry had been to him, how much Harry's love had protected him, came to Edward in the same thought and he said to himself: Harry was my father, and my mother too. Who then was Chloe, and who was Jesse? Would he ever discuss Chloe with Jesse? Was it possible that Jesse had taken out these old drawings of Chloe when he knew that Edward was coming? Edward laid the faded piece of paper on the floor. He thought, Oh God, I've got enough troubles – and he turned away.

He now looked at the big flat-topped desk. He felt uneasy as he did so, realising fully for the first time since his adventure began how improperly he was acting, doing exactly what Jesse had wanted him not to do, prying into Jesse's own private place, looking perhaps at his letters, or possibly worse at his unfinished work. The desk was untidy, scattered with sheets of paper, pads, notebooks, ink bottles, trays full of pens, pencils, crayons. Edward then noticed that it was dusty, *very* dusty. The desk, like the loom, was covered in dust. The desk was dusty, so was the easel, and chair beside it, and the palette and the pile of sketches on the floor. The pictures propped against the wall had high crests of dust upon them. The paint on the palette was hard and discoloured by dust. The studio was desolate, unused, abandoned. Edward, wanting to sit down, found another chair beside the wall, removed a sketch-book from it, and sat. He felt sick with fear and amazement. So Jesse was not only not here, but *had not been here* for a very long time. So Jesse had left them and they dared not tell him? Jesse was not the longed-for father, the healer, the hero-priest, the benevolent all-powerful king – he was indeed the devil, as Edward had been taught as a child. In any case he was not here, Edward had been deceived and made a fool of, Seegard was no longer Jesse's home, the palace was empty. Jesse had mocked *them*, and had now mocked *him*, Edward, coming so far on this vain pilgrimage from which he had hoped so much. Jesse was *really* elsewhere, in some quite other house, with other women, perhaps other children. Only his ghost was left at Seegard. But then why had *they* set up such a deception? It then occurred to Edward *they were all three mad*. Could that be? Or was *he* mad? He sat, holding the sketch-book in his hand. Looking down at it he saw a drawing, a beautiful calm not at all sinister drawing of a girl, fully clothed, standing beside an open window. She looked a bit like Ilona. It was then that it occurred to Edward that it was he who was mad. The deserted studio didn't mean no Jesse. Jesse had simply gone to paint elsewhere, perhaps moved his studio higher up in the tower, into a room above where the light was better, or different, where he felt different, starting a new phase, making a change. He jumped up, put the sketch-book back on the chair and made for the spiral staircase.

As his head emerged at the next level he saw at once that here everything was indeed different, the space had been partitioned, and what Edward could see had the air of the entrance hall of a flat. The floor was carpeted and an open door revealed a bathroom. There was a small table between two closed doors. The carpet was clean, the table dusted. Edward opened a door into a kitchen, and another into a sitting room. The next door which he tried refused to open. Edward pushed it and rattled it a little, then saw that there was a key in the keyhole. The door was evidently locked on the outside. He turned the key and opened the door. The room was a bedroom. The bed was opposite to the door, and lying on the bed, propped up on pillows, was a bearded man, looking straight at Edward with dark round eyes.

Edward thought later on that in that second of utter shock he had understood everything. He certainly came, very soon after, to understand much. He moved into the room, closing the door behind him. The man on the bed kept staring at him intently and moving his lips. His face expressed an intense emotion which Edward thought of afterwards, perhaps at the time, as a kind of apologetic distress, a kind of frustrated politeness, which was also expressive of deep grief. Edward, shuddering with emotion, approached the bed and stopped. The red lips, a little frothy, moved, but no sound came. The large eyes besought Edward to hear, to respond. At last a sound came out which, heard together with the pleading expression, seemed like a question. Edward grasped the sound. It was an attempt at his own name. He said, 'Edward. Yes, I am Edward. I am your son.' The helpless lips moved, adumbrating a smile, and a shaking hand was outstretched. Edward took the weak hand in his. Then he knelt down beside the bed and buried his face in the blanket. He felt the other hand touch his hair. He burst into tears.

'Please try to *understand*, Edward.'
'But why didn't you *tell* me —'

'We wanted you to feel at home here, to be quiet, to be peaceful, to be with *us*, to see what Seegard *was*, what it *stood for* –'

'We wanted the house to make its impression,' said Bettina, 'we wanted to establish you here first of all.'

'We wanted you to be *ours*,' said Ilona. 'We thought you might run away.'

'Why ever –?'

'If we had confronted you with it at the start,' said Mother May, 'it might have been too much for you. We were afraid you'd leave at once, simply hate the place and never find out how good it could be for you.'

'Is it true,' said Bettina, 'that you found the key yourself? Are you sure Ilona didn't let you in?'

'Of course I found it myself! Ilona has told you she didn't let me in!'

'Ilona doesn't always tell the truth,' said Bettina.

They were sitting in the hall at one end of the long table, near to the forest of potted plants. Edward had not spent long with his father. Jesse had not spoken again. Edward was still kneeling beside him when Mother May burst into the room, gorgon-faced with anger, and ordered Edward to go.

'And we didn't want you to see him like that,' Mother May went on. She was calm now, her face gentle and lucid. 'We wanted him to be more presentable.'

'You mean you'd have dolled him up like some sort of idol and let me catch a glimpse through the door –'

'No, no,' said Bettina, 'the point is he's not always like what you saw –'

'What we so much wanted you not to see,' said Mother May.

'Sometimes he comes to himself.'

'So it was true what we said,' said Ilona, 'when we told you he was away, but was coming back.'

'He has had absences all his life,' said Mother May, 'as long as I have known him.'

'You mean times when he's deranged?'

'No,' said Bettina, 'Mother May means – it's hard to explain –'

200

'He knows how to rest from life,' said Ilona, 'so his life can go on and on.'

'It's simply this,' said Bettina, 'sometimes he can talk perfectly well, and walk too. He walks about outside by himself –'

'And you let him?'

'He could go away, he could go anywhere.'

'But he's an ill man, he must be looked after –'

'He shams it now and then,' said Bettina. 'It's hard to say how ill he is.'

'Jesse was a conqueror of the world,' said Mother May, 'he was –'

'He is,' said Bettina.

'He is a great painter, a great sculptor, a great architect, a great lover of women, a supreme artist, a great human being. He cannot be as less than that either for himself or for us.'

'But if he's ill, and old –'

'He has his teeth,' said Ilona, 'and his hair, and his hair isn't grey.'

'You can't accept that he's old, that he's not as he was,' said Edward. 'But surely –'

'He isn't old,' said Mother May. 'At least he is, and he isn't.'

'You'll see,' said Ilona.

'How did he become ill, what is it, did he have a stroke or what?'

'Did he have a stroke?' said Ilona to Mother May.

'God, don't you *know*?'

'Illnesses have conventional names –' said Mother May.

'But something happened, he became different, and helpless, *when* –?'

'It was on a Tuesday,' said Ilona, 'I know because –'

'But *when*, years ago?'

'Some while ago,' said Bettina.

'But when – not that it matters I suppose –'

'It doesn't matter,' said Mother May, 'he has always been estranged.'

'All right, he's an artist – but this is *illness*. What does your doctor say?'

201

'We have no doctor,' said Bettina.

'A doctor has seen him of course,' said Mother May. 'But – of course – could do nothing. The condition is in some sense self-induced and beyond the understanding of –'

'But surely he can be treated, it looks to me like a stroke or a heart thing, blood not getting to the brain, not that I know anything, but I'm sure he could be helped, there are pills – he should come to London and see a specialist, they keep finding out new treatments – let me take him to London –'

'Indeed you do not know anything,' said Mother May.

Edward stared at the three faces confronting him. Once more they looked so similar, and in their concentration, older. Were not their fine blooming faces wrinkled, wizened like apples lying long in store become golden and a little soft? How old were they? Ilona did not always tell the truth.

'He doesn't need doctors,' said Bettina. 'Mother May is the best doctor. What she gives him does him good, it makes him calm.'

'You means she drugs him!'

'You can call any food a drug,' said Mother May. Her face was intensely, radiantly, almost hypnotically composed and bland.

'He isn't always calm,' said Ilona. 'He can scream.'

'So that's what I heard in the night, which you said was wild donkeys –'

'There are wild donkeys,' said Bettina.

'Of course he gets frustrated and angry sometimes,' said Mother May, 'and we have to restrain him. Once we had to get the tree men in to help us.'

'Oh, *no* –!' said Edward.

'Yes,' said Bettina, 'he was beginning to destroy his work. We had to stop him.'

'It took ages to get him up the stairs,' said Ilona.

'I don't understand,' said Edward. 'Look, do you think we could have a drink? I mean an alcoholic drink, some of that wine.'

'What about dinner?' said Ilona.

'Ilona, go and get some wine,' said Mother May, 'and just bring some bread too.'

202

Ilona departed.

'You mean you keep him a prisoner?'

'You keep saying he's ill and must be cared for, now you say he's a prisoner!'

'Of course he's not a prisoner,' said Bettina. 'We told you. He can walk sometimes. He can leave if he wants to. He doesn't want to, why should he. This is his home.'

'But what does *he* think? Wouldn't he like to go to London to have treatment?'

'No, he wouldn't.'

Edward said, 'I can understand your wanting him to be – more articulate – more presentable – before I met him –'

'We were waiting for that,' said Mother May, 'for his coming back. He does come back.'

'But you were wrong. You didn't understand *me*. You thought I'd give up, you thought I'd turn away from him, turn away from you. Of course I'm – disappointed – sorry, that's a ridiculous word to use. I so much wanted him to be –'

Ilona arrived with a tray, a bottle of wine and glasses, some bread and apples. Edward seized the bottle, which was uncorked, and poured out four glasses.

Ilona was deploying something which she had brought under her arm. She stretched it out, a piece of material with long trailing ends.

'What's that?' said Edward.

'It's a strait-jacket. You see it works like this.' She began to put it on.

'How *can* you! Stop it!' Bettina jumped up, dragged the thing roughly away, and threw it skidding off across the slate floor.

Mother May said, 'Bettina, please –'

Ilona, scarlet, her lips tightly closed, moved away to sit by herself further down the table. She covered her face with her hands. Bettina sat down. Edward pushed a glass of wine down toward Ilona. He said, 'You thought I couldn't bear the reality, but I can. I shall get to know him, I shall look after him. I'm going to have a real relationship with him. That's why I came here. He's my father.'

'The looking after is a burden best left to us,' said Mother

May. 'And please don't go to see him any more just now, it just excites him and confuses him.'

'He was glad to see me.'

'He didn't know who you were,' said Bettina.

'He did!'

'We will tell you when it's all right to see him,' said Mother May, 'I expect it will be soon. *Please* be unselfish enough to do what we want, we know what is best for him.'

'I'm sure he wants to see me, I'm sure I could help him. Couldn't you at least ask him? What do you think, Ilona?'

Ilona, who had been drinking the wine, burst into tears.

'Oh shut up, Ilona,' said Bettina.

'Why did you ask me to come here?' said Edward.

'We were sorry for you,' said Mother May. 'Simply that.'

'Why did you come?' said Bettina.

'For *him*. Because I was so miserable and I thought he'd talk to me and cure me. I thought he'd protect me. I thought he'd be wise and strong. And now – it's so awful – you're all *ashamed* of him –'

'Oh, really!' Bettina banged her glass on the table and walked away. The door of Transition banged loudly. Ilona, still audibly weeping, followed her. Mother May did not look after the girls, but kept her gaze fixed on Edward.

He looked at her quiet, intent face, radiant with concern and will. After two glasses of wine he felt drunk, desolated and faint. The black pain was back. 'Do you want me here?' he said. 'Shall I go away?'

Mother May reached across the table and tapped his wrist. 'We asked you here to do us good. And you will, you will – won't you?'

Edward was awakened that night by a loud clattering noise which left an after-sound of high ringing. He sat up in the darkness wondering if it might be thunder. He got up and opened the shutters and looked out of the window at the peaceful starry night sky. He closed the shutters again and went to the door and listened without opening it. Then he thought he'd put the chair against the door, couldn't find it, and discovered it was already against the door, where he must have put it on going to bed. He could not remember going to bed. He lay down again and promptly fell asleep and had a terrible hallucinatory dream about a black humpy monster coming up out of a lake. He was wakened again, in what turned out to be the grey grisly dawn, by the weird sound, very close, of a machine. At least it sounded like a machine, a harsh shrill jumbled rackety repetitive sound which stopped a moment, then started again, stopped then started. He staggered up and again opened the shutters. A swallow was singing just outside the window, sitting upon one of the wires that brought the 'unreliable' electricity. Edward banged the shutters and the bird flew away.

He went back and sat on his bed and remembered the loud sound and then the dream. Then he remembered the events of yesterday afternoon and evening. He had become quite drunk. After Bettina and Ilona had gone to bed he had, watched by Mother May, consumed some more of the wine. After that, after, he thought, saying goodnight (or did he just reel away?), he had gone along to Transition hoping to find Ilona, but the melancholy rooms were empty. Before going to bed he had actually made a short attempt at washing up and at sweeping the stone floor of the kitchen, always covered with potato peelings and onion skins from the impetuous cooking of the women. He recalled his last glimpse of Mother May, sitting alone at the table with an untouched glass of wine and the bread and apples. Had they eaten anything? He could not remember. He felt very peculiar indeed. He thought, here even the wine is drugged. He got dressed and looked at the dawn whose grey had turned to gold, a quiet lovely gold revealing all. The trees outside, the dark yews, the budding oaks, were motionless and solemn, potent, as if they had been thinking all night. Something in the quality of the dawn light made him feel the most terrible anguish and he thought about Mark and felt that he must have come to this place to die. Then he was overcome by an intense desire to see his father again, not soon but today, *now*: later they might find ways of preventing him. He looked at his watch. They would not be up yet. He must go at once.

205

Edward opened the door. The key was still in the lock outside, but had not been turned. The downstairs door, also with the key in it, actually stood ajar. Evidently there was, after the shocks of last night, some disarray. The bottle and glasses, bread and apples, were still upon the table in the Atrium.

Jesse, sitting up, seemed to be expecting him. He showed no surprise, but nodded his large head several times, opening his very red lips, and gazing at Edward with intent dark rather prominent round eyes. His eyes had a wet jelly-like appearance and seemed to be entirely dark, a reddish brown in colour, with no white area visible. They were gentle eyes rather like a cow's, yet also huge like the eyes of a tree. His nose was strongly aquiline. He had indeed still got his teeth and hair, as Ilona had said; the dark hair, though receding a little at the brow, grew into a copious crest and fell in long locks as far as his shoulders. The hair of his head and beard, which had been trimmed a little, was silky and dead straight. It showed no grey. His hands moved a little upon the sheet as if he were playing the piano, as he contrived, without exactly smiling, to nod his head. The hands were large and long-fingered, white and blue-veined, covered in long dark hairs which grew down as far as the fingernails. One finger wore, embedded in straggly hair, a big golden ring with a red stone. Edward noticed that the whitish-yellow pyjamas were badly frayed at the cuff and showed a long tear in one sleeve. The bed was disordered, the blankets falling off at one side.

Edward remembered afterwards that once he was in Jesse's presence the terrible *fright* which he had felt as he ran through the house left him entirely, and it was as if he knew, or were being told, exactly what to do. He did not speak, but moved forward and began to set the bed to rights, lifting up the blankets and smoothing out the sheet, accidentally touching the straying hands. Then he drew up a chair to the side of the bed and stared at his father, feeling suddenly like a favoured visitor, a necessary acolyte, someone summoned. He studied the big head, so close now, discerning squares and hexagons in the wrinkled skin. He became aware of a strong smell, a smell of urine, of sweat, of old age. Of course his father was not really old. Yet in spite of the dark strong hair, he seemed old.

Jesse was now hunching his shoulders and putting his head on one side with an air of whimsical thoughtfulness, almost playfulness. Edward took the near hand, the left hand, the hand with the ring, and, with the same sense of confidence, bent his head and kissed it. He released the hand which returned to its play.

He said, 'Father –'

'Jesse.'

'Yes –'

'Say – Jesse –'

'Jesse – oh – Jesse –' Edward felt an impulse to weep but knew that he must control it, stay clear-headed, as one entrusted with a message, or to whom important secret news was to be imparted. He had not expected Jesse to speak. Yet he had not not expected either. Everything seemed inevitable.

Jesse said something.

'Say it again.'

'You – didn't – come –'

The second time the words were fairly clear. Edward did not know how to reply. 'I'm sorry – I didn't know –'

'I wanted – you – I wrote –'

'I never had a letter.'

'Well – they didn't send – I wrote – I think – I forget –'

'I've come anyway,' said Edward, 'here I am and here I stay. I'm so glad –' He thought, I wanted to tell him about Mark, but of course that's impossible, it doesn't matter. I must keep him talking, I must keep *this* going on.

'They – the ones downstairs – the – the –'

'Your wife, daughters –?'

'No, no, the – what's word –'

'The women?'

'The women – fancy forgetting *that* –'

Edward was now noticing, through the hesitant utterance, Jesse's voice, his slightly drawling enunciation, his *accent*. He had been born in Stoke-on-Trent and still had an accent. This particularly seemed so surprising, so out of place, so very moving.

'It's nearly – the end – you know –'

'No, Jesse, no. You'll get better, you'll paint. Do you still paint?'

'No – can't concentrate – never mind – the paintings – I want you to have –'

'A doctor could make you better –'

'Listen – you have it all – the house – the paintings – the – the stuff –'

'Would you like me take you to London? We could see a good doctor.'

'My will – I've hidden it – over there –' Jesse waved toward a wall with a sort of metal square adhering to it, perhaps an old radiator.

'I want so much to help you,' said Edward, 'to bring you anything you want.'

'I'd like – yes –'

'Tell me.'

'A bit of –'

'A bit of –?'

'A bit of – skirt.' As he said this Jesse's face assumed a cunning almost leering expression. He giggled.

Edward said, 'Oh dear –!'

'I know – I can't – you can – I wanted to see you in your – in your – youth – And another thing –'

'Yes.'

'You look like –'

'Like?'

'Like – me –'

Edward took a moment to understand the point. He swallowed a gasp. 'Of course –'

'Don't mind. I wanted – to be sure –'

'You are my father,' said Edward, 'you *are*, before heaven, before the gods, nothing is more certain than that.'

'I see myself – in you – young. I liked her – so much –'

'My mother.'

'Yes. She'd dead – isn't she?'

'Yes.'

'I thought she was. I've got time – all mixed up – no one talks to me –'

'I'll talk to you.'

'Ilona used to – but she doesn't come – any more –'

'I'll tell her to.'

'They don't care.'

'Jesse, they do care. And I care. I love you.'

'Oh – love – I remember that! But now it's all black. I have drunk – and seen the –'

'Seen the what?'

'Seen the – Shakespeare –'

'Seen the spider?'

'Yes. He's always – at the bottom of the cup – looking at me. But spiders are good beasts – not to hurt – them –'

'I won't.'

'And – you know I think things – and can't say them – it's so terrible – those things – not frogs, the other ones –'

'Toads –'

'Yes. Look after them. Special. They climb up the ivy – to me – here. And the tall things – those tall plants – trees. Don't let them cut down – the poplar trees.'

'I won't. I'm sure they wouldn't do such a thing.'

'Oh – what they can do? When they thought I was – dying – they never came near –'

'I'm sure they –'

'They hoped it would be – all over –'

'Jesse, you –'

'They're ashamed – in front of the women – I'm a – a – you know – I'm just a load of shit – to be cleared away. Then they'll clean the room – open the windows –'

'Can you see the sea from here?' said Edward. 'May I look? Yesterday there was a mist.'

'Go and look. And tell me. I forget.'

Edward leapt up and went to the window. He saw the sea with the sun shining on it.

'What do you see?'

'I see the sea,' cried Edward, 'with the sun shining on it, and it's dark blue and all glowing like stained glass, and it looks so close, and there's a beautiful sailing boat with a white sail and – oh I am so glad – would you like to look, shall I help you?'

209

'No – I wouldn't see it – I'd see – something different. Your words – are better.'

Edward came and sat down. He took hold of the hand with the large ring upon it.

'That's for you too, the ring. You'll wear it – when I'm gone.'

'Jesse, I love talking to you. I wanted to tell you something – perhaps later on –'

'Come – some days –'

'You can walk, can't you? They said you could.'

'Some days – I can – could go a long way.'

'I'd come with you, if you liked.'

'They'll do me in.'

'What –?'

'Poison me – I expect – not to worry –'

'You're not serious! I'm here now, I'll look after you.'

'You'll stay –'

'Yes, yes –'

'Poor Jesse, oh, poor Jesse –'

'Don't.'

'Poor Jesse, poor child –'

'Jesse, *stop*, or I'll cry! You know they're not against you, that's an illusion!' A terrible pity for the maimed monster overcame him and shook him, and dread lest the pity should become visible.

'I know – what I know. There are terrible penalties – for crimes against the gods – I'll tell you one day – they're afraid of me – it's ap – ab –'

'Absurd – appalling – apparent – abhorrent –?'

'Funny how words go – they get lost – they're there and not there – they're in a black box – I'll soon be there too – I'll lie naked in that box – I forget what it's called –' Jesse began to pull off his pyjama jacket.

Edward's pity was now indistinguishable from fear, perhaps had been all along. He instinctively put out a hand to prevent Jesse from uncovering himself, then helped to pull the soft weak arms out of the sleeves. The ring caught in the tear and lengthened it.

Jesse now looked different, the wrinkles on his face seemed

to clear, to diminish until they were simply a hair-like veil spread upon a much younger face, which now looked calm and unanxious and lucid. The thick coppice of long straight smooth animal hairs which descended the chest was dark but a little flecked with grey.

'Don't worry – it's not time yet – for me to go. Leave me now – Edward – but come back –'

'Yes, yes –'

'Tell Ilona –'

'Yes?'

'No – nothing – she's a good girl – tell her that. I'd like you to marry Ilona.'

'But she's my sister!'

'Oh yes – of course – I forgot.'

'HOW DID HE know about the poplar trees?' said Mother May to Bettina.

Edward had descended from the tower to find the three women sitting waiting for him at the breakfast table like a grim committee. Even Ilona looked solemn. This morning, however, hungry after last night, they were all able to eat bran and oatmeal porridge, potato cakes with soya grits, oatmeal toast, apples.

'He creeps down and listens,' said Bettina.

'Down all those stairs?' said Edward.

'He can creep like a toad.'

'He said toads crawled up the ivy into his room.'

'I expect he goes up and down the ivy!'

'We asked you not to see him,' said Mother May. 'Why couldn't you wait?'

'He's my father.'

'He may never be better now,' said Ilona, 'so why wait?'

'But you aren't really going to cut down those beautiful poplars?'

'Yes,' said Mother May.

'We have to live,' said Bettina, 'we have to eat, we have to pay rates and taxes, we have to buy food and petrol and –'

'Have you any idea,' said Mother May, 'how much it costs to run a place of this size, a house a large as a palace –?'

'Yes, but aren't there other ways? He said to me, "Don't let them cut down the poplars."'

'We heard you.'

'I *love* those trees,' said Ilona, 'I think it's *terrible* to cut down trees –'

'You keep quiet,' said Bettina. 'You don't have to make decisions.'

'You don't let me make decisions!'

212

'Oh, shut up, Ilona.'

'Ilona, be patient with us,' said Mother May.

'Couldn't you sell a picture?' said Edward. 'Or some pictures?'

'They're keeping them till he's dead,' said Ilona. 'They'll be worth more then.'

'It's true that they'll be worth more,' said Mother May, 'so it makes sense not to sell any now. It's ridiculous to be senti-mental about the trees, they were planted as an investment.'

'But doesn't the fact that he doesn't want you to cut them down settle the matter – that he specially asked me –'

'Do not get the idea,' said Mother May, 'that you are a privileged messenger or interpreter of Jesse's wishes. He talks all kinds of nonsense and forgets it the next moment. You are a newcomer here, an *outsider*. You are new to a very complex and in some ways very old situation. You are blundering about in something you do not understand. It is not your fault. But you must realise this and be guided by us. You are our *guest*.'

'I can't understand your attitude to Jesse.'

'We are certainly not going to explain it to you!' said Bettina.

'He says you don't go to see him,' said Edward to Ilona.

'We won't let her go,' said Bettina.

'Why?'

'He lusts after her.'

'Oh – heavens –'

'I *want* to see him,' said Ilona. 'I want to *so much* – I'll go up with Edward –'

'No, you won't,' said Bettina.

'He's so helpless,' said Edward, 'I don't see –'

'He's not as helpless as you think,' said Bettina, 'sometimes he shams to put us off our guard.'

'You said he goes out, and you don't mind, you let him –'

'He could go anywhere,' said Ilona, drying some brief tears.

'Indeed he is much to be pitied,' said Mother May, 'he is full of impotent rage. There are no sane limits to the desire to conquer the world.'

'He was a god and has cheated us by becoming a child. It is

213

hard to forgive,' said Bettina. 'He is imprisoned in speech-lessness and cries with anger. To know so much and to be without words.'

'That is why he goes into trance-like sleeps,' said Mother May, 'when he can no longer endure his consciousness.'

'He really goes into suspended animation,' said Ilona, 'you'll see.'

'His soul wanders elsewhere,' said Mother May. 'He has always had this power, only now he uses it more often.'

'Sometimes we think he's dead,' said Ilona, 'only he isn't. His mouth falls open and –'

'Oh do stop!' said Edward.

'He will decide to die one day,' said Bettina, 'like an old sick animal who seeks a place, perhaps chosen long ago –'

'But he is *not* old!' said Edward.

'He is older than you think,' said Mother May, 'with him, time is unreal. Of course his *charm* remains. He has charmed you. He may try to use you –'

'He's *ill*, and he can be helped –'

'You keep saying so, but can you imagine him in a hospital ward?'

'Are we to treat him like a sick dog that one takes to the vet?' said Bettina.

'You don't know him,' said Mother May, 'you don't know his power, you have no conception of the greatness of his being.'

'Are you telling me he's still in charge?'

'In an important sense, yes.'

'You are saying contradictory things,' said Edward. 'You are confusing me, and you are doing it deliberately.'

'We would be deceiving you,' said Mother May, 'if we pretended the matter was simple.'

'He was a god in our lives,' said Bettina. 'Then he became a cruel mad god, and we had to restrain him.'

'They left him to starve,' said Ilona.

'Ilona, stop gassing!' said Bettina.

'Naturally at times he resents us,' said Mother May. 'We appear as an alien authority, we represent the diminishing of his world, the loss of his talents, his dependence on others. We

214

told you he once tried to destroy his paintings, break his sculptures.'

'Hasn't he a right to destroy his own work?' said Edward.

'No,' said Bettina. '*Think*.'

'He is a supreme artist,' said Mother May. 'He has been forever recreating himself. We, taking part in this process, have also to be his guardians, and the guardians of his work. We are responsible to posterity.'

'You need the money, is that it?' said Edward. 'Why don't you show Jesse off to the tourists? He's the most interesting exhibit here. They'd pay a lot to see him in one of his trances!'

'Please don't be offensive,' said Mother May, 'it doesn't help any of us.'

'You hide him away because he's a wreck and not a big romantic genius figure any more, and you send round false reports – I read in a paper that he was still painting – and now you want me to be your accomplice –'

'I suggest we stop talking to Edward,' said Bettina, 'we have already said too much.'

'You asked me here –' said Edward.

'We asked you here,' said Mother May, 'because we read that a young man had been killed and people blamed you.'

'You read *that*? No one ever suggested I was to blame.'

'We may have misunderstood,' said Bettina. 'The point is we just wanted to do you a kindness.'

'You mean it wasn't anything to do with Jesse?'

'No, of course not,' said Mother May.

There was a silence. The three women stared at Edward. He got up and walked away from the table, his sandals, Jesse's sandals, which were a bit too big for him, tapping softly, audibly, on the slated floor.

When he got as far as Transition he realised that Ilona was following him. He went on and was about to go up the stairs, but changed his mind and went instead into the Harness Room, which he also thought of as the Spider Room. Ilona came in and shut the door after her. She began to speak rapidly.

'Of course it was to do with Jesse, but it's hard to explain. I think Mother May wanted a change, any change –'

'I've certainly upset the ecology.'

215

'She wanted a new person around. They always wanted a son, not us girls. Only you're no good, you're too late, you weren't there when you were needed and anyway you had the wrong mother, it's all *mixed up* –'

'It certainly is.'

'And Bettina and I have been here too long, we can't help her, we're just like cats that belong to the house. In a way Mother May is like a Penelope who wants Odysseus to *go*, to be off on his travels again –'

'He can't go –'

'I don't know, perhaps he can, he –'

'But *you* can go.'

'I wanted to train as a dancer but he wouldn't let me, he wanted me here. Bettina had a young man, or sort of, but it was impossible and she wanted to go to the university, Jesse stopped it all, and as it is we're just bad painters, pretend artists –'

'Oh come, you've got your jewellery –'

'That's rubbish, you know it is, you didn't like it –'

'And Bettina can do all sorts of things –'

'She mends things, Mother May cooks – Bettina's jealous now because you prefer me –'

'Ilona, don't be silly! Jesse sent you his love. He said you were a good girl, he told me to tell you.'

'A good girl – that's nothing. There was something great here once, but we're just carrying it on mechanically in a pretend way. We can't seem to *do* anything any more, we can't even play the recorder any more.'

'But you played to me on that morning.'

'That's the only tune we can play properly.'

'And you used to weave.'

'Used to, yes. There was something, it's like remembering history, something long ago to do with salvation by work, and it was anti-religious and anti-God, that was a point, a sort of socialism, and like a kind of magic too, and being beyond good and evil and *natural* and *free* – that's what's so tragic, it was something beautiful, but the spirit's gone, it's gone bad, perhaps it was always sort of too deep a kind of knowledge, with something wrong about it, or rather we failed, *we* failed, he was too great for us – but that's what made Jesse so alive and full of power and *wonderful* as he used to be, as if he could live forever. And of course we had to be happy, and we *were* happy, I can remember that, and now we have to pretend to be happy, like nuns who can never admit that they made a mistake and that it has all become just a prison.'

'Why don't you leave?' said Edward.

'How can I leave? *You* can't leave. How could I?'

So I can't leave, Edward reflected later when he was by himself, standing in the middle of the floor of his bedroom, gazing at his unmade bed. The brief sunshine had gone, the wind from the sea was rattling the windows, the air in the house was humid, his clothes felt clammy. A rolled piece of paper was jutting from his pocket. He pulled it out and unrolled it. It was Jesse's drawing of Ilona which Edward had, he now recalled, picked up that morning as he came down through the studio. It represented Ilona as a child of twelve or fourteen. She had a surprised joyful look; perhaps that was in the days when they were all happy and believed in Jesse's magic. Her hair was done as it was today, the main central strands pulled back and clipped into a slide, the rest hanging free on each side. She was wearing an open-necked shirt-dress with flowers vaguely sketched upon it, which reminded Edward how much the girls' day dresses now looked like uniform. Even the woven evening dresses looked to him artificial, like pieces borrowed from a museum. He thought, women without men, they doll themselves up for me, but it won't do. Really they are dowdy, then cannot overcome a carelessness about their appearance, slatternly ways which have gradually come upon them. In the drawing Ilona's characteristic movement, her impetus forward, was indicated by a few lines representing the free folds of the dress. It was moving and extraordinary, how present Ilona was in the simple, probably hasty, sketch. Edward smoothed the paper out and put it carefully in a drawer, covering it up.

And why can't I leave, he thought, what keeps me here? Jesse, love for him, pity, duty. *My God, I said I'd stay.* And I

217

can't really trust anyone. I don't even know how old these women are or which is which. They are all elf maidens. Today as we were talking Bettina looked so old, perhaps *she* is the mother. Ilona looked old too, and so tired and wrinkled with anxiety, when she was with me just now. And Jesse, did he want me to come, ask them to bring me, does he really know who I am? Did he think about me in the past and want me, or did he, out of his *charm*, just *invent* it all as soon as he saw me? Was I brought here to help, to liberate his mind by talking to him, to be the guardian of his last days – brought here by them, by him, by fate? Oh how I shall disappoint them all! Is this a holy place where pure women tend a wounded monster, a mystical crippled minotaur? Or have I been lured into a trap, into a plot which will end with my death? I cannot leave. When Jesse said 'I want to see your youth' how could he not hate me for being so young and so alive? He is capable of rage and hate – and lust too perhaps. Have the women lured me here to punish me, to execute some communal revenge upon Chloe? I am the perfect victim, the fine upstanding youth with the wrong mother. Or is it just that, for some reason I shall never know, I have to take part in the final act of a drama which only incidentally concerns me and in which I shall be casually annihilated? God, how they frighten me, all of them. Jesse said they'd poison him. They could poison me any time. I'm always drinking those herbal draughts they put into my hands. Perhaps they are slowly depriving me of my wits, inducing hallucinations, like seeing that electric wire in Transition as the foot of a bird coming out of the wall. I thought I was mad because I was in love with Mark and couldn't go on living. Wasn't that why I came here? To lose the old hated self and be given a new one by magic. I was in love with Mark – and now I'm in love with Jesse. Is that my cure, my healing, my longed for absolution? One thing I can be sure of: there are awful penalties for crimes against the gods.

MIDGE MCCASKERVILLE WAS at Quitterne, the McCasker-villes' country cottage, sitting at her bedroom window. It was the afternoon, she hated the afternoon. Her knee was stiff, hot and painful, her hands were red and visibly grazed; she kept putting them to her cheeks to feel their roughness. She was near to tears, would welcome them soon, remembering the fall, and how, a day before, at Meredith's school concert, she had been moved to weep by the high sound of the boys' voices singing. Meredith's voice was not among them as he affected not to be able to sing. I'm always crying these days, she thought, rubbing her aching knee.

She got up and wandered about the room, touching her cosmetics which she laid out neatly like tools, then returned to the window. She had intended after lunch to make a big flower arrangement, but then it had seemed pointless. God, how restless I feel, she thought, I *can't* rest, all my limbs have that creeping restless ache. She had a feeling, familiar to her now, of needing to do something very odd simply to preserve her sanity. I want to do something, she thought, like break something or jump into a river or out of the window, it's like wanting to brush something off, like a purification. But how can I be purified? Any action which it is possible for me to perform is evil. And there is Thomas weeding the border. I hate the way he leans down so deliberately and then puts the weeds in a neat heap with all the roots together, he's so meticulous. And he wants to have a bonfire and then he always gets excited and looks stupid. He's not thinking about me. But he's a psychologist. How can he not know what is *streaming* through my head all the time?

Midge had wakened up that morning early, hearing the maddening hurtful singing of the birds, and at once thinking about the 'weekend' on which Harry was so much insisting and which now seemed impossible. Desire for Harry, for his embrace, most of all simply for the blessed relief and happiness for his *presence*, burnt in her now, making her rise again for another tour of her room. Only in Harry's presence was she collected and good. So was Thomas the cause of all her evil? Must she not have the strength to hate her husband and to join her lover? Perhaps it was so. Oh for freedom, to be out of this cage of lies and pain at last! She looked into her dressing-table mirror, at her beautiful hair and her distorted face, and for a moment opened her eyes wide and resumed her old insistent animated look which said 'like me, like me'. And was it she, whom everybody liked and petted, who was soon to cause such grief, such scandal and such chaos? She turned away from the mirror. 'You're always *moving* these days,' Meredith had said that morning. What had Meredith seen? What had he heard and understood? Perhaps nothing, she persuaded herself. The memory of that scene was already blurred. After the 'sighting' he had disappeared as if he had never been. She had said nothing to Harry.

Quitterne was a small pretty house, two red-brick cottages made into one, woodsmen's cottages perhaps since it stood in the middle of a wood. Civilisation, because of convenient access to London, had neared it, but its immediate sur- roundings were still unspoilt. The McCaskervilles had lived at Quitterne for twelve years. Their predecessor had put on a slate roof instead of thatch and made a gravelled drive, and surrounded the house with an area of rounded sea stones, black and glittering when wet, speckled and grey when dry. The garden, which had possessed rose beds as well as two long herbaceous borders, had been simplified by Thomas. There was now a plain lawn, showing off a fine copper beech tree, and one piece of flower bed up against the long box hedge which had been allowed to grow ragged. The wilder garden which blended into the wood was full of huge gross

220

rhododendron bushes, soon to be covered with mauvish blooms, and dotted about with wellingtonias and macra-carpas and a few elegant birch trees. The woodland, once so amazing to Midge, was of tall thinnish oaks and chestnuts, with a few big wild cherry trees, and places where filtering light had encouraged an undergrowth of ferny bracken. Among last year's brown debris where young shoots were emerging, patches of bluebells were here and there coming into flower, it had all seemed a paradise to Midge once, but now the little wild plants which used to please her no longer did so. She was alienated, frightened by the wood, tired by the stones. She would have preferred a pavement round the house and the (unthinkable to Thomas) complete removal of the copper beech. The dark intrusive tree exuded melancholy, even brushed the bathroom window with its drooping fingers. And now farther off in the wood where the McCaskerville territory ended some people called Shaftoe had built a horrible little modern house and a tennis court. Midge had heard the sound of falling trees and of distant alien human voices. Thomas and Meredith had been inclined to fraternise, but Midge had discouraged this. Thomas kept talking of retiring and living at Quitterne all the time. He said Meredith could have a dog then. At the thought of the dog Midge's eyes filled with tears at last.

Thomas had made his bonfire and the wind was blowing the smoke into the kitchen. Midge came out. Thomas's pile of weeds and winter cuttings had been rather wet, and Thomas had poured some paraffin on to encourage the now too violent blaze. Midge retreated from the heat. 'Keep back!' Thomas shouted to her, and to Meredith who had just come out of the wood. Meredith, who seemed to have grown several inches in the last week, stood by with his hands in his pockets with a slightly smiling supercilious expression, as of sympathy with childish antics. A little while ago he would have been dancing round the fire and rushing about to find things to burn. Now Thomas did the dancing. Red-faced, in an old threadbare suit and a flat cap, armed with a pitchfork, he circled the blazing fire, catching up mounds of falling burning twigs and hurling them back into the centre. A pillar of grey ash rising from the blaze was distributing itself, falling upon Thomas's cap and his clothes and his spectacles and his glaring sweaty face. What is he burning, she wondered, what is he *destroying* with such a fierce enthusiasm? She winced as she saw the force of the thrusting fork. What would happen if –? If what? If the customary modes of gentleness and concern and ordinary instinctive communication and *politeness* were ever, between her and Thomas, to break down? He was such a gentle polite man, so careful and so kind. Oh why can't I be *happy*, thought Midge. Isn't *that* the centre of the problem? I'm not happy, I'm miserable, I'm in hell, and that's all wrong, it isn't *me*. I *must* be happy, it's my nature, it's my right. That's what maddens me, what goads me almost into insanity, the feeling of that happiness, *my* happiness, existing so near, so very near, and I just . . . somehow . . . cannot . . . reach it . . .

'How's the poor knee?' said Thomas.
'Oh, better.'
'Let me look.'
They were sitting out in a moment of sunshine, their garden chairs with sagging canvas seats tilting a little on the uneven stones.
Midge displayed her bare leg with the scarred knee. Of course Thomas had fussed over her wounds, applied disinfectant, expressed sympathy. Now he was peering over his glasses in the way that irritated her. He placed his hand caressingly on the glossy unseamed skin above the scar.
'It's all hot,' said Midge, 'should I cover it up?'
'No, better leave it, it's clean. Poor darling, what a nasty fall.'
'It was stupid.'
'You are a juggins, you shouldn't walk in those high-heeled shoes, they're only fit for drawing rooms!'
'Yes – oh – all right –'
'Are you feeling well – I mean generally?'

'Yes, of course.'

'It's not the end of the month?'

'No, I'm fine.'

'You sometimes seem so –'

'So what?'

'Absent.'

'Perhaps I'm losing my identity. I never had much anyway.'

'An overrated commodity. Do I exasperate you sometimes? Sometimes I feel I lose you.'

'No, no. It's just that sometimes we seem to talk like strangers. I wonder do other married couples do that?'

'Never mind them. We have our way of talking.'

'I wonder how Harry and Chloe talked.' The urge to speak his name was suddenly irresistible.

'Oh those two –'

'You sound contemptuous.'

'Good heavens no. Other people's lives and *a fortiori* their marriages are great mysteries.'

'Even to you?'

'Especially to me – I've run through all the easy explanations.'

'But Harry –'

'Harry could have been a fascist –'

'You just see him as a bully?'

'I was going to say but actually he's a romantic. Well, I suppose fascists were, but he's a decent romantic. He's a disappointed leader. Of course he suffered from a famous father. It's like Willy's camel. He was romantically in love with Chloe and I'm sure they both played *that* for all it was worth. I don't mean this cynically. So much of life is acting – it can be disastrous, but sometimes it's a way of extracting some reality from a situation which would otherwise be beyond you.'

'So they were happy?'

'Yes, in their restless way. Don't you think so?'

'Yes, I suppose – Chloe was certainly a romantic. She's so remote now, poor girl.'

'Poor because she died young?'

'She never really loved anyone but Jesse Baltram. After all,

223

after *that* man everyone else would seem tame. She never got over being dropped by him.'

'Of course you never saw Jesse did you? I'd like to inspect that man some time.'

'Naturally she was grateful to Harry.'

'Well, he married a girl pregnant with another man's child.'

'Typical,' said Midge. 'He's so generous – chivalrous – wild – a bit stupid perhaps –'

'Self-destructive,' said Thomas. 'He wedded her remorse and shame and vindictiveness and self-hate. That was the smell that attracted him.'

'Don't be so psychological. She was very attractive in her tragedy-queen way. Why did he marry the other one then?'

'Because she was empty and virginal. Through her pure clear loving eyes he saw the great seas of the Antarctic and the circling albatross.'

'That's romantic enough. It's funny, I always think of Edward as Harry's son. Stuart is like a man with no father.'

'Immaculately conceived. A sinless absent mother, a virgin. A way of disposing of your father.'

'You think that explains it?'

'No.'

'Is Stuart really going to be a probation officer, is that the latest? Turn all criminals into a lot of Stuarts? I can't understand him.'

'Neither can I. He has a metaphysical urge. There are people who can only do one thing by running through everything. He's like a composer who has to invent the whole of harmony for himself. Stuart sees the machine of life that hardens the ego – sex, drink, ambition, pride, cupidity, soft living – he sees it as one big unitary trap, and his simple plan is just not to enter it at all. He dimly sees that this is a *cosmic* task. That's why he has to specialise in it.'

'He'll have a breakdown and cause a lot of trouble or become a psychopath.'

'Every nice girl loves a psychopath.'

'I wish he'd leave Meredith alone. I had that dream again last night about the white rider who turns to look at me. Or perhaps the horse is white. You said it was an image of death.'

'There's nothing wrong with that, life is an image of death. It is a study of dying.'

'I know you're awfully keen on death. I wish Edward would take more interest in Meredith. How is Edward, where is he? Everyone thinks he's here, where have you hidden him?'

'He has gone upon a pilgrimage to face an ordeal, his very own. He will be all right.'

'You aren't a scientist, you should have been some sort of romantic poet. I want to see Edward, I want to comfort him.'

'Shall we go for a walk?'

'Isn't it time for a drink?'

'No, not yet.'

'I'm too tired.'

'You need occupation.'

'So you keep saying, what am I supposed to do!'

'Why not pick bluebells.'

'You're a pixie, you're not human, you're elvish!'

While they were talking Meredith had approached, coming across the grass between the monstrous rhododendrons, his feet dewy from walking in the wood, making plimsoll marks upon the dry round stones. Yes, he has grown, she thought, he looks older, like he will look when he is twenty, when he is a student and has a girl friend. How terrible. Meredith, sunbronzed, his clean white shirt open at the neck, came and stood behind Thomas's chair. He had combed down his neatly cut hair into straight lines and checked his fringe. He looked straight at his mother with his cool abstract blue eyes.

Thomas was cleaning the bonfire ash off his glasses with a handkerchief.

Then Meredith, unsmiling, keeping Midge's gaze, put one finger to his lips.

Thomas had put his glasses on and was looking across the garden. Suddenly he leapt up with a cry and began to run across the stones and across the grass. 'Look, look!'

Midge, her face burning with distress at the dreadful gesture, ran after him. Meredith followed slowly.

An air balloon with blue and yellow stripes was silently, slowly, quite low down moving along just above the trees of the wood. The basket was clearly visible and the people in it.

'Oh, look!' cried Thomas again, excited, as he had been beside the bonfire.

Midge looked up at the beautiful balloon. Happiness. That was what it was. What she would never have. So lovely, so close, so out of reach. And Meredith had hurt her so cruelly, so much. She stared up at the moving balloon and the blue radiant sky beyond it through starting tears. The people in the balloon were waving. Thomas waved back. Midge and Meredith did not wave. Meredith was watching his mother. Midge turned away and went into the house.

'HAVE WE CONVINCED you?' said Mother May.

'Yes,' said Edward.

Jesse was lying on his back with his eyes open, breathing slowly and deeply, his red lips slightly parted as if about to speak. His plump arms and shoulders, visible above the sheet, were bare, his arms white and hairy, his shoulders white and hairless. His eyes now looking entirely round, were protruding, showing, it seemed, almost the whole of the orb, as if it were lightly resting upon the surface of the face. But these were not seeing eyes, or if seeing certainly seeing what was elsewhere. They were glazed, seeming a little crackled. Jesse's arms were stretched out relaxed upon the coverlet, the hands close, the fingers almost touching. Mother May took hold of one arm, pinching the flabby flesh, lifted it up and let it drop. The calm face did not alter. Edward shuddered.

'How long will he be like that?' said Edward.

'It's hard to say,' said Bettina, who was standing on the other side of the bed. 'It could be hours, it could be days, even weeks.'

'You don't try to wake him?'

'Of course not!'

'We don't let Ilona see him,' said Mother May, 'it upsets her. I mean, she knows it happens, but please don't talk to her about it.'

'I won't.' I wonder if they've drugged him, he thought, to prevent my talking to him? All conjectures seemed equally crazy. 'I'll go and finish my jobs,' he said, and went away down the spiral staircase, leaving the two women still looking at Jesse.

Edward do not however go to Transition, where he knew Ilona was. It was late afternoon, and some of the lunch things were still lying about on the table in the hall, things which Edward ought to pick up and carry. But he did not touch them. The routine at Seegard had, in the last day or two, quietly and imperceptibly, begun to break down. At any rate, Edward's part of it had, and Ilona had become, according to Bettina, 'even more scatter-brained than usual'. Saucepans were perfunctorily rinsed, not scoured, laundry failed to reach its destination, peelings lay undisturbed on the kitchen floor; strangest of all, two bottles of wine had appeared and stood shamelessly open upon a shelf beside the glass cupboard. At lunch, without comment, everyone had a glass of wine. So was it now a festival time?

Edward had decided, since it was impossible to talk to Jesse at present, to go for a long walk. Jesse had entered his 'trance' on the previous evening, the evening of the day of Edward's early morning conversation with him; but the women had only now yielded to Edward's sceptical questioning by giving him a sight of the spellbound sage. The door of the tower had, during the evening and the morning, stayed locked, and the key was not to be found. What Edward wanted now was to get out of the house, to get, for a while, right away, and if possible to reach the sea. He paused in the Interfectory, opened the drawer where he had tucked away the map, spread it out upon the table and studied it more carefully. The railway was clearly marked, crossing the tarmac road two or three miles beyond the Seegard turning, and veering toward the sea. Beyond where it crossed the road there were actually two stations upon it, one inland called Smilden Halt, the other upon the sea called Efthaven, no doubt the abode of the erstwhile fisherfolk. *Un petit chemin de fer d'interêt local*, as Edward thought to himself automatically. Before reaching Efthaven the railway ran for a mile or so right upon the edge of the coast. Clearly the thing to do was to find this railway and follow it. An abandoned railway usually kept its identity, raised up perhaps or in a cutting, still constituting a road, an unassimilated way through. He folded up the map and put it in his pocket where it jutted out as Ilona's picture had done, and went out into the Atrium.

Ilona was at the table, clearing away the lunch things which had remained disgracefully long untouched. She said, 'You saw him?'

'Yes,' Edward did not want to see Ilona, he felt awkward with her after her outburst yesterday in the Harness Room, and he passionately wanted to be by himself.

To his relief Ilona did not pursue the matter of the entranced Jesse, perhaps a painful one to her. 'Where are you going?'

'Out.'

'Are you cross with me?'

'No, Ilona dear, of course not. It's just that – it's all a bit much.'

'You aren't going to leave us?'

'No. You said I couldn't!'

'I just said that. Don't leave us. Don't leave us yet anyway. Don't leave me.'

'I won't.'

'I've got something for you.'

'What?'

'Just some nice tea, like you had the other day.' 'Tea-time' was not a Seegard custom, but Edward was sometimes given a hot cup of herbal 'tea' as a treat.

Ilona left the cup and saucer on the table and went away with her loaded tray.

Edward smelt the mixture and was about to drink it, then hesitated. Ilona's manner had seemed a bit odd, unnaturally casual, yet pressing, she had seemed especially anxious for him to have the tea. Supposing – well, supposing what? Edward quickly turned and poured the tea about the roots of one of the potted plants, a big glossy thing with long drooping branches.

Ilona returned. 'Did you enjoy the tea? Why, you've drunk it all.'

'Yes. Why not? What's wrong with it?'

'You know what that was?'

229

'What?'

'A love potion.'

'Don't be silly.'

'Really. Jesse made up quite a lot in a big bottle before he began to be ill. You're supposed to love whoever you see first after drinking it. But don't be alarmed – it was only me – and you love me already – anyway, I'm your sister.'

'OK, good joke! Now I'm going for a walk.'

'But you do love me, don't you?'

'Yes, Ilona, I do.'

'And you won't go away yet?'

'No.'

Ilona packed her tray and departed.

Edward looked into the cup, which he was still holding. There was a little bit of liquid left in the bottom. He looked at it for a moment, and then felt irresistibly impelled to drink it, and drank it.

Edward donned his mackintosh, closed the outer door quietly, and set off down the track. At the tarmac road he turned right. There was no one on the road and no car passed him. The flat countryside under low silver-grey clouds looked dull and mournful, as if bored and without occupation. The wind blew steadily, damply, over small trees already bowed to its persistent direction. Beyond low scraggy hawthorn hedges Edward could see, taller and sturdier now, the wet green shoots spottily tinting the muddy earth of the fields. The rain which had been falling earlier had ceased and the surface of the road gleamed blueishly in the subdued light which the clouds emitted as they bundled along. Edward's (Jesse's) boots made a sticky noise as he walked. Faintly, distantly, some birds were singing and other uttering anxious low cries. But the effect of solitude imposed itself on Edward's mind as a sort of silence. He walked and began to think about Mark and to try to concentrate his mind and picture again the events of that evening. What have I *done*, what did I *do*, he asked himself. But it was too difficult, and although he knew that it was possible to think in a better way, he felt too tired. He could feel his thoughts approaching some crucial, some really enlightening point, and then evading it and coming back to what was by now dull and familiar, so that he began to feel: what it this ceremony for? Then suddenly he found himself thinking about Harry, someone who had scarcely been in his mind at all since he had reached Seegard. The image of Harry rose, live and full of colour, and something stirred in Edward's heart, gratitude, love. He heard Harry's voice saying, Listen, you are having a *nervous breakdown*, you are *ill*, you will *recover*. Good old Harry, sane, beautiful, strong, *real* Harry, his father. Only Harry was not his father and had not cured him and could not. And Jesse, what could Jesse ever do for him? It was rather *he* who was now required to do something, something still shrouded and perhaps terrible. He was bound to Jesse, he loved him. And he had just said that he loved Ilona. He had new *responsibilities*.

Edward was so absorbed in these thoughts which moved, like the clouds, slowly, shedding dim yet vivid light, that he nearly missed the railway. He had in fact already passed it when he recalled having seen some long white gates. He returned some twenty paces and saw the gates, on both sides of the road, sunk off their hinges and grown over with brambles, but patently the gates of the level crossing. And there beyond them, just as he had pictured it, was the railway, the ghost railway line, a grassy road, quite distinct from the surrounding fields, leading away into two flat faintly misty distances. Firmly treading the brambles down Edward climbed over and sunk his boots into the wet grass. The grass in fact was not very long, had perhaps been scythed in the previous year, and made easy walking. Away from the road the railway was sunk a little between low banks on which great batches of palely luminous primroses were in flower. The sun appeared for a moment between the scurrying clouds, showing the details of the drooping grasses loaded with silver water, and the velvet texture of the primrose flowers. Edward felt as if his heart would burst out of his breast with a great inapprehensible anguish. He thought, how can I imagine things about 'recovering' or 'being cured' when what I simply am is *mad*, I have lost my *senses*, I walk along a mad thing, boiling with emotions and pain. Will it always be like this, all of my life, when I am alone, and when I see anything beautiful or innocent or good? And it's not just pain it's awful remorse, resentment, destructive hate. The sun was clouded. A little grassy path led up from the floor of the track to the top of the low bank, and Edward mounted it. Oh if only he could find *now* that the sea was in view, and run to it shouting. At the top of the bank however he could see nothing but more fields divided by little lines of small tormented trees, and a very slight rise, which could not be called a hill, with a neat copse upon it. Perhaps the sea was beyond that. He looked about, but although the work of man was everywhere to be seen in the form of meticulous cultivation, there was no other sign of humanity, no persons, not even a house or a barn to give scale and comfort to the flat faintly misty land. He walked on more slowly, kicking the longer grass aside.

It was then that he saw the girl. She seemed to appear suddenly as if out of a fold of the air, standing some four hundred yards off, motionless, her face partly turned away and clearly oblivious of his presence. Edward too stood still. He had at once recognised her as the one he had seen before, in the fen behind the house, how long a time ago, and whom he had, he now realised, completely forgotten about in the interim. There she was again, now in a moment of sunshine, with the vividness of a dream figure, with her short brown hair and her blue mac. Very cautiously Edward sat down in the wet grass with his hands about his knees and continued to observe her. He could not help feeling that it was very significant that now, especially now, after he had forgotten her, he should see her again. He wondered if, by some trick of the landscape, she were actually looking at the sea. She turned a little more away from him, moving one hand up to her breast, then to her neck, in what seemed to him a sad, even frightened, gesture; then she simply vanished. It took Edward a moment to realise that she had probably just descended to the level of the railway, perhaps at that point even lower, as from there she had, shortly before, as an apparition, risen up.

Edward got up hastily and plunged down the bank again to the shorter grass of the track, his mackintosh and trousers now soaking wet. He felt a breath of desolation which had seemed to be wafted to him from the girl, he felt frightened.

He wanted to run after her but dared not. He deliberately waited, breathing deeply, while the anguish which he had felt earlier spread its electrical discomfort through his whole body. He walked on slowly, then faster, then hurrying, but saw no one. About ten minutes later he saw the cottage. The cutting along which he was walking had gradually become shallower and, as he followed it round a curve, the building suddenly appeared, just beyond some clumps of hawthorn and elder, raised up a little just beside the track. At first it seemed to be deserted, even ruined. A large deformed yew tree, half overgrown with some creeper, completely obscured one side of it, and various spriggy plants were growing on the roof. Then as he came up the slight slope towards it he saw that a path had been cut through the longer grass, and in a moment he felt something hard, stone or concrete, beneath his feet. He realised that the little stone building was a station house, and that he was now upon the platform of Smilden Halt. He advanced cautiously toward the house, seeing now curtains in the windows, a cleared space before the door, a little fence and a gate with a board upon it saying *Railway Cottage*. Edward hesitate, breathing in the atmosphere of the ghost station. He knew that of course he had to go to the cottage and knock on the door. He felt dread and the hope that there would be no one there. He unlatched the gate and knocked on the door.

It was instantly opened by a tall rather fierce-looking woman with a strong gleaming face who peered at Edward through thick glasses which enlarged her eyes. 'Yes?'

'I'm so sorry to trouble you,' said Edward. 'I want to get to the sea. Could you tell me the best way to go?'

Before the tall woman could answer there was a cry, and from behind her, appearing indeed underneath her arm which was outstretched to hold the door, a smaller woman appeared suddenly, crouched like a monkey, a woman, a girl. She ducked out of the doorway, skipping forward and making Edward step hastily back. The girl was Sarah Plowmain.

'Edward!'

'Sarah!'

'Elspeth, this is Edward, Edward Baltram!'

'Oh, really,' said the tall woman in a cold repressive tone.

'Edward, how on earth did you know I was here?'

'I didn't,' said Edward.

'Surely you're not over *there*, are you, but you *must* be, and we didn't know –'

'He'd better come inside,' said the taller woman.

'No, he can't, he mustn't –'

'You've been shouting his name out loudly enough.'

'Edward, this is my ma, Elspeth Macran. She uses her maiden name. You know, she's a writer, I expect you've seen her stuff, Women's Lib journalism, she writes under the name of Elspeth Macran about feminism and so on, she's written a novel –'

'Do stop shouting, Sarah, and conveying senseless information. He had better come in. *That* is better, that he should come in, he's here and we can't make him vanish.'

'All right, I'll go in first and –' Sarah ran in again past her mother.

Elspeth Macran stepped back, and after a moment beckoned Edward inside.

It was darkish within and smelt of wood smoke and cigarette smoke, Edward began to see a big open fireplace where a few logs were burning, bookshelves with shabby books, shiny china ornaments, dried grasses in big jars, very worn rugs, and a table with a red cloth on it set for three. From the state of the plates it looked as if he had interrupted high tea.

'I'm so sorry to disturb you,' said Edward.

'Don't be silly,' said Elspeth Macran, 'don't talk about absurdities. Sit down, Sarah, stop frigging about.'

'Where shall I sit – I mean –'

'Anywhere.'

Sarah sat down at the table and actually picked up a piece of bread and butter, then put it down again.

Elspeth Macran stood with her back to the fireplace staring at Edward with her gleaming enlarged eyes. She was wearing a blue check shirt and a shabby tweed jacket. Corduroy trousers tucked into long socks gave a knickerbocker effect. When her face was not expressing strong emotion (which it often was) she could look imposing, even handsome.

'So you are Edward Baltram.'

'Are you really staying at Seegard?' said Sarah. She was now perched sideways on her chair, her short skirt hitched up revealing skinny bare legs and small rather dirty bare feet. Her small mobile face was bright with excitement, her mouth ajar with an involuntary grin of emotion.

'Yes.'

'But why, how?'

'Why not, they invited me, they wrote – and well – how is it you're here, I had no idea –'

'The explanation is simple,' said Elspeth Macran. 'I knew your mother, Chloe Warriston.'

'This was Jesse's love nest with Chloe,' said Sarah. 'You were probably conceived here, in the bedroom!'

'Jesse owned this house –?'

'No,' said Elspeth Macran, 'it was abandoned when the railway went, Jesse just used it. Then when he dropped Chloe she lived here for a short time with me.'

'With you –'

'I was a close friend of Chloe's. She was very unhappy and I came to her. Then she married that scoundrel Harry Cuno.'

'He's not a scoundrel.'

'She was a very unlucky girl. I liked this place and when the railway put it up for sale I bought it.'

'She bought it to spite Jesse,' said Sarah, 'she hates him.'

'So you know my father,' said Edward.

'I have never met him,' said Elspeth Macran, 'but I know a good deal about him, and I am surprised that you can bear to be in his house.'

'He is my father,' said Edward, 'and I love him.'

'That's got to be nonsense,' said Elspeth Macran.

'My ma hates men,' said Sarah, 'it's nothing personal.'

'You never saw him before, and he is now a babbling idiot.'

'A woman needs a man like a fish needs a bicycle,' said Sarah.

'He isn't,' said Edward.

'I hear he's dying anyway from lack of medical attention.'

'Edward, do sit now,' said Sarah. 'He may sit down, mayn't

he? Or do you think he'd better go? Sit *there*.' She pointed to a chair at the table.

Edward sat down at the table. He said to Sarah, 'You never told me –'

'About the cottage – I did, only you didn't pay attention.'

'Edward doesn't seem to be very good at paying attention,' said Sarah's mother.

'I remember now, only you didn't say it was so near –'

'Why should I? I never imagined you'd ever visit Seegard. Anyway, this has always been a sort of secret place, Elspeth liked it that way.'

'Why did they invite you?' said Elspeth, 'who wrote to you?'

'Mother May did – I mean Mrs Baltram.'

'"Mother May"!'

'That's what we call her –'

'You mean you and those half-crazy girls.'

'They are my sisters, and –'

'I want to see them,' said Sarah, 'I want to see them *all*, I'm wild with curiosity, can't you invite me to tea?'

'I forbid you to set foot in that accursed house,' said Elspeth. 'The place is dripping with evil and madness. Surely *you* must feel that, or are you already depraved?'

'It's *not* evil,' said Edward. 'It's a strange place. You don't know it and you can't understand it. There's something good and innocent there.'

'What did the letter say?'

'Mrs Baltram's letter? I wish you'd stop asking me questions.'

'What did the letter say?'

'She asked me to come. She said she'd read about my mishap in the paper –'

'Mishap. Did she use that word? That's priceless! You must have been out of your wits to accept such an invitation. Quite apart from the fact that Jesse treated your mother like dirt. Why do you think they asked you?'

'They were sorry for me. All right, why do *you* think they asked me?'

Elspeth Macran smiled, revealing very white false teeth. 'I

236

don't know, but not for your own good you may be sure. You don't imagine it was the old fool's idea? His mind has gone.'

'Don't be so aggressive, ma,' said Sarah. 'You'll reduce poor Edward to tears.'

'No, she won't,' said Edward. 'I think I'll go now. I only called to ask the way to the sea.'

'The way to the sea –!'

'I suppose if I just go on following the railway –'

Elspeth and Sarah were staring at each other. Sarah jumped up. 'Shall I get her?'

'Yes,' said Elspeth. 'She's been listening to the conversation. She may as well look at him. It may help her just to have seen the –'

Sarah darted across and opened a door. The girl whom Edward had now twice seen entered the room. Edward rose to his feet.

'This is Brenda Wilsden,' said Elspeth. 'Mark's sister.'

'Always known as Brownie,' said Sarah. 'Brownie, this is Edward Baltram.'

Mark's sister (Edward could at once see the resemblance) said nothing. She stared intently at Edward out of a big pale grave face, which might have been a boy's face, just as Mark's could have been a girl's. Her long head and large brown eyes and the thick straight brown hair which hung almost to her shoulders emphasised the 'Egyptian' look which she shared with her brother. She was less slim, less beautiful, however. She was wearing a shapeless dress and her hands were at her breast in a gesture like that of the earlier sighting. As she stared her face seemed to strain forward as if seen through a transparent muslin mask. She made the room motionless, standing there like a painted statue.

After a paralysed moment Edward began to speak, spewing out the sudden unpremeditated words. 'I gave him that stuff, he didn't know, he hated drugs, I gave it to him in a sandwich, I stayed with him, I only left him for twenty minutes –'

'It was more than that,' said Sarah.

'When I left him he was fast asleep and I thought –'

'Oh dry up,' said Elspeth Macran.

There was a silence during which they all stood still as if

holding their breath. Afterwards Edward thought of the awful scene in that room as being like one of Jesse's pictures, full of doom and dread and catastrophic forces held in suspense. The room actually seemed darker. Then Mark's sister turned and went back through the door.

'Go to her,' said Elspeth to Sarah. Sarah disappeared and the door closed. 'You'd better push off,' she said to Edward. 'Why did you have to turn up? She could have done without that. You aren't very popular here, I don't want to be unkind, I just wouldn't care to be you, that's all. You'd better run back to Mother May.'

Edward stood for a moment. Then he went to the front door and emerged into the amazing outside air, seeing with astonishment the landscape, just as it had been before, sunlit now, silent, empty, the sun picking out at a distance the soft pale green of a sloping field. He walked on a little bit along the platform, the way he had come; then stopped aware of sick pain and an intensity of emotion which nearly knocked him to the ground. He turned to look at the cottage, the little station house, so trim-seeming now, beside its big yew tree. He saw the clean finish of the stone. He began to walk back and stood beside the yew where, shadowed by it, there was a small square window. He peered in. Mark's sister was sitting in a chair, looking now not solid but like a dummy or bolster, head drooping forward. Sarah, kneeling in front of her, was twisting almost to the ground to look up into the hidden face.

Edward felt he might be going to be sick. He walked away, quickly now, along the platform and down the slope and on to the grassy track. He began automatically to walk back in the direction of the road. He felt dizzy. The sunlight kept coming in flashes and the air seemed to be full of tiny black insects.

When he had walked for a few minutes he heard someone calling his name and stopped.

Sarah was running after him barefoot upon the wet grass. She stopped a few yards from him and looked at him with an eager excited hostile face, like an animal checked in a pursuit.

'Well, what is it?' said Edward, in an odd harsh voice.

'You looked in. You spied on us.'

238

'I didn't know you knew Mark's sister,' said Edward.

Sarah spoke quickly. 'I knew her a bit, I knew Mark a bit, you weren't the only one. She was in America when you – when he died. When she came back I went to her and my mother visited her mother. We wanted to help. We invited her here. Then you have to turn up.'

'I didn't know –' said Edward.

'Well, don't come again, and don't ever try to see Brownie, ever. She doesn't want to hear your excuses. She hates you like her mother does. They'll never get over it. Just don't persecute her with your presence and don't write to her either. The least you can do is keep off. There's nothing you can do for her except be decent enough to leave her alone.'

'All right,' said Edward. He turned away and, without looking back, walked along the railway.

I would like to see you to talk about my brother's death. Tomorrow at five o'clock I will be in the fen where a line of willows runs down to the river, and there is a wild cherry tree leaning over on the other side.

Brenda Wilsden.

Edward crumpled the letter in his hand and stuffed it into his pocket. It was the day after his visit to Railway Cottage. The man who had given the letter to him stood staring at Edward with curiosity. The man was as tall as Edward, bearded and whiskered, his whole head liberally covered with an unkempt cascade of stiff weather-bleached hair out of which his ruddy large-featured face peered intently. His hair showed no grey, but he was not young, his dark eyes surrounded by deep wrinkles. His face and hair and indeed his whole person was covered with a fine fibrous dust which lodged visibly upon the shelving wrinkles. He wore a red shirt with a red handkerchief about his neck, and about his waist a wide leather belt with a brass buckle worn away and shiny with age. Edward did not need to be told that he was one of the tree men, when he had been silently accosted by him in the vegetable garden.

'Thank you,' said Edward.

The man still stood close, staring with evident curiosity, and Edward could smell his sweat and hear his breath.

'He's a cabbage now, in' he?'

'Who –?'

'He's a cabbage, a jelly, the guv'nor up there – in' he?'

'No, he isn't,' said Edward. 'He's ill, but he's not like that.'

'Had all the girls once. But that's finish now.'

'Thank you for bringing the letter.'

'Who are you?'

'I'm Edward Baltram.'

'You're the son.'

'Yes.'

'She just said, "the young chap", that's you.'

'Yes.'

'They'll eat you.'

'Who will?'

'Those bloody women. They'll carve you up. You better scarper before they start. So you're the son. God!'

Edward made a vague dismissive gesture with his hand, and turned away.

'He had all the girls,' the tree man called after him. 'Now he's senile, that's it, senile, poor old bugger.'

Edward walked quickly back to the house. It had been raining earlier, but now the afternoon was warm, the sun staringly bright, a sky full of harsh light was arched over the flat land. Edward stood in the hall and drew out the crumpled letter again but did not see it. He had of course said nothing at Seegard about his visit to Railway Cottage. He smoothed the letter out a bit, pocketed it again, and walked slowly along to Transition.

Ilona and Bettina were in the kitchen, standing at the long scoured wooden table.

'Did you get the lovage?' said Bettina.

'No, sorry, I forgot.'

'You're in a dream. Never mind. Just chop those herbs, would you.'

'Everything's dying,' said Ilona.

'And you, Ilona, go and fetch some more onions.'

'The swallows are dying, they don't come back any more.'

240

'I saw one this morning,' said Edward, chopping herbs.

'They don't come back to us any more. They used to nest in the loft of the stables. *Our* swallows are all dead.'

'Ilona – and take a basket, you dolt.'

'Oh, all right,' Ilona departed.

'Be careful with that thing, it's very sharp.'

There was a strong gentle sleepy smell of baking bread in the kitchen. Bettina, standing close beside Edward, was kneading cooked potatoes, rapidly making them into balls and rolling them in a circle of scattered flour. Edward saw her strong brown fingers dusted with flour crushing the soft potatoes one by one. He saw out of the corner of his eye a long strand of her reddish hair which had come down over her shoulder and curved over her bust hanging free and touching her arm. The sleeve of her brown working dress was soiled where she had turned it back at the elbow. Her arms were covered in golden down, matching the conspicuous long fine hairs upon her upper lip. As she worked she cleared her throat and sniffed in a preoccupied manner. He thought of the tree man, and wondered, why do those men not come and rape these women, how can they not? The automatic movement of the two-handled scimitar-shaped knife hypnotised him as he moved it steadily to and fro with a strong motion increasing the fragrant green mound of chopped marjoram and parsley. He let go of one handle to move the leafy stems nearer to him and suddenly felt an agonising deep pain in one of his fingers. The green leaves were instantly stained with red.

'Oh, you idiot,' said Bettina, 'put your hand under the tap, you'll make a stain on the table.'

Blood was welling up and streaming out of what felt like a deep wound. Edward turned on the cold tap and watched the blood and water pouring down into the old stained porcelain sink. Bettina was already scrubbing the table. Then she put the bloodied herbs into a colander. 'Just get out of the way.' She washed the herbs under the tap. 'Don't get blood on that cloth, please.'

'Well, what am I to do!' said Edward. 'It won't stop bleeding.' He felt like weeping. The wound was painful and felt dark and awful like a stab wound from an attacker. He could still feel the slice of the extremely sharp knife into the flesh.

'Put it over the sink. I'll get a bandage.'

Edward ran the water hard, trying to clear the blood fast enough to see the mouth of the wound. He thought, so I am wounded *now*, it would be *now*. But he could not make out which now it was, whether it connected with Bettina, with Jesse, or with *her*. He sat down abruptly on a chair, pulling his shirt down over his hand and watching the red stain spreading on the sleeve.

Bettina's brown hands appeared again, winding a white snaky bandage round and round his finger. The red kept on coming through and coming and coming.

He had known at once that Bettina's bandage had been a mistake. It had come out of an old dusty battered tin marked *First Aid* which looked as if it must have belonged to the first world war. There weren't even any proper medical supplies at Seegard. The piece of probably dirty, old-fashioned linen soaked with dried blood had simply stuck to the wound, and the finger (fortunately on his left hand) was stiff and hot and throbbing with pain. That morning (it was the next day) Edward had made an embryonic effort to pull the bandage off, but this was clearly going to be very painful and soon seemed impossible. He wondered whether the deep wound were not going septic or whether it needed stitches. Gangrene would follow, and an amputation. Should he go, but where, to a doctor? In any case today he could not go anywhere. Last night late, opening his door, he had heard the women arguing somewhere in East Selden, arguing emotionally with raised voices. He wanted to creep and listen but did not dare to. At breakfast he was informed that Jesse was still 'absent', unapproachably entranced. Earlier, Edward had planned, on this day, to insist on seeing him, perhaps trying to wake him. Only now, instead, he was standing beside the river, beside the line of willows, looking at the wild cherry tree.

There had been something weird, a little chilling, in Mark's sister's description of the place, as if it should not be possible to speak of that death, and then to follow it with a sort of poetic description. The place was easily identifiable because the line of willows was, in the area, unique, and ended at the river which, when Edward had first looked that way, had been invisible underneath the flood. This part of the fen was fairly dry now and, between intermittent pools, easy to walk on. A little beyond the willow however, scattered sheets of ready water began again and continued to the low horizon where, although it was a clear and fairly sunny day, no sea was visible. There were few trees so that the small leaning cherry tree, now coming into flower, was a landmark too. The river, broader here, contained between steep sandy banks, was running swiftly, the colour of Guinness, making, where it curved, circular eddies and little sheltered pools of more quiet water. Edward had of course been looking all about him, as, sick with emotion, he had come along, but had seen nobody. Of course he was early. But perhaps she had decided not to come, that it would be too terrible, that she felt too much hatred. Sarah had said that she hated him. Edward thought of the mother's letters. What a dreadful thing such hatred must be, surely it must aim to kill its object. He looked at his stiff finger and the blackened bandage. He sat down on the bank where there was a patch of grass and his heart too throbbed with pain.

Immediately there was, like a small explosion just above the water, a blue flash. Edward jerked his head and stared. There was nothing there. He saw the dark moving water and the luminous white flowers of the little cherry tree leaning downward, its branches extended over the river where at the curve they were reflected in a quiet surface. He blinked his eyes. Then appearing out of invisibility he saw, sitting upon a pendant branch, a bird, a kingfisher. At that moment the kingfisher flew again, very fast, skirting the sandy bank and dipping like a little dart into the stiller water where the river turned; then coming back to his perch on the tree. Edward could see the bird's strong beak and the fish which was instantly gulped down. He sat still watching the motionless kingfisher upon which the sun was shining, the small bird with its vivid blue wings and soft cinnamon-brown breast, sitting above the cherry flowers.

A shadow feel beside him and he jumped up. The girl was there, with her blue mackintosh and her wellington boots, wearing, not the trousers of his first sighting, but the shapeless dress which she had had on at the cottage, a rather shabby dress with a design of blue flowers. She stared at him with her stony brownish eyes, darker than Mark's eyes, as her brown hair was darker than his hair. Yet in her pale clear complexion and her large brow and thoughtful mouth and in some live intent expression of her face, she greatly resembled him, as if his face had been stretched into a larger mask through which, still, he looked out. The recollection of Mark's inspired godlike drugged face came before Edward, blotting out the girl. Then she spoke, looking past him. Her first words were, 'There's a kingfisher.'

Edward turned and the blue flash was off, disappearing round the bend in the river. 'Yes,' he said, 'he's – he's nice.'

The girl then sat down beside the river, her booted legs descending over the edge of the steep bank and her heels digging into the soft sandy earth. Edward, as it seemed absurd now to continue to stand, sat down near her, tucking his long legs sideways. The grass was damp and a coldish east wind had begun to blow. She began to tug off her mackintosh. Edward watched, checking the instinct to reach out a hand to help. Feeling the wind, or finding the operation too awkward, she decided to keep it on, pulled it back and buttoned it, frowning. In profile too she resembled Mark as she lifted her thick hair back and thrust out her lips in just his way. Yet she was less beautiful, and surely older; and would now grow, than him, older . . . and older . . .

She was silent, looking away from him down the stream, and he could see her swift breathing. He feared she might cry. The black sick faint feeling, which the kingfisher had interrupted, came back to him and he spoke hastily. 'Miss Wilsden, it is very kind of you –'

'Look,' said the girl, turning to him with a stern tearless face, 'my name is Brownie, everyone calls me that. And please let's not get too emotional.' She spoke in a firm clipped no-nonsense tone which reminded Edward of some of Sarah's women's lib friends. At the same moment he saw her and thought of her as 'Brownie'.

'You wanted to talk to me about Mark –' he said.

'No. Actually I want you to talk to me about Mark. That's different. I don't need to talk to you.'

'I'm sorry –'

'Sorry, I didn't mean to sound unpleasant. I just want you to tell me exactly what happened that evening. I can't make it out. I've got to be able to *think* about it. I wasn't in time for the funeral – or the inquest – I was on holiday and they couldn't find me – and people here told me a lot of different things – and – and speculated – Anyway, could you, if you would, just tell me what happened.'

'Are you older or younger than Mark?'

'Older.'

'That evening – you see –'

'No need to spin it out, just tell me briefly. I won't keep you.'

'Mark was in my room, and I gave him –'

'What time was it? I know it was evening, but what time?'

'About six. I gave him a sandwich with the drug in it –'

'He didn't know –'

'I was going to tell you. He didn't know, he didn't approve of drugs.'

'But you do.'

'I did. He went off on a – on a trip.'

'I detest and abominate drugs, I've never touched them, Mark and I agreed about that. Go on. Wait. Had you taken anything?'

'No. I was going to – to look after him –'

'And why didn't you?'

'Sarah rang up. Sarah Plowmain –'

'Yes.'

'And I went over to her place for about half an hour. And when I came back – the window was open and – he was – dead.'

There was a short silence. Edward, who had been intensely seeing Mark, so beautiful, so relaxed, smiling blond Mark in his disordered shirt lying on that sofa, now, as Brownie

245

slightly moved, saw instead the awful sunshine, the desolate bank, the dangerous river.

Brownie, who had been looking away, turned back and shifted her legs, breathing deeply, and said, still in her business-like tone, 'Could you describe what he was like on this – this trip – did he say anything to you?'

'Oh, he had a good trip.' Brownie made a sound. 'I mean – I'm sorry – he saw good things and – was happy – he was laughing – then he said –'

'What?'

'That things were all themselves – and everything was – one big fish – and that God was coming – like a lift. I know it sounds like nonsense, but the way he said it –'

'Yes, yes, I know about drugs. What else did he say?'

'That's all I can remember, there was something about spears of light – and flying –'

'Flying?'

'He said he was flying.'

'And you left him.'

'Yes, you see, he fell asleep –'

'Why did you go to see Sarah, she asked you over?'

'Yes. I expect she told you.'

'I want you to describe – to tell me why you went. It seems so odd. Are you in love with her?'

'No.

'But you'd been having a love affair?'

'No. But that evening – we did make love.'

'In half an hour?'

'Yes – or a little more –'

'You said twenty minutes at the cottage. Are you still lovers?'

'No, I haven't seen her since, except that time here – I wouldn't want to be her lover, not at all, it was all a sort of accident, our making love, I didn't intend it, it was her idea –'

'I still don't understand why you left Mark. You didn't have to go to Sarah, it sounds as if you didn't even want to.'

'I suppose I sort of did – she interested me – a bit – she asked me for a drink –'

'And you felt you might as well go.'

'I only meant – for ten minutes – and Mark was asleep – and I locked the door –'

'Were you drunk before you went?'

'No.'

'But you knew how dangerous – what that stuff is like – how one must *never* leave people.'

'Yes, I knew.'

'Then why did you go?'

Edward moved his legs, driving them down the bank and sending a shower of sand into the water. He almost shouted, '*I don't know!* How can I say why I went? I didn't know what was going to happen, I didn't know I was going to ruin my whole life –'

'*Your* whole life?'

'I didn't know he'd wake up and walk out of the window, I was happy, I was glad he had seen such good things, such wonderful things, and was asleep, he looked so beautiful and calm, like seeing a god asleep, and it was such a perfect evening, I though it would be fun to go and see Sarah, for ten minutes, I didn't think, I didn't imagine –'

'Yes, all right –'

'Your mother's been writing me the most terrible letters saying that I'm a murderer. You see I didn't tell them at the inquest that I'd given him the drug without his knowing, so I suppose people thought he'd taken it himself and that he took drugs and – your mother must have known that wasn't true – and she's been writing me these awful letters, lots of them, telling me I'm a criminal and she wishes I was dead, and that she hates me and will hate me forever – and you must hate me too, Sarah said so, and if you only knew how unhappy I am and how everything in my life is spoilt and *black* –'

'Why are you here – I mean here at Seegard. That seems odd too.'

'They invited me. I didn't know what to do with myself, I was going mad with grief – and guilt and – destroying myself – It was supposed to be a change. A psychiatrist told me to come.'

'A psychiatrist? Who?'

'Thomas McCaskerville. And I wanted to meet my father, I hadn't seen him since I was a child, I felt he might help somehow – It all happened at once, I can't make sense of it – but if you only knew how much I suffer and will always suffer –'

'Is it true that your father is dying of lack of medical attention?'

'No, of course not. But it's hard to explain – it's all so strange up there – Do you really want to know?'

'No.'

There was another silence. Then Brownie gave a long sigh and said, 'Well –' She shuffled her feet then turned awkwardly onto her knees and slowly got up. Edward hastily jumped up too. She said, 'Thank you.' Then she seemed about to go away, moving toward the willow trees, but paused, not looking at Edward. 'I'll ask my mother to stop writing to you. Perhaps she has already.'

'I don't know. The letters would all be in London at my father's house – I mean my stepfather's house – Look, I know you blame me terribly, you hate me, but –'

'I don't hate you, that's ridiculous. I suppose I blame you. If that means anything. I'll have to think. But that's my affair. I don't think you should destroy yourself or ruin your life – I don't think you can or will anyway – that wouldn't help Mark – or me – You're at the university, aren't you?'

'I was.'

'Well, go back, get on with your work, you could help other people in the future, stop just brooding about yourself, and feeling guilty. That's my advice anyhow. Thanks for coming.' She began to move away from him.

Edward said, 'Please stay with me, just a little while.'

'I must go.'

'Please stay with me, I must talk to you, I need you, don't leave me, please, *please* don't leave me.' He reached out and very gently touched the sleeve of the blue mackintosh near the cuff.

She started away from him as if to run off, then turned towards him, and tears streamed suddenly from her eyes. She said, gasping, through terrible sobs, 'It's that – I'll have to live all of my life without him – all of my life – and it's only just starting –'

'Oh *God* –' said Edward, standing helplessly beside her with his hands hanging.

Brownie had found a handkerchief and had with deft speed recomposed and dried her face, so that the quick storm seemed like a mirage. She said, in an almost calm voice, a little husky, 'Sorry. Must go.'

'Brownie, just say – oh Christ, what can you say – say you'll see me again – I'll go on my knees – I need you – you're the only person who can save me from hell – please *please* say you'll see me again – sometime – before too long – just say we can meet again, I beseech you, I beg you –'

'Oh – yes – all right – but –'

'Oh, thank God –'

Brownie's face suddenly changed again, looking past Edward towards the river, her lips parted. Edward turned.

A man was standing on the other side of the river near to the cherry tree, a bearded man standing with legs wide apart and looking towards them. Edward thought it was the tree man. Then he saw that it was Jesse. As soon as Jesse saw Edward he waved. Then he turned and began to pick his way along the bank over the hummocky grass.

Edward said the Brownie, 'Excuse me – that's my father.'

'What –? Can I help?'

'No, no. I'll tell you later if you'll let me. You did say we could meet again. I'm so glad about that. I can manage here. Thank you, thank you.'

She turned and went away along the line of willows.

Jesse had by this time gone quite a distance, walking upstream. His back could just be seen beyond some elder bushes as he continued on his way. Edward ran as fast as he could along his bank of the river. He shouted, 'Wait, wait for me.' He thought, I'll swim across.

Jesse paused and turned. He was wearing a rather dishevelled shirt, some sort of knee breeches, socks and boots. He stood there smiling at Edward. Edward understood the look of surprise on Brownie's face. For Jesse, though fully clothed looked extremely odd, his head, now seen in the open, being unusually large, his eyes also round and huge, and the knee breeches giving somehow the effect of shaggy haunches. Edward called, 'Jesse, stay there. I'm going to swim over.'

Jesse waved again in a nonchalant manner and began to descend the bank. Then, as Edward stared, he began to cross the river, walking upon the water. He came steadily across, taking carefully step after step, with the stream swirling about his boots, leaping sometimes up to his ankles. Edward, amazed, ran down to where the bank descended smoothly to a little beach and stepped into the water, reaching out his hand. Jesse, avoiding the proffered assistance, came ashore with a childishly triumphant smile. As he did so Edward saw, just below the surface of the fast river, a line of stepping stones to which he would not have liked to trust himself.

'Oh Jesse – you – oh I'm so glad to see you!' Edward suddenly overcome, threw his arms round his father.

'Used to be a ford here,' said Jesse, disengaging himself.

'You mustn't walk about like this,' said Edward, 'it's dangerous, you might fall, I must take you home, you mustn't be out here by yourself – come home now, please, with me.' He was afraid that Jesse would resist. However he allowed Edward to take his arm and they began to walk slowly back toward Seegard, whose weird ungainly form was illuminated by the now declining sun.

They had reached the green meadow where Edward had seen the yellow flowers when Jesse, who had been walking quite well, suddenly stopped and seemed disposed to sit down on the wet grass. 'Jesse, just come a little further. It's drier up there on the path.'

'I like it here.'

'Where were you going when I saw you?'

'Looking for those flowers – what they – cowslips – didn't find any.'

Edward pulled him a little and he walked on as far as the path, where he promptly sat down, then lay down, between two gorse bushes. Edward sat down beside him. He took off his mac and rolled it up inside out and put it under Jesse's head, which Jesse lifted to receive the pillow.

'Jesse, are you feeling all right?'

'Of course not. Smell, that smell, I remember it – the smell of gorse – like – like what – coconut.'

'Why, yes, so it is.'

'Who was that girl?'

Edward was surprised that Jesse remembered the girl. He answered. 'She's Brenda Wilsden –'

'Never liked that name, Brenda.'

'She's called Brownie –'

'That's better, nice –'

Jesse lay relaxed, gazing at Edward, his big furry spherical head propped up, heavy, lolling to one side, his arms crossed on his chest, his feet, in muddy ill-laced boots, crossed too. Edward noticed again the ring with the red stone whose wide gold band made the soft flesh bulge a little.

'Your girl?'

'No,' said Edward.

'You got a girl?'

'No.'

'Had girls?'

'Yes.'

'What were you talking about, with that Brownie?'

'We were talking about her brother. I gave him a bad drug and he fell out of a window and was killed, it was my fault. She wanted me to tell her how it happened.' In the short silence after this Edward wondered what on earth Jesse would now find to say. He had not been looking at him as he spoke, but now turned toward the propped head. The dark round eyes were looking at him with intelligence.

'Funny,' said Jesse, 'you looked so nice with that girl – in the sun – and you were talking about *that*.'

'I came here to tell you about it,' said Edward. 'It makes me feel so bad that sometimes I want to die.'

'You're not to die, no, no. I to die, not you.'

'You mustn't,' said Edward, 'I won't let you. Jesse, let me take you to London, we could see a doctor there who could help you – you're not old – please let us go to London –'

Jesse smiled, protruding his red lips out of their surroundings of luxuriant dark straight hair, hair which as it flowed shone like some strong self-confident plant. 'No. No.

251

It's all happening here.'

'What is happening?'

'Life and death, good and evil. I wouldn't go to London for that.'

Edward thought, no, of course, what I suggested is impossible, I can't quite see why, but it's *impossible*.

Jesse went on, and Edward was surprised at his command of the conversation.

'So you wanted to tell me – about the boy that fell?'

'Yes.'

'Why?'

'I thought you might help me, let me out of this – hell. Sort of – forgive me.'

'Has she, that girl, forgiven you, his sister?'

'I don't know,' said Edward.

'Then I forgive you.'

'Oh – Jesse –' Edward reached out and touched the back of one hand. Then leaning quickly forward he kissed the hand. The long hairs tasted salt.

Jesse, still gazing at Edward without visible recognition of the homage, said, 'I don't see young girls now – except Ilona – and she hasn't been around –'

'They won't let her. She loves you.'

'Oh I know, I know –'

'And I love you, Jesse. I love you so much. I must tell you. You could do everything for me, you could make me all over again –' As Edward found these words emerging from his mouth he felt a thrill of fright as if the words were actually little animals which had leapt out of his mouth and were now running about. He was hypnotised by Jesse's large protuberant red-dark eyes in whose depths he seemed now to see deep seas and sea creatures moving.

'Oh, well – I've forgotten it all.'

'What?'

'What I knew once – about good and evil and those – all *those* things – people don't really have them, meet them – in their lives at all, most people don't – only a few – want that – that fight, you know – think they want – good – have to have – evil – not real, either – of course – all inside something else –

252

it's a dance – you see – world needs power – always round and round – it's all power and – energy – which sometimes – rears up its beautiful head – like a dragon – that's the meaning of it all – I think – in the shadows now – can't remember – doesn't matter – what I need – is a long sleep – so as to dream it all – over again.' At this point Jesse's eyes closed for a moment and Edward was afraid he was actually falling asleep or going off into one of his trances. However he opened his eyes and said, 'As beautiful as fire.'

'What is, who is?'

'He is, I was once, no matter. It's all very close now. But you will live. You will be – all right. You're wearing my boots.'

'Yes, I came without any, they fit perfectly, I hope you don't mind.'

'So you're in my boots. Well, you're not involved, it won't touch you, when it comes. Perhaps spirits need a master – after all – if it isn't – too late. I used to know about that – I used to know everything – once. It doesn't matter. Perhaps I'll die of it, in the end, in the very end.'

'Of what?'

'Old age. Done my job, maybe. I'll think about all that – when I'm asleep. Help me up, dear boy. It's getting dark.'

When Edward raised his eyes from his father's face he saw that it had indeed got dark. The form of Seegard, the tower unlit, a dim light shining from the high windows of the Atrium, was outlined against a reddish sky. Then the other way, toward the sea, Edward saw as he rose that the sky was a dark clear blue, a blue full of the ink of the night.

Getting Jesse up was not easy. He seemed to have become abnormally heavy, his limbs falling about like leaden sacks. At last he was on his feet, leaning heavily on Edward, and they walked on very slowly toward the house. As they approached the stable yard a figure was waiting for them. It was Mother May. Edward began, 'I found him –'

Mother May thrust a strong arm in between Edward and Jesse, prising them apart. Her rough movement squeezed Edward's damaged finger, which he had forgotten, and which now began to burn with pain. He fell back, letting Mother

May take Jesse's weight and lead him on, trying to hurry him over the uneven stones. 'Oh come *along*!', Edward heard her say as she hustled him through the outside door into the Interfectory. When Edward entered the room the door opposite into the tower had already closed.

Edward walked out of the front door into the moist warm dark. Clouds must be covering the sky where there was no light, but the wind had dropped. He could smell the pine trees. He began to walk long the front of the house toward Selden. Supper was over now. Wine had been served. Jesse's escapade had not been discussed. Edward's mention of it was passed over with vague anodyne comments. 'Oh, he sometimes does that.' 'He can go quite a long way.' 'Some day he'll go off altogether.' Ilona, trying to say something, had been shut up and had burst into tears. She sat there at the table, her tears dropping into her bowl. It was not the first time Edward had seen this happen. He thought, they reduce her to childishness. But he made no overt movement of sympathy. Ilona's tears were ignored. And he wondered: did they *want* Jesse to go out, to get lost, to go away? Was it true that he was capable of becoming lucid and mobile and setting off for London or Paris, as they had more than once said? Today he had left the house with his boots on. Evidently doors had been unlocked, presumably no one had seen him go.

Edward was now in total darkness. The glow of the oil lamps through the high windows of the Atrium had been extinguished, wrapped up in an obscurity which was like some black velvet textile or soft inky stuff which filled space and touched Edward's face like ectoplasm. His feet, lacking confidence in this deprivation of sensory guidance, moved slowly and uncertainly, and he had lost his sense of direction. He suddenly came up against something, knocking into it first with his knee, then with his whole body. He exclaimed with fright. His exploring hands told him that he was up against the trunk of one of the ilex trees which he had imagined to be still many paces away. He felt the ridgy densely textured bark of the tree. He looked up, then round about, then stepped back a little. He could see nothing. He had lost all intuitive sense of his surroundings. The night sky, the arching trees, could as well have been the walls of a tiny black lightless room, an oubliette in the centre of which he was standing. He reached out again but could touch nothing. Then suddenly something took him by the throat, a frightful sensation that made him stagger and gasp harshly. He brought his hands up to his face. His legs, suddenly devoid of force, gave way at the knees and he squatted, losing his balance and about to prostrate himself as at the effect of a blow. One open hand found the ground and one knee, and he levered himself up and stood for a moment, legs wide apart, gasping. The sensation which had suddenly felled him was fear, pure contentless fear such as he had never experienced before. He was not capable of screaming. He checked the instinct to run as he knew he would instantly fall. He set off walking in long strenuous strides, his staring eyes wide open to the black dark, in what he took to be the direction of the house. After long moments he saw the lighted windows and a pale smudge lower down which came from the open door of the hall. He moved a little to his right and stretched out one hand to touch the stones of the wall, feeling their altering texture. As he approached the door someone came out of it and at once vanished into the dark. It was Bettina. Edward hurried in, then, in the light, paused to adjust his breathing. As he stood and breathed he heard behind him a weird high-pitched cry. It's only an owl, he told himself, but he made haste to close the door and get well away from it.

The supper table had not been cleared. At the table Mother May was sitting alone, and Edward saw before her a wine bottle and a half-filled glass. He sat down opposite to her, moving an oil lamp to illuminate her face. She had her calm young look, as he had first seen her, her face seeming entirely smooth and exuding, in the lamp light, a powdery golden glow. Her hair, glowing red and gold, was pulled back into a large neat bun, displaying the full intent gentle luminosity of her gaze, as she looked dreamily at Edward.

Behind him, outside in the fearful dark, other sounds were now arising, long wailing cries and shrieks. 'What in heaven's name is that?'

'Owls, of course.'

'I've never heard those sounds before.'

'They're mating. There are all sorts of owls and they have different cries. I meant to tell you, you must be careful going out at night, an owl could peck out your eyes if you came near its nest.'

'But why are they all suddenly shrieking together?'

'Bettina is calling them. She can simulate many birds' cries. She can make sounds higher than the human ear can catch. It's a sort of physical endowment. Jesse had it.'

Edward sat listening to the cacophony of wailing. 'Where's Ilona?'

'Gone to bed.'

Edward had wanted to see her and comfort her. He regretted not having done so at the dinner table. He found an empty glass and reached out for the wine bottle. The wine tasted delicious, fragrant and complexly sweet. 'What's this?'

'Dandelion wine.'

'I didn't know you could make wine out of dandelions.'

'You can make wine out of anything.'

'I've never had this one before, it's good.'

'What have you done to your finger?'

'I sliced it, slicing herbs. Look.' Edward began to pull the dark blood-stiffened bandage off. He was doing this, he was well aware, as an aggressive gesture, a reckless exposure, an exhibition designed to produce pity, fear and disgust. The bandage was stuck hard to the wound. A sharp pain shot through Edward's hand and up his arm. He wrenched the bandage off, feeling his flesh tear as if half his finger were being severed. He yelped, then gazed at the large raw wound out of which blood was promptly oozing, coming up fast in bright red globules out of the deep mouth of the cut and pouring down his hand and dripping onto the table.

'Here.' Mother May handed him a table napkin. 'Wait. I'll get something.'

Mother May returned with a steaming bowl, cloths, towel and a small box. Edward held his hand over the basin while Mother May, holding up his wrist, mopped the cut, staunched it a little, then covered it with a poultice of leaves covered with

256

a finger-shaped piece of linen and loosely tied with thread.

'That'll stop the bleeding and heal the wound. It won't stick.'

'Thanks. What is it?'

'Comfrey.' She cleaned the table carefully with another cloth and dried it, then put the basin on the floor.

Edward sat quietly inhaling the fragrant herbal smell from the basin. He was aware of silence. The concert of owls was over. Bettina was outside somewhere, standing or roving in the pitch dark. He could still feel the firm soothing grip of Mother May's fingers upon his wrist. Some white moths were circling round the lamp. He said, 'I want to take Jesse to London.'

'He wouldn't go with you.'

'Why shouldn't you all come?'

'It would be impossible.'

'Do you imagine you'd die if you left this place?'

'No, but I should very quickly grow old.' Mother May was staring at him with her large gentle lucid eyes. She poured some more wine into his glass, then into her own.

'You're all eternally young – except Jesse, and he –'

'Oh, he will never die, he'll simply metamorphose himself!'

'I wish I could help him, serve him. He did want to see me, didn't he?'

'Perhaps you imagine that you were the longed-for boy – your mother could have put that into your head – but don't be charmed by him. You realise he's crazy. He has all sorts of illusions, and he would tell you anything. He's just the wreck of a wicked old man.'

'He isn't wicked.'

'Pure wickedness never seems wicked. It's when it's mixed with good that it shows. He is an incarnation of evil. He has opened the door of evil and seen within.'

'What nonsense! You mean he ran after women.'

'He was my truth once. And if one's truth proves untrue . . .'

'I think you're just fed up with him because he's sick, and sick people are a nuisance!'

'He has betrayed us by becoming our child.'

257

'How can you talk like that, of course you love him, *I* love him – Or are you jealous because he loves me?'

'Does he? You are the blameless outsider, not tainted as we are by having known him as he once was. For that knowledge *he* cannot forgive *us*. You are fresh and unspoilt, you were never his gaoler, you never forced him screaming up those stairs. But be careful. He could maim you for life with his little finger.'

'I am maimed for life.'

'What you call suffering is nothing. You have never really suffered yet.'

'I can understand your resenting his having had other women. But I'm sure he never intended to hurt anyone.'

'If you are aware of nothing but your own desires you don't have to intend to kill, you just kill. Don't you even care that your mother was driven mad with grief? Of course he ran after other women, and after men too. You're the only bastard we know of. But there may be dozens of others.'

Edward did not like this thought. 'If I am the longed-for boy – why didn't you summon me sooner?'

'You are not very bright, Edward. Of course at the start Chloe guarded you like a tigress, she never let us near you, and Cuno would have kept us off too, but it wasn't just that. Can't you realise how complicated, how *dangerous* it all was? Jesse didn't want you to exist, he wanted Chloe to have an abortion.'

Edward was dazed by the idea of how very nearly he had not existed. 'Do you mean he chucked her out because of me, or she gave him up because of me?'

'You were a minor point then. When you did exist he pretended you didn't. He was tired of Chloe and you were thrown away with her. Later on if he mentioned you it was just to annoy us. And frighten us.'

'How frighten you? So you – the three of you – must have been against me?'

'Of course.'

'But you wrote to me, *you* did. It must have been to please him.'

'No. Just to make a change.'

'To make a change?'

'We were – becalmed – it wasn't good – it isn't good. We

258

needed a disturbance, a catalyst, we came to feel that any change would be better.'

'And have I been a catalyst?'

'Not yet.'

'Ilona said I'd stirred things up.'

'Ilona does not understand the situation.'

'But what change do you want?'

'You don't seem to understand it either.'

Edward thought, is it that they want him to die? But that's not anything I ever could or would bring about. *They* are crazy, not him. Groping for intelligence, Edward wondered if the wine were affecting his wits. He said, 'I'm sure you don't mean what you say about Jesse. Of course I was brought up by my poor mother to regard him as the devil –'

'Your poor mother was a bitch and a whore,' said Mother May calmly. 'She slept with everyone. Jesse wasn't even certain about you till he saw you.'

'My God,' said Edward. 'You mean you've discussed that with him?'

'Do you imagine you're the only person he talks to?'

'Did *you* ask me here because *you* wanted to look at me?'

'I've told you why. Just *think*.'

'Well, what am I to think? You say such odd contradictory things. I believe I have a real relation with the real Jesse. And you're wrong about my mother. And anyway my mother is my business.'

'She was my business when she tried to break up my marriage. She thought she could take Jesse away. Of course she failed. He went over her like a juggernaut, as he did over all the other poor waifs, I heard their bones crunch. She had a terrible life. No wonder she committed suicide.'

'She didn't commit suicide.'

'I hated your mother. I prayed for her death. Hatred kills. I probably brought about her death.'

'She died of a sort of virus.'

'A mysterious virus. The virus of hate.'

'You mustn't hate people.'

'I have a gorgon face,' Mother May continued to look at him with her calm lucid unwrinkled gaze.

259

'You conceal it well,' said Edward. But for a second he thought he saw something far back in her eyes like a little black thing peering out, and he was afraid. He went on, 'You said in your letter that you were sorry for me because of – what had happened – because of my misfortune – which you'd read about. But since I've been here no one has asked me anything about it. The only person I've talked to about it is Jesse.'

'You didn't bring up the subject. So we didn't.'

'Perhaps you're not interested.'

'We wanted you to tell us in your own time.'

'I think you didn't give the matter a thought!'

'We all have horrors in our lives which have to be lived with. We must all harden our hearts about the harm we have done to others, forgive ourselves and forget our deeds as the victims of them would do if they were righteous.'

'Oughtn't we to be righteous?'

'That belongs always to the future.'

'Is that all you have to say about it?'

'We have our troubles, you have yours. Men have to kill their fathers. Life has to go on.'

'What do you mean?'

'Only that you have to grow up, Edward. We are all in the hands of fate. That brother of yours, Cuno's son – '

'Stuart –'

'He knows what to do. Hasn't he given up sex?'

'He's mad.'

'Or good. Anyway he's extreme. That's what's needed now, extremes.'

'You're disappointed in me.'

'No –'

'Perhaps you wanted me to fail, you wanted Jesse to be disillusioned about me, that's why you asked me.'

'No – you just don't astonish me. You are a suitable companion for Ilona.'

Edward felt tempted to astonish her by speaking of Brownie and Elspeth Macran; but it was too dangerous a move. In any case he was beginning to feel rather drowsy and strange. Mother May's face, smooth and calm, now smiling a

260

little, was wavering and becoming larger and moving gently as in a wind. There was a ring of white moths circling rhythmically about the lamp. 'You're drugging me, aren't you, the wine is drugged, you're making me see things –'

'You have drugged yourself, Edward. Before you came here you drugged yourself for life. I know about these things. The effect of what you were taking never stops, it never leaves you. Do you know that? That's how you killed your friend, remember?'

'Don't – speak so –'

'Oh you and your troubles. You know nothing, see nothing. The question is, how much can you do for *me*? What can you do for me at this moment in my life – or am I to destroy myself before your eyes? How much can you love me – can you help me, can you love me, can you love me *enough*?'

Bettina came through the outer door, shutting it after her. She had undone her hair. She said the Edward, 'Flirting with Mother May?' She said to Mother May, 'Come now, come to bed and to sleep.'

Edward got up and walked unsteadily out of the hall. Looking back he could see nothing but the lamp shining through a cloud of moths.

MY DEAR STUART,

Dad, who is here, tells me you are proposing to chuck up thought. This has got me worried. You mustn't do it. Of course Dad may be exaggerating. Because of his old (you know) troubles he likes to think that everyone has extraordinary obsessions and is secretly *in extremis*. Maybe he has misunderstood. Maybe you are just momentarily fed up, as we all are sometimes. Thinking is hell. But just in case it's serious, let me beg you not to. It's a bad idea, it's an *abstract* idea. I don't want to enter into the moral good versus bad business. Not that I think it isn't the thing – I think it is *the* thing, for all of us I mean, but it's impossible to talk about, anyway in a letter, there isn't time, or rather it's that face to face one can keep on swiping out the bad formulations. (And you are seven thousand miles away, worse luck.) I suspect that goodness is too hard even to name and 'comes about' infinitely slowly if at all, as a scarcely visible result of watching a million steps. It can't be a 'programme', can it? Even if one enters a monastery it can't. Plato said it came by divine gift. Of course that doesn't mean it's a matter of luck. But you just have to work at something or other and be around. I wonder if even wanting it matters? (It would be too clever to say it was a positive obstacle!) My point is (I'm coming to it) that you'll be wretched, you'll be miserable, you'll feel useless, you're an intellectual, you'll miss thinking, you'll be *sick*: and if you drop out now, it's not all that easy (just look at the job situation) to get in again. So don't do it. If you want to be a 'social worker' why not try university teaching? It's just the thing. You have to nursemaid the kids all the time these days. Besides, reflect on this, the world is going most awfully astray (I see a lot of that here), and in ten years time we'll need all the decent men we can muster in positions of influence. (For your benefit I am avoiding the word 'power'.) I don't mean this in a narrow political sense. Perhaps the time for *narrow* politics is already over.

Meanwhile I live like a king here, anyway like a (which I'm not) hedonist. It's easy to do in America. (All right, if one's not poor, black, etc.) To be honest, I'm rather happy. Or would be if it weren't for certain, soluble I hope, love and sex problems. (These can't be avoided, you know, even by you!) New ones, not those old ones. (Of things displeasing to you I will of course not speak.) Everyone here is beautiful, the men, the women, tall, strong, clean, healthy, lucid-eyed. Why don't you come and visit me? We could talk of everything. Come and see the earthly gods before you give up the human race. Come and see *me*.

This is just a message. I'll write a letter later.

Yours,
Giles.

Stuart Cuno, sitting in the Parthenon frieze room of the British Museum, smiled over this letter from his friend Giles Brightwalton and stuffed it into his pocket. He was waiting for Meredith McCaskerville. They used to run. Today perhaps they would walk. There were things to be said. Nevertheless, the greatest part of Stuart's communication with the boy was wordless.

Stuart and Meredith met in various significant places, sometimes in an art gallery, sometimes in a park, often in the British Museum. It was like a secret assignation (though of course it was not secret). Across London they came, from points far apart, traversing time and space, coming closer, until suddenly at last they were in each other's presence. These, always somehow surprising and strange, meetings

263

were of quite long standing, since the days Stuart was 'uncle' and Meredith used to frisk like a puppy in his presence and paw and punch him playfully. All that had altered, painlessly and felicitiously in the substance of their understanding of each other changed. Now Stuart looked forward to the self-contained dignified straight-backed separate taller boy, his laconic reticence, his mystery.

At this moment, however, although aware of Meredith's imminent arrival, Stuart was reflecting that the questions raised in Giles Brightwalton's letter simply did not affect him at all. He would not miss the pleasures of being an 'intellectual' or an 'academic'. It was indeed with an intense relief, and without any sense of its being a cowardly action, that he laid down that burden. (Giles had not accused him of cowardice, but Harry had.) And as for being, in time to come, an influence, a power for good, Stuart thought (touching the thought with caution) that he was likely to have, by *his* path, more of such power. Was that then his aim? No. Harry had said that a religious man must have an aim. (There was no point in disputing the word 'religious' with Harry.) Stuart could only formulate his 'aim' in negative and exceedingly general terms. He wanted to avoid being bad. He wanted to be good. Was this unusual? Did he think he was exceptional? He had to be fundamentally and permanently alone, now at the beginning of his life, not only as celibate priests are alone, but as everyone is in the end alone. What had happened to make him live his life backwards in this way? That was another person's question. Nothing had happened, it was just so. He was surrendering his talents as monks do under obedience. He was not a monk, yet he was under obedience. Was it wrong to *think* about the matter in this way – or at all? He could not help thinking. But often he let his thoughts rise like smoke and blow away. Giles had said it couldn't be a programme. Harry had said it was all a sexual fantasy. Somebody had said there is no way, only the end, what we call the way is messing about.

Of course, he thought, *this* of mine is a matter of love and passion, which somehow denies time and yet also creates it, creates its own necessity and pace. It's a matter of looking elsewhere. Then I orient myself as I move. *This*, which he did not want to name, not with the abhorrent name of God, not either with the awkward dry old name of religion. He did not reject religion as he rejected God, but his private language excluded the word. It was a necessary passion, a necessary love, which was cunning so to station itself as to be attracted by what was holy. What an apparatus; and how difficult and yet how easy it all was. God had been convenient, a permanent non-degradable love-object, to use Thomas's phrase, automatically purifying desire. But it must all be able to happen without God. Could one not surely love everything so? Somewhere, in his weakness, there lurked the desire for a sign, for an indubitable light to shine so upon something. Yet did it not shine so upon *everything*? Upon evil too? Can one be a spectator of evil? To be a spectator of suffering was difficult enough: the mysterious awful untouchable suffering of others. Edward's suffering. The suffering of animals. The suffering of the whole planet burdened with hardship and injustice and unquenchable grief. The whole of creation groaning and travailing together in misery and sin. There was no solution to that, even at the end of the world no holy man in a cave, or working in a field or office, who knew the answer. Here were the negative things, the deprivation of understanding. To prise open a door of holiness and knowledge with a narrow but very pure instrument: had that once seemed to be his aim? Where on earth do such ideas come from, and such images, surgical, sexual? Is it a form of madness, or an ecstasy? The negation of such ambitions, such formulations, came as a kind of pleasure, like opening one's eyes into total darkness. Kneel and let the darkness flow over you, kneel and ask pardon for the sin of existing. Someone had described God as boiling over in the dark, a vast dark boiling of perpetually self-creating being. Something that Keats saw too. The mystical Christ walking upon the boiling sea. Christ in Limbo. Angels embracing repentant sinners in a picture by Botticelli.

Stuart was conscious of a feeling which he often now experienced of almost falling asleep yet of being intensely alert at the same time. What odd fragments of images came then, so vivid and charged with sense. There were the sort of things (but indeed they were all sorts of things) he had, he now remembered, told Edward to hang on to, talismans, sacraments, holy objects, existing in corners of the mind as they might in corners of a church or shrine. Surely Edward too had such things? Stuart had a mental picture of a small image of a god, or perhaps it was just a stone, upon a wet shelf of rock beside a fountain or waterfall. He could not recall ever having seen anything like this, perhaps he had dreamt it. What was it, this 'holiness' idea which he seemed to recognise as so ubiquitous and important? Was it perhaps dangerous, an ambiguous face of good, a blank face of sex? Where was Edward anyway and was it not time that he reappeared from whatever safe retreat Thomas, that magician, had despatched him to? Stuart felt a strong desire to see Edward, to help him. To *find out* how to. He had been no use to Edward at the start. Could he help him now? Could he help anybody? Sometimes he felt so alone with *this* that it seemed to cut him off from other people, and that couldn't be right. Would all that change when he found a job? Job: odd blunt word for it. He loved Edward, he loved Harry. He loved Meredith. Stuart was not dismayed by his sexual feelings about the boy. He had, or had had, more or less vague sexual feelings about all sorts of things and people, schoolmasters, girls seen in trains, mathematical problems, holy objects, the idea of being good. Sex seemed to be mixed into everything. Was this unusual? Was he perhaps 'over-sexed', whatever that meant? The mechanical superficial aspects of the desires characteristic of his youthful age he dealt with himself, privately and without guilt, easily blanking out any tendency to erotic fantasy.

His gaze began to articulate his surroundings of which he had not been aware. Stuart, not blessed with a classical education beyond the stage of elementary Latin, had rather unclear ideas about the Greeks with whom however he ardently identified. In an ignorantly attentive way, he knew the Parthenon frieze very well. He liked the young horsemen. He had always seen himself as a horseman, although he had never been on a horse in his life. By an odd quirk of association, the kind of association of floating fragments

266

which interested him in himself, he connected the idea of riding a horse with the image of his grandfather's death which Harry, without intending it to haunt the boy, had early imparted to him: the helpless swimmer, the white sail of the ghosting vanishing yacht slowly drawing away. Perhaps the connection came somehow through the Greeks, something dangerous and heroic and awfully lonely and sad, clearly delineated in a pure light. In Stuart's picture of his grandfather's death it was always early morning, with a cool clear sky and a calm sea.

The Parthenon procession was, in its stillness, so purposive, moving or waiting to move, prancing horses, swaying riders, all immobile, pressing forward, pressing onward, a procession to a mystery. No, it was not innocent; those careless young men were too beautiful. The gods, so relaxed, so calmly seated in repose, were not innocent either. The only blameless ones were the animals, the horses, and the sacrificial beasts lifting their fine heads, lifting up their touching unsuspecting heads to heaven; and one little boy, a page or groom, younger even than Meredith. Not innocent, but not evil either. These images belonged to fate. And rising up by an association of contrast Stuart saw a girl's plaited hair, plaits of hair severed at the nape lying in huge mounds. Did she plait it on the day she died, upon a day when she knew she would die? One might plait one's hair on any terrible day, like shaving before the scaffold. Oh it was the details, the details that were so unendurable.

And now Meredith had appeared, materialising in front of the line of riders, the soldierly boy, near, solemn, compact, dandyish in his dark clothes.

'There was an exhibition for blind people in the Museum,' said Meredith.

They were walking, perhaps aimlessly, perhaps led by the boy, and had crossed Tottenham Court Road. This took them out of Bloomsbury, both the area and the concept. The Museum was different of course, that was a palace of light and wisdom, floating like a great liner on that dark sea. Stuart did not like the handsome gloomy streets, full of memories of all those smart know-alls, people who had patronised his grandfather and his great-grandfather, and whom even Harry doffed his cap to. How Stuart resented that uncritical obeisance. Across the road was north Soho, reeking with sin of course, but also, in all those messy streets and real little shops, murmurous with humanity.

'There was this exhibition for blind people, sculptures of animals for them to touch, old stuff you know, Greek and Egyptian and Chinese, lovely animals. Anyone could come and touch them. I did, I touched them and stroked them, and a lot of people did, but not the blind people, *they* weren't there. I'd have liked to see the blind people touching the animals. But they weren't there. If I was blind I wouldn't go about. I'd stay at home. I wouldn't come to exhibitions for the blind. I'd be too shy – I'd be too proud, too ashamed –'

'There's nothing to be ashamed of,' said Stuart. But he knew what Meredith meant. How would he act if he were blind?

'People look down on cripples, they can't help it. I'd hide.'

'No, you wouldn't,' said Stuart. 'You'd be a different person, a braver one.'

'You think courage is a product of circumstances?' said Meredith in his harsh prim childish Scottish voice.

'Partly. But courage isn't just a thing on its own, it's part of your whole attitude to the world. With something awful like being blind you can't know beforehand how brave you'd be or what you'd do –'

'You might fail.'

'Yes, but one's always failing, there are infinite ways of doing that. Our courage and our desire to be good are tested every day –' Stuart was about to add 'every moment', but he refrained.

'You don't fail, do you? I can't see that you fail. You're the only person I know who's not all messy.'

Stuart wondered how to answer this. He said, 'I'm messy, only you can't see.' He thought, yet I do believe I'm different. What is this idea? Is it a good or bad idea? He also thought, I mustn't ever disappoint Meredith.

'Well, if it doesn't show that's everything, isn't it? Thoughts don't matter.'

'Oh yes they do!' said Stuart. 'They matter a lot. They make it easier or harder to *do* things. And anyway they matter in themselves –'

'Because God sees them? I don't believe in God. Neither do you.'

'They matter. They exist. And bad thoughts are better not existing.'

'I don't see how anyone can get rid of bad ones, they just come. I have *awful* thoughts. You've no notion!'

Stuart resisted the temptation to ask what they were. The boy was simply wanting to shock him, to make a little exciting emotional drama by eliciting a reproof. Stuart was increasingly wary of such 'advances' in his relation with Meredith. In any case filth is better not uttered, utterance gives it more reality and an easier lodgement. Stuart did not want to reflect about Meredith's bad thoughts, he even felt afraid to hear them. 'People used to pray,' he said, 'to get rid of bad thoughts, I've said this to you before. You should sit quietly every night and let them all fade away. See how unreal they are, based on false ideas and selfish attitudes.'

'I don't see how they can be unreal if they're there. You think I mean thoughts about sex. Some people say they don't matter, they're healthy.'

'You said they were awful. One has to judge one's thoughts. It's not all that difficult. Anyway you can try. Sitting still helps, get some distance and quietness in your mind, think of good things, perhaps.'

'Good things. Are there any?'

'Meredith, you know there are, and all sorts.'

'Do I know? I think everything in the world is covered with a sort of grey dust. Anyway, I can't see the point if there's no God. Is it true that Newton would have discovered relativity if he hadn't believed in God?'

'Who put that into your head?'

'Ursula. She said so at that dinner party, you were there, I was listening at the door, I always do.'

'I don't think so –'

'You'll say listening at doors is wrong.'

'Shut up. I don't think so. Mathematics is –'

'Stronger than God?'

'Such a powerful self-generating force. I doubt if the notion of explanation by deity would have stopped Newton if he had been capable of conceiving of relativity. It just wasn't possible for him to because of the whole intellectual context.'

'Is that why you gave up mathematics?'

'Because it's stronger than God? No.'

'Ought I to give up maths, history, Latin?'

'Of course not. Whatever can you mean? You must study as hard as you can!'

'I don't see – oh never mind – I won't be able to get a job anyway – except I will because Dad will wangle me one – it's nice to belong to the establishment. Dad told me you didn't like those posters in my room, so I took them down.'

'Good.'

'The ones of girls, and chimps on loos.'

'I can't think what you saw in that muck. And so unkind to poor animals to insult them with our human vulgarity.'

'There were such nice animals in that exhibition. Is that what's wrong then, vulgarity?'

'I hope you haven't been looking at any more of those filthy pornographic videos.'

'Dad told me not to. I told him I wouldn't.'

'But have you been looking at them?'

'Yes. All the others do. And I don't think Dad really minds.'

'I mind.'

'You didn't tell me not to look at the Greek vase in the Museum, with those satyrs chasing those nymphs.'

'That's a work of art.'

'I don't see why it's different.'

'It's beautiful, and –'

'You didn't like my looking actually, you pulled me.'

'I didn't.'

'So it is just vulgarity after all, not good and bad. It's whether something's beautiful or elegant not what it's about.'

'It *is* good and bad – it's how a thing is – presented sort of – it's the thought –' Stuart was not able to explain very clearly. 'And anyway, things connect. You not only looked at that muck, you lied to your father.'

'Is that worse?'

'It's deep. Don't start to lie, Meredith. Just don't *start*.'

'Oh I've started. I'm well on the way. I don't suppose he believed me anyway. He doesn't expect me to tell him the truth.'

'I'm sure he does. Don't talk about your father in that way.'

'Sorry. Of course I don't lie to you.'

'I'm glad of that.'

'But that's partly because I can predict you. I know what you'll say. I know you won't be *really* angry.'

'I wouldn't be too sure,' said Stuart. 'But – oh heavens – one can't win!' He laughed. He looked down at the boy, at the neatly combed hair disturbed by the breeze, the heavy silk locks, the evenly cut fringe, the birthmark, like the mark of a blow, glowing a little. Meredith looked up with his composed shrewd look, perhaps not sure what to make of Stuart's exclamation. He kicked a crushed Coca-Cola tin off the pavement into a pile of rotting cabbages whose odour mingled with the spicy smell of a little Greek shop. The Post Office Tower had come into view. As they talked they had been walking along crowded pavements, avoiding people, pausing, touching shoulders, crossing roads, hearing several languages being spoken, private in the middle of the human stream. Meredith stopped at a shop window.

'I say, look at *that*!'

Stuart saw what kind of shop it was, what sort of pictures were exhibited in the window. 'Come on, Meredith!'

They began to walk again.

'You looked,' said Meredith. 'I *saw* you look. You were *interested*.'

Stuart had indeed looked; and had, in passing such shops, looked before, for seconds only. The unnerving discovery was that he had instantly known *which* pictures were, for him, the 'interesting' ones!

'That's my problem,' said Stuart. 'Except that it isn't a problem.' Now as he walked on he was conscious of himself and of human obstacles, the hostile looks, the cacophony,

271

aware of himself as a fleshy pillar moving, as a tall thick man with a pale staring face and a little mouth and yellow animal eyes, a big ungainly animal lurching and obstructing people as he went.

'All this about what's good and what's bad,' said Meredith, 'what you go on about, it's just your thing. Other people don't think it's important. They don't think you can tell. They don't think it's the main thing in life.'

'And what do you think, Meredith?'

'Oh I don't matter – what I think – doesn't matter –'

'Because you're a child?'

'Because nothing matters.'

'Some things don't matter too much,' said Stuart. 'Other things matter absolutely. You'll find that out. In fact you know it already.'

'Shall I tell you how I know that nothing matters?'

'Go on.'

'Because my mother is having a secret love affair. So all is permitted.'

'*What*?'

'She told me not to tell my father, and I haven't. So you see, all is permitted and nothing matters. QED.'

'It's impossible,' said Stuart. As he looked down now he saw the boy's face disfigured by an expression he had never seen on it before. He repeated, 'Meredith, it's impossible.'

Harry Cuno was awakened suddenly from sleep by, as it seemed to him, a bright light shining on his face. He sat up in bed thinking that this must have been the light of the moon shining through a gap in the curtains. But now he could see no light; and as he sat there rigid he became convinced that he had been awakened by a bright electric torch shone for a moment upon his closed eyes. He felt extremely frightened. He waited a while in the dark room; no sound, no light. Then he heard a faint sound, a soft dark sound, then a clink, seemingly downstairs inside the house. He crept out of bed and stood shuddering beside it. The sound, repeated, now seemed to come from the garden. With tiny movements he edged to the window and parted the curtains a little and peered down. A very dim fuzzy light, it must be the first grey light of dawn, revealed the garden, and in it two figures. They were doing something very odd, they were stooping; as Harry watched with terror he realised they were *digging*, and had already dug quite a long deep hole in the lawn. He heard again the small clinking sound as one spade touched the other. He strained his eyes against the grey veil of the light. The alien awful intruders terrified him, what could they be doing in his garden in the dawn, strange people dressed in whitish robes, and with, he now saw, scarcely to be distinguished from the robes, long trailing beards. They were *old men*. And what they were doing, Harry suddenly now realised, was *digging his grave*. At the same moment he recognised the stooping bearded pair. They were his father and Thomas McCaskerville.

This of course was a dream upon which Harry was reflecting as he sat in a pretty little armchair which he had just bought in an antiques shop. He was sitting in a small flat, lately acquired, *the* small flat, to which he was going to bring Midge, the 'love nest' against which she had protested but to which she would now certainly come; just as certainly as she would come with him next weekend on the little trip (so brief, so *little*, as he constantly pointed out) which was to coincide with Thomas's conference in Geneva and Meredith's half-term with a school friend in Wales. Harry had not yet revealed to his beloved the existence of this flat. He had not yet furnished it properly, and he wanted it, when he showed it to her, to look so lovely, so perfect, so irresistibly enticing. And in any case one step at a time was the way. Midge would come on his weekend and they would be, for the first time ever, absolutely alone together, not in his or her house crammed with hostile ghosts, but in their private room, their new room, cleaned and burnished for them, a hotel room where they would be as a married pair, prefiguring their house, their home, their absolute being-together. That weekend would change her, as every little concession, and there had by now been so many, had changed her, moments in her long but so thorough metamorphosis from Thomas's woman

273

into Harry's woman. His touch of a transforming god was making her other, endowing her with new being, atom by atom remaking her, oh younger, lovelier, more alive. After the weekend she would accept the flat, it would seem natural, it would be desired. Harry knew that Midge, though she was absolutely in love, did not yet feel her need for him in the terrible imperative agonising way that he needed her. She did not *feel* her need; perhaps she took his enslavement too much for granted, perhaps he should frighten her a little? That tactic might come. He needed her as a drug addict needs his fix, without her he constantly fidgeted and groaned with longing. She was still held away, short of absolute surrender, by little threads of pusillanimous convention and by residual habitual unreflective scraps of affection for her husband. Thinking of this residue Harry clenched his fists and bit his lip. That too must be transformed, changed gradually into indifference, preferably into aversion, into hate. Lately she had said that she could imagine Thomas, but not Harry, being happy without her. That was progress. By hating Thomas himself he must make Midge do so. Already she did a bit. He must perfect her hate. Not that Harry desired this hatred upon which he brooded so for its own sake, as a trophy for himself or an adornment for her. It was simply a necessary part of the mechanism or chemistry of the change; a spreading stain perhaps, or a lever. And in this sense it might even be said that Harry hated Thomas without personal animosity.

And after this, he thought, we'll have a house in France, in Italy perhaps. This became so real in his mind, so immediately mixed with the warm spicy intoxicating smell of happiness, that he made an instinctive gesture of impatience. Why then this flat, this chair, these curtains, this television set, even a saucepan which he had brought and been so pleased with himself about, when they could surely now, so soon, *go straight on* to the house in France? How *maddening* her slowness was. After this weekend would not Midge do anything? Yet he had to perfect every step of the way to be sure there would be no relapse. Steady does it. And then he shivered as the thought of his terrible dream came back. He could not remember having ever thought of his father, his handsome happy loving father, or dreamt of him, as a hostile figure. How could his deep mind contrive to conjure up so vividly this ancient murderous apparition? How could he recognise such a being? Could ghosts be spiteful, must they not envy and detest the living? I'd be a spiteful ghost, he thought. Could they perhaps, metamorphosed into evil wraiths, do harm to those who had survived them? But of course the dream was not really about his father. It was his frightful animated image of Thomas as dangerous and old which had horribly clasped to itself the appearance of a father. Well, he did so at his peril, fathers must beware. But oh how crazy the mind is, ingenious, histrionic, wicked and deep. There were dangers, some visible, some hidden, and he was ready sword in hand to defend the woman he loved.

Harry felt now, and was conscious of feeling, as he had done in the past when at many moments he had believed in his power and his luck, when he had played cricket for his university, when he had stood for Parliament, when he had married Chloe knowing whose son she carried. All this, whatever the outcome, had been the stuff of heroism. About the girl from far away he felt differently; not that it had been a mistake, but it was just something natural, part of an ordinary life. If she had lived would he now be a very different man? Or would he have left her long ago? Piously he put away this bad thought, associating her image with that of his mother. Romula, he always thought of her as Romula, had liked Teresa. They were quiet women. Chloe belonged to the genuine stuff of Harry's life; as Midge even more imperiously did. Teresa was dead and Chloe was dead. Midge was alive, and life itself, making him in turn young, young as a young knight and as pure. On the previous evening Harry had done something very strange. He had gone through his desk, searched various old chests and drawers, found all the letters he had ever received from his first two wives, and hastily and without perusal burnt them all, putting matches to them in the empty hearth of his study. He then carefully collected up the frail ashes, still bearing traces of those two so different hands, put them in a bag and took the bag to the dustbin. He did not feel it was a crime. The past was erased, making the present and the future more to be. Midge deserved no less than everything, so far as he could give it, the whole of space, the whole of time. This was indeed a duty. He had lately remade his will, leaving adequate resources for the two boys, and the rest, including his house, to Midge. Thus did he capture and ensure the future. Harry always felt himself near to death; and supposing, as he and Midge were driving together, perhaps to that house in France, he were to be killed in an accident? Would she not feel pain when she found those letters, a particular extra unnecessary pain? This he would spare her, looking even beyond his own grave to care for her so tenderly with absolute devotion. The thought of Midge returning home alone and *not* finding the letters almost brought tears to Harry's eyes.

This thought of his death reminded him again of the dream, and now he remembered something else about it. In the dream he had been *young*, a young man, unmarried, unmade; and *they* had been *old*, very old, ancient like Druids, another race. So, he thought, it was their own grave they were digging and I was watching them from above. They belong to the past, I felt as I looked at them that I was seeing the past. It's the young against the old, Midge and I are young, Thomas is old, old. It was impossible to believe that Thomas was not much older than himself, Thomas was ninety, Harry was eternally twenty-five. No, he thought, I can't let my darling grow old with that man. Thomas already belongs to death, like my father, my poor drowned father. They are ghosts, as weak as paper. I tower above them. I have only to stretch out my hand and *take* the woman. Early in mutual love one feels able to exist upon pure joy, feeding upon it as upon the sacrament. Later that is not enough, even if an angel were to assure him that Midge would love him forever it would not be enough. He must have full and absolute possession. The door closed and bolted. Oh happiness, oh my God . . .

Harry leapt up. The sheer strength and energy of longing in him almost lifted him from the ground. He turned the television on, then loped into the little kitchen, knocking clumsily against the sink. He stood and stared at the saucepan he had bought, the kettle, the knives and forks, and smiled to think how it would amuse Midge to picture him buying these, and how she would chide him for buying the wrong kind. He turned on the tap and turned it on and on until a noisy raging torrent of hot steaming water pummelled the steel bowl and splashed the draining board and the window and Harry's suit. He reached out one hand into the hot stream whose rigid force resisted his thrust, then withdrew it quickly. The scalding water hurt his hand, re-animating the painful burn he had received when he picked up the hot coal when arguing with Edward. He hastily turned off the hot tap, turned on the cold and drenched his scalded hand and wrapped it in a towel; then jerked round in a shock of terror when he heard, close behind him, the voice of Thomas McCaskerville.

Damn, it's the television, he thought, I can't get away from the fellow even here. But what an odd chance. I shall make something of it. Two can play at magic. He went back into the little sitting room, nursing his hand.

Thomas's face, close up, peered purposefully forward into the camera, illuminated with a clarity of detail never seen in ordinary life. Harry stared at the big fox terrier face, radiant with energy and will and superior thoughts, the cold pale blue eyes enlarged by the thick donnish glasses, the neatly clipped fringe of light grey hair. The faint rabbinical shadow of the well-shaven beard. Harry felt he had never seen Thomas's face so clearly. The lips frothed a little as the words were framed and puffed out like pellets by the high didactic Scottish voice.

'So it is that we must live with death and see it as an illumination and a right, a final precious possession, ours as nothing else is upon this scene where all is vanity. The so-called "death wish" is not something negative, but one of our purest instincts. Every religion requires us to die to the world. Death has always been, in the wisdom of the east, the image of the destruction of the ego. What we see there makes the world nothing, and what the world sees there is nothing. Nirvana, the cessation of all selfish desire, the release from the tormenting turning wheel of illusory passions, is pictured as nothingness, the dust and ashes which all material and carnal goods are seen to be in the light of eternity which shines not

277

in a temporal forever but now, now with its justice upon every moment of our staggering rambling lives. Death is the death of the ego, and is in this sense a natural right, claimed too by those who decide to die to the world by the destruction of the body, the prison of the soul; thus the destruction of the body is the image of the liberation of the soul. And the liberation of the soul is the aim of true psychology. Death is the best and only picture we have of the fuller, better life for which, in our darkness, without understanding, we somehow yearn and strive. Death is the centre of life. We have to learn that we are already dead; the soul must learn it now, here in the present which is all we have, the lesson of its perfect freedom. We must hear the voice of the imprisoned soul, of all imprisoned souls, as they cry out in this age of perfected technology; when we can cure bodily sickness and send pictures through the air, but constantly tarnish and batter our thoughts and our desires with images of the sweet life, the full life, *dolce vita*, living like gods through the beauty of youth, the satisfactions of unfettered sex, the power and charm of wealth and great possessions, through having a brown suntanned healthy body, standing on a sunny beach with feet in the gently breaking waves. Is not this the very picture of happiness? Thus are we daily and hourly beguiled, made discontented and full of vain destructive wishes. It is from this that the experience of death sets us free, the discipline of death in life which we should not set aside as something reserved for helpless old age. What that time comes we may be unable to profit. The time for death is now.'

'Oh shut up, you silly old bastard,' said Harry, switching the set off. Thomas was annihilated, his big brightly coloured face blotted out, his precise high-pitched voice silenced. 'Why don't you kill yourself then, you crazy old fool? Not bloody likely. You live and thrive and fatten upon other people's death wish.'

Harry stood for a while, in the middle of the room, beside the pretty armchair. He thought, yes, how funny, that's exactly it. That's how it will be. That's where Midge and I will be standing with our young fine sun-bronzed bodies, on a sunny beach with our feet in the gently breaking waves of the warm sea. We'll be there. And we will be holding glasses of wine in our hands. And behind us there will be a bar, and a small simple excellent restaurant where we are about to have lunch, sitting in the speckled shade under a trellis of vines. And behind the restaurant there is a little town, full of squares and fountains. And in the little town there will be a picture gallery, and a small hotel with a view of the cathedral. And we shall be there, thought Harry, yes, we shall be there and *Thomas will be dead*. He will have been obliterated from our thoughts and our being as if he had died long long ago.

Then Harry thought, perhaps by then Thomas will be literally dead. What nonsense he was talking – he really looked as if he were mad. He's a *fanatic*. Perhaps he is actually intending to commit suicide. He is preparing us for his exit.

When he thought this Harry felt a momentary pang of admiration. Then he thought of his father. *Could* it have been suicide? No, no. *We* would never kill ourselves, thought Harry, *we* of the other race. Let *them* get out of our way. And he thought of Midge and how it would be, how they would be together in the little southern town.

EDWARD WAS ILL, really ill. He had been ill for two days. He lay in bed feverish, sweating, tossing, his lank dark hair plastered over his brow. His limbs ached horribly and no position gave comfort. He felt weak and frightened, ridden by illusions and dreams, tormented by sharp piercing anxieties. Supposing Brownie were to summon him and he could not come, supposing *they* intercepted Brownie's note and never told him? Suppose Jesse were asking for him? Suppose Jesse were dying?

Edward had seen Jesse again after the episode in the fen when Jesse had so strangely appeared when he was talking to Brownie. Could that have been a coincidence? Yet how could it not be? He was seeing meanings everywhere, portents, traps. He had seen Jesse on the next morning, peaceful, a bit drowsy, bathed in a kind of philosophic calm, though manifestly lacking words. Edward had sat for some time beside his bed, saying little himself, while Jesse murmured on disconnectedly, aware of Edward's presence but not looking at him. 'You looked nice together in the sun, you and that Brownie, bit of skirt, nice to be young, I too was young, I remember, I think – and Ilona, dancing – I hear it as music, as music. Don't worry, they have forgiven you, they have all forgiven you. It's getting dark – I'll go to sleep and dream it all over again – oh it won't stop, it never stops – round and round – where's Ilona, have they chained her up like a little dog? I think I hear her crying. I curse nobody, remember that. But oh the power – the power – the *dance* – it's so painful.'

Later on Edward began to feel ill. In the afternoon he was delirious. In the evening Mother May gave him a sleeping draught. He had terrible dreams, and the next day he was no better.

Now it was another afternoon, and a medical consultation was going on beside Edward's bed.

'I think it's malaria,' said Bettina. 'That day he was out in the fen he must have been bitten by mosquitoes.'

'It might be glandular fever,' said Mother May.

'Can't you find the thermometer? We did have one. Shall Ilona look again?'

'I've looked and looked,' said Ilona, 'I've turned the bathrooms upside down and the Interfec –'

'It's all that stuff you gave me to drink, and to eat,' said Edward, lying flat. 'It's not good for me. You're making me ill, so that I can't be with him –'

'Don't be silly,' said Bettina.

'It's fairy food, not fit for humans –'

'It's just the healthiest diet in the world, that's all!' said Mother May.

'You *know* we wouldn't hurt you,' said Ilona, 'we *love* you.'

'Oh Ilona,' said Edward, 'I want to ask you something –' Only he could not remember what it was he wanted to ask.

Later on, alone, he remembered. Had Ilona's feet really left the ground during that dance up at the *dromos*? Perhaps even then he had been suffering from some sort of sensorial disturbance. *Was* he being systematically drugged, was it possible? And how could he ask Ilona about that, about her bare feet sweeping the tips of the grasses and then rising above them? Wouldn't the question sound mad – or rather impertinent, impolite? If Ilona could dance on air was that not her business, perhaps her secret?

When it was coming towards twilight and Edward was alone he got up and walked slowly into his bathroom. He relieved himself and looked out of the window across the courtyard at the other side of Selden, East Selden, where the women lived. The women's quarters. He saw a lamp go on in Ilona's room and the idea of going over to see Ilona came to him. Why not? Because it was impossible. He stared, but could see nothing in the room, the sky was still too light, full of a darkish blue brilliant air which made everything look vivid yet also fuzzy and occluded, or perhaps it was his eyes. He walked slowly back and sat on the bed. He began to think about Brownie. He had been dreaming most dreadfully about her but could not recall the dreams. Now *everything* depended on Brownie. Of course it depended on Jesse too, but that was more obscure. Brownie was more urgent. Perhaps his sickness was simply *Brownie's absence*. What is that state called when you simply *cannot go on living* without somebody? Being in love. Was he in love with Brownie? Oh the yearning, the yearning was so great, he felt his entrails surge as if they were being drawn out. He leaned forward over the pain of it, holding his breast, holding his stomach. He thought, I *can't wait* until she calls me, perhaps she will never call me, I'll go over and see her tomorrow, I'll look for her till I find her. Or perhaps tonight.

He stood up and very slowly put his clothes on. It was possible to stand, even to think. He walked slowly over to the window and looked out over the pavement in front of the house and at the trees of the drive and the white flinty stones along it. He thought, I've been here for a long time now. The vivid evening light made monumental the turreted yews, the ash trees were already in feather and young oak leaves a pale greenish yellow, all very still in the quiet windless evening. Edward noticed all this detail as if it were important for him to know, as if he would be questioned about it later. He held onto the window ledge and cooled his brow against the glass. Then he saw something amazing.

A tall man had come quietly into the picture, into the empty picture which had been waiting for him, and had stopped as if asserting his sovereignty of it. He had come out from among the trees and paused at the edge of the terrace facing the house. For a moment, feverishly inhabiting his past fantasies, Edward thought: it's Jesse. It must be Jesse, coming quietly at evening as Edward had imagined him at first, when Jesse was so mysteriously and interminably absent: a tall figure, a king returning unannounced, confidently, to his kingdom. Then he thought, but Jesse's here, and anyway that's not him – it's someone quite else, and my God it's someone I know, it can't be, *it's Stuart*.

Edward rushed out of the room, flew down the stone steps scarcely touching them, and reached and fumbled with the West Selden door, now since his occupation usually left unlocked. He stumbled out, blinking, into the warm wide evening where there was an unexpectedly bright light, and stumbled on the uneven stones of the pavement.

The man came forward. The bright dark light illumined Stuart's commanding stature, his big pale face and amber eyes, his head with its cropped blond hair. He was carrying his cap in one hand as if diffidently, and in the other a small *suitcase* which he now set down.

'Edward, old man, are you all right?'

'Yes, of course, curse it,' said Edward, 'why shouldn't I be? What on *earth* are you doing here?'

'I think you're ill, hadn't you better sit down? Let's go inside and – What a weird place. We were all wondering where you were.'

'Come on,' said Edward. His immediate instinct, in his horror at the unspeakable advent of his brother, was to hide him, then to get rid of him.

Edward stumbled again upon the tones, for a moment resisted, then gave way to, Stuart's strong arm which was supporting him. They came in through the open door into Selden, and somehow in the half-dark got up the stone stairs into Edward's room. Edward lighted the lamp and clumsily dragged the shutters across with a clatter. He sat on his bed, checking an intense desire to lie down. Stuart stood.

'But why,' said Edward, holding his head, now conscious of an intense headache, 'how did you know, why did you come?'

'She wrote to me –'

'*Who* wrote to you?'

'Mrs Baltram. She said you were here and that you were disturbed and ill and that you – that you needed me. Of course I came at once.'

'Did you tell anyone?'

'No. Dad's away, and –'

'Mrs Baltram –' For a moment Edward couldn't think who this was. 'Oh yes – Mother May. But she *can't* have written to *you*, she can't have done – and I don't need you, you're just the absolute last thing that I need –'

'Here's the letter.' Stuart held it out, tilting it toward the lamplight.

Dear Mr Cuno,

My stepson Edward, your brother, is with us here. He is upset and unwell and would profit from your presence, if you had time to visit us here, where you would be a welcome guest.

Yours sincerely,
May Baltram.

'I would have telephoned,' said Stuart, 'only there was no number in the book. Hadn't you better be in bed, have you got the 'flu?'

'Yes. But –' Edward looked at the date of the letter. 'I *wasn't* ill when she wrote this – this proves that – or *was* I? Christ, why can't I remember –'

'I thought, I assumed, you'd asked for me –'

'No! I wish you at the devil! Everything here is all to hell, and now *you* turn up!'

'I'm sorry,' said Stuart. He sat down on the rush-bottomed chair and inspected the room, the vaulted ceiling, the canopied bed, Jesse's picture of the girl standing in the stream. 'It's a nice room. I like the ceiling. Since I'm here hadn't I better buckle to and help? I can, you know, I expect I can.'

'You can't,' said Edward. 'You're the last straw. Will you please go away, go home, *now*.'

'There isn't any bus, I looked at the timetable, they don't run after –'

'You can get a lift on the road.'

'Edward, do lie down. You *are* ill. How can I go away and leave you? Hadn't I better go and see Mrs Baltram? It seems a bit impolite to be sitting here chatting with you without making myself known to my hostess.'

'"Impolite", "chatting", God!'

At that moment the door opened and a light shone in from outside. Bettina entered holding a lamp in her hand. She had also lighted the lamp in the niche by the stairs which shone behind her, shining through her skirt. She was in her mauve and white evening dress with multiple necklaces glittering, faintly clinking. Her dark reddish hair hung down in a single thick plait, now drawn forward over her shoulder. The hair being drawn away revealed her sharp aquiline handsomeness. She moved into the room, making with one hand a gesture of homage to Stuart, who had risen; then she curtsied.

'Mrs Baltram?'

'No, I'm Bettina.'

'I'm Stuart —'

'Yes, we know. Welcome to Seegard.'

'She's one of the sisters, my sisters —' said Edward gauchely.

'May I show you to your room? Then supper is ready downstairs.'

'His room? Where?' said Edward. It was all like a hideous mocking charade.

Stuart had picked up his suitcase and followed Bettina out. Edward followed after and saw Bettina throw open the door of the big corner bedroom. The side window showed the hillside and the wood, dark against a darkened reddish sky. Bettina put down her lamp and closed the shutters on both windows and pulled the curtains. Then she lit a lamp which was standing on the table. 'We use these lamps you see — you can turn it off by just turning this little wheel to the right. We conserve the electricity for essential things like the deep freeze and pumping the water. There's your bathroom, there's hot running water. There's an electric torch in that drawer. I'll turn off the paraffin heater later on. Dinner in half an hour if that's all right?'

'Oh — thank you —' said Stuart, 'thank you so much.'

'I'll come back and fetch you,' said Bettina. 'Edward, what are you doing? You ought to be in bed.'

'I'm coming down,' said Edward. 'I'll show him the way.'

The thought of Stuart sitting downstairs with the women, the four of them together eating and drinking and talking about him, was utterly intolerable. Stuart's presence was not only an outrage, it was a violation of the laws of nature. It was an unforgivable territorial offence at which Edward wanted to stand and howl like an animal. He felt sick with jealousy and rage and shock. Stuart had been expected, perhaps they had been watching for him from the window and had run to turn on the paraffin heater. Perhaps it had been on all day.

Edward ran back to his room, leaving Stuart looking at Jesse's picture of the people sitting silently together paralysed by catastrophe. Mechanically he took off his jacket and put on the long oatmeal-coloured shirt which he wore at dinner time.

There was a little sound outside his open door and suddenly Ilona was in the room. She too had plaited her hair, schoolgirlishly in two flying plaits enlaced with ribbons.

'Oh Ilona – Stuart's here –'

'I know. I came to give you – to tell you –'

Ilona suddenly put her arms around him. Then he felt something cold on his skin. She had put a chain necklace round his neck. 'I made this for you.'

Edward had taken hold of her dress. 'Thank you – but –'

'Wear it tonight for me. I came to tell you –'

'Yes –?'

'Don't let anything frighten you. Remember, I'm your sister and I love you.'

'I feel so sick,' said Edward. But she was gone.

'Edward told us how much you would appreciate this place,' said Mother May. 'May I help you to some of our special food? We are vegetarians, you know. We have a carefully balanced diet, the best diet in the world, we often bore Edward about this, don't we, Edward? We use these wooden bowls. They are beautiful, don't you think? We always eat like this, picnic fashion, for simplicity. May I?'

'Please.'

Mother May had plaited her hair too, but had put it on top like a crown. The lamp light showed her face in shadowed detail, benign and calm, her eyes gentle, her mouth in repose, her expression eagerly, quietly attentive. Edward had never

286

seen her so pleased and radiant. A necklace of blue beads which he had never seen before circled her slim youthful neck. When she smiled he could hear the faint sound of a benevolent sigh.

Stuart was looking round, studying the high wood-beamed roof, the uneven stone walls, the tapestry. Edward was about to avert his gaze for fear of catching Stuart's eye when Stuart looked straight at him. In a signal apprehended only by Edward who knew him so well, Stuart indicated *amusement*. Edward thought, my *God*. He wanted to utter a little cry of aversion, checked his half-utterance into a cough.

'It's so wonderful to have you both here,' said Mother May, casting a loving look at both of them. She almost laughed with pleasure. There was something simple, almost touching, in her air of satisfaction. 'Will you have some wine? We make our own.'

'We make our own everything,' said Ilona.

'We don't usually drink alcohol,' said Edward. 'This is a special day.' He was suddenly acutely conscious of his long discreetly embroidered smock, Ilona's necklace round his neck, although he also knew that that was not what Stuart had permitted himself to be amused by. Perhaps Stuart was trying to reassure him. Edward did not like this either.

'No wine, thank you,' said Stuart.

'Fruit juice? Ilona, pass the jug. It's a mixture, Edward's favourite, apple and elderberry.'

'Welcome to Stuart!' said Bettina raising her glass.

'Where is Mr Baltram?' said Stuart. 'I don't mean Edward. Of course he's Mr Baltram. I mean – Edward's father –'

'He is not here just now,' said Mother May.

'Tonight it's just us,' said Bettina.

'You are very kind,' said Stuart. 'But – Edward – are you really better – shouldn't you –?'

'Yes, I'm better – thanks for coming, but really you needn't stay.'

'Oh, you must stay,' said Mother May. '*We* need you! Now we've got both of you!' She spoke jocularly.

'You'll never get away,' said Ilona.

'We need a moral Samurai,' said Bettina, laughing.

'You are an idealist, I know,' said Mother May. 'But seriously, you can help us –'

From somewhere beyond the hall, in the direction of Transition, there came a strange sound, increasingly gradually to loudness, as if a number of musical instruments were being twanged and jangled altogether, a crescendo sound as of an orchestra tuning up. Sudden silence ensued.

'It's for him,' said Bettina. She looked at Stuart with glowing eyes.

'The spirits bid you welcome,' said Ilona. Then she giggled and covered her mouth with her hands.

'The harp sound,' said Mother May. 'I am not sure what it means.'

Stuart sat very still, scarcely breathing, withdrawn into himself.

Mother May looked at him for a long moment, then looked at Edward. Edward saw her eyes asking something of him, some spark of reassuring communication, which he denied her by looking away. Then she said softly, as if whispering in the low unstrained whisper with which the good actor can reach the back of the gallery and which it seems that no one can hear except the person to whom it is addressed, 'Edward, my dear, you aren't well. Hadn't you better go back to bed?'

'OK,' said Edward, in a loud harsh voice, and rose abruptly scraping his chair back upon the slates.

Almost at once Stuart rose too. 'I think I'll turn in if you don't mind. I'm an early-bedder.'

He's being kind to me, Edward thought, already half way to the door. When he had passed through the swing door to Transition he paused however and listened. Mother May was detaining Stuart, asking what time he liked to get up, teasing him. Now Bettina was talking about breakfast arrangements. Now they were all laughing.

Edward went on more slowly. His legs felt weak and his mouth bitter. Transition was dark but he knew every step now. The lamp in the niche by the stone steps of Selden gave a dim light ahead. Then another light grew behind him and a footstep. It was Ilona. She was bringing a lamp which she set down on one of the shelves of the corridor. A lamp to guide

Stuart. Edward hurried, beginning almost to run.

'Edward – wait – don't be angry.'

'I'm not angry. I told you. I'm sick.'

'Don't be sick. Do you remember what I said to you?'

'Yes, Ilona.'

'You're my one.'

'How – ghastly –' said Edward. He went on up the stone steps and paused at the turning and looked down at his sister, with her silly beribboned pigtails and her plump cheeks and small peering bird-like face. He thought, she's going to cry. He said, 'All right, all right,' and ran on up to his room.

He lit the lamp and closed the shutters and began with frenzied haste to undress. He pulled his long shirt off, then found Ilona's necklace still dangling about his neck and tore that off, it was feeling strangely warm now, even hot. He got into his pyjamas somehow. His aim was to be able to pretend to be asleep when Stuart came up. He got into bed and sat there stiffly, massaging his aching legs and feeling the creeping perspiration which was covering his entire body, running in little channels down his chest. He thought, perhaps it's just kindness after all, she really wanted to help me, she loves me, they all love me, I need them so much and I've been so awful. What on earth went on in Mother May's intricate subtle mind of a mother, a wife, a stepmother, what could Edward frame of such a woman's mind? And he thought, perhaps it's for Bettina. That's what Ilona meant I suppose. She wanted to tell me she wasn't going to fall in love with Stuart. But Stuart could marry *either* of them and I *can't*! Then he thought but all this is *perfectly crazy*. Then he found, blundering towards it as in a crowded phantasmagoria, the image of Brownie, and he *prayed* to it: Help me, Brownie, help me. Then he realised he had forgotten to turn off the lamp, and as he was getting out of bed to do so Stuart entered.

'Ed, you aren't well. How are you feeling? Have you got a temperature?'

'No, of course not.'

Stuart sat down on the bed. Edward, back under the blankets, removed his long legs to the other side. He pulled the sheet up, peering over the top of it.

289

'This is a rum do here,' said Stuart. 'What do you make of it?'

'Nothing,' said Edward. 'It can't be thought about. It just exists.'

'What was that extraordinary noise?'

'Just some stuff falling over in the kitchen.'

'I see. They were joking. It sounded very odd. When is your father coming?'

'My – oh – Jesse – he's here, he's ill too, he's at the other end of the house.'

'I see. It was a *façon de parler*.'

'Yes,' said Edward, picking up the ridiculous phrase, 'a *façon de parler*.'

'I'd like to meet him. What's he like?'

'He's quite nice,' said Edward, beginning to disappear behind the sheet. He could see Stuart's kind animal eyes looking at him anxiously.

'Ed, you know I love you, I'll try to help. Or if you like I'll go tomorrow. It's all – for you –'

'Great,' said Edward, 'but I thought you loved everybody.'

'Don't talk rot. Don't tease me.'

'*Tease* you! Do you know how to turn off the lamp?'

'Yes, you turn the little wheel.'

'Well, could you turn it off, and then take yourself off.'

'All right. But remember –' Stuart's hand fiddled on top of the bedclothes, trying to find Edward's legs to touch, but Edward shrank away. 'Good night.'

Merciful darkness fell. Stuart blundered out of the door. Edward lay back into his bath of sweat, and began a twisting and turning which he felt would continue all night. He thought of tortured men in cages where they could neither stand nor sit. He missed the sleeping draughts which Mother May had given him on the previous night. Tonight they had forgotten.

The presence of Stuart simply made Seegard *impossible*, it simply ruined *everything*. Now *Stuart* would become the longed-for boy, *he* would be loved by the women, *he* would sit and talk to Jesse. He would probably be able to communicate with Jesse far more deeply than Edward. Stuart would understand, he would intuit Jesse's thoughts, he would tame Jesse, he would charm him, he would smile his kind feral boyish smile. Perhaps *that* was why Mother May, in her wisdom, had summoned him. Edward had failed, Stuart would succeed. This evening two people had told Edward they loved him – and there was nothing he could do with either love. These were useless loves. Tomorrow, he thought, I shall leave here, and I shall go to Brownie. He went to sleep after all and dreamt of Mark. Mark was sitting on his bed and holding his hand and smiling.

'EXCUSE ME,' SAID Harry, 'I see you're nearly finishing. Do you mind if we sit down at your table while you do?'

He was with Midge in the expensive, much recommended, carefully chosen restaurant in the little country town where he had booked a table for lunch, only they had arrived late and the table was gone, and Midge was tired and wanted to sit down, and the head water was not being at all helpful.

The man so addressed by Harry looked at him with interest. He was dressed in a brown suit of light-weight tweed with a herringbone design, with a waistcoat, and a watch pocket evidently occupied by a watch. He was wearing what looked like a Guards tie. His educated voice was not quite the sort of educated voice that Harry expected. He said thoughtfully, 'Well – I'm not actually – nearly finishing.'

Harry was conscious of Midge, some distance behind him, standing at the door of the crowded dining room, tapping her foot and being stared at by people at nearby tables. She had pulled her scarf over her head well forward to conceal her once-famous face, succeeding thereby in making herself more conspicuous.

'Well, could we just sit down? There isn't a table yet, and my wife is rather tired. You see, we did book a table only we were late and the bloody restaurant didn't keep it.' The word 'wife' came out easily. Harry and Midge had already had two days and two nights of their longed-for and indeed wonderful weekend, and were on their way back to London. At first Harry had shared Midge's anxiety about meeting 'someone they knew'. Now he didn't care a hang. He was winning the great game. The word 'bloody' was an instinctive appeal to the man he was addressing.

The man, who had a plate with some fragments of cheese in front of him, and an almost empty cup of coffee, looked at Harry with an air of detached not unbenevolent curiosity. He was in no hurry. He said, 'I don't *quite* see why you should come and join me. When one lunches alone one wants, at least I do, to lunch alone.'

Harry thought, God, a whimsical intellectual. He said, 'I quite understand, and I wouldn't usually ask such a favour, but as we've been let down and the head waiter won't help, I felt I had to fend for myself, and you're the only single person here, and as you've finished –'

'Ah, but I haven't.'

'Nearly finished, I thought you wouldn't mind if we just sat down and looked at the menu.'

'You could sit in the bar,' said the man.

'The bar's full,' said Harry, with exasperation beginning to sound, 'there's nowhere to sit, and my wife doesn't like bars.'

'I'm sorry to seem unsympathetic,' said the man, who had alert sparkling brown eyes, 'but I still don't see why I should agree to your suggestion. I value my table and my solitude. I don't see that the fact that I am a single person has any relevance.'

'Well, there are two of us and only one of you.'

'An argument from mere numbers is equivalent to an argument from mere force.'

'We won't disturb you –'

'You are already doing so.'

'And there's more space at this table.'

'There may be more physical space,' said the man, 'but there is not more psychological space. This is an expensive restaurant. One pays for its amenities, one of which is to be left alone to finish one's lunch in peace.'

People at neighbouring tables who had been staring at Midge had by now transferred their attention to Harry. There were smiles. Other conversations ceased.

The head waiter too had noticed the incident. He came up

and said to the man in an impersonally insolent voice, 'Have you finished your meal, sir?' Not that the head waiter was on Harry's side. His contempt for his clients was impartial.

'No, I haven't,' said the man. 'I think I'll have a liqueur. Could I see the wine list?'

Harry rose and marched back to the door. Midge had by now retired from the dining room and was hanging about just outside the bar. As soon as she saw Harry she turned and darted out of the front door of the hotel, making for the car park. Harry caught her up at the car. She was in tears. He opened the door and she got in.

'Oh why did this have to happen?'

Harry steered the car out of the car park and set off at random down the road. 'Well, you told me to do something!'

'Everyone was staring at us.'

'Don't cry, Midge.'

'My nerves are on edge.'

'It's because we're going home, back to London, that is.'

'Everyone was beastly to us, everyone was looking at us.'

'We'll find another restaurant, there must be something tolerable around here.'

'No, I don't want a restaurant, anyway it's so late now, no one would have us.'

'We could eat sandwiches in a pub.'

'You know I hate pubs. I don't want to be stared at any more. I feel everyone's against us.'

'Maybe,' said Harry, 'but we'll win all the same. What would you like? We've got to eat.'

'Let's have a picnic, like I said before, only you wouldn't. I don't want much to eat.'

'I do,' said Harry. 'I'm ravenous. And I've been driving for hours.'

'Well, you buy the stuff, buy anything you want, and a bottle of wine.'

'Two bottles. All right.' Harry hated picnics.

'Then we needn't be in a hurry,' said Midge, who had dried her eyes. 'My darling, I'm sorry –'

'I'm sorry too. It hasn't spoilt everything, has it?'

'Of course not!'

'We've been so happy. We will be so happy.'

'We *are* so happy.'

'That's what matters, isn't it?'

'I've quite recovered now. Look, there's a big grocer's shop, you can buy everything. I'll wait in the car.'

Harry went into the shop. He felt he had to give way to Midge now. The restaurant had been his idea. What had wrecked it, by making them so late, was his other idea of taking Midge to see his old school. Harry's spartan public school, which had been Casimir's school too, was situated in wild lonely very beautiful country, on the edge of a little town isolated among big silky sheep-dotted hills sparsely traversed by narrow winding roads between exquisitely constructed stone walls. The sun had been shining. It was a lovely drive, except that they had got lost. Midge was hopeless with maps. Then when they reached the school Harry wanted to go in and explore, show Midge his old dormitories, his old classrooms, the gym, the playing fields, scene of his triumphs. It was half-term. The buildings were mostly empty, some suitcases on beds, some parents and offspring strolling in the gardens. Harry led Midge in a daze through these rooms and corridors which were so soaked in, darkly, thickly, painted over with, the intense impure emotions of boyhood, places he still constantly visited in his dreams. Sickening himself with the excitements of memory, he kept Midge there too long, perhaps bored her, and made them late for lunch. Now, guilty, he felt he owed her the picnic which she had several times suggested and he had always adroitly evaded.

He returned to the car with a bag full of goodies and two wine bottles.

'Have we got a corkscrew?' said Midge, who had been studying the map.

They had not. Nor had they got a tin opener, knives, forks, spoons, plastic cups and plates, or paper napkins. After another cruise in search of these Harry was feeling very hungry and on the point of being cross.

'Harry –' said Midge, as they drove out of the town.

He knew from her tone that she was going to ask a favour, and he tried to swallow his crossness.

'Yes, my darling, my dear –?'

'I've been looking at the map, and, you know, the motorway passes quite close to Seegard.'

'To where? Oh that place where Jesse lived.'

'Lives. You can't have forgotten its name.'

'No. I just blotted it out of my consciousness long ago.'

'Would you mind if –'

'Yes, I would!'

'I don't mean call on them! I'd just like to drive somewhere near and see the tower. You can see it for miles across that flat land. I'd like to see that countryside again.'

'No, Midge.'

'Why not? We've been to *your* place and spent hours there. Why can't we just go round through that bit of country? We needn't go near the house, I'd hate to anyway, but I'd just like to look at the region.'

'Why?'

'Because I'd like to! You said this morning lovers give each other each other's *past*. Well, I want to give you this piece of mine.'

'You've never got over Jesse looking at you and saying "Who is that girl?"'

'Don't be silly. All right, I haven't! Good heavens, you're jealous!'

'Of course I am. It's ironic, I could die of it. Only I'm planning not to. Do you realise how much I suffer every day, every moment, at your being with Thomas? And now you're *going back* to him, back to your *husband*. Midge, we must decide. Listen, I've got a flat for us.'

'A flat?'

'Yes, a place where we can be entirely on our own, where there's no Thomas at all, where I can cook for you. We'll stay there tonight. Thomas won't be back till tomorrow. Meredith will still be in Wales –'

'I said I'd ring him.'

'You can ring him from the flat.'

'Harry – do be careful –'

'I won't be careful, I'm fed up with being careful, God, how pathetic, as I listen to myself, *begging* you to come to that little flat in the intervals of your life with Thomas. Midge, we love each other absolutely. Yes or no?'

'Yes.'

'You know about those tigers – what we said – the tigers of desire –'

'Yes.'

'We're closer now than we've ever been. You know that?'

'Yes.'

'Then have courage, my angel, my dear, it's all so near now, our happiness, one more move and we're *there* and *forever*. We must stop *pretending*. We *aren't* happy and that's a *scandal*. You say you hate telling lies and you've been bothered by people looking at you and about my calling you my wife, all right, let's stop it all, clear it all away and get in the clear. Please, darling, sweetheart, if you like I'll stop the car and go on my knees. Midge, you know it's going to happen, just stop putting it off, you know it's *got* to happen.'

He stopped the car. In the sudden silence the sun shone upon a field of damp pliant green grass and a group of dozy meditative black and white cows and the blue sign for the motorway. A church tower rose beyond some trees. A distant dog barked.

Midge said, 'Yes.'

'Well, don't look so grim and stony about it!'

'It's easy for you. I've got to wade through blood.'

'Whose blood? Thomas won't mind much, you know he won't. He'll *arrange* to recover! Anyway he has no blood. And Meredith is ours.'

'Yes. I love you. And it's got to happen.'

'So there.' Harry started the engine. He did not want now to press her further. He was feeling his way, oh so delicately, through the maze of her emotions, of her terrible dangerous hidden pain. He thought, she will come to the flat tonight. He said, 'My dear heart, we'll go anywhere you like, just show me the map. Where's that place?'

Midge pointed. 'About there, I think.'

'It's not exactly close to the motorway. About thirty miles. I don't call that close.'

'I do.'

'If it were a straight road – but look at the way those little roads wind about. Never mind, we'll go and take a very distant view.'

'I just want to see that flat land again, it's very strange and special.'

'It's funny, you look like Chloe today, perhaps it's the local air!'

'We could have our picnic there.'

'Oh we'll want to eat long before that!' Only Harry found that he was no longer hungry. He smiled as he drove along. He was feeding upon Midge's wonderful affirmatives.

At that very moment Edward Baltram was experiencing a miracle. (The second one that day.) He was holding a letter which had been put into his hand by one of the tree men, the man whom he had seen before. Edward had spent the morning in bed, giving himself over with a kind of relief to feeling ill. To his visitors, who appeared separately, Stuart, Mother May, Bettina, Ilona, he had enacted illness. He had not come down for lunch. Mother May had brought him a tasty anonymous soup which he had quite enjoyed. After lunch, surreptitiously, he got up, dressed, and sorted out his things, dividing his own clobber from the borrowed stuff. He did not know what to do with Ilona's necklace and put it inside a pair of socks. He looked at his suitcase, which now appeared so alien and old, but did not pack it. He sat on his bed. He was only playing with the idea of leaving. For how could he leave Jesse? The idea of kidnapping Jesse and taking him to London recurred, but with no picture of how it was to be done.

He went downstairs and into the Atrium. Here, near to the potted plants, stood the family group, Stuart, Mother May, Bettina and Ilona. They were looking up at the tapestry and Bettina was explaining it to Stuart. 'The fish represents a spirit which has escaped from its natural element –'

What rubbish, thought Edward.

They paused when they saw him.

'How are you feeling, old man?' said Stuart.

'A bit better. I think I'll just sit and read for a while in the Interfec.' It occurred to him that all four of them were gazing at him with meaningful looks. Well, not Bettina. Her look was unfathomable. They had clearly been talking about him.

Stuart and Mother May both started to say something at once.

'Sorry –'

'No, you go on –'

Mother May said, 'Jesse's a bit under the weather too. We thought you'd better not see him. He wouldn't want your virus as well.'

'Perhaps it's the same virus,' said Ilona.

'He's not seeing *anybody* at present,' said Mother May. She added, 'He hasn't *seen* anybody. We think it's better.'

'Much better, I'm sure,' said Stuart, staring at Edward.

Clumsy ass! thought Edward. But he was glad to know that Stuart had not see Jesse; it was humane of them to inform him. He went on across the hall to the Interfectory. They watched him until he had shut the door. Then he heard Bettina's voice resume.

He had spoken of reading simply as a ruse to get away, intending to go out through the back door and go walking by himself. He paused however, looking round the shabby room, so awkwardly full of a past the more distant and alien for being also fairly recent, the past of Jesse's youth and his prime. *I am here* . . . Edward automatically tried the tower door (locked) and did not trouble to look for the key (which would be absent). He wandered over to the fireplace and looked at the photograph of himself as Jesse. He wanted to cry. Then he began to look vaguely at the bookshelves which he had never entirely searched. It occurred to him that he had not, since arriving at Seegard, opened any book or even *considered* reading. Gazing dully at the shelves he suddenly saw the name of Proust. There before him was a volume of *A la Recherche* in French. He pulled it out. He looked into the front of the book and found Jesse's signature in what looked like a youthful scrawl. For some reason it surprised him to learn that Jesse knew any French. His heart began to beat with a new note, differently, as he opened the book at random. *S'il pleuvait, bien que le mauvais temps n'effrayât pas Albertine, qu'on voyait parfois, dans son caoutchouc, filer en bicyclette sous les averses, nous passions la journée dans le casino où il m'eût paru ces jours-là impossible de ne pas aller.* This sentence staggered Edward so much that he nearly fell down. It was a perfectly ordinary run-of-the-mill sentence in the midst of the narration describing some quite ordinary day's routine at Balbec, not particularly dramatic or significant, an *ordinary day* at Balbec – but Edward might just as well have been looking at the weightiest lines of a holy text or the climax of a great poem. Those nouns, *bicyclette, averses, caoutchouc,* those verbs, those tenses, that *nous,* that *impossible,* Albertine *filant* in the rain . . . Edward's stomach heaved with emotion and he sat down abruptly in one of the long low armchairs of slippery leather. The French sentence came to him with an extraordinary freshness, like a breath of clear air to a man just out of prison, like a sudden sound of a musical instrument. Intimations of other places, of elsewhere – of freedom. He felt as he read it a kind of invigorating self-reproach and a new sort of power. There too he lived, he himself. He was there.

He suddenly recalled someone saying about Willy Brightwalton that he believed in salvation by Proust; and for a moment Willy too, that old fat shabby figure of fun, appeared in the shed light as a messenger, a representative of something better. Better than what? He *could* rise, he could *get up,* he could *get out.* For there was elsewhere, as proof of it, this something else; and the unexpected emotion which had made him, a moment ago, nearly faint was, he now realised, pure joy.

He got up slowly. He had no desire to look at the book any more and he put it back in the shelves. All *that* belonged to the future. He went, as he had intended, to the door and along the back of the house. Now, after rainy weather, the sun was shining on the fen, making it steam slightly. The sky beyond was clear. From higher up one would be able to see the sea. It occurred to Edward that he had only seen the sea once since his arrival, on his second visit to Jesse when he had seen the boat with the white sail. On other visits there had been mist or low cloud. Surely the sea would be visible now from upstairs in East Selden; only East Selden was out of bounds. He considered another attempt to get across the fen, then decided to go toward the river, cross it, which should now be easy, and go up to the *dromos*. He went on past the ilexes and the greenhouses and the vegetable garden. He could now see the poplar grove covered in flickering golden leaves. The orchard was just coming into flower, the tight white buds edged with scarlet. It was here that he met the tree man who put Brownie's letter into his hand. The man, after handing it over, hung around in a pointed manner until it dawned on Edward that he wanted a tip. As Edward hastily handed it over, he thought how much more he would have been ready to give, had it been asked, for this letter.

Railway Cottage

Dear Edward,

I have been thinking about our talk. I am afraid I may have seemed rather hard and hostile. I needed so much to receive the truth about what happened, to know exactly what happened, the details, so that I could add it to the mass of that awful event, and *see* it, and take it in as much as I could. I had to feel I'd done my best to get it all and to live it all. Of course it's also a mystery and has to be lived with as a mystery. But it would have been unspeakably painful for me not to know, in some ordinary sense, as much as can be known about the events of that evening, and to hear it from you, in your words, in your presence. As you may imagine, I have heard some different accounts and speculations. I hope you understand. When we talked I was thinking of myself, and you may have thought me very selfish, as if I didn't realise how absolutely awful it had all been for you. I have at least gathered that you and Mark were very good friends, and that gives me a special feeling for you, I mean a kind feeling. It was good of you to be so frank and to answer all my questions. It must have been hard to do so – yet perhaps too it was a relief. You said you needed me, and I think it would be valuable if we talked again. Actually there's something else I'd like to ask you.

But I really have no idea how you might feel about this. I can a little imagine what a dreadful time you must have been going through, not only with people blaming you, but with you blaming yourself. You may feel, in spite of what you said at the river, that really our talk was enough and you don't want to see me again and be reminded or accused by my being me. You may wish in this matter to be by yourself. You said my mother had been writing you terrible letters. I'm very sorry about that. Please don't blame her but see that she needs help too. She needs to stop hating you – that hatred is taking over her life. It's possible that, indirectly, you could help me to help her. I don't quite see how, but it might be. I feel rather desperate sometimes. This note is also to say that tomorrow (Tuesday) morning I will be alone at the cottage. The others have gone to London and I'm leaving too on an afternoon train. If you felt like coming over, not too late, in the morning I'd be in. But if you don't want to, or perhaps can't, come I shall quite understand.

With good wishes,

Yours
Brownie Wilsden.

When he had read this letter through Edward became almost insane, overwhelmed by an intense emotion which was so mixed of pain and joy that for the second time that day, and much more intensely, he felt quite sick and faint. He ran, holding the letter, past the orchard in among the poplars, and pressed his forehead hard against the smooth bark of several of the trees. He laughed and groaned. He threw himself on the ground and rolled about, then lay on his back and looked up through the glittering twisting leaves at the blue sky. Then he sat up panting and read the wonderful letter again. It read to him like the order of reprieve. And yet at the same time he was remembering *the event*, summoning all his guilt, his deepest sense of his crime, all that mess of resentful misery which was still with him, unabated and unhealed. What he had taken for works of redemption had all been illusions, effects of magic. This was the real thing. The sense of a return to reality was so strong, like a fast translation, that he felt positively giddy. Here at last was a pure authentic voice, a good voice, speaking to him with authority. But he must not, and this was capital, expect too much, expect, indeed, for himself, anything. He must abide by the dry precise exactitude of Brownie's letter as by a legal document or deed of trust which said simply so much and no more. Yet he could not help, as he so chided himself, glorying in the letter. There was a sentence which he liked best and read oftenest. 'I feel rather desperate sometimes.' Did not that sound, the very least little bit, like an appeal? He thought, how can I be so meanly selfish as to let that please me! But he thought too, I'll put it all onto her, she will *deal* with it all. And he thought, and this thought began to blot out all other pains and speculations, *I shall see her again tomorrow.*

'The left wheel is still spinning,' said Midge.

The car had, ridiculously, become stuck in a grassy verge in one of the narrow lanes where they had again lost themselves after leaving the motorway. The earth had not seemed particularly damp or muddy when Harry had irritably backed onto it to turn, but the grass had concealed a shallow ditch. Now they had spent nearly an hour trying to move the car, putting newspapers, stones, twigs, even one of Harry's old jackets, underneath the wheels to make them bite. The car simply refused to budge. Midge was exhausted, red in the face from pressing things in under the wheels and pushing while Harry revved the engine, and helping him to dig away the earth which was like sticky toffee in the deepening ruts. It was now late afternoon and the sky had become overcast and the whole landscape darkened.

The picnic had been a great success. They had set off into the flat land intending to go to the sea. It turned out that Midge had no clear idea of where Seegard was, so there seemed no point in looking for it in what now seemed a large and thoroughly confusing area. It was always possible that they might spot the tower in the distance, but so far they had not done so. They had eaten the picnic on a little eminence, sitting on dry sheep-nibbled grass with a view of a large distant church which, without a guide book, they could not identify. Harry had bought sandwiches, salami, pork pies, tomatoes, cheese, biscuits, apples, bananas and plum cake. They ate a great deal of this and drank both the bottles of Spanish wine, pouring it into the glasses which Harry had bought at the corkscrew shop. Then they lay about on the grass for some time embracing each other. They had never made love out in the open before and the experience made them both very proud and happy. The landscape seemed to be entirely deserted. Then they fell asleep. After that they set off 'towards the sea', but were soon arguing about where it lay. Harry, who prided himself on his sense of direction, was reduced to driving at random looking for signposts, of which there were very few. Then after taking a turning down a road which degenerated into a farm track they had turned round, or tried to, and had thus become embedded in the grassy verge which had looked so reliably solid. Fortunately there was no urgent hurry about returning to London since neither Thomas nor Meredith would be home. Harry even thought privately that an accidental revelation might now do no harm at all. But he was affected by Midge's increasing distress and unnerved by her obvious fear; and the episode was now becoming thoroughly tiresome, with the darkening landscape and the lack of any signs of possible assistance.

'I'd better start walking,' said Harry.

'Yes, but which way?'

'I don't know! We haven't the faintest idea where we are. I wish to God we'd never set out over these God-forsaken mud flats. I'd never seen such an utterly pointless landscape.'

'I told you there was a marsh or fen or whatever they call it. You shouldn't have got so cross – if you'd only backed the car more carefully –'

'If we'd stayed on the motorway we'd be home by now, back at our flat drinking whisky! I've crammed the fridge with drink.'

'*Don't!* I'm *sorry!*'

'You stay here, get in the car if it's cold.'

'No, no, I'm coming with you. I'd be frightened here alone.'

'It's not dark yet. You'll get tired and slow me up, look at your shoes! You don't remember seeing a garage anywhere we came along?'

'No. I think there was a farm before we turned into the road we turned off to come here. And I suppose that track leads somewhere.'

'Just to a barn. I can see it. At least when it's darker we'll see a few lights.'

'Oh Harry – will it take so long? Must we have a tractor?'

'No, an ordinary car might do it, I've got a tow-rope in the boot.'

'Please, let me come, please!'

'Oh all right, but put your coat on, it'll be cold. Here, let's have some whisky now, there's a flask in the glove compartment.'

Standing beside the car they quickly drank the whisky, then set off together. Midge held Harry's arm to begin with, but he soon shook her off and increased his pace. Midge felt miserable and afraid and a little drunk. Fear of discovery, of blunders, of scandal, of being attacked and condemned and mentioned in the newspapers, fear of Thomas, misery about Thomas, was with her all the time co-existing with her sincere 'yes' to Harry's questions. The time would come, but not yet, neither could Midge see how. She could not help envisaging some kind of magical transformation, a rapid scene-change, whereby she *would have left* Thomas and be living happily with Harry – and with Meredith. Upon 'what Meredith knew' she refused to reflect, indeed had decided to conclude that he had understood nothing. Oh how would it be, that metamorphosis? Well, it *would* be, because it would *have to* be. Harry was right.

'Look, there's a cottage. I can see a light.'

They had been walking for what seemed a long time, and Midge had several times announced, and Harry had denied, that they would be unable to find their way back to the car. Even now the cottage was not near and they soon found that they had left the tarmac and were walking on a grassy track.

305

Once Midge slithered down an unexpected slope and they lost sight of the guiding light and the outline of the cottage roof against the fading sky where stars were already visible. At last they were close, fumbling with a little gate in a low fence.

'You go,' said Midge, pulling her scarf forward over her face. Harry turned up his coat collar and adjusted the cap with which, to please Midge, he had disguised himself. He went to the door and rapped on it.

Elspeth Macran opened the door and peered out. 'Yes?'

'I'm awfully sorry to bother you,' said Harry, 'but our car has got stuck in the mud somewhere near here, and I wonder if we could use your telephone to ring a garage?'

'We have no telephone.'

'Perhaps your car could tow us out! I've got a rope –'

'We have no car.'

Sarah, appearing beside her mother, said, 'Where's your car? We could help you push it.'

'Well, it's not very near I'm afraid, we've been walking for some time. Is there a garage anywhere near or someone who's got a car who could help us?'

'There's no garage. Our nearest neighbours, indeed our only neighbours, have a car but they're not particularly helpful people, and I doubt if you'd find the way –'

'I'll show them,' said Sarah.

'Would you like to come in?' said Elspeth. 'Is that –?' She vaguely motioned toward the figure at the gate.

'That's my wife. You are very kind, but –'

'What's your name?' said Elspeth.

'Bentley,' said Harry. 'Mr and Mrs Bentley. We won't disturb you. If you could just indicate the direction –'

'I'll go with them,' said Sarah, 'they'll never find it. They'll fall in the fen. Just wait a sec while I put my shoes on.'

'Better take a torch,' said Elspeth to Sarah, 'the mist's coming up.'

'Really, you mustn't trouble –' said Harry.

'Well, do you want to be helped or not? It's up to you.'

'It's quite close,' said Sarah. 'We'll take the short cut. Brownie's still in her bath, tell her I'll be back. Look, I've got two torches. Cheerio, ma, back soon.'

'Sarah, don't go in!' Elspeth called after them.

Sarah bounded out of the gate followed by Harry. Midge stood aside. 'Hello! Here, Mr Bentley, you take that torch and shine it on my heels. It's not far but it's a bit tricky in places and it'll be mistier further on.'

The sky had by now become quite dark and the stars were hidden by clouds. Great grey balls of mist, illumined by the torches, moved slowly by, nudging the walkers and obscuring the way ahead. Harry took Midge's hand and pulled her along, keeping the torch-light fixed upon Sarah's muddy shoes and the frayed ends of her jeans. Midge stumbled, trying to make out where to put her feet, her high-heeled shoes sticking in the thick moist grass which the torches vividly revealed. A chill wind was blowing, there were a few spots of rain. Midge began quietly and surreptitiously to cry.

'We're nearly there,' said Sarah at last, 'just up this slope. Here, Mrs Bentley, give me your hand. That's fine. Now we're on the level. Mind how you walk, it's a bit uneven. There's a door somewhere here, sorry it's so dark, I can't find it. Oh here we are, I don't think there's a bell.' Sarah banged on the door with her fist and called, 'Hello there!' There was a silence. She banged again.

Bettina opened the door a little way on a chain and said, 'Who is it?'

'It's me, Sarah, from Railway Cottage. I've got two people whose car has got stuck and they want a tow.'

Bettina shut the door, then opened it again a little wider and looked out.

'This is Mr and Mrs Bentley,' said Sarah, 'they want help with their car, they've been wandering around for ages.'

'I'm awfully sorry to bother you,' said Harry, 'but our car has got stuck in the mud, if your car could just tow us out –'

'They've got a tractor too,' said Sarah helpfully, trying to peer in.

'You'd better come in,' said Bettina. She opened the door a little more and Harry entered followed by Midge. Bettina, blocking the opening, said to Sarah, 'Thank you, goodnight,' and shut the door.

'Oh, thanks very much,' Harry called. He said to Bettina, 'Perhaps we could telephone –'

'We have no telephone.'

'I do hope this isn't an awful nuisance –'

'Of course it is a nuisance,' said Bettina, 'but we shall have to help you. Just sit down here for a minute.' She brought forward two upright chairs from the table and set them together beside the door. 'Would you like to go to the lavatory?'

'No, thanks,' said Harry. 'Sorry, Midge, would you?'

Midge sat down, dropping her handbag on the slates, and Harry sat down beside her. Dazed, they stared at a large dark open space which looked like the interior of a railway terminus. Midge did not recognise the room which she had last seen so long ago on a sunny summer morning thronged with gaily dressed and chattering people.

The Atrium was silent, and empty except for Bettina's receding figure, her swirling skirts almost touching the floor. It was lit by a single oil lamp near the door into Transition. Dinner, haphazardly rather late these days, had not yet taken place, though the table was set and some of the food already laid out 'picnic fashion' as Mother May called it. Harry and Midge, in their awkward place by the door, were almost in darkness.

'What a funny place,' said Harry in a low voice, 'they've let us into the barn. I'm glad to hear there's a tractor.'

A distant door banged, then Bettina reappeared carrying a lamp and accompanied by Mother May. Bettina was explaining, 'It's a Mr and Mrs Bentley, their car has got stuck, I expect they'll need the tractor. You remember when this happened last year we had to use the tractor. It would happen at this time of day!'

'Yes –' murmured Mother May.

Harry stood up.

The lamp approached.

Midge stood up. She had recognised Mother May. Then she recognised the whole scene. Her scarf fell back and Mother May recognised her.

Mother May said softly to Bettina, 'Bettina, go away for a moment, and keep the others out.'

Bettina handed over the lamp and walked back to Transition.

Midge made for the door but could not get it open. Harry said, 'What's the matter?' Midge said, 'This is Seegard.' Harry moved away from the light.

Mother May was trembling with excitement, her eyes, her gentle grey eyes, had become very large and were sparkling and her lips were moist. The lamp wavered and seemed about to fall. She threw her head back and stroked her hair with her free hand, unintentionally loosening some of the pins so that a loose tress fell down her back. She put the lamp down on the floor. She was breathing deeply. She was thinking, thinking.

Midge came back, also breathless, from the door. For a moment she looked completely wild, like a cornered animal, ready to fly senselessly or to spring upon her attacker. Then she became rigid, stony, staring, with her mouth open. Harry was thinking too. All three were thinking.

Mother May said to Midge, 'Do sit down. You must be tired.' Midge did not sit down, but looked away, taking deep breaths. With deliberate slowness she took the scarf away from her neck, shook it out, and put it in her pocket.

Mother May, who seemed now to have decided what to do, said in a low voice, 'Mrs McCaskerville –' She turned towards Harry. 'Mr –?'

'Weston,' said Harry with a smile, backing further away from the lamp light. 'The young lady who guided us here got the wrong end of the stick. My car is a Bentley, it's not our name. I was just giving Mrs McCaskerville a lift back to London when we had this mishap. I gather you have no telephone? That's a pity. We wanted to ring Mrs McCaskerville's husband and my wife to say we'd be late. As it is, if you would simply be so kind as to tow us out – we don't want to disturb your evening –'

Harry felt it safe to assume that he had not been recognised. There was something to be gained by further lies, little to be lost if they failed; and in any case he felt intensely disinclined to utter his name in that house.

'Wouldn't you like a cup of tea, something to eat?' said Mother May to Midge, smiling.

309

'I think we'd better get off at once. Don't you think?' Harry said to Midge.

Midge nodded and said, now smiling too, 'We really are so sorry to trouble you. I had no idea you lived near here, it's the oddest coincidence. It's so nice to see this house again. I was here once years ago with my sister. I hope your husband is well?'

'A little ailing.'

'I'm so sorry. Give him my regards.'

'I certainly will. I'll just fetch Bettina. She'll have the car ready by now.' She picked up the lamp and put it on the table, then left the room.

Midge said to Harry, 'What shall we do?'

'Brazen it out. It doesn't matter. These people don't matter. They won't talk, they've no one to talk to. They're crazy rustics, they live out of the world.'

'She saw me trying to bolt –'

'That was just natural shock! She was pretty shaken herself.'

'And she'll have recognised you, she'll have seen a photo or seen you somewhere –'

'I don't think so. It's awfully dark here and she was so stunned by recognising you, she scarcely looked at me. Anyway, what the hell – I'm not going to announce my name.'

'And your car isn't a Bentley, and –'

'So what, we can only try. Once we get moving we'll vanish out of their lives like a dream. They'll never make sense of this business, they'll be a bit mystified, perhaps they'll think it funny – they can never *know* anything. They'll forget it all – why should they bother –'

'You don't understand,' said Midge, 'she'll bother. She's interested, she's fascinated, she's playing with us. She won't let us get away with it.'

'Get away with what? I'm just giving you a lift!'

'I'm sure she'll recognise you –'

'I'll keep away from the light, I'll go outside the door. Just keep calm and we'll be out of this in twenty minutes.'

'We'll never find the car.'

'Oh stop moaning, put a brave face on.'

310

The outside door behind them suddenly opened and Edward and Stuart came in. Midge gave a little scream. She and Harry separated precipitately from each other and retreated. At the same moment Mother May entered from Transition, followed by Bettina and Ilona. The three women stopped, watching the scene by the door.

Edward rushed forward, 'Harry, Midge, how marvellous, you've found me! However did you know? Is Thomas here, did he tell you where I was? I've been ill but I'm better. Stuart only got here yesterday. Mother May, look who's here!'

'Well, who *is* here?' said Mother May.

'Why, it's my aunt Midge McCaskerville and my stepfather Harry Cuno. Have you met, of course you have. This is Mrs Baltram, we call her Mother May, and these are my sisters Bettina and Ilona.'

Bettina laughed. She said, 'First they were Mr and Mrs Bentley. Then he was Mr Weston. It's an evening for charades!'

Mother May, who had not recognised Harry, was by now so much in command of the situation that she was able to conceal the shock of surprise, and the immediately following shock of elation. She turned smiling to Bettina and said, rather loudly, 'Hush!' She turned back to Midge and Harry and said, 'In any case you are welcome, and now we've got all the identities straight I really must insist that you should stay and have some supper.'

Ilona said to Edward, 'Their car is stuck, we're going to help them.'

'But they'll stay to supper first,' said Bettina. 'They can't be rescued till they've eaten something, it wouldn't be right! Ilona, go and get some more plates and glasses, and some wine.' Ilona ran off across the slates.

'Oh yes, you must stay,' said Edward to Harry. He seemed not to have heard or taken in Bettina's remark. 'The food's all vegetarian, but it's super, you'll see. And I've got those two marvellous sisters. So Thomas told you! He said he'd keep it secret, but I expect he decided it was long enough. Have you come to fetch me? I can't come yet. I'm so sorry about the car. We'll all go and pull it out.'

311

Ilona had returned and was laying the table.

At the arrival of the two boys Harry and Midge had stood transfixed. Then they had looked at each other. Then they looked at Stuart. Midge pulled her scarf out of her pocket and put it round her head, then pushed it back a little.

Stuart, after standing quite still at the door with clenched hands, walked carefully, with lowered eyes, round the pair, who shrank back a little. As he passed he gave a kind of awkward ducking nod or bow. He set off across the hall as if to enter the Interfectory, then changed his mind and went and sat at the table. When Ilona began to set out extra glasses he smiled up at her and said 'Thank you.' He looked uneasily at his father, then looked away.

Harry said, 'Hello, Stuart. We're just going.'

Midge, looking at Stuart, uttered an extraordinary sound, a sort of long wail like an animal's whine or yelp. She sat down on one of the chairs. She said to Harry, 'Let's go at once, we'll find the car.'

'Don't be silly,' said Harry.

Mother May laughed.

Edward, beginning to realise that something was wrong, and what it was, ran up to Mother May. 'It's all right, you know, it's all right – But I think they do want to go, they won't stay to supper. I'll make up some sandwiches – Ilona will – I'll take them in your car – I can tow them, do it all – Bettina – just give me the car keys.' He ran to Bettina.

'You'd never find the way,' said Bettina. 'You'd be in the ditch too. It's difficult to drive in these roads, and the mist is up. I'll get the car out, or the tractor, if that's what everyone wants. We'll try with the car first, there's only room for two in the tractor. No doubt someone will let me know if there's a change of plan.' She left the room.

Edward, pulling at his lock of hair, said, 'Oh – oh dear –' He ran over to Stuart and touched his shoulder. 'All right, Stuart?'

Stuart smiled at him. A moment later he began playing with the cutlery on the table, setting it out in various patterns.

Edward went to Ilona and said, 'Do you think you could make some sandwiches?'

Ilona said, 'In a minute. I want to stay here.' She moved back against the tapestry so as to see the whole scene.

Mother May moved back to the table and sat down near Stuart, leaving Harry and Midge still standing near the door.

Harry said, 'I think I hear the car, we'll wait outside.' He made a move.

Bettina came in saying, 'I can't find the car keys.'

Mother May followed Bettina out again through Transition.

Edward said to Harry and Midge, 'Look, won't you *please* sit down? Come over here, eat something, have some wine?'

'No thanks,' said Harry, 'we really must be off.'

Edward said, 'Ilona, won't you make some sandwiches? Or just a bit of bread or something?'

Ilona seemed to be paralysed. She was leaning back against the tapestry, breathing hard, her hand at her bosom.

'Then I will!' Edward set off toward Transition but met Mother May on the way and turned back.

Mother May said smiling, 'We found the keys!' Then she laughed with the sort of half-stifled irrepressible explosive laugh of someone who has, in some solemn or pompous scene, suddenly glimpsed something funny. She said to the two at the door, 'Look *do* sit down. If you won't sit with us at the table at least sit on these two chairs.'

'Thank you, we'll wait outside,' said Harry. He went to the door and made another attempt to open it but failed. No one moved to help him. He came back and sat on one of the chairs. Midge, affecting to fiddle in her handbag, still stood. Then Jesse came in.

At first no one noticed him. The Interfectory door was in shadow and he moved in silently. He was leaning on a stick which after a moment made a tiny tapping sound on the floor.

Ilona, who was the first to see him, cried aloud 'Jesse!' and ran to him. Without attending to her he put a hand on her shoulder to support himself and looked round the room. Jesse was imposing. Huge-headed he stood like a magisterial prophet supported by an acolyte. He was dressed in dark trousers and an unbuttoned white shirt. His dark beard and hair were combed, his lips were red and moist, his large prominent round eyes glowed, he was barefoot. He looked

313

about him frowning upon the sparsely lit room into which the mist from outside seemed to have penetrated.

Mother May moved forward. She said, as if this were some ordinary social scene embarrassingly intruded upon by an ill person, 'Please excuse him. Come along now!' She pushed Ilona away, causing him to stumble slightly, and began to try to turn him round, but without seeming to notice her he resisted, half turning and looking back over his shoulder with his bright reddish-brown eyes. He looked toward the table, then suddenly forced Mother May away from him and advanced, thrusting his head forward and glaring. Then he said in a ringing voice, 'There's a dead man, you've got a corpse there, it's sitting at the table, I can see it.' He pointed his stick at Stuart. Stuart got up.

Jesse went on raising his voice further, not hysterically but in a tone of urgent command. 'That man's dead, take him away, I curse him. Take that white thing away, it's dead. The white thing, take it away from here.'

Bettina came in through the front door with her overcoat on. She went towards Jesse, then stopped beside Mother May and spoke to her.

Mother May said sharply to Jesse, '*Stop that, at once*, come along, come to bed!' Jesse flourished his stick at her and she retreated.

Bettina said, 'The men will have to deal with him. It's like that time when we had to have the tree men in.'

Stuart, who was still standing, moved back a little, still facing Jesse, like a man backing out of a royal audience. He bumped against a chair.

Jesse, no longer attending to Stuart, moved on into the middle of the room, looking intently at the ring of people who were staring at him. He stopped, then he seemed to tremble and dropped his stick, he uttered a low wailing sound. He said, not loudly, 'Will no one love me, will no one help me, will no one *help* me, will no one come to me?'

Mother May and Bettina, and Ilona too, had followed him, but he suddenly began flailing with his arms and they retreated hurriedly.

Midge pushed her scarf back from her face. She took it off

and dropped it on the floor. Then she took off her coat. She went toward Jesse slowly, turning her head to the lamp so that he could see her face, and stopped in front of him and put her hands upon his shoulders. She said, 'I love you, I'll help you. Dear Jesse, it's all right, it's *all right*.'

Jesse started, he hunched his shoulders, his mouth opened and trembled. He peered at her. She kept her hands firmly upon him, gathering him a little. Jesse said at last, almost whispering, 'Chloe – they told me you were dead – no one tells me the truth – now – I've been waiting for you to come back to me – such a long long time.' And he put his arms around her. Midge began to cry with audible sobs which were silenced when Jesse began to kiss her. With closed eyes, in rapt absorption, arms locked about each other, they stood there kissing passionately, kissing hungrily, quickly, unable to get enough of the longed-for food.

Mother May said in a tone of disgust but without emphasis, 'Oh what a vile mess!' She put a hand on Midge's arm to drag her away but the two figures were entwined together. Mother May and Bettina stood looking at them with an exasperated calm.

'Can't we propel them,' said Bettina, 'get him out of here anyway. Let her do it.'

Mother May said in a piercing voice, 'Mrs McCaskerville, could you please just help us to get him back to bed? He is seriously ill.' She began to prod Midge violently in the back. Jesse's bare feet began to slide forward upon the slates passing between Midge's feet, and as she moved, unable to sustain his weight, he fell down heavily, first sitting, then lying full length. He lay still with his eyes open, breathing heavily. Midge twitched herself angrily away from Mother May's hand.

Mother May called, 'Edward!'

Edward, who was still standing at the other end of the hall, ran forward and knelt, putting one arm under Jesse's arm. Mother May began to lift him on the other side, and Jesse, suddenly revived, began to scrabble with his feet and allowed himself to be pulled upright. He consented to be led toward the door of the Interfectory, only resisting for a moment to

315

point to his stick, which Mother May picked up from the floor. He did not look back. His arms still held on either side by Edward and Mother May, he disappeared. The door closed after him.

Harry, who had remained seated throughout this drama, got up. He glanced at Midge who was standing beside the door crying, her face in her handkerchief. Then he walked over to the table, sat down, and poured himself out a glass of wine. Stuart a little way from him also sat down. He put one hand on the table but was trembling so much that the knives and forks began to tinkle. He took his hand away and gave it to his other hand. He sat trembling, looking down at his clasped hands. Harry stared at him with curiosity.

'Well, son, sorry for this embarrassment.' Harry reflected that he had never called Stuart 'son' in his life before.

Stuart muttered, 'Oh don't worry, I mean there it is –'

'There, as you say, it is. Must be a bit of a shock.'

Stuart said, 'Meredith told me, only I didn't believe him.'

'*What?*'

'He said she – he didn't say who –'

'Meredith. Oh God.' Harry was about to ask: does Thomas know? Then he thought, what the hell does it matter what Thomas knows. He'll know everything soon enough. This is the end of Midge's marriage. This is the catastrophe I was hoping for. How I wish I'd told Thomas ages ago, as I wanted to, told him straight and not been meanly found out like this. It's a nasty bloody mess, not what I'd have chosen – still it's just as well really, it's all *happened* at last, and I'll just *keep* her now. I'm sorry about Stuart – but he'd have had to know anyway. And Meredith – of course it's sickening – But all I've got to do now is keep my head and be as ruthless as hell.

Bettina said to Harry, 'The car is outside. Hadn't you better get off? Would you like to go to the lavatory? Mrs McCaskerville, would –? No, all right.'

Midge, no longer crying, but with her back to the scene, ignored Bettina. She was standing, as if in deep thought, holding the back of one of the chairs.

'What about sandwiches?' said Bettina to Harry. 'Ilona, could you make some – Ilona –'

Ilona, who had pulled a chair away from the table to her place beside the tapestry, and was sitting with her face in her hands, did not move.

'No, thank you,' said Harry. 'Let's go. Come on, Midge. Goodbye, Stuart. Please thank Mrs Baltram –'

'If we can't do it with the car I'll have to come back for the tractor, but I don't suppose you'll want to – Ilona, you'd better go to bed.' Bettina picked up Midge's coat and scarf and handbag from the floor and put them on the chair beside her. Harry held Midge's coat while she obediently groped for the sleeves, he saw her desolate swollen face which yet wore a fierce strange expression.

Bettina repeated, '*Ilona*, go to bed. At once.'

Ilona rose and without looking at the company ran to Transition and went through the door, slamming it behind her.

Stuart, as if awakened by the noise, leapt up. He said to Harry, 'Could you wait a moment, please. I want to come with you, do you mind? Just wait, I'll get my stuff, I won't be long.' He ran off, following Ilona.

Midge turned furiously to Harry, 'We can't take him, we *can't!*'

Harry, coolly, said, 'I don't see why not, I don't see that it matters a hang. He knows all about it anyway, Meredith told him.'

'Meredith told Stuart – oh – no – I never told you – Meredith saw –'

'He *saw* us – what did he see? *Hell* – I told you we shouldn't be in your house –'

'It wasn't my fault!'

'Well, there you are. I expect Thomas knows by now. We're blown, thank God. We're on our own now, Midge.'

'Do you want to wait for him?' said Bettina, who was standing listening to these exchanges.

'Thomas needn't know – I'm *sure* he doesn't –'

'He soon will!'

'Neither Stuart nor Meredith will tell Thomas.'

'Won't they?'

'I don't want anything to happen yet –'

317

'But, Midge, think what's happened already!'

'Not yet – I don't *know* yet – not like this –'

'Do you want to wait for him?' said Bettina.

'We can't take Stuart, I won't have it!' said Midge, stamping her foot.

'Yes, we'll wait,' said Harry to Bettina. He said to Midge, 'Look, he's my son –'

'You say this *now*, to *me* –'

'He doesn't seem to be *persona grata* here, I'm not going to leave him behind in this hell hole –'

'You want to take him so as to compromise me further, so as to have a witness, so as to ruin everything –'

'You call it ruin, I call it liberation! It doesn't *matter*, don't you see –'

'He hates us, he'll bring us misfortune.'

Stuart appeared with his coat and suitcase. He said apologetically, 'So sorry to keep you all waiting.'

'Come on then,' said Bettina, and led them out onto the terrace, illuminated by the outside light, and across to the car.

'SO IT WASN'T Chloe –' said Jesse. He spoke quietly, dreamily. He was lying on his bed, in his shirt, holding Edward's hand.

Mother May was standing on the other side of the bed holding a glass of brown liquid.

'No, my darling,' said Edward. This mode of speech seemed suddenly natural. Of course Jesse was his father. But he was, as if now filled up to the brim, so much more: a master, a precious king, a divine lover, a strange mysterious infinitely beloved object, the prize of a religious search, a jewel in a cave. It was as if, in this sudden limp quietness, Jesse had gently, almost imperceptibly, imparted himself. Edward felt his heart bursting with reverence and love. 'But don't you worry, don't you grieve. That was Chloe's sister. Chloe is dead. She died long ago.'

'Of course,' said Jesse, 'I remember. She looks so very – so very like Chloe.' He was calm, more lucid, and peacefully rational than Edward had ever seen him. This change filled Edward with hope and joy.

'She did tonight. She looked just like pictures of her.'

'You can't recall your mother?'

'Not very well, hardly –'

'I can see her face in my mind so clearly. I loved her very much.'

Edward heard the car start. The sound diminished down the track and disappeared into silence. He said to Jesse, 'Oh don't be sad, dear dear dear Jesse. It matters so much that you

319

shouldn't be sad. I'm with you, I'll look after you. I've found you forever and ever. I love you.'

'They've gone,' said Mother May.

Edward began kissing Jesse's hands. Jesse smiled a little as if touched and embarrassed.

'Leave off,' said Mother May. 'Go along now Edward. I want Jesse to rest. I'll sit with him. He's had a shock. He's given us all a shock.'

'I'll see you tomorrow,' said Edward. He had such a strange feeling, the feeling of being terribly in love. The prospect of leaving Jesse was agonising. He stood up. 'Dear Jesse, dear sweet good Jesse, think of me in the night. I'll think of you.'

'I'll dream of you – Edward –'

'Tomorrow.'

'Yes, tomorrow.'

Mother May opened the door and Edward ran out.

The Atrium was empty, the table untouched except for Harry's empty wine glass. Edward hurried on into Transition and sped up the stairs into West Selden. He hurried to the end bedroom, knocked and went in. No sign of Stuart. Then he saw that the room was cleared, all Stuart's things had gone. Stuart had gone. This came as a weird unnerving surprise. He had, at that moment, depended on Stuart, wanted to talk to him about what had happened, wanted to know what Stuart thought, what to think himself. He felt frightened and alone. He went back to his own room and lit the lamp and sat down on the bed. So Stuart had gone off in the car. Actually it was just as well. Seegard was Edward's place and Edward's problem, Stuart was not a help, he was simply dangerous. Edward wondered if he was hungry and should go down to the kitchen and find something to eat, but he had not the will. He felt a bit sick and intensely upsettingly excited. And there was nothing left to do now but go to bed.

Or was there? He went into the darkened bathroom and looked out. East Selden was dark except for a little lamp light showing from Ilona's bedroom where the shutters had been half closed. Ilona was over there, by herself. Mother May was with Jesse. Bettina was out with the car. Edward felt, I *must* talk to somebody, I couldn't *possibly* sleep. What on earth happened this evening, what did it mean, how does it affect me, ought I to do something about it? Why were they there, was it because of me, will they say it's my fault, what *have* they been doing, whatever will Thomas think? Does Harry need me, does Midge need me, ought I to have gone with them, ought I to go tomorrow? But of course I *can't* go, I *must* stay. As he reflected, the whole background of his life now seemed in chaos. Midge and Harry turning up together, whatever did it mean? Perhaps it was all an accident, it needn't mean anything special. Yet why were they there, had they come to fetch him away, they didn't say so. Or did they? He couldn't remember. And Jesse calling Stuart 'a dead man' and 'a white corpse'. And Jesse thinking Midge was Chloe, and Midge kissing Jesse. It was all a nightmare. That image of her holding Jesse in her arms and kissing him so passionately upset Edward very much indeed. That would travel with him like a sinister icon.

Edward thought, I must see Ilona, and now's the perfect chance. He carried the lamp into the bathroom and looked at himself in the mirror. He needed a shave and a little impulse of vanity made him, before he checked himself, reach for his razor. He combed his hair, patting down the long dark front lock, and after reflection took off his jacket. He adjusted his shirt, opening another button. He thought he looked older, more gaunt and hawkish. He narrowed his eyes. Then he sprang long-legged out of the room and down the stairs.

The connecting corridor was pitch dark, with no light visible at the other end, but Edward had often looked along it in daylight and he strode confidently forward. At the end he touched the wall, pivoted around, and felt for the curve of the stairs which would, he imagined, duplicate his own stairs. He was right. His foot found the first stone step, and he silently padded his way up. At the top there was a faint sense of light, and after a moment his darkened eyes made out the dim smudgy streak of light at the base of Ilona's door. The silence, as he stood there, daunted him. Arms outstretched he tiptoed to the door and listened. No sound. He tapped softly on the door. Then again. He listened to his own fast breathing. Then he carefully turned the handle and moved the door.

Ilona was asleep. The faint lamp was upon a table beside her low bed. She lay on her back upon a reddish brownish surface which Edward took at first to be a sheet or quilt, but which he now saw to be her undone hair. The ribbons which she had woven into her plaits earlier in the evening also appeared here and there among the tresses. Her head was a little turned to one side and tilted back, with a hand and forearm twisted in behind it, in an attitude which might have expressed anguish had not her sleep set a seal of peace upon it. The other arm lay outstretched upon the disordered blanket with the palm open in a gesture of acquiescence or submission. Ilona's lips were open and her low slow breathing just audible. The closed eyes exhibited the long eyelashes whose light colour had made them, before, less conspicuous. In repose her small face had lost its animal pertness, the cheeks less prominent, the mouth without animation, childish, gentler. The sheet and blanket had been thrust down to reveal the delicate skin of her vulnerable stretched neck, the rounded embroidered collar of her blue nightdress and the shape of her small breasts. She looked, lying there, so helpless, so fragile and frail, as if it could hardly be imagined how she stayed in being at all.

Edward had closed the door and approached. For a moment he towered beside her, huge as his shadow. He felt amazement, then a deep pang of some sort of ashamed humility, and a new different chaste fear. His presence seemed dangerous to her, and he wondered if he ought not immediately to creep away. The bed, set against the wall, was small and narrow, low down, a divan, not a fine upstanding bed like his own. It was almost as if Ilona were lying upon cushions and coloured cloths piled upon the floor. Edward adjusted his own breathing and then very cautiously fell upon one knee beside her. Now he wanted to come closer, if possible to feel the waftage of her breath. His open anxious lips approached her lips. He paused, then drew back, and very quietly brought his other knee down to the floor and sat back on his heels. He felt an excitement composed of power and gentleness, conscious of their solitude together, of the house round about them silent and dark, and the dark clouded night outside the half-shuttered window.

Then Ilona awoke. He saw her eyes flutter open, close, then open again. She lay quiet a moment gazing upward. Then with a movement as swift as a leaping cat she sat up, recoiling against the wall. Edward quickly sat back upon the floor farther from the bed. Ilona's face, glaring at him, expressed intense fear.

'Ilona – dear – it's only me – don't be frightened – forgive me –'

She clutched her nightdress about her neck in a terrified movement, then tossed back the bed-clothes and thrust out her slim legs and bare feet. Edward rose and stepped back. Hastily she thrust her feet into slippers, then reached for a red dressing gown which was lying on the bottom of the bed and began awkwardly to drag it on. All this time her face was distorted in a grimace of mingled fear and annoyance. She buttoned the dressing gown with clumsy incompetent fingers and then stood up. She *whispered* to Edward, 'You *mustn't* be here, you must go *at once*.'

Edward got up too and said, softly but not whispering, 'Look, Ilona don't worry. Your mother is with Jesse, she said she'd sit with him, and Bettina has gone off with the others in the car. Stuart went too. There's only us.'

'They could come at any moment. How could you do this! You know you mustn't.'

Edward said, 'I don't know any such thing!' This was not true, he was intensely aware of being on forbidden ground. 'Anyway, why should we live by rules, who made these rules? I'm your brother. Haven't I any rights?' No, none, he said to himself.

'What do you want?'

'I just want to talk to you, do sit down for a moment, I won't stay long, Ilona, *please*, I'm feeling so upset and lost, I want you to help me just by letting me talk, I'll go soon I promise you. We'll hear the car, and Bettina will come in by the front door and if Mother May isn't with Jesse she's sure to be waiting for Bettina in the Atrium. They wouldn't want to talk up here.'

This entirely impromptu reasoning seemed to calm Ilona a little though it was probable she hardly understood it. She sat down on the bed and Edward sat, curling his legs, on the floor, not near her. Ilona gathered her hair carefully and stowed it behind her. She turned upon Edward a face of entire distress and said, 'You aren't going away?'

'No, what made you think that?'

'What happened tonight.'

'Well, what did happen tonight? My stepfather and my aunt suddenly materialised together. Bettina says they said they were Mr and Mrs Bentley.'

'I don't understand. That was Chloe's sister, who's married to –'

'Thomas McCaskerville.'

'And the man was Chloe's husband.'

'Yes, Harry Cuno.'

'Their car broke down.'

'Yes, but they were obviously together secretly. They must have turned up here by accident in the dark. If there is such a thing as accident.'

'I thought they'd come to fetch you.'

'So did I, till I started thinking. Never mind. I mean, never *you* mind. I just feel in such a mess as if I can't rely on anybody, and *that's* only just starting.'

'Jesse kissed her – I've never seen anything like it – he kissed her so much –'

'Yes. He did. Didn't he?' Edward felt strangely deeply upset, hurt, as if his mother had actually been present at the scene, as if her poor helpless ghost had been trying, in the person of Midge, to kiss Jesse, to touch, to embrace her precious faithless beloved. Edward had not, even now, reflected upon how his mother had been 'treated badly' by her lover. He did not want to have to think about all that. That kissing had been awful. It was exciting too. It was exciting in an awful way. And somehow it was all connected, connected with him, and through him with Ilona, with Brownie . . . *Brownie*. Tomorrow.

'Ilona, can I tell you something. You know about Mark Wilsden, don't you?'

'Your friend who fell out of the window.'

'Yes. Did Mother May tell you?'

'Yes, and we saw it in the paper.'

'You don't have newspapers here –'

'Dorothy sent us the cutting – you know, Mother May's friend.'

'Well, I've found his sister, and she's *here* –'

'Here?'

'Yes, she's over at Railway Cottage, where Sarah Plowmain and her mother live.'

'You've been over *there*?'

'Yes, don't tell the others.'

'But do you know those people, aren't they awful –?'

'I used to know Sarah. But, listen, I'm going to see Mark's sister again tomorrow morning, it's terribly important. She's been kind to me, she can help me, no one else can –'

'Can't I help you?'

'Oh Ilona, of course you help me, but this you must see is special –'

'You don't need me. You're going to her.'

'Ilona, don't be silly –'

'You'll leave us –' Ilona, putting her hands to her face, began desperately to cry. Copious tears ran through her fingers and down her cheeks, onto her neck and onto the embroidered collar of her nightdress and all down her dressing gown, staining it a darker red. She cried, pouring the tears out, and uttering a little whining keening sound.

'Ilona, don't cry, oh don't cry, I can't bear it!' Edward jumped up and sat beside her on the bed, putting his arm round her shoulders. He felt her thinness, her smallness, the fragility of her bones. She shrank from him and he moved back, removing his arm. He could smell the wet wool and the warm scent of her body, so lately asleep. 'Oh do stop, my darling –'

Ilona turned and dug under her pillow for a handkerchief, found it, and mopped her face and dried her neck. Still sniffing and crying a little she said, 'Will you take me with you

325

to London? Could I stay in your house? It would be just for a while. I'd find a job. Please let me come with you to London. I don't want to stay here, I'll die here.'

Edward felt an anguish of pity and love for her, and at the same time a sense of how impossible it was. He couldn't take Ilona to London and keep her in his room like a pet frog. She'd die *there*. And what job could Ilona find, what job could she ever find? He said, 'But you must stay with Jesse.'

'They won't let me see Jesse, they won't let me come near him. They're jealous. And tonight – he didn't even notice me.' She cried some more, then wrung out the handkerchief and watched the drops fall upon the little rug by her bed.

'Anyway, I must stay with Jesse.' Edward uttered this with instinctive vehemence, but it was a dark saying. He added, 'What makes you think I'm leaving?'

'You'll leave. You'll have to. You won't be able to stand it. They'll stop you from seeing him. You're bound to go, you'll follow *her*. You'll forget me. Nobody wants me.' The tears were coming again, like ever-renewed rain showers, Edward had never seen a girl cry so. He had never seen so many tears. Then he imagined that he had seen his mother crying when he was a very small child. So many women's tears.

'Ilona, don't, you're my sister and I love you, I told you so, remember.'

'Then can I come to you in London?'

'Well, it'll be rather difficult –' He thought, I can't imagine it, she'll die if she leaves here, and besides –

Ilona abruptly stopped crying. She got up and dropped the wet handkerchief in a corner and opened a drawer and drew out a large square of clean white handkerchief, carefully unfolded it and dried her hands upon it and put it in the pocket of her dressing gown. She said in a calm dull voice, not looking at him, 'All right, you don't want me. It was silly to hope. There's nowhere for me to go except into the river.'

'Ilona, don't talk such wicked nonsense! I've told you, I'm not going! And if I did, I'd always come back to see *you*. And later on, when things in London are a bit more sorted out, there's no reason why you shouldn't come to visit –'

'To visit! Oh you don't see, you don't *know*, what I want,

how *much* I want, how much I thought your coming here would make everything different and give me things to hope for – oh what does it matter. Go away, please, I want to sleep, and they mustn't find you here, they'd blame me.'

Edward heard the murmur, then the loud unmistakable sound, of the car coming back. He jumped up. 'There's the car, I must go. Ilona, I'll look after you, all my life, I promise – dear, dear Ilona, believe me –'

'Go on, go quick. I must put this light out.'

Before he reached the door she had turned off the lamp.

Edward opened his eyes. It was daylight. He had forgotten to close the shutters. He lay flat on his back, relaxed, vaguely conscious. Then he remembered the amazing happenings of the previous night, the arrival of Harry and Midge as 'Mr and Mrs Bentley', the apparition of Jesse, Jesse's curse on Stuart, then how he had held Midge in his arms and kissed her. He thought she was Chloe. How extraordinary. Had he dreamt it all or did it really happen? And then he had talked to Ilona and she had cried so much. And he had fallen down the stone stairs in the dark and hurt his leg. Then he had stood in Transition listening to the murmur of Bettina and Mother May talking in the hall. Near to the door he could have heard what they were saying, but the idea filled him with disgust and he limped back to West Selden. And now – how *awful* it all was, and what was he supposed to *do* about it? He sat up, pushed back the bed-clothes, and sat on the bed rubbing his bruised leg. He examined his cut hand, which had been healing since Mother May put that leaf upon it. Then with a flash he remembered: *Brownie. Today.*

He looked at his watch. It was already late, past breakfast time, he had overslept. Suppose he didn't reach her in time, suppose she were gone, suppose she thought he *didn't want to see her*, suppose he were to lose her forever? He began to dress in clumsy haste. Suppose *they* detained him. Suppose Ilona, out of jealous misery, had told him where he was going. Dressed, he went to the window to see if there was anyone outside on the terrace. He intended to slink straight out of the

West Selden door. A low heavy white mist was lying, its smooth surface a few feet off the ground. It looked as if a flood surrounded the house. Suppose he were to lose his way. God, he didn't *know* the way to Railway Cottage, he had only found it by accident! He must find where the old railway line crossed the road. But he had nearly missed it and could miss it again in this infernal mist. Anyway, that must be a long way round, there was surely a quicker way to get to the railway line. He must look at the map. But he had put the map back in the drawer in the Interfectory.

Edward stood in an agony of anxiety and indecision. He put his jacket on. He felt unwell, a little giddy and hazy in the head, he kept blinking his eyes, it was as if the mist had got into them. He went into the bathroom and wondered if he should shave for Brownie. He looked in the mirror. He looked a sight. Impatiently he shaved, moving the razor with painful slowness as if something were retarding his hand. He decided to put on a tie, then could not knot it properly and threw it down. He combed his hair and pocketed the comb. He still could not decide whether to risk going to fetch the map.

He opened his bedroom door and listened. The white silence of the mist had penetrated the house. There was not a sound. He went to the top of the stairs, then scurried back for his mackintosh. He went down as far as Transition and listened again. There was no one in the kitchen. He cautiously opened the Atrium door. The big hall was empty, the breakfast table partly cleared. He went as far as the table, and seeing bread, jam, a jug of fruit juice, felt suddenly extremely hungry. He had missed his supper last night. He quickly tore at the bread and drank two glasses of the fruit juice which tasted intoxicating like wine, perhaps was wine. He made up a jam sandwich and stuffed it in his pocket. He felt for a moment quite sick and as if his feet were not touching the ground, and he resisted a temptation to sit down by the table and rest his head in his hands. He went on to the Interfectory and entered the empty room. In a moment he had pocketed the map, and was running tiptoe across the slated floor to the main door when Mother May came in from outside. She stood aside as he passed her and swung out of the door. He

328

heard her call after him 'Edward!' as he ran, without looking back, across the terrace.

He wanted to get quickly away from the house and find somewhere where he could stand and study the map. He ran into the trees to the left, along beyond the greenhouses and the orchard, so as to put the poplar grove between him and the house. He pictured Mother May and Bettina running after him, calling. He ran, waist high in the white mist, half a man running away. Just beyond the poplars he slowed down, then stopped and listened. There was no sight or sound of a pursuit. He unfolded the map, which immediately began to fall about like a collection of small books loosely tied together with string. He knelt on the ground, wet with dew and mist, and laid it out, then savagely refolded it so as to see what he wanted. A footpath was marked leading off the drive toward the railway, but Edward had not noticed this path which by now had probably been closed and planted over by the 'nasty farmer' mentioned by Ilona. It was safer to go by the road. With the help of the map he could at least estimate the distance. He walked on parallel to the track over lumpy grass, screened by gorse and elder bushes and small hazels. He thought he heard a car. Then he certainly heard the sound of the river. He kicked his way through a mass of old broken bracken which was already stiffened by new curled shoots like little green walking sticks. Then there was the river bank and a path which he recognised. The mist clearing from the ground was diffused in the air and he could dimly see the slope of the little hill and the trees on the other side. As the map informed him, if he followed the river he would reach the road sooner, but at a point farther from his objective. On the other hand, he was afraid to walk on the track in full view, and once on the tarmac he could run. Why had everything suddenly become so difficult?

He decided he had better get back to the track after all. He looked at his watch. He had already spent a lot of time consulting the map and struggling along over the rough ground. *Time* was passing, he must *hurry*. He thought, almost tearfully, *I'm not well*. I feel so strange. I feel feverish, delirious, I've got a headache, I'd like to lie down and sleep.

Everything looks so odd. Perhaps it's just the sun, I can see the sun as a golden ball coming through the mist, only I mustn't look at it. There *is* a mist, isn't there, it isn't just my eyes? I shouldn't have drunk that fruit juice. Why was it there in that small jug? Did they leave it specially for me? They wanted to stop me from going away. I mustn't look at the sun. I want to sit down and rest for a moment, but I mustn't, I must get to Brownie, if I don't I'll never never find her again. He decided to follow the path a little further, hurrying as fast as he could. A clump of nettles looked to him like a green armchair, and he thought I'm inside a picture by Jesse! A leaf brushed his hand with a line of pain. He stopped, setting his feet wide apart and steadying himself. He looked at the river. He was just beside the 'bridge', where the water rushed through the leaning slatted fence and the horizontal bar made a precarious walkway. Clumps of cowslips were gathered near his feet, and down below the bank yellow irises were coming into flower, and wagtails were walking on the beds of floating water weed. He felt a desire to cross the river. Had he been *led* to this place, programmed to walk along that path? The brown water flowed purposefully, sleekly, less fast, taking hold of the slats of wood and passing through them smoothly without foam. There was a soft murmurous hushing sound. The water had a transparent look as of darkened glass. Edward looked down into the reeds which were growing up so greenly in the little gap between the fence and the bank.

Then he saw something amazing, something terrible. *He saw Jesse.* Jesse was down below him in the water looking up. He's gone mad, he's gone *mad*, Edward thought as the shock struck him with a vicious jab and he stepped back from the edge. He saw me coming and he's squatting there in the stream to frighten me. He came and looked again. It was different now. He could still see Jesse only he now realised that he was *under the water*. He saw his face and open eyes and a sort of smile, and his black hair and beard streamed out by the force of the water, also one hand, with the ruby ring clearly visible. Beyond the head there was a sort of black hump ribboned over with dead reeds, the water seemed still like brown jelly, and the eyes looking up like those of a sea creature. Edward thought, my God, *it's an hallucination*. It's like something I saw in a dream that night when I was drugged. *They* have done it to me. He knelt and reached his hand down into the water. As he disturbed the sleek surface the image vanished, but for an instant he could *feel the ring*, something soft and cold, then a hard band. Then this impression too was gone. Edward got up and stared down again, leaning his head forward, almost pitching into the river. He saw the brown water and the swaying of the young reeds but nothing more. The water was foaming and circling now and he could not see through it. He thought, he's not mad, *I* am mad; and he stepped back and began to run away along the bank.

He ceased to run and walked on for a few paces. The path had ceased at the bridge and the long grass impeded him and he stopped. Then he turned and came back. His mouth was open and his breath came in little anxious whining sounds. He stood again over the place and looked into the river, looked down into the water which had resumed its brown glassy transparency. There was nothing there. He sat and slid down the bank, digging his heels into the muddy edge, and balanced with the water over his knees. He looked again and made sweeps in the water with his hands. Then he edged along the bank, dabbing here and there with his feet, slipping into the stream almost to his waist. He climbed up the bank and ran and scrambled along the side of the river in the direction of the current for some way, looking among the reeds and the long streamers of cressy plants which wavered in the flowing water. Then he gave up and set off walking as fast as he could across the grass in the direction of the track.

When he reached the road he was still panting with fear and shock. He thought, this is awful, it's *hideous*. Will I go on being like this, am I *breaking up*? And he thought, no, *they* aren't poisoning me. It's my own doing. It's that awful drug I used to take, it'll never go away, never. What a horrible vision. I'm coming to pieces. *This* is what I've come to, this is where I'm being *driven*. And I thought I was recovering, I thought I was getting off. But of course, the punishment is automatic. And he thought, what can Brownie do against

331

this? I mustn't tell her, she's got enough of my troubles, she's had enough of me, she'll be horrified by me, I'll disgust her. Oh Brownie, poor poor Brownie. When he reached the cottage she was waiting for him, standing at the door.

'Edward, what's the matter, are you ill?'

'No, yes, I think I've got malaria.'

'*Malaria?*'

'Yes, there are malaria mosquitoes in the fen.'

'You're all wet and muddy.'

'I walked into a pool, perfectly silly. I thought I might be late.'

'Sit down here. Can I give you something? Coffee, sherry?'

'No, I'll be all right – in a minute.' He sat down in a low chair. He felt giddy and a cloud of blackness hovered over him, just above his brow. He said, 'I mustn't bother you, Brownie. I don't want to be in the way. You must do your packing.'

'I've done it. It's only a few minutes to the bus. Do have a drink. I'm going to have one.'

'All right, sherry.' The sherry, dark and rather sweet, tasted wonderful, like some drink rushed specially from heaven. He felt a little better. 'I feel all right now. Of course it isn't malaria, I just had a touch of 'flu, I'm over it really.'

'You're shivering. I'll light the paraffin stove. There.'

'Oh Brownie, Brownie –'

They looked at each other.

In the darker scene of the cottage room, where everything seemed to be stained by wood smoke or wear or age, Brownie looked older and shabbier, her hair less bright, her face somehow disorganised by tiredness or sadness. She was wearing a navy blue skirt and a brown jersey from the top of which a blue blouse confusedly obtruded. Her pale face seemed awkwardly large and naked, undefended by make-up or pretty hair or charm. She stood heavily, her feet apart, her hands clasped in front of her, staring down at Edward.

As she still stood, Edward made an effort to get up.

'No, no, sit. Shall I light the wood fire?'

'No, please not –'

'I didn't light it last night. It's a bit cold this morning. And the cottage is getting damp already.' She pulled an upright chair forward and sat on it, towering over Edward who felt uncomfortable and weak in his lower chair with its sunken seat and wooden arms. His long legs were uncomfortably stretched out, and his trousers steaming a little from the heat of the stove, which Brownie had placed close to him. He wanted to get up and find a higher chair, but did not dare to do this or to ask for more sherry.

'Thank you for seeing me –'

'Not at all –'

'You said you wanted to ask me something else.'

'Yes, two things actually – you must forgive my sort of probing – I feel I must get it all *clear* while I'm still able to see you.'

'Yes – of course –' It sounded to Edward as if . . . sometime very soon . . . their meetings would have come to an end forever.

'It may sound crazy to ask this – but – well – look, did you tell me the truth last time, about your giving him the drug without his knowing?'

'Yes! My God, if you don't believe me I'm lost!'

'Yes, yes, I know, I've just got to get another idea right out of my head. He didn't ask for it?'

'No!'

'But still he might have – for some reason – wanted to walk out of the window anyway.'

'I don't understand,' said Edward. He was feeling sick again, black, with an unbearable wretchedness closing upon him.

'I mean, you're sure it wasn't suicide?'

'Suicide? *No! Of course not!*'

'He wasn't desperate, nothing awful had happened to him, like losing his girl, or –'

'No!'

'He was, so far as you know, perfectly happy and OK?'

'Yes. He was very well, he was perfectly happy, everything was splendid with him. Oh God, I'm sorry –'

333

Brownie sighed. She was staring at the bright flickering window of the stove and had lifted a corner of her skirt which she was unconsciously kneading. 'Ah – all right – the other thing – excuse my asking, but did you have a homosexual relation with Mark?'

The question hurt Edward in a deep obscure way. It seemed to him for the first time that this was something which might have happened in that long future which he had, together with Mark, destroyed. 'No, I didn't. I loved him. But not like that.'

'And he loved you.'

'Yes. I think so. I'm sure.'

'But not like that.'

'No.' Can I be certain? thought Edward. God, how this hurt, this unexpected opening up of things that might have been, further torture chambers and caverns of pain.

'You see,' said Brownie, in her cool sad voice, 'lots of people have said lots of things, and someone suggested to me that you did have a homosexual relation and that you pushed him out of the window after a jealous quarrel.'

Edward cried out. He did now manage to get up out of his chair and stand before her. 'No! It's not true. How *could* it be true? Oh *Christ*! Who said that?'

'Nobody you know. Just someone who was speculating or guessing. It all *interested* everyone so much. A terrible complicated disaster excites people.'

'You don't think that, what you said?'

'No, I don't. I really don't, and I didn't. I just had to say it to get rid of it. It's gone now.'

'It's gone from you to me. I'll never stop thinking that people say that.' Edward instantly regretted these words. If there were a terrible thought, should *he* not take the burden of it, and be glad to take a pain away from her into himself? And did what he had just said mean that he cared more about his reputation than about Mark's death? He said, 'Oh hell, I'm sorry, I'm so sorry you had to hear such horrible – guesses and speculations –' He walked to the window and back, wanting to cry out and tear his hair.

Brownie, hunched and big on her chair, frowning slightly,

334

watched him. She crossed her legs and pulled her skirt down and sighed. 'So that's all – and I believe everything you say.'

'Well, that could scarcely be worse, the truth I mean. I deceived him and abandoned him, so I murdered him.'

'Don't talk like that please. Don't you see that it helps me if I can – can understand you and sympathise –'

'You mean if you can forgive me.'

'Yes, if you like to put it so.'

'Well, do you?'

'Yes.' She said it in a dull sad way.

Yet, he thought, how else could she say it? She gave him so much, was he to cry and complain because it was not more? She did not look like Mark today. Perhaps she was looking like her mother. He said, 'You are the just judge. Thank you – well – and so – I am finished with and can be sent away. What about your mother? You said I might be able to help her.'

'She goes on hating you.'

'Someone told me that hatred kills. Perhaps her hatred will kill me. Perhaps that might be the best thing, a kind of justice.'

'That's a rotten thing to say. Hatred kills the hater. My poor mother is almost mad with it.'

'So that's another of my crimes.'

'The consequences of anything can go on and on.'

'What can I do about it?'

'Nothing. I thought somehow you could help her but I don't see how. Let us say it doesn't have to concern you.'

He suddenly felt *she* hates me, *Brownie* hates me. But it can't be, *that* would kill. He said, 'Suppose I were to see her, or write to her?'

'No, I'll tell her some things you said – anything that's necessary –'

'So there's nothing more I can do for you?'

'No. You've been very patient.'

'Patient! God!'

Brownie got up and started rubbing her face with her hands, smoothing them over her prominent white brow, and tucking her listless hair in behind her ears. She yawned.

Edward stood back. His trousers were still wet, now hot and wet. Brownie turned off the paraffin heater. They moved toward the door. There was a pause. Brownie adjusted the collar of her blouse. Edward realised he had not, throughout their conversation, now over, really *looked* at her. They looked at each other for a second, then looked away. She said, 'Well goodbye, and thanks.'

Edward desperately tried to think of some way to continue the conversation, but could not. He felt a soft wet patch against his side, investigated his jacket pocket, and drew forth the remains of his hasty jam sandwich, now squashed into a red limp mess.

'What's that?' said Brownie.

'A jam sandwich. I forgot all about it. I must have crushed it against the chair. I put it – I hadn't time for breakfast –'

They might have laughed only they did not. Brownie smiled wanly.

'Can I throw it away somewhere?' He stood holding it out.

'I'll take it.' Brownie took it from him and threw it with some force into the wood ash in the fireplace. She rubbed her hand on her skirt.

Edward felt near to tears. The black miserable fear was about to overwhelm him.

'Shall I make you some sandwiches? Oh, I can't – I've thrown all the food away.'

'It doesn't matter. I'll have my lunch at – over there –'

'Goodbye then. Thanks for coming.'

They paused another instant and looked at each other again. Then each took a little step forward and, responding to the swift mysterious mechanism which so imperiously draws one human body to another, were clasped in each other's arms. They held together thus, strongly, violently, as if each would drive right through the other, their eyes closed, her head in his shoulder, his face buried in her hair, for some time. Then they struggled apart and Edward clumsily kissed her cheek, then quickly her lips, and they drew away.

Brownie looked quite different now. She was blushing and her face, alert, assembled, had a gentle almost apologetic look and she made a sweeping gesture with her hand suggestive of a bow. She looked hurt, touched, younger, almost timid. Edward felt a corresponding look on his own face. He felt like a subject who, after surprising his prince, wants only to kneel. Indeed he wanted to kneel and kiss the hem of her skirt.

Brownie turned away and said very softly as she turned, 'Don't go yet.' She went and sat down upon a faded reddish sofa under the window, overhung by dried grasses, and Edward came and sat beside her. He took her hand and, bowing his head over it, moved her knuckles to and fro upon his brow. He felt overwhelmed, split in two, by sudden physical desire and by an intense weepy humility. He drew his hair over her hand and hardly dared to look up.

She said, 'I don't have to catch that bus.'

He said, 'Oh Brownie, help me, love me. I love you.'

'I love you too, I think.'

Edward raised his head and looked into her dark brown eyes, darker than his own, which were so bright and gentle and truthful. He lifted a hand and put his finger lightly upon her cheek, he touched her mouth. He said, 'You pity me. You are consumed with wonderful miraculous pity for me. I am intensely grateful. I kiss your feet.'

He moved as if about to do so, but she held him. 'Edward – isn't it strange – we are the only ones who can help each other.'

'My God, you are so kind – so – so gracious, so precious – I can't find the words – like a great queen – you've got the one thing needful – like a magic jewel –'

'But you agree that we can help each other? Somehow, at least for that, we belong together. Don't get lost.'

'Yes, we can help each other. You can certainly help me. Oh my dear angel – it's not a cheat, is it?'

'No – I'm sure it isn't. I feel such – such –'

'Don't name it. I love you. I'm allowed to do that.' He took both her hands and began to kiss them, putting them against his cheek and feeling the kisses like tears.

The gesture suddenly reminded him of the last time he had seen Jesse, when he had kissed Jesse's hands, and Mother May had said 'Leave off', and Jesse had said, 'I'll dream of you', and 'Tomorrow'. It was tomorrow. And he had just seen, and for instants of time *forgotten*, that *terrible thing*. He sat up abruptly, his eyes glaring with distress and fear. Supposing it were real, true and Jesse were dead, drowned, and he had not saved him? Suddenly nothing in the world was more important than that he should run back to Seegard and make sure that Jesse was all right. Until he knew that everything, even the miracle of Brownie, was darkened and spoilt. If only Jesse was all right and Brownie was merciful and loving to him he could be healed. This was for real. Not what the women had been doing to him at Seegard which now seemed like a horrible charade.

'What is it?' she said. 'You look like you did when you arrived. You're sick.'

'No. But I've remembered something urgent. I must go back to Seegard.'

'Now? Can't you wait? I feel – maybe we'll never be like this again. I'm frightened. Don't go.'

'I've got to, Brownie. It's terribly important otherwise I wouldn't – I don't want to go. We'll be together again, of course – I'm so sorry –'

She took her hands away and stood up. The spell was broken. 'All right, if you must. I won't keep you. I can see it's important.'

'I'm awfully sorry. Will you be here?'

'I think as you're going I'll catch the bus after all, there's still time.'

'But we'll meet –'

'Yes, of course. Before I go back to America. Don't worry, Edward. This has been a good meeting. Perhaps we've done, in these few minutes, everything that is needed. Don't worry any more about these things, just leave them quiet.'

'Brownie, I – I'm sorry I can't explain – I have to –'

'Yes, yes, go, please.'

'Thank you, and – oh –' Edward ran to the door, stepped back towards her, then ran out. As he came out into the bright light he suddenly saw, quite close to him over some trees, the top of the Seegard tower. He could get there quickly after all, and perhaps get back again before Brownie went to the bus. Should he ask her to wait? The door had closed behind him. No, he couldn't. He had done everything wrong, everything in a doomed way. There was a curse upon him which only

338

those two could remove, and they had not yet done it. He began to run, first along the grassy railway track, then up the bank and across some slippery wet grass and over a little broken-down stone wall. The mist had cleared and the sun was shining into his eyes. The tower had now disappeared from view. He ran on, confident of the direction. But Edward had missed the path along which Sarah Plowmain had led Mr and Mrs Bentley, with the torch illuminating her heels. Soon he found himself climbing slowly through a muddy ditch full of brambles.

When at last he reached Seegard the first person he saw as he hurried into the Atrium was Mother May. She was sitting at the table and cutting lettuce leaves into long streamers with a pair of scissors and putting them into a large wooden bowl.

'Hello, Edward. What's got into you?'

'How's Jesse?'

'All right. Asleep.'

Edward turned and began to walk toward Transition.

'Edward!'

'Yes – sorry –'

'Come here. Sit down.'

He came and sat opposite to her at the table. Mother May regarded him with her calm long grey eyes. Then reached across and took one of his hands and pulled it towards her straightening his arm. Edward watched the movement of his arm as if it were something mechanical. Then he looked at Mother May's handsome head, her intricately woven mass of light red-gold hair, her gentle face and humorous quizzical mouth. He realised she was pressing his hand gently. 'Oh – Edward –'

'I'm sorry,' said Edward, 'I'm awful. I know I've let you all down. You've been marvellous to me. But I can't do it the way you want.'

'Do what?'

'Change. I'm just me.' The pressure of Mother May's hand reminded Edward of the weird conversation in which she had said to him, can you help me, can you love me, can you love me *enough*? He had forgotten the details of that conversation. He had been drunk. She had been drunk too. Did she recall it with embarrassment? She was unembarrassed now, full of power. He gripped her hand, staring.

'But we *have* changed you. Don't give us up. You need us, we need you. This is your home now.' She spoke with insistence, with authority.

'Oh yes, I suppose it is,' said Edward. Everywhere else was a wreck. Was it? Why not? He could not afford to throw it away. But he didn't want to think about these things now, he wanted to be alone.

She released him. 'Where did you go this morning?'

'Just down the track. Along the road.'

'You don't look well. You've got a fever. You ought to be in bed.'

'No, no –'

'Go to bed. I'll bring you up some soup.'

'No, I won't go to bed!'

He jumped up. His desire to be by himself was now so intense, he felt he would have thrown anyone who impeded him to the ground. He hurried away to the Transition door, and as he closed it saw Mother May looking intently after him. She called out, 'All right then, lunch in half an hour.' Edward fled.

Upstairs sitting on his bed he found himself remembering Sarah's words about Brownie. 'I went to her –' The idea sickened him. Sarah, like an inquisitive knowing little dog, had run to Brownie, to find out, to view her desolation, to take over the task of consoling her. Of course this was unfair. But he hated the notion of Sarah with Brownie, holding Brownie's hand, perhaps speaking of him. Jesse was all right, thank God, so why the hell had he mucked everything up with Brownie? That accursed hallucination seemed positively sent by the devil. If only he'd stayed with her, if only he hadn't so gracelessly run away, *anything* could have happened. Everything had suddenly become so good between them. She had said that she needed him, that they belonged to each other, she was ready to give herself. Christ, they might have gone to bed together! That would have been the *event*, the miracle, the healing, the perfect thing. He could have *had* that thing, binding him to Brownie

340

forever, she whom he wanted so much, oh so much – and he had disappointed her, chilled her, she may even have felt that he had disliked their embrace, that he was repelled by her, that he was making an excuse to get away. Oh *damn*. And now she was gone, to London, to God knows where, he hadn't even got her address. He couldn't go to her mother's place anyway. I'll go to London too, he thought, and find her and make it all right again. I'll go to London and take Jesse and Ilona with me. But as he thought it he knew that *that* was impossible. The pain of remorse twisted round and round in his entrails, remorse about Mark, remorse about Brownie, loss of all his happiness forever, loss, loss, loss. He went down to lunch.

Lunch felt curiously artificial. No doubt it was he who was alienated and turned into an actor. Ilona was silent, avoiding his eye. Bettina and Mother May were both watching him and seemed to take it in turns to jolly him along with trivial remarks. There were silences. There was no wine. It struck Edward that no one had said a word about last night, not said any of the natural things such as: What an extraordinary business! Fancy his thinking she was Chloe! and so on. But of course these were just the things they would *not* say. Edward, partly to annoy them, said conversationally to Bettina, 'So they all got away all right last night?'

'Oh yes.'

'And Stuart went too?'

'Yes.'

'Was it difficult to move the car?'

'No, it came out at once.'

'Stuart didn't stay long, did he?'

'No.'

'What did you think of him?'

'I'm afraid I saw very little of him.'

Edward subsided. After lunch he went up to his room. Now that he had time to think he began to wonder about the circumstances of his brother's departure. He searched about to see if Stuart had left him a note, then went to Stuart's room and searched. Nothing. He sat in a chair and looked at Jesse's disaster picture of people sitting on chairs. Then it suddenly came to him like a poisoned dart. *Is* Jesse all right? Hadn't he better go and *see*?

Edward ran downstairs and out of the West Selden door. He ran round the outside of Selden and into the stable courtyard and in through the Interfectory door. He tried the tower door. It was unlocked. Leaving it wide open he ran up the flights of twisting steps. Panting, he reached Jesse's door, knocked faintly, and thrust the door open. The room was empty, so was the bathroom. Jesse had gone.

'But you didn't see him go out?'

'No.'

Edward had searched the tower, then run through the rest of the house. He even went into East Selden, which was empty, and opened every door. He ran round the outside of the house. Then he began to shout. He had now gathered the three women together in the Interfectory.

Mother May and Bettina were both sitting upon the sofa and had unconsciously adopted identical postures, their hands, with fingers spread, upon their knees. Their long brown working dresses, pulled firmly down, came near to the ground. Ilona stood by the fireplace, fidgeting, shifting her feet, touching her face, patting her hair. Edward was striding up and down the room in torment.

'Who saw him last?'

'I suppose I did?' said Mother May, looking at Bettina. 'You didn't go in?'

'No.'

'When was that?'

'I'm not sure,' said Mother May, 'fairly early –'

'And he was asleep?'

'Yes.'

'Are you sure?'

'No. He sometimes pretended to be asleep so as not to have to talk.'

'What do you mean by fairly early? That was after I went out?'

'No, before. It was before breakfast some time.'

'Before breakfast? But you saw him again after that.'

'No.'

'So when I asked you how he was and you said asleep you were referring to what you saw hours ago?'

'Yes, I decided not to disturb him.'

Edward closed his eyes and groaned. 'Nobody saw him come down?'

'No. As we've told you.'

'Why did you leave the doors unlocked?'

'Edward,' said Mother May, 'we've *explained* to you, Jesse is perfectly able to walk, he often goes out, he came downstairs last night, and you yourself met him that time beside the river. He is generally much better at present, as you must have noticed. We don't always lock him in, if those doors were always locked he'd go berserk. We usually lock them at night, and at various other times, but not all the time. And we often forget. It's not all that important.'

'So both the doors were open.'

'Yes, evidently.'

'You didn't go up at lunch time?'

'No.'

'Why not?'

'Edward, he is an invalid. He had a very disturbed night. I stayed up with him for some time. I didn't get much sleep myself. I looked in in the early morning and I thought I'd let him sleep on. He doesn't depend on meal times! I was just going up to see him when you started shouting at us.'

'What's the matter with you?' said Bettina. 'Why are you making such a fuss? He'll turn up. Why are you in this state?'

'You don't think we should tell the police?'

'The *police*? Are you mad?'

'You say he was disturbed,' said Edward. 'He should have been looked after.'

'We've been looking after him for years,' said Mother May.

'Perhaps he's gone to London,' said Ilona suddenly.

'Most unlikely!' said Mother May. 'He'll just walk in. Edward, do stop this. You're just working yourself up. Go and rest. I told you to go to bed. You'll be delirious again if

343

you aren't careful. Forget about Jesse for a while. Then you'll find he's back again. He's not a prisoner. You'd be the first to complain if he was!'

Bettina got up. She said to Edward, 'I suppose you're still upset about last night.'

'Yes. *He* was upset.'

'He was pleased with himself!' said Mother May. She rose and went away through the door into the tower.

Bettina, after staring curiously at Edward, went through the door into her carpentry room.

Edward said to Ilona, 'Do you really think he's gone to London?'

Ilona refused to look at him. She shrugged her shoulders and spread out her hands and pattered quickly away into the Atrium.

Edward went into the courtyard and began going round the house again in ever widening circles. He went to the greenhouses, the garages, the wood store, he looked into various half-rotting sheds which contained old rusty garden tools and decayed wooden wheelbarrows. He imagined what it would be like to find Jesse sitting and smiling mischievously in one of those sheds. The sun was warm now and the jumbled singing of many birds filled the air almost with an obstructive network. He ran panting through the poplar grove as far as the river, and walked along the river bank as far as the slatted wooden bridge. Here he looked down into the water and tried to *remember* what he had *seen*. The memory image was already contaminated, overlaid and oblivescent like a dream. The only clear impression was the sense of having touched something hard, Jesse's ring. Edward leaned over seeing now the reflection of his own face. Was that perhaps what he had seen, and the rest imagined? He thrust his hand down into the cold brown water. His questing fingers touched something, a stone jutting out a little from the bank. He might have touched that. He began to walk back along the river, following its flow, and looking into all the reedy places. He skirted the celandine field where buttercups were now lifting their shiny buds like little hard yellow marbles. He came as far as the line of willows, then crossed

344

the stone bridge and followed a path up a slope of wild grass toward the wood. He came into the shade of the trees where last year's leaves were made golden here and there by the penetrating sun. Here the birdsong was almost deafening and so continuous that after a while he ceased to hear it. He reached the path which was so like a stairway made of the roots of trees, stepping upon the crackling brown fruitage of oak and ash and beech which lay before his feet like tiny sacrificial images of gods. When he could see the open light of the *dromos* ahead he slowed down. As he came cautiously between two trees into full sight of the space he saw what he now expected to see and knelt down as he had done before in the longer grass of the verge. Ilona was already there. She was standing near to the pair of huge yew trees at the far end. Surely she too was looking for Jesse. She stood quite still for some time with her back to him. Then she turned and walked back as far as the lingam stone, sat down on its base and put her head in her hands. Edward did not approach her. At that moment he *feared* any conversation which he and she might have together. He watched a little while, then rose and went back down the path and across the bridge. He began to wander about in the fen calling 'Jesse! Jesse!'

'He has metamorphosed himself,' said Midge, 'he has taken on some other form to renew his strength. He is lying in the woods in a trance, he has become something brown and small like a chrysalis, imperceptibly stirring with the force of a new life. You might have stepped upon him as you were tramping around.'

'Don't try to be funny about it,' said Edward.

'He has removed himself into invisibility, he has entered another dimension, he is entranced, transformed. He knows the herb lore. He has gone into the woods like a dog to find and eat the herb that rejuvenates and heals.'

'He may well have gone to London,' said Bettina, 'he did once before, to see his old painter cronies. He may have gone back to our old house in Chelsea, he sometimes thinks he's still there.'

345

'He's gone to that woman,' said Mother May, 'that Chloe.'

'Chloe?'

'I mean that other Chloe, your aunt, Mrs Bentley.'

'You're not serious!'

'You've seen Jesse rather down, he can be almost normal, he can be manic, he's certainly mobile – and he's cunning, half the time he's acting a part –'

'You mean he pretends to be helpless –?'

'Yes. He's unpredictable. We told you he might suddenly go off somewhere. He'll just turn up and wonder what the fuss was all about – *your* fuss that is, we aren't making any!'

'He'll think he was only away for an afternoon,' said Bettina. 'He has a different sense of time.'

'But where is he now? He can't be out of time. He must be somewhere. And if he's outside at night he could die of exposure.'

'We have had exceptionally warm nights lately,' said Mother May.

'Can't we *do* anything?'

'Well, what? You've searched the countryside, we've told the tree men to look out for him –'

'We could enquire at the bus,' said Bettina.

'I've already done that,' said Edward. 'I saw a bus up the road and I asked the driver. He said he'd have heard at the depot if Jesse had taken a bus. Of course he may have got a lift, or walked to –'

'Oh do stop,' said Mother May. 'He'll just come back. It's as simple as that. It's all happened before.'

Edward of course had not told the women about what he imagined he had seen. It was too terrible. He felt he would never be able to tell anybody about it, even after Jesse came back. For he did, somehow, believe that Jesse would come back. He could not bear to imagine otherwise. But supposing Jesse *had* been there, down in that water? Perhaps he had been going up to that strange place, or coming back, and had fallen? And suppose he was not drowned but had just that moment fallen and could have been revived if Edward had pulled him out? Edward imagined the scene, how he would have stood in the water, holding up Jesse's heavy head.

Could he have got him out alone, would anyone have heard him calling? What was the use of these tormenting queries? The fact was that Edward had believed, had *decided*, that he was seeing something unreal, and he had *gone away*. Yet he had also returned; and had found nothing there. But that did not prove anything. Jesse's body, or indeed Jesse, might have been swept away by the river a moment after he saw it. Yet that was most improbable. A large heavy body could not have been simply bundled away by that stream, it couldn't just disappear, and he had searched carefully for it very soon afterwards. If only he had not been so obsessively preoccupied with Brownie, so very very much wanting to see Brownie. Had Jesse died because Edward wanted to see a girl? It was Mark all over again. And down that way of thought madness lay.

Edward had not again suggested calling in the police. This was for a particular self-regarding reason. If the police came he would feel bound to help them by telling what he had 'seen'. Then he would also have to say that he had taken it to be something he had imagined. He could picture the laborious conversation which would follow in the course of which all that awful past would come out, drugs, violent death, every-thing. They would take him to the police station and keep him there and question him again and again. It would end with a hospital, with a psychiatrist, with a mental home, with electric shocks.

Edward had of course been over to Railway Cottage. Jesse might have gone there. Edward had broken one of the windows with a stone and climbed in. He searched the cottage, even the loft. What did he expect to find? He inspected the beds including the double bed where, according to Elspeth Macran, he had been conceived: the bed where, if he had not run away on that dreadful day, he might have lain with Brownie. But no, how could he have imagined such a thing, she would never have gone to bed with him suddenly like that. He told himself it was impossible. He had to comfort himself somehow.

It was now four days since Jesse's disappearance. Even the weather was strange, sunny and very still, with a golden-yellow moon at night. Before the moon came up the heavens were full of stardust, dim comets, falling stars. Then the moonlight was making the birds sing. Birds which Bettina said were not nightingales but sedge warblers sang loudly in the fen. And even before dawn the swallows poured out their rackety crazy song just under Edward's window. He had decided to go, to leave Seegard and return to London. He had even packed his bag, rolling up Jesse's sketch of Ilona in one sock and concealing her necklace in another. Yet every day he put off going because he thought: by the end of this day Jesse will have come home. He stood at his bedroom window, as he had done in the first days, looking down the drive, expecting to see his father appear. Oh my father – my father – he moaned to himself in the night, listening to the sweet forlorn singing of the birds. Oh my father, found and lost, come back to me. Edward was beginning to want to go to London to get, at least temporarily, away from Seegard. But he certainly thought it possible that Jesse had actually gone to London and that he, Edward, might discover him there. He recalled Jesse's saying to him about London, 'I wouldn't go for *that*,' that is to see a doctor. Did this not imply that he might go for something else? Here, he had searched and searched and walked and walked; in London there would be new things to do about it all, places to go to, people to ask, even people he could *talk* to. As he found himself thinking almost with yearning of Harry and Stuart and Thomas, he remembered 'Mr and Mrs Bentley' and wondered what on earth had happened to them. He also wondered whether Jesse might not indeed have gone to London after 'Chloe'.

It was now about ten o'clock in the morning. During the last four days the old Seegard routine had been largely resumed, as if they all had to take refuge in it. There was no more wine drinking. In intervals of his task of searching for Jesse, Edward washed up, swept floors, cleaned vegetables, fetched wood, and carried plates and laundry from place to place. He even, in silence, helped Bettina to pull down some rotten old shelves, full of woodworm, in a damp recess in Transition, and put up some new shelves which she had made. Soon, as he passed by, he saw that Ilona was painting the shelves. It seemed somehow incredible that they were *carrying on*. Yet what else could they do? He and Ilona had been avoiding each other. Edward argued with the other two, not with her. When such arguments began Ilona went away; and Edward did not seek her out because he did not want to hear her say what she was afraid of. Also he felt anguish and guilt because he was going to leave her behind, he didn't know how he could tell her this, and could not endure, either, to run away without telling. Of course there was no real question of taking her with him, even if she were willing to come. Even the idea of 'coming back to fetch her' had, at present, no reality. But I must tell her I'm going, he thought, I can't just slink away. Besides, I've got to *know* when Jesse comes back, and I can't trust anyone else to tell me. So he *was*, now, going?

He left the kitchen and went upstairs to his room, carrying some sheets which had been left outside the washroom, up as far as the airing cupboard on the landing. He looked out of the window to see if Jesse was coming. Then he quickly took off Jesse's boots and socks which he had got so used to wearing, and Jesse's pullover. He put on his own things and left Jesse's laid out neatly. He packed his belongings in his small suitcase and laid his mackintosh over the top of it. Then he ran down to look for Ilona.

He found her in the Atrium laying the table for lunch. She looked at him, then sat down. He sat beside her.

'I know what you're going to say.'

'I'm going.'

'Yes.'

'I'm sorry, Ilona.'

'Goodbye, then.'

'Will you let me know about Jesse?'

'I don't know where you live, I don't know anything about you.'

Edward wrote his address on a scrap of paper from his wallet. 'Will you let me know if – when Jesse comes back?'

'Yes.'

There was a silence. Ilona, sitting stiffly with folded hands, stared down at the table.

'Don't forget –' he was going to say: that I love you. He said
' – me.'

Ilona said, 'You're going away, that proves you don't care.'

'I do care! I'm only going to find him in London!'

'You won't come back.'

'Of course I will. I'll come to see Jesse. I'll come to see you.'

'I may not be here.'

Oh hell, thought Edward. He stood up and said, 'Don't be so silly! Of course we'll meet again. Damn it, you're my sister!' He tried to take her hand, grabbed her wrist instead, and then turned to hurry off. As he moved away something fell over his arm, clinging to him when he tried to brush it away. It was the pendant branch of one of the potted plants, the one into whose pot he had poured Ilona's love potion. Pulling himself free he called out, 'I'll write to you.' The door of Transition banged behind him.

In his imaginings of his escape Edward had always pictured himself creeping away on tiptoe at night, or in the mist, at any rate spying out the land first so as to meet no one. Now he didn't care a hang. He picked up his gear and ran down the stairs and out of the Selden door, crossed the terrace without looking round, and started walking down the track. He saw no one, no one called to him. As he came clear of the trees he saw that the sky was filled with flight after flight of wavering formations of migrating geese.

Just after he reached the tarmac a lorry appeared, and Edward thumbed a lift. Soon, sitting up high beside the driver, he was talking about football.

350

PART THREE

LIFE AFTER DEATH

'I'M NOT GOING to tell anyone,' said Stuart to Midge.

Stuart was back at his old digs, down near the river, off the Fulham Palace Road. Midge had suddenly turned up.

The drive back to London had been a silent nightmare. As soon as the tow rope had tightened and the car was back on the road, Midge had jumped into the front passenger seat. Harry had undone the rope and thrown it into the boot. Neither he nor Midge said a word to Bettina. Stuart thanked her and climbed quickly into the back of the car; he thought his father, who was revving the engine, was quite capable of leaving without him. Of course they got lost on the way to the motorway. Harry, grinding the gears, stopped the car, turned on the inside light and surveyed the map in silence. Stuart, sitting behind Harry, saw Midge's cold impassive profile as she stared steadily ahead. They jolted on, Midge and Harry sitting as far apart from each other as possible. Once on the motorway Harry drove at a steady eighty miles an hour. In London, he drove to Thomas's house where Midge got out and struggled to find her suitcase in the boot. Stuart jumped out to help her. As Harry drove away Midge was still searching for her latch key. Back in Bloomsbury Stuart followed his father into the hall. Not a single word had been uttered on the journey. Harry went up to the drawing room and turned all the lights on and found the bottle of whisky. He said to Stuart without looking round, 'You'd better find somewhere else to live.' Stuart left home on the next day.

Midge, who had not asked Stuart whether he was going to tell anyone, looked about his little room.

'So this is your monk's cell? Do you pray here?'

'Sort of.'

'Are you happy?'

'I don't know.'

'So you don't feel it your duty to tell Thomas about us?'

'No, but –'

'But what?'

'I think you should.'

'You think I should stop seeing your father?'

'I don't know about that. It's just the lies.'

'Oh – the lies –'

'And it affects other people.'

'Who for instance?'

'Meredith.'

'How do you mean?'

'He told me you were having a love affair, he didn't say who with, and that you had told him not to tell Thomas.'

'I didn't tell him.' After a pause she added, 'Well, I suppose I did. I put my fingers to my lips, like that.' She lifted her finger.

'It's bad for Meredith. A child can suffer terrible hurt and damage. You've involved him.'

'You think I'm corrupting him.'

'That's one reason why you ought to tell Thomas and not tell lies and conceal things. Whatever else you may decide to do about my father.'

'You hate this, don't you, you hate me for involving your father in this mess.'

'Well, I don't like it.'

'You're envious of people who can lead an ordinary life and have love and pleasure.'

'I don't think so. I just hate to see my father playing this sort of part.'

'Have you told him so?'

'No. We have not spoken about the matter at all.'

'But he asked you to go. So you don't fancy me as a stepmother.'

352

'I have never considered the idea,' said Stuart. 'I mean I'm not thinking about you in that way.'

'You don't think I'm going to marry your father? Why shouldn't I?'

'If you do, I shall see you in that light. I'm sorry, I don't mean to comment on all that. It's just the deception.'

'You assume Thomas doesn't know.'

'He evidently didn't know. Does he know now?'

'No.'

'But you'll tell him.'

'Only if you force us to.'

'I'm not forcing you.'

'Oh yes you are, you're putting on all your pressure, and your power, like rays.'

'Why did you come to see me?'

'I had to.'

'My father asked you to?'

'No. He doesn't know. Another deception.'

'Did he tell you where I was?'

'No. I got this address from your college.'

'But why did you come?'

'Because you were there. Because you saw us. Because you were in the car. Because you *know*. I'm having nightmares about you.'

'I'm sorry. Perhaps I shouldn't have come in the car. I just wanted to get away.'

'You were frightened of Jesse. He pointed his stick at you and called you a corpse. You ran away.'

'I felt I was doing no good there, perhaps harm.'

'I see what he meant. You sat in the back seat staring at us and it wasn't like having a human being there at all. You got into the car to punish us, to be a witness of our wrong-doing.'

'I don't think I did that.'

'Don't you know? I think you have a cruel streak. You negate everything, like death does. What did you say to Meredith?'

'When he told me? I said it was impossible.'

'Why impossible?'

'I didn't think you'd behave like that, or that you'd involve that innocent child.'

'You think I'm corrupting Meredith – I think you are. You want to have an emotional relation with him, you want him to be in your power, and you dress it up as morality, as if you were a kind of moral teacher or example. But you know nothing about children and nothing about yourself. You don't know how complicated and mysterious people are, you're a blunt instrument, you're hard, you're hardened by pride. Your relation with Meredith will end in a horrible hurtful mess. I advise you to stop seeing him – or are you too much in love?'

'I'm not in love,' said Stuart.

'Suppose I ask you to stop seeing him at once?'

'I hope you won't.'

'Suppose I – Oh never mind – You set yourself up so. I think you should return to the real world.'

'I think you should. I believe your romance with my father is some sort of dream. You can make it a reality by telling your husband. Then perhaps you can all see what to do next.'

'You know nothing, you feel nothing. Falling in love is a renewal of life. You seem to have chosen death.'

'I think you should renew your life by realising how much you love Thomas and Meredith.'

'Why were you at Seegard, was it some sort of plot? Oh how you've spoilt everything just by existing, by being there, by being you. What are you worth? What do you do all the time, lie on the bed? You pretend to be going to do something great, but you do nothing, you're a frightened ignorant boy who's afraid of real life. Why don't you go to a monastery and shut yourself up!' Midge who had been sitting on Stuart's bed got up to go. She had not taken off her coat. She even had a hat on which she now remembered, took off and put on again.

Stuart had been standing throughout the conversation. He moved now and put his back to the door. 'Wait a moment. Tell me really why you came. You didn't have to tell me all those things or to – expose yourself to my criticism – in this way.'

'What wonderful words you use. I wonder if you know how much you offend people all the time? I came because –

354

oh – you hurt me and Harry so much. I don't think he'll ever forgive you.'

'You mean by going in the car?'

'By being at Seegard at that moment and seeing us playing that part.'

'You mean pretending to be Mr and Mrs Bentley –'

'Oh you took it all in, you won't spare any detail!'

'It was an accident.'

'I don't believe you. I had to come because I thought I might, by seeing you and telling you how much damage you've done – how much you've hurt us – sort of brush it off, get rid of it, get rid of the nightmares. I can see you don't understand. You've become a nightmare figure, a horrible ghost. I wanted to see you as you really are, an idle stupid clumsy fool –'

Stuart stood aside and opened the door. He murmured, 'I'm sorry, I'm very sorry, I do understand. Please don't have any more nightmares.'

Midge passed him and clattered away down the stairs.

Stuart sat down on his bed. He did understand and he was sorry. He hated the idea that he could be, for anyone, a nightmarish ghost. He had been very upset by what Midge had said about Meredith. From his father's problem and from Midge as his possible stepmother he averted his thoughts. He rubbed his face and decided he needed a shave.

It was now several days since he had left home and he had become aware of how protected he had been by living in a pleasant house, the house of his childhood, with his father. As a student Stuart had lived in various digs, including the very room he was in now, but it had been different then, when he had had simple ordinary purposes. Then, it had been agreed to be a 'good idea' that he should live independently on his student grant, away, yet close. Now, although he did not imagine he was to be permanently banished, he was troubled by the circumstances of his enforced flight. He felt peculiarly alone – perhaps this was part of the process of 'growing up' which various people seemed to think he had

355

yet to experience. Thomas had warned him that he would be 'misunderstood'. He was also, now, able to judge how enlivened and upheld he had been by his 'decision'; and how vastly much remained to be decided. He recalled Giles Brightwalton's letter and Giles's clever humorous face. Would he ever be able to explain to Giles?

He wondered whether he would now have to face Edward's reproaches too. Had he let Edward down, had he, as Midge suggested, just been afraid and run away? Ought he to have stayed with Edward, with those women? He had left Seegard because something about its atmosphere appalled him. He felt as if he were breathing in falsity and would soon be *made* of it, as *they* were, as Edward even was coming to be. He had felt, as he said, that he could 'do no good' there. Yet was not all this just an intuitive impression, based partly on Edward's confused and exclamatory reactions? As for Midge, had he said too much, too little, the wrong things? He concluded that there was nothing he could do for Midge, 'a heart-to-heart talk' would have been unthinkable.

Stuart sat upright on a chair setting his feet slightly apart and folding his hands. He had still not made up his mind about training for a job. He had made an appointment with a 'careers' adviser. It was important to *start*, if possible, in the right place. His savings from his student grant would last a while. He must be patient; there would be signposts, vistas. Well, he was full of patience, *that* wasn't hard, and he felt no guilt about waiting. Midge had asked him what he did all day. He sat and thought. He sat and did not think. He walked. He slept well at night. He now began to think about Meredith. He dissolved Meredith. His face relaxed and his mind became gradually empty and was filled with a quiet indubitable darkness.

Midge, now holding her hat in her hand, was hurrying along, looking over her shoulder for a taxi, then down at the paving stones. She was afraid she would fall again, she felt sure she would. Her knee was still painful. She had come in a taxi, but now, in these shabby back streets, there was no sign of one.

She could not even find a bus stop. She did not want to ask the way, she had been crying. It was soon going to rain.

Midge had not seen Harry since that silent return from Seegard, and this fact tormented her. She had telephoned him from her house as soon as she judged he would have reached his, but when he answered he already sounded rather drunk, said Stuart was there, told her to go to bed. Then next morning she rang, and there was no answer. Then Thomas arrived back unexpectedly early, said he had decided to arrange some holiday, wanted to go to Quitterne. Midge wrote to Harry from Quitterne. It was a difficult letter. Midge was not a good letter writer, and could not, perhaps dared not, see what made this letter so hard. She was vague and incoherent, though she knew how much Harry hated this. He always complained that she never wrote real love letters. She was just beginning to imagine the effect upon Harry of Stuart's discovery, Stuart's awful *presence*. She thought, Harry will press me now, he'll pull everything down, and I'm not ready. He may even, without warning me, tell Thomas. He may come to see Thomas. These reflections almost made Midge want to stay on at Quitterne. The letter, once written, was also not easy to post. At last she managed to 'go for a walk' in the wood, and then run to a distant pillar-box. Meredith, who saw her writing the letter, had offered to post it.

Now, back in London since the previous night, she had, as soon as Thomas left for the clinic, telephoned Harry's house and got Edward, who had instantly asked her the surprising question, 'Is Jesse with you?' Edward said Harry was away all the morning, 'seeing a publisher or a lawyer or something'. Edward also said that Stuart had gone away, whereabouts unknown. The idea of going to see Stuart, vaguely in her mind for some time, had crystallised when she learnt that she was to have an empty London morning. The need, now, to 'do something about it all', was intense. She felt she couldn't just sit at home. Her exclamation to Stuart of why she had felt bound to see him was the true one. Of course she had wanted to be sure that he had not 'talked'. A sentence came into her head: a word from him could destroy us. But more than that she had needed to get rid of an obsessive image. Stuart, in his detestable role of witness and judge, had 'got into her'. She had to be able to dismiss him, to defeat him, and by voicing her contempt for his opinions to make it efficacious and real.

Midge was indeed having dreams, nightmares, in which Stuart's white face stared at her accusingly, as she had seen it staring when she was sitting on that chair by the door in that awful room, exposed, ridiculous, vanquished. In some dreams, when the pale horseman passed her by, he turned towards her and was Stuart.

But Midge also dreamt about Jesse. Jesse as a sea beast, covered in prickles and fur, like a sea lion, like a walrus, like a whale. Jesse coming to her, young again, and saying, I love you, marry me. And Midge in the dream would think, and I *can*, I am young and free, I am not married to anybody. Edward's question had stirred Midge and agitated her deeply. She felt now as she walked along Jesse's hot wet kisses upon her lips. She thought: *he is here*, and I shall see him again.

'EXCUSE ME, I wonder if by any chance you know where Jesse Baltram is? Someone told me he's in London, and I thought he might have come here to the Royal College.'

'Jesse Baltram's in town?'

'I'm not sure, I think so.'

'He hasn't been here. You haven't seen Jesse Baltram have you?'

'Jesse, that old rogue, is he around again?'

'I just wondered if any of you had seen him.'

'No, but tell him to drop in if you find him. He'll find a lot of his old friends still here.'

'And enemies!'

'Are you a painter?'

'No, just a –'

'I thought you might be one of his pupils.'

'He's too young to be Jesse's pupil, I was in Jesse's last class, this young fellow is a mere child!'

'Would you like a drink?'

'No thanks. I wonder if you could suggest anyone else I could ask?'

'Are you writing a book about him?'

'No.'

'It's about time there was a decent book.'

'But you like his painting? There are a couple of Jesses here.'

'Or were! They're in store now!'

'Anyone who has a few Jesses is sitting on a gold mine.'

'You might try his gallery.'

'Yes, try that place in Cork Street.'

'No, the lease ran out, the chap moved out to Ealing, name of Barnswell, try the telephone book.'

'Jesse wouldn't go near that poor sod now.'

'Still, he might know.'

'Well, well, I thought Jesse would never come back to London.'

'Can't you find out from his country place?'

'They aren't on the telephone –'

'Wait a minute. You look awfully like him. Are you his son?'

'Yes.'

'I didn't know Jesse had a son.'

'Just look!'

'You can't go away now, have a drink!'

'So you're not a painter? You must be!'

'No, I can't paint –'

'Have you tried?'

'No, but –'

'I'll teach you to paint.'

'Thanks, but I must go now.'

'Excuse me, are you Mr Barnswell?'

'What do you want?'

'I believe you used to handle Jesse Baltram's pictures.'

'Who says so?'

'Some people at the Royal College of Art.'

'How did you find this place?'

'I looked you up in the telephone book.'

'Are you a dealer?'

'No.'

'What do you want then?'

'I'm looking for Jesse.'

'I haven't got him. I hope he's dead. What do you want him for?'

'I'm just a friend of his.'

'Does he owe you money?'

'No.'

'Are you one of those toughs who go round collecting debts?'

'No.'

'Pity. If you were I'd put you onto him, if I knew where he was. He owes me plenty.'

'Have you any idea –'

'I imagine he's still rotting in the country, in that ugly nasty monstrosity he put up in those marshes, why don't you go there?'

'I think he's in London.'

'I wrote him enough letters there, he never answered.'

'What money does he owe you?'

'I paid him for some pictures he never delivered.'

'I'm sure he –'

'I took him up when no one ever heard of him, I made his reputation.'

'I'm sure he never meant –'

'He ruined my business. I used to be in Cork Street. Look at this dump.'

'I'm sorry –'

'I've still got some early Jesses. You interested in buying?'

'No, I'm not, actually –'

'They're not too pricey. Be a good sight pricier when he's dead. You could have a real bargain.'

'No, I –'

'Come on, it's an investment. I need the bloody money.'

'No, thanks – I wonder if –'

'Please yourself, if you don't want to be rich.'

'I wonder if by any chance you know his old address in Chelsea?'

'In Flood Street. I should think so. I was there all the time.'

'Could you let me have it?'

'Yes, on condition you let me know where he is when you find him.'

'All right.'

'What are you up to anyway? As if you'd say. Here's the address.'

361

'Thank you –'

'If you catch up with him you might just push him in the Thames. That stuff will be really up-market when the old swine is dead. Roll on that day.'

'Excuse me, I was wondering –'

'Come in.'

'I just wanted to –'

'Come right in. Drop your coat here, come into the drawing room. This is the drawing room. It used to be upstairs.'

'Thank you, I'm sorry to bother you –'

'No bother at all. Have a drink, sherry, whisky, gin? There's some Campari somewhere.'

'Well, thank you, sherry, but –'

'I hope you don't mind a dry sherry? I can't abide sweet ones.'

'No, fine, thank you. This *is* Number 158 Flood Street, is it?'

'Yes, sure. Sit down on the sofa.'

'Thank you –'

'How did you find my address?'

'I got it from Mr Barnswell in Ealing.'

'I don't know anyone in Ealing. I don't know any Barnswells either if it comes to that.'

'I wonder if you think I'm someone else?'

'How could you be someone else? I'm quite content that you should be you. Why want to be someone else?'

'I don't, but –'

'Are you at the university?'

'Yes, in London –'

'What are you doing?'

'French –'

'Don't you just adore Proust?'

'Yes –'

'I'm going to college in London too, next fall. I'm going to do psychology. How old are you?'

'Twenty.'

'Why, so am I, what a coincidence! What's your name?'

'Edward.'

'Mine's Victoria. Don't you think it's a pretty name?'

'Yes – but, look –'

'If you have a short surname you must have a long first name. My surname's Gunn. What's yours?'

'Look, I must tell you –'

'Do you know, I own this house!'

'You must be rich.'

'My pa is. He's given it to me. It's something to do with tax. Have another drink.'

'Look, Victoria, I just came to ask if anyone here could tell me where to find Jesse Baltram.'

'Never heard of her.'

'It's a he. He used to live here.'

'Sorry, lost in mists of past.'

'Would anyone else –?'

'Pa's only just bought the house. This ghastly wallpaper isn't our idea. The other people have gone. I reign in their stead. You are my very first visitor.'

'Where is your pa?'

'In Philadelphia making more money. I'll be living all alone here, except for Stalky.'

'Oh. Who's Stalky?'

'My grey pussy cat, he's still in quarantine, I miss him frightfully.'

'Could you give me –'

'He's all grey except for a little white spot on his front. He's cute. He thinks he's a human being.'

'Could you give me the address of the people who used to live here?'

'They left a bank address, their name's Something-Smith, I've got it upstairs somewhere.'

'Thanks, if you –'

'Why do you want to find this Baltram?'

'He's my father.'

'Why is he lost?'

'It's a long story.'

'Sorry. You must think I'm a funny lady.'

'I think you're a very nice lady. But you shouldn't have let me in. I might have been a rapist.'

363

'Well, there are rapists and rapists. Kiss me, Edward.'

Edward, nearly mad with remorse and grief, was kept going by hope. He kept picturing how wonderful it would be when he found Jesse. He kept praying, oh let me find Jesse, let me only find him and all will be well. He pictured himself telling Jesse about his adventures, and hearing Jesse laugh. In these visions Jesse was better, cured, rejuvenated, glowing with power and beauty. He had indeed metamorphosed himself, taken on another form to renew his strength. Sometimes Edward felt that this *must* be so, and that Jesse must be, not only alive, but somewhere *very near*. Jesse was simply teasing him by his absence, perhaps even watching him. He kept seeing ghost Jesses in the street, sometimes pursued them. Once he got off a bus and ran back having seen Jesse on a crowded pavement. The hope provided occupation, a *programme* for every day. Edward left early on his travels, came back late. He avoided Harry who was, he imagined, blaming Edward for what he had seen at Seegard, though of course no word was exchanged on the subject.

He had come back to a pile of letters, most of them from Mrs Wilsden. He glanced at each to satisfy himself that they were still simply hate letters, dated some time ago, from Sarah Plowmain complaining about various things, which he also did not read. Stuart had left a note with his address. Thomas had written asking him to come and see him. Edward did not feel ready to see either of these mentors. He wanted to find Jesse first and relieve his mind of the horror. If that really was Jesse, and not some dream or simulacrum, which he had seen in the river, he was guilty of a murder. A second one. He had left Jesse, as he had left Mark, to see a woman. The similarity of the two betrayals could not be accidental; and the torturing pain of these two crimes now mingled in his mind, each intensifying the other. He kept trying to make it less by telling himself that if he had really seen Jesse down in that brown water, then he had certainly seen a drowned man, a corpse, and not someone who could have been rescued. Jesse had looked so quiet, so strangely remote as if *calm*, not like a half-asphyxiated struggling victim. Yet suppose he had not been dead, but in one of his trances? Suppose he had just fallen in and, when Edward turned away, been instantly swept downstream and drowned later? The curious calmness of the image had contributed to Edward's immediate idea that it was an illusion, and to that he sometimes clung. He had at once taken it to be unreal, and did not that prove something? Alas, nothing except Jesse himself would ever be a proof; and without proof Edward would be condemned to eternal torment. Perhaps this was a punishment for what he did to Mark? He had, before, wanted a punishment, but not like this. He had envisaged a redeeming penance, not an intensification of guilt. Sometimes his only solace was the idea that he could always kill himself.

Edward was also torn by an intense desire to *tell somebody* about what had happened; and by the knowledge that if he told anyone, any single person, he would alter the entire world. He could then be accused. Well, was he not sufficiently accused by himself, would not other accusers all be less vindictive? Though he was demented by his secret and his solitude, the idea of anyone knowing was intolerable to Edward, as if with *this* the disgrace came: not only eternal pain, but eternal loss of honour. God, and he was still so young, bound to so long a suffering! He did not want to spend his life being pitied. He did not want to give away to any other person the power to reveal this second crime. No other person could be trusted. He could not now inform the police, he would be convicted of immoral and criminal concealment. He could not talk to Stuart, or to Harry or Midge or Ursula or Willy. He considered talking to Thomas; but Thomas would be so *interested*, so fascinated, Thomas would pursue the matter, making of it something more, something else, something (however long Thomas was silent) public. Edward could not let this terrible thing belong to another. His only hope of survival, if Jesse never came back, was to live with it and hope that it would somehow crumble. By imparting it, he would give it more life.

He thought of course, and all the time, about Brownie. He did not want to tell Brownie either, though it would at least serve as an explanation of his boorish departure if he could tell her the reason. If he confessed to her that would make an extra bond between them; yet the revelation could not but be 'too much'. Brownie had perhaps, though he might never know, forgiven him for what he did to Mark. How could he be forgiven? At any rate she had put her arms around him. If he told her he had done this thing as well, she would shudder away from him as from some damned and mutilated outcast. With all this however, in the poor confusion of his mind, he yearned for Brownie, he pictured her sitting in a chair while he laid his head on her knee and she gently stroked his hair. At times he desired her fiercely and embraced her in waking dreams, feeding on her kisses. But these desires were terrible to him, as glimpses of an inaccessible paradise. He did not know where she was, and his present task was to find Jesse. He could not go round to Mrs Wilsden's house. He thought of writing to Brownie there, but could not bring himself to compose the letter, which in any case her mother would probably intercept. What could he say about their last meeting? And if he wrote, he would dread receiving no reply or else a cool polite one. At present, it was better to wait and to keep even hope upon a leash. Brownie's emotion and her kindness were perhaps momentary impulses which later she would be glad to leave behind, together with her sense of having done enough for the man who had killed her brother. Yet hope, in the guise of faith, remained to him, and he felt sure that Brownie would not abandon him, and that soon somehow they would be together again. Soon, after he had found Jesse, he would find Brownie.

Anxiety does strange things to time. Every day dawned as the day when his uncertainty might end, so the end was kept near. Yet that would still be so if he had the peculiar doom of having to spend the rest of his life searching for his father. Ilona had said that she would 'let him know', but would she? She was probably angry with him, she must feel that he had betrayed and denied the love which he once said he felt for her. This thought hurt Edward with a special separate pang of guilt and sadness. In any case, could she write, get hold of a stamp, post the letter? And if he wrote to her would she get his letter or would *they* seize it first? Edward now regretted that he had not told Mother May and Bettina that he was going, thanked them for their kindness. He ought to have put on a pleasant and courteous demeanour instead of running off like a thief. He should not have appeared to treat them as enemies. His flight must suggest desperation, perhaps arouse suspicion. But what could they suspect him of? Even more terrible and dark thoughts had already begun to breed in Edward's mind as he went over and over the events of that dreadful day. As he had been going through the door Mother May had tried to stop him, she had cried 'Edward!' Did she know that Jesse had walked out? Were they hoping that at last . . . he had gone out to die . . .? Where they afraid that Edward might find him before he had had time to . . .? Or, where was Bettina? Was she perhaps at that very moment drowning him, holding his head down under water like someone drowning a big dog? When Edward had come back Mother May had said, 'He is all right. He is sleeping.' Did she mean – dead? After all they must have wanted him to die, because of the horror of his continued being. These thoughts were so sickening that Edward tried to bury them. He detested and feared them especially because he might be tempted to believe in them in order to exonerate himself. If *that* was how it was, then Jesse would have died anyway. He felt such awful pity for his father, and the pity was almost worse than anything. It was somehow in association with these nightmarish speculations, as it were as something of the same sort, that it occurred to Edward that he might go again to see Mrs Quaid. But he had lost the card with her address, she was not in the telephone book, and although he walked more than once round the streets near Fitzroy Square he could not at all remember where her house had been.

'LOOK,' SAID HARRY, 'let's not keep going round in circles. I'm not against your telling Thomas, I'm *longing* for you to tell Thomas, so long as it's part of your getting a divorce and coming to live with me *at once*. You must set the whole thing up together, say it all in the same sentence. I keep suggesting this and you keep hedging. I know you're frightened of telling him. If you like I'll tell him. Of course we can't go on just depending on the discretion of those two boys! But that brings out the absurdity which has been in this situation all along. When we fell in love I wanted to have it out with Thomas at once, only you wouldn't. You said you weren't sure. But you're sure now, and you still won't make up your mind – you're driving me *mad*!'

'I'm sorry –'

'Of course what happened at that ghastly house which you *would* go to – it's all your fault –'

'If you hadn't got so bad-tempered with the car and backed it into that ditch –'

'All right, my fault too, we've gone over all that. I know what happened, and Stuart being there, Edward wouldn't have been so bad, has been a frightful shock. I can see it's made you feel guilty! Pretty crazy reasoning to start feeling guilty when you're being found out! Well, I dare say that's not uncommon!'

'I've felt guilty all along.'

'Yes, but you're making a crisis out of it now, and I can't see why! Midge, your marriage is over. It was never what you really wanted.'

368

Harry and Midge were seated at a table opposite each other in the little flat, the 'love nest' which had so happily occupied Harry's time and thought, and was to have been a present for Midge, a joyful surprise. They were together in the tiny sitting room. They had not yet been together in the tiny bedroom. It was the afternoon of Midge's first London day since her return from the country. Harry had been out that morning discussing how to rewrite his novel with a publisher who had shown some interest. He had been annoyed and upset by Midge's disappearance to Quitterne which he felt she could have avoided. But his brief unavailability had other reasoning behind it, he had not studied Midge for so long in vain. He knew how awful she must feel about the Seegard drama. Of course he felt awful too, but had already put it behind him except in so far as it concerned his immediate strategy. The shock would make Midge retreat, want to tend and soothe her wounded consciousness, repair her lost face, rethink it all into some less disastrous perspective. Whereas what Harry wanted was yet more chaos, more violence, a final advance through the carnage. In all this he would have to manage Midge: to alarm her a little, then to force her. So he felt it would do her no harm to come back to London and not to find him waiting for her telephone call. The abstinence hurt him too of course, as he longed desperately for her company, and even now as they argued felt that deep rhythmic heartbeat of perfect joy which comes from being in the one right place, the presence of the beloved. Midge was looking, today, tired, worried, older, with a sad moving beauty which he knew that certain gestures of his, which he purposely withheld, would change into a happy beauty. She had her 'smart woman' look, in the plainest most expensive dark grey coat and skirt, covered with the tiniest faintest black check, and a blue silk blouse open at the neck and a narrow very dark green silk scarf. How long had she spent choosing it all that morning? Ages, he hoped. Her stockings were black with an open-work diamond design, her black high-heeled shoes shone as if her feet had never touched the ground. She was hitching up her skirt and crossing her legs and looking round the room. Harry hoped that she would start to make plans for the flat, adopt it quickly as *theirs*, their first home: a very temporary one, of course, representing an essential intermediary stage.

'What curtains should we have,' he said, 'plain or with flowers and things?'

'Plain,' said Midge, 'if we're having pictures. I like the brown carpet and the wallpaper. We could have a nice rug.'

'Oh Midge, I'm so glad you say that, you *believe* in the place! Darling, just believe a little bit more and we'll be home, safe in harbour. All that dreadful mix-up was a good thing really, it's moved things on a stage. It means we've got to go forward. It's a challenge, it means life, it means force, it means *avanti*! We must advance with our banners high! Oh Midge, what's the *matter* with you, you look so quiet and melancholy.'

Midge pushed her multi-coloured mass of hair, which the hairdresser kept so high and fluffy, back from her brow and shook it. Her mouth drooped at the corners. She said, 'An awful lot has happened somehow.'

'You mean at Quitterne? Thomas guessing? I'm delighted!'

'No, he doesn't guess – and that's so odd – it's important –'

'God, you don't mean touching!'

'He's so clever and he knows so much about people in a way. But he doesn't see this. He just doesn't see. He just trusts me. He's blind.'

'Well, what's happened if it's not that? Of course, yes, Seegard and so on, but that's not important in itself, it's just forcing us to do what we want to do!'

'You see, I think I had to go to Seegard.'

'Magnetised by Jesse's aura, yes, you said! Don't be plain stupid, my darling. Don't mix up the past with the future. But go on, why had you to go?'

'I suppose it was to do with Jesse –'

'You never forgot that moment when he said, "Who is that girl?" – and you couldn't help wondering – whether he mightn't have wanted you instead of Chloe.'

'Yes,' said Midge, throwing back her head. 'How did you know? Well, yes – but it's not that –'

'You had to triumph over Chloe! I know that's been one of your aims in life. Chloe dead and Jesse kissing you. And you've got hold of me as well. There's nothing more you can take away from the poor girl.'

'It was extraordinary –'

'Even though he's old and insane and thought you were Chloe!'

'Perhaps you can't imagine – but just to be *touched* by that man – let alone –'

'He grabbed you, he enveloped you, he practically ate you! Shall I take you back to him?'

'I don't want to see him again. That was enough.'

'I'm glad to hear it. Something's unsettled you. So it was Jesse, of course, I understand. You need to recover. But, my darling girl, don't let us waste any more time. We are larger, we are stronger, the world is ours. Compared with us all *that* isn't anything at all.'

'Jesse was a marvel –'

'Yes, good, but –'

'He was a beautiful miracle, but not connected with real life –'

'Good –'

'Except that somehow – I can't put this – he somehow – mopped up the past –'

'You mean your obsession about Chloe –?'

'Not just that – it was as if he touched me and then sent me away – like striking something and making it fly off at a tangent –'

'He shot you like an arrow! Good, so now we're both airborne.'

'It's not Jesse that's bothering me. It's Stuart.'

'Yes. His knowing is indeed, one might say, a damned nuisance! He might take it into his head to go and inform on us because he felt he ought to. And *that's* a very good reason why we should now tell Thomas all about it, in case Stuart does first! Midge, darling, *concentrate*, just imagine how we'd feel if Stuart did! We'd feel like miserable little criminals, mean little liars, found-out cheats – we'd lose all the initiative. That at least we've kept all this time, we've *chosen* how to play it, *we've* chosen. You're right to say Stuart is the problem. But once you put it like that, you're right up against the solution!'

371

'Stuart won't tell Thomas.'

'How do you know he won't?'

'He told me so.'

'He *told* you so?'

'Yes, I went to see him this morning and he told me.'

'You met him at my house, you came to look for me and –?'

'No, I went to see him at his lodgings, I wanted to talk to him –'

Harry jumped up, knocking over his chair, Midge backed her chair against the wall. The small space was still almost bare of furniture, the walls and windows bare. The plain dark brown carpet, approved of by Midge, alone drew the scene together into a room. There was a smell of fresh paint.

'You *went to see* Stuart, to *talk* to him – without telling me? What about? Did you go to beg him not to give us away!'

'Not beg – yes, I did want to know – but not only that –'

'What else for heaven's sake?'

'I wanted to *see* him –'

'You mean to stare at him?'

'Yes. And to talk too. I used to dream about him. At least I dreamt about a pale man on a horse looking at me. Thomas said it was death. I just realised, when I saw him, that it was Stuart.'

'All right, he's a gorgon, but Midge, you're mad, do you realise what it *does* to me, when you say so calmly that you went to Stuart and talked to him – after all *that*, and his knowing and his witnessing, and his sitting silent in the car, when we so wanted to be together –'

'That was why I wanted to see him.'

'You mean to tell him how upset you were! How can you have exposed yourself to *him*? Midge, I can't imagine this! I hope you told him to mind his own business!'

'Yes, but that wasn't what was happening.'

'You asked him not to tell Thomas, you begged, you crawled –'

'No, I didn't ask him anything. He said he wouldn't tell Thomas. He said he thought I should.'

'Confess and ask Thomas's pardon for a momentary aberration!'

'He didn't say anything about *us*, I mean he didn't mean to comment. He talked about telling lies and about Meredith. I told you that Meredith saw us, at least he saw me and heard you. I asked him to keep quiet. Stuart thought this was corrupting the young.'

'Meredith knew – yes – perfectly horrible –'

Midge was sitting tensely upright on her chair with folded hands like someone waiting in a hospital or law court. She spoke swiftly, monotonously, in a low voice, as if wanting to get the information across as quickly as possible. She looked at Harry's feet and every now and then shuddered a little.

Harry was aware that the entry of Meredith into the situation was dangerous and awful, but he did not propose to shudder about that now. It was part of the whole problem whose solution must and would issue from his will. He stood still for a moment, then kicked his fallen chair out of the way and began to walk to and fro in the small confined space.

He said, 'All right, I see how frightful all this is, and I'm sorry – I'm sorry for you, and for myself. We could have done without that bit. But since it's with us, Meredith and all, let's just make it into one huge packet of reasons for making our big move now, *today*. You stay here, I'll go and tell Thomas. Where is he, at the clinic?'

'I don't know.'

'You do know. Stuart's right, it's time to stop lying. I'm going to Thomas to tell him you want a divorce.'

'No, *no* – I can't now, not like that – Harry, don't go – *please* don't go –' Midge began to cry in an almost formal attitude sitting slightly forward with her elbow on her knee and her head bowed into her hand, with a kind of quiet, orderly, almost silent hysterics. 'Oh – oh – oh.'

Harry stood looking down at her. His broad smooth face was calm. He ruffled up his blond hair. He bit his lip a little in calculation. He said softly, 'Midge, we ought to do it now. Now's the time. You always wanted to wait for the time. Well, it's now. Isn't it? Isn't it?'

Midge ceased her gasping. She sighed a long dejected even rather exasperated sigh. She fumbled down for her handbag and handkerchief, her hair falling forward in a mass, revealing the whiteness of her neck. She mumbled, 'Harry, let's go to the bedroom.' Midge always used this phrase, never a more direct one, for their love-making.

'You're just trying to distract me,' he said. But he suddenly felt so tired and so full of desire. Why were they wasting their strength in arguing? Oh God, why did they have to be so unhappy?

'Harry, don't torment me.'

'All right – but we will – fix it all soon – and everything will be well. Darling sweetheart, my love, my own, don't grieve – I'll look after you until the end of the world, you know that, I love you.'

'Oh – I'm so tired –'

'So am I. Come on. No more fighting. Head up. Have a bit of style. And for God's sake don't go near Stuart again, well obviously you won't.' He opened the bedroom door. The double bed under its cotton quilt covered with masses of tiny flowers glowed expansively beyond. It took up almost all the room.

Midge rose and rubbed her eyes. She said almost sleepily, 'Well, I think I must see him again.'

Harry turned back. 'What on earth do you mean, *why*? There's no point, and you must be able to see how utterly I detest the idea!'

'Yes, but I must see him again. I can't bear his thoughts. I want him to stop the pain, that pain.'

'Midge, don't kill me with this *rubbish*. Think who he *is*.'

Midge yawned, distorting her face like a cat.

Harry stared at her. He came back and gently pulled her. 'You're tired, and you've gone a little crazy. Everything has been too awful. You'll get better. I'll look after you. Come this way, come with Harry. Into the deep river.'

DEAR MR BALTRAM

Thank you so much for your letter which has been forwarded to me by the bank. I am so sorry we are not at Flood Street to receive you! Now that the children are grown up we have moved out into the country! As you probably know, we bought the Flood Street house from your father whom my late father, who was in industrial design, knew slightly at one time. We were living in Hampstead before that, but the children always wanted to be by the river, I think children always want to be near water, I don't know why. I can remember meeting Jesse (if I may call him so, we always spoke of him familiarly!) on several occasions, and found him most impressive. After we moved in we invited him and his wife two or three times, but they never came! (Perhaps they were afraid we might have ruined the house. It certainly did look different inside!) We bought two of his drawings, rather odd but nice. I am so sorry to hear that you have lost touch with your father, that must indeed be most worrying. I am afraid that I cannot be very helpful, we never really knew Jesse and had no contact with his 'world'. I gather you have tried the 'obvious' places, like the RCA and the dealers. I expect he had some favourite 'pubs', but I'm afraid I'm not an expert on these! You asked about friends, but the only one I can remember being mentioned was a painter called Max Point whom my father spoke of as having been (if you understand me) a rather *special* friend of Jesse's. He told me not to repeat this, people were more secretive about such things in those days, but I expect it doesn't matter now! Anyway he may be dead, poor man. He lived on one of those barges on the Thames off the end of Cheyne Walk, his barge was called *Fortaventur*, I happen to remember, we thought it such a funny name for a little barge that never went anywhere! I'm sorry I can't be of more assistance to you. If I can think of anything else I'll write again. I hope and expect that by now you have been reunited with your father. As I said, we were disappointed not to be at home when you called! A nice American who made a lot of money out of I think toothpaste, something hygienic anyway, has bought the house, as I expect you've found out. It would have been nice to meet you. I wonder if you are a painter too? I often wish I was one, they have such happy lives. Perhaps we may meet one day. Let me know later if I can help in any way. My husband and daughters join with me in sending you our kindest regards.

Yours sincerely
(Mrs) Julia Carson-Smith

With this unexpected letter in his pocket Edward was stepping off the jetty onto a rather narrow and insecure plank which ran along between a crowded miscellany of large and small residential barges. There was nobody about to ask. The tide was in and the assembly of craft was well afloat, bobbing and knocking and gently nudging each other upon the gleaming water which was being agitated by a lively east wind. There was a sharp silvery northern light. The boats, drawn up in lines three or four deep on either side of the jetty, seemed deserted, as Edward walked cautiously along looking at the names. There was no sign of *Fortaventur*. He made out that access to the outermost craft must be gained by climbing over the boats in between, and was soon scrambling boldly across decks and jumping from one to another. The little hamlet of floating homes was full of variety, both in the form and size of the boats and in the evident life style of the owners. Some poor shabby hulks, with split and flaking woodwork, seemed ready to descend onto the mud never to rise again. Others were newly and gaily painted, with traditional waterway designs of birds and flowers, or with more modern abstract or fantastic decorations. Peering into interiors, Edward saw some furnished with a mere bed, or even pallet on the floor, whereas others were positive floating drawing rooms, with plush furniture, bookcases, and pictures on the walls. Here and there a curled-up resident cat betokened a continuous home life. The names were equally various, traditional or exotic. Edward's sadness, as his footsteps echoed through the hollow boards, was increased by realising how much he would have enjoyed this excursion if it were not for the doom which lay upon him. He had come out without a coat and the wind, racing up the river from the sea, and scribbling black lines upon the water, bit through his thin and scantily clad body. He was almost ready to give up, when upon a boat which appeared (as some of them did) to have no name he saw a white lifebelt hanging up with the word *Fortaventur* running round it in extremely curly letters. He jumped down from the rather higher deck of the next boat, landed with a thud, and stood nervously wondering if someone would now emerge from the cabin. No one did. Probably there was no one there. When Edward read Mrs Carson-Smith's letter he had vaguely recalled hearing Max Point's name mentioned somewhere together with the information that he was dead. Edward had come to the barges partly so as to occupy his time with something, with some *work* which related to his misery about Jesse, and partly just because of the name of the boat. He advanced to the faded blue door of the interior and knocked. As there was no answer he turned the loose dinted brass handle. The door opened upon darkness.

Edward stared in, seeing a long narrow room with curtains partly pulled. He blinked, then moved in, half falling down two unexpected steps. He stood again, smelling the damp wood. A husky voice from the far end said slowly, 'And – who – is – that?'

377

'I'm sorry to bother you,' said Edward, 'but I'm looking for Mr Point, Mr Max Point.'

'I – am – he.'

Edward could now see the interior in the dim light, and a man sitting at a table. The man looked very old, wrinkled, skinny, even emaciated, with a small bony red face, a short snub nose, and a bald crown. On the table there was a glass and a whisky bottle.

Edward advanced a little. The smell of mould now mingled with old sweaty textile smells and alcohol. He caught his foot in a hole in a threadbare rug. The narrow area was made narrower by quantities of pictures, canvases of various sizes propped and stacked against the walls, leaving a small corridor in the centre. Some of the canvases were damaged by long diagonal tears. Edward came and stood beside the table.

Max Point, sitting hunched, peered up at Edward with watery half-closed eyes. 'Have a drink. There's a glass. Sit down. What's the matter?'

'Please excuse me – I wanted to ask you –'

'Have a drink.'

'No thanks, I just –'

'What's the matter? I used to be a painter. Good for nothing now, only to die. I sit here, no one comes. I'm a liar, a woman comes, God knows who she is, welfare lady, brings me things to eat, otherwise I'd starve, see? Like a parrot – parrot in a cage, old party died and his parrot starved to death, one of the boats, didn't find him for weeks, parrot hanging upside down from its perch. They won't find me for weeks, and it'll be soon. You'd think a parrot would scream if it was dying of hunger, wouldn't you? Got no sense. When the old boy was alive that bird never stopped jabbering, then when he died it had nothing to say, it couldn't cap that, poor little bugger. Lady comes, I told you that, brings food – well, whisky's food, what I live on – got to eat – in order to drink – eh? Go out and get my pension, and the – the drink – necessaries of life, eh? The lav's bunged up, got to go outside, winter, summer, shit on the mud, the river takes it, the river bringeth, the river taketh away, it'll take me away one of these days – the river – takes everything away – in the end –'

378

The boat was gently rocking, very quietly and rhythmically rocking, like a cradle touched by a strong loving hand. The slightly irregular slapping of the water on the side made a soft musical counterpoint. Behind the table was an easel with a canvas on it, and a stool with a paint-smeared palette, a palette knife and brushes. Edward said, 'You're painting a picture.'

'Don't sneer at me – good for a bloody laugh – they all do – or did, they've forgotten me now, I'm the forgotten man. Do you know how long that picture's been there? Years. I forget how many. Five, ten. The paint's been dry ten years. All dried up and gone solid, like me. To paint you have to concentrate, *which* I can't do, see? But what are you doing here anyway, who are you? Have a drink. For Christ's sake sit down, I can't see you.'

Edward sat down. He felt a bit sick and a bit frightened, at the same time he felt such pity for Max Point that he wanted to put his arms round him. Perhaps the motion of the boat was making him feel so odd. 'I came here to ask you about Jesse Baltram.'

'He's dead.'

The promptness of the reply shocked Edward. 'I don't think so – he's somewhere in London –'

'He's dead. Take it from me. If he wasn't he'd have come back.' Some tears came out of Max Point's eyes and trickled down into the wrinkles on his red blotched face. 'Last picture I painted of him was from a bloody photo, painted him again and again and he got older every time. But he never came back. And now he's dead.' He put his hand against his wet nose, pushing the end of it up yet further. Then he suddenly sat up straight tilting the whisky over onto some papers which were spread out on the table. He stared at Edward. 'Who are you anyway, who the hell, let's look at you then.'

He reached out and turned on a lamp. After a moment he began to speak again, in a quite different voice, a clearer higher voice like that of a younger man. 'Jesse, you've come back after all, back to your old Maxie, the only one who really loved you, never had anyone else, I knew you'd come – that bitch May Barnes is dead, isn't she, she never mattered, someone said she's dead – Jesse, we'll be together again, like you said and I've hoped – that's love isn't it, you die without hope – you've forgiven me, I've forgiven you – You're the real painter, I'm a bloody sod, we never argued about that, did we – the only good thing in me is you – and you've been *here*, here in this bloody rotting boat all these years – God, how often I've seen you here and you weren't – and now it's really you – it is, it's true, isn't it, old man, old darling – touch me, hold me, make me young again, save me, my old magician, my king, my love –'

Max Point reached across the table and seized Edward's arm in a claw-like arthritic hand. Edward could feel the finger nails through his sleeve. He pushed back his chair, dragging his arm away. 'I'm sorry, I'm sorry, I'm not Jesse, I'm only his son, I'm Edward Baltram, not Jesse, I'm looking for my father, I'm so sorry, I know I look like him –'

'Jesse. Don't deceive me again – don't leave me now for the love of Christ. I'll die of it –'

'I'm not Jesse!' Edward cried, and leapt up, evading the poor skinny hands outstretched across the table.

'You're not Jesse – then who are you?'

'I'm his son.'

'You lie. He has no son. You've come to torment me.'

'No – please – I want to help you – let me help you.'

'Foul fiend, apparition, I know you, you've been here before, pretending to be Jesse. You can't fool me. Jesse's dead and you killed him, you devil. You killed him, and put on his skin, I know your ways, you've put on his face, underneath you have no face, only mud and blood and mess, I've felt you near me at night, pressing up against me, filthy vile ghost – and Jesse is dead, my beautiful Jesse is dead – go away from me, I'll kill you –'

Max Point jumped up and seized the palette knife from behind him. Edward saw the gleam of the blade and turned and ran toward the light of the half-open door. As he scrambled up the steps to the deck he looked back over his shoulder. Max Point had plunged the knife into one of the canvases.

*

380

'So he thought you were Jesse,' said Thomas.

'Yes, and then that I was the devil pretending to be Jesse. And he said that Jesse was dead and that I had killed him.'

Edward had changed his mind and come to see Thomas after all. The need to tell *somebody* had become too pressing; and Thomas was the only person he could tell. About Seegard, Edward had told everything, except of course about Harry and Midge, or about Stuart. He did not want Thomas to summon Stuart and question him. There was enough muddle without that. It was only after Edward had decided to talk to Thomas that he had really set up in his mind the clarified idea that his stepfather was having a secret love affair with Thomas's wife. The weird charade at Seegard, the arrival of 'Mr and Mrs Bentley', Jesse's incursion, Jesse embracing Midge, had almost seemed to Edward like a dream, a phantasmagoric prelude to what happened on the following day. Edward did not feel it his duty to inform Thomas, nor did he know whether or not Thomas knew or had known. Edward's own woes were of more pressing concern. All *that* was a mysterious and nasty blur on the side of the picture. But just as Edward had felt sad about not being able to enjoy the boats, he mourned a little that he could not now care more about his stepfather whom he loved, and about Midge about whom he had felt childishly romantic, and could not even be *interested* in this other drama which was taking place so close beside him. Another's pain is often, to the wicked heart, a consolation, only not in extreme grief. About Thomas he did not worry. Thomas was a man of power, whatever happened Thomas could look after himself. And in thinking this he was momentarily afraid for Harry, afraid for, after all in an important sense, his father. There were things it was better not to think about.

'And he called me an apparition. God, not only seeing one, but being one!'

'You think he said: Jesse's dead, *drowned?*'

'No, I think I imagined that, I tagged it on later – I just can't trust my thoughts and my memory any more. He said he dreamt about a false Jesse all bloody and muddy.'

'Well, let's leave Max Point –'

'That sounds so terrible,' said Edward, 'everyone's left him. Can't we do anything for him? He's all alone and drinking himself to death.'

'Well, if that's what he wants to do. People do awfully want to do such things and it's extremely difficult to stop them.'

'They ought to get him off the drink.'

'Would he be happy then? And who's "they"? You for instance?'

'I couldn't do anything. I mean social workers or something. He said some woman brought him food –'

'Then she has probably assessed the situation.'

'But I still feel – couldn't you go?'

'No. But I'll ring up the local welfare folk.' Thomas made a note on his pad. 'Now about you, who are going to thrive on disasters.'

'Thomas, don't make jokes.'

'I'm perfectly serious.'

'Stuart said, let it burn, but draw something good into it.'

'He wanted you to suffer, not to evade anything, then to find, in your own soul, truth and hope. That's what I want too.'

'He's religious, you're scientific, neither's any good when one's in hell.'

Thomas paused and looked carefully at Edward. 'You seem to attach importance to Point's seeing you as an apparition. Let's get back from there to what you thought you saw. Do you feel any clearer about it now? We've been talking for over two hours.'

'I'm wasting your time.'

'Shut up, get on.'

'No. I thought if I could only describe it to you, you could settle the question, at least I'd remember something crucial. It couldn't have been real – yet I touched the ring – I *think* his eyes were open – I'd had that drink, and I'm sure it was drugged.'

'And you said you'd been feeling ill, feverish? Does the fact that you didn't tell Brownie count for or against your believing *then* that it was an illusion?'

'Thomas, don't *muddle* me, I can't think like that – I don't

382

know – I'd already decided it was something awful –'

'Had you already conjectured that he might have been in a trance and you could have rescued him?'

'I don't *know* – I felt I couldn't commit myself by telling *anybody*, putting myself like that in anybody's *power*. If anybody knew everybody would know, or I'd think so anyway, and it would be a final doom, I'd be *branded*. And I especially couldn't tell her, I couldn't bring up something else, she'd see me as a diseased creature, a leper, bringing death everywhere. She'd stop seeing Mark's thing as an accident. She'd been so wonderful about that, but that was her special subject – telling her the other thing would have messed it all up –'

'It got messed up anyway.'

'Yes – I ran off, like someone who's got another appointment!'

'You'll meet her again. But do concentrate. From what you've said about that house you must have been in a pretty anxious state, under a lot of psychological pressure. The mad sage imprisoned by his wife and daughters, as you put it. The idea of Jesse's death must have been continually before you. Even, you say, the idea that they urgently wanted him dead and might be planning to murder him.'

'I shouldn't have said that. I never thought it and don't think it, I'm not that crazy. Oh if only I could *find* him. I don't even know if Ilona would tell me if he came home, if they'd let her. I'll have to go there. Oh if only I knew he was alive – then I could get back to Mark where it all began.'

'You speak of it as if it's a life task.'

'It is.'

'We'll see. I can't resolve this thing about Jesse for you, I wish I could. It seems improbable that it was real, and not some sort of hallucination, but the improbable constantly happens. We must wait. Meanwhile I have a suggestion for you, which is this. I think you should go back to your old digs for a while.'

'You mean – to that room?'

'Yes. Try it for a few days. You seem to have a deep feeling that you have to go through it *all*, as if you were living it all

383

through again, that's the picture of the "task". This, unless you do it, is a bit left out. Of course it will be very painful being there – but you must imagine it often enough.'

'All the time.'

'Well, go back, live right up against it, see it for real.'

'But they'll have let the room.'

'It's not let. I rang up this morning when I knew you were coming.'

'Oh – Thomas –'

'Think it over anyway. You don't regret having talked to me?'

'No. I trust you completely.'

'Good. By the way, I never asked you when exactly was the last time you saw Jesse before that river scene?'

'It was just the night before, when –' Edward flushed and bit his lip. He said lamely, 'When he came down suddenly when we were having supper.'

'What happened?'

'Nothing. He looked at us and went back again.'

'Nothing else? Is that true?'

'Nothing else.'

Thomas, staring through his glasses with his enlarged eyes, said, 'Mmm.'

Edward said after a moment or two, 'You don't think I'm *mad*?'

'No. Do you?'

'I have such mad ideas. I didn't tell you – when I was going up the hill to that strange place with the pillar – there were lots of little brown things on the ground –'

'Little brown things?'

'Yes, natural things, I mean like acorns, beechnuts, things like old chestnut husks, little dry brown things, very brittle. I stepped on them and they crunched and went to nothing – and I felt, I imagined, perhaps they, I mean the women, somehow put this into my head – that one of these – was Jesse – and that I'd crushed him and destroyed him. Then I began to think – perhaps this was out of a dream – that they were *all* Jesses, thousands, millions, innumerable Jesses. Isn't that madness?'

'It's *beautiful*,' murmured Thomas.

'You see they seemed like little talismans, little images of gods, if you see what I mean – and I was treading them under foot –'

'Yes, yes, you have travelled far. The soul responds, it gives back healing images. There is no end to its power to create new being. Perhaps in every grain of dust there are innumerable Jesses. Did you think that if there were so many it did not matter if you destroyed some?'

'I felt that I had destroyed *my* one.'

'The seed dies in order to live. Don't be afraid of your ideas, they are signals of life. Come to see me again soon. I must go to the clinic now.'

Edward stood up. For over two hours he had been studying Thomas's face, as if he were to draw his portrait, tracing his wavery Jewish mouth, scanning the neat fringe of his light grey hair, looking into the deep well of his glasses. With a sigh he turned away from Thomas, closed his eyes for a moment, then allowed the room to reappear, clear in the sunshine, some dust upon the desk, a speckled stone holding down a page of notes, books leaning sideways on a shelf, a little red figure which he had never noticed before in Cleve Warriston's picture of the mill.

Going down the stairs Edward saw Meredith crossing the hall. Meredith made a beckoning sign and Edward followed him into the drawing room. The afternoon sun shone through the climbing flowers upon the half-drawn curtains onto the tiny flowers upon the wallpaper, the formal flowers underfoot, and the roses and irises dotted in various jugs. The room smelt of roses and summer. The familiar room gave Edward a shock of pain, a woman's room, an old familiar room where he had indulged his childish love for Midge, a room not knowing of grief and fear, wherein, even now, she had arranged the flowers. He had not been there since the night of the dinner party when he had sat in a corner and pretended to read a book and Meredith had come and touched his sleeve.

Meredith said, 'It's Edward.'

'It's Meredith.' He's taller, he's older, Edward thought, he's capable of irony, he's capable of malice. How has he learnt, what does he know? Does he regard me as an enemy?

Meredith said, smiling, 'You've been seeing my pa.'

'Yes.'

'He knows everything except one thing, and that's the thing he keeps searching for while it's under his nose all the time.'

'That sounds like a parable,' said Edward.

'It's a novelty, like what you get at Christmas time. What do you know, Edward?'

'Oh stop it, Meredith,' said Edward, 'remember you're only thirteen.'

'Who says you can't go mad at thirteen? Can you do this?' Meredith suddenly did a handstand, his head went down, his elegantly trousered and now so long legs went up, his light brown hair flopped forward, his heels clapped together. Edward saw his spread hands upon the carpet, white with the weight. Then his elbows moved outward as he slowly lowered his head to touch the floor. He remained poised so for a moment, then in a whirl of legs and arms sprang upright. Looking at Edward now, his face was red and grim. He said, 'Go away. I've got a pain in my heart.' He did another handstand. His face, unintelligibly reversed, glared up at Edward. Edward went out, quietly shutting the drawing room door and the front door.

Why do I torment him so, thought Thomas, why do I keep sending him into danger? Suppose he goes back to that room and jumps out of the window?

He sat for a while holding in his hand the comb which he had automatically brought, together with a clean white handkerchief, out of the drawer of his desk. Then he began very carefully to comb his hair, feeling for the crown of his head and sleeking the silky hair down with his other hand. After that he pulled a little bunch of errant hairs out of the comb and dropped them in the wastepaper basket, put the comb away, and cleaned his glasses with the handkerchief. He set things in order on his desk. He straightened the pages of notes and the speckled stone which had come from Scotland. He set out his well-sharpened pencils in a neat row. He often wrote in pencil. He liked sharpening pencils and using different coloured ones.

He thought, most unlikely. Then he thought, all the same I must stop practising, I must retire, I really must stop it. He sat back in his chair. Thomas, who did not always tell the truth, did not have to go to the clinic. It was his research day.

He started thinking about the menopause, and how much false mythology this concept had generated. It was a favourite topic of many of his female patients, determined to connect their nervous crises with this phenomenon, and if they had no nervous crisis to induce one. In fact, he thought, there is no typical menopause, there are as many menopauses as women. A smattering of popular science caused so much unnecessary trouble, anxious schoolgirls counting the days to their exams, middle-aged women led to anticipate breakdowns by magazines picked up in their hairdressers. Of course there were cases. This was one subject upon which Thomas and Ursula Brightwalton were in agreement. He wondered if Midge thought about it and whether the prospect was worrying her? Ought he to say something, in general terms of course? It was characteristic of their marriage that they did not discuss such things. Thomas's puritanism, both Catholic and Jewish, shunned physiological conversation about sex. Some couples made verbal directness, even coarseness, a part of their intimacy. Thomas and Midge had retained a sort of shyness which Thomas valued. Of course, as a doctor, he tended his wife and said what was necessary, but not as chat. He loved his wife deeply with a dignified and reticent passion and continually felt how fortunate he was to be married to her. His ancestral sense of the absoluteness of marriage had never, in their long relationship, been shaken, he took their permanence for granted. He was never worried by the luncheons with men friends from her 'model' days, which she amusingly (not always unmaliciously) described to him afterwards. Their life together was orderly and ceremonious. As a young wife she had matched her ways with his, being in love with his authority. Later the difference of age between them had seemed to disappear. It will no doubt appear again, thought Thomas, but we are past danger.

Midge had seemed restless lately, short-tempered with him and with Meredith in an uncharacteristic way. Their love-making, dependent on mute signals, had over many years decreased in frequency and lately ceased, no doubt temporarily. Thomas, who certainly did not desire this state of affairs, had said nothing. He wondered if he should talk to Midge or continue to rely upon the telepathy which had always made them so close and happy together. He decided to reflect upon the matter. He recalled Ursula saying, long ago, that of course Thomas ought to have married a busy Scottish body who was always in the kitchen, and Midge ought to have married a rich industrialist with a yacht who would enable her to have a *salon* full of the rich and famous. A joke of course, and another false generalisation. The same was true of Ursula's idea that Thomas was an autocrat and a bully. *We* are happy, he thought *we* know what 'living well' is. Meredith was one proof of that. Thomas, who, in his work, so skilfully talked and probed and pressed, did not do so at home. He did not 'confront' his wife or his son. He had very rarely been overtly angry with Meredith or chided him harshly; but when Thomas was displeased Meredith knew and knew why. The child's intelligent eyes, at an early age, met his in a silent compact. Sometimes alone together, Thomas writing, Meredith reading, they would raise their heads and look at each other, unsmiling. Later, alone, they would smile.

Thomas despatched a missive about his wife to his unconscious mind and turned his thoughts to Mr Blinnet. Mr Blinnet continued to puzzle Thomas. He sometimes found himself considering the theory apparently held by Ursula that Mr Blinnet was an impostor. Yet of what kind? With what motive? If he simply enjoyed spending his money year after year to deceive Thomas did not that in any case betoken an abnormal state? He had come to Thomas after ineffectual hospital treatment by drugs. (He had refused shock therapy.) Mr Blinnet apparently lived a normal life, he enjoyed a private income which he managed by himself, he drove an expensive car. He was (it seemed) entirely without family and had never been married. Everything about him was normal except that he was mad. (Thomas had met similar cases of which Mr Blinnet's was the most striking.) He had frightening delusions, he was persecuted by laser beams, by telepathic probes that entered his brain, by aliens with ray guns, by packs of mad dogs which followed him in the street. He was particularly afraid of dogs. He also had a continuing fantasy about a dead woman who was growing into a tree. This woman was sometimes described as his wife, whom he had killed, intentionally or accidentally, and (in various versions) buried on a common, sunk in a lake, burnt in an oven, or dismembered and strayed in the sea. Yesterday he had handed Thomas a long poem on this subject. Mr Blinnet often wrote poems, dull banal insane poems, the fantasies of the insane are usually inertly uninventive. His latest poem (he was much given to assonance) began, 'So she grows old in her grave under the tree, so she grows cold in her skirt of earth, yet still grows from her clothes of mould, sprouting from the dirt of her clouts, I have found her above ground as a green mound' (and so on, rambling without form or conviction). Was Mr Blinnet a homicidal maniac in a period of repose? He did not seem to be that kind of madman; but suppose he were not a madman at all? Suppose Mr Blinnet, a sane man, had committed a serious crime, and had then set up an elaborate pretence of being insane, for use in court should the law catch up with him? Ingenious – but would such a long deception be necessary? Mr Blinnet would seem to be of the stuff secret agents are made of. He was indeed very like a secret agent as portrayed in a film, whose appearance so perfectly belies his real nature, which yet, to the discerning eye, looks slyly through. Mr Blinnet's calm beautiful face was like that of a simple sage or holy man, yet the eyes, caught sometimes unexpectedly, were watchful, even amused. Mr Blinnet, for all his sufferings with sprouting corpses and laser beams, often enjoyed a secret joke. If it was all a charade, why did he need to go on, how could he? Of course he loved Thomas. (Thomas loved him.)

Thomas's thoughts returned to Edward. Edward wanted Thomas to tell him whether that vision of Jesse was an hallucination. Thomas could not. He was inclined to think it was. If a drowned man had been there what Edward had *seen* would have had a different quality and the idea of hallucination would not have arisen. It was important that Edward had classed it in this way at once. But what was the use of speculating? Time might show something. It was better for the present to let Edward *occupy* himself with his continued ordeal, until he could feel that he had *done everything*. In the end he would tire and come back and fall unconscious at Thomas's feet. Then another phase would begin, a convalescence in which Edward's youth, his simple and robust nature, his instinctive desire for happiness, would effect his cure. But it would be a serious mistake to start this process too soon.

Thomas felt tired. He had been concentrating upon Edward. Now he would concentrate on his book and forget Edward. I must stop, though, he thought. I've *got away* with it so far. I might be found out at any moment. I long to be free, art and reason have led me to this place, from now on I'll be guided by desire. I can't go on exercising this ingenious skill, this power, bending and contorting people's lives like a Japanese flower arranger. It must come to an end – before something goes wrong, before I lose what, after all, I still treasure so much, my reputation, my – honour. What poor Edward has lost, and seeks. For me, there could be no authority, no magisterial healer. Then he thought, how much I would like to discuss some of these things with Stuart. Could that happen? Perhaps later. But first of all I must retire from all this, I must *let it go*. We'll live at Quitterne, and I'll *think* and I'll write. Magic must come to an end. Of course Theseus must leave Ariadne and Aeneas must abandon Dido, Athens must be saved, Rome must be founded, Prospero drowns his book and frees Ariel, and the Duke marries Isabella. And Apollo tames the Furies. Thomas sat for a while and then added half aloud, 'And flays Marsyas.' He smiled.

'I WANT YOU to teach me to meditate,' said Midge.

'I don't know how,' said Stuart, 'I just do it. I mean, there are those very long disciplines – I just invent it for myself, perhaps all wrong. You must ask someone else.'

'You want to get rid of me.'

'No, I just can't help.'

'You *must* help. You're supposed to be doing good. Is it because it's personal?'

Stuart said, after a pause, 'I doubt if I could help anyway, but as it is – I mean my father being involved – I feel it's better that we don't talk.'

'Who else can I talk to? Surely you have a special duty, a special obligation. You're the only person who can see it all. You must help me to *think*, no one else can. I want to tell you everything about myself and about the situation, telling you would make so much difference – then I could make the right decision. Don't you want me to do that?'

'Yes, but –'

'Aren't you even *interested*?'

Stuart considered. 'Yes, I am "interested". But that sort of interest is a mean low instinct and one I can't follow.'

'You think it wrong to imagine other people's sufferings?'

'No possible good could come of your telling me all this.'

'How do you know, why are you so certain, why not *try*, what are you afraid of?'

'I'm able to see all sorts of bad consequences, which

perhaps you can't. None of this conversation should be happening at all –'

'How can you say anything so dry and heartless –'

'It's a device, it's a way of putting off telling Thomas.'

'You mean if I don't tell Thomas you will!'

'No. I won't tell him.'

'Ever?'

'That question doesn't arise. Thomas is bound to know sometime soon. My father might tell him. It's better if you do. Once the secret doesn't just belong to you and to my father it's just very likely to come out somehow –'

'I suppose Edward might tell him. Or those devils at Seegard might send it around. But – it doesn't mater – I feel as if he knows already –'

'Do you think so?'

'No, he doesn't know, but as you say he's bound to, so there it is. What I want is to understand what I've done – that's what I want to talk to you about – and about it all, and what such things mean anyway. How can I judge? I need you, I need your help, I beg you to help me, I want to confess, I want to pour it all out in front of you –'

'I understand, but pouring out is just what won't help. It's no use telling me. That's just a diversion, another emotional experience, a way of experiencing – of continuing – that relationship – Go to Thomas. Telling *him* is what will make everything clear and real. You've been living in some sort of dream – that's how I see it anyway – until you tell Thomas you won't know what you are doing. Once you've told him you'll be a different person.'

'That's what I'm afraid of.'

'Part of you is afraid. But you *do* want to be another person, to stop deceiving –'

'You seem to think a woman can love no one except her husband. You think any other love is worthless – but it may be the most valuable thing in the world. And it happens all the time. You just want to separate me from your father. The whole thing makes you sick. Can't you be objective?'

'Yes, it does make me sick,' said Stuart, 'but that's not the point. The point is to tell the truth. Telling a lot of lies,

392

particularly systematic lies, gradually detaches one from reality, one can't *see*. My own view, which isn't important, is that this thing with my father is wrong – there's Meredith to consider, and –'

'Don't be vile, don't be so crude and boorish, you're envious, you're spiteful – you don't understand, how can you –'

'All right, I can't, I'm sorry and it's no use trying to make me understand, I'm not involved at all and I mustn't be.'

'You're afraid of your father.'

'I don't think so. I'm sorry I said just now it was wrong. The deception was wrong. It's only when it's all in the open that you will be able to see what's been done and what to do next. It's no use recounting it to me, that's just for thrills, you just want a distraction, like going to the cinema to forget your troubles, it's a fantasy.'

'You call my telling you the whole truth about this business a fantasy?'

'Yes. You can't and wouldn't. It's with Thomas that the truth can emerge, not with me. *This* is just setting up an emotional atmosphere, some sort of disturbing pseudo-connection –'

'I see – what *you* are afraid of is an emotional relationship with me. Do you feel you are in danger?'

'No. I feel you are in danger.'

'You flatter yourself. Do you think I might fall in love with you?'

'No, of course not! I mean you could just become addicted to endlessly talking about yourself to somebody – anybody –'

'It sounds like analysis!'

'In a way that would do you no good. It's just continuing the dream, the untruth, and putting off what has to be done –'

'You think I might disturb you.'

'No!'

'You said it was "disturbing".'

'Please let's not argue like this –'

'I'm not arguing, you are. I just want help. You set yourself up as something amazing – you've created this sort of – vacuum – all round you – you can't complain if afflicted people rush into it. Is your idea of holiness driving everyone away? You ought to be on a pillar.'

'It's only – you –'

'I'm so special – perhaps a temptation!'

'No. You know what I mean. Let's stop this conversation, it's such a mess –'

'You hate mess. Where there are people there's mess.'

'Look, this involves *my father* – I can't discuss his – his –'

'Adventures.'

'With you. It's not seemly.'

'I love your vocabulary.'

'He would – rightly – dislike it. That's one good enough reason for asking you to please go.'

'It's the other reasons I'd like to get at.'

'You just want a nervous emotional scene, a plucking at the nerves, it's no use –'

'If you're so anxious about not hurting your father, why did you travel back with us in that car?'

'That was a mistake,' said Stuart, 'I regret it. I just wanted to get away.'

'Mistakes have consequences. Oh Stuart, help me, just a little, any little thing could help me. Don't be so cruel. I want something you can give – just give me something – like a sort of absolution – no, I mean some forgiving understanding, compassion, *feeling* –'

'I'm sorry for you –'

'That's something.'

'But I can't help you. Please don't ask for anything here, it's the wrong place.'

'So there is nothing you have to give to someone who is mad with grief?'

Stuart reflected. 'In this context – nothing.'

'Oh you – devil – you and your mistake –'

'I don't want to make any more, here.'

'It's too late. You think a single slip might demoralise you. You've got to be perfect even if everyone else perishes. At least I'm beginning to know you better!'

They were sitting in Stuart's little room, he on the bed, she on a chair. They spoke in low voices. Oblique watery sunshine entered through a spotty window which Stuart had closed when Midge arrived unexpectedly. The walls were a tear-stained pale green, the shiny new linoleum, which rose to obstruct the door, a more vivid green. There was a washbasin and a thin white towel. There were papers on a small table, pamphlets, forms to be filled in. Stuart's broken-backed suitcase, half unpacked, the lid fallen back onto the floor, was visible in the fluff under the bed. The wainscots were lightly piled with dust. The room was cold and smelt of unwashed clothes and damp.

Stuart felt cold and awkward. He had been shaving. He had been vigorously dashing cold water onto his face, and his hair was wet. His shirt was undone. He had tried to button it up but the buttons felt wrong and he had not wanted to look down and check them, Midge had so immediately started her attack and he had had to concentrate. He looked at Midge with his amber animal eyes which he could make so cool and unexpressive.

Midge, who had tossed her coat onto the floor, was soberly dressed; she wore a brown skirt and a white blouse and very little make-up and no jewellery, but her neat leather belt and her shoes somehow, like a distinguished signature, guaranteed and illuminated the smart ensemble. She sat gracefully, turned a little sideways, her skirt unconsciously hitched. Her small hands, with darkly red-painted nails, wandered nervously as she talked, along the hem of her skirt, over her knees, up to her throat, to her hair, like two anxious harmless little animals. She was no longer slim, but she looked, now, well composed, elegantly caparisoned, young, alert like a young soldier in a spotless rig. She constantly drew back her thick mane of bright hair, tugging at it nervously.

'Stuart, don't you understand what I'm saying to you, what this scene is all about, what it *means* when you *have* to see someone, when you want more than anything in the world to talk to him, to be with him? I love you. I've fallen in love with you.'

It was true. It had happened, Midge later realised, in the car coming back from Seegard, when she had so much felt that she did not want to touch Harry, *must not* touch him.

395

Gradually she had felt her whole body change, first dreadfully chilled, then slowly warmed, by the rays which came from behind. She had sat stiff at first with mingled horrified fear, misery, anger, embarrassment, remorse. She wished Stuart away, dead, never to have existed, his dreadful consciousness, his *knowledge*, utterly extinguished. She apprehended his big white clumsy body, so close behind her, heavy in the back of the car, as a contaminated corpse, full of a fatal disease, disgusting, dangerous. Then after a while she began to feel simply tired, surrendered to a hopeless quiet sense of 'it's too much'. Then a physical warmth began to steal over her and somehow, without altering her posture, she relaxed and let herself be warmed. She was conscious of an aura of emotion, unfocused desire, new desire. How could that be? There was a physical effect, a happening, as if her whole body were being remade, as if by radiation, the atoms of it changed. She felt soothed, as if ready for sleep, yet was also intensely alert, alive. She was, had been as she later thought, aware that it was Stuart who was in some way affecting her, simply by his proximity doing something to her. What did it mean when something like that happened? But nothing like that had ever happened to her, this, like herself, her altered self, was entirely new. She was not tempted to turn round, to turn round would have been *impossible*. As she sat there staring ahead with wide open amazed eyes, conscious of Harry's profile in the dark car and of his jerky angry movements as he drove, she breathed deeply and meditated upon what was so indubitably going on. It was as if this were something beyond personality, a cosmic chemical change wherein he was a pure force and she was a pure substance. So strong was her sense of the impersonality, the ineluctable objectivity of the happening, that it could not have occurred to her then to wonder if Stuart too were in any way conscious of it.

When, back in London, Thomas had taken her away to Quitterne, she was glad to go, to *rest*, to find out what had happened to her. Of course she would have to go to Stuart to tell him, but first simply to see him, to be in his presence. That was clear. But now she began to see everything else as well. Had the dangerous proximity, the *being* of Stuart, fatally

396

damaged her love for Harry, that beautiful mutual desire which she had cherished so, which had filled her consciousness and glorified her body and dictated her meticulously organised timetable for nearly two years? It was surely impossible that she could have stopped loving Harry, of course she loved him, but was it now *different*? Dreamily, alone at Quitterne with her husband and her son, segregated in an absolute interval, she tried not to worry about that, or about what she would do, but simply to indulge and protect and strengthen her awareness of Stuart. It was as if Stuart had already been given to her, as a subject to be *thought through*, in its entirety. She summoned all her memories of him from earliest childhood, she meditated upon him, she collected him. She was relieved, though at the same time hurt, when, in London again, she had found Harry absent, not anxiously and lovingly waiting. She had not planned to see Stuart on that morning, she had not *envisaged* seeing him, but Harry's absence had served as a signal. By now however Midge had begun to see what a terrible situation she was in. She had been agonisingly touched by Harry's little flat, by his familiar beseeching, by the pressure upon her of his utter ignorance. Old deep habits of love and loyalty fought for life against the new revelation. How could she not still love Harry, how could he not be her absolute? She felt an agony of tenderness and pity, which came as a new intensity of her awareness of her lover, while at the same time, even as she talked to him, she was planning her next encounter with Stuart, wondering how soon and with what mien she was to go to him again. Letting Harry make love to her had been touching and strange, as if *he* were now young and to be looked after, and she fled from thought by falling asleep before the end. She promised to telephone Harry, to fix something, on the next day, but did not, and went to Stuart instead.

'Oh don't be silly!' said Stuart. 'Go home.'

Midge rose and flew to the bed and sat beside him, and for an instant her skirted leg touched him and she felt the warmth of his thick body through his shirt. Stuart leapt up and retired to the window, jostling the table and knocking his papers to the floor.

'Midge, don't talk such absurd nonsense –'

'Stuart, listen, don't say anything hasty, I know it sounds mad, I know it's a surprise, but it's something *real* – don't just reject me, *think* – I know you want to live your special life and have no sex and never marry, I respect that, I *love* that, I only want to be with you sometimes, I only want you to *accept* my love, think of me as a friend or a servant, I could be useful to you. You want to do good things, good works, so do I, my life has been so idle, so useless, so full of vanity, that's why you mean so much to me, if you understand *that* you must let me be with you – I could be your helper, your secretary, I'd cook for you, do anything, it's not impossible, please just realise how *little* I ask, I only must be connected with you, not separated, not utterly sent away, I simply want to *give* you my love –'

'Stop it,' said Stuart. 'You don't really believe or feel any of this, you don't even understand it, it's just emotional babbling – you're having a nervous crisis, you're suffering from shock, from finding me and Edward at that place – naturally you resent my having been there, and this is just a peculiar way of attacking me – you'll see that tomorrow, you'll feel different – of course I wish you well, I hope you'll make the right decisions and be happy, but what you've been saying is simply senseless – you're not yourself – go away and rest – go, please – I'm going to open the door now.'

Midge slithered off the bed and was at the door before him, keeping it closed. 'You've killed my love for Harry. It's over. Aren't you glad? I'm alone now, I'm yours, you must take responsibility for me, you must *know* what I feel, you must recognise me and acknowledge me. I have to exist for you and be in your life, this *has* to happen. It's your doing, you provoked it all, you have these feelings too, I can sense them. It all happened in the car, I could feel you drawing me, you must have been desiring me then, in the car.'

'Sorry,' said Stuart. 'I did not desire you then or at any time, I have no such feeling. Please don't delude yourself. Now go home and take an aspirin and go to bed. I can't do anything for you. Even listening to you rave is doing you harm.'

'You are moved, you are excited, you care about me. It

can't be all on my side, something so strong, so vast. Falling in love is a miracle, it's a renewal of life – you must feel something – you made me love you – I shall have to tell them all – Harry, Thomas, Meredith –'

'Midge, please, please, don't tell more lies and hurt more people. All this stuff is false, what you speak of isn't there, *I* am not there. If you want to change your life go back to Thomas, if you want a miracle and a renewal look for it there. If you just stop telling lies and go home you'll find that you're really happy at last, you can't have been happy in a deception. I don't believe what you just said about your love for my father, but if things are somehow changing that's a good thing, you'll feel free –'

'Free! Don't mock me. Can't you see how much I'm suffering, are you human or not? Oh – you don't see, you don't understand – I'll write to you, I'll explain it all –'

'Please don't write, I won't read your letter, I won't reply, please don't start anything –'

'Start anything! It's started. You have the key of my will. Only you can stop this terrible pain. Please, will you just touch me, your touch can heal – don't refuse it, don't deny your gift – hold my hand, I beg you, if you don't it will wither and drop off – I'll burn it, I'm burning, all my body is burning – oh for Christ's sake save me, comfort me, touch me –' With that Midge stretched out her hand. It hung in front of him, near his unbuttoned shirt, poised like a motionless hovering bird.

Stuart took hold of her hot hand and felt how her fingers clasped, her nails pulling his skin, her hot palm caressing his knuckles, as if a warm feathery bird of prey had pounced upon him. He closed his eyes so as not to see her flushed excited face and moist lips and eyes. He pulled his hand quickly away and stepped back. Tears came streaming from her eyes and fell onto her white blouse and down between her breasts.

Stuart said, 'I'm sorry.' He pulled at the door handle, moving the door to thrust her aside, and ran away down the stairs. Once out in the road he walked fast with long paces until he came to a place where there were bushes and a few trees and a seat. Partly concealed he sat down, looking back along the road. He wanted to see Midge leave.

After about five minutes she came out of the door. She looked up and down the road. Stuart was not sure whether she saw him. She turned away in the other direction. When she was out of sight he waited a while, then walked back slowly to his lodgings.

EDWARD PUSHED UP the sash window as far as he could, then placed a chair under it and mounted on the chair. He looked obliquely down, then, stooping and holding the sides of the window, leaned out. He saw the pavement, the railings, the darker rectangle of the basement area. On that night the light had been on in the basement flat. Why had they not heard? Perhaps they were in the back room with the television on. Now it was afternoon and the sun was shining. The bottom of the open window was only a little above his knees. He had always pictured Mark walking out of the window; perhaps because he wanted to think of him as feeling, at that last moment, happy and all-powerful. He wanted to think of him as somehow, somewhere, really walking on air. It would not be easy to walk out, one would have to bend down, to clamber onto the sill, then straighten up, outside the window, leaning forward and stepping outward . . . What had it felt like at that moment, and when had Mark realised, had he ever realised –? What sense did it make to wonder what he had intended? One might leap forward into the air. Or simply crumple up and tumble head first. Had he screamed as he fell? How had he missed the railings? Smiling, he walked, sailed out like Peter Pan. That was the first play Edward ever saw, and it still held for him the greatest moment of all theatre, Peter's appearance at that loft nursery window, looking in out of the dark night at the sleeping children, alien, excluded, sinister. No ghost which ever later walked in Edward's shuddering imagination had been more terrible than that

401

flying boy. Edward found himself suddenly swaying. He got down hastily from the chair. The idea came to him: supposing tonight, after I fall asleep, Mark comes flying through the darkness and lands upon the window sill and very quietly pushes up the sash . . .

Edward felt so sick with fright and yearning and the old misery that he had to sit down, not upon the chair but upon the bed: the very bed that Mark had lain on that night, relaxed and happy, talking such sweet nonsense and smiling up at Edward. He bent forward over the pain which was changing now into an appalling love urge, an agonising 'if only'. If only it had all been a bad dream, if only Mark could come to him now, real, not dead, not a ghost, laughing, happy, beautiful, making silly jokes in French. God, how happy they had been, both of them, and they *didn't know*. In paradise and *not knowing*. Oh how love tugs and pulls, beams itself, shapes and embraces, so certain of the reality of its object, as if it could create it out of nothing. But when its object *is* – nothing? To love the void. Edward, to distract himself with a different mode of grief, pulled from his pocket several letters from Mark's mother which he had found waiting at home but had not yet looked at. He had taken them away because he felt he *ought* to read them and had not yet nerved himself to do so, but also because he did not want to leave them where anyone else might be tempted to look at them and see therein Edward's blackness, his utter irrevocable disgrace and shame. Edward told himself that Mrs Wilsden was half out of her mind, needed help, should be pitied, but her hatred came to him all the same, just as she seemed to wish, in pure shafts of crippling torturing accusation. Mrs Wilsden's tone and style had changed slightly but the content was much the same.

Why have you come intruding into my life, why do I have to think about you all the time, why is my mind blackened by your hateful image? I am in hell and my grief will never end. To my last day I will think every moment of his death, picture it, live it, this wanton wilful death, this theft of a whole life, a whole good sweet life of joy and loving, leaving a hole in the world, a bleeding gash. *I saw his body*,

402

broken by you, broken. You have left him behind, left him and forgotten him, as you did upon that night. I hope you fall out of a window. If only my hate could kill you – or better that you should lose what you love most and feel what I feel, be where I am.

'But I *am* there!' Edward cried out aloud, crumpling up the letter. He glanced at the others, not reading them carefully, just to make sure that no miracle had occurred, no letter that began, 'Dear Edward, my anger against you is over, it has run its course, I realise you have suffered too, you have suffered enough, I forgive you.' There was no such letter, those healing words would never come.

Edward had heeded Thomas's command and returned to the terrible room, had moved in with a suitcase and rucksack containing books, though he was sure he would never work there, and could not yet see how he would ever work again. The landlady had been pleased to see him. She referred to the room as 'the death room' and said she had had difficulty in letting it because people thought it unlucky. It had even already acquired a reputation of being haunted. Edward had gone in order to obey Thomas, because it was something to do, a move to make, a part of the 'work' which he now did instead of that which he would never do again; and also so as to get away from Harry, who evidently wanted him out of the house. Of course nothing was said between them. But Edward, observing Harry's irritable unhappiness, felt awkward and guilty before him because of what he had witnessed at Seegard. But now, as he sat on the bed with the crumpled letters at his feet, it seemed such a terrible mistake to come here all alone, where he would die, or go mad in the night struggling with a ghost which was trying to lead him to the window.

And everything was jumbled up together, a cramming of grief and fear together in his heart, for there was still no news of Jesse. Ilona had not written. Edward had found no trace of him in London, could think of nowhere else to look, so even this task which had filled his time was coming to an end. He still wanted to find the medium, Mrs Quaid, feeling blankly that she might help him somehow, but the house where she had lived seemed to have been simply removed from the map. She had probably moved elsewhere and he would never trace her. Or perhaps all *that* had been a dream, a spirit that came to him in a dream? Much worse, there was no way of finding Brownie. He almost began to wish that she had gone back to America and that somebody would tell him so. He could not go to her mother's house. He sent a letter to her Cambridge college but there was no reply. He must try to conclude that she did not want to see him, she had got what she wanted from him and did not want to follow up her impulse of pity, perhaps now judged it would be no kindness to him since really she felt so little. She might well regret that strange display of emotion. And he had left her so brusquely, almost rudely, without even asking her for an address. She may have decided that her company simply caused him too much pain. It seemed that there was nothing now for him to *do* except to *suffer*. Had Thomas intended that? Did Thomas know what he was up to, or was he just trying out random ploys like shaking a faulty machine? He was not God after all. Edward resolved to stick it out for one night, perhaps two, and then if he was still alive, go elsewhere. But where? He could not go to stay with friends, he had no friends, now, he was too ashamed. He would have to tramp looking for lodgings or go to a cheap hotel. He would have to keep going home just to see if there was a letter from Brownie or Ilona, but he dared not believe that these longed-for letters would ever come. Sooner or later, as he was beginning to realise, he would have to go back to Seegard. Sometimes he saw, in lightning flashes of hope, Jesse alive, Jesse at Seegard, where he had been all the time, the women laughing at Edward's relief, cherishing him, welcoming him, as at his first coming. But now more often, as he conceived the inevitability of his journey, he saw the return to Seegard as something awful, some final sally into the dark.

Edward had been sitting on the bed for some time, shuddering and trying to cry or to resolve to do something ordinary like going out to eat something, when Stuart came in.

'Hello, Ed, are you all right?'

'Don't be stupid.'

'Why did you come back here?'

'Thomas suggested it.'

'Oh. I see why.'

'I don't. I'm going mad.'

'Then it's just as well I came.'

'How's Harry? Of course you've left home too.'

'Very morose. I went to see him.'

'I can imagine your lack of conversation.'

'Yes. He told me you were here. I put that plant back in your room.'

'What plant? Oh, thanks.'

'I'm worried about Midge. She's in a bad way.'

'How long do you think that business has been going on?'

'You mean –?'

'Mr and Mrs Bentley.'

'I don't know. Do you think Thomas knows?'

'I can't imagine he does.'

'Why?'

'He'd *do* something.'

They were silent a moment, picturing what Thomas might do.

'I'm not sure,' said Stuart, 'Thomas might just wait.'

'For it to be over? No. Oh hell, I don't care, I feel so bloody miserable, I feel like killing myself.'

Stuart went to the window and closed it and removed the chair to the other end of the room and sat on it.

'Not that way. I'm not suicidal really, I wish I was, then I could see an end to it all. God, how unhappy everyone is, why can't people be happy. Are you happy? Yes, I suppose you are. Why shouldn't you be? You're *innocent*.'

Stuart considered. He said, 'I think that at some level, deep down, I'm something *like* happy, I'm not sure if that's the word – but at another level I'm awfully bothered.'

'Bothered! Christ, I wish I was bothered!'

Stuart got up, took off his black mackintosh and the scarf of his now-abandoned college, threw them on the floor, and sat down again. He was wearing a dark corduroy jacket over the neck of which the open collar of his not-too-clean shirt rambled a little. His short blond hair stood raggedly on end.

405

Sitting with booted feet apart he looked robust and sturdy, almost monumental, by contrast with Edward's thin twisted figure. Edward's shoulders were hunched, his legs entwined, his hands restlessly rising to push back his dark lock, then returning to clasp and wring each other.

'Ed, I wish you'd go and see Midge, she likes you.'

'Did you come to tell me that?'

'Not just. You could help her and –'

'Thereby help myself, by thinking creatively about somebody else. I know. It's no good, I hate everybody. Well, I don't hate you, you're a phenomenon. Christ, you're my brother. But what's the use of my seeing Midge? Have *you* seen her, did you call sympathetically with a bunch of flowers? No. I'm no use. I'm sick, I have no being, all my substance has been slashed to bits, I'm a rag, a piece of screwed up paper, a bit of black muck in a drain, I wouldn't *exist* enough for Midge to *notice* me.'

'You're existing now.'

'You're making me exist. Thomas can do it too. Otherwise I'm a whingeing shadow. What do you want me to do anyway? Take Midge's attention off Harry by making her fall in love with me?'

Stuart looked startled. 'Oh. Do you think that might happen?'

'Midge is wild. She might suddenly hate Harry for the Seegard business. She might do anything. Even confess to Thomas. But I don't know, it's no use my going near her, I've got too bloody much to cope with in my own soul, such as this for instance –' Edward picked up several of Mrs Wilsden's letters and threw them at Stuart's feet.

Stuart looked at one of the letters, then at another. 'Poor thing, how awful for her, how terribly she must be suffering.'

'I knew you'd say that! What about me?'

'I mean, how dreadful to suffer through hating. But she'll recover, she'll see it differently, she'll suffer differently. It doesn't make any difference to you, I mean so long as you wish her well and don't hate her back.'

'How do you mean, no difference?'

'Well, it doesn't give you any new information about what actually happened. You have to think about that in your way, not in her way. She's not the voice of God or justice or anything. She can't touch you or harm you. She's an unhappy person reacting in a violent manner. Of course you're connected with her, you have duties, to think of her, pity her, help her if you could – you're connected forever. But that doesn't mean she's your judge. You don't hate her, do you?'

'No, of course not, but –' Stuart's reply muddled Edward. He felt dissatisfied with it. 'What those letters say – it's a menace, it's a curse –'

'She can't curse you, Ed. That sort of power doesn't exist. The destructive bit is all in your own mind. Or do you think she'll arrive with a gun?'

'No, I suppose not. But hatred can kill all the same. She can make me hate myself. I could accidentally fall under a bus because I thought she wanted me to and because I agreed with her, I could curse myself.'

Stuart gazed at him, frowning. 'You shouldn't be alone here. It's one of Thomas's bright ideas, but he's not always right. He thinks about things in a dramatic way. Don't see it all as a drama or a riddle. There isn't any riddle.'

'Yes, there is. My riddle. My very own.'

'Come back soon, come home or come to my place. Well, I'm going to move out actually, we could look for somewhere together. You've made such a point of suffering, it's enough, come back and rest, be *quiet*, you're stirring yourself up so all the time, you've been through it all –'

'I haven't – not yet – perhaps never –' It occurred to Edward that Stuart did not know about Jesse's disappearance. He resisted the temptation to tell him. *That* was part of it all – it had to be connected – somehow. Connected – like his eternal connection with Mrs Wilsden. He considered asking Stuart if Jesse was with Midge, but the question would sound crazy, and if Stuart had seen Jesse in London he would have said so. Of course Midge had denied that Jesse was with her, but he might be there secretly. Edward had better go and find out for himself. He said, 'Perhaps I'll go and see Midge.'

'Good, it'll be something for you to do.'

'What are *you* doing, if it comes to that? Have you planned your life yet?'

'Not really. I might take a teacher's training course. I could get a grant.'

'Teach sixth-form maths? You'll soon be back where you started!'

'No, not that. I'd have to learn a lot of new things –'

'You're daft!'

There was a soft knock on the door. Edward, startled, frightened, called, 'Come in.' A girl came in. The girl was Brownie.

Edward and Stuart looked up. Edward suppressed a yell of joy. He said to her, 'Hello. This is my brother, Stuart Cuno. He's just leaving.' Then to Stuart, 'This is – a student – someone I know – Betty er –'

Brownie advanced. Stuart edged round her. They looked at each other and Stuart bowed slightly and then went out of the door. His heavy feet receded down the stairs.

Brownie and Edward stood like statues. Edward had suppressed his impulse to rush to her crying out, and now found himself wondering what to say. He made a vague welcoming gesture and said, 'How did you find me?'

'I thought you might be here.'

He wondered why she thought that. 'Please sit down.' He thought, we are a thousand miles from each other, all that closeness, all that *ease*, has gone.

'Why did you say I was someone else?'

'Because I couldn't bear anyone to know that we know each other.' The idea of Stuart knowing was intolerable. Why? Because Stuart would *think* about it, have expectations, wonder about the future. But *no one* must do that, even Edward must not. Too much was at stake. If he lost Brownie, if she went away, if she rejected him or detested him: that must not be known. He could not bear, after all *that*, that people should also know that he had known Brownie and lost her. That, with all the other things that they knew, would be too much. About Brownie, about Jesse, these must be secrets, secret matters, locked away.

'Why not?' said Brownie. She walked over to the window and looked out, but did not open it.

'You know what room this is?'

'Yes.'

'You haven't been to it before?'

'No.'

Brownie returned from the window and sat on the chair vacated by Stuart. She put her handbag on the floor beside her. She was wearing a brownish tartan skirt and a floppy woollen cardigan over a striped shirt. She pulled her skirt down and wound the cardigan about her. The sun was clouded over and the room was cold. Edward sat down again on the bed.

'Oh Brownie, I'm so desperately glad to see you, I've wanted to see you so much –'

'But why don't you want other people to know –?'

Edward was about to say: in case I lose you, but the words were presumptuous. How could he not lose her? Or rather, how could he lose what he had never had? He said, 'I don't want this, our knowing each other, gossiped about, it's too precious.'

'I see, yes.' She said after a pause, 'Are you living here, then?'

It occurred nightmarishly to Edward that she might think he had just returned to his old room as a matter of course, that he *didn't care*. He said carefully, 'I felt I had to face it, that it would be a good thing – I'm not staying long – just long enough to –' He floundered.

Brownie looked at him with a heavy long tired face, with a thinned drooping mouth. There were wrinkles and discoloured flesh about her eyes and she looked as if she might have been crying. Her hair had been a little jaggedly cut shorter, perhaps she had chopped it about herself with hasty scissors. Her large face looked naked and vulnerable, strained, almost ugly, with its prominent bare brow. She looked like a clever woman, an older woman, not connected with someone like Edward. Her stony brown eyes questioned him, then looked disconsolately away.

Edward felt again that sickness of being, that awful clawed-away unreality which he had spoken of to Stuart. He thought, she'll go away and we won't have really talked at all, this time she'll go away forever. 'Brownie – please, *please* –'

'I know. I'm sorry. I'm just in a state of shock.'

'Forgive me. I know. Seeing this room. You felt you had to. I can't help calling out to you. Oh if you knew how full of nightmares my head is, it's full of spiders.'

Brownie considered him with a softened expression. 'Spiders are nice animals. They do no harm.'

'These ones are poisonous.'

'I know. I'm just making conversation. Be patient. Is my mother still writing to you?'

'Yes.'

'In the same way?'

'Yes.' Edward thought, my God, she mustn't see those letters, she might ask to read them, she'd see such a terrible blackened picture of me in those letters. But the letters were nowhere to be seen, Stuart must have taken them away.

'My mother is suffering frightfully, she's scarcely sane.'

'I – yes – I'm sorry – I wish I could – are you living with her?'

'No, I'm staying with friends, with Sarah Plowmain, at her mother's place.'

'Oh – Sarah –' The remembrance of Sarah was painful, unwelcome, and the idea of Brownie intimate with Sarah, talking to Sarah was utterly sickening. Edward recalled his glimpse through the window of Sarah kneeling in front of Brownie and comforting her. He wanted to kneel down now in front of Brownie and comfort and be comforted. But the distance seemed insuperable, the posture impossible.

'You see,' said Brownie, 'my mother sort of – hates the sight of me – for being alive while Mark is dead – she always loved him more.'

'Oh my God!' Can't these things *stop*, he thought, is there *no end* to the consequences?

'She will get over it of course. She loves me really. That love will endure and the hate will go. She will stop hating you too. Don't be – afflicted by it.'

The word 'afflicted' fell in front of Edward like a portcullis.

410

He could think of nothing to say for a moment and kept shaking his head in a slow stupid way as if making some silent observation. He felt leprous, untouchable with misery, *dull* with it. Brownie could not give him the *life* that he longed for and hoped for. He felt, like a man in instant danger of death, that he must do something at once, make some effort to save himself. He was afraid that at any moment she might say goodbye and he would be unable to stop her. He must at least keep her talking, hold her mind against his like a healing leech.

He said, 'I wish I could do something for your mother, but of course there's nothing I can do. Perhaps I could do something for her without her knowing, without her ever knowing – well, that's nonsense isn't it. I must start thinking about doing something for someone.' He thought of Midge for a second.

'Are you studying, reading books?'

'No.'

'Shouldn't you? You're doing French, aren't you?'

'Yes – like Mark –'

'Get back to work, that's best.'

'What did you do at Cambridge?'

'Russian. I'm writing a thesis on Leskov.'

'You're lucky to know Russian.'

'You could learn it, it's not hard, it's a marvellous language.'

After an empty silence Brownie picked up her handbag. 'Well, don't worry about my mother –' It was a preface to departure.

'Brownie, come and sit beside me here. *Come.*'

She came and sat beside him on the bed and they sat awkwardly together side by side, fumbling for each other's hands and trying to look at each other. Then with sudden agility, Edward swung his long legs up onto the bed and somehow bundled Brownie round with him as he lay back. For an instant he terribly feared her resistance, but none came. Brownie dropped her handbag and clumsily humped herself in full length beside him. They lay face to face, breast to breast, her heavy shoes knocking his ankles. Edward sat up

411

for a moment, took his shoes off, then hers. She lay still and her warm feet aided him. She had now half buried her face in the heavy counterpane which covered the bed. He lay back and caressed her hair and laid his hand across her shoulder. Intense relief and an infinitely gentle desire which was relief and worship and gratitude flowed through his relaxed body. He put his lips against her cheek, not kissing, just touching. Her cheek was hot and wet. 'Brownie, I love you.'

She said, muffled, 'Edward – dear Edward –'

'I need you, I love you, you need me.'

She pushed him away a little, turning her head to look at him, their faces suddenly huge, flushed and made strange with emotion, smeared with her tears. 'Yes, we need each other – but it's because of Mark.'

'We're bound together. You love me, say you do.'

'Yes, but it's because of Mark.'

'It's a miracle. You don't hate me, you love me.'

'Yes, but –'

'You've said "but" three times. Don't kill me now that you've said you love me. Just love me and give me life. Oh my darling, oh my joy, my Brownie, will you marry me?'

'WHY DID YOU come here?' said Elspeth Macran. 'Hasn't she got enough troubles without your intruding?'

'Come away, Stuart, come and talk to me,' said Ursula Brightwalton.

'I'm sorry. I wanted to talk to Mrs Wilsden alone,' said Stuart. 'I can come back another time.'

Mrs Wilsden was sitting at a table in the darkened room. There was a teapot on the table. Elspeth Macran was sitting next to her. Ursula had risen when Stuart was ushered in by Sarah.

'Why did you let him in?' Elspeth Macran asked her daughter.

'I just arrived,' said Sarah. 'He said he wanted to see Mrs Wilsden. I didn't know you were all here.'

'You're a fool,' said Elspeth Macran. 'And put out that cigarette.'

'He just followed me in –'

'I'll go,' said Stuart. 'Perhaps I could come tomorrow.'

'No, you can't come tomorrow,' said Mrs Wilsden. 'You came to say something, say it. Don't *you* go,' she said to Ursula and Elspeth.

'We certainly won't,' said Elspeth.

'Have you come as an ambassador?' said Ursula.

'Tell him to sit down.'

'Sit down, Stuart.'

Stuart sat down near the door, near to the lamp which gave the only light in the room. At the far end, where the table was,

413

the curtains had been pulled against the fading evening sky. Ursula resumed her seat on the other side of Mrs Wilsden. Sarah squatted on the floor near the fireplace. The lamplight shone on Stuart's blond hair and dazzled a little in his narrowed eyes. He stared uneasily at the three figures at the table.

'Yes, as a sort of ambassador,' said Stuart, 'only no one knows I've come, no one asked me to come, I just thought –'

'You just thought you'd come,' said Elspeth.

'Yes. It's about the letters.'

'What letters?' said Ursula.

'Mrs Wilsden has been writing letters to Edward –'

'Could you address me?' said Mrs Wilsden.

'I'm sorry. I – naturally I'm worried about Edward.'

'Poor Edward!' said Elspeth.

'I wanted to tell you – Mrs Wilsden – that my brother –'

'He isn't your brother,' said Elspeth Macran.

'That my brother is suffering very much. He is really in awful and continuous pain, very unhappy, very guilty –'

'We're delighted to hear it!' said Elspeth.

'Of course I'm not excusing what happened –'

'It didn't happen, he did it,' said Mrs Wilsden.

'I just wanted to say two things to you,' said Stuart.

'Make it brief, Stuart,' said Ursula, 'use your head.'

'One is that if you want to know that he is deeply sorry and suffering extremely, he is. The other thing is that – I wanted to ask you – please – not to write to him – those letters –'

'Did he show you the letters?' said Mrs Wilsden.

'Well, yes, he showed me some –'

'So he's showing them about to make people *pity* him!' said Elspeth.

'What did you say in the letters, Jenny?' said Ursula.

'He only showed them to me,' said Stuart, 'and he didn't want pity, he feels as wretched about it as you could wish. I only felt that – enough had been said – and I wondered if you could – if you write to him – say something milder – like that you knew how sorry he was. He's very much at the edge.'

'You mean he might kill himself?' said Mrs Wilsden. 'Let him do it then. Why should I stop him?'

'He's not likely to kill himself, but he's almost mad with grief.'

'Why should I care about his grief? I have my own –'

'He's young –'

'So was my son.'

'I know,' said Stuart, 'that it must be very hard for you to stop hating him, but I feel that you should try – perhaps – because –'

'Really, this is the end!' said Elspeth. 'Don't you agree, Ursula? This puppy has come here to preach to Jennifer!'

'Go on,' said Mrs Wilsden.

'It does you no good,' said Stuart, 'to write him those bitter accusing letters – I know you will never get over what happened –'

'Stuart –' said Ursula.

'But if you could try to – to make some gesture to Edward – to show that you know he feels so guilty and ashamed – some sort of forgiving gesture – anything, a few lines, a little note to say – if you could do that – you would help him to make better sense of it all, to *see* it all properly – and perhaps you would help yourself to be less sort of extreme – you'd feel new things. Sorry, I'm not expressing this very well –'

'You want me to make him stop feeling guilty, to feel it doesn't matter, that it was just an unimportant mistake?'

'No, I don't mean that, he couldn't possibly feel that. It's just that despairing self-destructive guilt or spiteful hatred are sort of – black useless bad conditions – which destroy the life which should – come back in a new better way – to people who have committed terrible crimes or been terribly injured.'

'The blackness is his,' said Mrs Wilsden. 'Let him drown in it. How can you come here, here to *me*, and whine because your brother's unhappy? Do you want me to help him to dream it didn't happen?'

'I don't mind his being unhappy,' said Stuart, 'I mean I do, but that's not the point. He'll feel guilty all his life, anyway he'll feel responsible, he'll remember forever, every day. I don't want him to dream anything, he's in a dream now, a dream of guilt and fear and hate, which your letters help to keep going, I want him to wake up and look at it all in a real

415

way, and if you were to be the tiniest bit kind to him it *would* wake him up, it would be like an electric shock, he'd see the world again, he'd be able to live it and remake himself. As it is he's living in a fantasy.'

'You detestable complacent prig,' said Elspeth. 'We've heard about you, pretending to give up sex and going round being holy. Don't you realise what a charlatan you are? What you really enjoy is cruelty and power – cruelty like what you're doing to our friend. Get out of here.'

Stuart did not move. He was concentrating on Mrs Wilsden. 'Please forgive me for coming and talking like this –'

'You overestimate my power to give electric shocks to murderers,' said Mrs Wilsden. 'He sold drugs.'

'He never sold drugs!' said Stuart. But he was not sure.

'I don't want to talk to you,' said Mrs Wilsden. 'I find you a horrible and hateful person. You can only do hurt and harm and I am sorry for the people you will have power over in your life. You came here to bully a woman. Well, you have failed. You want me to "forgive" that boy, that man. I cannot will to forgive.'

'I don't see why not,' said Stuart.

'He has done me terrible damage, destroyed my life and my joy, and done so deliberately. I am surprised that you dare to come here and torture me by mentioning his name. You are more than impertinent, you are sadistic and cruel, as Elspeth said. Now please leave my house.'

'I am sorry,' said Stuart. 'I meant well.' He got up, blundering against the lamp.

Sarah leapt up and turned on the centre light in the room. It seemed now to be almost dark outside. Stuart saw the three women sitting in a row like magistrates. Elspeth Macran, thick glasses balanced on her long nose like a huge-eyed bird, Ursula neat, almost in uniform, with her bright inquisitive eyes, and Mrs Wilsden looking younger than the other two with a big large-browed haggard face and a lot of tangled fairish-brown hair.

Sarah opened the door and Stuart went out into the hall and stood confused. Sarah threw the front door wide open, revealing an unexpectedly bright evening outside. Stuart stumbled down three steps and set off along the pavement. After a few moments he was aware of a person, like a little ragged boy, running by his side. It was Sarah, in jeans and tee shirt, her hair clipped short, her small sallow gipsy face glaring up. She seized the sleeves of his jacket and held on. He stopped.

'How *could* you come and torment that poor woman?'

'I'm sorry,' said Stuart. 'I wanted to stop her writing those letters. They don't do her or Edward any good.'

'God, you're stupid. Look, tell Edward to stop messing about with Brownie Wilsden. He's been seeing her. What the hell does he think he's up to? I haven't told Mrs Wilsden. If she knew *that* she'd *die* of rage. How can you be so insensitive, how can he be so bloody? He can only harm Brownie, she's terribly unhappy, her mother's turned against her, he'll just mess her up still more, he'll drive her out of her mind. And tell him from me –'

'Yes.' Stuart looked earnestly down.

'Oh never mind. I'm glad he's feeling guilty about Mark. But what about me? Why doesn't he feel guilty about me? I can think about that night too. He's gone off, I wrote him and he didn't answer. He's a bloody criminal. Tell him I hate him forever. Tell him to take himself away and get himself seen to. No one has ever been really kind to me ever, my childhood was a desert and a desolation, I don't fit in anywhere, I've fallen out of everything, I don't really exist, no one cares. Everybody's predatory, out for themselves. I used to want to meet you because you sounded different, you sounded special. I made up to Edward because of you. But you're awful, you're so crude and pleased with yourself, you'll only do harm in the world, and I'll tell you one thing, women will always detest you, they'll smell you out and hate you. Tell Edward to stop meddling – oh I know you think I'm jealous –'

'I don't –' said Stuart.

'But it'll kill Mrs Wilsden if she knows he's even met Brownie. Can't he do one decent thing? What's your religion?'

'I haven't exactly got one,' said Stuart.

'Either you're religious or you're not. You believe in

nothing. That means you believe in yourself. Have you got any scars on your body?'

'No –'

'I had a dream about you. But that was before, when I thought you were a good man or something. What a con! Goodbye forever. Tell Edward – oh never mind – fuck it all.'

Sarah let go of his cuff, which she had been holding onto as if suspended from it, and scudded away. Her small feet, emerging from the tight jeans, were dusty and bare. She reached the house and vanished inside. Stuart heard the door bang. He walked on.

A few minutes later a car began to slow down beside him and stopped a little further on. Ursula leaned over and opened the passenger door.

He got in.

'Shall I take you home to Harry's?'

'No, I'm not living there now.'

'Where then?'

'Look, there's no need for you to drive me –'

'*Where?*'

He gave her the address and they drove on.

'How's Edward?'

'In a poor way.'

'I gather from Elspeth that he turned up at her cottage, he was staying at the Baltram residence. Thomas sent him of course. I can imagine how much good that did! They say the old man there is dying from lack of medical attention.'

Stuart said nothing. He did not want to have to tell Ursula about his own visit to Seegard about which he felt confused, even almost ashamed.

'I'll go and see Edward and get him back on pills. I bet he's lost them or chucked them by now. I suppose *he's* at Harry's?'

'No,' said Stuart, 'he's living in his old digs, in his old room, where it all happened.'

'*That*'s Thomas's idea too? It has his trade mark.'

'I think so. Harry just told me when I called in.'

'Have you quarrelled with Harry?'

'No.'

418

'Everyone's behaving so oddly these days. I'm the only sane person around. I've been away at a conference in California. I thought they were all crazy *there*. But if I take my eye off you lot – How are you? Have you heard from Giles? Willy told him to write to you.'

'Yes, he wrote me a marvellous letter.'

'Which you paid no attention to. But how *are* you?'

'All right –'

'Let me give you some advice, young Stuart. Don't *wait*, don't sit around thinking about doing good and wondering what's the best way for you to do it, go and do some for a while. Do some voluntary work with miserable afflicted people. I could suggest some things. I haven't a moment now, will you telephone me?'

'Yes. Thanks Ursula. I'm afraid I messed things up today.'

'You certainly believe in shock tactics.'

'I'm sorry now –'

'Oh don't be, it's original, who knows, everyone has been pussyfooting around, the change might do her good. How can one know what to do with grief like that? The human mind is a bottomless mystery. Only people like Thomas imagine they understand it, and my God they're a menace. It's just luck that Thomas hasn't killed anybody yet. He's simply taken over Edward's fantasy! That's called therapy. It's the same with that old crook Blinnet. Thomas is fascinated by other people's dream life, he's lost all sense of reality. All the same I can see he's losing his grip, he's losing his confidence, and that's vital. They can only function if they're supremely confident, like God. Could you give me Edward's address?'

After Ursula dropped him at his lodging Stuart stood a while on the pavement wondering if he should walk to a café where he sometimes had supper. A walk might do him good. He felt upset and tired and hungry. He decided it would be better to stay in his own room and cook something on the gas ring. He could sit quiet there. He was glad to have seen Ursula, though he felt no impulse to 'have a good talk' with her, as she had

419

hinted that he might. He began to mount the stairs, pleased with the prospect of being alone. However his troubles were not yet over for that day.

The door of his room was open. He went in, and in the subdued evening light saw someone there, standing in the middle of the room, a man, no, a boy. It was Meredith.

'Look, I've waited *ages* for you.'

'Sorry, I've been away –'

'Of course you have, I saw that! I went to your dad's place. He wasn't pleased to see me. He gave me your address and slammed the door.'

'I'm glad you've come. I could give you some supper, but – What is it?'

'What is what?'

'Why have you come? Just to see me? There's nothing wrong I hope.'

'Of course I haven't come just to see you. That's not how we work things, you and me. We don't just drop in, we make appointments. We don't meet in each other's houses, we meet in mysterious public places, improving places, like the British Museum or the National Gallery.'

'Would you like some Coca-Cola?'

'No. I'm in a state.'

Stuart sat on the bed. Meredith stood looking out of the window.

'What's this state you're in, tell me.'

'It's about you.'

'I'm sorry to hear that –'

'And my mother. You know I told you she was having an affair and you said it's impossible. Well, it isn't impossible and it's with your father. Did you know?'

'Yes.'

'So you told a lie.'

'I didn't know then,' said Stuart. 'I found out since. Does your father know?'

'I don't think so. He lives in a world of his own. He and Mr Blinnet sit on a cloud together and play harps. But that's not the point, I mean about your dad. It's about you.'

'How, about me?'

'My mother's upset about you, and I don't know what it is. What is it?'

'I think she's upset because I know about her and my father. I found out by accident.'

'But what did you do to her, you must have put some sort of spell on her?'

'What did she say?'

'Oh all sorts of things. Something or other was all your fault. It sounded as if *you*'d been seducing her! I couldn't make it out.'

'But – why did she talk to you?'

'I talked to her. I shouldn't have, I think. But it all *hurt* me so much, it got inside my head, I couldn't bear it. I suppose I wanted her to say it wasn't so, even if it was. It was just hell, it is hell. You were right, it's impossible, only the impossible is possible. I didn't ever dream that she – it's incredible – and so terrible. I felt cut off from her – and from my father because he didn't know –'

'What did you say to her?'

'I just said I knew and I thought it was horrid. And then I felt I'd done something so dreadful to my mother. She was so miserable and sort of – squashed – I wished like hell I'd held my tongue. And then she started talking sort of wildly – I was scared stiff – as if she'd gone mad – and then she told me I mustn't see you again –'

'She said that?'

'Yes, but that's nothing. She said it before, and I just said, "Don't be silly" and she took it back. But then she went on about you as if you mattered a lot, as if you'd sort of taken her over. You didn't make a pass at her or something?'

'No,' said Stuart. 'Meredith, please calm down. I just suggested to your mother that she ought to tell your father, and stop this thing with mine –'

'That's all is it! But she's in love with him, isn't she? Or with you, I don't know. Perhaps you're both after her.'

'Meredith, stop this. You know perfectly well that I wouldn't –'

'How do I know? I don't really know anything about you. Sometimes I feel you aren't really there the way other people are. You're a pretty peculiar chap. You're ambiguous, or ambivalent, somebody said. My mother said you're a bit mad, she said that earlier. Everyone says that actually. She warned me against you. She said it would end badly. You've led me on to be dependent on you, you've tampered with my affections, you want to dominate me. I'm older now, I understand. I mustn't see you any more, I don't want to see you any more, you're sentimental about me –'

'Shut up,' said Stuart. 'You don't believe any of this nonsense. I haven't done anything to your mother except tell her what I thought. She asked me what I thought and I told her.'

'She came to you.'

'Yes, I wouldn't have said anything. And I certainly don't intend to tell your father. I just hope and believe that this deception will end soon. And I'm not sentimental about you, I love you. You're old enough to understand that terminology. Meredith, there's nothing wrong here. Don't let other people –'

'She thinks you're after me. I know about these things.'

'Don't be utterly silly. We're free individual people not cases of something or other. We've known each other for a long time and we've trusted each other, you know I'm not –'

'I don't want you, it's all gone wrong, it's become a nightmare, and it's your fault.'

'I'm very sorry about your mother –'

'She came to you, I hate you –'

'Stop being hysterical, don't shout!'

'You made me get attached to you, you wanted to control me –'

'I may have wanted to influence you, but –'

'I don't want to see you any more *ever*!'

'Meredith, *wait* –'

Meredith's wild tears were flowing. He threw himself across the room toward the door. Stuart tried to stop him, grasped at his waist then clutched his coat tails as he struggled free and slipped away. Stuart ran down the stairs and out into the street, but the boy, fleet of foot, was already disappearing in the gathering evening dusk. Stuart ran a little way after him then gave up. He returned slowly and went upstairs to his room and closed the door. Then he sat on the floor leaning against the bed as the room grew dark.

'IT CAN'T ALL have been smashed by that sorceress at Seegard or because Jesse kissed you and set you off, sent you off at a tangent as you said, that is made you temporarily insane? Well, I can imagine you suddenly thinking you were sort of in love with *him*, you said you'd been thinking about him all your life, and being jealous of Chloe, and –'

'It's *not* that, I *told* you –'

'*That*'s the shock, that's what's unhinged you, but you'll recover –'

'It's nothing to do with Jesse or – it's nothing to do with anything –'

'That's impossible,' said Harry. 'Everything is to do with something. What I cannot and will not believe is that you can even *imagine* that you're in love with Stuart. That *not*.'

They were at Midge's house, not upstairs in 'their' room but sitting in the flowery drawing room. Thomas was safely away all day at the clinic. They sat facing each other a few feet apart, and each face was gaunt with the horror of new truth, as if blown back and bared by a great wind. They stared, sick, biting their lips and sometimes trembling. Midge was wearing no make-up except for a dab of powder on the end of her nose. Harry was wearing a dark red bow tie with his black leather jacket which, Midge had told him once, made him look young and desperate.

'You can't love him,' said Harry, 'it's not possible, I won't believe it. What is loving him, what does it consist in, do you want to go to bed with him?'

424

'I don't know – I suppose I do –'

'If you don't know and you suppose, you're not in love.'

'It's not like an ordinary thing of wanting to make love –'

'Wanting to make love isn't ordinary, wanting it like *we* want it isn't.'

'It's just that he's so remote, he's strange, I can't imagine – I want to be with him, to touch him, to talk to him, to be – in an absolute tension – with him –'

'Midge, do you know what you're talking about? Do you know *whom* you are talking about and *to whom*? I don't suppose this is an ugly joke designed to hurt me, but it feels like it.'

'You *must* see that I'm in earnest,' said Midge. 'I can't help hurting you just by telling you the truth. You used to say that I evaded the facts and wouldn't speak straight. Well, my speaking straight now proves how much in earnest I am. Only something very extreme would make me behave like this.'

'Or a mental breakdown. I think you are literally mad, the strain of our love has made you go mad. You'd better ask Ursula for some pills! You'll recover. Only don't drive *me* mad in the interim. You've invented the one thing in the world that would hurt me most of all.'

'I didn't invent it.'

'Think who this person *is* on whom you profess to be fixated!'

'Who? Oh – your son – yes –'

'You'd forgotten? You think it doesn't matter?'

'Yes – but – I don't feel him as anyone's son, he's just himself.'

'Are you feeble-minded? *I* exist, look, I'm *here*. We've been happy utterly devoted faithful lovers for two years, we are planning to marry –'

'I feel so changed –'

'Midge, do you want me to hit you? There's a whole world invested in this. We've been loving and truthful and tender and passionate with each other. We didn't regard this as a casual adventure. Did we?'

'No, but something has happened –'

'I still think it's Jesse. The thing about Stuart is just a by-product, it's *shock*, that's what it is, *shock*. I even thought it might be a good thing, your meeting Jesse like that, even the ghastliness of Stuart and Edward being there, I thought it might *jolt* you into telling Thomas. If only you'd let me tell Thomas then, when you started talking about Stuart on that day! If only I'd been brave enough to leave you at the flat and go straight to Thomas and tell him, whether you liked it or not! I've let you rule me all along because I love you. Christ, I've been such a coward, you've made me a coward. If I'd told Thomas *then* you'd never have developed this thing about Stuart at all.'

'No, I was already in love with Stuart, only I didn't tell you, I fell in love with him in the car, when he was sitting behind us. He *made* me do so.'

'You mean he deliberately – you said he hadn't tried to –'

'No, he didn't, he hasn't, it was just his *being*, like a sort of radiation –'

'We're getting all mystical now. You make me sick, oh so sick, as I've never been with you before. You are destroying it all in front of my eyes, all our precious perfect love, making yourself hate me, making me hate you. It's like something mechanical. I feel like killing you.'

'Harry, I'm desperately sorry. Don't you think I'm miserable too about this?'

'I shall certainly kill him.'

'I'm being very brave, so brave, because of him. He made me feel how unworthy it all was, how rotten, untrue to Thomas, untrue to you –'

'You mean you never intended to marry me at all!'

'I don't mean that –'

'You're in a masochistic trance. It's the sort of thing Thomas could explain. You've been feeling guilty for two years and now Stuart finding out has crystallised it all into a manic fit of self-abasement. All right, feel guilty if it pleases you, only don't call it being in love with Stuart. He occasioned it. He doesn't have to be the love object too!'

'That's how it is,' said Midge, gaunt and pale with the effort of this explanation which had been going on repetitively for some time. 'His being so different, so separate and

426

entire and not messed up into things, I couldn't help it, he was a revelation suddenly just as himself – not what he said or meant – just *him* as if he *was* the truth –'

'Like Jesus Christ. I shall vomit. Can't you see him as he is, a timid, pretentious, pompous, conceited, abnormal neurotic?'

'I love him,' said Midge.

'And you no longer love me?'

'Harry, I don't know. It's different, it has to be because everything's changed. I feel cut off from you. You must have felt that at the flat.'

'I did, but I thought it was a temporary thing. I still think *this* is a temporary thing. It can't be otherwise. We've so tried and tested each other, we've *achieved* each other – Or are you going to marry him!'

'That's not the question. Nothing's in question, I told you, he rejects me.'

'Then are you not mad? What are you going to do with this alleged love? Go on loving in vain for the rest of your life?'

'I think, later on, he might let me work with him, help him in his work – his helping people –'

'Midge, you're pathetic! I can't take you seriously.'

'You must take me seriously, we aren't as we were –'

'I can't recognise you. Who is speaking?'

'I'm glad you say that. I feel that I've changed, I've got confidence, certainty. I can tell the truth. I've always been afraid of saying what I really thought, I've evaded direct questions, always hidden in half-truths. All those endless lies had got into me so that I couldn't talk properly to anyone, as if I had no truthful language at all – it made me into a puppet, something unreal, *we* were unreal, I've often felt that.'

'You never felt anything of the sort. We are the reality of the world, everything else is mere appearance. Midge, we love each other, we've said it a thousand times, said it clear-eyed and in the truth. Don't distort the past. Our love is eternal and forever.'

'It seemed so. I didn't conceive that anything could happen so fast. Now I feel a kind of relief. Though I'm very miserable too.'

'But all this is *false*, don't you see, this thing about Stuart, it's play-acting, it's dreaming, it's wicked fantastic dreaming, Stuart is nothing, he's a simulacrum, a corpse, like Jesse said, he's death itself. You admit he rejects you. If you leave me now you'll be dead for the rest of your days. You'll crawl back to Thomas. You'll be an object of derision and contempt. Have you no pride? Do you want to die?'

'Yes, I think so, I mean I just don't care about –'

'I never thought I'd see you as a weak sentimental lying clown, spineless, timid, *stupid*, you are *stupid* – I wonder what Thomas will make of your new fantasy life?'

'I think Thomas knowing would have killed our love at any time.'

'So you deceived me?'

'No. Well, I deceived myself. I was afraid to tell him.'

'Because you thought if you confessed to him and he forgave you you'd realise you loved him after all – is that it? I thought the opposite – that if Thomas knew it would break your relation with him absolutely, it would snap. If he knew, you'd be mine in an instant. Hell, why do I use the past tense, that's what I think now. When he knows, you'll be mine.'

'Why haven't you told him then?'

'Don't make me raving mad! Because you didn't want me to!'

'I think you're afraid of Thomas. We both are.'

Harry lowered his head almost as low as his knees, breathing hard, and groaned. Then he said, looking at her with his hardest look, 'Well, *now* you'll tell him? Or shall I? Perhaps you'd better. You can explain about Stuart, which is dark to me. Or will you tell him about Stuart and not about us? Or vice versa?'

'I shall have to tell him everything now.'

'Oh God. Maybe don't tell him just yet, give us time to sort this other business out first, give yourself time to *recover*. When we're perfectly together again we'll tell him.'

'Let's not get in a muddle –'

'That's your funniest remark yet.'

'You *are* afraid of him.'

'The fact is, we haven't either of us the slightest idea how Thomas will react.'

'It is all rather outrageous. After all, you're his best friend –'

'Have you just thought of that, damn you? You're not the only one with guilt feelings! I love you too much to trouble you with mine, I swallow all that by myself.'

'Harry, you've been good to me –'

'Yes, I'm *afraid*, so maybe it's best to get it over and sort out all the wreckage afterwards. Not that I see what he could do to me, change me into a toad. I don't see what anyone could do to me now, if I lose you, Midge, I'm done for – I'll drown.' He saw the quiet empty boat, sailing itself, slowly yet too fast. He said, 'Well, when will you tell him – today, this evening?'

'I – I expect so –'

'You can't face it. I'll tell him.'

'No –'

'Suppose he wants a divorce? Will you expect me to be waiting for you?'

'No, I can't –'

'I will be of course. When the storm breaks you'll run to me, when you've told Thomas, everything will be destroyed except your bond with me. We'll be all right, Midge, let's go to him together.'

'No –'

'My dear, my heart, I love you, you love me, you can't undo our love, we belong utterly together till the world ends, we are one person, we've tested our love and it's real, it's strong, it's good. I see it now, Stuart simply *represents* Thomas, that's why you're so confused, you're anticipating the shock of confronting Thomas, you're enacting it beforehand – so, don't you see, the real shock when it comes will be *less*. Isn't that how it is? Please don't be crazy any more, be the old Midge, see, it's only me, Harry, your love and your sweetheart. Don't fail me now, don't kill me with grief. You'll recover, it's the shock, it's the strain, it's a derangement, you're ill, you're not yourself, you're in a dream. *Wake up*.' Harry rose and moved the few feet towards her. He pulled her up, grasping her dress at the shoulder with violent hands. He shook her roughly to and fro, then threw her back into her chair. Her head met the back of the chair with an audible crack.

Midge put her hand to her head, staring up at him, and tears came into her eyes. She said, whispering, 'If only you hadn't taken him in the car, I'd have gone with you to the flat – but it's too late now.'

There was a sound outside in the hall, Harry moved away and Midge rose, adjusting her dress and mopping her eyes. Then someone knocked on the drawing-room door. As Midge went towards the door it opened and a bald man came in, not immediately recognisable as Willy Brightwalton, since he had, advised by a wise American, given up brushing his wisps of hair across his crown, cut them off, and surrendered himself to tonsured baldness. He was also suntanned and thinner. Midge cried out, 'Why, Willy! Welcome home.'

Willy advanced, kissed her on the cheek, and put a bag he was carrying down on a table. 'Hello, Midge, dear, I hope you don't mind, I hoped I'd find you alone, I mean find you, at this hour in the morning. The door was open so I came in. Hello, Harry, I was going to call on you too, bit of luck really. I just got back yesterday, I feel awfully funny, my body clock says it's midnight or something. I came nonstop from San Francisco, stayed awake all night watching a film, didn't get a wink of sleep. Ursula wanted me to stay in bed all day, but I felt far too restless and bouncy –'

'Are you glad to be back?' said Harry.

'Well, yes *and* no. I had the most tremendous fun in California, Giles drove me all the way down the coast, and we saw whales, big grey whales, migrating, quite near to the land, and seals and sea otters, you'd have loved it, and we drove down to Mexico and we saw the Grand Canyon and numerous deserts. They love deserts over there. We glimpsed Ursula, she was at a grand conference you know in San Diego, but she didn't stay long, she hates America, I don't, I must say it suits me, one does feel more free, or perhaps it's just being in another university and feeling irresponsible. I was lecturing on Proust and met some pretty good Proustians, both faculty and students. We had a Proust-reading marathon to raise money for ecology, it was terribly funny, they called it a Proustathon –'

'How's Giles?' said Midge.

430

'Spiffing! That word's part of an act I put on to amuse the Americans – it came out quite naturally. He's in cracking form. He's published an article which has become quite famous, I couldn't understand a word of it!'

'Do you think he'll stay there?'

'I fear he may. I hoped he'd go to Oxford, but *tout casse, tout lasse*, still it's not all that far away nowadays. He's thinking of buying a house with a palm tree and a swimming pool, everyone has a swimming pool there, I've done a lot of swimming –'

'You look very well,' said Harry.

'Talking of Proust, how's Edward?'

'I don't know,' said Harry, 'he's moved out. I think he's all right.'

'Oh – and Stuart? I told Giles to write to him. Dear me, I've picked up endless Americanisms. I say "guy" and "do you have" – Has Stuart given up his crazy plans?'

'I don't think so.'

'Oh dear. I've got some stuff from Giles to give to Stuart. And presents for everyone. I've just brought yours round, Midge darling, may I unload? I'd have brought Harry's if I'd known.' As Willy began to unpack his bag Harry sat down beside the table, staring at Midge, who avoided his gaze.

'That's just some candy. And a bottle of Bourbon for Thomas, not that he drinks much, he's awfully hard to find presents for, Giles wanted me to buy him a disastrous American tie, that was a joke of course. Here's a pair of funny stockings, the girls there wear them, it's the fashion, very pretty girls, I must say, a bit tall for me though. And here's a blouse and two dresses, one of the faculty wives took me to a shop which she said was the *dernier cri*, please excuse her accent –'

'Oh Willy – what perfectly lovely things – what a darling dress, and that one, such perfect colours, and the little fluffy blouse – how awfully kind of you –'

'I hope the sizes are right. I'm so glad you like them. They're absolutely you, aren't they. And that's a little necklace, it's just glass, but I thought it was rather cute.'

'Willy, you've been *extravagant*, thank you so much!'

431

'Well, that's the lot, glad to have given satisfaction. By the way, what Sunday paper do you get? I don't suppose you ever see this one, it's rather on the "popular" side. A friend of Ursula's left it for her, she's away again, on a course, always learning something. I had a look at it – this would interest both of you – there's an article about Edward's father – look, there's a photo of him when he was young, looking exactly like Edward. I haven't had time to read it actually, perhaps we could have it back, I'm sure Ursula would like to see it.' Willy spread the paper out on the table. Harry picked it up.

Midge said, 'I've got to go out soon, Willy, but let's meet before long and you can tell us all your adventures.'

'I've had plenty, I can tell you, I got mugged!'

'No!'

'Very mildly. A guy with a knife asked for my wallet. I didn't argue! And then when we were at the Grand Canyon –'

'Willy, you must go, I'm longing to hear but it must wait.' Midge escorted Willy out into the hall. 'I hope you bought some clothes for yourself too. What a fine coat, is that new, it's camel-hair, isn't it? Goodbye, and thank you so much.'

The door closed. Midge stood for a few moments breathing deeply. She looked at herself in the mirror which hung above the big Jacobean chest on which people put their coats. Her face was shiny, but no one would have guessed it was from dried tears. Her dress had come apart a little at the shoulder, but it didn't show much. She went back into the drawing room.

Harry said, 'We're blown.'

'What do you mean?'

'Mrs Baltram has written about us.'

'*Written about us?*'

'Yes. She's going to publish her memoirs, all about Jesse's love life, and they've printed the most up-to-date bit which features Edward and us.'

'But – I don't understand – what does she say – does she give our names?'

'Pretty well. Look, read this bit.'

I may mention here a more recent example of Jesse's extra-ordinary power of bring about coincidences and of drawing people to him by will. Madness surrounds genius and an electrical psychological band surrounds great men. Edward had been with us for some time and was becoming, in the unpolluted natural atmosphere of our home, less disturbed, when two surprising things happened. His step-brother Stuart turned up, whether inspired by curiosity or some desire to help I cannot say. He seemed a rather simple though well-intentioned youth, but if he came to 'do good' to poor Edward he had little time to effect this because of the drama which followed hard upon. It was a foggy night and rat-tat on the door and behold a couple, a man and a woman, who announced themselves as Mr and Mrs Bentley. Their car had become embedded in the fen, a not unusual accident, and we were asked to help pull it out, which of course we agreed to do, we often play the role of Good Samaritans. About this time Jesse made one of his evening appearances, suddenly entering the hall like a king in full beauty, holding his stick like a sceptre and gazing imperiously round. A sudden scream, a cry of 'Chloe', and my lord was embracing the woman who was it turned out *Chloe's sister*. She had thrown herself upon him like a leaping cat. This character has, you will recall, already appeared as a schoolgirl in this story, I recounted how she turned up one day with Chloe and sat mum at our table, intimidated to be in such unusual company and staring about with her mouth open. Jesse enquired who she was but paid little attention to the answer, she was a plain little girl. The resemblance in later years to Chloe was more perceptible though slight, however Jesse saw it and was translated back in time. The pattern was completed when it turned out that 'Mr Bentley' was a relation of Stuart's! Undismayed we pulled their car out of the fen and sent them on their way complete with Stuart. Jesse, none the worse for his time-trip, went to bed and had forgotten the episode the next morning.

Midge laid the paper down. 'But – will anyone notice – I mean she doesn't say our names –'

'Of course they'll notice. The news will go round. Everyone

433

will read this. Someone kindly brought the paper to Ursula! It's headed *Jesse Baltram's Harem*. Jesse's suddenly famous. And so are we.'

'Harry, I don't understand – we don't take this paper – Thomas won't have seen it – and it just says a relation of Stuart's –'

'Stuart hasn't any relations who know you except me. Or do you expect us to invent one? God, why did it have to happen like this? It's no good, this will be discussed at every dinner party, in every gossip column. The implications are as clear as crystal. We needn't argue any more about who's going to tell Thomas. The world will tell him.'

At that moment there was the soft sound of a key in the front door, and a step in the hall. Thomas entered the drawing room closing the door behind him. When he saw Harry he stopped, opened the door again and pointedly stood aside. Harry walked out of the door and out of the house.

Thomas went to the table, saw the open pages which Midge had laid down, and threw on top of them a copy of the same Sunday paper and of a popular daily paper. He said, 'I suppose "Mr Bentley" is Harry?'

'Yes.'

'With whom you've been having a love affair?'

'Yes.'

'Did you go to that place to show yourself and your lover to Jesse?'

'No, it was an accident.'

'How long has this affair been going on?'

'Two years.'

'*Two years?*'

'Yes.' Midge moved over to the window, threw open the door onto the balcony, and sat down near it. Thomas followed.

'Did Meredith know?'

'Yes. He saw me and Harry here. He knew we'd been making love.'

'You mean you made love here, in this house?'

'Yes, in the spare room. We used to meet at Harry's place before Stuart moved in.'

434

'And you're in love with Harry?'

Midge hesitated. 'Well – I was – yes.'

'What do you mean you were? Do you want a divorce so you can marry him?'

'No.'

'Why not?'

'I don't want to marry him,' said Midge. She began to cry a little, keeping it in control, averting her face.

'You want him as a lover not a husband? Does he want you to get a divorce?'

'Yes.'

'You say you don't want a divorce but if, as it appears, you love him and not me wouldn't that be sensible? Please say what you want.'

'If *you* want a divorce –'

'Are you expecting me to accept this liaison, which incidentally is now public knowledge? In case there was any ambiguity a well-known gossip columnist has named names. Do you want to go on being my wife and his mistress, is that it?'

'No. My relation with Harry is now over. It ended before I knew about that article. I was going to tell you. I hope you'll believe me.'

'I don't think I do. I think you're just defending yourself after the shock of being found out. When did the relation end, as you say?'

'I think – it was a few days ago.'

'When you realised you could not conceal it any longer. You decided to say it was over. To help yourselves over a difficult time and then resume. It doesn't sound like a coincidence that "you think" it ended a few days ago! Please be honest and tell me.'

'It was because of Stuart.'

'Stuart? Of course, he was there, and Edward. And Meredith knew. Weren't you afraid Meredith would tell me?'

'I asked him not to.'

Thomas, standing near her, one hand stretched out to touch the wall, was silent a moment. He said, 'You have defiled everything. But just let me understand. Edward and Stuart

435

have been discreet – and Meredith too . . . But no doubt you felt you could not rely on their discretion forever. Hence this change of tactics. To hide your relationship more securely by pretending it is over?'

'No, no – it was *Stuart* – he told me I ought to tell you. He wasn't going to tell you. He said I ought to.'

'But why should that have altered anything? Look, I just can't believe that a relationship which has lasted for two years under difficult circumstances can suddenly dissolve like that. Deception on that scale demands a great deal of thought and energy and – commitment. It must have been the major part of your life, your chief activity. You must have felt you were really married to Harry. Why should Stuart matter?'

'Because he made me see. He made me feel different. I fell in love with Stuart. I'm still in love with him.'

Thomas looked at her carefully. He moved away from the wall, took off his glasses, took out his handkerchief, then stuffed the handkerchief away and put the glasses on again. 'What does that mean, what can it mean? Have you told him?'

'Yes. I love him. I went to him, I want to be with him. I want to work with him, I want to work for him, I want to change my life.'

'So now you don't want to live with Harry you want to live with Stuart?'

'Yes, but – I must see Stuart again, I must –'

'Have you told Harry this?'

'Yes.'

'You'd like Stuart to be your lover? What does Stuart think about it?'

'He doesn't want me, not like that. But later I might be with him in his work, I want to change, I want duties –'

'Duties – oh – my dear Midge – Anyway you want to leave me and Meredith?'

'Not Meredith.'

'But me?'

'Only because you won't want me now.'

'Do you expect me to beg you to stay? I won't do that. It would not be fair to you. You must decide what you want to do. You may well be happier without me. I don't understand this Stuart thing. I don't think it's a deliberate deception, but it's some kind of psychological device. Aren't you relieved in a way that I know?'

'Yes.'

'Precisely. It must have been nervous work. You're suffering from shock because Stuart knew and because he dared to judge you. To save yourself you had to embrace your executioner. I can imagine that Stuart was an obstacle, after your secret life had been working like a charm, something really hard at last. You'll get over Stuart and run back to Harry. He'll console you. Isn't that what will happen – my dear – wife?'

'No. I don't think so. Oh you're so *cold*. You never do anything natural –' She lifted her head with her wet mouth open a little. She had stopped crying.

'What do you want me to do, shout and break things? I've only just, an hour ago, discovered what you and your lover have known for years. I've only just found out that my happy life has been based on a mistake. I'm just not inflicting my suffering on you in the form of rage.'

'I don't think you really care all that much.'

'Of course I do, it will damage my practice! Who will take their troubles to a man who can't even understand his wife? How do you imagine I feel about being made a public fool of? This sort of bespattering publicity changes people, and it's only just beginning. Journalists will be on the telephone, photographers outside the door. It'll be like the old days for you, only you won't enjoy it this time.'

'You are cold and detached, you *think*, now you are not even being serious, you don't care. You have never really *seen* me at all.'

'I may be a fool, and I may have been an imperfect husband, but I have loved you very much and I do love you very much. Only you must not expect me to bare my heart to you now, at this moment, in this situation. I find you with Harry, he runs away, he has nothing to say, you offer no excuse, there can be no excuse. I am confronted with the monumental fact of your passionate love for somebody else and your cold-blooded willingness to deceive me. Now I have to protect myself and I am beginning to do so at once. I am not going to let you and Harry maim my life. I am very deeply hurt. My conception of you, my thought of you, was so precious –'

'You took me for granted.'

'Of course. I trusted you completely. My home, my marriage, was one place where I did not have to be suspicious. My love for you was an absolute resting place. Now I learn that you have been lying to me systematically, anxiously watching my plans in case they interfered with yours, arranging your timetable so as to be with your lover, longing for him, thinking about him, even as you spoke to me being with him.'

'It didn't feel like that,' said Midge.

'You mean you didn't think of it as lying. Your sense of his presence made me unreal, so how could I be damaged! You resented my existence, you looked past me at him. You excused yourself because your love for him was live and real, and your love for me was old and withered.'

'I was in love.'

'That is supposed to let people off.'

'I'm sorry – I didn't expect it.'

'I don't want to talk about it,' said Thomas. 'Having a scene now would be no use to either of us. I don't want to stir things up to satisfy your emotions. You had better stay here and sort yourself out. I won't be in the way. I'm going to Quitterne, when I've packed a case. You decide what you want and let me know later on. I won't put any pressure on you, and I will help you to carry out any plan you make. You are free to make up your mind. One thing though. If we part company, or when we part company, Meredith stays with me.'

'We'll make civilised arrangements,' said Midge, her tears beginning again. 'But please don't go away yet – you haven't understood –'

'Civilised! We are far far beyond civilisation! How I wish it hadn't been Harry.'

'Thomas, please don't be so angry –'

'Do you call this anger? I wish you well. I want you to be happy.'

Thomas left the room, Midge sat moaning into her handkerchief. A few minutes later his steps came quickly down the stairs and the front door opened and closed. Midge sank to the floor beside her chair and abandoned herself to sobbing.

BROWNIE HAD NOT said yes to Edward's question. But she had not said no either. They had not made love. Not there upon the bed where Mark had lain in his happy drugged ecstasy before he got up and floated out of the window. They had sat and talked about Mark. Though neither of them exactly said so, his presence in the room quietly contradicted any pleasure they might have had in each other's company, at the same time constituting that strange ambivalent bond. 'It's because of Mark.' 'Yes,' Edward had said, 'but it's not just because of Mark.' 'It might be, that might be its deep meaning.' 'Well, if it's deep enough – that wouldn't be bad, would it?' 'It would be – if we were just substitute Marks for each other – blotting him out.' 'But we couldn't blot him out.' 'No, so perhaps he's a barrier.' 'What would he have wanted?' 'We can't make sense of that question.' This discussion, whose logic eluded them, began to frighten them both, and they stopped it. They talked more simply about Mark, Edward talked about the college, Brownie about their childhood.

Now Edward was going to see her again. They did not want to meet in that room a second time. They could not go to Mrs Wilsden's house, or to Elspeth Macran's, and Edward could not envisage bringing Brownie to his own home. He and Brownie both felt secretive about their painful necessary extraordinary relationship. They did not want yet to expose it to the scrutiny of the world, not yet, until they had themselves riddled out what it was. They were secret homeless lovers, not

440

even yet lovers, and that homelessness and deprivation was somehow too a part of their relation, their pact, something which made it for the moment in an essential way provisional and innocent.

Today they were to meet for lunch in a pub suggested by Brownie in Bayswater, not far from, but not dangerously near, Elspeth Macran's house. Edward did not want to suggest anything. He wanted to come where *she* said, and there was a soothing charm in the idea of their both making their way through big indifferent anonymous London to that meeting place where they would sit as invisible people in their private corner. The idea of meeting in a pub was good too, it suggested, perhaps, a new phase, a beginning of ordinariness, wherein their relation, less strained, would become more full. Edward, much too early for the rendezvous, was walking through Soho. He liked long walks through London, the action of walking dulled and calmed his too active mind. He had not entirely given up hope of finding Mrs Quaid, though he thought it most likely that she had simply moved on. He could hardly, in memory, now believe she was absolutely real. It was more like remembering a dream. He decided to walk to Bayswater through the back streets north of Oxford Street, passing near to Fitzroy Square on the way.

Edward had not told Brownie about Jesse, at least he had not told her about his 'hallucination', or about Jesse's disappearance and the London search. He had spoken vaguely about his stay at Seegard. Brownie had expressed no curiosity about it. There were other things to talk of. There had been no letter from Ilona. He did not now expect one. How could Ilona write him a letter? It was almost as if he now believed her to be illiterate. If she ever did write, Mother May would censor the letter and would stop any note saying, 'Don't worry, he is back.' As long as Edward *did not know*, Edward would be bound to return to Seegard. The place was by now becoming grotesque and dark in his imagination and he feared the idea that he must go back to it. Everything changes so in one's mind, he thought, and there was so much that was irreducibly awful in his own. Sometimes he imagined how things, some things at least, might turn out well. He would suddenly find Jesse, perhaps meet him in the street. That would be somehow typical of what happened with Jesse, it would be right. So Edward as he walked along looked at the people he passed, often seeing false Jesses and experiencing the sharp stab of a quenched hope. Or else Ilona would write after all, saying casually, 'Of course he's here', sending Jesse's love. Or else Edward would go back to Seegard and, as he imagined it, creep in, unlock the tower door and run up the stairs and into Jesse's room and into his arms. He lacked Jesse, he missed him, he longed for him. And then came back the awful fear, the guilt, the secret which only Thomas knew. Would he ever, in some happy future, sit with Brownie and tell her all about it? In that telling the hallucination would become something almost trivial, something seen at once as an illusion. Then as his hunted mind came back again to Brownie, he felt: but there is no future. It was like looking in the mirror and seeing nothing there.

He had now spent two nights in his old room. There had been an efficacy, what Thomas believed in, but it was over, had done what it could, perhaps only in the meeting with Brownie there. It afforded him no more wholesome thoughts. There were evil spirits there, spirits of guilt and terror. Most of all, Edward was now afraid that in the end he might begin to hate Mark, to see him as a demon who had ruined his life. An evil Mark was sometimes in the room at night, standing beside Edward's bed. Why should not Mark desire revenge? He had ruined Edward's life, but Edward had taken his life away entirely. This was a new and dreadful idea, emerging from the mass of poisonous spiders with which he had told Brownie his head was crammed. He must find somewhere else to live. He thought of returning home, but he felt afraid of Harry. He could imagine, from the automatic workings of his own imagination, how much Harry might, simply because of what he knew, hate the sight of him. Harry would bitterly resent any 'loss of face' and any witnesses thereof. Edward wondered, but without any lively speculation on the matter, what had happened to Midge and Harry. Living isolated in a world of his own, Edward had not seen any newspapers or 'naming of names'. He thought about Midge and about how

442

he ought perhaps to go and see her, but he reflected that she too might find him hateful, and he did not feel strong enough to risk it. If he were rebuffed now he would weep.

So Edward walked along, watching the people pass, suffering a vivid phantasmagoria of hope and fear which moved faster and faster through his exhausted mind. Because of the evil spirits he had been unable to sleep. He saw Jesse at Seegard, sitting up in bed waiting for him to come. He saw Brownie in the pub telling him that she would no longer see him, that she had realised that she could never forgive him. He saw Ilona dancing upon the tips of the grass. Then he saw her drowned in the river, rapidly swept along towards the sea, her long hair dark like river weed. He saw Harry leaning forward and saying, 'You are *ill*, it is an *illness*, you will receive help, you will recover.' He saw Thomas's gleaming spectacles and his neat fringe and heard Thomas's Scottish voice saying, 'In every grain of dust there are innumerable Jesses.' He saw Stuart's yellow eyes full of love and judgment.

Edward walked on and on; then he stopped. He had seen something which he had passed by and which had registered in a violent flash upon his mind, not understood at first. He turned back and walked slowly, looking at the houses. Then he saw it, quite small, a little yellow card pinned onto the wood at the side of a door. *Mrs D. M. Quaid, Medium.* Below it another card exhibited the reverse side. *DO THE DEAD WISH TO SPEAK TO YOU?* Edward put his hand to his throat. He had been looking for Mrs Quaid, but now he felt afraid, he trembled. Had he been *led* here, and if so for some evil purpose? If he saw her again would he *go mad*? It seemed to him now that he had simply forgotten how awful, how weirdly unsavoury, it had been up in that room, what Mrs Quaid did and what she was. How could it be a good thing to see her again? Had he not better go on, ignore the little yellow card, take to his heels and run? He had in his imaginings thought of Mrs Quaid as a tool, a means to an end, a *method* of finding Jesse. What Mrs Quaid might really do and say, what terrible thing she might reveal, or seem to reveal, what lie or sickening image she might plant in his mind forever, was now vivid in his imagination. Mrs Quaid was dangerous. But

443

of course it was now impossible to go away. He pushed the door. It was open. He went in.

When he came to the door of the flat it was closed and, he tried it, locked. There was no notice on it. It was not a seance day. There was no bell, so he tapped on the door, first softly, then loudly. After a long time the door was opened on a chain and someone peered through the slit. 'Yes?'

'I wanted to see Mrs Quaid,' said Edward.

'She's not here.'

The door started to close, but Edward had put his foot against it. 'Mrs Quaid, please let me in, please. I'm a client of yours. I came to a seance. You helped me a lot. I know it's not the right day, but I *must* see you.'

Mrs Quaid undid the chain and Edward pushed the door. He had recognised her voice with its slight Irish tone. Her appearance had changed. She was much thinner. She was not wearing her turban and straggling grey hair clung to her neck and strayed over her hunched shoulders. She stood in the hallway, stooping, the neck of her dress hanging open and her beads hanging free and swinging. She looked sideways at Edward, then shuffled away along the corridor. He closed the door and followed her into the large room where the seance had been held. The curtains were partly pulled and the room was obscure. The chairs, no longer arranged in a semicircle, had been pushed away, some on top of each other, into a corner. Two armchairs stood beside the fireplace where a small lamp was alight and an electric fire occupied the empty grate. The television set, unveiled, stood opposite one of the chairs. Mrs Quaid, stooping, shuffled along, trundling forward like a hedgehog, picked up a bottle which was standing on a small nearby table, and after some hesitation put it into a coal scuttle. She sat down in an armchair, and stared up at Edward, twisting a strand of grey hair round and round her finger. He fetched an upright chair from the other side of the room and set it near her and sat down. He did not fancy the other armchair. During his excursion Mrs Quaid's eyes had closed.

'Mrs Quaid –'

'Oh – yes – what did you want?'

'I want –' What did he want? Edward had not prepared the necessary speech. He said, 'Last time I was here you said something about a man with two fathers. Well, that was me. Do you remember?'

'Of course not,' said Mrs Quaid. 'I am but the vehicle. The spirits speak, not I.'

'Well, a voice spoke to me, it spoke my name and told me to come home. I think that was my father. Well, I went to him, I went home, but now I've lost him again. I don't know where he is, he may be dead only I don't think so, and I thought you might help me.'

'There is no seance this week,' said Mrs Quaid, 'and anyway they only talk with the dead, so unless he's dead there'll be no communication.'

'But there was a communication and he was alive. If you could only get in touch with him again –'

'I don't know anything about that. People imagine all sorts of things, they hear what they want to hear, they see what they want to see, it's not *my* fault. Not everyone is able to understand the voices that come from the other side, not everyone is worthy.'

Edward saw that Mrs Quaid was shuddering. She had put the shawl which had been on the television set round her shoulders and pulled it close up to her neck. Her face was thinner and her white scalp showed through the scanty limp grey locks. Her head, bowed forward so that her eyes, turned up, could barely see him, was nodding compulsively, her long glittering earrings scraping her gaunt neck. With a fussy movement she released the shawl and pulled out the beads which had disappeared inside her dress. She arranged the shawl underneath the beads, tried to tie its corners in a knot but failed, and peered up at Edward with an old cross sad thin-lipped face. It occurred to him that he had not really seen her face on the last occasion, it had been a blank underneath the big jewelled turban.

'Are you ill, Mrs Quaid?' said Edward. 'Can I help you?' He stood up and moved nearer to her.

'Of course I'm ill. But it doesn't matter. It's not catching. What did you say you wanted?'

445

'About my father. I can't find him. He's lost. His name is Jesse –'

'I can't help you. It's not what I do. You have to wait for the spirits. They decide. It's no use saying to them find the boy's father.'

Edward sat down in the armchair. He said, 'If you could just try – I could come to a seance next week –'

Mrs Quaid had closed her eyes and now lay back in the chair her head lolling a little. Her breathing became audible. Edward thought, hell, she's fallen asleep. And how dim the lamp is, she must have put something over it. And the television is on, only I never noticed, there's a picture but no sound. Edward lay back in the chair, breathing in the dust which his movement had raised. He began to look at the television screen. The set was badly adjusted and some shadowy things, perhaps branches of trees, were jigging about. Then the light became brighter, a strong grey light composing a steadier image. There was a line across the screen which Edward soon interpreted as the horizon. He was looking at the sea. He thought, it's a monochrome set, they look awfully dull after colour, or perhaps it's an old film. But there's a lot of light, like a rainy afternoon when the sun's coming through the clouds. The picture changed, showing the edge of the sea, small waves silently breaking, drawing pebbles back after them. The camera moved along the beach, showing sand dunes with wispy grass waving in the wind. Edward thought, it's very soporific, this sort of picture, how slowly it moves, with silent waves breaking and silent wind blowing. Now there was an estuary, the mouth of a river, land on the other side, poplar trees, reeds, birds rising, some big geese heavily getting themselves up, their wings beating on the water. I'd like to hear that sound, thought Edward. The camera was moving inland following the river bank, passing a little stony beach, the river was becoming less wide. Then there was a group of graceful willow trees reflected in the smooth water, and beyond them something jutted out, a wall, like a broken jetty, reaching out into the stream. Then suddenly the camera became still and there was a man. He was standing a little way from the bank, with his back to

Edward, a tall man in dark clothes. Then he moved and turned round and the camera focused on his face, a young man with straight dark hair falling across his brow. Edward did not move except that his finger nails dug into the arms of the chair. As the face came closer Edward thought, *but that's me*. Then he thought, no it isn't, *it's Jesse*. But what's happening, they must be showing some old film about Jesse, what a coincidence, how strange, how *awful*. Jesse was pushing back his lock of hair with one hand, and now walking away toward the river bank. He paused at the bank looming down into the water. Then he turned round again and smiled at Edward.

Edward woke up. There was a strange regular sound. He was lying sprawled in the armchair in Mrs Quaid's big room, the television screen was blank. Mrs Quaid, sitting opposite him, illumined by the lamp, was asleep. The sound he had heard, and which had perhaps awakened him, was her snoring. Edward sat up. There had been a film about Jesse. The television was switched off. He must have dreamt it. He stood up. Then a fear came to him, a terrible sickening suffocating fear like he had had out in the dark that night at Seegard. He made for the door, was unable to open it, twisted the slippery handle to and fro, then wrenched it open. He closed the door of the room behind him, got to the door of the flat and closed that behind him too and went leaping down the stairs. Out in the street he felt almost incredulous, amazed to find ordinary daylight and people walking about on the pavement. He began to walk too. He looked at his watch. It was after four o'clock. He had slept for hours. Then he remembered. *Brownie*. He began helplessly to run, but he knew it was no use, the pub would be shut now. She would have waited and waited and then gone away. He had missed her, he had lost her.

IN HER FIRST instalment of 'memoirs' Mrs Baltram treated us to a recent piece from her thrilling diary (upon which she tells us the 'memoirs' are based), brought in as an example of the 'electrical band', to use her words, which she says surrounds her husband. Some might describe the goings-on at their country residence more simply as evidence of a disorderly life. Mrs Baltram seems to think that being a genius excuses every excess, and being married to one every indiscretion. One almost begins to be sorry for the poor man who is, we gather on other evidence, a sick and senile recluse who gave up working years ago. He appears nevertheless, as of now, as her 'lord', 'a king in full beauty', 'a sorcerer upon a flying horse' and so on. Mrs Baltram's rather banal prose has its purple patches, spurred onward by hyperbole and sugared by sentimentality. She tells us she has 'had to survive', hints that she has 'had her consolations', there are 'penalties attached to marrying a genius'. There certainly are, it seems. The second instalment now tells us in some detail how poor May stood aside while Jesse, 'his eyes ablaze', carried his model Chloe Warriston up to his room. ('Of course to be Jesse's "model" meant only one thing, there was a long line of tawdry maidens' etc.) If they keep up this standard the 'memoirs' promise to be, and are no doubt intended to be, an orgy of indiscretion and revenge. Every page glows with malice. Mrs Baltram is expert in the art, practised it must be admitted by almost every biographer, of seeming to utter warm assessments

448

and even adulation while quietly and ruthlessly diminishing the object of attention. Perhaps we all want to diminish those whose stature accuses us of being small. Few however are able (or willing) to mount such a rich operation of belittlement. Mrs Baltram emerges as an obsessive diarist. The diaries from which her saga derives might indeed make more interesting, even more attractive, reading. Perhaps in due course we shall be treated to the diaries as well! As 'literature' Mrs Baltram's complaint, judging by the first two extracts, seems likely to be worthless, but as a social document it may well be of value. 'May Baltram knew everybody', the effusive introduction tells us. I suppose scandals about the love affairs of clapped-out painters are good for some mileage. Just how good a painter Jesse Baltram was seems, judging from the controversy his wife's writings has already stirred up, to be a matter of considerable dispute. She has certainly made publicity for her own hoard of pictures by enticing references to 'late erotic works not yet known to the public'. The discerning sociologist, now and in the future, will no doubt treat these ramblings as a text for the psychology of women who imagine they are liberated and are emphatically not: a phenomenon of our age. Mrs Baltram has suffered no doubt many stings and arrows of jealous pain. She has clearly planned a plump revenge upon all those pretty models who warmed Jesse's bed. (See the treatment of Chloe Warriston in the current offering.) What she suffered from even more bitterly however, and which she would be reluctant to admit although her epic seems to reek of it, is envy. She was a little woman married to, however one regards him, a considerable man. Her revenge on Jesse for being famous, attractive, talented, charismatic, everything she was not, is likely to be a thorough one. However we need not feel too sorry for Mrs Baltram. She is onto a good thing. After two more newspaper instalments to whet our appetite we are promised the publication of volume one of the memoirs. This book (and there are more to come) will be a best-seller. There is even talk of film rights.

Thomas McCaskerville was sitting in his study at Quitterne reading an article on May Baltram's memoirs by Elspeth Macran. He had also read the second instalment of May's 'ramblings'. He had been alone at Quitterne now for two days. A journalist had rung up on the first day, after that he had silenced the telephone. He had however made some calls, to the clinic to postpone his patients, and to the boarding school where Meredith was to go in the autumn to ask if he could be admitted now. (They said he could.) He had written and received no letters concerning what had happened. He had sent no signal to *them*. He wondered when Harry would come to see him. Harry would *have* to come to see him; Thomas willed him to come and had only to continue his punishing silence to compel him to do so. Thomas wanted to see Harry here at Quitterne, he wanted Harry to come to him under a nervous compulsion as, what – a suppliant, a penitent, an enemy? Whatever it was, Harry would be tormented into coming by an agonising increasing anxiety about Thomas. Thomas had planned no strategy for this encounter. He knew that when the time came he would find the right tone, the words, the mask. Until then Thomas would not move in the matter of Meredith. He must, till Harry came, till he could thus *find out* something, be simply silent and absent. Of course there could be no question of speaking to anybody else. When he had received information, then he could begin to act. He wanted to get Meredith out of that house. He wanted him to be somewhere absolutely else, on neutral territory, where he could be attended to without – it seemed incredible how much had changed – having to treat with alien powers. It was hard on Meredith to translate him so rapidly. But it was hard on Meredith anyway. The idea that his son had 'surprised' Midge and her lover in Thomas's house was detestable to him, his wounded imagination kept returning to it to supply an endless variety of detail, and this alone could make him feel that he would never again have clean thoughts. He had always been quietly strict with Meredith, Midge had sometimes accused him of being too severe, but this regime was contained within a deep wordless understanding between himself and the boy who was so like

450

him. Thomas respected the laconic dignity of his son and gestureless love passed between them. Against this bond, against the possibility of either silence or speech, an obscene offence had been committed. However Thomas did not conceive of any loss of the boy; in the face of whatever might be, he and Meredith were one.

Thomas was able, now, to *think* about Meredith, and about Harry. He was able to 'take up positions'. About Stuart he decided not to speculate, content for the present to regard him as an aberration which would pass leaving Harry in possession. He could not think about Midge, in relation to her he was a raw mass of suffering. His mind, unable to sustain coherent understanding, fell apart into craven incredulity, bleeding deprivation, sobbing childish misery, tragic attitudinising, cold cruel curiosity, and rage. He was astounded to discover how much anger he was capable of. Of course 'anyone could have told' Thomas, and indeed he told himself that it was likely that his young wife would attract admirers. She was so pretty, so animated, so well-dressed, so unlike the person whom younger Thomas had expected and *wanted* to marry. She was, for him, an improbable wife, a marvellous visitation, a strange juxtaposition, and that had been for him a source of joy never of uneasiness. Her falling in love with him, and she had indubitably been in love with him, was a proof of the abundant unpredictable richness of life, an overplus of quite surprising delight. She gave him a happiness which he had imagined to be unattainable, even alien. Within him now his love, intact, even his happiness, his ignorant incredulous happiness, remained to torment him, a huge trembling sensibility which could suffer but not diminish or die. I love her, I love her, he said to himself, sometimes covering his face and moaning. Why cannot that be enough to be the whole of reality?

He accused himself, and tried ingeniously to accuse himself more and more. Why had he not, somehow, defended her, kept her safe? Why had he, with his professional knowledge of so many surprising secrets, never conjectured that his wife might look elsewhere? He was perfectly aware that she had acquaintances about whom he knew little, about whom indeed he never even questioned her. He had been inattentive, self-absorbed, his love had been sleepy, he had not only taken her for granted, he had taken his love for her for granted too. No doubt it was also a kind of vanity, a sense of his superiority to any possible rival, a prevailing consciousness that people were always a bit afraid of him and would never dare to cross him. But then, in his defence, his love, his happiness would cry out that he had trusted her so perfectly, with a perfect childlike simplicity which reigned here, and here alone, inside the achievement of his marriage. And then his terrible anger would conjure up the hateful *pair*, the tormenting *they* who had so utterly destroyed his joy and poisoned his mind and crippled him with pain. He could, he felt, have so much better borne an honest loss, a truthful departure. And how much easier too with another man, a stranger, any man but that man whom he had so full-heartedly liked and trusted.

He pictured his wife's face, so radiantly full of lively sympathetic self-satisfaction, of what he had read as absolutely innocent *joie de vivre*. Had he regarded her too much as a happy dependent child? That Midge, his own dear loving private Midge, could have planned and executed a long cold-blooded deception . . . He reflected upon the details of it. He did not dare to doubt the passionate need which had even led his wife to deceive him in his own house. Two years, and how they must have longed for each other. The loving telephone call as soon as Thomas had left the house. The anxious careful planning of timetables. The casual questions about when Thomas would be away, where and how long. The fine calculation, the ruthless scheming which went on behind those familiar smiles. The different face that looked beyond his shoulder as he embraced her. Yes, the ruthless *will* that made him into nothing. The whole full-blooded flow of another life happening in the interstices of his presence to her. So rather he himself, his claim upon her, represented the dull lifeless interval, the tedious and hateful routine to which she returned unwillingly from a bright place of passion and tenderness, with its own private language, its luxuriant mythology and secret codes of love. Thomas saw it now, that other place, as a tented camp, full of activity and joyous bustle, rippling pennants and high silken canopies and stirring trumpet calls and drums. All the colour of life was *there*, while *here* had been drained down to a monotonous grey. Two years; and he had not even noticed, not seen or felt, the relentless process which had been depriving him of what he so utterly relied upon and so much loved.

Thomas recalled that he had indeed noticed and reflected on Midge's recent 'moods', and had decided not to worry! He decided now that he should not review the intimate details of their marriage seeking for 'causes' of what had happened. The causes were no doubt multiform, probably deeply hidden, at any rate not to be probed or brooded over at present. Not everything is improved and clarified by being dug up. Thomas had left his own puritanical shyness undisturbed. He valued chaste instincts and held them, in himself and others, apt to promote happiness and the strong orderly passion of real loving. He had always felt, between himself and Midge, a deep and authoritative sexual flow which mocked the vulgarity of text books. She had loved him, needed him, teased his solemnity, clung to his strength, admired, esteemed and trusted him, given him her lively beauty and the entirety of her physical presence. Or so he had imagined; how far back should he now dare to look and see it all as false?

Thomas was not used to misery, his deep grief at his parents' deaths had not been like this. It was as if there were a great void where his love for Midge had been, and yet how could that possibly be – it was just that he was suffering in a new and dreadful way, like the invention of a new torture, *real* suffering, his love transmuted into absolute pain. How could he, Thomas, suffer so? He was also not used to uncontrollable anger. He felt at times a rage, which might become obsessive, against the conniving pair, amazement and shock at their treachery, and against Harry sometimes a violent disgust amounting to hatred. Thomas was aware that he must soon check and dissolve these destructive emotions; but he lacked any compelling vision of the territory beyond. His pride, his dignity, deeply wounded, demanded aid, redress. A resigned forgiving surrender which the world

453

would interpret as weakness? (So he cared about the world?) A solitary meditative 'generous' understanding, likely to be indefinitely prolonged? A cool plan of campaign to destroy his rival? And regain a sulky hostile consort? There seemed to be no solution. No good would come of rushing to London, he had, for now, to wait upon events, hope for miracles, discipline his mind. His love for Midge, twisting and turning, grown violent and wild, tormented him at times with visions of happiness and joy which were proffered by his craven imagination as a cheating solace, how it would all somehow painlessly 'come right' in the end. I love her, I want her, he cried again and again. But he could not have what he desired so desperately and, above all else, his dear wife back as she once was, tender and true.

These repetitive thoughts, already forming themselves into the mechanical patterns which Thomas recognised and dreaded, were halted by a sound from outside the house, coming to him through the open window, the sound for which he had been waiting of car tyres upon the gravel. Thomas rose and watched from the window as Harry alighted. The car door closed with a discreet click. As Thomas waited for the bell to ring he combed his hair.

'I believe you don't care,' said Harry.

'It would be convenient for you to think so.'

'You don't want a divorce?'

'No, of course not.'

'So you don't mind?'

'I now know you are a callous liar,' said Thomas, 'am I also to put you down as a fool?'

The emotional shock of the meeting for both of them had been even greater than they expected, so that they had spent the first twenty minutes talking almost at random to conceal their agitation. Both were determined to keep calm, to reveal no weakness, to dominate, to win. They had not expected to be overcome by a kind of floundering confusion which landed them in sudden moments of blankness and anti-climax. So far from being too dramatic, the scene was proving, from the point of view of any progress it was likely to make, not dramatic enough. Thomas had an advantage in being less dependent on alcohol, which he was resolutely not offering to Harry, whose need for it in a crisis was even visible in his restless gestures and roving eyes.

'We've got to be calm about this,' said Harry, 'be sane and destroy as little as possible. I hope we can remain friends.'

'Of course we can't,' said Thomas, 'you seem to be incapable of thinking. What did you want anyway?'

'What do you mean?'

'You came here uninvited, presumably to say something. Could you get on with saying it?'

'God, you are a cold fish,' said Harry. 'Why pretend that you're surprised that I came, didn't you expect me, didn't you want some explanation, some account of it all, or did you just intend to get on with your work and ignore it?'

'Why have you come running to me? Do you want me to comfort you?'

'Hell no! I should have thought you were the one in need of comfort.'

'My wife informed me, and I believe her, that she no longer loves you. She does not want a divorce. I should have thought this leaves you with no alternative but to get out of our lives. I certainly don't want to go over the details of your defunct love affair. Since you appear to have nothing to say I suggest you go. I see no need to talk to you and I don't want to see you again. I've finished with you.'

This speech was delivered with a venom which surprised and daunted Harry. He realised how, with a double-think which now indeed seemed naïve, he had expected Thomas, while certainly upset, even angry, to be also somehow still his old self, ironical, cool, helpful, sympathetic, full of patient understanding. Harry had come to Quitterne because, as Thomas had discerned, he had to, the need to see Thomas, simply to be in his presence was, now that all was known, overwhelming. He needed the comfort, the relief, of having *seen* Thomas and found him, even if not actually forgiving, calm, detached, ready for quiet rational talk. But Harry also needed, before finally determining his own strategy, to find out what Midge had said to Thomas, and to do this without letting Thomas know how little she had said to him. He had, since the revelation, been with her and talked to her but without being able to understand her. She was like a wild thing, restless, very disturbed, averting her head, exclaiming rather than conversing. He had telephoned her house on the evening of the revelation but got no reply. He dared not go round for fear of Thomas. The next day she answered the telephone, told him that Thomas had gone to Quitterne and that he might come and see her. He came, full of hope, and found himself sitting with her in the drawing room like a visitor, like a suitor. The shock of Thomas's arrival still hung in the room, the papers flung upon the table, the door flung open. Harry was already beginning to regret that he had not stayed and faced Thomas at once, though he realised too that he would have been paralysed and, terrible to admit it, ashamed. If he had stayed he could at least have got, what he now felt sadly without, a general idea of the situation. It was only when he saw Midge again that it occurred to him to wonder whether she had told Thomas about Stuart. He hoped she had not, he hoped and sometimes felt sure that 'the Stuart thing' would pass, perhaps very soon, and that all would then be just as he desired, as he had in his imaginings pictured the time 'after Thomas knew': Midge in shock, shedding tears of relief, running to Harry, staying with him, settling at last into the joy and rest of being entirely his. With anguish he stared at her, studied her, as she walked about the room, sighing and disordering her hair. She told him, without being asked, that after Thomas's departure she had gone round to Stuart's lodging and found him gone, the room vacated, no address left. When Harry rang in the morning her first question had been about Stuart, whether he had come home. When Harry came to her she let him take her hand, but asked him how she could find out where Stuart was, who could she ask? She showed, as she flung about the room, no consciousness of Harry's distress, his grief, his fear, his need for reassurance which now he dared not voice for fear of prompting some awful dismissal. It was better, for now, if she accepted his presence as that of an old friend, someone with a right to be there, almost like a doctor. At any rate she did not at once send him away, and twice exclaimed in the course of what was virtually a staccato monologue punctuated by his soothing murmurs, 'Oh Harry – Harry –' as if she felt he could help her somehow; and this gave him hope. 'Thomas has gone.' 'Where can I find Stuart? I could ask his friends.' 'What have I done, oh what have I done.' Harry said things like, 'Do be calm, don't worry, I'll find Stuart, don't worry about Thomas, just rely on me, don't forget me, everything will be all right.' He said nothing about his intention to visit Thomas. Once or twice he framed and reframed in his mind the question: what did Thomas say to you? What did he do? But he did not utter it, it was too awful a question to intrude upon her extraordinary state of mind. During this time, and when he saw her again the next day, he formed the view, and there was some comfort in it, that she was actually temporarily insane; and in his double-think image of his meeting with Thomas he included some unimaginable conversation wherein he *consulted* Thomas about Midge's health.

Another idea which had hovered in Harry's head as, in an anguish of haste once he had realised he had to see Thomas, he drove too fast along the motorway, was that there was to be a reconciliation scene. Harry would dominate the interview, sympathising with Thomas who, having lost his wife, had understandably run away. In this posture Harry could admit a degree of guilt and could even, in some carefully worded formula, ask Thomas's pardon. After that they could talk like men of the world. But now, as he looked across the desk at Thomas's face and heard the tone of Thomas's voice, such gestures were impossible. It was war. So Midge had told Thomas she no longer loved Harry. Or had she? Thomas could have invented that. And had she told him about Stuart?

Harry replied, 'It's not true that Midge no longer loves me, that's your invention. Why do you keep referring to her as your wife? Her name is Midge. And why did you run away from London if you really believed that she wanted to stay with you? What you say doesn't make sense. I had a long talk with her yesterday and again today. Of course she had been in a state of shock, but she's getting over it, she is deeply and permanently in love with me, which perhaps is something you can't imagine. She was never really in love with you, she was never really *married* to you. She and I have discussed all this of course, I know what things were like, I know everything. She was always afraid of you. That's why we had to tell all those lies which I detested so. All right, we were at fault there and we're sorry. With me she's a different being, she's happy, she's free, you wouldn't recognise her. You're a psychiatrist, you must know when someone's unhappy, you have seen how restless and resentful and discontented she was. With me she's *at home*. You must realise you've lost her, don't fight it, let her go, she'll go anyway, she's gone. You ran off and left her because you realised she wanted to be with me and you couldn't stand it. You've given in, you've surrendered, you recognise that she'd gone for good, she's mine. I didn't want to say all this, I wanted to be generous, even to say I was sorry, but you've forced my hand. She's said so many things about you which no one who loved you could possibly utter, she said you were cold, without any tenderness, without any humour, she said you neglected her, you bored her –'

'Those are lies,' said Thomas, 'foul contemptible lies.'

'They aren't actually. If you really thought she'd left me why did you go? Why did you leave her, why did you leave Meredith, you don't even seem to care about him. She's right, you're cold, you don't deserve that wonderful woman, I think you don't really want her, why don't you face it? Good God, you're supposed to be good at conducting interviews with disturbed people, you don't seem to be doing very well with this one. Of course you're the victim this time, you're the patient, don't you see, *you've got nothing to say.*'

Thomas, red in the face, sat still, staring at him, visibly trembling. Then he drew in his lips and lowered his gaze and took off his glasses. Harry thought, I've won, I've won her, she's mine! He's speechless with rage but at least he's speechless. Perhaps he does want to get rid of her after all, why didn't I see this earlier, why didn't I believe it – I've won, I've won!

With deliberation but quickly Thomas pushed his chair back and opened a drawer in his desk. Harry sprang to his feet.

At that moment something happened in the room. A brown flurry crossed it diagonally and recrossed it drawing quick jagged lines in the air. There was a soft whirring sound, then a loud bump. A robin had flown in through the open window, flown about, and then crashed against the glass.

Thomas leapt up, he said to Harry, 'Close the door.'

The bird was beating its wings painfully against the window pane. Thomas attempted to open the window wider, but the sash was stiff. Harry said, 'Mind him, mind him.' The robin flew away from the window and began rapidly circling the ceiling, occasionally thumping its frail small body against the walls. Harry came to help Thomas and raised the window a little further. The bird, after fluttering for a while in a top corner of the room, fell down onto the floor behind a pile of books where it stayed ominously still. With an exclamation of distress Thomas began to pull the books away. Harry kept saying, 'Oh go out, go out, that way, that way.' As the books began to collapse round about it the robin rose again, collided with a wall and came to rest on top of a cupboard, looking down with its bright brown eyes. Then, with an air of decision, it flew downward and out through the window, and with a graceful movement of freedom swooped, then rose and perched on the copper beech tree, looking back toward the house.

'I was afraid he might get caught in the sash,' said Harry.

Thomas drew the window down a little, then closed it. Not looking at Harry he said softly, 'Go away, go away.'

Harry said, 'Were you reaching for a gun?'

Thomas after a pause said, 'No, of course not.'

'Thomas –'

'*Go away.*'

'I'm sorry.'

Thomas made a gesture as of taking note of the statement and opened the door. Harry went out. The sound of his car followed almost at once. Thomas stood still a while, then opened the window again and let in the song of the birds.

Later he wandered downstairs and out into the garden, crossing the uneven grey pebbles onto the grass. He walked on a little into the edge of the wood where the light green haze still showed the blue sky and distant rhododendrons were blurred with mauve and pink. He thought, how typical of Harry to imagine I was reaching for a gun when all I wanted was something to clean my glasses! But if he still thinks I was, let him. He lives in a world of romance, romanticised violence. The gun idea, Thomas reflected as he walked along a path between the dead flowers of the bluebells, was in a way a right one. I could have killed him at that moment. Why? Of course what he was saying was nonsense – or was it, was all of it? It was a stream of the most deadly and awful insults. But I couldn't reply, I couldn't say this and this is untrue because – and I couldn't just shout I love my wife, I won't give her up. Violence seemed the only response and for me it was impossible. He was right, I have nothing to say, he was simply winning. Good God, I might have burst into tears. As he thought this he found he was still trembling with anger and shock. That robin was providential. Also, though whether this was a good thing or not Thomas was not able to decide, the incident had enabled Harry to say he was sorry and Thomas, at least, with a wave of his hand, to receive the utterance.

Already the red-brick wall of the Shaftoes' house could be seen through the greenery and Thomas turned back as he always did at this point. How to its depths his life had changed he was now beginning to understand. Would he have pure quiet free thoughts ever again? He felt intense piercing unhappiness. Not despair, the weakness and relaxation of despair would have been a relief. He felt alert, active, capable of decision, but in anguish.

The word *lâcheté* came into his head, a word he had always felt to be more expressive than the English 'cowardice'. He said to himself, *je suis un lâche*. Why had he abandoned Midge, left the house, left Meredith behind? Harry was right to pick on this as a winning point. It now seemed just as clear to Thomas that he ought to have stayed as it had seemed then that he had to go. Had he left to save his dignity? Or because he was afraid that disgust at Midge's treachery might make him hate her? *Could* he hate her as, just now, he hated Harry? It was a terrible thought. He had run away from her as from

460

his own violence, so as not to find himself detesting the sight of her. Suppose he were to go back now and find her gone, fled, would he not have himself to blame? But of course she would not leave the house so long as Meredith was there, Meredith would, simply by his existence, counsel her well. It never occurred to Thomas to wonder whether Meredith might take sides against him. He did wonder how and for how long what Meredith had seen would affect, perhaps embarrass, his relations with his father. Would they ever speak of it? How endless and horrible the consequences were.

Thomas had been waiting for Harry to come. Harry had come and something had happened. Now it was Thomas's move. He thought, I ought to go back to London and be with Midge. I need to know whether Stuart has actually killed her love for Harry, as she said he had. Such a thing was possible, and though Thomas had never seen anything quite like it he had seen similar things, he could see how it might 'work'. He wondered if he should go and see Stuart. If Stuart was, with whatever results, a 'temporary craze' for Midge, it might be wiser to leave him alone for the present. Or was Thomas simply reluctant to appear before young Stuart in the role of the husband of the woman who loved him? Surely Stuart would act with sense and discretion, probably just run. Or would he? Was it conceivable that, however inadvertently, he might *encourage* her? I'm a calculator, he thought, a manipulator. I set things going and leave them, such as sending Edward back to that room. I'm a careless gardener, I plant something and go away. I said the 'right things', that is the clever things, to Midge and left her to digest them.

As he came into sight of the house a large car drew up on the gravel. For just a moment Thomas thought it *must* be Midge, come running back to him, and he felt a shock of joy. Then a familiar figure wearing a trilby hat stepped slowly out of the car. It was Mr Blinnet. Oh God, thought Thomas, this breaks every rule in the book. He ran forward.

EDWARD WAS STANDING outside Railway Cottage. The sun was shining and a slight haze, a sad rather dusty golden afternoon haze, hung over the flat land. Perfectly still in the windless light, white cow parsley and mauve blooms of tall grass hung above the railway cutting. A mass of little bright blue flowers were growing at Edward's feet: their name, long forgotten, flashed into Edward's head: germander speedwell. A large *For Sale* notice was propped up in the yew tree. The window which Edward had broken on his previous visit now hung wide, a little off its hinges. He climbed in, his foot sinking into the damp spongy surface of the sofa which had been moved against the window. Rain and storm had evidently entered, and even in summer sunshine the room smelt of mould and the cold of unuse. Most of the furniture had been removed leaving the sofa and a couple of broken chairs and a worn rug. He crossed the room, hearing his feet sound on the bare floor, and looked into the bedroom where the old iron bedstead remained upon which Jesse and Chloe had once so warmly lain wrapped in each other's beauty. He returned to the main room. The place was bare, rotting, ruined, soon to be overtaken by weather, by nature, by fungus and green intrusive shoots. As Edward stood and listened he fancied he could hear the soft murmur of this intrusion, the yew trees scraping against the window, the ivy lifting the slates, the insects working deep inside the wood. He shuddered and let himself out of the door, closing it carefully behind him. He pushed the broken window back into place, jamming the warped wood. Then he descended to the level of the track and set off again, trying to recall the map and ignoring the path to the right which led to Seegard and along which on that fateful night Sarah Plowmain had trotted to lead Midge and Harry to their doom.

The grassy track went on, curving gently, becoming as it proceeded more overgrown with nettles and clumpy sorrel. It also began to rise slightly and Edward could feel under his feet the hard stony surface on which the grass was growing. The cutting fell away and he could see, turning to look back, fields of shimmering reddish barley, and beyond them an extraordinary tract of colour, a yellow which exuded itself in intense powdery light seeming to make the summer sky behind it dark by contrast. This must be the fields of rape which Ilona had spoken of. The colour reminded him of something: it was the violent terrifying yellow of Jesse's abstract pictures. As he turned and went on he saw, rising above some trees not far away, the tower of Seegard. He was now bearing to the right upon a snake-like eminence, walking a little above his surroundings upon a low embankment on either side of which the earth was marshy, dried mud with watery cracks irregularly covered with wiry marsh grass. Small ragged willows, elders and hazels still obscured the view ahead and the soft warm hazy air, gently vibrating with light, flickered in Edward's eyes. The flat creamy flower-heads of the elder, covered with bees, exuded a strong smell of Seegard wine. He had hastened from the station to the bus, and then directly from the road along the rail track to the cottage, keeping well away from Seegard. He had had little to eat and felt empty and a little giddy and the sound of the bees seemed to be resounding inside his empty head. He was carrying his jacket and sweating in the heat of the afternoon. Then suddenly, passing out of the trees, he saw the sea appearing quite close to him on his left, a calm glittering light blue; and when he stopped in a new silence he could hear it very quietly touching the shingle. A faint cool air came from it, too gentle to be called a breeze, but giving relief from the inland torpor. Edward reflected later that if on that very first day when he was looking for the sea he had simply trusted his own sense of

463

direction and his *knowledge* that the railway coted the shore and must lead to it, had he not stopped at Railway Cottage, he would not have met Brownie, and would not, on the day of his 'hallucination', have been in such an agitated hurry that he did not stay to understand what he had seen; might indeed have been with Jesse that morning, so that Jesse would not have left the house and become lost . . . Thoughts which it was better not to think.

In spite of the sick frightened preoccupation with which he travelled Edward could not help feeling eased by seeing the sea and stepping down off the grass onto the clean stony shingle, the brown smoothed flints of the sea shore of which Ilona had told him. He marched over the crunching stones, then stood a while and watched the small waves breaking, affectionately pawing at the land, and heard the faint rhythmic swish of their fall and the grating sound of their withdrawal. Black and white oystercatchers were running along the verge of the water uttering their trilling fluty cries. But he could not enjoy the sea today, it filled him with loneliness and foreboding and sorrow, and the clear curving line of the horizon did not inspire in him its usual magisterial calm. Today the sea's magic was other, alien and dangerous in the sunshine, its blue very cold. He went on, first beside the water, then returning to the raised bank of the railway which was easier to walk on. After a little while he could see the beach ahead of him crossed by a stone wall and a line of white broken water stretching out into the sea. This must be the little harbour of the 'fisherfolk' Mother May had mentioned, whose village 'fell into the fen' after the great storm and flood which also put an end to the railway. The harbour when he reached it seemed almost intact, both piers, one straight, one crooked, enclosing a space of calm water where some terns were fishing. The shattered remains of the station platform appeared suddenly beside him but of the village itself he could at first see no trace. Then gazing about he began to discern here and there whole large fragments of stone walls, leaning over at strange angles as in mediaeval pictures of destroyed cities, surrounded by watery pits and overgrown by ivy and wild buddleia. Edward did not pause, however, indeed he had now begun to run, as he could see the river estuary not far ahead.

The railway track turned slightly inland but Edward ran straight on, running upon fairly firm grass and leaping over occasionally stony grassy humps. The river, which had disappeared from view behind high reeds and willows, now opened at his feet so suddenly that he nearly fell in. He stopped and looked at the wide exceedingly calm expanse of purposively moving water, reflecting blue sky and some tall poplars on the other side. Edward stood there and his legs positively ached with a desire to stand still, to turn back. Then he felt the fear again, the terrible black choking fear which he had now felt twice before. His diaphragm was pierced, the lower part of his body filled with blackness. He panted for breath. Breathing deeply he forced himself to move forward, to walk slowly upstream, gauging the diminishing width of the river and looking over the bank into the reeds which grew in clumps of varying size in the stream, joined here and there by white comfrey and yellow irises and floating beds of water crowfoot. He kept looking for a certain formation of willow trees, but there were many willows, like and yet not like what he could recall. Then he saw where the stream had made a little beach with stones, and some way beyond it was visible a stone structure jutting out into the water which he saw at once must be the remains of the bridge or causeway upon which the railway had crossed the river. Edward, panting again and with his hand at his throat, walked on a little and then stopped. He was dizzied with gazing down into the dark reedy water. He thought, I must have passed the place and *there's nothing there*. Oh let there be nothing and let me be free to go home. I've tried, I've tried. But would that be freedom, would he ever now be free? He thought, I'll do another fifty yards and then go. Then he saw the willows, at least a cluster of willows which seemed to stir his memory in a new way. He went on more quickly until he was near the trees then knelt down on the bank, peering intently over the edge. At first he saw only his own reflection, the dark shape of his head thrust out over a space of water. He began to see more deeply down among

465

the reed beds, moving a little upstream, still upon his knees. Then he saw Jesse.

He knew the terrible thing that he saw was Jesse because – how could he doubt it – this was where Jesse himself had told him to look. Also, strangely floating up almost to the surface, was a pale bloated hand with a ruby-red ring upon it. What was below was darker, a rounded bundle trussed in tangles of weeds. Obeying an instant compulsion Edward reached down and touched the hand. It was soft and very cold. He touched the ring and then, still as in obedience, he drew it off. It came away smoothly with ease, and he put it on the middle finger of his left hand which he only now remembered was where Jesse had worn it. Then he staggered up, turned away and tried unsuccessfully to vomit. His sounds of woe broke what had seemed a silence but was now full of the song of birds. He sat down in the grass with his back to the river, holding his head in his hands. Then he got up and went back and leaned out over the reed bed. It was still there. He could now see the hump of the shoulders, the big head bent forward, some hair moving in the water. Tears streamed down Edward's face and he began to sob, standing there leaning over the edge of the bank. His tears fell among the reeds and into the river. He sobbed loudly for some time, uttering his dreadful anguish as a cry for help. But of course there was no one there to hear him. What should he do, what was he going to do, he now at last wondered. Should he attempt to pull the drowned body out, could he do so? Forcing himself against a sickening repugnance he knelt again and leaning down felt for the humped shoulders and tried to take hold. As his hands slipped over muddy textile and touched flesh he had an instant fear that the dead man might suddenly grip him and pull him in. He felt the weight but could not move what he now saw to be deeply embedded in tangled reed stems and roots and water weed. He would have to get down into the river and unwind . . . He could not do it. Besides, if he set the thing free it might be instantly taken from him by the force of the stream and swept away into the sea.

As he sat back again on the grass and blinked his eyes against the light he wondered: *is this too an illusion?* He stood up and shook his body like a dog, pinched his hand and his arm, and looked all about him at the empty landscape, at the open mouth of the river, at the configuration of willows, at the broken stone stump of the railway bridge. Then he looked down carefully, observing his perceptions and his state of mind. This was certainly no dream, it felt quite unlike the other occasion. But did not *this* prove the other real, that other vision when Jesse had seemed to look up at him through the water and smile? Or could *that* perhaps somehow prove that *this* was unreal? It's certainly not unreal, thought Edward. As for the other – perhaps I'll never be certain – I mustn't think about it now. Then he turned about sharply, with a sudden impression that there was someone standing behind him. But the fen was flat and empty as before.

He noticed that he had stopped crying but his face was all wet with tears. He mopped it with the back of his hand. He thought, I must go to Seegard and tell them. Oh God how awful. Then he thought, but suppose when I bring them back there is nothing there? Supposing it all happens over again? I should go raving mad, I should hurl myself into the sea, I should start swimming and swimming looking for Jesse. He put his hand over his mouth and turned away. He thought, anyway I'll mark the spot. He had thrown his jacket down on the bank. He picked it up and mounted it like a little scarecrow upon a stick, conspicuous above the grass. Then he set off following the river inland and was soon able to see, closer than he had expected, the tower of Seegard and the high roof of the barn. At the same moment he caught sight of a figure, a man, coming towards him, a tall man with a beard. Edward said to himself, it's Jesse, it *must* be, it was an hallucination after all, a second one . . . But this idea lasted for a second, and he recognised, now near to him, one of the tree men, the one who had brought him Brownie's letters. Edward thought, I won't say anything. Then he thought, people might suspect me, that man will see my marker and –

Edward said to the man, 'I've just found the body of Jesse Baltram, he's drowned, he's in the reeds, down there just beyond the old railway bridge, I've left my jacket on a stick –'

467

'The guv'nor? Are you sure it's him? Is he drowned then? I thought he might be when we heard he'd gone.'

'Why did you think that?' said Edward.

'That'd be just like him, that'd be the way he'd choose to take himself off. I'll go and have a look at him. Are you going to tell them up at the house?' The man seemed pleased and excited.

'It was an accident,' said Edward.

By the time he reached the main door of Seegard the sky had become overcast. The tower was surrounded by screaming swifts. He opened the door and entered the Atrium which was huge and dark and felt chilly after the warmth outside. He remembered how it had looked to him then, on his first evening, and for a moment he seemed to forget or not believe what he now knew and had come to tell. Oh let it be over soon, he thought, let it be over soon – whatever it is that is now at once to come. He called out. Only when he had called did he hear what he had said. 'Ilona!' Silence. He walked across the slates which were cold and felt damp and sticky underfoot, and opened the Transition door. 'Hello!' No one. He thought, can they all have *gone*? He walked back to the Interfectory door. The room was empty. He thought, there's no fire burning, then he thought why should there be, it's summer now. The news he had to bring was eating him like a fox. He went to the tower door expecting it to be locked, but it opened and he went into the large downstairs 'exhibition room' where there was a subdued but very lucid light. The room was intensely quiet. He was about to call out again when he saw that two people were standing on the other side of it gazing at him, Bettina and Mother May. The canvases had been moved about, some propped against the wall.

'Hello, Edward,' said Mother May, 'we're checking our catalogue of the pictures. You're just in time to help us. Are you all right? We're so glad to see you, aren't we, Bettina? We wondered when you'd come back.'

As Edward came towards them he felt his throat closing up,

468

as in dreams when one tries to articulate but cannot. He sat down on a chair close to them.

'What's the matter, Edward?' said Bettina. Their repetition of his name sounded menacing. They stood looking down at him with curiosity.

Edward had automatically opened the buttons of his shirt and passed his hand over his throat and chest. He had run most of the way from the river and had been panting and sweating. He felt now as if, since he had entered the house, he had been holding his breath. He look long deep breaths, shivering with emotion.

'Edward, what *is* it?' said Mother May, but she sounded more curious than anxious.

'Jesse,' said Edward.

'What?'

'He's dead, drowned.'

'What do you mean?' said Bettina.

Edward thought, do they know, have they always known? 'I found his body down by the estuary, caught in the reeds. He's dead.'

Mother May and Bettina looked at each other. Bettina said, 'Let's move out of here, shall we?' It sounded like a suggestion to adjourn for coffee.

The two women moved towards the door. Edward, gasping for breath, and idiotically carrying his chair, followed. He left the chair at the doorway. Bettina stood aside to let him pass into the Interfectory. Then she quietly closed the door, locked it, and replaced the key on the chimneypiece. Edward sat in an armchair, then pulled himself up again, the two women sat, he stood by the fireplace.

'Now what *is* all this?' said Mother May severely. 'Do calm down.' Today she and Bettina had their hair done in identical styles, every pin matching, the long heavy hair bunched in a long neat bun suspended upon the back of the head, showing the neck at the back. They were wearing their day dresses and long blue aprons. They stared at him with their similar youthful faces.

'He's dead,' said Edward. 'I saw him. I saw his body down near the mouth of the river. If you come I'll show you. This

469

time it's not a dream.' Of course it wasn't last time either, he thought or was it, what did I decide? Oh let them start *believing* me.

'You are not yourself, Edward,' said Mother May, 'please talk to us more quietly. Have you eaten today? Did you have any lunch? Bettina will set out something for you.' Bettina did not move however.

Edward was thinking, why on earth did I tell the tree man? Now if he's *gone* I'll never know and I'll go mad. The tree man might want him not to be found, he might think someone would blame him. He said, 'If you will come I will show you. But hadn't we better ring up – oh of course we can't – tell the police, get an ambulance –' Oh God, he thought, what's the use of an ambulance, am I not sure he's dead, or was that last time? He said, 'It's true, it's *true*, he's *dead*, why do you *torture* me by *pretending*!'

'We aren't pretending,' said Bettina.

'Where's Ilona? She'll believe me.'

'Don't talk so fast, Edward,' said Mother May, 'it's not easy to hear what you're saying.'

'Where do you think he is then, if he's not dead and not in the river?'

'What an odd question. We don't know where he is and I think you don't either –'

'I saw him just now with my own eyes, I *touched* him, look, look!' Edward thrust forward his left hand displaying the ruby ring.

The women rose and came forward, gazing at the ring.

'Is that Jesse's ring?' said Bettina to Mother May.

Mother May turned away. She said, 'It may not be your fault, but you have brought death into this house, you killed your friend, you came here with your stained hands, you brought death with you, Jesse saw him sitting beside you at the table –'

'Oh –!' Edward ran out of the room and across the Atrium, pounding the slates and continuing to moan as he ran. He slithered and crashed against the door, got it open, and rushed out into the air. The avenue was dark but the sun was shining on the yellow fields beyond the ilexes. Edward ran across the

470

terrace, and into the avenue. He wanted to find *someone to tell*, someone in authority who would believe him, anyone who would *do* something. Then he decided he must first go back and see if it was *still there*. He turned round and began to run back the way he had come, only now the country looked different and he was not sure which way to go. Tears came into his eyes and he howled out aloud, 'Jesse, Jesse, Jesse!' Perhaps he should simply go up to the tower and see if his father was sitting as usual upright in his bed and smiling? Perhaps that was why they did not believe him?

Then he saw, coming across the grass from the direction of the river estuary, a man, then a group of men following, carrying something, carrying, he saw as they came nearer, a body upon a stretcher. They had covered the face with Edward's coat. Mother May and Bettina had come out of the Atrium door, and they saw the funeral cortege. The tree men were bringing Jesse home. As they came nearer Mother May began to scream. Edward could see her struggling with Bettina, who wanted to lead her back into the house.

'YOU'VE DONE NOTHING but cause trouble, pain and strife, that's what your good intentions amount to. Why have you come back?'

'I'm sorry, Dad,' said Stuart. 'I suppose you saw the evening papers?'

'Yes, about Jesse Baltram being dead. So what?'

'I was worried about Ed. But he's not here?'

'I don't know where he is. What have you done to Midge? Did you summon her and accuse her?'

'I didn't summon her, she came.'

'I don't believe you. You bewitched her. And you did accuse her.'

'I said something about not lying – I can't remember what I said –'

'You can't remember what you said! You casually wreck other people's lives and you can't remember how! And you've done permanent damage to Meredith by your sentimental tampering.'

'Who says so?'

'Midge does. He cries all day. Children of that age never recover.'

'I haven't harmed him. Perhaps he's upset about other things.'

'And now his crazy vindictive father has sent him off to boarding school so that he can cry somewhere else. Are you pleased to think that you make children cry?'

'Don't be angry with me, Dad. What is Midge going to do?'

'So that's what you came to find out, you're after her.'

'No, I'm not, I'm not going to see her again –'

'When you've made someone thoroughly wretched by your prodding you say you won't see them again! You desire her.'

'No –'

'You came here to discuss her.'

'No – you mentioned her –'

'I didn't, you asked what she was going to do. I'll tell you. She's going to be an anchoress.'

'A what?'

'A female hermit. She's going to live alone in a bed-sitter and give up sex and do good to people.'

'She won't be able to,' said Stuart.

'She can try. Waiting for you to come. You've changed her, you've made her natural life cease to function, she's become a pathetic automaton.'

'That's nonsense,' said Stuart, 'she's in a state of shock, it's the idea of Thomas knowing. It's not me, it's being found out. She'll recover.'

'You think everyone will recover, you're wrong. *Are* you seeing her?'

'No, I told you – Hasn't she said?'

'She says she can't find you. I don't know if that's true. She lies, everyone lies.'

'Dad – she isn't *here* is she –?'

'No. So you did come to look for her! She's at Thomas's place. Thomas is in the country.'

'When she's got over the shock she'll probably leave Thomas and come to you.'

'You'll try to stop her.'

'No –'

'Why did you come with us in the car then if you didn't want to come between us? You've made a dead set at destroying our relationship. You disapprove!'

'I disapprove of deceit, I haven't otherwise tried to do anything –'

'Yes, you have. You think you've got a hold on her, you'll never let her alone now. You're jealous. You were always jealous because she loved Edward and not you. You were jealous because I loved Edward and not you. Admit it.'

Stuart considered this. 'Yes, a bit –'

'So you see –'

'But that was a long time ago when I was a child, and I never thought you didn't love me, you did, you do.'

'Is that an appeal?'

'No.'

'You need some lessons in psychology, the fact about human nature is that things are indelible, religion is a lie because it pretends you can start again, that's what made Christianity so popular –'

'I don't know about that,' said Stuart. 'I think religion is about good and evil and the distance between them.'

'These extremes are fictions,' said Harry, 'false opposites which invent each other, decent people don't know about either. Your good and evil are bad dogs better left to lie. Evil has a right to exist quietly, it won't do much harm if you don't stir it up. Everywhere you go you're an intruder. You'll go through life making trouble, you're *dangerous* –'

'Please stop –'

'You'll come to grief in the end and the sooner the better. Midge's simple life act is supposed to impress you, she thinks she'll be worthy to help you in your work, then one day you'll seize hold of her –'

'Oh Dad,' said Stuart, 'don't keep talking like that, don't keep trying to argue with me.'

'I'm not trying to argue! We all have smutty thoughts, you have vile fantasies, don't deny it, you're repressed –'

'That's a ridiculous word which I utterly reject.'

'You're getting angry.'

'You're trying to make me angry but you won't succeed, listen –'

'Of course Midge will get over this rubbish and come to me, she's mine – I just terribly resent your interference.'

'Listen, I came to look for Edward –'

'What good have you ever done Edward? You never tried to communicate with him, you don't know anything about him. You're too self-satisfied and opinionated and bloody clumsy to communicate with anyone.'

'But I wanted to say something else.'

'What, for Christ's sake?'

'I want to come back here, to this house – may I?'

They were in the drawing room of the house in Bloomsbury. The evening sun was shining in upon the faded green panelling. Stuart was standing, still wearing his mackintosh, it had been raining earlier and he had been walking about for a long time before deciding to call on his father. Harry was sitting at his desk where, with the help of a bottle of whisky, he had been writing a letter to Midge. He had swivelled his chair round and was aware of looking, in the focus of Stuart's cold stare, dishevelled, even drunk. He felt for a moment almost tearful with rage and unable to speak. He said, 'It's no accident that you've damaged me –'

'What?'

'It's no – Oh damn you, no, you can't come back here, I hate the sight of you, that's all, keep away! Hell is somewhere near here and you're a devil –' Harry got up and stepped forward and steadied himself by moving his chair and holding onto the back of it. Stuart did not move. 'Get away, don't stand so near me –'

'Dad – please forgive me – I meant no harm – may I ask you –'

'Christ, have you understood nothing, don't you know what hurts people – you've hurt me so much – you've hurt my life – deeply – get *back*, get *out* –'

Harry lunged forward, swinging both his hands. He was almost as tall as Stuart. One hand pummelled the wet mackintosh and slid downward, the other clawed across Stuart's face. Harry lurched and almost fell and Stuart retreated.

'Sorry. I'm going.' Stuart went quickly to the door and paused a moment, Harry inhibited an impulse to call him back. Stuart went out and closed the door. Harry picked up a glass paperweight and hurled it at the door where it cracked one of the wooden panels. He sat down, blundering, almost missing the chair, seized his letter and crumpled it up. He had, for the moment, no language, did not know how to address Midge at all. Her incomprehensible withdrawal from him, combined with some continued need of him, her acceptance of his presence, her maddening repetitive exclamations about her state of mind, aroused in him a terrible inexpressible violence; he was tormented by anger, by desire, by hope, by visions of her sudden return, the door opening, her outstretched arms, her loving face. He slid from the chair, knelt on the floor and then stretched himself out face downward on the floor. He said aloud into the carpet, 'She must come to me, she will come to me, she has nowhere else to go.'

Stuart, going down the stairs, heard the paperweight hit the door and interpreted the sound. It reminded him of something. Oh yes. Edward throwing the Bible after him. People were always doing that it seemed. Once outside the door he had covered his face with his handkerchief, his nose appeared to be bleeding. He went into the cloakroom off the front hall and soaked his handkerchief with cold water and mopped his face. His nose was painful and he wondered if it was broken. How did one know whether one's nose was broken? He touched it gingerly. Blood continued to drip into the basin. He washed out his handkerchief and, holding it wet in his hand, stepped out of the front door into the sunshine. Holding the handkerchief away from his side and occasionally mopping his nose with it, he walked as far as Tottenham Court Road and started along Oxford Street. His nose stopped bleeding and felt better. He squeezed the wet reddened handkerchief over the kerb and rubbed it over his nose and mouth, and put it in his pocket.

He walked on, awkward, avoiding people who stared after him. His immediate objective was a certain church north of Oxford Street which he liked and where he could sit in quietness. He entered the high dark secret church with its musty spicy numinous smell and sat down, then knelt down. There was no one there. He breathed more slowly, more deeply, ceasing to hear the sound of the traffic, letting the intensity of the silence affect him. His heart, which had been racing after the distressing scene with his father, slowed down. The clouds of strong emotions began to disperse leaving a calmer sadness. Then this sadness was submerged in another deeper sad feeling. *There was no one there*. Of course he had never imagined there was, never in his life believed in God for a moment, it had never seemed to matter. There was no one to talk to, no one to give, in the last resort, perfect help, perfect love. Stuart had never especially expected people to love him, never depended on love. He had loved his father and known at the same time that his father loved Edward more. He had not minded that as much as they imagined, they, Harry, Thomas, Edward perhaps, anyone who bothered to think about it. Perhaps this separateness, this cutoffness, this determined notmindingness had to do with the absence of his mother, the earliest truth in his life, the absence of complete love together with the haunting idea of it not as a real possibility but as an abstract, an invisible sun giving light but no warmth. The notion of explaining himself, even of knowing himself, was alien to Stuart, and he had never framed any theory of the sort which was so natural to the mind of Thomas. Indeed he thoroughly disliked such theorising. He did not often think of his mother, he tended, not irritably but with a sad firm gesture, to banish her image. But now when it came to him in the empty church he somehow connected it, and knew then that he had done so before, with his conception of himself as a sort of 'religious' man with a dedicated destiny: that or nothing, that or smash, and since not smash or nothing, then that.

Stuart frowned. He did not care for this connection of ideas. What was the matter with him, was he becoming weak? It occurred to him to wonder if it mattered that there was no God. It had always seemed to him to be essential that there be none. He had never looked for a Him or a Thou, or tried to reconceptualise the old deity into some sort of nebulous quasi-personal spirit. 'God' was the proper name of a supernatural Person in whom Stuart did not believe. The quiet church, which he had often visited and from which, after the scene with his father, he had hoped for something, now seemed hollow, wrong, the wrong place. Am I giving way, thought Stuart, is it smash after all? Am I *deeply* troubled, daunted, by being told that I do nothing but harm? This place used to calm me and encourage me because it made everything that I wanted seem clean and innocent, as if it guaranteed the existence of holiness or goodness or something and connected me with it. But I don't need that sort of connection, it's a separation not a connection, it's a romantic idea of myself, as if I imagined I was robed in white. It's not that I thought I'd got anywhere or learnt anything or that people should notice me – but I did expect to be somehow immune from doing harm. I've lived with my own thing, with *it*, for a long time, longer than I've told anyone or really measured myself. *It* can't have gone wrong, I know that, *it* can't change or stain. Perhaps I'm just realising, now that I've *started*, that if I do anything at all I can do evil. If I can't communicate with people this isn't just an innocent awkwardness it's a fault I must overcome, but overcome in my *own* way which I haven't yet found out. Oh, if I could only have a sign. I know I can't, but I keep coming to places like this and kneeling down as if I expected something, some pleasure perhaps. (At this he rose from his knees and resumed his seat.) I must do without all this. That's the sense of my idea of *work*, my problem of it, which I haven't solved yet and which *they* think I'm wantonly putting off and perhaps I am. I'm enjoying an interim when I can feel that I have, in some ideal secret sense, achieved everything when I've really achieved nothing. I haven't let myself take in that I've got to do it alone – I'm alone and will always be alone, not in a romantic way, but in that *other* way, which perhaps for *me* is an illusion, I can't even know that yet. Because *it* is certain doesn't mean that *I* can travel. I may be condemned not to be able to help people. I must learn to try, but that sounds wrong too. Do the nearest thing, refrain from stupidity and drama, not just be small and quiet, be nothing, and let the actions come right of themselves. Then he thought, I can't make sense of it – oh how unhappy I am suddenly – like I wasn't before.

Frightened by his thoughts Stuart jumped up and hurried out of the church without looking back. Behind him he heard some footsteps, perhaps of a priest who had emerged from the vestry. He hurried back to Oxford Street and went on walking in the direction of Oxford Circus, walking, a tall man, among the people, swerving and tacking to avoid touching them, looking over their heads, walking like (he suddenly felt, and it was a terrible image) a man seen in a film, when the star is seen walking alone in the crowded streets of New York (it had to be New York) filled with the magical significance of his role, happy or unhappy, an image of power, of the envied life, surrounded by other actors who are, by contrast, devoid of being; and it is all false. When he reached Oxford Circus, Stuart went down the steps into the Underground station. He wanted to get back to his new digs and shut the door. He wondered, am I simply ill, is it 'flu? Am I seriously ill, will I die young, is *that* the solution? What idiotic thoughts. Perhaps I'm just hungry.

He began once more, as now often, too often, to relive those extraordinary final hours at Seegard, his father looking so white and wretched, averting his eyes and pretending to be calm, calling Stuart 'son', then Jesse with his big shaggy head and glowing eyes like a witch-doctor in a superhuman mask, shouting, 'That man's dead, take him away!' And all this time Stuart had sat at the table silently watching it all; no, he had risen for Jesse. He was the passive hated witness, a corpse sitting there, everywhere an intruder, as his father had said. This was the condition for which *work* was the cure, but would he ever really achieve it? He thought, I sat quietly at the table, I sat quietly in the back of the car and I felt terrible and small like a vile bacillus. No, I didn't feel that at the time, I was just paralysed, I was very frightened of *him*, in the car I was thinking more about *him* than about *them*, as if he were really powerful and dangerous. And now he is dead. Poor Edward.

As Stuart stood upon the platform waiting for the train he felt a new and dreadful feeling of shame, a shameful loneliness and sadness and grief, as if he were both banished from the human race and condemned for eternity to be a useless and detested witness of its sufferings. This was what he had felt and foreseen when he had found the church so repugnant and so empty, and with this he returned to the scene with Harry, Harry's rejection of him, Harry's misery and hatred, the blow in the face which would be remembered forever.

As he thought these thoughts, standing upon the station platform, feeling a little giddy as with hunger, he was looking down into the black space below him, the vault underneath the rails. Stuart had sometimes imagined how, if someone were to fall down there, he would jump down after them and pull them up just as the train was roaring into the station. Now, without any image, he gazed down onto the black sunken concrete floor of the track. Then he saw that there right down at the bottom something was moving, as if alive. He frowned and focused his eyes. He stared. It was a mouse, a live mouse. The mouse ran a little way along beside the wall of the pit, then stopped and sat up. It was eating something. Then it came back again, casting about. It was in no hurry. It was not trapped. *It lived there.*

This revelation was taken in by Stuart in a moment. It entered him like a bullet. It exploded inside him. He felt about to fall. He stepped back from the edge of the platform. He found a seat and sat down, leaning his head against the tiled wall. What had happened, was he having some sort of fit? He gasped for breath, feeling his whole body change. An extraordinarily peaceful joy ran through him, a thrilling consciousness of the warmth and pace of his blood, running through all his veins and arteries down to the minutest vibrating threads in his finger tips. A light shone in his eyes, not painful, not like a flash, but like a shrouded sun which warmed his body until it glowed as if it too were all radiantly alight. He rolled his head to and fro against the tiles, half closing his eyes and sighing with joy.

'Are you all right, son?' A burly figure in overalls was leaning over him.

'Yes –' said Stuart.

'You got blood on your face. Have a fall or something?'

'No – thank you so much – I'm all right – I'm really – all right.'

EDWARD WAS BACK in London. He had waited, standing in the avenue, long enough to see the body of Jesse, together with its bearers and mourners, enter the house. Mother May and Bettina, both weeping, entered last. Then he ran away down the drive and along the track to the road. It was only when he reached the road and stopped hurrying that he realised that his jacket was left behind. By now *they*, wailing beside the body, would have lifted it to look on Jesse's face. Fortunately Edward's keys and money were in his trouser pocket. He began to feel cold. There was distant thunder and it started to rain. He set off walking toward the station, but the bus picked him up when he had gone a mile. He wondered briefly whether it was his duty to telephone the police and decided it was not. A train had been cancelled and he had to sit for a long time, in wet clothes in a cheerless waiting room, his body aching with restless misery. It took tediously, agonisingly, long to get back to London, to his room, or rather to Mark's room as he now thought of it. He considered going back to Bloomsbury, but he was afraid to miss any message there might be from Brownie. There was none. It was evening. He had eaten nothing.

He wondered whether he ought to have stayed at Seegard. His desire to get away *at once* had been intense and imperative and he later wondered what it was: simply fear? He did not want to have to see that thing again. There is primitive fear of dead people, the ugly unnatural dead, the polluted dead who spread sickening vapours, the envious

481

dead who drag the living down and smother them. Edward remembered the terror he had felt when touching that wet humped weight. But it was not just fear which made him run, it was a curious painful sense of propriety. It was not for him to stand by and watch the women crying. He did not belong to that scene. He had been a visitor at Seegard, not a part of its substance. And he felt too with an intensity that was almost comforting that he had said his final farewell to Jesse down at the river by the willow trees. There was no other farewell to be said. He had done his duty, completed his appointed task, his last service to the ladies of Seegard. He had performed the rite which, evidently, was to be performed by the son for the father. He had found Jesse in his secret place. Standing around with the tree men while the wife and daughters did things to the corpse, sent messages, made arrangements, made a meal perhaps, he would have gone mad with misery. Nor did he want to witness Ilona's grief, or risk being the one who had to tell her. But he was sorry not to have seen her, and this alone he regretted.

On the evening of his return, although it seemed shocking to be hungry, Edward had gone out to a pub and eaten sandwiches and drunk a lot of whisky. Then he came back to the room which smelt of emptiness and absence and went early to bed and into a deep sleep. He awoke next morning to a frightful new form of unhappiness. His father whom he had sought and found and sought again was dead. In his crazy searching round London he had, he now realised, hoped and somehow believed that his father was alive. Now Jesse was dead and there was *nothing to do*, the story was over. Mark was dead and Jesse was dead too. They had made a pact together against Edward. It was, he suddenly felt, almost a comfort to return to the old familiar pain of Mark's death, as a distraction from the new awful pain of Jesse's. Am I getting used to Mark being dead, he wondered. Then he looked about the room, at the bed, at the chair, at the window, and the old horror rose up afresh. He thought, I *must* find Brownie. He had left London on the day after his failure at their rendezvous. Surely she would write or come to see him, she *must* have known that only some terrible accident could have stopped him from arriving. He decided to wait all day in the room in case she came, but the agony of waiting was too intense. He went out, leaving a note on the door of the room, another on the front door, and a message with his landlady. He walked the streets of London, and could not help still looking for Jesse among the people who passed by. He went to the pub where they had arranged to meet and stayed there, getting drunk, till closing time. He went round to Mrs Wilsden's house, he remembered her address from her numerous letters. Of course he did not dare to ring the bell, but he hung around at a distance watching the door. He sat in a café which commanded one end of the road and watched till his eyes glazed. Of course Brownie had said she was staying with Sarah, but she might well have gone back to her mother. He considered going round to Sarah's house, but could not make up his mind to, he felt too ashamed. He went back to his rooms, then to the nearby pub and then to bed. A note left with his landlady turned out to be from Stuart giving his new address. He did the same on the next day and on the next. Then he thought of Mrs Quaid. Mrs Quaid had found Jesse. Might she not find Brownie?

On this occasion Edward had no difficulty in finding the house. The sun was shining and the day had established itself as a warm summer day, a London summer day with a London light and dustiness and haze of green trees and resonance of sound and emergence of colour which can seem, according to one's mood, so genial and festive and full of spacious celebration, or so stifling and oppressive and full of ghostly nostalgia. Edward saw how tired all the trees looked already, their leaves drooping and grimy, and the streets were full of sad echoes. As he approached Mrs Quaid's house he felt a now familiar sense of danger, and of something shady and disagreeable, even bad. The street door was unlocked as usual and he pushed it open and went soft-footed up the stairs. Mrs Quaid's door was shut and he stood outside it for a while, feeling a sudden revulsion, unable to decide to knock. At last he knocked, timidly, indecisively. There was a long silence. No one came. Edward, looking at the worn dusty carpet, the banisters sticky with dirt, the dense mass of particles floating

483

in the air, revealed by the sun shining through a landing window, felt sick with a pointlessness and loneliness which deprived him of his sense of himself. He felt a fright at not existing, a feeling of the entirely precarious nature of identity, such as healthy people leading ordinary lives sometimes receive as a sudden quick glimpse of insanity and death. Since it did not matter what he did, he tried the handle of Mrs Quaid's door, found the door unlocked, opened it and went in.

The corridor inside was dark, all the inner doors being closed. In the light from the landing Edward began to fumble along the wall searching for an electric switch. As he was doing this the door at the far end which led into the big room opened and an indistinct woman with a cap on her head and a necklace round her neck stood in the doorway. Edward said, 'Mrs Quaid –' But he had realised at the same moment that it could not be Mrs Quaid. His hand found the electric light switch. The woman at the doorway took a step towards him and said, 'Edward.' It was Ilona.

'Oh my God!' said Edward. For a moment he actually considered whether he had not become mad, whether he had *transformed* the image of Mrs Quaid into that of Ilona in his mind. He closed the door behind him and sat down on a chair against the wall.

'Edward, dear, however did you find me?'

'*Find* you,' said Edward. 'I wasn't looking for you. You can't be here, it's impossible. This is a crazy place full of ghosts and hallucinations. It's not you. You look different.'

'I've had my hair cut off.' What Edward had taken for a cap was Ilona's hair, cut close to her head.

'Oh Ilona, I can't bear it, I can't *bear* it –'

'That I had my hair cut? They did it very well –'

'No – being *mad* like this, everything being *mad* –'

'Edward, I'm so glad to see you. Don't sit out there like a cat. Come in, come here.'

Edward got up and followed her into the big room which looked almost exactly as it had done on the last occasion, the chairs piled on each other in a heap in the corner, the armchairs by the fireplace. A table had been pulled into the middle of the room. The thick furry curtains had been thrust well back and the room was full of bright light, Edward could see through the window a sunlit wall close by, a tree beyond.

Ilona did indeed look different. Her closely cut short hair made her look boyish and also older, almost sophisticated. Her green dress which was narrow and smart and rather short added to the impression. She wore high-heeled shoes. Only the necklace, one of her old ones, looking oddly out of place, recalled her previous persona. 'Look, let's choose a chair and sit down. I'll have this one, you can have this one. I don't like those armchairs. Let's sit at the table. I've been writing letters.'

Ilona pulled a chair out of the heap and set it at the table near the one on which she had been sitting. They sat down and looked at each other.

'Ilona, you left them –'

'You mean them at Seegard – yes –'

'You couldn't bear it – what happened – Jesse –'

'Oh I left before that – I left after you went, almost at once – I've been in London for ages.'

'Ilona! But you do know – about Jesse being dead –?'

'Of course, I read about it, it was in all the papers.'

'You *read* it in the *papers*?'

'Yes. Edward, please don't be so intense.'

'I don't understand. And you haven't been home? I can hardly believe you've left Seegard. I feel you must still be there, as if you couldn't leave –'

'As if I'd crumble to pieces in the outside world? As you see, I haven't.'

'And you've been in London all this time and you didn't tell me, didn't get in touch –'

'I was going to – I wanted to get a job first.'

'You came to London all by yourself?'

'Yes! I'm not such a silly girl as you think.'

'But – look – why are you *here*, why *on earth* are you *here* – were you expecting me?'

'No – why are you here if it comes to that? How did you know where I was?'

'I didn't. Mrs Quaid lives here. I came to see her.'

485

'Then you didn't know – she's dead.'

'Oh – I'm so sorry – how awful –' It did indeed seem to Edward something awful, something uncanny and doom-laden. He said, 'She's dead too', as if death were catching and Jesse had infected her. 'But she can't be dead. I mean I saw her a few days ago.'

'She died a few days ago. She must have died just after you saw her. The funeral was yesterday only I couldn't go. She's had cancer for ages. But you know her, do you? How do you know her?'

'I came here to a seance – that was before I came to Seegard – I never told you because it was so weird and extraordinary, I felt rather secretive about it – and a voice told me to – to come to my father –'

Ilona, the new Ilona with the cut hair, was looking at him intently. 'You mean you got a *message*?'

'Yes. Well, it seemed like that. Then Mother May's letter came. I didn't tell about the message, I didn't want her to feel there was any reason except her letter, and anyway it would have sounded perfectly mad –'

'How strange – I didn't know you knew Dorothy – Mrs Quaid –'

'I only saw her twice. The second time I – oh never mind – But you still haven't said why *you're* here, here today in this house? Did you come to consult her – too?'

'I live here.'

'You –?'

'When I came to London I came here, I had to have somewhere to stay. Dorothy Quaid is an old friend of Mother May, she knew her at the art school, she used to teach textile design before she developed her gift. She's the person who used to take all our jewellery and stuff to London to sell.'

'You mean she knows you – she knew you all – she knew Jesse – she's been to Seegard?'

'Yes, I said, she's an old friend.'

'So that explains it – or rather – it doesn't – I'll have to think – and you've been here all this time –'

'How did you come across Dorothy?'

'That was by chance – if there is such a thing. A girl called

Sarah Plowmain gave me a card, she's the daughter of Elspeth Macran who used to know your mother, I think – Oh dear dear Ilona, I'm so glad to see you. I was so sorry not to see you at Seegard on that day – but of course you'd already gone earlier –'

'What day? Have you been at Seegard?'

'Yes, didn't you know? I suppose they don't write and it's all just happened. I found Jesse.'

'You mean you –?'

'I found his body. Oh – did the papers say anything about that? I haven't seen any newspapers, I've been rather –'

'No, there was nothing about you.'

'I suppose they didn't want to bring me in – they didn't say – I found his body in the river – I –'

'Don't tell me about it now, please.'

'I'm sorry, I don't want to upset you.'

'I'm not upset. Of course I am upset. But I knew he was dead. Ever since he disappeared I knew that he was dead.'

'*How* did you know?' said Edward. He stared at her new closed grown-up face.

'Just a feeling, an intuition, a quite certain feeling.'

'He was in the river. What do you think happened?'

'As we shall never know,' said Ilona, 'it's better not to think.'

'You don't imagine – well, you're right. Better leave it. I feel – such awful grief and shock – I kept believing he was alive.'

'I got over the shock earlier. I cried then. I'm over it now.' As she said this Ilona's eyes filled with tears and she bowed her head over her beads.

Edward got up and touched her shoulder, touching the soft cool material of her dress, then he touched the sleek hair which glittered so in the bright sunlight and felt so smooth, he felt the warmth of her head and wanted to stroke her gently, but his gesture remained awkward and unfinished. Ilona shuddered, then got up, found her handbag on the floor, took out a handkerchief and blew her nose. They resumed their seats.

Ilona said, 'What did you think of my mother's memoirs?'

'Oh,' said Edward, 'has she published them? I haven't seen –'

'Something came out in a newspaper. I expect someone will show you.'

'I've been awfully out of touch. So I expect you'll go back to Seegard now?'

'No. But I'm leaving London.'

'Where are you going?'

'Paris.'

'*Paris?*'

'Yes. I've never been there.'

'But, Ilona, you can't go to Paris alone. I'll come with you.'

'I won't be going alone.'

'Ilona – what have you been doing since you came to London. Did you get a job?'

'Yes. I'm a dancer in Soho.'

'You don't mean –'

'Yes, I'm a stripper.'

'How *can* you –'

'Very easily. You must come and see me. Don't be shocked. Look, here's a card, it's called the "Maison Carrée". It's a job, I had to do something to earn money, I couldn't just go back and say I couldn't – and the only things I can do are dance and make jewellery – and –'

'Dance – yes –' Edward recalled what he had seen in the sacred grove. 'You're a wonderful dancer.'

'How do you know?'

'You must get a real job, with real dancing, in ballet or –'

'It's too late for ballet. Maybe I will get another job later on. Things happen quickly in Soho.'

'But did you go to Soho on purpose?'

'I didn't really do anything on purpose. I thought Dorothy would help me to get a job in the jewellery trade. She was always rather fond of me, you see. Then just as I came she got much more ill – that was so terribly sad – though of course we knew it had to happen – I didn't expect it –'

'Poor Ilona –'

'She was such a nice person –'

'Don't cry, I can't bear it –'

'Oh such a lot has happened to me –'

'What else?'

'Edward – you know what attracts poltergeists?'

'What? Yes.'

'Well, I wouldn't attract any now.'

'Oh my darling,' said Edward. But he already knew.

'You see – I asked you to look after me – and you wouldn't – and now someone else does –' Ilona's eyes, which had filled with tears, now overflowed, her mouth was wet and she mopped her chin with her handkerchief, she looked defenceless and childish like the old Ilona.

Edward jumped up again. He felt such an intense desire to protect her, to gather her to him and shield her, together with a dreadful hopeless remorse, and he groaned to think how much in the future he would suffer for this too. He even said, 'It's too much, it's too much –' He stood near her wringing his hands.

'Oh don't worry,' said Ilona, dropping her soaked handkerchief on the floor and trying to dry her face with the back of her hand, 'I'm all right. I'm going to Paris next week with Ricardo, he's one of the people at the strip joint.'

'But they must be awful people.'

'Ricardo isn't, he's gentle and – he's in theatre really –'

'I suppose he's Italian.'

'No, he's from Manchester, he had a terrible childhood.'

'Ilona, I'm so sorry.'

'Don't be. And they aren't awful. There are all kinds of other people. It's all somehow happened as it had to happen, I'm pleased with how it happened.'

'But what about Mother May and Bettina?'

'They don't need me. They're strong. I have to follow my own path now. Of course I'll go back to see them later on.'

'Dear dear Ilona, dear sister, I wish you'd let me help you now, I'm so unhappy, I need someone to love and look after, don't go away with Ricardo, stay with me.'

'No, no, it wouldn't do. Look, I've got to go soon. I have to rehearse something, I'll get in touch with you when I come back. I've no idea when that will be, and I'll have to find somewhere else to live, but I'll get in touch, really.'

Ilona had risen and moved toward the door. Edward followed her. He said, 'I can't bear your going away, now that

I've found you, I can't bear it, please stay, I love you.' He stared down at her cap of beautifully cut red-golden hair, like the shining fur of some delightful animal, and was able now to reach out and place his hand upon her. He stroked her hair, and as he touched the round of her head he felt through his fingers the electricity of her whole body. He drew his hand firmly down onto the back of her neck, and then stepped away. They looked at each other.

'I'm glad to see you, Edward. There's something I want to say to you. In those memoirs, just the bit they published, I've know for years my mother was writing some sort of diary, she never showed it to us, she says somewhere that she has had consolations –'

'Consolations?'

'Love affairs. Jesse had love affairs. She says she had too. Of course it must have been long ago.'

As Ilona paused, making this sound like the end of her statement, Edward said, 'And – go on –'

'Just that.'

'I don't understand,' said Edward.

'Leave it then, better leave it anyway, I must go, I must bathe my eyes and put my make-up on.'

Edward stared down at her upturned face, so small and lean without the great mass of hair. He said, 'Oh *no* –'

'Leave it. It's like that other thing.'

'Are you saying that Jesse might not be your father?'

'He *might* not be. But we'll never know. So it's no use imagining.'

'Now you've said this how can we not –'

'Bettina resembles Jesse and I don't, but of course that doesn't prove anything –'

'We could have a blood test – but no, Ilona, no – we can't start *investigating* – it's unthinkable –'

'I agree.'

'How strange. Jesse once said he hoped I'd marry you. I reminded him you were my sister. I wonder if he thought you weren't.'

Ilona shook her head and said nothing.

'Is there anyone you think might be your father?'

490

Everything they were saying was so terrible. Edward thought, we must stop this.

'No. There was a man, he's dead now, I think he was Jesse's lover, and then Mother May took him away, but I haven't any reason to think – it's just that I somehow remember about him – he was a painter, his name was Max Point.'

Edward was about to cry out at the name, but stopped, covering his mouth with his hand. He would have to think about that one. He said, 'I suppose – not now but later – we could ask your mother –'

'No, we couldn't. No, no. She couldn't bear it. She might say anything.'

'You mean we couldn't believe her, or she mightn't be sure, or –'

'She couldn't bear it. And if it all got confused.'

'No, I see what you mean, we can't, better to leave it alone. There's nothing to be done.'

They stared at each other with a long sad stare, lips parted. 'Anyway,' said Edward, 'I love somebody else.' It struck him as a bizarre thing to say, what did 'anyway' mean?

Ilona sighed and turned her eyes away. 'I wanted to say it to you – now it's said and gone.' She went back to the table and picked up her handbag. 'I must be off, I've got a lot to do, I've got to get some contact lenses and buy some clothes and go to the club. You know, Jesse's a sex hero since those memoirs – you look just like his picture – you can have any girl in London.'

'Ilona, don't talk like that! I'll see you before you go to Paris?'

'Better not. I'm glad we met here. We'll meet again later. I'll know myself better later. You could come and see me dance, but just to watch, don't try to –'

'I don't think I'll come,' said Edward. 'I don't want to see you dance there. I'll see you dance at Covent Garden.'

'I shall never dance at Covent Garden. Goodbye, dear Edward.'

They looked at each other again. Then Edward came and took her round the waist as if they were to dance together then and there. He kissed her on the cheek, then on the lips.

'Oh Ilona, sweetheart, be my sister, I shall need a sister as the years go by.'

Ilona pulled away and opened the door. 'I'll just go and wash my face, and fix my make-up, I'll be away in a minute.'

'I'll walk with you –'

'No, I have to hurry. Just stay here for a little while, then go. I'll unlatch the door, close it when you leave.'

'Where can I write to you?'

'You can't. I'll write. I know your father's address, your stepfather's address, I looked it up. Goodbye.'

'Goodbye.' Ilona was gone.

Edward thought, she's afraid Ricardo might see us together in the street and not believe I was her brother! And he might be right! How this will torment me too – it will *torment* me, why did she *say* it! I want her so much as a sister and now – He tried to recall Max Point but could see only a red face and a bald head. Ought he to go and see him again? Ought he to have told Ilona about him? It was all wild fantasy anyway. And Ilona was likely to have enough troubles.

Edward had sat down in one of the armchairs. He began to think about gentle Ricardo with his terrible Manchester childhood. He ought to have asked her how old Ricardo was. Twenty, fifty? Which would be worse? Edward became aware that he was facing the television set which was looking at him with its big blank hypnotic eye. He leapt up and scudded across the room. He saw the card of Ilona's strip club upon the table and pocketed it. He stood still and listened. The traffic was audible but there was other noise too. The flat was murmuring to itself with faint sibilant sounds as of slightly moving textiles and creaking furniture and falling dust. The flat was lonely, mourning, empty. Or was it empty? Was it not extremely likely that Mrs Quaid was still around somewhere?

Edward left the room, turned out the light in the corridor, closed the door of the flat behind him, and ran down the stairs and out into the street. He began to walk again toward the pub where he was to have met Brownie. He stayed there till closing time but of course she did not come.

SHE HAD SEEN it again in dreams, that beautiful terrible sexless stare. She thought a lot about death and was comforted by a sense of its nearness, its possibility which quietly and reassuringly nudged her. She checked her sleeping pills, poured them out into her hand. Thomas had given them to her. Perhaps, it occurred to her to wonder, that meant they were strictly non-lethal? Thomas would not have feared her suicide, but he probably gave her whatever he gave his patients. If so they must be compounded not to kill. She put the pills away. She had not intended to take them anyway.

After going to Stuart's lodging and finding him gone Midge had given up searching for him, or rather could not at the moment think of any way of finding him. She was sure however that she would see him before long, she waited for him. She wanted very much to be in his presence, to have him look at her and speak to her, and to talk to him about her 'better life', to explain what it would be like and hear from him some, even the smallest, word of acknowledgement of her intent which would confer reality upon it. From others she could expect nothing but scorn, but *he* would be able to discern the grain of truth in her confused and darkened 'new being'. Out of the collapse of her double life, a life so customary, so well adjusted, as to seem real and almost dutiful, she fled to her new vision as to the only exit; one which Stuart, in destroying her world by his existence and his knowledge, had at once also provided. She wanted to talk to him about how it would be, in that happy simple future time.

493

It all depended on him, and when he understood he could not fail.

Meanwhile, comforting herself with pain, she went over and over the details of the catastrophe, convincing herself of its horror and completeness and of her guilt with which she could do nothing except somehow leave it behind. It was as if there was nothing left in her life up to now with which she could either rest or work. The guilt, the disloyalty, the lies, the hurt and harm done to others, must be seen as real. But Midge, in attempting so to see it, did not consider it as a place where there were for her any stepping stones, any possibility of reconstruction, renovation, explanation, acts of healing. The collapse was, she reckoned, too complete for that. She could not do good, and only stain her hands further, by going back, however well intentioned, into that mess. Better, as well as easier, to leave it all behind like a house fallen down, destroyed utterly in a conflagration, wrecked by a bomb. This also meant that she need not, at present, think in any awful detail about the future. Thomas could not morally or legally take Meredith from her, so Meredith would be with her too in that better future. Meredith was away now at his new school. He had, with an amazing and disconcerting calm, organised his own departure, obeying Thomas's written commands. He had left a list of books and clothes to be sent on after him which Midge had not yet had the strength to look at. She had had no 'talk' with him and he had tacitly made it clear he wanted none. There was no prolonged emotional farewell. She cried a lot after he was gone, but was relieved that he was out of the house.

A more immediate and agonising torment, one which confused the reckoning up of her sins and which had led her to shake and pour out the bottle of sleeping pills, was the notion, indeed the knowledge, that she had only to send the briefest word, give the slightest signal, to Harry to reinstate the whole splendour of their love in a new situation of freedom. Was it not now, as Harry indeed had said, exactly what they had wanted, had they not been given by chance what had seemed, to her at least, so impossibly difficult to achieve? Thomas knew and had gone away 'leaving her free to decide'. Perhaps he really, as Harry had speculated, did not mind, felt relief. The old barriers which had seemed so strong had suddenly vanished. Nothing now prevented Midge from running to the house in Bloomsbury. She did not now have to look at her watch, to calculate, to lie. All was known, lies were over. She had only to speak, to utter one soft word, for it all to rise up like a magical palace, a city, full of trees and flowers and singing birds and marble steps leading upwards in the sun.

She had asked Harry not to try to see her again for a little while. He persisted in treating her as temporarily 'ill', and feigned the gentle bracing cheerfulness of one humouring an invalid. Only Midge could see the terrible fear in his eyes. Putting a calm face on it he said he might have to be away in any case but would certainly come and see her at once on his return and hope to find her 'better'. Midge had not said to him, do not come again. When *this* possibility, which she still kept at a distance, came too close she would suddenly ask herself, so am I never to see him any more, never, as we once were? She had felt a curious relief, almost pleasure, in talking to him about her feelings for Stuart, as if Harry had already become an old friend or confidant. But such meetings were possible only on *his* assumption, only endurable for her because of a double-think whereby Harry was not yet lost. Sometimes when her mind came out into the open and darted to and fro before returning to its refuge with Stuart, she wondered if she were really mad not to want more than anything in the world to see Harry and to make his happiness. Perhaps her illness was just a total annihilation of the sexual urge, something which might come about unexpectedly through a chemical change. The electrical force which had, for two years, bound her in all her thoughts, in all the lively predatory impulses of her feelings, all the vibrations of her physical being, to this one man, had been switched off. But no, sexual desire had not vanished, it had only changed. Midge *yearned* for Stuart's presence, his face was constantly before her, usurping the place so long occupied by Harry's; and Midge depended from it as from a floating vision which alone saved her from a fall to death. She continually pictured, treasured, cosseted, brooded over that saving image, seeing the pale unsmiling face and the yellow-amber eyes which were changing as she looked from coldness to oh such gentleness. She caressed that face with her thoughts but never in fantasy touched it with her lips or hand; only sometimes she did imagine herself kissing the sleeve or shoulder of his jacket, and this was exquisite. In spite of such indulgences there was something abstract in her desire, and this too, half apprehending it, she treasured. She wanted, panting and thirsting for it, his presence, for him to *look* at her, to *speak* to her, him as himself with all his commanding being, his authority, his separateness, his inaccessibility, his unconnectedness with other people, the sense in which he would never be connected, and yet could, without connection, yet *be*, for her, not just for her, yet totally for her.

Of course Thomas was also 'in her mind' all the time but obscured by a dark cloud. She often reminded herself of the coldness of his departure. 'Do you call this anger? I wish you well.' She had said some cruel things to him but could not now remember what they were. She had appealed to him, but could not imagine how she could do so now; nor could she imagine his wanting to see her again except to arrange a separation. She was conscious of a great deal of 'stuff', perhaps just an accumulation of time, her past, her marriage, which lay aside, with Thomas, and would at some point have to be 'dealt with'; but this too was in shadow. He retained, and would probably use, when that reckoning came, a vast capacity to hurt her, and when she thought of this she trembled. She dreaded seeing him again and avoided picturing that scene.

Edward was sitting in the dark. He was at the 'Maison Carrée'. The tiny auditorium, entirely filled with men, was entirely quiet. Their intentness was unruffled by the slight restlessness of ordinary spectators, nor did it resemble the spellbound silence which attends great 'moments of theatre'. It was as if they were all avidly, motionlessly, hurriedly *eating* what they saw. The pale expressionless faces, dimly visible in

496

the light from the stage, stared privately forwards and, in their determination to remain, while ravenously concentrated, anonymous, seemed to resemble each other, composing an audience of clones. Furtive, shrunk into themselves, no gesture, no slightest twitch, proclaimed an individual. Blasphemously simulating the selfless contemplation of the mysteries of art or religion, they sat tensely still, while inside each head a small machine of secret repetitive fantasy noiselessly whirred.

Edward, detached at first, was already becoming part of this silent community. He too sat, incapable of shifting or turning his head, his blank face strained forward, his mouth pouting a little with attention. He had found a seat at the back. He was very anxious that Ilona should not see him. She had suggested that he should come, but he could not conceive that she had meant it, she wanted only to demonstrate that she was not ashamed. Suppose, on seeing him, she were to forget her 'act', cry out, burst into tears? It was a vile place; yet quickly he allowed himself to become interested in the predictable routines of the girls, not all of them very young, with their bright false smiles and jerky provocations. The music, sometimes dreamy, sometimes noisy, streamed through his head, and it was as if a part of his being had fallen fast asleep while another part was intensely, meticulously alert. He almost forgot why he was there, and began comparing the girls with each other. None of them could *dance*; only one or two who evidently *enjoyed* undressing sent a tiny whiff of simple reality out into the breathless stench of the auditorium. But Ilona, how would it be when *she* appeared, what would happen to the audience when they saw a real dancer, the triumph of grace over gravity? Would they not *wake up*, turn to each other in amazement, cry out, weep and confess their sins?

Now a grinning girl in a silver top hat and a sequin shift was jiggling and wriggling to and fro, awkwardly manipulating a black silk shawl with simulated coyness, then dropping it and jauntily kicking it aside with black high-heeled shoes which beat a noisy rhythmless tattoo upon the boards. The sequins fell to the ground revealing a thin little

497

body covered by three stars. As the girl flourished the top hat and tossed it away, then hopped around to reveal her back and discard the stars, Edward suddenly realised that *this was Ilona*. Was she shamming? No. *She could not dance.* He lowered his head. When he looked again she was jumping about naked, smiling a strained stretched smile out into the dark. Her nakedness was pitiful, touching like that of a child, pallid, clammy, bare, the human form revealed in all its contingent absurdity. It was shameful and tragic. What in the other girls had seemed simply ugly and vulgar, here shone out as something sublimely obscene, like an exhibition of a deformity, which at the same time was little, pathetic, soiled and childish. He began to stare at her, to inspect her body, her long thin neck, her bony legs, her small pointed quaking breasts. He closed his eyes. The music indicated the end of the act, the stage was empty. Edward got up quickly and went out into the street.

'Edward, I'm Glad you've come,' said Midge. 'I so much wanted to see you.' She had not particularly thought of Edward or imagined she would be able to talk to him, but now that he was here she felt relief, as if he were unique, the only person she could talk to easily.

'Midge, I'm sorry,' said Edward. 'I meant to come –' He did not say he had been told to come. 'I've just had a lot of troubles – And I thought, you know, Ursula would be with you –'

'Why Ursula?' said Midge. 'Men always think women flock together at such times. No one has been near me, it's like having scarlet fever. Anyway Ursula is at a conference in Sweden.' Midge owed this information to a long very carefully worded letter she had received from Willy Brightwalton, in which he made a point of indicating that he was alone. Willy did not say either that he would gladly leave his wife to run to her side, or that were he free to do so he would at once offer her his hand. He said however, tactfully, eloquently, everything else about how deeply he cared for her, grieved for her, sympathised with her, desired, in any way she could oblige him by mentioning, to serve her. He asked her to let him know at once if she wished to see him. He signed himself 'your Willy'. Midge had not replied to his letter and he had not, at any rate yet, appeared at the door uninvited. Willy was a timid man and was not only, like many people, afraid of Thomas, he was also afraid of Harry. A similar tactful paralysis evidently affected Midge's various old lunchtime acquaintances. She had received no other letters. The telephone occasionally rang but she did not answer it in case it was Thomas. She was shunned in a way which augmented her resentment and her shame without affording her the energy of defiance. She was glad to see Edward.

Midge in her desolation looked, Edward noticed, as meticulously casual as ever. Her straight navy blue linen dress which might have been the uniform of an expensive school was changed by some indefinable air of its wearer, together with a light blue cravat, into the head-turning outfit of a smartly dressed woman. She seemed to have lost weight. Her face, as if touched by the sun, bloomed and glowed, and seemed to owe its translucent smoothness to no art at all but merely to youth and summer weather. With her skirt tucked up and her dark-stockinged legs crossed she faced Edward and patted her hair into an affecting disarray. She might, with her calm words and suave looks, have seemed almost composed had it not been for the hard line of her drooping mouth, and her frightened eyes which signalled so clearly to Edward 'Oh help me, help me, care for me.'

'Did Thomas ask you to come?'

'No.'

'Did Harry?'

'No.'

'I can't believe anybody now,' she said. 'Well, whose fault is that?'

'I haven't come as an ambassador,' said Edward, 'if that's what you mean.'

'You know Jesse Baltram's dead? Of course you do, it's in all the papers.'

'Yes.' No account of Jesse's death made any mention of Edward. In a way he felt wounded. That was Mother May's doing, to keep him henceforth out of the picture. He felt jealous, as if some right of possession had been violated. But on reflection he was relieved. It would have been terrible to have to talk about *that* to police, to journalists. He would never cease to recall what had happened, but he did not want to have to speculate about it in any ordinary way. Later on perhaps he might tell Thomas.

'Are you sorry, does it matter to you?'

'Yes, I'm sorry,' said Edward.

'But of course you didn't know him, except you saw him as a small child.'

'I saw quite a lot of him at Seegard.'

'But you were never at Seegard.'

'Yes, I was, I was there for a short while, I was there when you and Harry came that night –'

'*Were* you?' said Midge. 'I must be going crazy. Yes, I remember now. I just blotted you out!'

Yes, thought Edward, it's all blotted out, no one will know that I came to Jesse and loved him and that he loved me. It will be as if it had never been. Perhaps I shall stop believing it myself.

'It was a shock,' Midge went on. 'One doesn't expect people to die. And somehow I thought I'd see him again. But in an odd way too I was pleased, it took me out of my own troubles for a moment. I suppose it's an old trace of jealousy, I was jealous of Chloe because that man loved her. Now they're both dead. Doesn't that sound callous? Jealousy lasts forever.'

'Does it?' said Edward.

'Yes. Bad news for the young. Would you like a drink? No? I've stopped drinking. I imagine you've heard about me and Stuart?'

'You mean about you and Harry? When you turned up together at Seegard I assumed –'

'No, I'm talking about Stuart, that I've fallen in love with him.'

'Look, Midge, I'm a bit out of touch, I've been entirely on my own, I thought you and Harry –'

'Yes, I was having an affair with Harry, but suddenly, that

time at Seegard, I fell in love with Stuart, Thomas knows about it all now, he's gone away, I don't want to see Harry, Stuart won't see me – I feel everyone must know, but perhaps they don't.'

'Wait a minute –'

'Harry wanted me to leave Thomas, then when Stuart saw us together with all those pathetic lies about Mr and Mrs Bentley he killed something in me simply by looking –'

'You loved Harry, and now you love Stuart? But surely you don't love him just because he killed something –?'

'Yes, I do, exactly. I think I'll have a drink after all, will you? It's just that I suddenly saw how sort of dead it all was, as if death were looking at me and making things dead –'

'But did it all happen in an instant?' said Edward, accepting sherry.

'Not quite. It began in an instant and it went on in the car driving back. I could feel Stuart sitting behind me like a block of ice. Everything I'd *wanted* just became worthless, as if I didn't want *anything* any more. And then when I got back I realised that what I wanted was Stuart. I mean as if he had made a great void and nothing could fill it except him. This meant I had to go to see him and talk to him – I offered myself to him, not just as sex –'

'What does that mean –?'

'But as, I can't explain it, as a complete gift, I wanted to change my life so as to work with him, I still want to, to do some good in the world –'

'But what about sex? I know Stuart's given it up, but with you on the scene – I must say I'm *amazed* –' Edward felt the amazement warming him, or perhaps it was the sherry. Midge looked more animated too.

'He was cold. He told me to stop lying, to tell Thomas all about Harry, you see at that time Thomas didn't know, he only found out from that newspaper –'

'What newspaper?'

'May Baltram published an article about Jesse and she brought it right up to date! She actually described that evening at Seegard, how Harry and I arrived incognito, how they found out who we were –'

501

'Oh Midge – in a newspaper?'

'Then the gossip columnists took it up. Apparently she's written her life story in volumes, all about Jesse's love life, all about Chloe, yards of spiteful stuff, and it'll all be printed, she hates everybody. She's probably writing lies about you at this very moment.'

'I don't believe that. But she described what happened, and Thomas read it? What a rotten way for him to find out –'

'Yes. I was very sorry about that. I was just going to tell him.'

'What else did Stuart say? Wasn't he *tempted*? What an extraordinary business!'

'Tempted? Of course not. He told me it was all an illusion.'

'But you want him, you desire him? That's being in love.'

'Yes – but it's impossible like that – it must be in the other way –'

'I don't understand this. I suppose he told you to stay with your husband?'

'No. He didn't say that. Just that I should tell everyone the truth –'

'And leave him alone! It doesn't sound as if he's done you much good.'

'Oh he has, he has – such good – like a revelation –'

'Sorry, Midge, I can't buy this – let's get it clearer. Were you very much in love with Harry?'

'Yes, very much, and for a long time, I wanted to be married to him, only I couldn't see how.'

'But could this stop so suddenly? It isn't that you just decided you preferred Thomas? This idea of your being in love with Stuart seems to me perfect nonsense, it's daft, it's false, it can't be so, it must mean something else! What did Thomas say?'

'He thinks I'm still in love with Harry. He thinks this is an episode in my love for Harry. A sort of shock effect.'

'Have you been seeing Harry?'

'Yes, but not in the old way.'

'How rotten for everybody! God, what a mess. You know, I think Stuart's a red herring.'

'How do you mean?'

502

'He's not part of the thing at all, he's just an external impulse, a sort of jolt, a solid entity, something you bump into. It's all just happening in your mind. Your thinking you're in love with Stuart is just an effect of things breaking up, of seeing an open scene, you're surprised by your own ability to see things differently –'

'It doesn't feel like that,' said Midge. 'I want to be *with him*, and he may never want to see me, and when I think that I don't want to live – and it prevents me from thinking about them –'

'Them?'

'*Them*.' Midge found difficulty in putting it otherwise.

'You mean Thomas and Harry? That's just it. It's an escape from choice. And thinking you love Stuart gives you a new kind of energy and makes a holiday from having to sort out the other thing – which you'll have to go back to – wait, wait, you said everything you'd wanted became worthless. Perhaps there was a revelation, but you'll have to judge it – you'll have to *see* it all – perhaps Stuart has done something for you –' Edward was getting quite excited.

'I *can't*,' said Midge, 'I can't judge, I can't see, I want him to comfort me – it's all awful – *I*'m awful –' She began to cry so quietly that it was a moment before Edward noticed that her cheeks had become wet.

'Oh darling Midge, don't cry, let me comfort you, let me hold your hand.' Edward pushed his chair up close to hers so that their knees were touching. He took hold of Midge's hand, and the next moment her head fell heavily against his shoulder. He leaned over until his long lank dark hair was mingling with her fair fragrant hair in which he could now see so many strands of different colours. He put an arm round her shoulders and cradled her until she drew back. He felt, which he had not done when he had so much admired her when he entered the drawing room, a sense of her whole body, its weight, its warmth, its softness, its being covered by clothes.

'Lend me a hankie, Edward.'

'Here. Now let's sort it out together. Don't worry about Stuart. In some way you'll do him good. You'll have shaken him. He'll have to try, he'll have to think what's best to do, and of course he'll see you again and want to be your friend. There's a bond between you.'

'You think so?'

'Yes. So that can be good for both of you. But this being in love is an illusion, in a sense it *must* be, it's a momentary flash. Stuart's external, it's all in you, Stuart's nothing, he's power-less, he's an unreal element, I mean he's just a happening, you've invented him. In the way *you* imagine it you're not really connected at all. Harry and Thomas are real. And Meredith is real.'

'I could get custody of Meredith in a law court – oh what a nightmare it all is – and Thomas was so cold –'

'He would be. He's so used to not showing his feelings he probably had to withdraw a bit. Poor old Thomas, after all it's pretty rough on him. You know how much he loves you, you must know that however cold he is. Where is he incidentally?'

'At Quitterne. He went away and left me – to decide what I wanted –'

'And what do you want?'

'I don't *know* – You think Stuart won't hate me? I want to change my life –'

'You have changed it. You've stopped having a secret love affair. If Stuart made you feel it was awful perhaps that was the right feeling. You can go on changing your life, you can do lots of good, after all what's stopping you, what's stopping any of us from doing lots of good –' Edward paused for a moment, impressed by the idea he had just uttered – 'Of course Stuart won't hate you, he's crammed with good intentions, don't worry about Stuart, it's his thing that people don't have to worry about him, it's as if he isn't there, if he's done something to you it's because that something was ready to happen anyway. If you really hate the thing with Harry and you realise Stuart can only be an inspiring friend, just look around and think what real things are left, plenty I'd say. On the other hand, if you're really still desperately in love with Harry –'

Midge, who had been looking intently at Edward and still holding his hand, suddenly stood up and put her hands to her face. She had heard the soft click of a key turning in the front door. Two people had that key, Harry and Thomas. She said to Edward, 'Go and stop him. Then tell me which it is.'

Edward darted to the drawing room door and closed it behind him. The man in the hall was Thomas.

Thomas looked at Edward with a strange expression, intense and searching and at the same time mischievous, as if it were Edward's birthday and Thomas had brought a secret present for him. He did not seem to be surprised to see him. 'Hello, Edward.'

'Thomas, she's in there. She asked me to find out which one it was –'

'I'll announce myself. How are you?'

'Better,' said Edward. Was he better?

'Good boy. Come and see me here tomorrow.'

'I'm going to Seegard tomorrow,' said Edward. This too had just come into his head. 'I've got to,' he said, 'I won't stay –'

'Well, come and see me very soon. Did you go back to that room?'

'Yes – you were right – but it's enough –'

'Go to Harry, he may need you. I'm glad you've been with Midge. Now buzz off.'

As Edward passed Thomas, Thomas's right hand gripped Edward's left. As he opened the front door Thomas was pausing at the drawing room door and looking back at him. Edward went out into the street closing the front door behind him.

SEEGARD IN THE bright soft afternoon sunlight looked different again, like an overgrown parish church with its stout tower and irregular nave. The light was kind to it, smoothing in the streaky stains upon the concrete of the tower, making the soiled surface seem old, giving it a hazy golden-brown patina like lichen-covered stone. The yellow rape had faded but other fields were shimmering with barley and stiff blue-green wheat. He thought, I have seen the seasons change and the year turn in this place. Along the track wild roses were profusely in flower, some with stiff petals, large and pink, some small and frail and almost white like scraps of paper. The cow parsley was over, which Ilona called fretty chervil.

Edward stopped just before he came to the avenue of trees, and looked about and listened. He could hear a lark and a distant cuckoo, but these sounds scarcely disturbed, even accentuated, a deep warm silence which hung over the land and the house. He could not hear the river. He went slowly forward, stepping upon the pavement, until he came to the last feathery ash tree. Then he stopped again. The main door into the barn was shut. He looked at the windows of Selden, at his own window, then up at the tower. The idea of being covertly observed disturbed him. He felt guilty, an intruder, someone who might legitimately be shot at. He had prepared, even for himself, no explanation of his visit. He had now twice run away without a word. How would this be viewed? Had they noticed, did they care, were they even there any more? As soon as he had seen Thomas Edward had realised

506

that it was *essential* to go back, not to try to find out 'what had happened', but simply to make peace, to establish himself as acceptable and real, and then make a more dignified and considerate departure. *They* must do this for him, be kind to him, meet him without anger, accept him as a mourner, bring a certain period of time, a certain drama, to a quiet close, set him free. After *that* the question of his further connection with Seegard and its inhabitants might become an ordinary question which could be rationally considered.

Free to do what? To return to the beginning, to his guilt and anguish about Mark, go back to that as an interrupted task? Settle down to a lifetime of unanswered questions about Jesse? He had certainly not come to Seegard seeking some total clarification, there could be none. See Midge again and find out what she had decided? Talking to Midge had felt somehow good, perhaps simply because it had aroused some ordinary animal-like curiosity about the world outside himself which had been dead for such a long time. Look after Harry, talk to Stuart? Follow Ilona to Paris? He felt miserable about Ilona; supposing something awful happened to her in Paris? Was this yet another radiant source of guilt which would travel with him? He proposed not to think too much about that. The urgent thing, the real thing, which was now his *duty*, was to find Brownie, to be *with* Brownie, to *immerse* himself in her presence as in a healing spring. How feeble his attempts to find her now seemed, how pusillanimous, slinking about near her mother's house, ashamed to go to Sarah's. He had been so tired, suffering from a sort of moral lassitude. He had lacked an energy and a courage which he would perhaps regain if he could make his peace with Seegard. Then he would bang on her mother's door, interrogate Sarah, find her friends in Cambridge, follow her to America if necessary. Then indeed nothing should prevent him from finding Brownie and *marrying* her.

Edward tried the door of the Atrium, it was open, he stepped inside. He had expected to suffer from shock, but had not anticipated the electrical wave of emotion which rushed at him and over him as he quickly closed the door and took a step into the huge room. He trembled, then sat down quickly on a chair. There were two chairs standing together near the door in an unusual position, and as he sat he realised that these were the chairs upon which Harry and Midge had sat, like disgraced prisoners, on the evening of their disastrous apparition. No one had moved the chairs. He got up at last and placing his feet cat-like upon the slates moved to the table. There were some clean plates piled upon it, and a cup with some liquid in it. He walked to the door of the Interfectory and peered in. The room was empty, sleepy, shabby, untidy, smelling as usual of decaying books and dirty ancient cushions. He went to the door into the tower. It was unlocked and he went through into the big ground floor 'art gallery' room. This was different. Jesse's pictures had all been taken down and stacked against the walls showing only their backs. He hastily returned to the hall, he had begun to feel he was looking for Jesse, walking less cautiously now but still unable to break the silence with any cry of 'Hello!' or 'Where are you?' As he padded towards Transition he noticed that the tapestry of the girl pursuing the flying fish had been taken down and was folded into a thick pile beside the wall. Perhaps it had already been bought by an American. The potted plants had also been moved, pushed much more closely together in their corner so that their branches were bent and overlapping, some had been broken, they looked dusty and drooping too, perhaps forgotten and unwatered. He thought, Ilona watered them. One of them seemed to be dead; it was the one into which he had poured Ilona's love potion, and which had grasped at him with its leafy arms when he had been about to leave the house on his first flight. He paused to pity it, then hurried on to Transition. The kitchen was untidy, some crockery left in a wash-bowl. The big stove was out, but the deep freeze 'large enough to contain a human body', was purring. In the wash room there was a pile of clean towels. Edward checked his instinct to pick them up and take them to the airing cupboard. If he found no one he would not want them to know that he had passed through the house like a ghost. As he opened the door into Selden he heard a stutter of sound which he took to be a swallow singing, until he realised it was Mother May's typewriter.

508

Edward sped along the west corridor and out onto the terrace by the door in the façade. The sound of the typewriter, also reminding him of what Midge had told him, made him feel unready to confront Mother May. He did not trust Midge's account of the matter, but the idea of someone writing about his mother, perhaps about him, dismayed him very much. He recalled the way Midge had said, about Jesse and Chloe, 'now they're both dead'; and for a second his mother's ghost appeared beside the path he was following, opening its arms and uttering a soundless shriek. Edward hurried on. The person he wanted to see was Bettina. But perhaps by now she too had fled. He passed the ilexes and the orchard. Here too things had changed. The poplar trees had been cut down. The felled trees lay, neatly denuded already of their branches, long smooth poles aligned in the grass. The tree men had cleared the scene. At the river the grass had grown so high along the bank that he missed the slatted bridge at first and had to retrace his steps. He crossed easily over the sunken level of the docile more gently flowing stream. The wood was darkly shaded and the saplings upon the hillside, through which he had passed so easily before, were now in full leaf, forming sticky screens which picked at his clothes and sprang back at his face. His feet discovered the little path which was overhung by plants and scarcely visible. He could feel the tree roots and little woody icons underfoot. He thrust his way in, seeing the sunlight beyond, and came out onto the level of the *dromos*.

The sun, shining into his face, dazzled him as he began to look and to move toward the yellow lingam stone. Someone was sitting on the low fluted column which formed the pedestal. It was Bettina.

'Hello,' said Edward, 'I thought you might be here.'

'Hello Edward,' said Bettina, 'I thought you might come.'

Bettina too had cut her hair, though not so short as Ilona's. It fell thick shaggy and uneven almost to her shoulders. She had probably cut it herself savagely, very quickly. He pictured her with angry eyes, armed with long scissors, staring into a mirror late at night. He found himself saying, 'What did you do with your hair, all the stuff you cut off?'

509

'I burnt it.' She was wearing one of her 'good' flowery dresses, not woven, but made of light cotton, which she had hitched up over her knees revealing long slim brown bare legs and sandalled feet. She sat leaning forward, her long necklace swinging gently. As Edward looked she pulled her skirt down.

After a moment's silence he said, 'Those plants need watering, the ones in the hall.'

'Yes. Yes.'

Bettina with short straight hair looked younger, cleverer, foxier, like some casual stylish boy who might be pointed out as a brilliant student. Edward saw her now for the first time as separate, lonely, someone with a private individual future, not part of a trio, and his heart was touched. Also he saw her likeness to Jesse, and with a strange pang her likeness to himself, as he read or conjectured a reciprocal vision in her face, as she narrowed her light grey eyes in the sunshine and thrust back her untidy hair. She did not smile, but regarded Edward with a not unbenevolent curiosity. She said, 'You're wearing Jesse's ring.'

'Yes. It's mine. He gave it to me.' Surely that's true isn't it? thought Edward. There was no other possible answer. He was not going to surrender the ring. He said, 'I see the poplars are dead.' He had meant to say, 'cut down'.

'Yes, we had them cut down.'

'Surely you don't need the money now?'

Bettina continued to stare at him and did not answer.

Edward sat down on the grass, it was warm. 'Why is the grass here always so short?'

'The tree men put sheep in.'

'Why did May ask me to Seegard?'

'She felt she had to, after she got Thomas McCaskerville's letter.'

'*Thomas McCaskerville's letter?*'

'Yes. Didn't you know? He wrote to her about what had happened to you, saying you were depressed and needed a change. He suggested we invite you, so we did.'

'You mean it wasn't your idea at all?'

'No. Did you imagine we suddenly felt we wanted you?'

'Yes,' said Edward, 'I did. This rather changes things.' So it was Thomas's doing all along. Perhaps Thomas thought he would run away and wanted to be sure he knew where he'd run to. And Edward had so much needed, still so much needed, to feel that there was somewhere where he was longed for.

'I don't see why,' said Bettina. 'We could have said no. We welcomed you. We were glad to see you.'

'Were we?'

'Edward, why do you think I'm your enemy?'

'I don't. Yes, I do.' He was afraid of her. Yet what could she do to him now that Jesse was dead?

Bettina did not repeat her question or deny that she was his enemy. She sighed and turned her head.

At least Jesse had wanted him. That couldn't be taken away. 'Jesse wanted to see me, he wanted to see me very much, he said so.'

'He may have said anything. You probably didn't realise how far away he was. He didn't even know who you were. He kept saying, "Who is that boy?" and we'd tell him, and he'd forget again.'

'No,' said Edward, 'he knew who I was all right. He said he wrote to me. I never got any letters. I expect someone destroyed them.'

'He was rambling. He couldn't have written a letter. He couldn't paint, he couldn't write. The only thing that really struck him was when he saw you with a girl. That upset him, it made him jealous.'

'How do you know?'

'He told us. Of course. He told us everything. Who was the girl, by the way?'

'Mark Wilsden's sister.'

Bettina did not display any interest in this. 'Why have you come here now?'

'To see you. And about Jesse.'

'What?'

'About his death. I don't understand it. Was it suicide?'

'What do you think?' Bettina got up and mounted onto the fluted plinth and stood holding onto the pillar with one hand.

'Or was he murdered?'

511

'You mean by us? Edward! Why not by you?'

Edward, beginning to get up too, paused on one knee. A slight breeze was blowing Bettina's skirt and her hair. The sun was sinking behind the trees and the air was cooler. He wondered, could Bettina have *seen* him find drowned Jesse and pass on? If that was what happened. 'Why me?'

'You were the new factor in the situation, the dangerous newcomer, everything had been the same for a long time, it seemed nothing could shift it, then when you arrived a lot of things happened quickly. Probably it wasn't your fault – any more than it was that your friend fell out of the window. Some people just bring disasters about.'

'That's nonsense,' said Edward. 'You wanted him to die. I didn't.'

'It's not as simple as that,' said Bettina, 'it's true we couldn't bear to see him decaying in front of our eyes –'

'I remember now, May actually said that she'd written to me because she thought I could make things change!'

'You call her May now, do you? His senility was spoiling all our lives, it went on so long. We hated to see him fading, we pitied him.'

'Perhaps you destroyed him out of pity.'

Bettina looked down at Edward who was now standing near her. 'You can be absolutely sure of one thing. Whatever happened it was what Jesse wanted to happen.'

'That sounds like an excuse.' But it was what Edward wanted to think too.

'You disturbed him,' said Bettina, 'you talked about taking him to London. He had to die here.'

'You're sure you didn't help him to die?'

'You mean by leaving doors open? He couldn't have died an ordinary death. Something came to fetch him.'

'I don't understand.'

'Perhaps you were involved after all. Or rather your brother was. He was a portent, just a sign.'

'Jesse said he was a dead man, a corpse.'

'There was a collision of forces.'

'You don't mean Stuart *did* anything to Jesse?'

'No, no, it was all happening in Jesse's mind, an

apprehension, an alien magic, your brother was something external, an unconscious manifestation, a symptom not a cause. Something quite accidental can seem to exorcise the gods one lives by when they are departing anyway.'

'Are the poltergeists still there?'

'They've gone. They were Jesse's. Not anything to do with me and Ilona.'

'You think Jesse got a – a message – that it was time to go? So it was suicide?'

'You simplify everything!'

'Was that why May invited Stuart? I hadn't changed things enough, so she asked him.'

'It's just that a lot of things happened,' said Bettina, 'and I dare say a lot of other things made them happen.'

Standing near to her now, looking up at her sunburnt face and neck, Edward had an urge to seize hold of the skirt of her dress. The fear he had felt earlier had turned into a nervous excitement. He knew he must try to use this perhaps last chance to make Bettina talk. He had been clumsy, there was some better question, some key question, which he ought to ask, which would elicit the answer to the riddle. He could not find it. He asked instead, 'Did you burn him, like your hair?'

'No, we buried him.'

'Where?'

'Here.' Bettina jumped down from the pedestal and strode past Edward toward the two big yew trees which made a cave of darkness at the end of the glade. Edward followed. At the very end of the grass something long and dark was lying on the ground, or rather was set in the ground so that the surrounding grasses leant over and covered its edges. It was a large slab of black slate. Edward peered down at it. There was something carved, a few letters. JESSE. Edward and Bettina looked at each other across the stone.

'It's a piece of slate which was left over from the floor of the Atrium.'

'It must weigh a lot –'

'The tree men carried it. One of them is a stone mason, he carved the letters. As you see they're not very regular. They carried Jesse too.'

'So he's – here.'

'Yes.'

'In a coffin.'

'Yes. The tree men made the coffin, just a simple one. They are quite clever.'

They looked at each other. Then they looked down at the stone. After a few moments Edward said, 'I can't believe he's dead. I was looking for him in the house.' Already the earth had invaded the sides of the stone a little. Later on, if no one tended it, it would become covered with earth, overgrown with grass, lost. He said, 'Does May think he's dead, do you? Or do you think he's lying in the earth like a chrysalis and will come back to life and return?'

'He will not come back in our lifetime.'

Edward looked at Bettina who was still staring down, her face was very sad, yet with a beautiful relaxed repose. Taking in her words, which seemed so curiously appropriate, so quietly in place like words in a burial service, he wondered, is she mad, am I? Seeking something to say, he said, 'Perhaps people put down stones like that to keep the dead from rising.'

'If he came back now he'd be really mischievous, he'd be bad.'

'He has to wait?'

'To refill his being. I miss him terribly, agonisingly.' It was the conventional words which sounded strange.

'And May – how is she?'

'I can't measure her suffering. She is in a chaos of misery, she is degrading herself with grief.'

Edward recalled the typewriter. What did Bettina think about the 'memoirs'? It was possible she knew nothing about them. 'I miss him,' said Edward, 'I shall always miss him. I shall always think about him and love him. Of course he knew who I was, he thought about me, he wanted me to come, he loved me.' He thought, so they have buried the monster. With what rites did they lay him to rest?

Neither of them spoke for a while. Edward could no longer concentrate. The key question which would unlock the riddle had drifted away, no longer present even as an occluded

514

something. He found himself glancing at his watch. 'Well, I must go. I must get a train back to London. I have to look after my father.'

'Goodbye, then.'

Edward wondered if he should say something about Ilona, but decided not to. He said, 'Thank you – for talking to me – I hope – well, of course – we'll meet again – I'll come here – maybe –' But he could not find in his heart any wish or intention to come back. He searched for some suitable valediction. 'Will you be all right?'

Bettina smiled. 'You told Ilona we were elf maidens. Elf maidens look after themselves!'

Edward raised his hand in a kind of salute, like a gesture of homage. As he began to move away Bettina, seeming to forget him, stepped onto the slate and turned her back, looking away into the darkness under the yew trees. The movement seemed to him deliberately sacrilegious. For a moment he thought that she was actually going to *dance* upon the stone. If so, that was a dance which he must not witness. He hurried across the grass and began to run as quickly as he could down the pathway.

An idea which had come to him earlier was now growing in his mind. Of course he 'had to believe' that Jesse had known him and loved him. But was there not perhaps a proof? He bounded quickly across the swaying bridge and ran through the poplar grove, leaping over the smooth trunks of the felled trees. He went round the back of the house to the stable yard so as to enter immediately into the Interfectory. Glancing towards the fen he saw that the celandine meadow was now in full bloom with buttercups and white clover and misty tinges of red sorrel. He hurried in through the Interfectory and through the door into the tower. Here he slowed down and mounted the spiral staircase panting for breath. In the studio and 'nursery' nothing had changed except that the 'toys', which had been lying randomly about, had been pushed into a heap against the wall, and in the studio one of the tantric pictures of the beginning, or end, of the world had been set up on the easel. He did not pause to look, but hurried on up the staircase into the quiet carpeted 'flat' above, which seemed such an utterly different place. The hall of the flat was as neat as before, the doors closed. Edward, determined not to stop or pay attention to his frightened heart, reached the bedroom. There was no key in the lock this time, the door was unlocked. As he opened the door he prepared himself to see Jesse still there, propped up in bed, gazing at him with those jelly-like round eyes, and he felt ready to faint. But of course the room was empty, tidy, clean, the bed covered with a patchwork bedspread. The bed, which had been made invisible before by the disordered bed-clothes and Jesse's huge presence, now seemed so narrow and so small. It looked like a room in a country hotel, pretty but impersonal, where the last guest's messy disorder had been tidied away in readiness for the next guest.

Edward went straight to the window. Yes, there was the sea, a dark glowing blue spotted with emerald. And, oh, upon the sea there were crowds and crowds of sailing boats with huge-bellied spinnaker sails, striped in all colours, reds and blues and yellows and greens and blacks, moving slowly in different directions, crossing and passing each other with the elegance of a slow dance in the bright evening light. He thought, it's a sailing club, there's going to be a race, or rather the race must be over now. And suddenly he thought, there are people out there in a totally other world, people laughing and joking and kissing each other, men and pretty girls opening bottles of champagne. He turned back to the room, seeming now so small and quiet and lonely and sad. He wondered if the women had made that patchwork quilt, working silently together in the winter evenings. The white radiator which Jesse had indicated, an old-fashioned square metal object, probably not in use for years, with no pipe connected to it, was bracketed onto the wall, and Edward noticed that it had been dusted. There was a very small space behind it, into which he inserted his fingers from above. Nothing. Probably there had never been anything except in Jesse's mind. He knelt and pushed his fingers upward from below behind the cold metal. After some shifting to and fro his finger tips touched something which moved, but which it was impossible to grip. He was able to push it up a little and then, exploring from above with his other hand, he got two fingers onto it and drew it upward. It was a small folded sheet of cheap lined writing paper. He unfolded it. *I, Jesse Aylwyn Baltram, hereby bequeath everything of which I die possessed to my dear much loved son, Edward Baltram.* The will, written in a rather shaky Italic script, was dated about two years earlier. The witnesses, signing below with awkward hand, were Tom Dickey and Bob O'Brien. Clearly these were tree men whom Jesse had called in secretly, perhaps one day when the women had gone to market, or met deep in the wood on one of his walks by himself.

Edward sat down on the bed and looked at the document. A great explosion of surprise and joy and horror opened out around him like a bomb cloud or doom-laden martyr's aura. How wonderful, how terrible, how marvellously significant, how frightfully painful: what on earth was he to do? After having read the thing through several times concentrating on each word he folded it again and put it in his pocket and sat staring at the window where the sky had assumed a denser softer more velvety blue. He thought, well at least this proves that before I came Jesse was thinking about me – and loving me. I believe he did write to me, as he said, only they intercepted the letter. But the will – did he really mean it, or was it just a passing impulse, a momentary gesture of spite against his captors? Edward said aloud, 'Jesse, what shall I do?' As he spoke, he touched the ring, and wondered if he would, some time in the future, do this again. There was no revelation. He reflected that of course May, with her suspicious mind, might have imagined that Jesse would want to play this trick, and would have made him update his 'proper' will at intervals. Or perhaps she thought that no such 'whimsical' will could defeat her claim in a law court. Were there to be law courts then? Did Edward want to sneak in and disinherit May and his sisters? Of course not; though the idea of being fearfully rich formed itself for an instant like a little golden spark in Edward's mind. But he didn't need money, did he? He could earn his living, and he'd probably inherit something from Harry. What disgusting thoughts, all about lawyers and money. Of course he might make a generous arrangement, just keep a bit as a memento – but that was still about lawyers and money. Or just flourish the will in front of their noses and then tear it up? That would leave them with a moral dilemma – not that May and Bettina would stand much nonsense from a moral dilemma – well that was unfair, how little he knew them really, they had always been acting a part with him. Better to destroy it at once. What did Jesse want? Perhaps nothing in particular, perhaps just to send Edward a message, and he had done that. The will had performed its only good important task of *reminding* Edward, for he had always known it since the first moment when he had opened the bedroom door, that his father knew him and loved him.

He got up, straightened out the bed, and went to the door, he did not look back or go again to the window to see the coloured ships circling in the evening light. He closed the door behind him and went with orderly haste down the spiral stairs. In the Interfectory he found a box of matches on the chimneypiece and burnt the will in the fireplace. He instantly regretted that, without further reflection, he had performed so irrevocable an action.

He now urgently wanted to get away without any more encounters. As he finished breaking up the papery ashes with a poker he saw, staring into the corner of his eye, the photo of Jesse, Jesse as Edward, Edward as Jesse, hanging on its nail low down on the wall. He lifted it off, looked at it, and decided to take it with him. *I am here, do not forget me.* In the Atrium he hesitated, then went over to the corner where the poor plants had been so roughly crowded together and felt one or two of the dried-up pots. He had an impulse to fetch water for them, but the urge to escape was too great. He picked up the cup of liquid which was on the table and smelt it. It was one of May's herbal brews. He poured it into the pot of *his* plant, the one that seemed to be dead. He thought, either this will cure it, or else put it out of its misery.

As he made his way out he saw that something which had not been there before was lying on one of the two chairs by the door. It was his jacket, cleaned and folded, which he had last seen covering Jesse's dead face. Edward picked it up and went out banging the door behind him. As he did so a piece of stone the size of his hand leapt out of the wall beside him. The enchanter's palace was already beginning to fall to pieces.

I AM ON a golden chain, thought Midge. I have been taken back into history. I have allowed myself to be trapped by morality. Her captors were her husband and her son.

It was high summer at Quitterne. Midge was sitting upstairs at the bedroom window watching Thomas mowing the lawn. Head down, grey hair flopping forward, without his glasses, he appeared to be propelling the big yellow machine which in fact propelled itself, making great play with it when at the end of each journey it had to be turned. Neat stripes of darker and lighter green were appearing upon the already sleek turf which was now half covered by the shadow of the copper beech. Thomas, dressed in old corduroy trousers and a sloppy open-necked blue shirt, looked younger, altogether more impromptu. He paused at intervals to wipe the sweat off his glowing sun-reddened face. Beyond him red and white roses posed in the quiet sunny air against the tall shabby box hedge where intensely blue delphiniums with black eyes were also in flower. Thomas, pausing in his toil, looked up and waved. Midge waved back. She had cooked a splendid lunch. She had washed up. She had rested. She had put on a different dress.

Midge had made her decision. She had made it, when it came, so quickly that looking back it sometimes seemed as if it must have been a matter of chance. Supposing that confident key in the door had been Harry's and not Thomas's? It was all chance or else the opposite, something arranged by God. Edward's arrival for instance. The talk with Edward, so quiet, so *sensible*, had itself been a necessary event. Edward had been the new ingredient, the mediator. No one else could have done it. He was the closest person who was not horribly involved, a candid intelligent well-intentioned on-looker, an old friend, he was unique. Talking to him about Stuart she felt she was telling the story for the first time. Telling Harry, telling Thomas, had not been, could not be, truthful narration, but a form of warfare. Taking it in, Edward had, quickly and intuitively, touched her state of mind, pressing its structure at vulnerable and unstable points. His cry 'it's mad, it's daft, it must be false!' about her love for Stuart had startled her like the war cry of a new force. It was possible to see 'the event' in a different light, not losing faith in it, but receiving in relation to it, more space, more play. Stuart had seemed so authoritative, so complete, something lethal making all her previous existence worthless, inspiring that terrible craving, that pain, which could only be alleviated by his presence and feared like death itself the possibility of banishment. Edward, who had been suffering so terribly himself (this fact only occurred to Midge later) appeared here on the side of the ordinary world where absolute choices between life and death did not take place, where reason, gentleness, compassion, compromise brought about viable ways of life. Of course she would see Stuart again, of course he would not reject her with loathing. From this point she could see her sudden passion not as false, not as a 'psychological device', but as an impersonal happening which was not quite what it had seemed, but something to be reflected on, worked on, compatible with other things. Of course she could never live with Stuart, work with him, do good with him as she had intended, all that was a dream, not an empty lying dream, but a pointer of some kind. Well, there was always plenty of good she could do if she wanted to. And when she was this far along Midge was already imagining how Stuart might be her friend, perhaps laugh at her, and by then – he wasn't God after all. The intense relief of *not* facing death, as if Stuart by rejecting her could decree her end, filling her with gratitude to Edward, made the image of Stuart less huge, less final, more human. Edward had said Stuart was something external, something bumped into. It was all in her own mind, something she was doing to herself. So she could do things – even *make use* of what had happened?

What had happened had been in effect a means by which she had separated herself from Harry, a light in which she had been appalled by the last two years. But did this change in Stuart's image which was also, was it not, a self-preserving flight from death, leave her as she was before, however for the moment separated and appalled, still Harry's mistress? Could not the Stuart drama be regarded as a pointer to the truth and realism of – acknowledging Harry and marrying him, *thus* ending the evasions and the lies? Was the separation from Harry perhaps a cleansing period which would *return* her to him, truthful resolute and unashamed? Or was Harry over? Would she be taken back into history, rejecting as an episode the shocking, the revolutionary, the entirely new? So complex and so swift were the thoughts, condensed yet clear, which Edward had occasioned by his awkward intuitive words, by his very presence. After a paralysis of misery and fear Midge's mind flew about like a bird seeking freedom. Am I calculating, she wondered, can I calculate? If I stay with Thomas I can be friends with Stuart, but not if I go to Harry. If I leave Thomas I might have to fight for Meredith. I've never really thought about . . . Meredith's unhappiness . . . Harry always said it would be all right. Yes. Meredith is an absolute, Stuart is not. Edward had said, doesn't that leave you with the real things? He meant Meredith and Thomas. Yes, they were real. Stuart was a dream. Harry was . . . Had Stuart permanently killed her love for Harry? Had not her delays and her falsehoods themselves been evidences that she did not love him *enough*? Could she make *that* sacrifice for Harry, to destroy her home, her marriage? Evidently not. And, evidently, the long affair had not unmade her home and her family. And Thomas . . . didn't she love him? Yes. Oh how she was weighting the scales now, doing it deliberately, and seeing everything except the ultimate *why* she was suddenly seeing in this new light. When it came to it (but why was it now coming there?) Harry too, like Stuart, was a dream, something that couldn't *be*, and had she not known this all along? Those two awful years, and

522

they had been awful, had proved it so. But surely all that love and joy had been something real? Well, it was past. Then when Thomas arrived it was as if she had expected him: such a gentle quiet unfrightening loving Thomas. It was as if he too had been thinking and thinking, approaching her in his thought, and their two thoughts had brought them, at just the right moment, together. (This was something which Thomas said later on.) He had even begged her pardon and kissed her hand. That he kissed her hand somehow impressed Midge very much. After that they embraced and Midge cried a lot and Thomas cried a little. And after that they talked for hours. And Midge could see that her decision had been made.

I deceived my husband, Midge thought, and now I have betrayed my lover. I handed him over to Thomas, tied hand and foot, gagged and helpless, I did not look at his beseeching eyes. I told it all to Thomas as if it were the story of a catastrophe, a bondage from which I had escaped (but I *did* feel I was escaping, I *did* feel free), something awful which had happened to me and which he was to sympathise with, and he did sympathise. He did more, he *protected* me so carefully at every point where I might have felt shame or resentment at having to tell such things to anybody. He *made* me tell them, yet at once they were turned into something else, as if as soon as they were told, as soon as they came out of my mouth, they were metamorphosed from black into white. And Midge had a picture of black pellets emerging from her mouth and being changed into white sweetmeats, white bread, white moths, doves. I suppose that's what happens when people confess to a priest. And that was how I betrayed Harry. I sold him for gain. And yet I had to, I had proved to myself that there was no other way to move, it was what I wanted more than anything to do. And when I was talking to Thomas I knew that I loved him and had always loved him and my not-loving-him had been a necessary fake. Or perhaps too I was falling in love with him again in a new way. The not-lying made everything so completely different, and of course not as it once was. And if I had refused what was then possible I would have unmade myself and been taken to hell by a black serpent. Why do I think this, has Thomas put all these notions into my

523

mind? There are such strange things there too. Are they out of his old Scottish-Jewish mind, full of monsters? Or are they my monsters? I must not be afraid now, but oh the pain, the pain of it all. Of course I didn't tell all of it; and since the telling of it made it something different perhaps I didn't tell any of it. And of course Thomas understands that too. He knows when to press, to hold on with a grip of iron, and when to relax, to make light and air, to withdraw to a great distance so that he is only a tiny figure the size of a matchbox. I suppose that is his kind of cleverness, or is it wisdom, I don't know, the cleverness for which I love him. But he thinks he was a fool not to have guessed, and I hate to think of that. And there he is now, he has finished his mowing and is putting up a badminton net.

How has it all happened, she wondered, because it *has* happened. Or am I still in danger? Do I have to know that ultimate *why* or *how* before I am not in danger? Is it all ultimately a matter of instinct? When Thomas kissed my hand I just knew. Perhaps it's impossible after all to explain, really to tell the truth to anyone, or to see it all oneself. That's what God is for, to make our lies truth by seeing into the heart. But that's something we can't know. I cheated Thomas really, I told him everything except one thing, not a particular thing, not like a fact, but I kept something back like a precious jewel, I stole one thing from the casket when I handed it over. *That*'s what Thomas knows, but he won't say, he'll just watch. And I misled Stuart because I said I no longer loved Harry and that Stuart had killed my love for Harry when what he had really killed or maimed was my desire for sex. And that comes back. How awfully strange it all is now, as if I can suddenly see everything in my life, it's not quite in focus but it's very vivid, and I can sit here with folded hands and look at my life. It's as if I have nothing to do now, Thomas and Meredith will do it all. I still love Stuart, but it's a quiet subjective sort of love, I don't want to shoot myself and fall at his feet. I frightened him, poor boy. Thomas said Stuart was a 'negative presence', a catalyst. A handy thing to be, he said, a good catalyst. He said I'd put it all onto Stuart, like an ass's head. He said in a little while I ought to write him a kind letter. Stuart will want everything to be all right, and I'll help him and there will be a bond between us. Such things did Midge say to herself for consolation and to keep her mind calm and clear while she was suffering the terrible pain. For the secret which she still carried with her was that even now nothing in the world prevented her from going back to Harry. His love for her was still there waiting, like a great warm house, a spacious beautiful sunny landscape. Her love for him existed too, crushed into that tiny radioactive capsule, tumour, gem or speck of poison.

Of course the fierce little thing would slowly lose its potency, fade and dissolve away into nothing, or rather be changed into some identifiable but harmless piece of tissue. But now, a slight shift in the particles which determine events and she could be far away, with Harry, in the south of France, sitting in a café and looking at the sea, or on an island in Greece, or in an exquisite white Italian city perched on a hilltop. The banality of her imagining made her sigh. That was not the stuff of her great love which had now been almost entirely transformed into pain. Now that she had made her choice she had the fearful *leisure* to rediscover all her old attachment and experience it, alone. Thomas could not, in that secret place, help her, though he knew, he saw, her suffering and was humble and gentle in its presence. He saw where it was and regarded it with his cool blue eyes. Stuart had said stop lying and you will see where you are, if you stop lying and go home you will be happy. It was not as simple or as fast as that; though there was, she knew, a lightness in the future which had been absent from her life for two years. Be patient, Thomas had said to her, be quiet, do not be made unhappy by your unhappiness. Welcome it in. Welcome it! Sometimes it devoured her, her substance preying upon her substance, her own cells blackly infected and turned to burning ill. She had written to Harry. She had not told Thomas this, but he knew. She had written such a short letter, she couldn't write letters, saying that it was over and they must part, they were already parted and she was sorry. It was no use trying to explain. But the little letter, when she read it through, was as she had wanted it to be, perfectly clear. What

525

she had not told Thomas and he did not know was that she had at once had a reply from Harry which she was keeping hidden in her dressing table.

Midge sat relaxed at the window, all her limbs limp. She was an invalid. She was waiting for the signs of health which would gradually appear, touching her whole body and her aching soul with little gentle caresses. She could wait and breathe and be patient as Thomas had told her to. She would cook and clean the house and bring in flowers, aware that all the good things she felt sure she was destined to do would perhaps after all turn out to be the dull old familiar things, the duties of her family and her home. She could not have survived that rupture, that desertion, that flight, that had seemed so beautiful in the unreal prospect of it, to leave Thomas behind and Meredith torn in two, and live a new free life with Harry, casting off the past. It had only seemed possible because it was really out of the question, something not really imagined, a fantasy coexisting with a reality which excluded it. How could she have done it to Meredith: the choices of which to hurt, the painful embarrassed visits, the car driven mutely from the door, each parent unable to talk about his life with the other; the silent loneliness and the terrible cultivation of indifference and withdrawal. Sometimes such fates could not be avoided, but here it would have been wanton. I wish he hadn't known, she thought. But he would have found out later. And he is so grown-up now, with his clever conscious eyes, and how *intelligently* he and Thomas have worked together to *entangle* me in their love and, it seems incredible to think of it in that way, their *gratitude*. And Thomas says they haven't discussed it, and I believe him, *they haven't exchanged a word*. How alike they are! And she smiled, for of course it wasn't just for Meredith that she had thrown away that of whose charm and beauty she dared not think, it was for Thomas. She had tried to learn to hate Thomas in order to have the strength to leave him. It was difficult to credit, even to remember, those states of mind. Now she was free to discover all her old feelings for Thomas, or rather to find out what had been happening to them, as if she had come back to find them grown, developed, refined, and most evidently powerful. Had she not always known that Thomas was better, stronger, more lovable, more interesting? Thomas had won the game.

I was in love, thought Midge, I was *mad*, but I *was* in love. It was a self-authenticating experience, as *he* used to say; was it not unfair to call it a dream? Only not everything has a place in life, and there was no place for this. Was it just the long lying that ruined their chances? Supposing they had told Thomas at the start? But the start was so exciting, so confusing, no statement could possibly have been made, it was all an unutterably brilliant present, there was no future, the present was the future, how could they have reflected and planned? Later on the structure of falsehood was already there and it seemed at every moment impossible to tell Thomas, and equally impossible not to intend to tell him. They were both waiting for a sign. Well, the sign had come. Did she still wish, as she often had wished, that she had met Harry first, never married Thomas, that it had all been different? This wish, which had seemed so full of substance, now seemed empty. But something, the undeniable past itself, could not be destroyed. Would she, one day, feel sentimental about it? She would not forget that she had loved Harry and the remembered love would become in time harmless. Meanwhile the possibility of Harry would remain for a while, rejected yet active, like a benign curable tumour. The word was frightening, some tumours destroyed their owners. Death could come; but I won't die of that, she thought. Death was everywhere, its rays were falling upon herself and upon those she loved and upon the whole earth. She recalled her dream of the white horseman, and the curious effect which Stuart had had upon her, the killing of her ordinary life, the annihilation of her instinctive desires, the sense of utter deprivation which had been too a kind of unearthly joy. She realised that this intense feeling had passed, was already remote even absurd, yet was also something she would not forget.

The sun was declining and the shadow of the copper beech had covered most of the lawn, where Thomas and Meredith were playing badminton, enthusiastically but very badly. Now Meredith's dog, a golden labrador puppy with a talent to amuse, had seized hold of the shuttlecock. As the players pursued him with shouts of laughter she was aware of something moving in the sky. It was the air balloon with blue and yellow stripes which she had seen once before, and she felt an impulse of pleasure, remembering how unhappy she had been then.

Midge left the window and opened a drawer in her dressing table and took out a pair of stockings in which she had concealed Harry's letter. She wanted to read it just once more.

I cannot and will not accept what you say. Please be clear about this. I will not accept it and you do not mean it. This is, how strange, my first love letter to you. Ever since that day after Ursula's party when we looked into each other's eyes, looked away, looked again, and *knew*, we have been so close, so often together, we have lived without letters. I wanted to write to you, to consume the pain of absence in writing, but you were so afraid of Thomas. Now that doesn't matter any more, I don't even care if Thomas reads this. I love you, I *love* you, and I possess you and will not give you up. And you love me, and you *love no one else*. Do not deceive yourself, my darling and my queen, do not falter now when the way is open for us at last. I love you, I live by and in your love, my life rests upon your love. I have had to live from day to day, every day you were still with me was paradise regained. But I hoped, and you hoped, that the time would come when we would live in eternity, just us two absolutely together. My knees shake, they give way when I think about you, I lie struck down to the floor as I was on that first day. Do you realise how rare this is, mutual perfect love? With my body I thee worship. We know, which is given to so few, perfect happiness, perfect joy. You cannot deny this, to do so would be a deep wicked lie, not like the lies we had to use to protect ourselves, to protect our precious love, and which we hated so, I hated so, they were never my fault. I should have stayed with you on that day when Thomas arrived, when he knew, I regret that, I am sorry, I was a coward, fear of Thomas has undone us all along, let it not do so now when at last there is no need. Oh my love, my sweet dear love, my every instinct is not to hurt you, I would fight with demons, with God himself, to save you from any smallest hurt or harm. And now I seem to be accusing you. I *do* accuse you, of untruthfulness, unfaithfulness, lack of courage – lack of courage at the very moment when it is most needed and will be most rewarded. We are so close to our happy ending, to achieving what we have worked and suffered for and have a *right* to, our freedom together. You have had a shock – two shocks – Thomas's discovery and your little mad fit about Stuart, which I hope and believe is over. (*That* I could not credit or countenance. I now realise that I took it too seriously!) You may feel that you want to rest. But, my love, my angel, this is no moment for resting. We must *work*. We must establish our true home, where we shall live forever immortal as the gods, where we shall fly our indomitable flag – you remember about the flag? Midge, do not delay now, do not be *idle*, I cannot believe that you, with open eyes and who have experienced both, could now prefer the second best, the tenth best, to the best! If you did you would regret it bitterly, as the years passed, inside the emptiness and loneliness of your marriage. You would grow old quickly if you stayed with Thomas, *he* is old. Don't let sheer weakness, sheer senseless convention, for it is *entirely* senseless now; don't you see, keep us apart for another day. I am waiting for you, hour by hour, minute by minute, *waiting*. We shall have Meredith, he will be ours, we have agreed, we know. Don't be afraid! How can he not prefer us, and our happiness and our gaiety and our freedom, to the austerity and dull harsh Scottish gloom of Thomas's world? Thomas is a melancholic. We can live anywhere, in the coloured places, in the sun, as you always wanted. We can travel to the east. You said how much Meredith wanted to go to India. He can go to India with us. We'll be a happy trio, a happy family, we'll *enjoy* life. *We* won't live in the dark. Don't delay, don't any longer live without all those *good* things, so *many* of them, which in your deepest heart you *desire*. Oh follow your desires, your own, your very own. Not only the utter perfection of our bodies together –

529

let *them* speak for us – but also a universe of rich harmonious endlessly various and ever renewed happinesses for us and for Meredith – My dear dear love, I kiss your feet, and beg you to end this agony of uncertainty for both of us. I feel I shall die of this pain, die of your absence from me – *imagine* what it will be like when you run to me, into my arms, and when at last we can go away together without needing any falsehood or fearing any discovery. Don't you see – we have been *given*, what we could not boldly seize, *permission*, I mean moral permission, to do what we *want*? Don't feel any guilt about it. You won't hurt anyone much, only Thomas's *amour propre*. He has deep feelings, but not in his marriage, as you said once. But if you destroy me – I don't mean I should commit suicide or die of grief, I should live on and perhaps even try to fall in love with somebody else. But any other love would be a shadow, a fake, compared with this reality which we have achieved together, this world-revealing certainty which we have shared, my princess, my gentle sweet darling, my one and only. Midge, nobody in the world can make you *be* as I can.

I ought never to have let you go away, I regret this and ask your forgiveness on my knees for this and any other fault which I have unwittingly committed. Once it was *known* I ought never to have left your side. The crazy thing about Stuart came like a cloud between us at the crucial moment, as if some devil, perhaps out of Thomas's deep mind, had come to confuse us. If it had not been for that you would have run to me the moment, the second, that Thomas found out. Your weird obsession with my son, so uniquely hurtful, upset me too much, as I now see, impressed me too much, I should not have believed it. It was a neurotic fancy that you ran into rather than face the immediate task of breaking with Thomas. *Come to me* – and let us live, where you always wanted to live, in the truth and the light. Oh God how much I love you. There is nothing in me but that love. Do not destroy me, Midge.

H.

Midge read the letter again, with tears in her eyes. It moved her terribly. How it conjured him up, with his sweetness, his beauty, the authority of his love, his *absolute charm*. He was right, they were perfectly suited to each other. But it did not follow that they could ever be happy together, and happiness was so much the point. Rightness and goodness of course; but happiness . . . that was essential . . . And even now, while she was still so ill with it all, she had tasted it a little, witnessing the joy of Thomas and Meredith. She and Harry had deceived themselves about their future, as they had deceived themselves about the importance of Thomas and Meredith. She read between the lines of the letter, so touching and so ardent, that perhaps Harry realised too that something, he could not tell exactly what, had broken their compact. Midge was not sure exactly what it was either, and when the break had come. Was it to do with Stuart, that cloud which had arrived so strangely at just that time, and had not left her as she was? Surely Stuart was a symptom or a sign, not a cause. What Harry said about Meredith was wrong, almost a lie, something which he wanted to believe. Tears fell from her eyes, tears for something wonderful which had had to end and was gone into the past where it would fade and not be remembered as she remembered it now. How could one resist such a lover, how could one have resisted him? She was fortunate to be, when it ended, in another place, a real place, a place which she had really never left, inside an innocent love. Poor Harry, he had gambled everything, while she had always kept something back. But then that was part of how she had failed and made him fail too. It was hard to think about.

The letter had arrived three days ago and she had intended to destroy it at once, for fear of Thomas finding it, and for fear of being tempted to read it again, but she could not. She had now read it several times. Yesterday, with a terribly beating heart, she had run out to post a note which just said, *No, I am sorry. No.* As she did this she was pierced by the thought: he *will* find someone else, and I shall have such a terrible long pain of jealousy. My pains are not ending, they are beginning. Her hand nearly failed her and turned traitor as she reached the letter out to the pillar box – and imagined Harry opening it, and what different letter she might have written. Yet when it was done she felt better, more free, as she had not felt free for two years, more completely herself. Harry's letter must now be destroyed. The idea of keeping it and reading it at intervals was horrible to her. It was already dead. She had killed it.

She took it downstairs and burnt it in the grate. She had just finished crushing the ashes with her foot and was standing looking down when Thomas entered, and she moved quickly away.

Thomas, who had of course found and read the letter soon after its arrival, guessed what she was doing, saw the traces of tears and gazed upon her with particular tenderness and pride.

'Thomas –'

'Yes, my darling –'

'Now you're retiring would we have enough money to go to India with Meredith?'

'I don't see why not.' (Thomas, perhaps it was a Scottish characteristic, was in fact far better off than he had ever let on to anybody, even his wife.)

Thomas was in an extraordinary state of mind. When he was alone he gazed at himself in the mirror and even made faces. He had spied on his wife, watching her through a window he had seen a look of touching animal pleasure on her face as she ate a cheesecake. He tracked her, like a keeper tracking a sick animal. He watched her for symptoms of health. He felt that his general understanding of human psychology had broken down. Where the individual mind is concerned the light of science could reveal so little; and the mishmash of scientific ideas and mythology and literature and isolated facts and sympathy and intuition and love and appetite for power which was known as psychoanalysis, and which of course did sometimes 'help people', could make the most extraordinary mistakes when it left the paths of the obvious. Wild guesses, propelled by the secret wishes of the guesser, could initiate long journeys down wrong tracks. The person he found most puzzling was himself. Why had it seemed so essential to run out of the house after he had confronted his wife with the proofs of her infidelity? He had left her with cold words. He seemed instantly concerned with his dignity. He even talked about damage to his practice, not because he cared about it or even thought it would occur, but because he wanted to set up an instant barrier of ironical coolness and 'practical considerations', not only to protect himself but to hurt her. He could not have stayed and argued, produced a 'natural response' with shouts, commands and prayers, that would have been painfully out of character, he did not want to be forced to become another person. He had been incapable of any direct response also perhaps because he needed to despair at once. The shock of discovering what another man (less orderly, less trustful, less self-confident, less self-absorbed) might have found out sooner had been so intense, an utterly new kind of shock which paralysed distant and unpractised regions of his being. He felt he had to be alone to recover *himself*, and to make himself capable of sustaining with dignity and rational calm the total collapse of his marriage.

Harry had pretended to think that he was cold, uninterested in his wife, prepared to give her up. Midge was supposed to have said he was humourless, untender and boring. Prompted by Harry, Midge probably had said those things. He could imagine how instinctively they must have connived together to protect themselves by belittling him. Thomas was resolutely concerned not to imagine the details of those 'two years'. There was no need for *that*, and here he could truthfully tell himself that there were mysteries which could not be fathomed and must be left alone, in the old parlance, 'left to God'. His imaginings, when not vulgarly obvious, would be wild, and in either case falsities. It was a kindness to Midge not to pursue her in his thoughts into that place, so frightful to him, so painful to her. Surely he would meet Harry again. Their lives were bound together by other lives: Edward was Midge's nephew, Meredith's cousin. Besides, he did not want altogether to lose Harry. He allowed himself to imagine how agonisingly intolerable Harry must have found his mistress's sudden 'fancy' for his son. Would

Thomas one day, perhaps soon, be helping Midge to construct some easy, friendly relation with Stuart? *Could* they all meet, and let it not be seen in any of their brows . . .? He hoped so. The future, that must be endured, and meanwhile left quiet in the dark.

Thomas was not afraid. He was allowing himself to feel happy, sometimes he wanted to shout with it. Such positive self-conscious happiness was rare in his life. Patiently, without pressure, largely without speech, he would rework his relationship with Midge, his love and her love, and feel at times her questing fingers seeking for his in the same dark. He had confidence in her return, and for a time would have to be the quiet tactful spectator of her unhappiness and slow recovery, letting his happiness teach and tend her. In this task Meredith would be his wordless telepathically close accomplice. Thus they would heal her, Meredith's joy and relief, imaged in the crazy friskings of the puppy, was a constant source of reassurance, almost a proof. Meredith liked his school, he was growing up, he was clever and wise. This too was the future. Thomas felt that, through no merit of his own, he had escaped a terrible shipwreck, and was now able to sail on, more securely as every day passed with its interests and events which were not connected with the alarms of the recent past. So, other things could happen, ordinary life could go on. But something far from ordinary had taken place which would have totally obsessed Thomas had he not been otherwise concerned, and which even as it was caused him much anxiety. It concerned Mr Blinnet.

Mr Blinnet's unscheduled arrival at Quitterne had been immediately prompted by Thomas's unprecedentedly abrupt cancellation of their next session together. This shock to Mr Blinnet's system occasioned changes in his state of mind which might have come about anyway or might perhaps never have come about at all. When Thomas had rushed forward to Mr Blinnet's car he had at once tried to persuade his patient to return to London, promising to see him as usual in a few days. Mr Blinnet would have none of this. Thomas then asked him into the house and gave him a cup of tea, hoping that he would soon calm down and go away. For it was clear that Mr

Blinnet was very upset, he even took his hat off. Thomas was very upset too, and had to go upstairs to comb his hair. Then Thomas, who wanted a drink, offered one to Mr Blinnet. Soon after this Mr Blinnet began to reminisce about his life in terms which he had never previously used. It emerged from these, and Thomas gradually became convinced, that Mr Blinnet had actually committed a serious crime, and that the more detailed part of his story of mental aberration was fictitious. Thomas could see, as in a film, the pale round face of his erstwhile patient changing before his eyes until he was confronted with an entirely different person: someone clever and determined enough to succeed, in a long relation with an experienced therapist, in simulating mental disorder. (When Thomas expressed surprise Mr Blinnet said impatiently, 'It's all in the books after all!') In fact, and this rescued Thomas from complete dismay by interesting him a lot, Mr Blinnet's sane fantasy had been so wholehearted that it had become a compulsive addiction; and in this sense, to some small extent, Mr Blinnet was 'genuine'. This was worthy of study.

The original idea had been the one which Thomas had long ago mooted and rejected: the refined elaboration of a legal defence to be used if the crime ever came to light. It would probably have worked too, thought Thomas. What, to the eye of a jury, could be madder than Mr Blinnet? He imagined his own ardent defence of his patient in the witness box. Yet had Mr Blinnet been quite clever enough, had he simulated just the right kind of madness for this particular crime? A psychiatrist acting for the other side might have caught him out in some crucial error, some revealing slip. Thomas was already conjecturing what such a slip might be. He was fascinated by his own credulity. What a pity, he recollected, that he would never be able to publish a paper on the subject. As it was, that afternoon's work left them both in a serious quandary. It was not that Thomas felt a duty to telephone the police. His professional secrecy could remain unbreached. The nature of Mr Blinnet's crime was such that it was not in the least likely to be repeated, in fact strictly speaking could not be repeated. Mr Blinnet was not a public menace, and Thomas did not believe in retributive justice. It was just that their relationship, whose intimacy had been sterilised and confined by the ethics and atmosphere of therapy, was now suddenly set up in the middle of ordinary life, engendering new obligations, new problems, new emotions. There could be no talk now of 'transference'. Mr Blinnet was in love with Thomas. Thomas had acquired a new friend, a close friend, whom he could not abandon. Now that the mask of crazed obsession, originally simulated, later habitual, had been removed, Mr Blinnet's face expressed a refined intelligence. What am I to *do* with him? Thomas wondered. Announce he is cured and introduce him to everybody? Mr Blinnet had no plans for reducing his dependence upon his healer. Whatever am I to do? thought Thomas. Well, that too was the future and another story.

IT DOESN'T ADD up, thought Edward. Ilona said it was telepathy, not that that explains anything. Mrs Quaid could have 'read' that I was worrying about Jesse – except that then I wasn't. So it's independent of time, is it? And of course she knew Seegard so it was in her mind too. But then the television? That could have been just a coincidence, there was an old programme about Jesse, perhaps Mrs Quaid had a tape of it, and I'd imagined the background, the sea, the estuary, places I'd thought about and wanted to get to, just as I was falling asleep? I did go to sleep, didn't I? As for finding Jesse's body, the mouth of the river was a pretty obvious place to look. There's a funny feeling about all that business, he thought, it's all very intense and brightly coloured, yet difficult to recall, like a dream, I mustn't *worry* about it. I worry because I want to feel that Jesse arranged it all, and that's a sort of nonsense.

'By the way, Ed,' said Stuart, 'there are some letters for you upstairs, Harry put them in a drawer in your bedroom. Sorry, we forgot yesterday.'

Edward and Stuart were home again, back with Harry at the house in Bloomsbury. Edward had arrived the previous night, letting himself in quietly with his key, hearing Stuart and Harry talking in the kitchen. They had been glad to see him and had asked no questions. They fed him. He went to bed early and fell asleep at once, vaguely aware of Stuart looking at him and turning out the light. When he woke up in the morning he felt that he had never slept so long and so deeply. He recalled no dreams but seemed to experience his sleep in memory, as if he could remember having lain in a deep black warm pit. The sense of home-coming, which he had not expected, touched his heart. The kind surprised faces of his father and his brother made him, in his relief, realise that he had imagined that they would be angry with him. Why? Because he had run away, disappeared, refused their help, quarrelled with them, killed somebody. He had fled to Thomas, then to – But now all that was over. He was starting again, with nothing in the world left to do except to find Brownie and *be* with her – tell her everything and lay all his burdens down at her feet. So he had felt as he crawled up the stairs to his room and fell into the pit of sleep.

After his return from Seegard Edward had spent two more nights at his lodging, in *that* room, in case Brownie should come there. The passing hours and her not coming made him feel sick and mad, and when it grew dark he began to think about Jesse lying there alone underneath his stone between the yew trees. He imagined Jesse lying there with his eyes open, breathing quietly. Then he thought about Mark Wilsden's mutilated body which had been burnt. He went to bed exhausted but could not sleep. Late the next day he went home. The familiar house, the old familiar sound of his father and his elder brother talking, downstairs, in another room, about other things, made him, with an instinct he constantly checked, feel secure as he had felt in childhood. The azalea which Midge had given him 'to cheer him up' so long ago was back in his bedroom, no longer in flower, a little green tree. He woke feeling stronger, able to decide things. He decided that he would go to Mrs Wilsden's house and ask for Brownie. Nothing was left now except Brownie, that was all that remained of his task, his ordeal, his penitence, that was all and everything, for everything depended on that.

'Where's Harry?' said Edward. He had made himself some coffee in the kitchen, then discovered Stuart sitting reading in the drawing room. The sun shone into the green room, paling the green panelling as if one could actually see it fading, sparkling upon the gilded cupids who were holding up Romula's mirror. Stuart was sitting in the box-like armchair beside the piano reading a book. The atmosphere shot Edward straight back into the past. It was the first day of the summer holidays. Free, nothing to do.

'He's in his study,' said Stuart, 'telephoning his publisher.'

'His publisher?'

'Yes, isn't it splendid? He's written a novel and it's to be published! He's ringing up Italy, the publisher's got a villa on the bay of Naples with a view of Vesuvius.'

'I shall write a novel one day,' said Edward, 'and I shall have a villa in Italy, or at least know someone who has.'

'How are you, Ed, better?'

'I don't know yet. I've been at Seegard.'

'I'm sorry about Jesse.'

'Yes. What's happened about Midge?'

'She's down at Quitterne with Thomas. She seems to have chucked Harry.'

'Oh. I never understood that business. So we're all back home here. What are you going to do?'

'I've decided, I'm going to be a schoolmaster.'

'Just like that?'

'I've got to go to a training college first, I've got a grant, and –'

'Oh. Well done. I'll just go and look at those letters.'

Edward legged it up the stairs. He found the letters in a drawer and sat down on the bed and spread them out. He looked for Brownie's writing but it was not there. There was an unsigned postcard of the Eiffel tower from Ilona saying, *Back soon, hope see, your loving sister.* There were several typed envelopes, two letters from Mrs Wilsden, and one in a vaguely familiar hand. He opened this one first.

My dear Edward,

I just thought I'd write to say how pleased we all are with you because of what you did for Midge. She told me all about the whole thing on the telephone. You were exactly right, you were calm and wise, you gave her 'room to turn round', those were her words, what a gift to be able to give to someone who's 'up against it'! She's *so* fond of you and you were really the only person who was close to her that she could talk to! You made her understand her 'real feelings'. You ought to be a psychiatrist, you'd be a jolly sight better than Thomas! You simply said, 'Look, let's sort it out together' and you did. Then when you said 'Stay with Thomas', it was clear that this was right! Well done little Edward! Come and see us soon, won't you? We were sorry to hear about Jesse Baltram. Not that you knew him, but it must have been sad. I hope and believe that you are better. Time heals, dear Edward, youth heals. You must be ready now to see that it wasn't your fault and to forgive yourself. Everyone else has forgiven you long ago, or rather never blamed you at all. I expect you've heard our wonderful news about Giles. We'll tell you all about it when we meet. Willy sends his best love and hopes you're reading Proust! With very loving love to you, dearest Edward,

Yours Ursula.

Edward threw the letter onto the floor. He did not remember saying 'Stay with Thomas'. Perhaps Midge imagined it afterwards. He opened two of the typewritten envelopes. One contained an invitation to a party from someone called Victoria Gunn, the other an invitation to a dance from someone called Julia Carson-Smith. Edward could not think who these people were and threw their letters on the floor too. The next letter was from Sarah Plowmain.

Dear Edward,

I'm sorry you got that awful letter from me hinting at dire things. I thought I was pregnant and I decided I must have an abortion and I was going to write to you and say it was all your fault and you had now killed someone else, our first child. However it turned out to be a false alarm and that child which caused me such frightful worry never existed at all! Even after this time interval I'm still suffering from shock. The imagining of that child was so intense (I even thought I ought to be finding out how nappies work!) and I told nobody and I couldn't bring myself to dream of 'consulting' you, I felt it was all my own affair, my future, my university degree, my life. And I felt angry with you because you'd rushed into my room and started it all and rushed out again and dropped me. And you didn't answer my other letter and I felt abandoned and I'd said how unhappy I was and you didn't even reply! Of course I'm relieved about the 'child' but I feel sad too because of course in the end I probably wouldn't have destroyed it. I miss it, and feel now almost as if it had died! Everything has been a mess lately and what hasn't been has just made me envious! Ma is in a permanent state of excitement and indignation about May Baltram's memoirs (I expect you are too! I refrain from further comment!). She is going to write her own memoirs and a big book on feminism. (Of course I didn't tell *her* what I thought was going on inside me!) I feel so depressed. I've given up smoking. You know, I think my father's death is just catching up on me. I wish I'd cared more about him. I might have given him something to live for and made him love life after all. Edward, I'd like to see you. Nothing to do with sex, I'm fed up with sex, I think I need friends. It's only lately occurred to me that sex prevents friends – it does for women anyway. I hope you'll be decent enough to reply to *this* letter. I've never done you any harm. I hope you've got over the Mark business. Of course I know one never gets over etc. etc. etc., but in a way one does and should.

Love from Sarah.

Edward read this letter through and crumpled it up and dropped it. He was about to destroy Mrs Wilsden's two letters unread when he thought he had better look at them. The first one was familiar, Mrs Wilsden was beginning to repeat herself. 'Murderer ... blackness ... loss ... forever ...' Edward picked up the second one, opened it, glanced at it, and as it was already slipping from his fingers began to take it in.

I have written you some terrible letters, terrible letters out of my terrible grief. I felt that you should realise what you have done. I am told that you do. Nothing can bring my son back. One has to live with such things, every day,

541

every minute. I had to write those letters to you. Now it seems less necessary. I know you won't forget ever in your life. But I must gather up my grief and not spend it in vain accusing. I have been asked to say, and I do say, out of the sincerity of deep sadness, that I forgive you. Perhaps it is pointless to use those words, but after having written those letters I feel I may owe it, if not to you, then to someone or something else. I imagine your state of mind and I pity you. As you may know, I am soon going away, and some peaceful gesture may be appropriate as one surveys one's arrangements and one's life. And an angel has spoken on your behalf.

Jennifer Wilsden.

Your brother's visit did some good. Tell him.

Edward could scarcely believe that anything so wonderful had really happened. He read the letter through again very carefully, scrutinising and weighing every word. Yes, it was a good letter, a beneficent letter, an order of release. The reference to Brownie could only be the opening of a door. A door! He could go straight round now this very moment. Knock on Mrs Wilsden's door and find Brownie! He had been dreading confronting Mrs Wilsden, and even more the likelihood of failure, of being sent away with curses and learning nothing. Now, though his visit might be embarrassing, Mrs Wilsden could hardly deny him news – or sight – of that angel who had spoken up for him! Indeed it seemed to him very likely that Brownie was actually there, in that house, waiting for him to come. She had felt it necessary, before seeing him again, to persuade her mother to forgive him.

Edward could not contain his joy. The metaphor was apt. He felt as if he were bursting with it, it was running out of his eyes and ears and mouth and the soles of his feet. He stood up and covered his eyes and his brows with his hands holding himself hard lest he crack with emotion. He breathed deeply and stood quite still for a while. Then he went to his wash-basin and began very carefully to shave. His hand trembled. He looked at his mad grinning face as he stretched his lip for the razor. He ought to have washed his hair, but there was no time. He dried his face and drew back the long dark locks from his forehead. How dark and bright his eyes looked. He took off his cotton jersey and began looking for a tie, kicking aside the papers on the floor. He noticed the last unopened letter, with a typed envelope, which was lying on the bed and thought he had better glance at it. It was from Brownie.

My dear Edward,
   I am very glad that I saw you and was with you. It was something so essential for both of us, it came about in such a beautiful way, and it did so much good, I am very very grateful to you for your sincerity and frankness, your love and grief for Mark, and the affectionate support which you have given to me. You will by now have had my mother's letter. I am so happy for her that she was able after all to overcome that awful violent bitterness. She is in all ways better. Our mourning for Mark will never end, but it will change, become gentler and wiser and less extreme. You have helped very much in this. We *had* to meet. I am sorry I didn't see you at that pub when you failed to turn up. Of course I know only something very urgent could have prevented you, so please don't worry about that. I'm so glad we met in that room – Thomas McCaskerville wrote saying you were there – seeing that window was an experience I had to have, and it was a special blessing that I was able to have it with you. I feel that together we have 'gone through' so much, as if there were a set of things which had to be done, a sort of ritual which had to be completed, for Mark, and for ourselves; and without you this would never have been, for me, complete. I thank you and bless you with all my heart.
   I expect you will have heard by now that I am going to marry Giles Brightwalton. We have known and loved each other for ages, but Giles kept thinking that he was really homosexual. (He even thought he was in love with your brother at one time – I don't know whether your brother knew.) Now at last he has entirely made up his mind. (I said nothing about him earlier, because then there was nothing to say.) We are going to be married next month and live in

America, where I hope to get an academic job, and my mother is coming too. By the time you get this we shall have left England. Everyone seems pleased. Willy was especially clever about it all. I think he got alarmed when I wrote to Giles about meeting you! Giles was alarmed too! My mother, who always wanted me to marry him, is overjoyed. I think this is what made her able to forgive you.

Edward, I hope you won't be hurt in any way, I'm sure you won't. It was Mark who brought us together, and our mutual affection, which I hope will remain, flowed in and through him. Giles knows about this, but I won't talk about it to anyone else, it's our secret. I was relieved actually when you didn't come to the pub. It was a sort of comfortable sign. My mother and I will be living in the New World and we shall leave Mark behind in peace. And I hope that you too, dear Edward, will be at peace, feeling no guilt or self-destructive distress about the past. No one was to blame. Life is full of terrible things and one must look into the future and think about what happiness one can create for oneself and others. There is so much good that we can all do, and we must have the energy to do it. I was so sorry to hear of the death of your father. It was a blessing that you were with him near the end. Giles joins me in sending love and good wishes. We shall hope to see you, here or over there, before too long. With my most affectionate and humble thanks,

With love,

Brownie.

Edward found that he had, while reading the letter, been panting, incoherently exclaiming, choking for breath. For he saw at once that it was not the letter he had been waiting for. He stood, feet well apart, controlling his breathing, and when he had looked at the letter again and was sure he had understood it all, he put it down on the chest of drawers beside the azalea, and lay down on the bed. So Brownie was gone. She had been taken from him and had vanished. She had been a dream of reconciliation and love, and she had finished her task. He had believed in her passionately,

544

reverently, she had been for him the touchstone of all reality and truth. Yet in a way she had never, for him, existed at all. She had needed him for her 'ritual'. He had been of service to her as a part of Mark, a remnant, a relic. She had written about him to Giles. She was not really part of Edward's story after all, it had all been contrived and imagined. Even her visit to Mark's room had been organised by Thomas. And he had failed her twice, three times, after she had done so much and come so far. She had been relieved when he did not come to her at the pub, it was a 'comfortable sign', an indication that she need not feel guilty about having 'loved' him, while all the time she loved somebody else. So, after all, when he had thought there would be some significant and healing end to his guilt and his grief, he was presented with a simulacrum, which indeed he had fashioned himself. It was not the order of release. The light fell on those who waved goodbye, leaving him behind in the dark, the old dark full of miseries and ghosts, which he had but briefly been away from in a dream. With a demonic accuracy, the pain of jealousy had been added now to all the others. Jealousy lasts forever. Bad news for the young. And he recalled his dream about the butterfly, the psyche which flew about and could not get out of the window, and fell down dead upon the floor. Edward lay limp upon the bed with folded hands and tears gathered behind his closed eyes.

At about this time Stuart too was reading a letter which he had just received by the morning post.

My dear Stuart,

I am so very sorry I startled you with that curious 'declaration of love'. It all seems very strange to me now, I suppose it's what Thomas calls 'a psychotic episode', and I certainly owe you an apology! Please don't worry about me or about my state of mind, all that is definitely over! As you know, I am at home as usual with Thomas, and have discontinued what was always an uneasy and unhappy relationship with your father. All that has been put away into the past, and I hope will not affect continued relations between our families. I rely on you for help in this. Please don't feel upset about anything to do with me. Really you didn't do anything to me, it was all in my mind. You weren't part of what I was going through, you were just an external impulse like a bump or jolt. I thought you were affecting me in some way, but you weren't really, you were a negative presence, a sort of catalyst. Because of your unworldly withdrawal I was able to see my situation, and you brought about things which didn't really concern you at all. I put it all onto you like an ass's head. My thinking I was in love with you was just my being surprised by my ability to see things differently. So it was all my doing, I'm so sorry! Edward was perfectly sweet, very sympathetic and kind. Please give him my love if he's with you. Meredith sends love and says cryptically 'it's OK', which he says you'll understand. He's awfully grown up now he's at boarding school. Thomas is with a patient, he's still got one or two, but if he were here he'd send love too. After a little while I hope we'll meet again. With all best wishes and love,

Midge

Sitting in the box chair in the drawing room with his book on his knee Stuart read this letter through twice. Then he raised his head and looked at how the sunshine was throwing shadows of leaves onto the shutters. He sat still a while, thinking, with his pretty lips pursed and a little intent frown above his puzzled yellow eyes. Then he relaxed and began to smile. He was glad about Meredith; and he liked the bit about the ass's head.

The mouse. And the spider. Who had talked about the spider? Thomas. Well, the spider mattered too. There are signs everywhere, everything is a sign. There are no ordeals, or else everything is. And no way, only the end, as somebody told him.

He decided he should go upstairs and find out how Edward was getting on.

When Stuart reached him Edward was sitting on the edge of his bed with a lot of crumpled paper round his feet. He looked terrible.

'How tired you look, Ed. Here, I've brought you some coffee and today's *Times*.'

'Thanks. Put them on the thing, the chest of drawers. No, give me *The Times*. I hope there's been an earthquake with ten thousand dead.'

'No, I'm afraid not. I've had such a nice letter from Midge, she sends love. She says you were so kind to her, you were wonderful.'

'So everyone thinks I'm wonderful. Except Harry. I don't suppose he does. Does he hate me? He was quite polite last night.'

'Of course he doesn't hate you!'

'He was pretty angry with you, wasn't he?'

'Yes, he chucked me out twice. But when I came back again one evening – Well, he was sitting in the drawing room looking crazy, he'd been drinking and he hadn't shaved and his hair was everywhere and his eyes staring, he looked like something out of Bedlam, you know, those pictures of mad people – like what I thought a madman looked like when I was a child. I said something and he simply ignored me, didn't even look at me. I just sat down – he was sitting by the fireplace and I sat here, and we just sat together in silence for quite a long time. Then quite suddenly he seemed to come together, and he said, "I'm sorry, Stuart –" and then we talked a bit and everything was all right between us. I knew it would be. And he's awfully glad you're back – So you see –'

'How nice everyone is,' said Edward. 'I'm wonderful and everyone is nice. And you're going to be a schoolmaster.'

'Do go down and talk to Harry – when you feel like it – just –'

'Yes, yes. So we're all gathered together.'

'And Willy rang up to say he was looking forward to your being back next term and were you getting on with some reading. I suppose you know that Giles is going to marry Mark's sister?'

'Oh that, yes. I've known about that for ages. I mean that

it was likely. It's splendid, isn't it.' It occurred to Edward that of course no one knew about his relationship, his *love* relationship with Brownie. Brownie hadn't talked, and he hadn't. It was 'our secret'. What a good thing it was that he had never told anyone. He could do without public commiserations and sympathetic looks – without the *shame* of having lost her.

'I think it's such a good thing,' said Stuart, 'I've always been very fond of Giles, he's such a splendid chap. And I'm told she's stalwart. I think you don't know her? I haven't met her.'

You have though, thought Edward, in that room where I said she was Betty something. I don't suppose he'll remember. When he meets her as Mrs Giles Brightwalton she'll be so bloody transformed by matrimonial happiness and the USA. Yes, she's stalwart all right. Stuart's vocabulary was often curiously apt. As he talked Edward was idly turning the pages of *The Times*. Suddenly something caught his eye.

'Stuart, old chap, could you please bugger off?'

'Right oh. Come down soon.'

As Stuart disappeared Edward was studying a short entry in the obituary column.

Max Point, who died last week, was a member of the Jesse Baltram circle and a friend of Baltram. His early painting shows the influence of Baltram's 'mythological' subjects, but he is best known and esteemed for his mature portraits in the style of Soutine and Moteszcicky. His paintings of the Thames, beside which he lived, probably attained most popularity and may be seen in provincial collections. The Tate Gallery possesses, but has rarely exhibited, a portrait of Baltram by Point. This will be on view during the promised and eagerly awaited Jesse Baltram exhibition. Max Point, who painted little in later years, was certainly a versatile and underrated artist. It is time he was rediscovered.

Edward sat staring at the obituary, letting it stir up such a mixture of intense and painful feelings. He remembered the silvery northern light upon the river and Max Point's face in the brown darkness, distorted as perhaps in one of his portraits in the style of Soutine. He recalled how he had said to Thomas somebody should do something, and Thomas had said why not you. He had meant to go back. Then he remembered that this was perhaps Ilona's father, and that he had never spoken of him to Ilona. Better so. Ilona too had been seeking her father. Now he was dead. And Mark was dead and Jesse was dead and Mrs Quaid was dead and Edward's first child was dead, or rather had never existed. And my Brownie is dead, he thought, or never existed. And I am dead too.

Except of course that I'm not and am alive and suffering. I am in love with two dead people and one lost one. I shall never be happy again because everything in the world will remind me of Mark, and I shall always be wishing that I could undo the past, when so little needs doing to it in order to give me a happy life. Stuart said let the fire burn. It has burned and burned and me with it, burning alive and screaming. Chin up, put it behind you, there's nothing deep, God isn't watching you, personal responsibility is a fiction, you're simply ill, it's an illness, you will recover, think of it as a spiritual journey, your image of yourself is broken, there is life after death, you will thrive on disasters, suffer, don't evade anything, live in pain, reach out and touch something good, remorse must kill the self not teach it new lies, hope only for the truth, the soul must die to live. All right, all right, all right. But the awful fact was that he had not moved an inch, all movement, all journeying, had been an illusion, he was back at the beginning, back with Mark, back in hell. I'm branded, he thought, I'm walled up, I'm crawling with cockroaches, I stink of misery and evil, I haven't any being left, it's all been scraped away. I'm a raw rotting wound. It seemed as if something was happening, but I was having a dream, now I'm back in reality, I felt it touch me as I read that letter, I'm back where I started. It was *all* magic, all those ideas people had, all the words they said, everything I hoped for, the spiritual journeys, the redeeming ordeals, the healing draughts, reconciliation, salvation, new life. It was all hallucination, everything that seemed good and ordinary and real. That wasn't for *me*. The light which I saw wasn't the sun. It was just a reflection of the fires of hell.

The uprush of these thoughts was so fast that Edward gasped, then moaned, then got up quickly pulling his shirt away from his neck and opening his mouth. He felt as if his mouth was full of sulphur and went to the basin to wash it out. Leaning over he felt sick. A blackness hovered above him as if he might faint. He opened one of the drawers of the chest intending to lean upon it, saw Jesse's ring which he no longer wore lying inside, and shut it hastily. He went to the window and opened it. The sun had gone and a wind was tugging the dusty leaves of the trees in the gardens round about. They already looked tired of summer. Behind it all lay the derelict dirty horror of London, doomed city. Now I *am* ill, thought Edward, except that it's the soul, the soul. The soul can die. I saw that in my dream. He wondered if he should run downstairs and ask Stuart to help him.

Harry was in the kitchen washing up. He had refused Stuart's assistance. He was thinking about his parents. That is he was thinking about Midge, which he did all the time, and at another level he was thinking about his parents. Had they been happy, had his father had love affairs? It seemed very likely. When he could have found out he didn't care. Had his mother resented all those sacrifices she made, becoming a typist instead of a pianist, to serve that blond handsome egomaniac? She thought he was a genius. The sense of the distance away of their world made him feel giddy. Of course the simple fact was that Casimir hated music. Harry hated it too. He had an early memory of the sound of the piano in the drawing room, always sad, conveying pointlessness, annihilation, death. How pretty his mother was, with that gentle apologetic face and pale fluffy hair frizzed by the hairdresser, and little feet in shining high-heeled shoes which gave Harry his first conscious erotic experience. Lying on the floor under the piano he had watched the jerky irregular powerful movements of those little feet upon the pedals, and listened to the soft mechanical sounds which the pedals made, so much

550

more exciting to him than the music of Bach or Mozart. After Casimir died the piano was heard again, but it had lost its heart. The music had no more authority. Teresa too, the girl from far away, had sat in that drawing room on that sofa and Harry had watched his young wife watching his young mother. Teresa had played the recorder before they got married, but Romula's piano silenced her. They had got on well, though Romula was jealous. She moved out of the house into a flat. But the house rejected Teresa, she was never really its mistress. Casimir never met Teresa. Would he have found her attractive, would he have teased her and called her his wild colonial girl? She was not wild. She was a hard-working student who had saved up to come to England to do a diploma. He never saw her parents or her homeland, not even the albatross could make him take that journey, and he could not now remember why he had loved her. It was all so long ago and she had lived so short a time, it was as if he had killed her. She hovered in his memory as something undefiled, not quite of this world. Perhaps he had been enchanted because she had loved him so much and with so virginal a love. He was her first and only lover. So young and unmade, she had seemed to crystallise for him a brief idealism, out of what was confused before and cynical after. Chloe, whom Romula never knew, was another matter. Chloe was like him. Oh God, why had he not instantly discovered Midge when Chloe died – little Midge living down in Kent, whom Jesse had noticed and said, 'Who is that girl?'

Midge was perfect, right, his right woman, his mate. Oh why did he meet her so late, and why had he now, for such bad muddled reasons, lost her? For he had lost her, Harry had given up hope. He had been out-manoeuvred, out-witted, cheated, mystified, baffled, made a fool of by Thomas, Stuart, Edward, chance, fate, Midge herself. He would get his own back on them all. He would find another perfect woman and marry her. He would dumbfound Thomas, dazzle the boys, and cripple Midge with jealousy and rash regret, paying in full for the pain which he was suffering now. There were other women. He could even recall having had that thought, as if it were the very same thought floating back in a capsule, after

Teresa died, after Chloe died. Had he had it before they died? No, he had been faithful, perhaps because he was not, in either case, tested for long. There were women in the world! He might even have one in view already. But oh the pain, the longing, the absence, the sheer physical torture of a desire which had grown, out of perfect satisfaction, so habitual, so strong, and so precise. Harry knew that he was not the type of a martyr. He would not die of love, he would, in time, cheer up, look about, find other sports and joys. He would write another novel, he already had some ideas. He would not fall out of his boat and see it drift away faster than he could swim. All that, knowing the future, he knew. What a strange thing is a man's life. But this knowledge did not ease the present anguish as he looked down at the plate which he was holding and realised that he would not be with Midge, *his* Midge, his beautiful perfect lover, ever again in the world.

'Dad, I wish you'd let me do that.'
    'No, I like it, it's good for me.'
    'Shall I go to the shops?'
    'No, I'll shop. I'm going to do some serious cooking.'
    'Oh splendid!'
    'You and Edward need some decent food, you boys never eat. Where is Edward?'
    'He's talking on the telephone.'
    'Who to?'
    'I don't know. When are you going to Italy?'
    'Friday. I may stay a bit, I want to work on my next novel.'
    'Oh good. You'll be beside the sea?'
    'Yes. From my bedroom window I shall see Vesuvius.'
    'That should be inspiring. What's he like, your publisher – he must be very nice to invite you –'
    'Oh very nice. He's a she –'

Edward had dialled Thomas's country number. He got Meredith. Thomas and Midge were out to lunch with some people called Shaftoe. Edward talked to Meredith. His precise slightly raucous voice was made by the telephone to sound like Thomas's. Later their voices would be indistinguishable. Edward suddenly recalled the awful dinner party at the McCaskervilles' when he had sat in a corner and pretended to read a book and Meredith had come up and touched him. He talked to Meredith about his school, about the dorms, the masters, the games, starting to learn Greek. He talked about Meredith's dog. He put the 'phone down and went back to his room.

The mad black fit had passed, leaving ordinary misery behind. I suppose I'll get better, he thought, I suppose I won't always be totally wretched. I must be a bit better if I can even think this. I wonder if the madness, the terror, the horror will recur at different times in my life, coming back as if it had never been away, prompted by some other dreadful happening? Perhaps there will be many of these catastrophes I can't conceive of now, perhaps I am doomed to have an unlucky life. But this is a senseless idea which I reject. I suppose Brownie will fade, I think I never let myself fully believe in her, I *pretended* that everything depended on her, but that wasn't really our situation. Our relationship was always strained and willed. We never got past the stage of using each other to placate Mark. The word 'placate' brought with it the image of a sad envious ghost knocking at the doors of life to hold the dimming attention of those whom he loved, who loved him once. I wasn't to blame, said Edward to Mark, it wasn't my fault, I never wished you any harm, we are parted now, and you will stay young and I will grow old, and I won't forget you, but I can't let you destroy me. My life belongs to others, those who are here now and those who are to come. But oh Brownie, dear dear Brownie, whose real face he would never see again. He had not made love to her in that room, it would have been a sacrilege; and yet by that very sacrilege he might have won her. If he had done *that* could she have left him? But these too were senseless thoughts which must be banished. All that time she was yearning for Giles who was yearning for Stuart.

Edward opened the drawer and looked at Jesse's ring. He took it out, and reaching farther in drew out Jesse's sketch of

Ilona, and the chain which Ilona had given him, and the photograph of Jesse which he had stolen. He propped up the photograph and the sketch, put the chain round his neck, and last, with some misgivings, put on the ring. It was like a religious ceremony. He tested his feelings. No warmth, no vision, quiet relics. It occurred to him that he might put the ring on to the chain and wear it round his neck, like Frodo. The idea amused him. He put the relics away, let them rest; and he wondered whether in the future, in some emergency, he might not, with greater expectation and with more remarkable results, put on Jesse's ring. Jesse had always been more of a lover than a father, he had not finished with Jesse and, like the women, could not entirely believe that he was dead.

'I've got to survive,' he said aloud. He began to pick up the papers which were lying on the floor and put them in order on the bed. He folded Brownie's letter and put it in his pocket. He wanted to destroy it, it was ghostly material already, something uncanny and awful which he would dread ever to come upon in years to come. Yet he could not destroy it today. He would do so tomorrow. Perhaps when he read it again he would see it as a false letter, full of evasions and excuses. He suddenly realised that he would have to answer it, to say 'it's all right, don't worry, be happy'. He would have to congratulate the happy couple. It might sound insincere, but they would not notice that in their joy! He tore up Mrs Wilsden's first letter and pocketed the second. It meant less to him now. She had only 'forgiven' him because she was so pleased about Giles and Brownie. He looked at Ursula's letter, it was a 'nice letter' but he threw it in the wastepaper basket: it had occurred to him that even Willy had worked against him, alarming Giles by the idea of a rival. So, in a way, Edward thought, I brought about Brownie's happiness after all! Will this ever console me? He uncrumpled the letter from Sarah, understanding it for the first time. The letter smelt of incense and brought back that little dark room where Sarah had seduced him while Mark Wilsden's life was being taken away. Now for the first time Edward recalled that he had enjoyed the seduction. Well, he had explained to Mark that it was not exactly his fault, and it certainly wasn't Sarah's fault. Perhaps Mark bound him to Sarah as he bound him to Brownie. He thought, I have a responsibility to her, I'm responsible for her, she's unhappy, I must go to her; and he felt a stirring of curiosity, so often a motive to benevolence. Then he looked at the other two letters which had seemed so mysterious. Who on earth was Victoria Gunn, who wrote so familiarly, like an old friend, inviting him to a party to celebrate the liberation of someone called Stalky? The address was Flood Street. Of course, that was the dotty American girl he had met when he was looking for Jesse, and Stalky was her cat who had been in quarantine. But who was Julia Carson-Smith, writing from an address in Suffolk? Why she was the person who had lived in Jesse's house and knew about Max Point. Her note accompanied a formal invitation card. *We are giving a coming-out dance (rather old-fashioned but rather fun!) for our youngest daughter Cressida, and we do so hope that you can come! I enclose instructions how to find us. A special bus will meet the 2.45 train from King's Cross.* I'll be there, thought Edward. I'll talk to Sarah, I'll drink with Victoria, I'll dance with Cressida. There are girls in the world. It's as Ilona said, there are all kinds of other people. I'll start studying again, and I'll learn Russian, and I'll write a novel. I'll write all about what has happened to me, or rather not about *it*, but about something terrible that I'll *invent*. I'm so full of terrible things, enough for a lifetime of writing! And so, as Thomas said, I'll thrive on disasters. Am I wiser now, or just more hardened? A picture of ordinary happiness came to him suddenly as a blue sea and a jostle of boats with huge coloured stripy sails. He thought, it's not like what Thomas said about new being and so on, it's more like what he said about the natural ego growing again! But he said there'd be some sort of evidence left behind. I must ask him about that sometime. Maybe I've just got so tired of it all I'm letting go and nature is curing me! Anyway I'll try to do some good in the world, if it's not too difficult, nothing stops anyone from doing that.

He picked up Ilona's postcard, and her face came back to him as he had first seen it on that wonderful first evening at

Seegard, the 'festival' they had made for his arrival. He remembered the taste of the wine, unlike any wine he had ever drunk. And Ilona, with her mass of hair falling down her neck and her mischievous shy look. All the innocence and charm of Seegard came back to him with that memory. Had it all been proved an illusion? What had Seegard done for him, was it an irrelevant interval, a corrupt mystery, a good enigma, a journey to the underworld? He felt now that, whatever it was, it was a huge business, so huge that it would take him years and years to think it out; and it occurred to Edward for the first time that there could be experiences which lasted a lifetime through, constantly changing, never disappearing; as of course Mark would never disappear. And as he thought this he thought of his own long long future; and of Mark and how his future was ended. He had assisted too at the end of Seegard, had perhaps even, as Bettina had suggested, helped to bring it about. He had disturbed Jesse, he had produced Stuart, he had broken it all up by being a novelty, a portent, a spectator, an *alien*. But still everything that happened must have been what Jesse wanted. Of course I'm thinking about it in two quite different ways, thought Edward. In a way it's all a muddle starting off with an accident: my breakdown, drugs, telepathy, my father's illness, cloistered neurotic women, people arriving unexpectedly, all sorts of things which happened by pure chance. At so many points anything being otherwise could have made everything be otherwise. In another way it's a whole complex thing, internally connected, like a dark globe, a dark world, as if we were all parts of a single drama, living inside a work of art. Perhaps important things in life are always like that, so that you can think of them both ways. Of course one *works* at things in one's mind, one doesn't want to think that what happens 'does nothing' or 'doesn't matter', as if it was wasted, it's much more comforting if it's part of one's fate or one's deep being somehow. Perhaps that working is a kind of magic, like what made Stuart run away. It's dangerous, but I don't see how we could get on without it.

And Ilona, what on earth was happening to her in Paris? He looked at her postcard. Was she all right, and was it his fault if she was not? He decided not to worry. She would soon be back, he would meet the new strange Ilona, and they would talk and talk about their adventures, and in the future he would *look after her*; after all he was her elder brother. Why had he imagined that Seegard had come to an end which he had brought about? That was sheer conceit. Seegard was still there, it was a house where people lived, he had a mother and a sister there, he would go and see them one day, he would go with Ilona and there would be a festival. He would go and swim in the sea. They were not his enemies, they were out, they were free, they were ordinary women now. May was unhappy, 'in a chaos of misery', she might need him, she might be pleased to see him. He recalled May's 'Can you love me enough?' It was a fair question. Interesting unpredictable Bettina might need him too. In a little while he would go to them in peace.

But Jesse was dead, he could not be visited, and did not, however much he might work or be worked in the mind, belong to that open and accidental scene any more. And yet, Edward thought, Jesse three times interfered between me and Brownie, and not only when he was 'still alive'. Well, Jesse was a mystery, he had joined the things which go on and on in a life and are in a sense eternal. I did find my father, thought Edward, and he was a magician. Is magic bad? Stuart would think so. It was as if a storm raged about Jesse, but in the middle of the storm it was calm. And as in a vision Edward saw Jesse in the calm centre, diminishing into a tiny radiant sphere, and in the middle of the sphere there was a child. I love him, thought Edward, *he* has done me no harm, only good, he is alive in me, he needed me, I am responsible for him, I will keep him as a secret, a mystery which I will study and by which I will not be dismayed or made afraid. He is innocent. And then suddenly in his mind he saw his mother Chloe, as she had stood beside the path and opened out her arms and shrieked. He thought, I'll talk to Harry about her, I'll find out all about her, I've never done that. Perhaps I'm responsible for her too!

And Brownie, would there always be a special bond between them, fashioned by time into something pure and good? Brave abstract words. Perhaps Brownie too would become one of the eternal things. At any rate he was sure that the deep confused pain he felt about her now would pass. He could distinguish between pains, he who had had so many. This was not an illness of his whole being, it was a clean wound which would heal.

'So we're together again,' said Harry, pulling the cork out of a bottle of champagne, 'us against the rest.'

They were in the drawing room. Stuart was cutting open a carton of apple juice with a pair of scissors, and carefully pouring it into a glass jug.

'But we're not against the rest, are we?' said Stuart.

'I am. Edward, drink this, it'll do you good.'

'Thanks.' Edward drank some of the champagne. It tasted heavenly.

'I meant to tell you, Ed,' said Stuart. 'I saw something written on a wall near the British Museum, it said *Jesse Lives*.'

'I saw that too,' said Harry, 'and *Jesse Baltram is king*.'

'What does it mean?' said Edward.

'It means your father is a sex hero!'

'I thought it was rather touching,' said Stuart, 'he means something to people.'

'My sister said I looked so like him, I could have any girl in London!'

'Good on you, Edward,' said Harry, 'I drink to you!'

'What's this place you're going to?' said Edward to Stuart.

'It's a teachers' training college, I can do a short course. I have to have a diploma.'

'I suppose you'll teach sixth-formers?'

'No, little children.'

'You mean ten, eleven?'

'No, eight, six, four.'

'You must be mad!' said Harry.

'You see,' said Stuart, 'things must be got right at the start –'

'You mean computers? I thought you hated them!'

'No, I mean thinking and morality –'

'You sound like a Jesuit, indoctrinate them when young –'

'Computers, OK, but that's just mechanical. You can teach language and literature and how to use words so as to *think*. And you can teach moral values, you can teach meditation, what used to be called prayer, and give them an idea of what goodness is, and how to love it –'

'Stuart, you've opted for power after all! I thought good men were powerless. You're a power maniac, just like I said!'

'Of course the problem is how to do it,' said Stuart, 'it's all in that, the *whole* problem is in that – I'll have to learn – and meanwhile I'm going to do some voluntary work with some of Ursula's people –'

'It sounds wonderful,' said Edward, 'but nobody will let you.'

'I think they will,' said Stuart. 'Of course I'll have to get experience first and work out a system and interest other people. I'd like to have a school of my own.'

'There you are,' said Harry, 'Stuart as boss! You won't last long in the education world, in fact you'll never start! You'll never make a schoolmaster, they'll laugh at you. You're really a masochist –'

'Well, let them laugh, perhaps I'll laugh too. I'll be experimenting, searching, it seems to me that the basis of education –'

'You'll be searching all your life,' said Harry, 'I'm afraid you're a "seeker", I never could stand seekers, they cause endless trouble. You'll never find your place, you'll always be a beginner – Don't you agree, Edward?'

'No,' said Edward, 'I think Stuart is more like a monument, he just exists and that's a good thing, he's an unmoved mover. But seriously, I think he could have a lot of influence, he might become a great educational reformer, we certainly need one.'

'No one can avoid muddle,' said Harry, 'no one can avoid corruption, the pure dedicated life is an illusion, the mere idea of it is a damaging lie, look at all the wickedness priests cause, they're as messy as we are only there's a conspiracy to keep it dark. The idea of goodness is romantic opium, it's a killer in the end. Stuart's a menace, he's a simplifier, he's got no imagination, he's got no sense of drama –'

'Wait a minute,' said Edward. 'Those aren't the same –'

'As you said, he's a monument, he's static, he's like those Greek philosophers who thought nothing moved and all was one –'

'Perhaps he's got no unconscious mind,' said Edward.

'Everybody's got one, that's why religion is an illusion.'

'There's something he hasn't got.'

'Well, it's not sexual urges, he's my son, he'll break out!'

Stuart had been laughing. They all laughed. Watching the two tall men together Edward saw how much they resembled each other. Stuart had grown older. How had he managed to do so, experiencing nothing?

'If you do ever get your education theory going and have your own school, I'll invest in it!' said Harry. 'So you'll sit at a desk now and learn things? What will you learn, what's that book you've been reading?'

'It's a novel by Jane Austen called *Mansfield Park*.'

Harry and Edward roared with laughter.

'You see, I have to do a paper in English literature –'

'You're reverting to childhood. You're nothing but a six-foot child!'

'I can't put it down, it's awfully good –'

'Of course it is, silly! And what are you reading, Edward, what's that book you're reading?'

'Oh – Proust –' Edward had been looking for the passage which had so amazed him at Seegard about Albertine going out in the rain on her bicycle, but he couldn't find it. He had turned to the beginning. *Je me réveillais souvent de bonne heure.* What a lot of pain there was in those first pages. What a lot of pain there was all the way through. So how was it that the whole thing could vibrate with such pure joy? This was something which Edward was determined to find out.

'And this time next week you'll be looking at Vesuvius out of your bedroom window,' said Stuart.

'We'll come and join you,' said Edward.

'No you won't!'

'A lot of gods live around there,' said Edward. 'There's an entrance to Hades. Or is that at Etna?'

560